DRIFT PATƎRN

By

JOJ RⱢT PAJIT

"Mathematics is the language
with which God has written the universe."

~ Galileo Galilei

grey gecko press

Published by Grey Gecko Press - Pensacola, Florida.

www.greygeckopress.com

Printed in the United States of America

Design by Grey Gecko Press

Library of Congress Cataloging-in-Publication Data
Padgett, George Wright
Drift pattern / George Wright Padgett
Library of Congress Control Number: 2022946970
ISBN 978-1-9457605-4-9
First Edition

For my father for exposing me to the world of science fiction (and specifically time travel stories).

What I would give to travel back in time to place this book in your hands.

PROLOG

(Prologue)

<u>ONE</u>

August 9, 2012

LUCI **G**AUDIANO **CLOSES HER EYES.** The twelve-year-old allows the numbers to form in her mind with the softness of a flower bud opening in a warm beam of sunlight. A constant stream of summer air pours in through her slightly cracked backseat window. It feels good allowing it to play in her long, dark curls of hair. "Ah ha, 1,510,010,620!" she announces triumphantly. Though she is certain of the calculation, the girl opens her eyes to ask, "I'm sure 520.89 multiplied by 2,898,904.98954 equals 1,510,010,620. Am I right?"

"Nope, you're way off," her mother says from the front seat, making an effort to conceal the calculator app on her phone screen.

"What do you mean?" the twelve year old demands, leaning forward as much as the seatbelt will allow. "Yes, 1,510,010,620 *is* right."

Her mother grins, caught in her fib. "Why do you even ask?"

"She likes to hear that she's right," the father answers, shooting a quick glance into the rearview mirror. "She wants to hear you say it. I don't blame her; it is pretty impressive."

"Gimmie another one," Luci says. "In the trillions this time."

"I don't think this calculator can go that high. Anyway, we'll be there in a few minutes, and my battery's about to die."

Her mother turns to her father driving. "I don't know why you pay that Tim Callahan guy to do the taxes. Luci could do it for you in a fraction of the time, and for free."

"Better than that," he says, "I say we head to Vegas before school starts back up and make a killing having her count cards."

The remark earns him a playful punch in the arm from her mother.

"Papa," Luci says, exasperated, "they won't let me on the casino floor until I'm twenty-one.""How do you even know things like that?" her mother asks, looking back to face her.

The girl shrugs. "Just do. In 3,401 days, I turn 21."

The man laughs as he merges into a small cluster of traffic. "It's a date then."

"You'll have her do no such thing," her mother scolds him.

He ignores the chastisement. "Seriously, though, Luci-poo, I think you should consider joining that Mathletics thing. You've really got a gift."

"I told you not to call me that anymore."

"Call you what?"

"She doesn't like to be called 'Luci-poo,'" her mother says.

"Since when?"

"For a while now," Luci answers sharply. "It's baby talk, and I'm almost thirteen."

"Your birthday isn't until December, but even then, you'll always be my Luci-poo."

"Papa!"

He rolls his window down to motion a car to cut in front of him. "Look, I'll make a deal with you."

"I don't like your deals."

He suppresses his laughter. "I'll make a deal that I won't call you that if you join the Mathletics Club that Mrs. Richards keeps emailing us about."

There's a pause as Luci goes on the assertive. "How's about I make a deal with *you*? Think of three super high numbers this side of a million. I'll multiply the first two in my head and divide by the third and have the number for you before we get to the dog shelter."

"I feel like I'm being hustled."

Her mother shifts to him. "I think you are."

"So, what do you get if you do this?" he asks.

"*When* she does it."

"Will I have to stop asking you to join Mathletics Club?"

"I want Pepé."

"What's a Pepé?" he asks.

She runs her fingers up and down the edges of the seatbelt. "He's the little black and white one . . . at the shelter."

He shoots a look over to the woman. "You let her name one of the rescue dogs? That's a *bad* idea."

She raises her hands in mock surrender. "No, this is the first I'm hearing about it."

"Please, Papa," Luci interjects.

"Luci-p—" he catches himself before adding the offending cutesy suffix. "Luci, I told you that we can't get a dog right now; it wouldn't be fair to it. The apartment's too small."

Luci pleads, "Pepé is small and could stay in my bedroom. I'd keep him in there and he'd never leave."

Her mother softly interjects, "Luci, that's not a good life for a dog, big or little."

"When I said I'd think about it, we were talking about moving to a house with a yard," he says defensively.

"Your father's promotion means we'll need to stay in the city for a while longer for him to be closer to the project."

He adds, "But it's definitely something to consider for the future."

"For the future?" Luci scoffs. "That's the same thing you said last month when we went to work at the shelter." She clenches her rolled-up Sudoku magazine. "You keep changing it."

"Well, I guess it's like Yogi Berra said: the future isn't what it used to be."

"That doesn't even make sense. You always say that when you want to break a promise."

"I never promised," he says, looking over his shoulder at the girl. All humor is gone from his voice. "I said we'll see what the future holds."

Her mother attempts to cool the situation down. "Luci, you know that we love the dogs at the shelter, all of them. It's just not the right time is all."

He nods. "When things get a little more—"

At first, Luci thinks it's an explosion until realizing the car is spinning out of control on the bridge. She's mercilessly yanked to the side until being violently restrained by her seatbelt. Not only does the harness forbid any additional movement, but the force of the band slamming her back squeezes the air from her lungs. Her head jolts back hard against the seat. Loose fragments of broken windshield glass sprinkle her lap and the seat beside her.

As the whirling subsides, her mother wails her father's name. "*Anthony!*" The sound is mournfully horrifying.

Luci, seated directly behind him, can't see his condition. The panic in her mother's voice makes her panic. *What's wrong with him?* She can only see the dark curls of his hair and his head slumped forward. "Mama?" she feebly utters, gingerly massaging the deep soreness in her chest.

She doesn't answer, only screaming hysterically through her hands covering her face at whatever she sees beside her.

A second impact jolts them.

There's no spinning this time, but Luci feels the crunch of the collision in the front quickly followed by the jolt of a stiff impact to the back of the car.

The ghastly clamor of metal scraping and contorting shifts her mother's attention from Papa's state to what's happening on the other side of the windshield. Luci makes out the top chrome mesh grille of a truck through the cracked spider's web of glass, a fractured image kaleidoscope of horror.

Mama screams "*No!*" so loudly in the confined space that Luci clasps her ears. The girl sobs, trying to understand why this is happening to them.

Her mother turns to her, crazed eyes wide with fear. "Luci, we've got to get out! The driver's pushing us over the guard railing!"

"What?" Luci asks shaking her head. "Who—"

"Just undo your belt. There isn't much time!"

Luci's hands are not her own. The adrenaline raging through her tiny frame makes her fingers twitch and spasm. "I can't . . . I can't get it!" she shouts. "I'm sorry, Mama."

There's a sickly sensation of the car's angle shifting as the front end begins to lift off the asphalt.

"I'll help you, baby," she shouts, "as soon as I get mine off."

The truck engine growls and revs its mechanical fury. The demonlike shriek of oversized tires grinding against the bridge pavement flinging gravel in every direction is terrifying.

Luci, crying, frantically grapples with her seat's harness, but it's no use.

The car's already at an impossible angle common only to queasy carnival rides.

Her mother shouts her name as the car begins to tip and thrusts her hand in the backseat. She squeezes Luci's hand like a vise, preventing her from snapping the buckle loose. "Keep it on!" she shouts. "We're going to fall!"

Luci experiences a queer sense of weightlessness as the car goes over the edge of the high point of the bridge.

The sensation doesn't last.

The back of the car slams into the water with a ferocious thunderclap, snapping Luci's head forward in her seat for a third time. The taste of iron in her blood flows from her freshly busted lip into her mouth.

The roar of lake water into the car's interior through Luci's partially opened window and the shattered windshield replace the noise of Mama's wails. It's unexpectedly cold, and Luci stiffens to the chill. The vehicle sinks quickly. Sunlight from overhead fades from the cracked windshield as their descent speeds up. Luci's heart pounds in her ears as water rushes in, sounding like manic applause. Splashes of cold water pelting her in the face stifle any cries for help.

She coughs uncontrollably, triggering her lungs to gasp for any lifegiving oxygen that can be found. Bubbles forcefully escaping upward to the surface mockingly assault her ears. The rapid descent abruptly halts when the back of the car embeds in the sandy floor of the lake with a shuddering thump. Intolerable water pressure smashes against her like a suffocating lead blanket.

Luci finally frees herself from her seatbelt, but bright stars of light swirl around in her vision, confirming she's running out of time. Her lightheaded disorientation of floating in darkness is petrifying, but she must press through the fear. She knows if she slows even for a moment, she will die—and she's the only one that is still awake enough to do anything for the three of them.

The front of the vehicle steadily lowers to the lake floor basin. Luci floats against the car's roof. Her oxygen-deprived lungs burn in agony. The nose of the vehicle reaches the lake's sandy bottom with a sluggish thud, leveling off.

She swims downward, groping in the darkness for the door handle. Bright sparks of light crisscross in her eyes as every cell in her body aches, screaming out for precious air.

The horror that she's going to die in this water cage grips her heart.

She wrestles with the slippery handle. Above ground, the door would open easily, but at this depth, the outside pressure's too great against it.

Luci's lungs feel like they're on fire, and her muscles revolt against her commands, drifting into a semi-lethargic state. She is losing this fight.

With the little strength she still possesses, Luci scrambles to position her back against the door. She snatches the handle behind her and pushes off the seat with her tennis shoes to gain leverage to open the door.

Luci rejects that this is how she dies—it can't be. She pushes her back against the door for a final time.

It is not enough. Her world goes black.

TWO

"THERE SHE IS," THE MAN with sparkling blue eyes says. "My name is Daniel."

Luci struggles to keep her eyelids open. She wants to ask why the small room they're in is shaking from side to side, but there's something covering her nose and mouth. She tries to remove it but can't raise her hand to her face.

"Blue-eyes" must see her panicked expression; he leans in closer. His speaking is over-enunciated. "You were in a car accident and went into the lake . . . but you're okay now."

Equally frightening, Luci discovers that she can't turn her head to the source of the other voices in the small space, nor can she determine the source of the electronic chirps and beeps.

Daniel "blue-eyes" is smiling at her, but it's not a true smile. It's too big to be real. "We performed CPR and stitched up a nasty laceration on your leg. You're riding in an ambulance now to the hospital. We just want to do a little checkup there to make sure that everything's good." The smile expands.

One of the other voices mentions something about blood pressure. Another calls out a dosage of *Zosyn*.

Luci tries to ask "blue-eyes" about her parents, but she's too sleepy to form the sounds.

So sleepy . . . so slee—

THREE

LUCI'S THROAT IS AS RAW as if she has gargled thumb-tacks, making breathing painful. Opening her eyes requires surprising effort. She anticipates seeing Daniel "blue-eyes" hovering over her, but instead, an antiseptic white ceiling slowly comes into focus, revealing that she's no longer in transport. The plastic tube in her nose partially obstructs her view. When she attempts to reach for it to pull it out, she discovers the quilted restraints by her side won't budge. *"Why am I still tied up?"*

Claustrophobic panic sets in as she realizes she can't move her neck or body. Tears stream down her face as she calls out, "Help me . . . someone please . . . I can't move." The pressure on her bruised ribs makes her instantly regret trying to shout, and she lets out a pitiful moan.

"Ah, good. You're awake," a gravel-worn voice responds from an unseen corner of the room. "My name is Ms. Schofield."

The cervical collar preventing Luci from turning her neck blocks her peripheral view. She runs her tongue over her swollen lip. "What is all this stuff . . . all these tubes?"

"Hooked up to an I.V. machine—for antibiotics is my guess," Schofield answers. "You have a pretty serious cut along the length of your leg."

Luci startles at the unexpected sound of wooden chair legs barking as they're scraped across the floor toward her. When the chair skids to a stop, Schofield's leathery face comes into view, the eyes like tiny dark marbles. "Hello, sweetie."

She disappears for an instant as she bends down and then returns. Looking at a clipboard, she smacks contemplatively. A pointy tongue pushes a piece of hard candy from one side of her mouth to the other and back again. "It says your name is Luci Ann Gaudiano. Is that right?"

"It's pronounced *Loo-chi,* not *Lucy.*"

Schofield makes a note with a Bic pen, mumbling to herself. Her overdone lipstick and makeup scheme makes her look like one of those women during the French revolution she's studied in history class.

"Why . . . why am I here? Where are my parents?" Luci has never felt so claustrophobic and vulnerable in all her short life.

The marbles look up from writing. "Standard stuff. They just want to observe you for a bit is all, and, like I said, get antibiotics fighting anything in that lake water you swallowed or that may have gotten into that cut."

"Where are my parents? I need to be with my family!" Her bruised chest punishes her again for this outburst.

"Doctors are just waiting for the CT scan to come back." The candy shifts to the opposite cheek. "Shouldn't be too much longer. You've been out of it for a while."

"I . . . I want my family," Luci croaks.

A weird smile forms on Schofield's face, revealing tiny teeth. They're not baby teeth, but they're not quite full grown either. "Oh, my dear Luci, it says there is no outside family. You belong to us now."

"What do you mean . . . belong to *who?*" Luci scoffs in panic, pulling hard against the foam restraints binding her wrists and forearms. "Where's my mother and father?" She ignores the ache in her chest in order to shout, "I want them!"

"Your parents are dead."

PORT I

(Part I)

<u>ONE</u>

ҺU TERITѲRI UV KOLѲRODѲ

3 MⱠLƵ NѲҺƗST UV ѲRѲ SITI

MΔ 22, 1863

⊖

PRƗ-ҺⱠ NѲ KѲWU

SECURITY MINISTER POL CAVAZOS WIPES at beads of sweat racing down his plump face. He tries to convince himself that everything will be okay once the stagecoach makes it to Denver City. There's nothing of any importance in this obscure interval juncture, making it the perfect point in the past to hide the device he's stolen; nothing here but dirt and a noticeable lack of dentistry among everyone that he's encountered since his arrival thirty-two and a half hours ago.

The dusty ground quakes beneath twenty-four horse hooves as the carriage bumps along. His meaty hand clings to the overhead leather handhold to steady himself. The air is stiflingly hot; it must be over a hundred degrees inside the musky compartment, but he doesn't dare pull the burlap curtains back inviting in more dust.

Not prone to doing his own "field work," he recounts he was forty-six the last time he took a leap skip to another time interval that was active, over nine years ago. The only redeeming quality of this irksome journey is that it could be the turning point in the struggle against his adversaries, *L'inversione*. Though uncertain of what he's snatched from them, he knows it must be important, and *he* has it now, not those insane anarchists.

Cavazos is the rickety charter's sole passenger, but he feels more of a prisoner as the Concord coach unmercifully bounces all 443 pounds of him around. Despite this abuse, he pounds the ceiling of the cab with an open palm. He shouts above the noise for the Pinkerton men to go faster. Though the reinsman doesn't reply directly, there's a sharp crack of the leather ribbon followed by the whinny of one of the horses outside.

Cavazos glances over at the dark steamer chest opposite him, the sheer weight of it keeping it solidly in place. He wonders about the function of the mechanism inside for the thousandth time, tempted to pop the brass latches open again for another look.

From behind, there's the sound of rapid galloping out of synch with the team pulling the coach. He swallows hard and removes his pristine cowboy hat, risking a peek out the left side window—bandits! Two riders on the left and a third advancing on the right give the coach a wide berth to avoid being swept up into the wake of its dust plume.

The explosive crack of a rifle from the Pinkerton positioned directly above Cavazos's head startles him. He's impressed that the gunman managed to move from the front to atop the coach with all the bouncing around the vehicle is doing. The masked trio is indifferent to the warning shot. The rider on the right thrashes the horse's reigns and hastens its charge.

Cavazos dives back into the cab, his heart pounding wildly. Another shot erupts from overhead—this one's not a warning. At least Cavazos is getting what he's paid for with the two Pinkertons. He gnaws at the knuckle of his index finger. Preparing for the worst, Cavazos yanks the wallet from his jacket pocket and shoves a wad of bills into his boot. An instant later, realizing his folly, he inserts a small portion back into the billfold so the thieves won't suspect anything's missing. Hopefully, the coachmen can subdue the bandits, but Cavazos can't take the chance of being stranded in this era without currency.

A third report of the Pinkerton's rifle cuts through the chaos. Still bumping around in the coach, Cavazos glances at the steamer chest. How will he explain that its contents can't possibly have any value to the thieves of this period? He gives into the urge to peek out the window on the right side. The horse and rider close in.

The horseman produces a rod-like object from a side holster longer than a rifle of the period. Cavazos instantly recognizes the familiar sight of a churka blaster. His heart sinks, and he swallows hard as the masked man extends it in his direction. As security minister, Cavazos knows the weapon's capabilities; he ordered the design specifications himself. He's paralyzed with fear, unable to retreat into the safety of the cab. His mind races, trying to figure out how they found him here. He'd taken so many precautions.

The rider steadies the churka, aiming it at the rifleman. He fires an uninterrupted blast of concentrated energy. The heated blue glow lasts for a full two seconds before the slain Pinkerton topples from the roof of the coach.

The shooter narrowly misses trampling the dead man with his steed. Cavazos shoves away from the ledge of the window and falls prostrate on the floor of the coach. Judging by the chaotic manner that the coach is weaving, the stage driver knows something bad has happened to his partner. This is confirmed when the driver yells out the name of the slain defender.

The unmistakable aroma of sulfur from another churka blast fills Cavazos's nostrils. There's a bump. It lifts and slams the coach back down as wagon wheels tumble over the dead driver. Something's happening under the carriage. There's a rumble beneath him like a great sword being unsheathed from a scabbard. The wooden reaches detach and slide away from the rear axles as the stagecoach begins to slow. The stomps and whinnies of the team grow more distant as the horses flee in fear.

Without warning, Cavazos's world turns sideways as the driverless carrier plows into an embankment. After a brief period of weightlessness, what's left crashes down on its side.

White spots explode in his vision. Something is wrong with his arm . . . something bad. He hollers out in pain, certain that the limb is broken. He won't find a heal kit in this interval. Everything slows, contrasting the relentless pounding of his heart. A shaft of sunlight pours in from overhead as dust motes swim wildly, circling in the beam. Moments before, it was the left window. Now, with the coach on its side and the burlap curtain gone, the opening acts more as a sunroof. The spinning of a squeaking wagon wheel eventually slows to a halt.

TWO

April 9, 2032
Baltimore, Maryland
[39.2903848/76.6121893/4.603.391.857/2374:36:22]

BΛLTIMOR-MƎRRILAND

ΛPRIL 9, 2032

⊖

PRƐ-Hɫ NꞫ KѠWU

Luci Gaudiano's lecture concluded nearly an hour ago. Even so, there's still a half dozen or so well-dressed stragglers milling about under the outside awning of the Baltimore theater. They exchange stories and jokes, not recognizing the thirty-something five-foot-three brunette in a grey sweatshirt shuffling by as their evening's speaker. Luci pauses to remove a Cubs baseball cap from one of her two overstuffed gym bags and secures the hat firmly on her head. The rain dwindles to a trickle as the marque lights reflect in shimmering puddles on the sidewalk.

There's a limo parked at the curb. A tall, burly man emerges from the front right side of the vehicle. "Dr. Gaudiano?"

She offers a faint nod and shushes the man before the small cluster of people behind her take notice of them. Across the street, a lanky silhouette of a man ducks slowly backward into the shadows of an alley.

The driver reaches for the cumbersome bags, but Luci pulls back, asking, "What happened to the other driver who brought me here from the airport?"

"Uh . . . mechanical failure. The vehicle was towed away from here while your talk was going on." He pops the trunk. For the second time, his attempt to help with the bags is refused.

The small but strong woman heaves them into the cavernous trunk with a thud and slams it closed. She wipes the drops of water from the trunk onto her faded jeans and extends a handshake. "I'm Luci. No need for the formal *Doctor Gaudiano* stuff."

The husky seven-foot man glances down at her hand as a bewildered expression forms on his doughy white face. "My name is Royse . . . Royse Timmons." He adds the obvious, "I'm your driver tonight." Absently tugging at a small ruby rectangle on his earlobe, he chides, "I thought I was going to have to go in there and find you."

Luci considers the comment, and while it's awful customer service bordering on rudeness, she lets it go because as of this moment, she is officially on vacation. She offers a non-threatening shrug. "What's the rush? The car rental place you're driving me to is less than twenty minutes from here."

Royse motions to the side of the limo. "There's someone who's eager to meet you."

The big man pulls the door open, and Luci is shocked to see that another passenger already seated inside. A figure wearing a bright orange rain slicker leans forward into the glow of the overhead dome light. His wrinkled but muscular hand pulls back the hooded cowl, revealing an older man somewhere in his late fifties or sixties. The weathered face, prominent nose, and dark olive skin lead her to guess the man's nationality is of Middle Eastern descent. "Hello, Dr. Gaudiano. My name is Enos Macer, and I've come from a long way to meet with you this evening." He chuckles slightly. "Yes, farther away than you can possibly imagine."

Luci instinctively takes a step back, bumping into Royse, who's already closed the gap behind her. "Dr. Gaudiano, please," Royse says, gesturing for her to take the seat opposite the older man.

Invitingly patting the seat with his palm, Macer says, "We haven't much time and must be on our way."

"Not much time for what?" Luci asks, tensing up at the unexpectedness of the situation.

The smile melts from the old man's face. "We need your help in saving what's left of the world."

THREE

March 3, 843 BC
Naşibina, Turkey
[37.0696439/41.213997/4.603.388.8223/3615:11:51]

NΛΛBƎNU-TꓱRKꓱ

MΛℂ 3, 843 BC

⊖

PRꓱ-H± NΩ KΩWU

THE SOUND OF THE TEENAGE girl's sandals slapping against calloused heels with her every step echoes throughout the spacious chamber. She follows a crooked path formed by stumpy candles, and their tiny flames flicker and dance as she skirts by them. She cautiously moves across the intricate pattern of the mosaic tile so as not to startle the figure staring out the open window at the other end.

The lone silhouette draped in a long, ornate cloak as dark as ink clicks on a handheld translation device. "So . . . the message from Malom?"

The girl halts some twenty feet or so from the window, purposefully leaving a suitable distance between her and her mysterious employer. The smell of cooked meat rises from the street market three stories below. "Yes, Cyphor," she answers, pausing to remember the details of the transmission. "The exact words are, 'He's taken back the final part of the ESTA, and you should meet him at the interval he put your . . .'" Her mind goes blank, and she bites her bottom lip trying to remember the name of the odd machine.

Her eyes shift from Gicul's back to the chamber's foreign and most audacious fixture. Running half the length of the right-side wall is the twenty-foot-long and four-and-a-half-foot-high tube. A few days ago, Gicul informed her that the sleek, iridescent outer shell was made from a strange material called "*plastic*," an otherworldly substance smoother to the touch than sanded wood treated with oil. The front section contains two tilted back-to-back seats reclining at extreme angles.

"Longchair," Gicul finishes the girl's statement, finally turning to face her.

"Yes, the *longchair*," she says in agreement, turning to look at Gicul's feet peeking from beneath the floor length garment. "The longchair *coordinates*." She struggles to form the unfamiliar word in her mouth.

Gicul doesn't respond.

After a brief silence, the girl chances a question of her own. "You'll be leaving then?"

"Yes. The moment you played Malom's message, notices went out alerting my enemies as to the time period interval that I'm in." Gicul pauses. "You must never return to this building, and, for your sake, never mention your visits here over the last two weeks to anyone." Gicul advances to the longchair and runs a hand across the transparent plastic covering that serves as a type of cockpit roof to the seats. "Even when you're old and have grandbabies bouncing on your knee, you must tell no one of me and that I was here . . . *never*. It's for your own safety and protection."

"Yes, Cyphor. I will tell no one."

"Your payment's in the bag on the entry table by the door."

FOUR

April 9, 2032
Baltimore, Maryland
[39.2903848/76.6121893/4.603.391.857/2374:39:41]

BALTIMOR-MƵRRILAND

ΔPRIL 9, 2032

⊖

PRƐ-Hɪ NꞼ KꙨWU

"Please, Dr. Gaudiano," Macer says, urging her to enter the limousine. "We'll talk on the way to your transport kiosk."

Luci turns, looking for the small cluster of lecture attendees under the awning, but Royse's big frame blocks her view. "The car rental place?"

Thunder rumbles across the night sky.

Royse gently nudges her. "It's about to rain again. You should get inside."

She warily complies and takes her seat inside. "Mr. Macer, do I know you?"

"By proxy. I'm the sponsor of tonight's lecture." As he nods to Royse to close the door, Luci notices the same type of ruby rectangle fixed onto his ear as the driver. "I arranged for you to be here over two years ago when I was visiting 2030 Luxembourg. Although there wasn't enough time to travel to this country to find you, I had plenty of time to pay Vincent DuPont a sizable donation to coordinate tonight's event."

Luci dismisses the odd statement, avoiding the obvious question of why it taken him two years to make it from Europe to the states. She shifts in her seat, crossing her arms, self-conscious about her appearance. She would have never changed into her casual clothes if she'd known about this rendezvous.

"Dr. Gaudiano, I work for an organization that requires your expertise, and we need you for a special project."

"What expertise?"

In the dim interior light of the car, Macer's eyebrows rise like two bushy caterpillars standing up from the table. "Your mathematical gift with codes and patterns, of course. Trust me when I say that we know a lot about you . . . everything, in fact. Ph.D. from the Department of Mathematics at Stanford, a resident of the city of Chicago, thirty-three years of age, parents died in an automotive accident when you were twelve, and you're unmarried."

Tiny hairs on the back of Luci's neck come to attention as she wonders why a stranger would have this level of detailed information about her.

Royse gets behind the wheel and calls to the back of the limo, "Sir, Shar says we have thirty-four minutes."

"What's a Shar?" Luci asks, studying Macer for anything that would tip her off to his involvement as a CIA or FBI agent.

Macer ignores her, choosing instead to reply over his shoulder to Royse, "Well, then, I suggest we make haste, Mr. Timmons." He turns his attention back to Luci. "I also know that the reason you requested being driven to the car rental kiosk instead of to the airport for a flight home is that you're not going back to Chicago, at least not for a couple of weeks."

Luci gnaws at her bottom lip as she wonders why this guy is being so theatrical. "Yeah, so?"

Outlines of buildings and lights zoom by through the window as the vehicle picks up speed. "You're headed just a little south of a place called Atlantic City to a small, sleepy town, maybe a population of ten thousand or so."

A knot forms in the pit of her stomach. She presents her best poker face, but everything inside tells her that something's off about this. She can't put her finger on it, but Macer doesn't seem to be FBI or CIA. Figuring he already knows the details, she makes a calculated bluff in hopes of masking the nervousness creeping up her spine. "Yeah, that's right. It's my college roommate's beach house in Ventnor City. How—or better said, *why*—do you know all of this?" She removes the baseball cap and tries her best to casually massage her scalp, but a tiny bead of sweat forms on her top lip.

He smiles, and laugh lines spring from the corner of his eyes and mouth as the creases on his forehead grow more defined. "It's my business to know things . . . for the sake of the project, of course."

"The project that you *still* haven't told me about." Her heart rate is climbing. She can't hold it in any longer. "Do you work for the government? Is that what this is?"

In the flash of signal lights, she catches those eyebrows rise again. "Yes, you could say that . . . but it's not for the government in the way that you know it."

This guessing game is annoying. What's going on here? Luci's tired and spent; she's just given a lecture to fifteen hundred people and isn't in the mood for some unorthodox interview, regardless of who this man represents. "Look, Mr. Macer, I'm getting a little bit freaked out here by all the research that you've done on me. I don't mean to be rude or ungrateful, and I appreciate whatever part you had in hosting tonight's event, but now isn't the best time for whatever you're offering. Don't get me wrong . . . kudos to your investigators who found out all that stuff about me, but I'm renting a car and heading to the beach house for some much-needed R & R."

She doesn't want to blow this if the potential for real grant money is a possibility, so after a long sigh, she regroups. "I'll be back in my office Thursday the 22nd. Leave a message or send an email, and I'll be in touch. Again, I don't mean to be rude or dismissive here, but it's just that it's been an odd month, and

I desperately need some time to reset." Her mind meanders to the unwelcome face of Michael, her fiancé. She mentally corrects herself—recently-made *ex-fiancé*.

The increased speed of the limo snaps her back to reality. "Hey why is he driving so fast?" she asks, looking out the darkened window. "Where are we going?"

"You'll see," Macer says in such a cryptic manner that it makes her queasy.

The noticeable absence of billboards indicates that they've detoured off the route to the airport, and something's definitely wrong here. Luci nervously bites the inside of her cheek as a form of self-punishment. In this day of roadways crammed with self-driving vehicles, she should've known someone dispatching a limo service for her was off. "I demand that you tell me where he's taking us, Mr. Macer." Every report she's ever heard of women being abducted flashes in her mind. "What's going on here?" She swallows hard while pressing the Slim-Phone on her wrist to activate a call to 911.

"I'm afraid your device has been neutralized," Macer says, casually pointing at her wrist. "We didn't want any . . . interruptions."

An unsettling panic washes over her as she mashes the buttons of the wristband more forcibly.

He's right—the phone is dead.

Luci's mind races; her pepper spray is in her backpack in the trunk with no way to get to it. She chastises herself for being so stupid. No matter how tired she was, she should've never let her guard down while traveling in another city.

Macer grabs the car's handhold to brace himself as the speeding vehicle unevenly sways from side to side. "Dr. Gaudiano, if you'll just—"

He stops short as Luci wrestles with the door handle.

"Let me out of this car!"

Her heart beats wildly. She's got to get out of here. She tries to visualize how she'll drop and roll from the speeding car.

Macer's voice is calm and even. "We mean you no harm."

A marble-sized knot forms in her throat. She tries to push it down with a gulp of thick air. "What . . . what are you going to do to me?" she demands through gritted teeth. She wonders if she could gouge out his eyes with her fingernails but dismisses the idea, having no solid plan beyond that.

"Dr. Gaudiano, I *promise* that you are in no danger here from Royse and me. I just want to have a brief chat with you. I have a proposition."

She tries for the handle on the opposite door, but it doesn't budge either. The opening behind Macer into the driver's area of the limo is too tiny for even her small frame to squeeze through. She lunges to scratch at his face and eyes if she can get to them. Macer snatches her wrists mid-way as if he's anticipated the attack. Luci screams in frustration as he squeezes her wrists tightly. His strength surprises her.

"Sir, are you okay back there?" Royse asks, stealing a quick glimpse over his shoulder before shifting his attention back to the road.

Macer stares into her eyes. "Yes, Royse. We're doing fine."

It's unnerving to her that his response is so even and without the slightest bit of effort. He pumps his grip on her as he asks in a soft but deliberate voice, "Are you quite done with all of this?"

She inhales sharply and bites her lip while surrendering a defeated nod. How could she have been so stupid? No one sends a car with a driver in this day and age. The image of the pepper spray in her bag in the trunk flashes across her mind again, but how can she get to it?

Luci massages the circulation back into her wrists as she rattles off a series of random numbers. She mumbles to herself as if invoking a mathematical mantra of sorts.

Macer is stunned to silence, studying her.

She quietly multiplies, subtracts, squares, and divides the figures aloud until enough of the fear is shoved to the back of her brain for her to form an escape plan. She plays along. When they reach their destination, she'll have more options. She'll demand her bag, saying she needs it for feminine hygiene reasons. When she gets it, she'll blast the old man in the face with the spray and kick him in the crotch. When the bigger man moves to help him, she'll run. She'll humor this Mr. Macer, whoever he is. She'll play along and ask questions until the precise moment presents itself to strike. She inhales a deep breath to steady herself. Attempting to keep her voice from quivering, she says, "So, since I'm obviously stuck in here, let's discuss your project or offer . . . or whatever it is."

Hard rain pummels the roof of the limousine, forcing Macer to speak more loudly. "Dr. Gaudiano, as unbelievable as this may sound, we really do need your help in saving the world. I'm not exaggerating, I assure you."

An exasperated breath escapes from her lungs. If she'd been drinking something, she would've involuntarily spewed it onto Macer's orange rain gear. "Yeah, right," she says, the words filled to the brim with sarcasm. "You must be out of your mind. I thought you were speaking metaphorically when you said that before. I had no idea that you were being serious." So much for playing along, she thinks.

He leans in, and as he does, the plastic of his rain slicker squeaks a little. "I am completely serious."

The ruby rectangle on his ear catches the light. This invokes the unsettling thought that he and Royse may be members of some cult.

"You have an amazing gift for solving difficult number sequences," Macer says in an even louder voice to compete with the noise of the car barreling down the highway and the rain relentlessly striking the roof.

"Number sequences, huh? Like a code breaker, Alan Turing-type stuff?"

He shifts on the seat. "Not exactly code breaking, but dealing with sophisticated formulas that I guess could sort of be like codes."

There's no pause from Luci. "You got the wrong girl, pal. Breaking codes isn't what I do." She reminds herself that this is the opposite of what she should be doing. She needs to play along and act like she'll do whatever they want.

His eyebrows rise as he rebukes her, "Yes, well . . . Royse here is not really an automobile driver, but he's driving, isn't he?" Before she can respond, he says, "You're good with patterns—unparalleled to anyone in your field, in fact. That's what we need. *You're* what we need."

"Yeah, okay . . . sorry," Luci responds, trying to appear as sincere as she can. "Please continue." She contemplates how the hard rain may give her an advantage when it comes time for her to make a break for it. As best as she can determine from the architecture outside, they're on the outskirts of the city entering the warehouse district.

Macer smiles, and the crow's feet around his eyes scrunch up. "Dr. Gaudiano . . . Luci, I need you to pause and suspend the analytical part of that fantastic brain of yours for a minute. What I'm about to relay to you will seem impossible to your rational mind at first, but if you give me a chance, you'll discover it's all true, every bit of it. And in a few minutes, I can prove it."

She crosses her arms, tucking her tightly balled-up fists into her pits. "Em . . . okay. This code that you want me to crack, what's it do? Bank vault system, security codes, nuclear warheads, what? And how sophisticated is it?"

Macer grips his chin to stifle a genuine chuckle. "Oh, nothing like that."

As the vehicle begins to slow, he pinches the rectangle on his ear. "Pardon me a second, please."

As he speaks and his intonation changes, Luci realizes it's a communication device. "Shar," he begins, "how much time do we have left?" He pauses briefly. Luci doesn't hear a reply but knows there is one by Macer's nodding head in response. "I agree, we're striving for an amiable solution. That's desired, but contingencies ought to be in place should the situation call for it."

Her stomach clenches as she catches him shift his eyes from her as he utters the word "*contingencies*." Exploiting the break in eye contact, she tries her wrist phone again, but it's still dead.

He looks back in her direction. "And Shar, I'd like you to get the validation item after all." Macer massages his forehead with the tips of his fingers. "And keep a tight clock. We don't want to be trapped here for the next few weeks."

When he disengages the conversation, Luci asks, "What's a *validation item,* and what did you mean about getting trapped?"

He holds a hand up. "Just a precaution, a little *bonus,* if you will. But we'll get to that." He looks over his shoulder through the opening to Royse. "I'd like a moment before we go in, okay?"

Royse doesn't look back. "I'll just pull up near the main entrance of the warehouse. We should arrive there in about two and a half minutes."

"That'll be adequate."

He shifts his gaze back to Luci. "There's no easy way to begin what I'm about to tell you, so I'll just dive in."

Her stomach clenches as the sky rumbles again.

Macer interlocks his fingers and begins. "DPM—*drift pattern mathematics.* The papers won't publish until 2041, and the first use of DPM isn't deployed until twenty-two years after that in 2063."

"I've never heard of drift pattern mathematics," Luci says, studying Macer's face to determine if he's a liar or just plain insane.

"Yes, I know," Macer says, nodding. "No one knows of it . . . *yet.*"

"What does it do? What's the theorem?" Something inside her perks up. She attempts to suppress this obscene thrill, but at the same time, she's famished to know something new, even if it's a theory from a suspicious source.

"I'll get to that in a moment. Imagine if, halfway through the twenty-first century, a breakthrough technology was developed that harnesses DPM. Hundreds of self-regulating machines deployed into the stratosphere, what you would regard today as weather satellites. These systems are able to *skip* or leap forward in time up to seventy-two hours and transmit back precipitation events." He pauses allowing the words to sink in.

Luci grips the ball cap in her lap as she processes the concept of something jumping forward in time by seventy-two hours.

Macer continues, "Consider if, at first, it was used for luxury purposes. Imagine if you planned an outdoor activity like the one with the sticks and the holes in the dirt ... uh ..."

Her head is still swimming from the previous statement about the seventy-two hours thing, but she manages an answer. "*Golf.* You mean golf?"

He snaps his fingers. "Yes, that's it, the golf. If one knew the exact time the rain would begin and end, you would plan your respite around it. Within a few years of the release of this technology, foretelling meteorological occurrences goes mainstream. People subscribe to services—"

Mesmerized by the concept, Luci butts in, "The ability to know future weather would change some many industries: agriculture, airlines, resorts ..."

Macer smiles. "The science at the time was still in its infancy, but it didn't remain confined to weather reports for very long. Where we come from, people moving through intervals are common weekly and sometimes daily occurrences."

"Time travelers?" Luci blurts out as her rational mind slams on the brakes.

He nods. "Yes. We call them *sitters* because of the transport compartment, but time travelers. Anyway, crews of men and women from your future routinely leap skip into the past and back to your future."

"Seriously? You're talking about traveling through time?" She scoffs, glancing at the back of Royse's head, trying to determine if he's laughing in the front.

Macer continues as deadpan as can be, "That is precisely what I'm talking about. DPM. Drift pattern mathematics is the foundational theorem that time travel is built on."

A burst of genuine laughter overtakes her, and it takes a moment to recover. "Oh, you guys are good," she says, barely able to breathe. Some of the tension drains from her body as she scans the interior of the limo. "Is this being filmed? Is this for SYFY.net or some TruTV streaming channel?"

Macer doesn't break from character. Luci is impressed by his commitment to the gag. She leans over and gives him a playful punch on the arm, but his stoic expression doesn't waiver.

"Sir," Royse says as the car slows to a stop, "we're here. Shar reports that we have about twenty-five minutes."

"What happens in twenty-five minutes?" Luci asks, returning the ball cap snuggly to her head. "What's inside that warehouse, a surprise party or something? Is Tim behind all of this?"

"The four of us—me, you, Royse, and Shar—have to be out of here," Macer says, ignoring the second question. "We must return to our time in your future."

"So you're from the future? What year?" That they're continuing the farce mildly irritates Luci. When Macer hesitates to answer, she says, "Hey, you can give up the make-believe, alright? If you're not going to take me to a car rental, fix my phone so I may call an auto-drive cab to there. It's been a long night, and I have a three-hour ride before me."

A disturbing thought pops into her brain. What if her notion that this is all a gag is her mind constructing a self-coping mechanism? She's intelligent enough to know she's capable of such a thing, because if all of this *was* real, it'd be too much to bear.

Macer sighs. "I realize that all of this is probably overwhelming, but as someone who's a pioneer in the field of mathematics, there's something you should know. Einstein got it wrong, at least in part."

"Come on, the jig is up," Luci says, trying to ignore the queasiness returning to her stomach. "It's over. I'm on to the prank or whatever this is."

Macer persists. "Unlike the fictional stories of H.G. Wells and his contemporaries regarding leap skips—or *time travel*, if you will—there are limitations to where and when one may go. The universe has seemingly randomly pre-determined points in time one may travel to. We call these intervals." He rubs at his forehead again. "Think of an elevator shaft in one of your high-rise twenty-story buildings. The elevator rider can exit at any of the twenty stops, but they can only get off at those openings. He or she wouldn't physically be able to leave the compartment halfway between floors. The exit options are pre-determined before the rider ever steps into the box. Now imagine a building that extends forever in both directions. That's what a leap skip is like, extending forever into the past and future."

Though she knows it's preposterous, the concept of time travel limitations is intriguing. "So, one couldn't go back in time to see Lincoln deliver the Gettysburg Address or the Titanic leave port or stop Hitler's rise to power?"

"Precisely—unless, of course, there's already a skip point juncture there." Before she can ask, he informs her, "And there's not."

Her brow furrows as she processes the data. "And the warehouse here is one of these random skip hole things or something?"

"We use the term *interval juncture*, but yes, it's an opening for a very brief period of time. This one was only open for 134 minutes and will close in—"

"In approximately twenty-three minutes," Royse interjects from the front.

Macer closes his eyes to rub them. "I funded the lecture so we'd know exactly where and when to find you and have time enough to return here. We've gone to tremendous lengths to bring you back with us."

"So the countdown is how long we have left before, what, it seals up for good?"

"Yes, that's right. There's another one that will open in a couple of weeks, but it's halfway around the world from where we are now," Macer says. "I'd prefer that you come willingly, but—"

Luci cuts him off. "Willingly? You can't expect that. You kidnapped me!" She adds the qualifier, "Again, provided that any of this is real."

"Oh, this is real—as real as it gets, I assure you." The annoyance at continually being cut off shows on Macer's face. "And kidnapping would imply that there's a ransom. There's not. I want to appeal to your humanity, Dr. Gaudiano. The fate of millions depends on your coming back to help us. Remember how I described a time corridor? What I didn't tell you is that it's being destroyed. To use the elevator analogy again, there are *'floors'* that we used to be able to get off on that are gone to us now—obliterated as if they never existed."

Luci ponders the data she has so far and moves to debunk it. She must debunk it and prove to herself this isn't real. The gatekeeper of logic within her demands that it's impossible. Her question comes out slowly. "So, if what you say is true—and that's a big *if*—what do you need me for? I don't get it. This drift pattern thing is already published in your future time. I mean, it's out there for everyone, right? So for me, in my time, at this very moment I . . . we can go to the library and look up Johannes Kepler's laws of planetary motion. I don't have to go visit him in his time interval or whatever you call it." She lifts the wrist with the computer band on it. "Even, better, I can Google it right here. You have the internet in the future, right?"

Macer's answer comes out as an obligatory mumble, "Yes, we have a knowledge repository similar to the ARPANET of this interval."

"Then why don't you look it up and have your future computers bang out the math and be done with it?" With a sarcastic smugness, she adds, "Royse didn't need to consult with Henry Ford to drive us here tonight. Why do you need a mathematician from your so-called past to solve the broken time doors thing for you if you already have the equations somewhere?"

His expression sours. "It's a little more complicated than that. Something's wrong and what we have isn't enough anymore. The math we have rounds the numbers up or down.

That's the way the formula was constructed. And while it's worked up until now, something's changed and the exact non-rounded numbers are required."

This revelation excites her because it's something that's relatable to her field. "You're talking about Goldbach's Conjecture!"

"I don't know what that is," Macer admits, "but you should come with us to see if you're right. We'll bring you back once you're done. We must bring you back for this to work."

She goes on to explain as if she's sixteen again and answering a question in the Caribou Mathematics Contest. "Eighteenth-century Christian Goldbach. The issue is that the result of rounding the following value up to the next integer cannot be determined: 10–n, where n is the first even number greater than 4, which is not the sum of two primes, or 0 if there is no such number, right?"

"I honestly have no idea what that means, but the fundamentals of DPM in layman's terms is like if you lean against a lamppost on the corner of Main Street on a Tuesday morning at 8:00 AM and then return there twenty-four hours later, you're not in the same spot in the universe. Though you may be at the same geographical spot on the Earth and the lamppost is relatively the same, the planet is in a different spot than it was 80,000 seconds ago."

"Eighty-six thousand four hundred," Luci offers.

"What?"

"It would be Eighty-six thousand four hundred seconds in a twenty-four-hour period," she answers.

Macer continues with an acknowledging nod, "Right. So anyway, the Earth is rotating, moving around the sun, but the sun and its planets are also spiraling through the galaxy, and galaxies spin around the universe. Everything is in a constant state of flux, hurtling through space. One also has to consider continental drift. Due to the shift of the tectonic plates, the landmasses are in a constant state of flux too, and they're not moving at the same rate of speed. It may not seem like much, but what was formerly Europe was in a different place two hundred years ago from where it was eight hundred years ago. All of these are factors in the drift pattern."

Luci rubs the nape of her neck. "So it's a way to pinpoint the precise location of the lamppost on Main Street today and where it was a month ago and where it will be hurling through space a decade from now."

"That's only one aspect of it, but there's a lot more to it." He pauses before adding, "But fundamentally, that's one of the major parts of it that we need you to solve. Until recently, the numbers could be rounded up or down within a hundred thousandth of a second, but not anymore. The metaphorical corner where the street lamp was has been obliterated."

"Destroyed by who and why?" Luci asks.

He thinks on this, finally offering more of a proverb than an actual answer. "War finds every generation. Only the tools of our destruction change."

He utters the words with such contempt that they hang on the air like frost.

Finally, Luci says, "What you propose sounds nearly impossible. Even *if* the drift pattern was real, what makes you believe that I can crack something like that anyway?"

There's a pause as something odd happens. The older man turns to Royse before answering as if to gain confirmation from the subordinate. Royse gives a slight shrug, and Macer looks back to Luci. "Again, this is very real, and I know that you *can* do it and *will* do it because you wrote the drift pattern a long time ago . . . or better said, you *will* develop it in your future nine years from now."

Unexpectedly, he grabs the door handle and shoves it open. He looks back in at her as he pulls the hood of the raincoat over his head. "Come on. I wish to show you something."

FIVE

May 22, 1863: The Territory of Colorado
1 mile northeast of Oro City
[39.2508223/106.2925242/4.603.391.688/4828:21:17]

HJ TERITORI UV KOLORODO
1 MɪL NOHɪST UV ORO SITI

MΔ 22, 1863

⊖

PRɪ-Hɪ NO KOWU

CAVAZOS CONTEMPLATES PLAYING DEAD AND staying in the busted stagecoach, but then he remembers *who* and *what* he represents to the city. His blood boils at the audacity of these sanctimonious anarchists. The haze of dust inside the cab makes his eyes water as he tries to right himself in the sideways carriage. The effort results in blinding pain. After a few seconds, he winces, grits his teeth, and makes another attempt. Part resolve to punish the culprits and part sickening curiosity forces Cavazos to extend his head through the window, now positioned above him. He nurses the injured arm against his chest, keeping it as immobile as possible.

"Good afternoon, Councilman," a masculine voice behind him calls out, mocking his predicament. "Now, you wouldn't have any weapons in there, would you?"

More out of spite than courage, he turns to face the trio on horseback. "Who do you think you are? I'll have every one of you—"

"Just answer the question, sir. Do you have any weapons with you in there?" The tone is less friendly.

Cavazos steals a glance down inside the coach at the steamer trunk. As far as he knows, it's not a weapon. If the riders are only after him, he can abandon it and return later after this is sorted out. "No weapons . . . I have no weapons in here."

"Are you the only one in there? No cybos?"

Cavazos grits his teeth and thinks that if he'd been traveling with his cybo guards, these criminals would already be cooked from the inside out. "No, I'm alone in here. It's just me."

The trio's horses shift in place, the effect of unspent adrenaline. Still, the riders hold them in a tight formation. The female culprit of the three says something to the others but too softly for Cavazos to make out. He looks her over; she's too stocky for his tastes. He consoles himself that the flat-faced woman is probably a lesbian anyway. Streams of sweat trickle down his face, but he doesn't dare wipe it for fear that any movement may be mistaken for aggression, and each rider has a churka at their side.

After a tense silence, he calls out, "Hey, I'm hurt over here! I'm pretty sure my arm is broken." He scans their faces but can't get a read on what's happening, and that's alarming. "Did you bring a heal kit to this interval with you?" He hates to sound weak, especially in front of this trio of twisted nihilists, but the pain in his arm is intense, and pride is a luxury he's willing to suspend to end it.

The slender man in his mid-forties looks to the butch woman. She gestures to the ground, and she and the larger man dismount. As they soothe their horses, the man remaining on horseback says, "I'm Noah Beaumont, and these two are my colleagues from Relicus City." The woman takes calculated steps toward the stagecoach, fixing her churka on Cavazos. The big man and youngest of the three holsters his in a side catch of his animal leathers and approaches the coach more casually.

Beaumont points at him. "Jonn here is going to help you down, so don't try anything."

Cavazos acknowledges with a nod of the head. "Do you have a heal kit or not? I'll be more lenient on whichever the three of you gives me a kit." The offer invokes a shared chuckle from the trio, a sound that makes his stomach tighten into a knot. He blurts out, "What do you want?"

The question goes unanswered as Jonn scales the busted coach reaching for him. The woman continues moving like a predator, searching for an optimum angle with her churka. Jonn grabs Cavazos roughly by the shoulder, sending more white dots of pain across his vision. He gasps but refuses to give him the satisfaction of crying out. He grunts in a voice that only the man can hear, "Young man . . . *Jonn*, if you get me out of this, I'll see to it that you're rewarded. Fry these other two for me, and you'll never have to work another day in your life."

Jonn spins Cavazos around to face him. With a smug smile, he points at the severed lobe of his right ear. "I'm sorry, but I don't think so, sir."

The absence of a one-inch ruby stud piercing tightens the knot in Cavazos's stomach. "Where's . . . what did you do with your Viatorio?" he stammers.

Jonn ignores the question. "Let's get you down before the boss gets here."

"Huh, before . . . who's coming? Is it Cyphor Gicul, is he here?"

Without answering, Jonn deadlifts him up and out of the stagecoach opening. More pain shoots through Cavazos's body as he slumps to a sitting position against the upturned coach. He shouts to Beaumont, who is still on horseback, "Do you work for him . . . for Cyphor Gicul?"

Beaumont looks over at the woman, who appears to be the group's de facto leader, for a second time, then tucks his churka into the side catch holster with nonchalance and nudges his horse to advance. The animal slowly trots up to where Cavazos sits, and Beaumont guides it in a pacing motion before his captive. The unique equine scent of the beast distracts

Cavazos as he reflects on a time in the future when animals like this won't exist.

Jarring him back to reality, Beaumont says, "You know, my late father worked under you many years ago when you headed up the Ministry of Information." He clicks his tongue. "But that . . . that was a long time ago."

The mention of his position of importance emboldens him. Looking up at Beaumont, he commands, "Son, I demand that you answer my question! Do you know who Cyphor Gicul is or not?"

The ruby rectangle of the Viatorio is missing from his ear. Beaumont shrugs. "Can't say that I've ever met Gicul, but we *do* work for his same purpose, for *L'inversione.*"

The group's name makes Cavazos's jaw clench. "If you free me and help set a trap for Gicul, I won't order you to a Carcerium chamber or cybo reconditioning. I'll act as if this never happened. In fact, I'll make the three of you heroes and name a city holiday in your honor. No one has to know about any of this."

The woman answers for them, "That's a generous offer, but how exactly would you both keep us anonymous and at the same time name a day of honor after us? Sounds like some of those New Australia lies if you ask me."

Before Cavazos can respond, Beaumont jumps back in. "Thanks, but it's not up to me anyway."

"Then who's it up to?" Cavazos growls with no attempt to mask his frustration.

"Oh, he's on his way," the female of the group butts in. "He'll be glad to see you, though I suspect you may not be as happy to see him."

The sardonic way she delivers the line sends a chill down Cavazos's spine more intensely than the throbbing agony of his arm. He goes on the offensive. "You murdered those men I hired. They were residents of the interval. Furthermore, you killed them using non-interval tools. That's a violation of article six of the edict."

She speaks again. "Article six, huh? Yeah, well, while that *is* very unfortunate, some costs and certain actions are necessary to achieve our goals to set things right. But *you* shouldn't have involved those men. You put them at risk when you hired them, which I believe is also a violation."

Beaumont lifts his hat to wipe his brow and snugly returns it. "She's right, but then again, we've broken a lot of rules to get to you today." He points to his own severed earlobe.

"It's here!" Jonn shouts from within the coach. It's obvious to Cavazos that the best locks that money could buy from this interval were no match for whatever device Jonn used on it.

As if brought to life, Beaumont quickly dismounts from the horse to join his partner. The woman moves directly in front of where Cavazos sits, never lowering the churka.

With the Jonn and Beaumont occupied inside of what's left of the coach, Cavazos makes a desperate plea to her. "I beg you to let me out of here. You can have whatever's in the case. Just let me go. I'll give you anything."

She speaks for the first time where he can hear. "Yes, I bet you would. The problem is that we already have what we want now, so you have nothing left to bargain with." She takes a few steps forward, angling the churka dangerously at his heart. The barrel is only inches away. "The fact that you forced us to track you down and chase you through this forsaken interval just compounds our aggravation. We've been waiting for you to arrive here for nine and a half months and are none too happy about it. We've got four and a half days before the twin of the juncture you came through occurs, and it can't get here fast enough for me." She presses the end of the weapon against his arm, igniting a wave of anguish. "I say take a look around at this blue sky, Councilman Cavazos, because these are probably the clouds that you're going to die under."

Tears stream over his puffy cheeks. "Please, don't. It doesn't have to be this way. I'm sure that we can find a compromise. I could remain here . . . here in this interval. Just let me live."

To his astonishment, she takes a few steps away from him. He gnaws his bottom lip, wondering how he's convinced her. Her boots scrape across gravel as she takes more steps away from him, but the weapon remains fixed on his heart. She smiles a wicked smile. "Like the man said, it's not up to us. It's up to the one who's coming for you."

The way she gleefully says it chills him despite the Colorado heat. Who is their boss that's *coming for him,* and more importantly, how much will Cavazos have to offer to buy him off?

SIX

April 9, 2032
Baltimore, Maryland
[39.482315/77.069092/4.603.391.857/2374:54:08]

BΛLTIMOR-MƎRRILAND

ΔPRIL 9, 2032

⊖

PRƗ-Hɫ NΩ KⱯWU

ROYSE SHAKES WATER FROM THE large umbrella and leans it against the inside metal entrance door of the warehouse as Luci and Macer continue walking through the cavernous area. The rain sounds like applause, and Luci flashes back to the start of her lecture in the theater a few hours ago. The analytical regions of her brain run through the events of how she arrived in this defenseless situation. She chastises herself again for not carrying the pepper spray that her fiancé Michael had given to her. Macer refused when she asked to get her bag from the trunk, saying that she wouldn't need it where they were going. She neglected to form a contingency for this response and was forced to go along with it. She assures herself that whatever is really going on here, she'll be able to debunk it soon enough and be on her way. She simply needs more facts to process.

Other than the rain striking the roof, the only sound is their footsteps echoing off the dusty concrete floor up to a high ceiling that disappears into the darkness above. The combined smell of petroleum, grease, rust, and mildew is a strong indicator that whatever this place was originally used for, it's been out of service for a while. At the other end of the deserted space hangs a naked lightbulb. It dangles from a long extension cord double-wrapped around an overhead beam.

Below the light is a figure bent over a cheap folding table. A flickering glow from a device illuminates a woman's face. She looks up as they approach and regards Luci as if she's seen a ghost, but the woman had to know she was coming. The woman stammers a bit, her voice echoing throughout the area, "Sir, we have a little under twenty minutes."

The battered pressboard table she stands behind is like an island in a sea of nothingness. The lone item is a device that looks like a translucent computer tablet vertically balanced at a seventy-degree angle. As they reach the table, Macer asks the woman, "Did you get it?"

She peels her eyes away from Luci long enough to verify something on the device. "He's sent it, and it's nearly here, sir. Once it arrives, I'll queue it up and have it ready to activate in a few minutes." The woman is strikingly exotic in appearance. A no-nonsense short style of platinum white hair frames the girl's white porcelain face, petite nose, and mouth. Her eyes shine a brilliant emerald green. It's hardly a surprise that there's a rectangle ear stud peeking out from her sharply cut hair. All three of the strangers have one. Though her elven features make it hard to tell, Luci guesses she's in her mid-twenties. If Luci didn't know better, she'd think she was looking at a human-sized version of an albino Tinker Bell, except for those mystical green eyes—that's definitely not an albino trait.

"Luci, I'd like to introduce you to someone," Macer says, motioning for her to come around from the table. "This is Luci Gaudiano. And Luci, this is my technical officer of sorts for today's leap skip, Shar Ryson."

Dumbfounded by the woman's appearance, Luci forgets that the woman is complicit in whatever's going on here and extends her hand by reflex. She quickly pulls it back in as Shar offers a bow. "Yes, Luci, I'm pleased to meet you. It's an honor."

Though she can't put her finger on it, something is peculiar in Shar's delivery. Luci's response is awkward. "Uh . . . yeah, thanks . . . I guess."

Luci faces the man beside her. "So, what's really going on here, Mr. Macer?"

"Please call me *Enos*. I insist."

Shar's eyes widen at the request and how quickly the girl catches herself and returns to the odd-looking device.

Royse approaches with two metal folding chairs. He sets them up facing each other and then takes his place behind the one intended for his boss.

"That won't be necessary, Royse," Macer says. "We're not going to be in here for long."

Shar says, "Sorry to interrupt, sir, but the validation item just made it through."

"Perfect," Macer says, dismissing her with a nod and wave of the hand. Shar disappears into the darkness. A moment later, a shaft of light on the far side of the warehouse shines briefly as she opens a door into another room. Luci notes this—it may be an exit route out of here. Royse's large frame is a motionless statue behind his boss, but his eyes continuously scan the area. The tension is real, leaving Luci wondering what they're so afraid of. If no one knows she's here, why are they so on guard?

"What's going on, Enos?" Luci asks, scanning their faces. "Why is everyone so tense?" This can't be real, but these people are genuinely wound up about something. And true or not, that can be a volatile mix. "Do you feel that we're in danger from something?"

Macer nods to Royse, who says, "We may not be the only ones who have come for you this evening."

The response is so sincere and matter of fact that it winds her. "Who else is after me and *why*?"

Royse answers for him, "There are those that want us stopped and hope to see that our mission fails tonight."

Luci looks at Macer, who's studying her reaction. "Another group from the future like the three of you?" The idea of being the object in some twisted game of capture the flag sends a shiver down her spine. "What do they want me for? Are they doing drift pattern things too?"

Macer says, unblinking, "No, they want to execute you."

Her knees weaken a bit, but she manages to find her footing and not fall face first into the rickety-looking table. Before she can utter another question, Macer adds, "They want the opposite of what we need you for. They want to prevent your work on drift pattern."

Luci's eyes don't blink as she studies him for any trace that his response is a joke told in poor taste. "You're saying that these people want to kill me to stop the drift pattern from being created?"

He answers without any preamble, "Yes."

Royse leans toward Macer. "Sir, Shar says the item's ready."

"Wait, I have more questions," Luci protests as Macer heads in the direction that Shar went off to minutes ago.

Without glancing back at her, he says, "Dr. Gaudiano, we really must be going. And not to alarm you, but we really shouldn't be out here in the open. It truly is a risk for any of us to stay in one place too long."

Royse reaches for her elbow to nudge her along, but she jerks it back swiftly. "You don't want to alarm me?" she says with a raised voice. "You just told me people from the future are coming to kill me. That's pretty alarming."

Royse says in a reserved but firm tone, "It's time to go. You can ask questions later." He grabs Shar's device from the table and uses the light of the glowing translucent screen like a lantern behind Luci, lighting the trio's steps.

Luci walks quickly to catch up to Macer. "I need to know something before we go any further."

He continues moving to the other side of the warehouse, maintaining his stride.

"Mr. Macer, wouldn't it make more sense to wait until I figured out this drift pattern thing for you to visit me? By coming to me now before I've solved the equation or whatever it is, is a little like getting the winning Super Bowl quarterback while he's still in diapers learning to walk. You said I develop this DPM thing in 2041. Why are you here today instead of nine years from now?"

Macer stops and is clearly agitated as he turns to Royse. "This was a lot easier before."

Royse acknowledges the statement with a shrug. "To be expected, sir. Everything was further along for that, and there was no convincing to be done. Plus, Shar was the one—"

Macer cuts him off, "Yes, but I just thought . . . I don't know."

That they speak as if she's not standing there between them annoys Luci. "Hey, I'm right here," she says, snapping her fingers. "What do you mean that it was easier before?"

Macer takes a step and positions himself uncomfortably close to her. She goes to step back from him, but Royse closes the gap like a human wall behind her. Macer speaks evenly. "Dr. Gaudiano . . . *Luci*, my hopes are that you would be a willing participant in this . . . *endeavor*. I find it so much easier when members of a team cooperate of their own will and desire, but make no mistake about it, you *are* coming back with us voluntarily or by force."

Luci nearly jumps out of her skin when Royse puts a firm hand on her shoulder.

A wide, crocodile-like smile forms on Macer's face in the dim glow of the device Royse holds in his other hand. The angle of the light from behind her distorts the old man's expression into a gargoyle-like caricature. Macer takes another step toward her. His chest nearly brushes up against her. She can smell his breath and feel the heat of his exhale as he whispers, "I understand your disbelief up to this point. You're a scientist, and none of this has been proven out to you yet. I can appreciate that, I really can. But what I'm about to show you is going to change all of that."

Without shifting his eyes from her, Macer removes the raincoat and lets it fall to the concrete floor. He rolls up the sleeves of the tan jumpsuit he's wearing. "You'll find all of this is going to work out much better for you if you simply do as I say. Just do what you're told and have a little faith in me." He takes a step back from her and asks in normal volume, "You can do that, right?"

She is a swirl of emotions; anger, fear, confusion—each one vying for center stage. She knows now is not the time to fight, so she grits her teeth and answers, "Yeah, I can do that."

"Good," Macer replies with such force that it startles her and echoes throughout the area. He turns on his heel like a swivel and heads to a large wooden door in the corner. Macer reaches to touch his earlobe. "We're coming in, Shar. Activate the longchairs." He turns again to address Luci. "I've had a recording sent from my interval, a conversation captured on video that you'll find interesting."

"What . . . is it?" she asks as butterflies congregate in her stomach.

Macer stops at the door and faces her in the bluish light of the computer pad. "Let's say that it's the proof you're looking for from someone whom you have no choice but to believe."

The butterflies twist into knots inside her. She resists the urge to run. Luci's innate compulsion to seek out answers overrules her sense of fight or flight. She's got to see this through. What could possibly be on the other side of the door that makes this man so annoyingly certain that she'll believe in his time-travel fairy tales?

SEVEN

May 22, 1863: The Territory of Colorado
1 mile northeast of Oro City

[39.2508223/106.2925242/4.603.391.688/4828:29:29]

HU TERITΘRI UV KOLΩRODΩ
1 M±L NΩHΞST UV ΘRΩ SITI

MΔ 22, 1863

PRΞ-H± NΩ KΦWU

JONN AND BEAUMONT LOWER THE steamer from atop
the sideways coach. The trunk lands in the dirt beside Cavazos with a thud. The plume of dust it kicks up causes him to
cough. Cavazos begins to complain but stops, distracted by
the sound of heavy, rhythmic clomps of horse hooves. A fourth
rider approaches, kicking up a dust trail in the distance.
Cavazos's chest tightens as he remembers Beaumont's claim
that he'll regret seeing whoever this is. He wonders if Cyphor Gicul himself is approaching until he remembers that
Beaumont said that he'd never met the elusive terrorist
himself and he knows whomever this is.

A kerchief covers the unidentified man's face as his horse
gallops evenly at a deliberate pace. A sharp tug on the reins
makes the animal rear up several yards from the overturned
stagecoach.

He dismounts without a word, and the woman breaks her
stance and rushes to his side. She says something in his ear,

nauseating Cavazos when she gestures in his direction. The figure nods but doesn't advance.

Jonn and Beaumont startle Cavazos by climbing back down the side of the coach. Both grab a handle of the trunk and shuffle to drop it at the stranger's feet. The woman opens it, and all three back away, giving the newcomer room. He takes a step forward, bending slightly to peer inside.

Satisfied, he closes the trunk and instructs the woman in a gravelly voice, "Ley, take Jonn and go clean that mess up on the road. Dispose of the bodies in the interval's proper custom and then rejoin us at the ranch house."

The rough voice is familiar to Cavazos, but he can't place it. His heart thumps wildly, his throat constricting as he tries to swallow. The two companions obediently ride off as the man with the covered face takes his time moving closer to him. When he finally makes it to within four feet of Cavazos, he crouches down and runs his fingers absently through the dirt. Noah Beaumont comes to his side with the churka he's reclaimed from the horse saddle.

"Noah, we won't be needing that," the man says softly. "You know that Pol and I are old friends." He brushes the dirt from his hands. "Very old friends."

As the man removes the kerchief, Cavazos places the voice and gasps, "Malom Roderick?" He nearly chokes on the name in fear. "How . . . how did you break out of the—"

Malom removes his hat, and long salt-and-pepper-colored locks of hair pour down, matching the growth of beard stubble. "Funny story, really. It was you who inadvertently tipped Gicul off and helped me escape from the Carcerium, but that's a different conversation."

"Gicul? Wha . . . what are you talking about? What are you going to do to me?"

Malom leans forward and mashes his index finger against Cavazos's forehead. The man's perfectly aligned, oversized teeth distract Cavazos as he begins to speak. "You remember what I told you, right?" He sighs. "But you know, Pol, can't we just enjoy this moment? I mean, the poetic beauty of it all? It's not always best to rush things. Let's not get into a big hurry into that other business, okay? You see, I've become a patient man thanks to you. Being locked away in the Carcerium has made me very patient, in fact." He springs from his crouch and scratches the back of his neck. "Whew, my knees can't take that for very long anymore." Malom draws a pistol on Cavazos before the injured man knows what's happening. "Stand up, *councilman*."

Cavazos totters to his feet, still nursing his arm. "Is that thing real?"

The question amuses Malom, and he turns the revolver in his hand to the side and back again. "Wouldn't be much of a threat if this relic wasn't." As if needing to explain himself, he says, "Old habits die hard, I guess. Article six of the edict and all."

"You can't kill me," he declares as boldly as he can muster, but his eyes lock on to Malom's gun. "You said Gicul broke you out. How'd he do it? Who is he? Is he hiding here in this interval? I want to see him to make a deal. I want to talk to your boss."

"Who is *he*?" The question is followed by a snide smile. "For you being the city's security minister, you certainly don't know much. You've spent so much effort and resources to find one person and still come up emptyhanded. Well, it's a bit of a disgrace. Do you even know what you have in the trunk? What you took from Cyphor and us? What that old technology can be engineered to do?" He leans in a little more. "You should have come to our side when I offered, but instead, you went and stole that from us after killing a number of us in cold blood."

"I don't have to know whatever that thing is. The fact that you and Gicul had it is enough for me, whatever his twisted plans are."

Malom addresses Beaumont, who's remained motionless behind him the entire time. "Noah, I saw a pond a quarter of a mile back. Take the interval animals there to refresh. When you come back, we'll fasten the trunk on the black one."

"But sir, will you ..." Beaumont catches himself and makes the correction. "Yes, sir."

"We'll be fine here until you get back," Malom offers in his friendly tone. "As I said, we're old friends."

Cavazos watches him ride off over Malom's shoulder. "You could just leave me here ... here in this interval. Gicul will think you've killed me because I'll never leave. He'll never know. Tell him it was ... tell him I was killed by some marauders that came over from New Australia."

"New Australia?" Malom asks with raised eyebrows. "No, I think you know why that lie won't work."

"Just let me go, damn you."

Malom sighs. "Pol, you know I can't do that. You know how this time-skipping stuff works. I have to end this here to ensure the future and stop Macer." He shakes his head slowly. "I have to end it here ... end you."

Cavazos swallows hard, his mind frantically searching for a way out of this. An idea pops into his head. "Look, to show I'm sincere about not going back, I have something for you."

Malom's eyes narrow to suspicious slits. "What is it?"

"Around my neck ... let me get it, okay?" Cavazos stammers, but there's a slow hope creeping into his heart.

Malom nods and motions with the pistol. "Take it out ... slowly."

Cavazos releases the grip from the injured arm and cautiously removes a necklace. After fumbling to get the chain over his head, he produces a thin black onyx rectangle as long as his index finger. "It controls the cybos. Take it. I won't need it, because I'll be here in the past—no cybos here. Just let me live, I beg of you." He sniffs, his efforts to hold back emotions lost, and weeps openly. "I don't want to die here," he blubbers.

Malom doesn't receive the item from Cavazos's extended quivering hand. "You should have listened to me, Pol. I gave you a chance . . . a chance to stop it, to end the whole thing . . . so billions of people could be saved in the past and in the future."

"Billions of people saved? You're insane, it's impossible!" he shouts, spittle flying from his lips. "You don't know what will happen. I've told you there's no way to be sure even if you could do it." His throat constricts as tears gush. "Gicul's theories are madness . . . they're not sound." His voice breaks. "Just take this from me and let me live out my days here. Just leave, and you'll never see me again." His heart races. "You won't get away with it!" Cavazos screams, making his throat raw. "Whatever you're planning, you won't get away with it. Chancellor Macer will find you again and lock you in another Carcerium chamber, this time with a pain motor . . . in perpetuity!"

Malom calmly shakes his head while making a tsk tsk sound. "I'm disappointed in you, Pol. Don't you see I've already gotten away with it? If it weren't true, then they'd be here already, your boss Macer and a whole legion of his modified cybo abominations." He turns the gun in his hand again as if appraising it, judging its weight. "You know, in the end, killing you probably won't make a difference at all, at least if Cyphor and *L'inversione* succeeds. It'll be as if it never happened, none of this. But for the moment, while I'm still here, it's amazing how satisfying it is to see you squirm, and that's gotta be worth something."

Cavazos presses his back against the wood of the destroyed coach. "You're insane! All of you are insane!"

Malom nods pensively as if contemplating his words like a recently delivered diagnosis. "If that's true, you made me that way. You made me go insane." He cups his free hand to his severed earlobe as if he's just heard something. "Hear that?"

Cavazos is genuinely shocked and confused as he strains to listen. "I don't hear . . . what . . . I can't—"

Malom removes the hand from his ear, and the smile on his face contorts to a grimace that displays all his teeth. "Exactly. That's the sound of nothingness. No one coming to save you, not Chancellor Macer, none of your cybo guards, no Directorate, nothing. Only the sound of oblivion." He clicks the pistol's hammer back with his thumb. "Nothing—nothing to stop me from doing . . . *this*."

Pol Cavazos never hears the gunshot that erupts into his face.

EIGHT

April 9, 2032
Baltimore, Maryland
[39.482315/77.069092/4.603.391.857/2375:01:52]

B∧LTIMOR-MЯRILAND

∆PRIL 9, 2032

PRɪ-Hɪ NΩ KⱣWU

IT TAKES A BIT TO acclimate to the painful brightness of the fluorescent lights in the medium-sized room. Judging by the various wall items, charts, regional maps, goal calendars, and the like, the area once was used as a sales office for whatever was manufactured at this facility. Instead of furniture or cubicles, there are two unfamiliar imposing structures running diagonally across the room. Positioned crossways from the bottom right corner to the top left are two separate pristine shafts of highly reflective white plastic.

At first, Luci thinks that they're unpainted props from a webisode program she's streamed called *Tron Defenders*. Often, the characters of the show battle in "light cycles." Resembling two-wheeled motorcycles, the vehicles on the fictional program emit walls of colored light that solidify to block their opponent in. The racers speed around one another until the loser is destroyed in a fatal crash.

Closer observation reveals more differences than just the color. Firstly, it's not a cycle at all—there are no wheels. The "cockpit" is also different, allowing for two passengers instead of one.

There's a narrow enough space for Shar's smaller body to maneuver between the corner and the plastic front nose of the compartment.

"Here it is, sir," she says, handing a disk the size of a thick drink coaster to Macer. In a matter-of-fact voice, she adds, "We're past the quarter mark at thirteen minutes, forty-six seconds."

She turns her back to them and slides open a panel in one of the long plastic tubes dominating the space. The sound of digital chirps ring out as Shar works.

How they got these things into the room is a mystery; the only door is the one to their backs, and it's much too small.

Luci's ship-in-a-bottle mystery is suspended when Macer says, "These are what we call *longchairs*. The technology within them, plus drift pat-tern mathematics, allows for temporal navigation, or what is commonly known as a leap skip. We don't skip for anything as trivial as weather information any-more. All those time satellite devices were decommissioned a long, long time ago anyway." He's preoccupied with activat-ing the coaster-size device in his hand. Macer twists it, and the disc expands like a stumpy telescope in his palm.

To her amazement, the device hovers in place chest-high in the air.

"Ah there we go," Macer announces with satisfaction. "As I said, Mr. Einstein got a lot right, but he couldn't be more wrong about faster-than-light travel."

A holographic image roughly the size of a shoebox appears in the air between them. Luci's blood runs cold. Unless Macer is a masterful close-up magician or she's been slipped a hallu-cinogen, whatever is happening here isn't an elaborate prank.

The paused image is of Macer sitting behind a futuristic-looking desk. The vantage point that it's "filmed" at is from over the shoulder of someone with dark hair so their face isn't visible.

"What is this?" Luci asks softly as if in a trance.

"It's taken from a recording made a couple of days ago in my office."

Luci shifts her eyes from the frozen digital image of him to the sly look on Macer's face.

He rubs his chin. "The three of us come from a place in your future called Relicus City. I hold a high office there, and because of that, it's standard procedure that all of my meetings are auto recorded. I can mark them private or confidential, of course, for sensitive matters of the city. The point is that I want you to tell me if you recognize the story the lady tells me here."

Addressing the device, Macer utters the command, "Activate file."

The recording of him begins to speak as the hologram comes to life mid conversation. "It's of the utmost importance that we be clear."

The voice of the person opposite of him agrees. "Yes, Chancellor, I learned that lesson long ago."

Luci shudders, recognizing the voice. When she gasps, Macer nods, smiling victoriously.

"It's me!" she says, finding it increasingly harder to breathe.

Luci listens more for confirmation, but it's undeniable. As odd as a person's voice sounds aloud to themselves, she knows this to be hers. In preparation for tonight's lecture, she recorded and listened to herself talk a dozen times to perfect the cadence and timing of her talk.

On the hologram, Macer interlocks his fingers and leans slightly back in the chair as he listens to the woman on the recording.

"I was nine years old . . . that was third grade for me at Lakeview Elementary. The last week of the school year, we had what they called a 'fun day' one afternoon. It was like an outside activity day with various contests—hundred-yard dash and whatnot. There was this one booth where they were giving away this porcelain doll. Someone had made this beautiful miniature taffeta dress from hand. It looked like one of those hoop dresses from the Victorian period or something.

Anyway, all that you had to do to win it was to guess the number that they were going to draw later that afternoon."

Luci knows exactly where this story's headed. Her hand covers her open mouth as the voice on the video explains, "So I wrote my name on the side of the pre-cut slip of paper and wrote a bold '99' and placed it in the jar with the other entries. Later, when they drew the random number, it *was* 99. The teacher went through all of the slips to see who came closest to the number. I was elated that I'd guessed it. I've never been lucky like that. It was incredible. I daydreamed of giving the doll to my mother. She loved stuff like that, and this was a one-of-a-kind dress. I imagined the look on her face."

"What happened?" Macer on the video urges.

"They looked at my slip of paper, and because I'd written my name on it sideways, they couldn't determine if I'd written a '99' or a '66'. If only I'd underlined the number, they would've known, but I didn't, and Hailee Blake had printed an '88,' so they gave it to her." She shrugs, adding, "Since then, I've always made certain my communications are abundantly clear."

The image freezes, and Macer reaches for the floating device. "Have you ever told that story to anyone?" He collapses the disc on itself. "I mean other than me, obviously."

Luci stares at the ground, frozen in place. "I feel like I'm going to be sick." She struggles to set the unfathomable concept of time travel in her mind, but there's no compartment to tuck it into. Normally, she's euphoric at discovering new things, but she only feels drained and emotionally sucker-punched by this revelation.

Macer breaks the silence to ask again, "Who else knows of that story?"

Her voice is barely a whisper as she slowly raises her eyes to his. "Not anyone, not even my mother. I was too embarrassed to tell her." She feels the walls closing in and gnaws at a cuticle. "This . . . *this* is all real . . . what you said . . . time travel?"

A smug smile forms on his face. "Every word of it. You see, you've obviously already come with us." He holds up the disc.

Taking a step toward her, Macer places it in her hand. It's cold to the touch as he gently clasps her fingers over it. "You can trust me, Luci. We need your help. Millions of lives are at stake."

She's dumbfounded. Too many conflicting ideas ricochet around her brain. Finally, she latches onto one. Looking down at the device in her hand, she utters two words. "Why now?" She opens her palm as if to offer it back to him. "Why are you here? What happened before?"

The response surprises him. "What do you mean?"

Shar interrupts, "Sir, less than ten minutes remaining."

Luci ignores her, focusing only on Macer; she can feel her mind is closing in on something. "You never answered my question from before—why now? Why do you need me now? In fact, you still haven't adequately answered why you need me at all." As the thoughts begin to fuse together in her mind's eye, her words gain traction. "Why are you here today? Why did you come to this point in time instead of later?"

Macer's bushy eyebrows climb up two inches on his forehead. "I already explained to you that one can only leap skip to pre-determined intervals that are established by—"

She doesn't allow him to finish before delivering another verbal blow. "What happened to the other version of me . . . the video version of me?"

A metal clang rings out through the room, making everyone tense. "Sorry, sir," Shar says, bending to pick up the tool she's dropped. Her eyes shift, and she reports, "Sir, nine minutes, seventeen seconds."

"Five hundred fifty-seven seconds, huh? What happens if I refuse to go?" Luci asks defiantly.

"You won't refuse," Macer answers. "Anyway, let's be amiable about this."

"Or what?" Luci snaps back.

Royse sighs in frustration, "You saw the thing . . . on the video. You're in his office."

"But I have a choice, right?"

"Of course, my dear," Macer says, gesturing to steady Royse. He double taps the hologram disc in her hand. "But obviously, you decided *'yes'* or we wouldn't have this."

"I don't get how this works. If I have any free will in this and decide not to go, you'd have no video to show me now."

"Luci," Macer begins, "you've got to trust that—"

"So, maybe a better question is what went wrong?" she says as her eyes dart around the room as if the answer is printed on one of the old sales charts. "Or are you going to tell me that I'm going to meet myself? Am I going to be working on drift pattern with another Luci version?"

Though he offers a faint smile, Macer's response is tense as if she's made a faux pas or something. "We really don't have the time to go over it all right now."

"I need to know—I need to understand," Luci pleads. "If you've done all of this research on me and spent any length of time with any version of me, you'd know that I have to understand how things work."

Macer lets out a long, resigned sigh and says, "Well, it doesn't exactly work like that. You won't see yourself. Long-chair technology and the U-curve will overlay this version of you onto the one that's on this message. It's called *identity convergence.*"

"So, what, is it like painting a wall with a different paint color—it's the same wall underneath?" Something about this doesn't add up to her. Another announcement from Shar punctures Luci's thoughts as the young woman nervously reports, "We're under the five hundred mark at four hundred sixty-one seconds."

"If I leave with you tonight, run the math so you can recalibrate your equipment or whatever, and then you bring me back here to right now like nothing happened, right?"

Macer nods his head *yes*, but Luci catches Shar shoot a glance to her and quickly back down.

"What? What is it? What are you not telling me, Enos? Shar, what's really going on here?"

Macer begins to answer, but Shar cuts him off. "This is a unique interval."

"In what way?" Luci demands, shifting attention to her.

"It's a unique interval in that it has an echo. There's what we call a *twin* that will occur in . . ." She checks something on the screen. ". . . in two hundred fifty-eight hours, twelve minutes, and thirty-two seconds. It'll last for seventeen and a half minutes near a fish market in a place called . . ." She checks the device. ". . . East Timor. It's very rare to have another interval so close in time."

At first perturbed with being cut off, Macer is pleased with Shar's reply and reinforces her statement, "Normally, the intervals don't fall that closely to each other. For instance, when is the next one after that, Miss Ryson?"

Shar answers in a clinical tone, "The next one after that won't occur for another three years, five months, twelve days, and twenty-two minutes." She looks at Luci. "And it will be open for all of twenty-six minutes and eighteen seconds located in the Arctic Sea."

Macer's eyebrows rise. "So, you see that it's really important that we get moving here."

Luci shakes her head. "I'm sorry, but this is all too much for me to process. I need more information. Why can't you come back to take me in eleven days? Why can't you just get me from . . ."

"*East Timor*," Shar volunteers. "It doesn't work like that. Due to a chronal reciprocity—"

"I don't care what you have to do." Luci feels her heartrate climbing. "I'm not ready to go. I need more answers. Look, I'll hide out until you come back. I'll be safe. That'll give me a chance to—"

"Sir," booms Royse's baritone from behind her, "should I go ahead?"

Luci spins around. Something as thick as an old-time roll of quarters is in his hand. He twists a button on the device and shrugs, looking past her to his boss.

"What's he doing?" Luci asks, turning back to Macer with widened eyes. "What's in his hand?"

"It's okay, Mr. Timmons," Macer says, beaming a smile as bright as the midday sun. "She's right."

"But, sir," Shar protests.

Macer gestures, and the woman falls silent. "Miss Ryson, I'm certain that you'll be able to accommodate the doctor's request, and we'll plan to retrieve her in a week and a half."

Luci should feel relieved that Macer's agreeing to her request, but something's still off. She turns in time to see Royse nod, but he continues to twist a metal ring on the device. She knows they won't kill her, but what is he doing?

"Enos," she says, advancing to him, "do I have your word?"

He gives a slight bow of the head. "Of course." He points to Royse. "Put that thing away and make sure the warehouse is still clear before we head to the vehicle."

Luci hesitates, clutching the hologram disk in her hand tightly enough to cause pain. Finally, Royse responds, "Yes, sir. I understand." He makes his way past her to the door. "I'll be right back."

No one speaks, creating a pregnant pause.

Finally, Shar breaks the awkward silence. "Two hundred fifty-one seconds, sir."

"Thank you, Shar."

"It's all so unbelievable," Luci says, still attempting to process and qualify all that she's heard and seen. "I can't get over this."

"Yes, I can appreciate how news of this can put one a little of balance," he says, motioning Luci to the door. "Just remember, Doctor . . ." He grabs the door handle. "You really didn't leave me any option."

The imposing form of Royse is poised and ready with device in hand in the open doorway.

Luci screams, pleading, "No, please don't!" Her heart spikes in fear as she hurls the hologram disk at his face.

It rebounds off his shoulder, and Macer shoves her forward into the clutches of Royse's massive free hand.

The injection into her neck is quick.

Across the room, Macer's voice rings out, "You'll see that I'm right, Dr. Gaudiano. It's the only way. Now you'll have a pleasant, mellow little dream, and we'll speak on the other side."

Luci's legs go limp. Royse firmly catches her. Through increasingly blurred vision, Luci makes out Shar rushing over to assist. Those brilliant green eyes ... but there's so much shame in her expression.

Luci can't recall what all the fuss had been about. She feels fine now. Why had she made such a big deal of it all? A warmth envelops her, and in the haze, Shar and Royse's faces distort, and they look like ... babies. His hairless, perfectly round, bald skull looks exactly like an infant's head. Their muffled voices deteriorate into indistinguishable sounds. She smiles at the children. She wants to ask the two babies where their mothers are at. The question remains as how they got here.

She decides to take care of these infants, at least until their parents return from wherever they've gone off to. Luci determines that when she's a mother, she will never leave her newborn's side, not even for a moment. She will care for these two for now. She extends her heavy arms out to the baby that had been Shar. Then the world turns sideways as color slides off everything in the room and then goes dark.

NINE

March 22, 2191
Relicus City
[6.217012/127.792969/4.603.388.823/1932:36:27]

RELIKUS SITI
MΛȻ 22, 2191

THE PRESSURE PUSHING AGAINST LUCI makes her feel as if she is deep under water, invoking a panic in her. An impenetrable blackness envelops her. Every movement is a sluggish undertaking. Through an act of sheer will, she slowly tilts her head back at a shimmering grey blob floating far above her. As she attempts to raise her hand to it, her arm lethargically responds to the command as if pushing upward through a vat of molasses. The pulsating shape grows brighter as the distance closes between them. The pain in her head changes from a slight twinge to a throbbing ache in direct proportion to the increasing size of the blob, but she can't turn away. The shape transforms into a light—faint at first, but soon, it grows as bright as the sun, making her head feel like it's on fire.

There's a voice—a female voice—that sounds far away. "Luci?"

She's alarmed that she can't respond. The light is rushing at her; the pain intensifies.

The voice speaks again. "Luci, are you awake?"

A hand softly rests on Luci's shoulder. The stimulus helps her to partially reconnect to the external world. She wants to ask Michael about who is in their bedroom, but then she remembers that he wouldn't be in the bed with her, not since the breakup. Luci struggles to open her eyes but only manages two thin groggy slits.

The voice is clearer now. "Luci, if you can wake up a little more, I can administer something for the headache that you're having."

Luci responds with slurred words, "Something for my head?" Her lips feel like rubber.

"Yes, I know, but you have to be more alert before I can give you anything. It'll work better." The voice is soft and pleasant, almost musical to the ear.

Her eyelids feel as heavy as anchors, but she manages to force them open a little more. The room is vibrating, swimming and spinning in all colors of the spectrum. It feels like hot coals have replaced Luci's brain. Thirsty—she's so thirsty. Her mouth is cotton.

"Just a little more," the woman encourages her.

Luci is good with voices, and she recognizes this one—the countdown woman with the porcelain-doll features, Shar. As she fights to focus, she realizes she's groggily staring into the woman's brilliant emerald eyes. Everything comes back in a rush, and her fear competes with anger. She's regaining control, but her question still comes out clumsy. "What . . . what did you do to me?"

"We had to leave," Shar says in a sorrowful tone. "There was no choice."

As Luci comes to, she realizes she's not in the warehouse office and shudders in disoriented fear.

Shar leans over her. "You're alright. Here, this will help with the pain and disorientation."

Luci attempts to pull back from the injector, but her body is lead, and she feels the sting of the prick before she can avoid it.

Shar pulls away from her neck. "There, that'll help right you." She places the instrument in her pocket, but not before Luci sees it. The device is similar to the one that Royse used to put her under, maybe even the same one.

Shar's smile is warm and genuine as she informs her, "It has a little bit of a soother in it too for anxiety. You've been through a lot—it will help." She offers a plastic cup. "Feeling better?"

Luci gulps the water until it's gone. There's a faint metallic taste, but she doesn't care. "I feel like . . ." She sits up in the ovoid-shaped bed and turns her head from side to side, waiting for an aching aftereffect. She does it once more but only suffers a mild dizziness. It's miraculous. The pain is gone without a trace. "Wow, that's good stuff. Even my head is cleared up."

Whether it's intended or not, the bed looks like an egg to Luci, an oval with a section of its outer shell removed. She scans the windowless room. It's a frosted white Plexiglass cube with soft light coming from the floor, ceiling, and walls. It's warm, like being inside of a dim low-wattage lightbulb. There's an open doorway in the left corner. Even though there's no visible medical equipment, she asks, "Is this a hospital?" She shifts on the bed, allowing her legs to dangle over the side, and glances around. "This room is small and empty like a recovery room. Where are we? What is this place?"

Shar looks puzzled and slowly repeats the word as if it's foreign to her lips. "Hospital? No, we did a leap skip to Relicus City. You're safe here. I told Chancellor Macer that I wanted to be here when you revived . . . that I wanted to be the one to give you the fegg instead of it being dispensed from a machine so you wouldn't be scared. I know your aversion to that kind of thing."

"How do you know I'm scared of needles? Wait—are you guarding me?" Luci feels her blood pressure rising despite the soothing sedative in the shot. "Is that Royse guy out there in the hallway in case I try to escape so he can give me another shot?"

The question clearly catches Shar off guard. "What? No, Mr. Timmons is the chancellor's man, like a protector. The chancellor is taking care of official business. You've been asleep for a long time."

Luci gnaws her bottom lip at this revelation. "How long was I out?"

"For a while." Her emerald eyes gaze at her with an unblinking stare. "I . . . I wanted to be here when you revived."

"You already said that," Luci responds, slightly irritated. "Why was it important to you to be here when I woke up?"

Shar hesitates before she answers, "I wanted to . . . I was the one that got you before . . . not the chancellor and Royse. You might say that we became . . ." There's a peculiar pause as Shar searches for a word. ". . . *friends*."

"From when you got me a few days ago?" Luci asks.

"Well . . . sort of," Shar begins. "I wanted to tell you that I . . ." She looks down at the floor.

"What is it?" Luci runs her fingers through her hair, wondering what's happened to her Cubs ball cap and her computer wristband. "Just tell me."

Shar sighs. "I need to tell you something about Chancellor Macer and what happened from before."

Luci feels queasy, but not from the aftereffects of the drug.

Shar leans in. "Luci, you need to know—"

Something enters the doorway, cutting her short. At first, it looks like a narrow trash receptacle like those commonly found outside of an office building. The notable difference is that the three-foot-high and one-foot-wide gunmetal capsule floats a couple of feet off the Lucite floor. It looks like an oversized floating bullet. She can hardly believe her eyes. "*Was there a hallucinogen in that shot?*"

The object glides noiselessly up to the side of the bed, causing Luci to scoot back from it instinctively.

"It's only the domestic attendant," Shar explains, crossing her arms. "Think of it more as a concierge or butler from your time."

"So this isn't like a guard sentry or something?" Luci asks, eyeing the hovering robot suspiciously. "Are we in the future— my future?"

"Yes, Dr. Gaudiano. Yes we are. It's UNIFON 2191."

That the answer is delivered in such a matter-of-fact tone is a punch to Luci's heart. "What is UNIFON?" She speaks in a whisper to herself, struggling to absorb the outlandish concept. "One hundred and fifty-nine years in the future. Everyone I know is dead . . . all of them, dead for a long time." Her eyes fix on the glowing floor. "And here I am . . . all alone . . . again."

Memories from when she was twelve swell up, but she's become very adept at pushing them back down into the small compartment of her being. She bites the inside of her cheek and then exhales slowly as she gazes back up at Shar. "But wait, that's not right." She blinks quickly. "After I finish doing what you all want of me, I can go back, right? I mean, you get me back into to one of those shiny chair things and we zip back like none of this ever happened, correct? You said something about East Timor."

Shar nods, her eyes fixed on her. "That's what the chancellor said. You'll be returned just a little over week after the talk you gave."

The floating robot moves to the corner, and she asks, "What were you saying about Enos Macer to me a minute ago?"

Shar answers, "I don't know what you mean." Her brilliant green eyes flick up and to the left.

"Shar, I need you to level with me, woman to woman."

"Yes, Luci—I mean, Dr. Gaudiano?"

"I need to understand what's really going on here. What are you holding back?"

Shar nods. "A revolutionary named Cyphor Gicul is destroying the interval juncture openings, but we don't know why or how."

"I still don't get why that is such a big deal," Luci says. "Humans have existed for several millennia without skipping through time as you say."

"We don't leap skip to simply visit the past for recreation or as tourists. It's about the survival of the human race."

Luci reads the intense expression on Shar's face. It's obvious the young woman is conflicted as to what to say and what not to reveal. Luci feels bad for her until she remembers that it's she who is the victim here. She wonders if this is the beginnings of Stockholm syndrome that she's developing. She determines that she must keep focus; she must stay on target if she's going to make it through this. "Okay, so everyone keeps mentioning 'survival of the human race.' How is that? What do you all mean?"

Shar takes in a deep breath and then exhales, choosing her words delicately. "It really should be Chancellor Macer to go over all of this with you."

"It's alright," Luci encourages her, feeling something's on the verge of bursting open in the conversation. "I need to know. Give me the big picture of what we're up against."

Shar sighs and glances over to the bot before turning back to Luci. "A long time ago, there was a bitter war between the nations that existed back then. I don't remember their names, but they're gone now. The conflict grew out of control, and then several nuclear exchanges took place." Her face lights up. "China . . . it was one of the names . . . and something else." Her expression turns grave again. "Though the missile launches began with the major nations, in the end, every country that had access to a weapon used it. The record of it states that at that point, the fighting didn't last for very long, but the burning period after it lasted for many years, what's called *Hi no Kawa*."

"What?"

"*Hi no Kawa*, but there's many names for it—*Nat i brande*, The Night of Ten Million Fires, *Enjō Pembakaran*—but it's all the same. It's the day the world burned."

It's as if all of the oxygen in the room disappeared, and there's a sickly stillness. Luci slides a wayward strand of hair from her eyes. "How long ago did this *Hi no Kawa* happen?"

Shar pauses to calculate. "It was about thirty-five years into your future—no, wait, thirty years." Shar's voice is cold and flat as her eyes fix on the corner of the bed. "When *Hi no Kawa* was over, only one eight hundredth of the world's population remained. In a few decades, the planet went from over ten billion people to an estimate of less than thirteen million scattered souls, and then many of those died off later."

Luci's mouth moves. "Nine billion nine hundred eighty-seven million lives."

Shar allows the statement to linger as if doing so will give the number a chance to evaporate. She speaks so softly that her voice is a reverent whisper. "An unforeseen consequence of the fallout was the damage to the topsoil and below in the oceans. Even most of the insects died. The nutrients required for plant growth had been extinguished by radiation and other poisons. Nothing can grow from the ground anymore. Within a decade after *Hi no Kawa*, all the animals were all consumed as food. This was because there was no feed or grain left." She finally looks up to Luci. "This is the world that I was born into. Until I was twenty-two, I'd never seen a living mammal other than a human—they simply don't exist in this time. The first leap skip that I ever did was the first time that I saw a feline and then a horse that wasn't holographic."

"You don't have any animals here?"

"No, all of them died or were consumed by the survivors to stay alive, since no crops could be harvested."

Another wave of despair hits Luci. She had forgotten about Marcus H., her slobbering bulldog with the gimpy paw. Her neighbor is pet sitting Luci's rescue mutt for the two-week period she's supposed to be at the beach house. At least she was to do that over a century and a half ago. She wonders if she'll ever see Marcus H. again.

"So, you see, Dr. Gaudiano, we leap skip for food, going into the past to stay alive, to survive."

Shar studies Luci's expression, allowing this to sink in before continuing. "What was left of humanity came together out of necessity. They pooled their resources to expand leap skip understanding. The basic premise had been at work for a half century through drift pattern mathematics." She gestures to Luci. "Your drift pattern. The chancellor's father, Waleen Macer, led the team that eventually figured out how to successfully leap skip a human. The journeys were just for a few days at first, but once they had a fundamental understanding of leap skip technology, it eventually led to being able to go back years, then decades, then centuries. They built Relicus City with materials they scavenged from the past. Waleen Macer was and forever will be a hero."

"You say they skip back into the past. Do they ever go into the future?" Luci asks.

A confused expression fills Shar's petite face. "There's no food in the future. Teams farm it in the past and send it through to this interval."

"But aren't you the least bit curious of what the future holds for your people? Don't you want to skip forward?"

Shar's posture stiffens even more. "Forward is prohibited—article two of the edict." As if to block a response, Shar adds, "The longchairs are constructed with a FTT failsafe that restricts Future Temporal Trespass."

"Okay, I get it, I guess, but I don't understand why, if you possess this remarkable ability to skip back in time, you don't just send everyone backward in time hundreds or thousands of years before this *Hi no Kawa* thing takes place. I mean, why not colonize some forgotten past that wouldn't even be noticed? Why go to the trouble of sending food and supplies from the past instead of just setting up back there?"

Shar freezes, and Luci studies her, wondering why she looks embarrassed. No, it's not embarrassment. It's the look of shame. But why?

Luci verbally prods her. "What am I missing here, Shar? Surely I'm not the first one to ever come up with this as a solution. Why not colonize the past before *Hi no Kawa*?"

Shar returns her eyes to the floor. This time, Luci bends to enter her line of sight. "Is it some kind of edict or code thing like the 'no going into the future' rule or something? Or is the thought of abandoning this time plateau considered irresponsible?" Luci reaches for the woman's shoulder. "Shar, help me out here. Are there too many people to take back into the past? What is it?"

Shar mouths a word. It's spoken so softly that Luci can't hear it.

"What'd you say?" Luci asks.

"Sterilization." Shar says slowly lifting her head to meet Luci's gaze. "The reason that sitters can't bring soil from the past, the reason we can't plant seeds we gather from other intervals is because the trip through time sterilizes them."

Luci shrugs. "So, what does that have to do with—"

Shar cuts her question short. "Everything that we carry through in the longchairs or skip barges becomes sterilized . . . everything." She pauses and then adds with a quivering lip, "Including people."

Luci doesn't catch on at first, but then the horrifying pieces of the puzzle snap into place. She gasps and throws her hands over her open mouth. Though she doesn't feel different, traveling through time to the future period of Relicus City made her barren.

TEN

LUCI'S MIND INSTANTLY REJECTS WHAT she's just been told. "You're saying that anything you bring through time is sterilized?"

Shar's head bobs a slow yes.

Luci tries to turn down the static in her mind. "So this happens after how many journeys?" A panic rises in her heart. "How many . . ." She searches for the term. "Shar, how many skips do I have until—"

"Only one," Shar says in a whisper, though the impact of it feels like the answer is shouted through a megaphone. "It's already done."

"No, no, no . . . you're lying," Luci says, covering her mouth. "Tell me the truth." A lump forms in her throat. "Why would you say that? Why would . . ." She pleads with her, "I agree to help with the drift pattern equations. You don't have to do this to me. I'll do what you all want. I'll help." Fighting to hold the panic in check, she asks, "Does it revert back when I'm returned to my own time period?"

Shar's voice trembles. "I'm sorry, but it's true. There's no way to reverse the effects of the leap skip."

Luci's springs up from the bed, pacing. Her head is in a cloud of confusion. "No, this can't be happening. This can't be real." Hot tears swell in her eyes, and her pulse beats in her ears. A solution forms in her mind, causing her to stop abruptly. "Wait, there's another version of me from another time. Why couldn't I get my eggs from future me and—"

Before Luci can finish, Shar shakes her head somberly. "Leap skips don't work that way. Both versions of the subject would have to converge at a time-neutral point using two exclusively independent longchairs. I'm so sorry. I know being a stretch . . . having a child was important to you."

Through gritted teeth, Luci says, "You don't know anything." Her words bubble up like acid. "How do you know anything about what I would want . . . what I would ever want?"

Shar looks wounded. "From before. It wasn't a few days ago. That's what I wanted to tell you." Shar slides her hand from her cheek to the ruby rectangle on her ear. "Yes, sir?" She's all business now. She looks at Luci, but it's clear she's speaking to someone else. "Yes, I'm on my way."

At first, Luci thinks it's a bluff, a ploy to get her off balance, but when Shar spins around and heads for the doorway, Luci demands, "Wait! What did I say to you the first time I was here? What happened to me?" Her frustration mounts. "Answer me! Please answer me."

Shar stops in her tracks. With her back still to Luci, she says, "Luci . . . Doctor, I'm really sorry for before. I know this may not make any sense to you, but I want you to know that I'm sorry anyway." Shar takes a step and stops again. "Just keep yourself alive and stay safe. We'll be back when it's time."

<u>ELEVEN</u>

WITH SHAR GONE, LUCI COLLAPSES face-down into the egg-shaped bed. The combined shock of everything prevents her from concentrating on self-soothing with her random math exercises. Only once in her life has she experienced such bottomless despair. She refuses the impulse to openly sob for two reasons: she's self-conscious about the hovering machine in the corner and she's never been one to wallow in self-pity. The accident that took her parents from her when she was twelve delivered her from any of those self-indulgent tendencies.

Still, she feels a deep sense of remorse, and a dark, empty hole envelops her. There's something else—a pulsating, black rage growing in the pit of her stomach, anger that's she's been violated. Something has been stolen from her—her possible future. They might as well have gutted her and ripped a kidney from her insides.

Without warning, thoughts of her ex-boyfriend, Michael, move to the forefront of her mind. After three and a half years, she broke it off with the unofficial fiancé thirteen days ago. There wasn't a fight so much as a weird and eerily calm disagreement over children.

How bitterly ironic to her now is that it all was about having children.

She felt ready.

He did not.

The conversation had the cold, peculiar semblance of a business transaction. The equation between them simply didn't match up, leaving them no rational reason to continue. That it was handled so clinically surprised her and stung a little. They even shook hands instead of a final embrace or kiss.

She made the conscious decision to not harbor any resentment toward him. It wasn't that he broke a promise or anything; he was always clear on the topic. She was the one who changed.

The concept of a family has always been in the back of her mind, but at age thirty-three, the idea has sharpened closer into focus. She wasn't obsessing, but she feared she was on the threshold of doing so.

For years, Luci has known the consequence of a pregnancy to her work and repressed the urge to contemplate such trivial things. Being female in the academic world had always been an uphill climb. Her gender meant that she was often required to be better and work harder than her male colleagues, and sometimes even that wasn't enough. Any sign of femininity was quietly considered a badge of weakness by many, a twisted admission of inferiority.

Though it was never said aloud to her, the cultural undertow of it always worked against her, trying to pull her down backward under the sea. She suspected that her gender in the mathematics community was discreetly observed as the equivalent of a cripple competing in the high jump, and nothing screams, "*I have a uterus!*" louder than being knocked up.

Despite all of this, the seed of the idea took root in her heart at some point. For what it was worth, she's more than demonstrated her skill and more than earned her place at the boys' table, but a baby . . . that would be too much for them.

There was no rational reason for her to forfeit the life she knew for motherhood. Where did such an illogical desire come from? She considered that her subconscious may be working against her, attempting to restore and repair the family that she has been deprived of because of the accident.

Up until now, the prep work for the lecture has served as a distraction from the Michael breakup situation, but now that that is over, she wonders how she'll be. Life is never as clean as math, but even so, that the possibility of motherhood has been snatched away while she slept is difficult to process. All of that is gone to her now, an option that is no longer viable—with Michael or anyone else.

A knot forms in her throat, and Luci sniffles and sits up in the bed. The concierge bot hovers at attention in the corner. An unexpected guilt sweeps over her, guilt for not attempting to run sooner when they were in the main warehouse. She probably would have been recaptured, but what if she was able to get away? This is the worst of all of it, the realization that she allowed Enos Macer to extinguish future possibilities for her and barely offered a whimper as it went down until it was too late. Luci's rational mind catches up with this train of thought, reminding her that there was no way for her to know time travel rendered her eggs infertile.

She's not guilty—Enos Macer is!

She rises from the mattress, ignoring her stomach twisting like the handles of a vice. If the robot in the room with her is recording everything, it could be transmitting live back to Macer now.

"Are you listening, Macer?" she asks, advancing on it. "Who do you think you are? You don't decide for me!" She recognizes the futility of confronting her captor in this way, but an unquenchable anger short-circuits any possibility of rational thought. "I hope you can hear me through this thing, because I want you to know something. Unless you restore me to the way I was before, I refuse to do anything for you! Not a single equation until you prove that you'll send a doctor back with me to harvest my undamaged eggs from before." She's unaccustomed to such an avalanche of emotion overtaking her. It's frightening not to have control, but she can't stop.

She lunges at the cylindrical casing of the robot. It's cold to the touch as she grabs it. "If you'd been smart, you'd allowed me to stay in my time and work on the drift pattern for you there, but you didn't, and you drug me across time, killing my chance to ever have a . . ." She hesitates, picturing the faces of her dead mother and father, and finally utters the word, "*family.*"

The concierge releases a low-voltage charge through its outer shell. It doesn't hurt her, but it's enough to shock Luci into releasing her grip. The machine exploits this and zips through the doorway before she realizes what happened.

"Come back here, you son of a bitch!" Luci scrambles to follow, still shouting, "You can't make me do anything for you! You have no leverage! There's nothing left to take from me, nothing left to barter with. I don't care if all of your people starve." It's a lie; she does care, but the momentum of her pain-induced rage gets the best of her. As she exits the brightly lit cube of a room, the light fades. "Everyone knows that you can't subtract from zero. It's fundamental math. And you have zero left to take from me! You should've—"

She stops mid-rant as the realization that she's in a future environment hits hard.

Outside the doorway, an awestruck Luci surveys the area. She's on a catwalk overlooking an open-design loft below. Shafts of sunbeams pierce the oval windows at the top of the domed area like rods of light. A quarter of the way down from the peak glass walls, an enormous aquarium encompasses the entire circle down to the bottom. These tiles are illuminated in the same manner as the floor in the bedroom. She makes her way to the end of the balcony to a spiral staircase as if in a trance, pausing as she passes a bathroom on the same level as the bedroom. She returns her focus the area below. Slightly off center of the expansive glass bubble is a kitchenette pod with low walls made from highly reflective material like plastic. Beside it, a white table sprouts up from the light floor like a flat mushroom and is surrounded by a trio of chairs.

Halfway down the staircase, Luci realizes it's not really an aquarium, and the sight takes her breath away. The bottom three-fourths of the flat are submerged in water. Remembering the time she drowned, she resists the urge to race back up to the safety of the top level. The absence of any visible fish or sea life confirms Shar's statement about the demise of the animal population due to severe radiation and consumption.

On the ground level, Luci spots a single door and rushes to it. There's no knob, but she's streamed enough science fiction shows to know to place her hand on the small protruding rectangle situated to the right of the entrance. There's a soft tone as the plastic pad glows pinkish red and then reverts back to white. She tries her other hand, but it yields the same result.

She looks behind her at the far back top of the igloo-like glass enclosure. "Robot, unlock this door." When the concierge doesn't respond, she shouts, "Robot, or whatever you are, I command you to come here!"

As the machine slowly glides downward, Luci notices the area to the right. It's a second bubble dome that wasn't visible from the top of the stairs. The upper half of the space contains the bedroom and bath. Beneath it is a large circular pit with a curved sofa and several soft chairs. All four of the seats, including the sofa, face a large bowl-like object positioned in the center. She notes the dark metal basin with a circumference larger than an inflatable kiddie pool back home. Nearly three quarters of it is filled with liquid; it gently sloshes in the container, making a bubbling sound.

The bot stops a few feet from the door and hovers in place.

Luci makes a perturbed gesture to the door pad. "Well, open it, R2-D2."

When there's no reaction, she commands it in an agitated voice, "I order you to open this door."

The lack of response is infuriating, but her rage begins to cool and she can reason again. If the concierge is monitoring her for Macer, it makes sense that it would ignore this command.

She needs to come up with a plan. Luci strategically scans the room for options. The only thing she has to bargain with is herself. They won't risk something happening to her, so

that's her leverage. She moves about the area into the kitchenette. Anything that can generate heat will do. The hovering bot
follows at a safe distance. The technology in the small pod area
is strange and abstract to her.

"Robot, how does one heat up food in here?" Luci asks.

The machine comes closer but doesn't offer any verbal
response.

After a few frustrated, unsuccessful attempts to activate
something that she may start a fire with, Luci gives up on the
idea. Setting a fire in hopes that the door would automatically
open was a longshot anyway; if this place were anything like
the smart houses of her time, the flames would be extinguished
before she have a chance to flee, or the robo-butler would've
snuffed it out anyway.

She returns to the palm pad at the door. It responds with
another soft tone and disappointing pinkish red glow. If only
she'd watched Shar's exit instead of collapsing in a fit upstairs,
she'd at least know how the door mechanism worked.

"I've gotta start making better moves if I'm going to survive this experience," she mumbles to herself while staring up
at the curved glass ceiling high above her head. She quickly
dismisses her self-flagellation as it dawns on her that if the
roles were reversed, she'd never abandon a prisoner in an area
that they could easily walk out of. No, for the time being, she's
trapped here until she can acquire more data.

"Where would I go anyway?" she says aloud, finally feeling her heart rate return to something close to normal. She
reasons that even if she were to get free, it's not as if she could
steal a car and drive back home to Chicago. And if what she's
been told has any truth to it, Cyphor Gicul's band of revolu-
tionaries would love to snatch her up and slit her throat.

Luci repeats the name "Cyphor Gicul" a few times as she
makes her way to the large circular pit sitting area. Something about the name is oddly familiar, but she can't determine how. She's never known anyone called Cyphor. She takes
a seat on the overstuffed sofa, watching the hundreds of bubbles

dance in the area's centerpiece, a dark metal basin. The sway-ing movement of the liquid is hypnotic. Luci changes from the couch to a position of sitting on her knees before the enormous bowl. She's sweating and leans in to wash her face.

A voice from across the room shouts, "Stop!"

It's Macer. He rushes to her in alarm.

The dark red Nehru jacket with embroidered R insignia on the side is quite a contrast to the coverall jumpsuit that Macer wore the night before. Royse trails quickly behind him, wearing a nondescript black shirt and trousers.

Macer declares, "That's a very sensitive piece of equipment, and you could gravely hurt yourself."

Luci glances at the bubbling pool, but there's nothing. She rises to her feet. "Why did you do this to me? You knew the consequences of time travel would eliminate any chance of me bearing children."

Macer stops on the other side of the basin from her and is quickly joined by the floating concierge bot.

His hesitation to answer frustrates her. "Did you tell the first version of me when I came here before? Did you tell *that* Luci what the trip did to her?" She manages force her anger down this time. She must remain calm and get more data.

Macer inhales sharply and wipes his forehead with a cloth from his pocket. "Yes, you're right," he says with a minimal shrug of the shoulders. "It was wrong of me not to give you the choice. Truth is that she—the other you—wasn't told of leap skip side effects because it never came up."

Luci tries to ignore how Royse has positioned himself beside her, looking ready to pounce if the situation calls for it. She does her best to nonchalantly take a few steps away from him, though it likely won't make much difference if he decides to grab her again. "So where is she—the other version of me? What happened before, making you feel that you were forced to come and snatch me after my lecture last night?"

"Like I told you in the warehouse, identity convergence occurs and U-curve overlays this most current rendition of the subject. That eliminates the previous incarnation."

"Yes, you did say something like that, but you know what you didn't tell me? You never told me why it was necessary." Her hands ball into fists at her sides. She tries to uncurl them to appear more relaxed than she is, but they remain knots of flesh. "You said you'd explain it all on the other side, because we had to go right then. Well, here we are, on the other side of the skip, so start talking."

Macer's bushy eyebrows rise in surrender as he lets out a resigned sigh. "A madman who goes by the name Cyphor Gicul leads a group called *L'inversione*. Their stated goal is to prevent *Hi no Kawa* from ever taking place." Macer's dark eyes burrow into her, and the tension in his face displays every wrinkle and crack like lines on a worn map. "We cannot deny that the war and its outcome was horrible, but the fact is that we've risen from the ashes like a phoenix and rebuilt something ... something worthwhile here. I'll show you proof of that in a little bit. Anyway, something happened when you were here before ... the *other* you." He plops down in one of the seats on the opposite side of the circle from her.

A shiver runs through her body. "Something happened ... like what?"

He gazes absently into the bubbling fluid between them.

"Tell me," she demands. "I have the right to know. It must have been something pretty bad if the other Luci was willing to allow me to write over everything that she had done with fresh experiences. How far did she get with solving your drift pattern thing?"

He runs a hand over his bald, veiny head to massage it. "She never even started."

The revelation winds her. Luci stammers, "Why? What did she say? Did she refuse to do it?"

Royse motions for her to sit. She reluctantly complies while staring Macer down.

The dark beads of his pupils fix on hers, and she can't look away. "She didn't say anything," Macer says softly above the gurgling of the basin. "She died."

Before Luci can utter a word, he adds, "She was assassinated by Gicul's second-in-command."

She covers her mouth. Was this what Shar was about to tell her?

Royse takes a seat beside her as he says, "That's why we had to get you here quickly. We had to make sure you were safe away from Gicul's cult of followers. It was just a matter of time before they would have done a leap skip to your interval and eliminated you a second and final time."

Macer doesn't admonish his interruption and only nods sorrowfully. "Yes, this is true."

Luci's feels as if she's been dunked in ice water.

Macer leans forward with elbows on knees. "I understand how overwhelming all this is, but we've taken precautions this time to ensure your absolute safety, and the man responsible for your murder has been apprehended and will never be set free. Furthermore, only a select handful of people know that you're here now. Even in your own interval, everyone will think you're at your friend's beach house in New Jersey for a couple of weeks."

The truth of this makes her feel even more desperately alone.

He stands. "I'm confident that your expertise will solve what's happening here, and we'll even be able to put an end to Gicul and his followers. We'll return you to your time, and you'll continue on with your life."

She rises, and it triggers Royse to stand too. She shakes her head. "Continue on as a barren woman," she says defiantly. "You still had no right to do that to me. But I think that there's a way to make it right ... there's a way to fix what you've done."

Macer exchanges a curious look with Royse and then shifts back to Luci. "Really? And how is it that I can make things right as you say?"

"You have time travel at your disposal," she begins and stops short.

"Yes, go on," Macer says, though the tone is condescending.

"Okay, look," she says, attempting to present her demand. "Unlike males who can generate millions of sperm at any time, females are born with all of the oocyte egg cells that they'll ever have in their lifetime. Approximately eleven thousand of these die every month prior to puberty, and after that, only around eight hundred ever mature into a viable ovum, or egg. That works out to be four hundred per ovary."

"What's your point?" Macer asks. "You said you had a way for me to 'fix' your sterility. It sounded like a demand of sorts. What is it? What are you asking?"

"So when all of this is over, you send a physician back with me to before I came through the skip when my eggs were still good and extract some for me to use at a later date."

"Okay, but it won't make a difference," Macer replies with indifference.

"Why do you say that?"

"Not to be crass, but the other version of you, the later one, she didn't have children either, and she was brought here at a much older age in your timeline—past typical childbearing years." He lifts a hand in mock surrender. "But I'll honor your request and do as you've asked."

She's stunned that the negotiation was so easy. "Wait. How do I know that you'll keep your word?"

Royse takes a step toward her. "You'll show him respect."

"No, it's alright, Royse," Macer says with a disarming chuckle. "Dr. Gaudiano here is a woman of science who has devoted herself to a career in dealing with things that she can prove. That's one of the things that makes her so good at her job." Macer turns and heads for the entryway as he speaks. The concierge bot trails him as he walks, no doubt recording every word. "Unfortunately, this isn't a formula that can be balanced into an equation. No, this is the stuff of humankind. It's only my promise to do something." He talks more loudly to compensate for the distance between them. Returning with a satchel, he's all smiles. "You see, we're just going to have to trust each other."

Royse moves to the side, making room for Macer. The older man reaches into the satchel and produces a stack of some type of cloth material. "Luci," Macer says affectionately, "as I said in the warehouse, all of this will go so much easier if we work as friends instead of adversaries. I'm sure you'll solve the equations more quickly if you approach the project as our ally and collaborator instead of as a captive prisoner holding out as long as you can, hunger strikes, and all that type nonsense."

He tucks the items under his arm to bend and lower the satchel to the floor. "I know, in our haste, I wasn't able to be completely truthful to you or go into details of what we're up against, and for that, I apologize. I am truly sorry, but the issue of leap skip sterilization was a minor concern to us compared to the extreme probable risk of you being murdered in your own interval."

He cautiously steps forward, offering the stack of light blue fabric, but Luci's mind is a million miles away. "But Shar said that it couldn't be done . . . for me to go back to the same exact time."

She instantly detests the part of herself that is so quick to betray Shar in order to get at what she wants. Shar is the only one of her three captors that has been the least bit kind to her. Exposing Shar's comments to her boss isn't who she is. Could it be the stress of everything finally revealing who really lurks in Luci's core? Her heart sinks with guilt and the prospect that maybe she is this cold.

Macer's smile grows even larger as he thrusts the garment at her again. "I wouldn't worry too much about anything that Miss Ryson said. She's a lovely girl and a talented technician, but she doesn't know everything, and this is one of those things beyond her scope."

Luci absently receives the clothes. She plays back the memory of her discussion with Shar, about the possibility of reversing the sterilization. "It's just that she seemed so convinced that—"

"Yes, I'm sure she believed in every word of whatever she told you, but you should trust in me, not her."

Luci did it again. She looks down at the bundle of clothing in her arms, vowing to herself no more Shar talk. "Okay, Chancellor, so trust . . . what is it that you're entrusting to me?" She looks up at him for an answer. "You said that we have to have to trust each other."

"Yes, well . . ." he begins as his grin fades, "Relicus City is dependent upon you to solve the current crisis, and in a way, even more critical are your actions when you return to your interval."

Royse nervously shifts his weight from one foot to the other, which gets Luci's attention. "What is it?" She turns to Macer. "What?"

"If, for any reason, you were not to create DPM in our past, this city would be extinguished before it ever has the chance to be."

"Because *Hi no Kawa* would not occur?" she asks. "But how would I be here in this moment now if everything hasn't occurred? Obviously, everything goes according to the way you know it to be. Otherwise, you wouldn't exist to get me in the first place."

"Actually, that's not entirely accurate," Macer says. "Movement in the past doesn't 'lock into place' in the present or future until the subject commits to it. A man standing at a fork in the road but hasn't chosen a path is allowed to go either way. Once he commits to his choice and begins to travel down the road, the action solidifies, for lack of a better term. He commits, and then the universe responds accordingly."

The explanation dazes her. "So everything is not settled yet? This is different from all that we know about space and time."

"Yes, well, the people before Copernicus believed that the sun rotated around the Earth, but mankind later found out there was something different at work." He shakes his head. "Whether *L'inversione* were to succeed in taking your life or you willfully don't submit the drift pattern theorem when you return, either way, the city would cease to exist. That's the part that I have to trust you to do, following through with DPM no matter what."

"We've taken measures to ensure this," Royse interjects.

The politician's smile returns to Macer's face as he gestures to for the man to be silent on the subject. "Ah, but that's a conversation for another time. For right now, I'd like to promote some good will between us. I've arranged for a special visit for you today. I want you to see what's at stake, what we're fighting for, so to speak, in hopes of inspiring you to achieve great things while you're our guest here." He points at the bundle in her arms that Luci forgot was there. "Those garments are something more appropriate for where we're headed. It's important that we don't draw attention to you being here. *L'inversione* could have spies anywhere. We must be extremely cautious."

She shakes her head. "I just don't get it. What's the motivation of *L'inversione?* I mean, if they succeed, then everyone here loses, right? This whole place disappears because it will have never happened. How does that serve them?"

Macer extends his palms upward. "Exactly. Hence the name of their group: *L'inversione.*" He shakes his head at the preposterous concept. "Leave it to say every generation through time has been plagued with charlatans, religious zealots, and small-brained, suicidal nihilists."

"It's religious?"

"Honestly, I don't know. Like I mentioned, we've captured one of Gicul's lead men. Though he knows he'll never be free, he's resistant to any of our questions. Even if the war was preventable, which I doubt it is, there's no reasonable evidence to support the theory that *Hi no Kawa* wouldn't occur again in some other form—a worse event that would destroy the entire human race. That's a gamble that I'm not willing to take."

This is new information to Luci. "They really believe that the nuclear war can be averted?"

"*L'inversione* have either deliberately or inadvertently sabotaged several interval junctures. Their stupidity is only matched by their recklessness. If they manage to accidentally damage the city's pathway to our food supply, we'll return to a period of barbarism, and then . . ." His gaze intensifies even more. "I'd expect that those who did survive would eventually starve too, but only after cannibalizing the flesh of their fallen neighbors."

The idea is gruesome and hangs on the air. Luci holds the clothing tightly to her chest. "Do you have other food source intervals or farming outposts?"

Macer shakes his head. "There was no need. The Grange is all that we have. When my father Waleen and the others established it, there were no crazies like Cyphor Gicul threatening to erase everything we'd built."

"But what of New Australia? Were you at peace with them back then?"

"We didn't even know of their existence until a few years ago," Macer answers. "There was no practical reason to spread out our efforts over multiple intervals." He massages his temples. "And the threat of Gicul and *L'inversione* has come up so fast that there hasn't been time enough to consider alternatives that would feasibly satisfy even the basic daily food needs of the people."

Eager to shift the subject, Luci remarks, "I still don't get how stopping me from developing the drift pattern fits into their objective of preventing a nuclear holocaust."

The two men exchange a curious look, and then Macer addresses her. "I thought that you would've figured that out by now, my dear. DPM . . . your drift pattern theorem is what set the war in motion in the first place."

TWELVE

AT MACER'S BEHEST, A STUNNED Luci heads upstairs to change into the outfit he's provided. She mechanically ascends the spiral staircase, attempting to process this new revelation.

For what feels like an eternity, Luci looks at herself in the digital mirror of the bathroom. She studies her own unblinking eyes, wondering if hers is the face of the woman that killed the world, a modern-day Pandora. Was she culpable for the fate of nearly ten billion people? Physicist Robert Oppenheimer's Fat Man and Little Boy had extinguished the lives of two hundred thousand people; this was fifty thousand times that. Would the world have been better off if she'd died in that car crash alongside her parents on that balmy August afternoon? As it was, she escaped with only bruised ribs and the cut to her leg when she was dragged from the submerged vehicle. Of course, those were the physical injuries; the real damage doesn't always show up in an x-ray.

"Doctor, are you coming?" Royse yells from the lower level.

A weary sigh escapes from her and shouts back at the closed door. "Yeah, I'm fine. Just a minute."

She's surprised that her bundle from Macer isn't anything like what Shar wore. It's a long grey-blue dress made of coarse material swathed around a fine white underdress. Both of these garments wrap around some sort of headpiece, leather shoes, and a knotted leather belt. She discards her jeans and t-shirt and tries to make the best of the snug-fitting garb. It reminds her of the costume she wore in her high school's production of Hamlet.

Still processing the weight of the world, Luci slowly descends the spiral staircase in an emotional stupor.

Royse stops his pacing when he sees her.

Trying hard to avoid tripping on the narrow full-length dress, she scans the room. "Where's Macer?"

"He's outside speaking to someone." Before she can ask, he adds dismissively, "Don't worry, it's one of the select few who knows about your visit here." Royse moves over to her. "Hey, sorry about before . . . you know, last night and all. We were running out of time, nothing personal."

Her teeth clench together, and she doesn't give him the satisfaction of accepting his apology.

Royse plows through the awkwardness by changing the subject. "You should go ahead and put the guimple on and use your hair to conceal that you don't have a Viatorio."

"A what?" Luci asks.

He taps the device on his ear. "One of these. I expect you'll get your Viatorio later today or tomorrow, but for right now, it's better if we don't draw attention to you, and the absence of one will certainly make you stand out."

She puts on the head garment. Adjusting it, she makes a sardonic observation. "I look like Lady Marian from Robin Hood or a high-fashion nun with all this stuff on."

Ignoring her tone, he clinically answers, "It's called a kirtle. It's a requirement for one to be properly clothed for the interval they're visiting in case they encounter any of the residents from the period."

She grabs the hem of the skirt and lifts the bottom a few inches off the floor. "So, what is this for, medieval England?"

"No, eleventh-century Spain," he answers, unenthused. "The twin mountain monasteries known as Yuso and Suso."

"Monasteries . . . why there?"

"You'll see," Royse says.

"You said it's important to be properly dressed for the time period, but you can't go dressed like that. Or am I going there alone?"

"No, the three of us are going there together." Royse moves for the door. "I'll change at the station. The chancellor and I have lockers there."

She's seen how Royse worships his boss and knows how he'll likely support any lie and half-truth that Macer rattles off, but she decides to give it a shot. "Royse, I need to ask you something," she says without the coolness in her voice now.

He stops and turns to face her with a surprised expression. "Yes, Doctor?"

Luci gnaws at her bottom lip before asking, "Chancellor Macer said I caused the war. Is that true or is he just trying to guilt me into doing all of this?"

There's a pause as Royse's forehead furls. The pensive look on his face and delay makes her sick to her stomach. With a sigh, he says, "It's the truth. I mean, you didn't cause it, but arguments of the use of DPM did trigger *Hi no Kawa*."

She considers this, attempting to determine if he's lying or not. She can't tell if his expression is too hard to read or if he's simply telling the truth. Somewhere, there must be a database or something where she can research the information for herself.

Finally, she says, "Maybe you can answer something more personal for me, a question not related to the war."

He shrugs. "What's your question?"

"Do you have a family? You know, spouse, kids." She catches herself before saying pets, given that no such thing exists here.

He looks relieved to discuss something less dismal. "No, never oathed. And yes, a family would've been okay, but it wasn't that big of an issue for me since I was appointed to be the chancellor's Level One Protector." He catches himself mid-shrug and allows his shoulders to lower more slowly. "It's a security thing. If I had children or a spouse, someone may be able to get to me through them, compromise me to get to the chancellor. I took a vow to serve him."

"Why does he need protection? Who's out to get him?" she asks, wondering if Cyphor Gicul is out to kill him too.

"Our current system government is fresh—just a few decades old, in fact—and as to be expected, there are some that feel that they should have been selected to lead or appointed into positions of authority but weren't. Because of that, the chancellor has many enemies, some cowering within the city, some in New Australia."

This is more new information to her. "What's New Australia? Could Gicul be from there?"

"It's a pocket of survivors outside of our city. Maybe a few million or so, we don't know for sure. The chancellor doesn't think there's any affiliation with Gicul though. Cyphor Gicul seems to know too much about Relicus City." His eyes look past her to the ground as if the answer's marked on the floor. "The little that we do know of Gicul indicates that he usually avoids our interval, doing leap skips to less frequented areas to avoid detection and capture."

"But can't the longchairs be tracked?" Luci asks. "Shar said there was something in them regulating where they went."

Royse looks back up at her. "That's true, but a man named Malom Roderick, a pioneer of Longchair technology, was swayed by Gicul into overriding the tracking capabilities. He's the one that the chancellor mentioned that's locked up."

"So Gicul literally could be anywhere." The comment comes out more barbed than Luci intends. "I mean, how do you know that he's not in Spain right now waiting to attack us?"

Royse looks wounded and reacts defensively. He points his index finger at her. "Look, I've managed to protect Chancellor Macer now going on five and a half years. I've devoted myself to his safety. We will find Cyphor Gicul and put an end to all of this Undoing nonsense." Royse turns as he squeezes the

Viatorio on his ear and places his hand on the door's palm reader.

Luci takes note of the activation protocol for later.

The door slides open with a swoosh as the change in air pressure hisses around them. There's a faint smell like that of ammonia but different. She faces out of the mouth of a tubular glass enclosure. Fifteen-foot-high horseshoe-shaped fasteners line the submerged corridor, and glittering sunlight cuts through the waves above. The light dances a hypnotic pattern on the black mats of the walkway. A hundred or so feet down the glass hallway stands Macer with his back to them, talking to someone.

Concentrating on clearing the bottom of her dress over the raised door threshold, Luci nearly stumbles into the monster directly to the right side of the opening. She gasps, horrified by the grotesque appearance of the hunched-over, greyish creature. It's a thing of nightmares, and it's moving toward her.

"Wait, wait, wait, wait," Royse sputters in a desperate voice as the ghastly being focuses a futuristic rifle of some sort on Luci.

She staggers a few steps backward from it, only stopping when she collides into the curved wall of the corridor. Royse moves with amazing speed placing himself between it and Luci collapsed on the floor. Her heart pounds at the sight of what must be one of Gicul's assassins.

"Stand-down code one seven twenty-nine!" Royse yells frantically, mashing at his Viatorio. "Protocol 9-F bulwark nikto!"

The creature instantly slumps over in place as if awaiting another command.

Luci makes it to her feet, spurred on by pure adrenaline soaring through her system. "Sweet Jesus in heaven, what *is* that?" she asks in a voice loud enough to echo throughout the corridor.

This is the source of the pungent stench. To Luci, the sickly-sweet stink of ammonia is like an epoxy coating on a swimming pool. She instinctively covers her nose with her sleeve to keep from retching, gawking at the monstrosity. It's difficult to determine its height, since the creature's hunched over, but it's easily taller than she is.

"The chancellor's gonna have my ass for this," Royse says sourly. He glares at her. "We were in such a rush that I forgot to notify it of your leave clearance for permission to go to the Grange."

Luci can't turn away from the hideous abomination before them.

A dingy plastic sheeting, yellowed over time, covers much of the thing's body. Its arms emerge from the tarp, strapped with dark, rubber, elbow-length gloves that match its boots.

The most shocking feature is the face. A stained damp and dripping cloth like burlap conceals the forehead. It loosely runs along the side of the face like oversized muttonchops. Large ovals have been cut away from the mask for the glassy, vapid eyes to peer through. Though the skin is grey, Luci suspects this was once a person of African descent due to the prominent flattened nose and likely a male, judging by the scattered whiskers sprouting from its chin.

"But . . . it's on our side, right?" she asks, muffled by the sleeve of her dress.

"Huh? Oh, yeah, it's a cybernetic sentry," Royse explains. "They're called Cybos." He points to the rod weapon. "And it's got a churka."

She can tell by the sadistic tone in his voice that her shock and revulsion please him, but she can't take her eyes off the guard. Its mouth is cracked open, exposing rotted, discolored teeth as it "breathes." To Luci, it looks more like a dog panting in slow motion, but unlike a canine, this creature's tongue has been cut out.

"Everything alright down there?" a nasally male voice asks.

"Yes, sir!" Royse yells in an agitated but booming voice. "Everything's under control."

"Who's that?" Luci asks softly, her heart rate finally settling.

"The city's minister of security. He was the head of the cybo deployment project about a year and a half ago. The name's Cavazos."

"Pretty impressive once you get past the sheer ugliness of the thing." Royse boasts like a used car salesman ready to close a deal. "Don't be fooled by it being slumped over like that; these things are very fast when the circumstance calls for it."

Luci's strength gradually returns to her. ""It's human though, right?"

"It once was, but hard to still say that after the subject has gone through processing. Its physical abilities have been enhanced beyond normal human limitations to serve us. Like I said, looks can be deceiving. These are fierce fighters when it comes to it."

"But is it *alive*?" Luci asks, slightly embarrassed that she's affected by it the way she is.

"It responds to direct commands and initiatives, but other than rudimentary tasks, there's no conscious thought taking place in there."

She manages to peel her eyes off it to finally look at Royse. "But who was he and how did it become this way?"

"It became this way because somewhere along the line, it couldn't comply. There are no executions in Relicus City. Enemies of the state are either jailed in Carcerium compartments or reprocessed into a cybo rather than taking human life."

Luci scoffs, "So lobotomizing your enemies and gloating as you force them to perform slave labor is more humane than letting them die with dignity?" Her eyes wander back to the hunched cybo. "I'm sorry, but that's messed up."

Royse counters sharply, "Unlike the interval that you come from, we in Relicus city use every resource, even a life that would try to corrupt or destroy what we've built here."

It saddens her that anything would be forced to exist in a state like this. Luci gestures to the cybo with her free hand. "Did you know him?"

Royse snorts. "Of course not, and it's not a '*he*' anymore anyways. Don't humanize it like that." He adds dismissively as he moves to her, "Look, it probably was a reprobate from New Australia that came over here to attack us or something. Anyway, whatever it did, it's been punished for it and has a chance to serve for the betterment of Relicus City."

He blocks her view of the cybo, pointing to the Macer at the end of the corridor behind her. "Now, if you will, please."

A compulsion for having the last word, Luci begins to walk but says, "It's still not right. I don't care what *he* did. Nobody deserves to end up like that."

The conversation at the other end of the corridor intensifies, growing louder. Macer's back is to them as they approach. "Pol, I don't care about your protocols. You have to keep this covered for me. It's not like there's anything of any value there anyway."

A dumpy, heavy-set man dressed in similar clothes to Macer glances over to Luci and Royse as they approach. She finds it curious how anyone can be obese in a time of food scarcity. Did she misunderstand what Shar said about the conditions here? The man's dark eyes lock onto hers from about fifty feet away. A scowl forms on his face as he looks back at the chancellor. "Enos, it's just that if we—"

He's cut off by Macer's raised voice. "Pol, if you can't do it, perhaps I should appoint someone else that can! No one is stationed there, so nobody's going to know unless they find out from your technicians. So are we clear on this?"

Cavazos shoots a look back at Luci and Royse as they approach. She averts her eyes, sensing his embarrassment at being chastised in front of them.

"There is a way that I can modify the report and suppress it," the man says through gritted teeth, "but only for about a week. Then it'll come out."

"Hopefully, that is all we'll need," Macer says triumphantly. "So go and get it done." He makes a point to pat him on the shoulder harder than a friendly acknowledgment.

The overweight man offers the best bow he can manage without toppling forward before turning to leave. "Yes, sir."

Macer spins to face Luci and Royse walking up. She catches a flicker of hatefulness in the older man's eyes. Then his bushy eyebrows shoot upward, and the hundred-watt smile flashes at her. "I'm so sorry that you had to witness any of that." He droops his head slightly. "Sometimes you have to get a little aggressive for people to take you seriously." He snaps his fingers a few times. "But that's over, and I'm eager to show you my city."

The stranger waddles down the corridor.

"You look splendid, my dear," Macer says with an ever-widening smile.

Luci isn't fooled by the mask of his fake warmth. "I don't appreciate being imprisoned and watched over by that cybo thing."

Macer offers a faux wounded expression. "But you're not a prisoner here, as I've said before. You're my guest. And as for the security, it's for your own safety."

"Is everything alright, sir?" Royse asks guardedly.

Macer's eyes shift to him. "Reports are that the Pakpattan interval juncture is gone."

"We lost another one?" Royse scratches the back of his neck. "Pakpattan . . . that doesn't even make sense. There's nothing there—no people, no outpost, no nothing."

"I agree, Mr. Timmons. That's exactly what I was telling Security Minister Cavazos."

Royse quietly asks, "Sir, do we still want to do this then?" He twirls a finger in the air indicating Luci.

"Yes," Macer answers firmly. "We proceed with the plan. I think it will do the doctor good to see everything in context, to experience firsthand what she will be saving through her work, both Relicus City and the Grange." The smile disappears from his face, and his words become acidic. "And Royse, don't think that I don't know what just happened down there between the cybo and Dr. Gaudiano. I'm surprised that I have to tell you this since it *is* your job, but her safety should be given the same importance priority as my own."

Royse lowers his head. "Of course, Chancellor."

THIRTEEN

LUCI FOLLOWS HER GUIDES INTO the same compartment that Cavazos retreated into moments before. It's the size of a freight elevator, and Luci takes her place beside Macer. Royse positions himself in front, facing the door as it closes. As the lift ascends, she adjusts her headpiece. "Royse said we're going to some monasteries in Spain?"

"Yes. Actually, just one. We call it the Grange. It's where all of our food is grown and harvested. If that interval were to ever close—"

He doesn't finish the sentence, interrupted by the opening of the elevator door.

Before she's able to ask how all their food is supplied from a monastery farm, Royse steps through onto the platform outside and presses his index finger against his lips. The sharp smell of saltwater fills Luci's nostrils as she and Macer remain in the elevator compartment. She wills herself to stop fidgeting, realizing the nervous act is compounding her stress.

After a few tense seconds, Royse gestures the "all clear" for them to join him. The trio moves outside, down a curved white platform as long as the corridor they were in before. It's like the pier of a boardwalk constructed from a type of plastic instead of wooden boards. Luci thinks of the boardwalk in Atlantic City back home, where she was supposed to be at today—a place long in the past from here. Normally, the sound of water gently lapping against the support beams thirty or so feet below would be soothing to her, but not today.

Even the warmth of the midday sun on her face and ocean breeze blowing through her dark hair cannot ease her growing tension; there is someone, somewhere intent on taking her life. It's obvious to her that Royse is anxious too. Like an ever-vigilant guard dog, he alternates scanning from left to right, up and down with every other step.

At the end of the curved walkway, the top of a stationary dome peeks above the crest of the water. Luci suspects that, like the domicile they've just left, the main part of the structure is submerged. She glances back to the one behind them. If the outer dome is any indicator, the one they're headed to is triple in size.

Macer declares, "*That* one is my home." They take a few more steps before he adds, "Though I haven't seen very much of it lately—I've spent most of my time in my office the last few weeks, what with this Gicul crisis and diplomatic problems with New Australia."

"Are you at war with New Australia?" she asks.

The answer comes slowly. "Technically, no. We have a treaty."

"But Australia? How far away are they from here?"

Royse motions to speed up the pace.

Macer gestures to the water. "Relicus city, where we are, is in the Pacific Ocean near the equator, approximately fifty-three hundred miles from them."

The dress she's wearing wasn't designed for haste. Luci concentrates on keeping the pace without stumbling and falling flat on her face.

Macer says, "Essentially, it's only us and New Australia that have managed to restore any semblance of society, and yet we fight. Despite everything that's gone before, our two nations stand against one another."

"Come on," Royse commands from the front.

Luci lifts the hem of her skirt a few inches for more mobility. "How many of them are there, and why would they be your adversary?"

"Best estimate is there's a million or two of them out there," he explains. "It's strategic for them to withhold their exact numbers from us. We don't tell them, but our census numbers of citizens in Relicus City tops the six million mark. There's a peace agreement in place between us, but I find it absurd how we're like conjoined twins fighting over who gets to eat the last piece of Jehasi bread." Feeling the need to explain, Macer adds, "It's a bread that's like a thick paste . . . not very good."

The population number catches Luci's attention and forces her to slow. "Wait—so you farm food for six million people at a monastery in eleventh-century Spain? How's that even possible, time travel or not?"

The question peps Macer up. "You'll see soon enough."

Though she knows it's in vain, Luci protests, "I'm so sick of everyone telling me that."

As they make their way along the outermost part of the curve, a glint of sunlight catches Luci's eye. To the side of Macer's quarters is a platform supporting a hefty machine. As they approach, Luci realizes it's a vehicle of some sort easily as large as a helicopter.

Luci points. "What is that?"

Royse speaks above the battering wind noise off the sea. "It's a drobine, the chancellor's personal transport." He continues scanning for any signs of danger.

Increasing his pace even more, Macer says, "Royse will fly us to the longchair hangar a few kilometers from here."

Luci nods her head in acknowledgement, but she's looking beyond the dome of Macer's house at other bubble structures in the distance; thousands, maybe hundreds of thousands of them, lay across the water like floating pearls. Though it's difficult to make out through the soft haze, a vertical building of some sort defiantly dwarfs them all in the distance.

Royse rattles off some technical jargon as he leans against the strange-looking bladeless chopper. He pinches the Viatorio on his ear, communicating to some type of flight command somewhere. The craft is an elongated bubble held in the middle of a perfectly round upturned horseshoe. A series of crisscrossing cables suspends the passenger compartment in place like a spider's web that's snagged a clear pebble in the center.

Royse ends his transmission and touches a panel on the side of the four-person craft. The left side of the shell folds down, transforming into steps. Macer and Luci enter first, and then Royse finds his place behind a virtual console. As Luci sits, the bucket seat startles her by wrapping a mesh harness around the top half of her body.

Macer's seat does the same for him as he informs her, "You may adjust that if it's too tight."

Slightly embarrassed, Luci brushes off her surprise, saying, "I have an aversion to being strapped into things."

"Trust me, you'll be grateful for the harness soon enough," Royse says as the virtual panel before him comes to life. The steps return to a translucent state as they retract with a pressurized hiss and fold back into the craft to form the side.

The drobine lifts in silence. It effortlessly shoots upward from the platform, and Luci feels her stomach left behind. She glances through the glass roof enclosure as the giant horseshoe apparatus shifts its angle slightly, affecting the pitch of the pod. It propels them through the sky without any visible moving parts.

Macer taps the window on his right to get her attention. He proudly announces, "You're getting a view of Relicus City that most people never see this far out."

From the air, a pattern to the city forms that wasn't visible below. If the intricate hexagonal grids were a net gently floating atop the brilliant blue green shimmering water, Macer's place would be a node on its outermost strand.

"This is amazing," Luci says. "How did you all do this?"

"Through an act of sheer will," Macer responds without missing a beat.

She pulls her gaze away to meet his eyes. "No, I mean where did you get all of the materials . . . all the construction?" She points through the glass. "I mean, how did you build all of this on the ocean in the middle of nowhere?"

Macer's thick eyebrows rise. "Oh, yes," Macer says dismissively. "About that." He pauses, rubbing his forehead as if to jumpstart a memory. "I believe your interval called them the Arab United Emirates, or something like that. Shortly before *Hi No Kawa*, investors from there endeavored to build a floating resort with a nearby amusement park."

She nods. "So you built on top of it?"

"No, the construction site was many kilometers from here, too far from the vortex. We moved the materials here. The Emirates even had constructed a small airport for all the guests they expected to peddle their services to."

"It's incredible, really," Luci says, "all that you've done here."

"I and those with me have nearly fulfilled the legacy began many years ago."

Luci nods. "Started by your father, Waleen, right?"

The mention of the name disrupts his oration, but he quickly recovers. "Yes, my father, Waleen and his contemporaries . . . and now the torch of that leadership has been passed to us."

The magnificence of the city zipping by hundreds of feet below them takes Luci's breath away.

As the drobine effortlessly glides in the direction of the center of the city, the hexagon frameworks bunch up in smaller groupings. The bubble domiciles, all relatively the same size, form tighter clusters as they close in on the city's middle. Every so often, the craft zips over a more conventional structure, a building like from Luci's time period, but none exceed a height of three or four stories tall.

Macer explains, "This . . . all of this is why you're here. This is what you're saving."

Situated in the center hub of the city, one structure towers high above the rest. The impossibly tall, gleaming building casts a long shadow like a sundial across the dome clusters below. The base of the structure is unique from anything Luci's ever seen, like giant tree roots stretching out in every direction.

Macer points. "That's where we're headed."

"Here we go," Royse announces from the cockpit. "Making our ascent to the tower now."

The craft angles sharply upward. Even in the pressurized cabin, Luci's ears pop. "How tall is it?"

Macer is pleased by her astonishment. "The top of the spire is nine hundred forty meters. It had to be." Macer corrects himself, "Well . . . the portal threshold is located nine hundred fifteen meters in the sky, but there are two office levels above that."

"The time door is just floating up there?" Luci asks, grateful for the chair harness that's securing her in place as Royse said she would be.

Like a patient teacher, he explains, "We don't choose their placement, in the same way someone doesn't get to choose where Mount Everest is located. In fact, quite a number of the interval junctures are unreachable because they're thousands of feet below the earth or sea way up in the thermosphere. Minister Cavazos has said he'd even heard of one in the belly of an active volcano."

"But how do you know that the portals are there?" Luci asks.

"Drift pattern mathematics identify not only when but where they're located, like an astrophysicist of your day finding black holes in space without ever actually seeing one through a telescope."

She resists reminding him of Dr. Katie Bouman's shot during the second decade of her century.

Macer gestures to the handhold lowering beside her. "You're gonna want to grab that."

"What, huh? Oh . . ." she replies, taking his meaning. She clutches it just as the drobine turns at a sharp angle and sails vertically upward parallel to the building.

The *g*-force prohibits any further conversation from her as she's pressed into her seat by an unseen pressure. It feels like an elephant is sitting on her chest, forcing her heart to the bottom of her medieval costume footwear.

Eventually, the craft returns horizontal. Royse guides the hovering vessel as gently as a butterfly into one of four open bays.

FOURTEEN

"Wow, that was intense!" Luci exclaims, gasping as the drobine hatch retracts with a pressurized hiss. A uniformed man and slender woman wearing similarly designed outfits to Macer's approach from a distance. They cross the cavernous landing bay to the craft. Macer exits first down the steps while Royse completes the vessel's shutdown protocols. The woman's greeting echoes throughout the area as she rushes up to him. "Good afternoon, Your Excellency."

Luci hikes her long dress up to her shins and cautiously descends behind Macer.

His tone is all business, devoid of any warmth toward the woman. "We have three for the Grange today."

She offers a submissive nod. "Yes, sir. Mr. Timmons alerted us. Two longchairs are being prepped."

Luci feels a slight unease that the uniformed man standing at attention has the same type of churka weapon that the cybo held outside of the guesthouse doorway. She's never liked guns, and though this future weapon is radically different in design from the rifles back home, she suspects its purpose is the same: to end life. Luci looks past him to the massive opening in the side of the building Royse flew them through. The city is even more breathtaking from this dizzying height. The bubble structures shine like little iridescent dots on the sparkling blue water below. The sight of it reminds Luci of looking out from the observation deck of the 108–story Willis Tower back home in Chicago and makes her feel homesick.

Gazing upon the glittering city below, she's reminded of Macer's statement that there's some six million or so lives down there whose fates rest on her ability to solve an elusive math problem. What if her DPM discovery was a fluke, something that she stumbled across?

And what of the "victims" of DPM, her mathematical principle? What does she owe them? Briefly, she contemplates lifting the long hem of her skirt to her knees and making a mad dash for the bay opening. Surely her suicide would prevent *Hi no Kawa* from ever happening. What did Royse mean earlier about taking measures in her interval? Were her friends and colleagues at risk if she forfeited her life? Could Macer simply send a crew back to her lecture and snatch her all over again? The memory of Shar's final admonition to her that she "must keep herself alive" pops into her mind.

The time to act passes.

Royse rejoins them, and the party briskly walks across the area. To Luci, the combination of the row of small glass offices and the highly-polished tile floor looks like a car dealer's showroom, minus any vehicles on display.

To her relief, the man with the churka doesn't follow them through the large door at the end of the area but rather stands at attention outside.

"This is one of the things that I wanted you to see," Macer says as the four of them step onto an extended escalator that stretches farther upward than modern engineering of her time could fathom.

She cautiously peers over the side of the handrail. A hundred feet or so down is a busy canyon maze of conveyor belts shuffling containers the size of tall minivans in every direction. Scattered workers in white jumpsuits and head coverings move throughout various station points, but the operation is almost entirely automated. A dull churning sound drones on as the containers push through the intricate labyrinth to their destinations.

"All of that is food?" Luci asks, noticing for the first time the cybos perched on various planks extending from the walls.

"Forty-nine metric tons a day," Macer says. "It all comes through here and is distributed throughout the city. Remarkable, isn't it?"

Luci doesn't look up to where he's standing, her eyes fixed on the production below. "And all this . . . it feeds a city of six million?"

Macer descends the wide escalator steps until he's on the one Luci occupies. "Every gram of it."

After a couple of minutes of the steady climb, Luci says, "I have to admit, I'm impressed."

Macer smiles. "I knew you would be, and this is only the distribution processing plant. This is how we get the food to the city. The true magic happens in the other interval. Wait until we go to the Grange interval and you meet Bru."

She looks up at him. "This is amazing, but . . ." Luci hesitates, feeling a lump form in her throat.

"What? What is it, my dear?" Macer asks as his bushy eyebrows climb upward.

Tears well in her eyes. "We don't even have everyone fed in my time. Scores of people go hungry. It's just that I still can't get it out of my mind that this . . . all of this is because of me . . . because of something that I had a hand in creating. Ten billion people, Chancellor . . . a ten followed by nine zeros. All those people dead because of something I did."

Macer sighs and puts his hand on her shoulder. Luci resists the urge to pull away from his touch. The escalator continues to carry them upward in silence for another minute or so.

As they reach the apex of the climb, Luci says, "I just wish there was another way . . . a chance to avoid the *Hi no Kawa* war that causes all of this."

"Well . . ." Macer begins as the four of them take turns emptying onto the platform, "there's not."

The response is so unexpectedly curt and unflinching that Luci is taken aback.

Before she can respond, the attendant announces, "Sir, they're almost ready for you inside."

"Very good," he replies, moving to the door the woman ushers him to.

As Luci falls in behind Royse, her mind wanders to Macer's motive for bringing her here. Why risk exposing three of them to an attack by Gicul just to give her a tour of the city and show off the Grange? It makes no sense until she remembers that while he's a leader of a city of six million, he's a politician first. Politicians—the good ones at least—always had an innate sense of what a person wanted at their core. They were masters at sniffing this out and then finding a way to deliver whatever it was to them in order to get them to align with their goals.

Luci rebukes her transparency to him, but a part of her—a large part—is unashamedly thrilled to receive new information to process, taking to it like a cat to catnip.

As did the man with the churka, the attendant waits at the door and doesn't enter with them. The ceiling of the medium-sized area stops about twenty feet up, considerably lower than the areas they've been through since their arrival to the station. Four cybo sentries stand with backs to the entrance, two positioned on the left and the right. They remain motionless and at the ready, each behind separate hinged glass cases that look a little like dunking booths. It takes a moment to register the absence of the foul smell that she's come to associate with these pitiful creatures, and she is grateful for whatever marvel technology contained in the enclosures has filtered out their stench.

Along the left and right walls of the dimly lit room sit a dozen small half-cubicles. Each of these half squares is occupied by a man or woman who gazes in silence into a personal water basin as wide as a sink. They pay no attention to the entrance of the trio at first. The entire scene is surreal to her. Except for the odd bowls in the center of the desks, it reminds Luci of air traffic control stations she's seen in the movies.

Another major exception is that there are no radar screens or any visible computer devices.

A thin man in his thirties rises from one of the cubicles to approach Macer. He's got a port-wine-stain birthmark that runs from his chin to his cheek like an upside-down question mark. Luci wonders how appearance-conscious the people of this future time are and if the mark makes his him uncomfortable in social settings. As he walks over, Luci notices that a clear trough smaller than a rain gutter runs along the back ledge of all the booths. There's a clear tube that empties into each worker's respective pod bowl. Workers occasionally lean forward and sip the bubbling liquid from the desk basin with a straw-like apparatus.

Before she can ask about the peculiar practice, Royse nudges her. "One's about to come in."

"One what?" Luci asks, more confused than ever.

He points to a platform at the back of the room and says one word. "Longchair."

At first, the black waist-high stage platform looks like the top half of a giant set of pearly-white dentures. Nine longchairs arranged side-by-side with their bulbous fronts point into the room. Six of the fifteen slots are missing. This leaves gaps in the giant row of teeth as if the mouth it belonged to has had them knocked out in a brawl.

Royse nudges her and points to a digital display in front of one of the gaps. "Looks like it's coming from 1923 Argentina."

"What's in Argentina?" Luci asks.

Royse shrugs. "Never been there myself."

"So these don't just go to the food processing area?"

Royse shakes his head. "Of course not. Longchairs can leap skip to any sanctioned interval point. In fact, the two on the end are the ones we used in order to leap skip to your interval yesterday evening."

"I don't remember this place," Luci says.

"Yeah, well . . . you were unconscious."

Macer beckons to Royse across the room, and Luci follows him a few steps behind.

The technician with the birthmark and olive-colored skin that Macer's talking to looks uncomfortable; he avoids eye contact with Macer, choosing to stare at the floor.

Royse approaches. "Is everything okay, Chancellor?"

Macer nods, but he speaks softly and through gritted teeth. "Royse, this is technician archivist Benold Jesper." The chancellor acts as if he's brushing something off the shoulder of the technician's dark-green uniform as he continues in a low but firm voice. "Mr. Jesper claims there's no record of my return from the Grange a few days ago."

Royse cracks his knuckles while glaring at Jesper. "That's impossible. We didn't take a leap skip to the Grange last week. I accompany the chancellor everywhere he goes, and yesterday was the first leap skip we've done in a while. You should check again."

Jesper fidgets, wiggling nimble fingers at waist level, typing on the air. It appears as if he's wearing brass knuckles made of black rubber.

"I'm sorry, sir," Jesper says softly to match the conversation. "There's no R.O.R., Record of Return." He reaches for his Viatorio. "The longchair was returned by auto retrieval."

Macer looks around the room, studying the faces of the crew taking notice of them. "I know what R.O.R. stands for. Obviously, there's a mistake since I'm standing here in front of you." He turns to Royse. "Mr. Timmons, do I look like I'm at the Grange to you?"

Royse comically squints and mockingly tilts his head as if to get a better look. "You know, Your Excellency, I'm probably not as smart as all these technicians in here, but I'm pretty sure you're standing next to me—that is, unless we're both still at the Grange."

Jesper lowers his head again but manages to say. "You did a leap skip by yourself the other day. Mr. Timmons wasn't with you."

Luci cringes, wishing she could do something for the humiliated worker, but what?

"I see," Macer replies even more pompous than before. "And when did this leap skip supposedly occur?"

"Four days ago at 14:36."

Macer mock contemplates this. "Hmmm . . . Royse?"

The big man reaches in his pocket, slides his own set of the rubber knuckle things over his fingers, and pinches the Viatorio on his ear. After briefly air typing, he says, "No, that's not right. You were dedicating the new statue at that time." He returns the virtual key bands to his pocket. "And I was with you there, Chancellor."

The expression on Jesper's thin face is a mix of confusion and fearful apprehension. "But . . . the R.O.R . . . it can't—"

Macer extends his hand and pats him warmly on the shoulder for a second time. "It's okay, Benold. Clear the error. Print me some new stitch for the Grange."

His reply is a feeble, "Yes, Your Excellency."

Luci is embarrassed for the flustered man, wondering if a mistake *was* made here. Something about it all feels off.

Royse asks Macer, "Are you sure you don't want me to retrieve your stitch from your locker instead of printing new ones? I'm headed there for my outfit."

"No, Royse. Benold here will take care of me. Right, Benold?"

Luci finds Macer's gushing charm unsettling for some reason.

"Is Mr. Timmons accompanying you today?" Jesper asks.

Royse answers before Macer can. "I told you, I go everywhere he goes."

The tech nods, but his expression betrays his doubt.

Royse places his massive palm on the man's other shoulder. "I suggest you let it go."

Still all smiles, Macer adds, "We'll also have the lady joining us today."

Relieved to move onto other business, Jesper asks, "Name?"

Before Luci can answer, Macer holds his hand up chest high.

Jesper sheepishly adds, "You know I have to record the entry for chrono census purposes."

Luci tries to answer again, but Macer butts in. "I think that you can make an exception for today."

The whipped tech crosses his arms in frustration. "But Chancellor, if I leave it blank, I could lose my job." He adds, pleading, "I'd suffer a point deduction fine from my points account if nothing else."

Luci can tell by Macer's demeanor that this is the final straw. "Affect your point pay . . . lose your job, huh?" Macer asks coolly.

Jesper tries to reclaim his words, but it's too late. Royse moves in between him and Macer, grinning. "I told you to let it go."

To Luci's amazement, Macer steps around Royse's big frame and commends the technician. "Well done, son." He puts his arm around Jesper, still speaking softly to avoid making a scene. "It's dedication to order, attention to detail, and persistence that Relicus City was founded on." He gives a warm squeeze of his arm around him. "Well done."

Jesper's confused expression matches Luci's. "Uh . . . thank you, sir," he says.

"Who's your second here, Benold?" Macer asks, scanning the room with his extended index finger.

"My second?" Jesper stammers.

"Yes, who's in charge when you're away?"

"She is," Jesper volunteers while pointing to a young female worker dressed in red sitting in the fourth tray spot.

"Splendid," Macer says, patting his back. "I'd like you to go with Mr. Timmons, and he is going to put in a notice of accommodation to the section director on your behalf. We'll see if we can get a job for you that pays more points."

"Thank you, sir, but all I was—"

Macer turns to the big man. "Royse, be sure that you inform the director that I recommend that Benold be considered for immediate promotion."

"Consider it done, sir," Royse says, leading him away.

"What just happened here?" Luci asks in protest.

The response from Macer is curt, but the smile never wavers. "This is city business, nothing that you need to concern yourself with."

Luci's not convinced. "But where's Royse taking him?"

Macer ignores her and gestures to the woman in red. "Miss, if you'd come here for a moment, please?"

The cautious woman steps forward, to Macer's satisfaction. He gently takes her hand.

She's nearly blushing. "Yes, Your Excellency?"

"Congratulations, Miss. You've just been promoted to whatever Mr. Jesper used to do up until five minutes ago. Contact your director and tell her the good news and that I said so." He lets her hand slide out from his grasp. "But before you do, I need help with a special project. First, print me up a fresh set of stitch for me to wear, and then set up two of the longchairs for a leap skip to the Grange. The lady will go with me, but only note two sitters in the manifest log— myself and Mr. Timmons. You can do that, right? It's very important, a special project for the city."

The woman nervously adjusts her knuckle bands and looks over as Jesper is discretely manhandled out of the area by Royse.

"Pay Mr. Jesper no mind. He doesn't work here any longer," Macer says. "Don't worry, he's been promoted too. A very exciting day here for all of us."

"I suppose I can do that . . ." she begins, "if it's for the good of the city."

"Great," Macer says, snapping his fingers. "Then no more delays."

As Luci takes the scene in, there's an unexpected pop sound as loud as a champagne bottle opening.

Macer tries to calm her. "It's just the noise from the long-chair coming in from a leap skip to this interval."

"Why did it pop?" she asks. "Is it something about the craft adjusting to the existing air molecules in the room?"

Macer's eyebrows rise. "Who told you that?"

"No one," she answers with a shrug. "It's just that I assume that a small amount of the atmosphere comes over from the longchair's skip interval of origin; otherwise, the passengers wouldn't be able to breathe, and the vessel would collapse in on itself from the pressure."

When Macer's mouth drops in astonishment, Luci knows that he's impressed with her deduction. In contrast, the disinterested expression of female technician in red tells Luci that this fact must be common knowledge to the workers in the station. To keep Luci's identity secret, Macer attempts to downplay and mask his amazement, but Luci catches a glimpse of it as she continues. "It makes sense," she explains. "The existing air molecules and the ones enveloping the longchair collide in a tiny explosion of energy."

"Yes," Macer says, having composed himself. "As harmless as static electricity. Pardon us a moment, please."

Macer and the newly promoted lead technician leave Luci as they trail off to the young woman's cubicle.

Even though she expected it, Luci is still amazed by the sight of a longchair now occupying one of the slots that was vacant before. Other than the cork popping sound announcing its arrival, there's nothing to indicate that it wasn't there the entire time—no heat, glow, steam, or sound, nothing.

The roof of the longchair pod slides open, and a woman climbs out wearing a bright green strapless tassel-fringe dress. The felt cloche hat on her head matches the elbow-length gloves. Luci thinks she looks as if she's just come from the dance floor doing the Charleston—who knows, maybe she has. Luci's mouth drops. She knows this waif of a girl. It's Shar. She has brown eyes instead of green. Luci assumes it's colored contacts. Also, her hair is dark, not platinum white, which is understandable considering where she's just come from, but she's certain that it's her.

Luci rushes across the room and up the platform stairs to greet the only other woman she knows in this interval. The flapper woman reenters the longchair for something she's forgotten inside as Luci hurries down the aisle. She calls out, "Shar!" as the woman emerges through the pod roof and back onto the staging platform.

Now holding a clutch bag, she turns to face Luci, but it's not Shar. This revelation causes Luci to take a step back.

The woman descends the steps and then heads over to one of the technician cubicles. She thinks on how the flapper woman will never bear children, never celebrate being a mom on Mother's Day—if that's even a thing here.

After a few minutes of Luci's silent desperation, Royse and Macer emerge from the changing area and join her on the platform. In their new costumes, the men can pass for old-world monks if one ignores the Viatorio devices on their earlobes. She won't ask about Benold Jesper's promotion—that can wait. They'd probably lie to her anyway.

Royse offers a grandiose gesture to the longchair pod as the lid slides open. "After you."

She cautiously steps down into the seat. It feels like leaning back on a lounge chair rigged into a strange sarcophagus.

Macer whispers something to Royse. The big man nods and then helps him down into the front seat. Though her view is obstructed, Luci knows Macer's in place when the top glass of their longchair slides closed.

Macer speaks over his shoulder from the front seat. "The leap skip may be a little disorienting at first, but don't panic. You'll be okay."

By force of habit, Luci scrambles to find a seatbelt until she realizes longchairs can't exactly crash into anything. She's grateful that the seats face opposite of one another so Macer can't see her anxious gaffe. The roof of the longchair pressurizes with a soft hiss and resounding click. "Do I need to do anything?" Luci asks, trying to distract herself from the mild claustrophobia setting in.

"No," comes the answer from the front. "Trips to the Grange are routine. Everything is programmed in and ready. We'll be there before you know it—don't worry."

But Luci does worry. She pictures the young face of technician dressed in red and wonders how many interval skip launches she's administered. Luci calls out over her shoulder to Macer, "Couldn't you have waited until we returned to promote Benold Jesper? He seemed to be a more experienced operator."

"We'll be fine," he answers from the front.

An unfamiliar voice through the longchair's inset speakers gives Luci a jolt. Once again, it's good that the pod seats aren't facing each other. The soft computer-generated speech welcomes her and announces the intended time period destination along with the geographical location of the leap skip they're "sitting" for. Luci thinks of the pre-recorded safety messages provided by the Chicago Transit Authority on the L-Train as static electricity gently washes over her skin in waves.

The system continues, "As a cautionary reminder, please know that sitters are subject to all laws and customs of the chronus-interval they are attending. Any violation is prohibited by Relicus City mandated edicts and will result in punishment from an appointed tribunal."

A muffled pop on the outside of the "craft" alerts Luci that the system is pressurizing a thin layer of air around the pod like she and Macer previously discussed. Her mind attempts to console her fast-beating heart by reminding it that she's done this once before; granted, she was unconscious, but this isn't the first time.

Luci is startled by a burst of incredibly bright light as if a picture has been taken with flash bulbs. Then everything goes dark, and it's the most obscure black she's ever seen. Macer is quiet in front of her, so she assumes this, too, is routine. She remembers back to when she was nine and the family visited an underground cave hundreds of feet beneath the earth. At the halfway point, the guide told everyone to remain motionless as he clicked off the interior lights of the cave to demonstrate how dark it was. It was terrifyingly exhilarating as everything went black. Young Luci waved her hand in front of her face, and as expected, she couldn't see a thing. By comparison, the all-consuming nothingness she experiences in the longchair reduces the darkness in the cave to a dark shade of grey.

Then, through the window at the far end of the stretched-out longchair is a pinprick of emerald-green light. It unfolds and expands, resembling a train tunnel. The rational part of her mind knows and argues it's not, but the "tunnel" is perfectly round and spinning counterclockwise. The emerald light at the end grows brighter.

Luci experiences a brief sense of weightlessness, and then the impossible happens. The windows above and to the right and left stretch and distort. They elongate like taffy and stretch and twist until finally silently snapping off the craft. They return to their rectangular shapes, but beyond the opening of the longchair. Luci's respiratory rate increases as three shapes become six, then twelve, then twenty-four.

They continue to subdivide until the entire tunnel is lined with thousands of spinning rectangles of blue-green and amber yellow. Luci imagines herself in a rolling kaleidoscope made of shimmering glitter mixed with pulsating shards of glass; all reflect the brilliance of the expanding emerald light. It feels as if the longchair is stationary while everything else rushes by where the windows once were.

She looks down at herself—that was a mistake. The glittering isn't confined to the outside of the longchair cabin. Her form also pulsates from the opaque color of her skin and medieval clothing to a translucent wash of millions of dot-sized mirrors. She gasps and feels for her legs as the swimming lights revert to her normal form and then disappear again. As she continues to alternate between being there and not, she reflexively covers her loins. She's able to feel her hands, even when they disappear from view and back again. *"Can I feel the longchair ruthlessly zapping at my ovaries, sterilizing me at a microscopic level, or is it just psychosomatic?"*

The sides of the compartment vanish from view, interrupting her thoughts. To test it, Luci extends a hand—as expected, the enclosure is physically there, just not visible. Trillions of spiraling rectangles shoot past her view in a blur. Luci feels as if she's simultaneously falling and being catapulted upward through a bottomless well. Every few seconds, a quivering ring of light ripples from behind her, headed into the rhythmic flashing of the emerald pulse. The vibrating rings alternate from a bright violet-fuchsia to aqua blue-green. Instantly, the impossible darkness reappears . . . and then normal light.

FIFTEEN

August 16, 1044
La Rioja, Spain
[42.2870733/2.539603/4.603.388.823/5485:18:18]

LΔ RΩHΛ-SPΔИ

ΛGUST 16, 1044

⊖

PRɪ-Hɫ NΩ KΩWU

LUCI IS FINALLY ABLE CATCH her breath as she studies her hands, which have returned to a steady state of opaqueness. "Wow, that was intense!"

In contrast, Macer's reply from behind is placid. "The leap skip? Yes, the first few times can be a thrill. Believe it or not, like with anything, it becomes mundane after a while."

The hatch slides open, and Royse helps Macer onto the platform from the longchair. Finally, he assists Luci. Judging by the hay and sunlight shooting through the ramshackle wooden construction, they're in the rafters of a barn.

"The chancellor speaks five languages," Royse boasts. "It's unlikely we'll encounter any of the interval's residents, but if we do, let him do the talking. He can always say that I've taken a vow of silence, and you . . . well, you're a woman. There's not much for females to say in this interval."

As Luci wonders if she should be offended by the statement, Macer chimes in. "It works out in our favor that any area Mozarab monks living at Suso are hermits that have a tendency to avoid others. Still, Royse is right to be cautious as we make our way there."

"What's that over there?" Luci asks, pointing at a different-looking longchair from the two that brought them here.

"That was one of my father's," Macer says. "It's a bit of an antique by today's longchair standards, but it still gets the job done."

"But why is it here?" she asks.

Royse busies himself with the external panel of the transport he came in. "You're going to want to step back a little," he says. "I'm sending this one back."

Before Luci can ask what Royse means, Macer answers her original question. "The older one over there has a one-to-one path."

"What does that mean?"

"Unlike the longchairs that brought us here today," Macer explains, "it has only one destination, my home and back. Sometimes Royse and I use it rather than going into the city."

"Sir," Royse courteously interrupts, "I'm sending in thirty. Please stand clear."

"Luci, please step this way," Macer says, motioning to her. "Maybe it's nostalgia, or maybe I'm just some sentimental fool, but I do enjoy taking that model from my office to here and back. Another challenge with the early design was how every leap skip required a passenger be aboard."

Royse calls from behind them with bravado, "So you can't do this!"

The more modern longchair Royse had been fiddling with makes a popping sound and then vanishes from sight.

"Don't worry, Luci," Macer says. "We'll take the prototype one back. There's no need to be concerned. For all intents and purposes, it's just like the other units."

She looks at Royse. "I guess we don't have much choice now."

"It wasn't my idea," Royse answers under his breath to her.

Luci quickly pieces together that the source of Royse's irritation is that he won't be traveling with them on the return trip, since his longchair will skip back to the Spike instead of Macer's home.

They descend the creaky wooden stairs of the hayloft in what has become their standard order: Royse in front, then Macer, and then Luci.

She asks, "So this isn't the Grange?"

"No," Macer answers, pulling the cowl of his monk garb over his bald head. "The Grange is an underground facility beneath the monastery. It's a brief stroll from here. That's the reason for the stitch."

"The clothing?"

Macer answers, "Yes. In the event we encounter any residents of the interval, we want to be careful not to disrupt things. We have a non-contamination edict."

There's a cybo posted near the barn door on the ground level. It's hunched over, dressed in a loose-fitting monk's tunic with a churka modified to look like a thick walking stick with a bulbous head. She tries her best to ignore it as they move past, but the stench of it forces her to cover her nose with a sleeve.

Royse slides a board to the left, revealing the same type of plastic door pad as the one back in Macer's guesthouse. He places his hand on the palm reader and taps his Viatorio. A vertical slat slides down, revealing a trio of other churkas that have been modified to look like wood. He lifts one from the rack, and the panel slides shut again.

Royse resumes his protection mode as he steps through the barn door, searching the outside for anything that's amiss. The intense look on his face causes Luci to suspiciously scan the area for attackers as well.

It's near dusk, and recent rainfall has left a dewy freshness in the country air. Careful not to slip on the slick grass, the three descend the hill to a worn dirt pathway that's turned to mud. Luci wonders how proficient Royse is with the blaster. If assassins have been dispatched to this interval, they could be hiding in any of these trees to ambush them. Just how good is the big man leading them with a churka?

Macer says to Luci in a hushed tone, "The color green—I suspect many citizens of Relicus post for jobs here just to see the trees and foliage. So much green."

Arrays of insect and bird noises celebrate the watering of the trail's lush foliage. Maneuvering over and around mud puddles, Luci tugs the back of Macer's frock and says in a hushed tone, "Wouldn't it be easier to just have the longchairs appear at the monastery?"

Macer softly answers Luci as they methodically follow the bodyguard's steps, "Longchairs placed too close to the source of the vortex are disruptive, since they aren't a constant. They leap skip from juncture to juncture. In contrast, the chrono portal for the Grange remains open, flowing like a river from this interval into ours. It never stops."

Luci rehearses this new concept aloud. "So the portal thing for the food is similar to tossing barrels into a flowing stream, and they just follow the current—in this case, the time current downstream to your interval?"

"In the simplest of terms, yes, something like that," Macer says. "The vortex points are in a constant state of forward dispensation."

Royse pauses in front as if he's heard something. He scans the area, the churka an extension of his arm. Luci's heartrate speeds up, but only the sound of bug noises register in her hearing.

Royse points out a plump brown rabbit in the tall grass on their left side.

Experiencing a slight bit of relief, Luci swallows and continues her questioning of Macer. "So you can't skip back in time to gather food that you harvested from last year or, for that matter, even a week ago."

"Right. Not even containers that were sent and delivered as recently as last night. A vortex like the one in the Grange is in a constant state of flux, moving in linear time, closing each microsecond as it passes by. There is a direct one-to-one correlation between the time here and in Relicus city; a quarter of an hour here is the same measurement of a quarter hour there." He pauses to concentrate, stepping over a section of a fallen tree. "Even after all of these years, we still don't know what causes the intervals or the few vortex points."

This mystery excites and intrigues her. She embraces the distraction from any unseen foes in the forest. Luci rushes a step to get closer to Macer. "And you don't know why they're placed where they are?"

"The best theory that I ever heard was from Lucius Bunn. He was a man that worked with me—well, really, Waleen, my father. He suggested that time was like cloth—say a garment of some sort—and in that fabric there were buttons sewed in, holding it all together. Intervals would be that tiniest of spaces between the button and the buttonhole that the universe allows us to slip through." He reaches for her hand and guides her over the obstacle of the fallen tree.

Luci nods in appreciation. "You mentioned in the warehouse that the intervals don't necessarily open into monumental moments in mankind's history, so if you wanted to meet Julius Caesar or Winston Churchill, you couldn't."

"True," Macer answers. "We can only leap skip to where the universe allows us to go."

"And you can't return to the same exact moment in time twice? If you're in one of these forward dispensation chronal energy things we're about to see?"

"The vortex—*yes*, this is also true," he answers softly as he scans the area.

Royse pauses again, but no rabbit emerges this time.

Luci speaks in an exaggerated whisper. "So, to use a word picture example, someone riding on a passenger train from my time could move from one of the very back car compartments to a front one as the train rolls down the tracks. After a few minutes, they return to the compartment in the back of the train." She pauses to navigate around a wide puddle. "But even if the passenger returns to their original seat in the back, the same exact one from before, they're not in the same place as they were because the transport has progressed down the rail."

"Yes," Macer says. "That's a sound example."

There's something about it all that makes Luci's brain itch. Academia has taught her to be certain of her understanding before she exposes a fallacy. "Let me make sure I've got all this. Longchairs skip from fixed points and arrive at fixed points except if they're too close to an open vortex like the one we're headed to see, and this is because . . ."

As she searches for the adequate terms, Macer interjects, "Due to how the dominant chronal energy attributes take precedence."

She repeats the phrase *"dominant chronal energy attributes,"* committing it to memory.

Macer jumps in. "This is why we can't leap skip from here to anywhere but back to Relicus City, and the duration we spend here will be relative to our return there."

His confirmation slides the puzzle together in her mind. The conclusion is simultaneously exhilarating and disquieting. "Then you've got a problem," Luci says in a somber voice. "If I understand all of this . . . even if I do manage to solve what's destroying the interval openings across the world, and even if there's a way to keep this 'river of time' flowing into the future, eventually, it's all going to run out anyway."

For the first time, Macer stops in place to look at her. The abrupt halt makes Royse take notice, and he hurriedly backtracks to them. "What's wrong, sir?"

"It's okay, Royse. What do you mean, Dr. Gaudiano?" Macer asks with widened eyes.

Luci's stunned by the panicked look on his face and glances down at the mud on her shoes. "Well, what century is it today . . . where we are, what's the year?"

"It's 1044, August in 1044. Why?" Macer says, taking an anxious step in her direction.

She looks up at him. "This is 1044, and Shar said that the Night of Ten Million Fires, *Hi no Kawa*, occurs around the year—"

"The year 2068 PH," Royse butts in. "*Hi no Kawa* begins in 2068."

"Okay, so 2068, which means this place and any production ceases at that time." She pauses to calculate. "That's one thousand and twenty-four . . . so the city's food source ends around year 3200 . . . 3215 to be exact."

Royse and Macer look at each other, and then Macer confirms, "A thousand years into the Relicus City's future?"

"Yes, if the food processing area we're headed to right now doesn't survive the catastrophic nuclear event in this place's future, you're done," Luci says, slightly perturbed by their smugness. "What makes you think you'll be able to grow food in Relicus's future if you can't grow it in 2191?"

Macer pauses. "You bring up an important point, but we're more concerned with what's happening now. If Gicul succeeds, there won't be any future."

Luci mutters to herself the line that her father used to say. "The future isn't what it used to be."

"What do you mean by that?" Macer asks.

"Nothing," Luci answers. "Look, you should send a scouting party as far into the future as they can go to see how things are. Perhaps there's some technology or something that—"

"Absolutely not," Macer says. "A leap skip into a future interval could have dire consequences to the city."

"But why? What's the problem with that?"

"It's illegal," Royse blurts out. "Article two of the edict. That, plus longchairs have built-in FTTs to keep anyone from taking a leap skip forward."

"That doesn't make any sense," she protests. "It's a law that your society made. You can change it. He can change it—he's the chancellor." Luci feels like she's pleading, but she doesn't back down. "I'm not saying to give everyone access, just a few trusted emissaries like Shar or you, Royse. You two just go and report back how things are, how the problem got solved. Surely that'd be allowed, given what's at stake."

Macer shakes his head and answers in a somber voice, "It could be too disruptive."

Luci's voice comes out louder than expected. "How do you know that New Australia isn't already doing something like this, that they haven't skipped ahead into the future?"

"They haven't," Macer answers a little too quickly.

"You know this because they told you or something? How can you trust them? Even if there's some treaty or something, how do you know?" She adds, "Where do they get their food from? Do they have a Grange interval too somewhere?"

"It's inconsequential," he says dismissively.

Luci guffaws. "How can you say that? The possibility of another food source, I know they're your enemy or whatever, but that's huge." She can't believe this. "What is it that you're not telling me? How can I help if you continue to withhold stuff from me?"

"I'm withholding nothing," Macer says, pointing his index finger at her face. "In fact, the reason we took the leap skip here should be proof that I'm trying to be as candid as I can be with you for the sake of the city. But a leap skip to the future wouldn't serve what we brought you here to do." Macer motions to Royse. "Come on, let's get going."

"Whatever," Luci grumbles under her breath and grudgingly follows.

THE THREE TRAVEL IN WARY silence for a few minutes until they reach the foothills of the blue-green mountains. Sprouting up from a small clearing among golden wheat fields is the stone structure of their destination. Macer turns as Luci approaches and puts his index finger to his lips. She nods her understanding to remain silent as she joins them on the stone pathway. The building has two naves separated by horseshoe arches. Unevenly spaced shafts of natural light pierce the area terminating on the rock floor. The trio enters the main doorway and moves into the square-segmented chapels inside.

Though they're only whispers, Macer's words echo off the cool, hard stone surfaces. "La Rioja is where the first words in Castilian Spanish were ever written down. This is the birthplace of the Spanish language. Two centuries from now, Gonzalo de Berceo will write the first poems in the Spanish language." Macer points at one of the open areas to the right of them as they walk past. "In fact, his remains lie in the Romanesque chapel, or better said, he will be put to rest one day down in there."

Royse steps past them, reaching for a spot on a nearby column. After a quick search, he slides down a small, flat panel masterfully disguised to match the color and texture of the buttress. He repeats the gesture he did in the barn of activating the palm reader while tapping the Viatorio affixed to his earlobe.

The soft hum of a machine engine makes Luci turn around, searching for the source. She realizes it's coming from under the ground, but something else catches her attention. The ends of a tapestry are slowly curling up into themselves like an old-fashioned window shade. The slab behind the wall hanging gradually lowers at an angle until it forms a ramp downward into an area brightly lit with artificial light.

"Wow!" Luci exclaims with a soft chuckle.

"We shouldn't linger," Macer says, urging her down the stone slope.

With Luci in the front and Royse in the rear, the three proceed down a hallway lit by panels in the floor. Luci recognizes the material used is the same that led out of Macer's guesthouse. She pauses, looking back as the ramp returns to a vertical position, sealing them in with a thud.

"We're almost there, Doctor," Macer says, indicating for her to continue.

She spots an opening on the right side at the end of the corridor up ahead. Luci detects a familiar stench even before they come within fifteen yards of the doorway, the sickening, putrid scent of a cybo. She wonders why, with all their technological advances, they can't find a way to remove or better conceal the stink of these loathsome creatures. She fakes needing to adjust her medieval garment in order to allow Macer to go through the opening before her, but Royse waits.

As Luci hurries past the cybo sentinel, she bites her lip upon realizing that it's female or at least *had been* female at some point in the past. They move into a vestibule lit from the floor as in the apartment. Royse approaches another palm reader pad on the wall, and seconds later, the door slides open with a pneumatic hiss. "Welcome to the Grange, Doctor."

SIXTEEN

Luci steps forward a few feet to clutch the cool safety rail in both hands and brace herself. The unexpected vastness of the area below is dizzying and a sharp contrast to the eleventh-century structure bearing a smaller footprint above. She's at the edge of a five-story balcony overlooking an enormous complex bathed in warm, pinkish LED light. Endless stacked rows of tightly arranged metal racks extend upward from the concrete floor; they easily reach thirty-feet high. All of the deep trays are filled to the brim with perfectly situated vegetation beneath slowly oscillating fans.

Royse moves to the corner, where there's a lectern-like control panel. The podium chirps and beeps as he presses buttons. When the steel mesh floor beneath Luci's feet jolts and begins to lower, she realizes that the three of them are standing on a large square lift platform. As it descends, Macer joins her side and gestures to a worker below in white coveralls. The figure in a hairnet and rubber gloves casually keeps pace with a robotic pallet mover as it glides along the edge of row after stacked row. "Due to a generous point compensation, serving here is in great demand by residents back home—that and the honor of helping to feed everyone."

Luci recalls Benold Jesper's desperate concern for his *"points"* back at the station and deduces that *points* must be some sort of Relicus City incentive.

The worker and robot disappear into a long row of vegetation as Macer says, "Our *farmers* here have a duty tour of six months at a time. They work three weeks on and have a week off back in the city."

Luci thinks of the parallels of offshore rig workers and the people serving here. She scans the area, focusing on the two dozen or so technicians carrying out various tasks. "They stay on site for three weeks then?" She doesn't say it aloud, but the irony that all the workers rendered infertile are fertilizing and growing plants for harvest isn't lost on her, all for what Macer refers to as a generous compensation of points.

"Yes, the living quarters are three levels below this farm floor, under the nuclear generator quads." Macer pauses to press his Viatorio. "Director Mandal is on her way to meet us. I've instructed her to give you a proper tour." He adds a statement that Luci finds peculiar. "I think you'll really like her."

Luci gazes over to Royse. His posture is more relaxed, which indicates that the threat risk is at minimum in this place. In fact, he looks bored enough to make Luci wonder if there's any risk at all.

They're nearly two thirds of the way down to floor level when she notices a shorter figure than the one before. This one is dressed in yellow coveralls and approaches from the towering racks of plant life. The dark-skinned woman stops at the edge of the platform and tugs at her ear. She acknowledges something with a nod and softly says something beyond Luci's hearing.

Macer exits the lift first and motions for Luci to follow. The older woman's kind, smiling face resembles Luci's high school trigonometry teacher, Mrs. Chopra. The instructor bore the same dark complexion and Indian features as this woman. For the first time since Luci's abduction, she wonders if any cultural identity remains for this future people. Is family lineage and heritage even a thing here in this culture of desperation and survival? Has the racism of the past died with *Hi no Kawa*?

The woman removes her hairnet, revealing a dark mound in a tight bun while offering a slight bow. "Hello, I am Bru

Mandal. Welcome to the Grange." The smile on her rectangular face is warm and unrehearsed, unlike Macer's many masks.

Before Luci can respond, the stocky woman adds, "I know who you are, but there is no need for any of the crew to know you and why you are visiting us today."

Macer steps forward. "The director is right, no need for rumors to start a city-wide panic." He turns to the woman. "I have some business to tend to. Bru, deliver our special guest to Royse and me in section four when you're done."

Luci does a double take at him. She catches herself about to protest when she realizes that this place *must* be secure, and being without the two of them for a bit may be a good thing. This may be an opportunity to learn more about what's really going on without them continually shutting down her questions.

Bru answers, "Yes, Your Excellency. I will bring her to your office." Another subtle bow accompanies the woman's words.

The two women stand in place while Royse joins Macer, and they head off, looking like monks on their way to prayer.

"He has an office here?" Luci asks.

"A small one, yes," she answers and then adds, "Small by a chancellor's standards, that is."

Luci gazes at Bru, trying to detect the intent of the comment but doesn't sense any sarcasm or spite in her.

Bru's smile grows, and in a cheery tone, she says, "Okay my lovely. Let us begin."

"Do I need to change into a jumpsuit?" Luci asks, still a little self-conscious of her costume.

"We are not going to do any actual crop handling, so no, that will not be necessary."

When Luci goes to remove the head covering, Bru abruptly pulls her hand away, explaining, "Uh . . . Mr. Timmons said you have not been fitted for a Viatorio yet. It is best not to draw any attention that it is missing." The soft, grandmotherly smile returns. "We do not wish to attract any unwarranted interest in you, Doctor. I have posted on all active personnel V coms that we have an inspector onsite today, so it is likely that most everyone will try to stay clear of interacting with you. So act *supervisor-like*." She goes on to explain, "Normally, everyone here is fairly cordial, but hopefully that will keep them from you."

Luci secures her headpiece more firmly. "Thanks . . . I guess."

In a determined voice, Bru says, "Anyway, we should get started, my lovely. We only have a limited time today."

Luci agrees, and the two approach the towering stacks of soil trays. "This level is known as the farm floor. It's two hectares large."

"*4.94211 acres or 215,278.3116 square feet.*" Luci can't stop the automatic conversion in her head.

"It is home to over two-hundred and fifty different types of plants. And then there is the micro-algae; very high in proteins, carbohydrates, and omega-3 fatty acids and such."

Luci notes the pride in the woman's voice and offers to her, "That's very impressive."

Bru pauses to accept the compliment and then resumes, "So, for the plants, instead of forcing seed down through soil, they're positioned in trays stacked thirty-two feet high. As you can see, there is no sunlight, so the plants instead bask in the pink-orange glow of Aug-Lights. Their tray fans continuously spin as regulated amounts of fertilizer is dispensed every few hours."

"It's all automated then?" Luci asks.

"Not exactly," Bru says. "Not yet anyway. Maybe someday. The growing trays collect thirty thousand data points on things like temperature, humidity, CO_2, and oxygen levels. The technicians on the level directly beneath this one analyze these metrics in real time. They mine the data to determine batch growth level and the time for optimum harvest."

Under the pink glow of a faux sunset, a lanky man in yellow coveralls approaches. Luci is astonished to see a floating container the height and length of a bookcase trailing behind him. A drawer extends out to his chest, revealing rows of segmented trays. The technician makes a selection while pinching his Viatorio with his free hand. He turns and presents Bru with a leafy clipping. The director receives it and grabs her own Viatorio. A silent moment passes between them before the man nods and moves on with the hovering container following.

"Sorry," Bru says, tucking the sample in a pocket. "I had to sign some things."

Luci wonders why the face-to-face was necessary at all since the transaction was obviously virtual except for the sample vegetation.

Bru catches Luci's gaze transfixed on the floating case zooming along behind the man like an obedient pet. "I'm guessing that you must not have cargo suspensors in your interval?"

"Cargo suspensors?" Luci turns back to her host. "No. In Chicago, we have *5 Guys and a Van Moving Company*."

A blank expression lingers on Bru's face before she jumps back into the rhythm of her tour. "Vertical farming uses ninety-eight percent less H_2O and less than half the fertilizer of a traditional farmstead from pre-*Hi no Kawa* farms from centuries ago. Since the greens grow indoors, there is no exposure to pests, which eliminates any need for pesticides."

"Wow," Luci responds, genuinely impressed while observing a worker using a forklift-type crane in the distance to stack some trays.

"We maintain complete control of the plant life, tailoring the lights to specific spectrums and intensities. The ventilation is regulated, temperature of the roots, and sprays of nutriated water meticulously applied. By adjusting the algorithm, farm technicians can theoretically make the plants sweeter or boost levels of vitamin A, whatever is needed or desired."

Luci follows Bru as she breaks off from the walking path along the racks and heads for a transport. It looks like an extended golf cart with twelve plastic bucket seats facing outward from the sides. The wagon moves on long track treads instead of tires, absent a driver and steering wheel to distinguish the front and back of the vehicle.

Luci wrestles her period dress into place as the two of them take their seats with a handful of other workers. Seconds later, the driverless cart is in motion, taking them deeper into the facility.

The travel wind blows against them, but Bru's hair bun remains undisturbed and neat. She continues, "The rows of greens sit under infrared light, the spectrum undetectable by the human eye, but the plants can *see* it."

Though nothing's said, Luci can feel the other passengers perking up. She can sense their curiosity about her, the "*special inspector,*" and how they're probably wondering why she's still dressed in the maiden costume instead of standard-issue coveralls. She looks coolly at those facing her; the stare delivers the intended effect, and the few workers nervously break eye contact.

Bru carries on as if she's given a thousand such orientations. "Without the challenge of nature's changing climate, we enjoy year-round growing seasons indoors, using significantly less water, no need for pesticides, and avoidance of biological invaders that cause diseases like salmonella, escherichia coli, and listeria."

After a half minute or so riding in silence, Luci asks, "What are the main crops grown here?"

"These racks are mint. Over there is kale, basil, and then lettuce."

"No, I mean the overall production," Luci says.

"Oh, that would be soybean, South Asian jackfruit, and the micro-algae I mentioned before."

"What's Jackfruit?" Luci asks and instantly realizes her mistake even before the workers begin whispering to themselves.

"Inspector, do you mean what is the *size* of the Jackfruit we harvest?"

"Yes, that's what I meant to say," Luci remarks, grateful to Bru for the save.

year 1941. The first problem is it is situated in the Atlantic Ocean off the coast of what you would call Florida in between Puerto Rico and Bermuda—"

"You mean the Bermuda Triangle!" Luci blurts out.

Bru's expression doesn't change.

Luci tries again. "Where all the ship and planes disappear at . . . you know, the Bermuda Triangle." She quickly realizes this is a reference that Bru is unfamiliar with. "I'm sorry, please go on. You said the vortex is on the ocean."

Bru resumes, undaunted. "Worse than that, the termination juncture where it empties is a kilometer and a half in the sky above an irradiated area in the desert of the Sudan. And then there is the vortex that begins in fourteenth-century Antarctica with a flow exit point thirteen hundred meters underground in irradiated Pingdingshan, China in 2133."

The mood of the conversation turns grim, but Luci's need for knowledge forces her to press on. "And there's no way you can synthesize food back in Relicus city?"

Bru shakes her head. "Not to the output levels needed to satisfy over six million people. While there are some who tinker with this for personal enjoyment, the results are not enough to keep one alive."

The statement reminds Luci of two things: her college days when she grew tomato vines on the balcony of her apartment in Chicago and, more recently, her ex-fiancé Michael's obsession with beer microbreweries. While both were fun, neither yielded enough product to justify the effort.

"Was that your second question?" Bru asks, bringing Luci back into the present.

"Huh? No, I wanted to ask about New Australia. What do you know about them, and what is their food source?"

Bru switches the small case from hand to hand and tightens the grip on the handle. "New Australia is a mystery even to me, and *I am* a member of the Directorate. All that I know is there was an attack on the city about seven or eight years ago by them, and we were unprepared with no defenses in place.

Fifty or so lives were lost in the attack before those marauders made off with a bunch of food." Bru attempts to offer a reassuring smile, but the expression doesn't hold. "But my lovely, you do not need to be concerned. They will not come to the Grange. You are safe here. I'm not even sure that they know about this place, though the chancellor has work being done to fortify the vortex, just in case."

Luci clarifies, "My question was more about how many of them there are and where they get their food from."

"I am sorry, but the truth of it is we have very little information about them at all. My guess is that they leap skip back and gather food from pre-*Hi no Kawa* intervals since they are not doing what we do with the vortex."

The answer is baffling. "How much can be carried in a longchair?" Luci asks.

"Not much, but there are larger transports than longchairs—skip barges," Bru answers. "But something like that still would not come close to the amount that we process and ship from here at the Grange." The smile returns. "Come. I will show you the best part of what we do."

As they approach the deck, Luci notices that the design of the control pedestal on the left-hand side is similar to the lift she rode on at the entrance. This platform is significantly larger than the other and is noticeably missing handrails.

"Stay clear of the sides," Bru instructs her, flipping a toggle and activating their descent. "It is actually used for freight transport."

Luci adjusts her stance to maintain her balance as the platform lowers and increases in speed.

Bru looks over at her, shrugs, and gives a playful wink. "It is not made to haul people, but it is the fastest way to get to where we are going."

She reaches over and hands Luci the small case. "Here. Take this, please."

Luci awkwardly grasps it while concentrating on her balance. "What is it?"

"It is for the chancellor. Tell him that is the only one and the last one for a while."

"What is it?" Luci questions, remembering that Bru is supposed to deliver her to him at the conclusion of the tour. Is she a part of *L'inversione*? Has Luci been duped into thinking this person was just a grandmotherly old woman when she was an assassin? "Is it a device or some-thing?" she asks sternly. "I don't know that I'm the one who should be—"

Bru waves her off. "Just give it to him for me, please."

"Wait . . . are you leaving me somewhere?"

"No, I am taking you to the vortex of the chrono portal."

Remembering the discussion on the way from the barn with Macer, Luci asks, "Isn't that dangerous . . . I mean, if we get too close?"

She grins. "Trust me, you will be fine. We need you too badly to risk anything happening to you."

As a soft wind brushes across Luci's face from the descent, she still wonders what she's agreed to deliver to Macer. She questions whether she's completely misread this woman next to her.

The lift comes to a soft stop on a landing pad. "What is this? I need to know if I'm going to take it to him." Luci holds up the case, being careful not to shake it.

"Why are you so suspicious, my lovely? If the chancellor is occupied or not in his office when we are done, I will drop you off. I know he is not leaving without you, so I asked for you to deliver it to him is all."

"Is it money, like a payoff or something?" The perplexed look on Bru's face prompts Luci to ask, "Do you have money here?"

"I do not know what this *money* is."

"You all don't use money in Relicus City? How do you buy things and conduct commerce?"

"Oh, you mean *points*," Bru says, stepping off the platform. "How could my points be put into a container? The case contains an avocado."

"An avocado?"

"Yes, it is a fruit, which is botanically an oversized berry containing a single seed—*Persea americana*, a member of the flowering plant family *Lauraceae*."

"I *know* what an avocado is," Luci says, following her.

Bru explains in a matter-of-fact tone, "They take up too much water and space to make mass production worthwhile with our current technology, so tell him it is the last one for a while."

Luci looks at the case, muttering to herself, "Avocado. Un-freakin'-believable."

The low, rhythmic rumble of machines churning fills the dimly lit area. Luci follows the director up a ramp leading to a catwalk far above the processing zone. Much like in the "the Spike" building back at Relicus City, most of the work here is automated. A mystifying maze of conveyors and lifts abruptly start and stop, swing food product around, sift it into containers, and seal them at blinding speed. Robots fused with multicolored straps pull and lift containers through to their destinations, making it appear more like conveyor belts with metal arms. A handful of workers patrol the equipment and check status readings, but it's nothing like the throng of technicians on the farm floor.

"Forty-nine metric tons a day, right?" Luci asks.

The director stops and turns as if she's been insulted. "Who told you those figures?"

"Uh, Macer . . . I mean, Chancellor Macer did back in Relicus City."

She scoffs. "Hmph. Before you give that to him," Bru says, pointing at the avocado case, "inform him daily production here is 36.8 tons. He is only off nearly twelve tons." She shakes her head and moves to cross a gangplank intersection.

Still slightly annoyed, Bru explains, "So, anyway, he wanted me to show you the processing plant here. As you can see, its flow layout mirrors the one back at the city. In here, we assemble, pack, and send to the vortex canal one level below."

The term *"vortex canal"* reminds Luci of the river analogy between her and Macer.

Looking over the edge with her, Bru allows Luci a few seconds to gaze upon the hypnotic movement of the plasti-crates through the system. Next, they cross over to the other side of the immense area without speaking. Along the way, Luci reminds herself that somewhere hundreds of feet over their heads rests an eleventh-century monastery made of stone. She makes a promise to herself that if she makes it out of this alive, she'll return to the monastery as a tourist of her time one day, though she knows it's unlikely that she'll be able to penetrate the Grange then.

They make their way to another elevator—this one is of normal size. "One more stop to go," the director announces as they enter the compart-ment. She pauses to press her Viatorio. "Yes, sir," Bru says to the air.

Luci concludes that a director of a plant like this probably isn't required to answer *"sir"* to many people and wonders if it's Macer on the other line.

Bru's gaze fixes on Luci as she replies to the com, "Yes, you may send it, but I don't see the point of—" She shrugs in mild exasperation, but her voice remains neutral. "That will be fine. We're going down there now. I will V you when we are headed back up to your level."

Luci knows the call is concluded when Bru sighs and shakes her head to herself. The elevator doors slide to a close in response to Bru pressing her Viatorio.

"Macer?" Luci asks sympathetically.

"He is sending something to me now. Just a second, please."

After a moment, Bru sniggers and says, "Always a flair for the dramatic with that one, just like his father." Before Luci can respond, Bru says, "He wants me to ask you something." Her eyes look past her as if reading invisible letters in the air. "He wants me to ask you if you're familiar with a nineteenth-century Swedish munitions manufacturer Alfred Bernhard Nobel?"

Searching for the question's relevance, Luci tilts her head slightly. Her answer begins slowly. "Yes, Nobel established an award program recognizing achievements in academic, cultural, and scientific advances."

"Correct," Bru agrees with raised eyebrows. "The article that the chancellor sent me says that Nobel amassed his fortune by producing explosives. It says that many died as a direct result of his scientific discoveries and exploits."

Luci knows where this is headed now. She resents Macer for forcing Bru to serve as surrogate bully. Knowing it's not her fault, she allows her to continue.

It's clear that Bru is paraphrasing much of the article she's required to relay, but there are bits that feel as if she's straight reading to her. "But Mr. Nobel was given a second chance by fate for his legacy to end with a good name. In 1888, Alfred's brother Ludvig died. The newspaper of the day mistakenly ran a long, scathing obituary of Alfred Nobel, thinking it was his death. Alfred read it, horrified that the writer condemned him as a 'merchant of death.'"

The elevator doors open, but neither of them exit the compartment while Bru continues, "The newspapers of the day described him as a man who had made it possible to kill more people more quickly than anyone else who had ever lived."

In an effort to draw this sloppy, non-subtle exchange to an end, Luci chimes in. "Yes, it was clear to Alfred that if he didn't do something, this would be how the world remembered him. He knew that he couldn't bring back the lives of those his science had destroyed, but he was able to do something positive for the future of mankind."

Luci gets cocky. "Did he tell you that scientists even named the synthetic element nobelium after him? So I am given the chance to clear my name of ending most of the life on the planet."

Bru shrugs and says apologetically, "His motives *are* pretty transparent sometimes."

The two of them stroll down a dimly lit grey corridor.

"I'm sorry about that," Bru says. "I understand that they've already told you about *Hi no Kawa*."

"Yes," Luci responds hesitantly. "Director Mandal . . . do you trust him?"

"Trust whom?"

"The chancellor," Luci says. "There's something about him that I can't quite . . ."

Bru laughs the question off. "I would never say it to his face, but he can be as impatient at times as his father Waleen was, but *of course* I trust him. We would not have anything without the both of them, and that is a fact." She quickly corrects herself, "I mean, certainly, there were others who helped create what we have in Relicus City—those of us that serve on the Directorate—but Waleen and now Enos Macer are the visionaries that have brought us to where we are today."

"And the reason I'm here," Luci adds flatly.

Bru whispers emphatically, "Yes, why you are here. Malom Roderick's gang and Cyphor Gicul have to be stopped at any cost before they're able to achieve their goals of destruction and extortion or whatever they are up to."

Luci locks in on this new term to describe the motive of the anarchists. "What do you mean by *extortion?*"

"Just a theory that I have about the things that have been going on lately."

"What?" Luci asks. "I promise not to tell anyone if you're afraid that—"

She scoffs. "My lovely, I am far too old to be concerned and give any energy to what people may think of me. It is just that I question what Gicul is really up to."

"Why . . . how do you mean?"

"As a city leader, I am privy to some very classified information such as the intervals that have been destroyed by Cyphor's group up to this point. As best as I can tell, most of them are skip point junctures that serve no real function to Relicus City."

"So what's your theory as to what he's doing it for?" Luci asks, intrigued.

"I think it is a demonstration that he *can* do it. I think Cyphor, whoever he may be, is trying to show us that he has the capabilities to obliterate a skip point juncture into nothingness. If his goal is the Grange, why not start here? Why not take out the longchair skip point in the barn a few miles from here and keep anyone from coming or going?"

Luci thinks on this. "Terrorism only works when people fear what may happen?"

"Exactly. I believe that the end goal is for him to declare that he will destroy the longchair portal in the barn and thereby trap the workers here unless his demands are met. Everything else that he is doing is just a demonstration that he can make something like that happen."

The concept is not without merit to Luci. "Have you told Macer any of this?"

"Yes, but the chancellor is convinced that *L'inversione* are modern-day zealots who want to destroy what we have built by preventing *Hi no Kawa*. Even if things could be undone, I just cannot see that anyone would hate their existence to the degree that they would erase themselves forever. No one is that crazy."

Luci quietly contemplates how she'd considered jumping from the 270th floor of Relicus City's tallest building just a few hours ago to prevent the *Hi no Kawa*. A new idea then floods her brain, superseding the previous morbid thought. "Wait, you send large containers back and forth from here. Why couldn't the Grange staff personnel travel that way? Has Gicul ever destroyed a vortex before?"

"No," Bru answers. "I believe a chronal vortex would have to have both ports eliminated simultaneously for that to work. I admit that is something beyond my expertise. We do have a nice young man working on how to fortify the vortex openings right now. Maybe you can chat with him about the science of it." She adds, "I don't see any reason that people couldn't be transported back and forth through the vortex."

"You may want to mention it to the chancellor." Luci says. "Have him also alert Royse to protect against stowaway invaders."

"Stowaways? How?"

"*L'inversione*, or even marauders from New Australia, could come from Relicus City to the lower levels of the Grange by hiding in the empty containers that are sent back."

"I see," Bru says with contemplative slowness.

When they reach a door, Bru presses her Viatorio and places her palm on the door reader, and the door slides open.

They pause in a brightly lit antechamber that may have served as an office at some point. Now it's a blank white room with a door on the opposite side. As her eyes acclimate to the difference in brightness, Luci says, "I've only spent time with three people since I've arrived here: Royse, the chancellor, and a woman who skipped to my time to get me named Shar Ryson. All three of them told me that no one knows where Cyphor Gicul and Malom Roderick are."

"Well, that is partly true," Bru responds, returning to her normal speaking voice. "No one knows the whereabouts of Gicul; Malom is a different story. He is locked up." She frowns. "A shame, really."

"You know him?" Luci asks, eager to gather more information.

The old woman nods. "Malom once served on the Directorate. He and I were colleagues many years ago. A pleasant fellow, very smart . . . until he went mad from too many leap skips."

"That can happen?"

"To some people. It's very rare. You have nothing to worry about since you only have a few leap skips to do what we need you for." She smiles. "I promise."

"What do you know about Gicul? Who is he and what does he look like?"

Bru shakes her head from side to side. "No one knows. No one has ever seen him and lived." She scratches her forehead. "I mean except for Malom, I guess."

"How do you know they're not one in the same . . . that Malom Roderick *isn't* Cyphor Gicul?"

"Impossible. Malom is sentenced to a Carcerium chamber by Councilman Cavazos for . . ." There's an odd pause as the director chooses the right phrase. "He was punished for *crimes against the city*."

Luci rubs the fabric on the sleeve of her blue dress. "How do you know he didn't escape somehow?"

"No one escapes Carcerium—it is impossible because of how it is set up," Bru says somberly.

"I don't understand," Luci says. "How can there be no way out?"

"The best way that I can explain a Carcerium cell without going into too much detail is that it is an area smaller than this caught in a time loop."

Before Luci can ask more, Bru opens the door, and a wash of aqua blue-green light pours into the space. Luci instantly recognizes the same flickering colors from the leap skip that she, Macer, and Royse made an hour and a half ago. The two women empty out onto a claustrophobic tile walkway that reminds her of an empty subway terminal in Chicago, not that they're ever completely empty like this.

Floor-to-ceiling transparent containment barriers made of glass or super plastic run along the left and right side. Large containers the size of railroad boxcars noiselessly slide along through an alternating mix of bright silver ripples of chronal energy, the channel on the right flowing in the opposite direction of the left. Bright violet-fuchsia rings spiral through the tubes enveloping the containers and then ripple down the chute. The rhythmic pulse is considerably slower than that of the longchair experience, and the intensity of these emerald flares fade in and out instead of strobing at seizure-inducing speed.

She follows the director down the walkway, cautiously moving past cybos perched in guard boxes every two hundred yards or so. The creatures' heads nearly touch the low roof of the confined space.

Slowing her pace, Bru explains, "You may think it strange, but I find this area of production very soothing."

They're at the end of the of the production canal; a tangible reverence descends over them. Luci subconsciously removes her headpiece and holds it in her hands. Both women watch in silence as massive plasti-crate after plasti-crate fades from view into the swirling vortex like a ship sailing into a fogbank out of sight. Even though Luci's rational mind grasps that she's observing the containers leap skip 1,147 years into the future, it's like watching a video loop of a sleight-of-hand magic trick being performed. Each time one disappears, her heart flutters slightly as if it's the first time she's witnessed one vanish.

After a bit, Luci turns and joins Bru on the other side of the walkway, watching the intake vortex. One after another, the huge plasti-crates appear out of thin air and begin gliding down the slow-moving conveyor belts for refilling. "You're right, it's very soothing to watch for some unexplained reason," Luci says. She notices their partial reflections transparent barrier. Luci realizes without her hat, they're the same height and nearly indistinguishable in the distorted reflection other than the yellow and blue color of their garments.

In a mesmerized voice barely above a whisper, Bru says, "For me, it is sort of like watching an infant sleeping . . . softly inhaling and exhaling."

In an unexpected move, Bru affectionately puts an arm around Luci. She tenses at first but allows the gesture, welcoming the comforting touch.

Bru says, "My lovely, you really should keep the hat on. There are monitors down here, and you know . . ." She gestures to her Viatorio.

Luci complies and puts the headpiece on one-handed while holding the case with the avocado.

Bru turns back to the intake vortex. "I guess this place and what we do here is sort of my baby, since becoming a stretch is not an option for me."

"A stretch?"

"A *stretch* . . . you know." With her free hand, Bru pantomimes the plump belly of pregnancy. "Someone who gives birth."

"We have a different name for it in the interval I'm from," Luci says. "We call someone that gives birth a *mother*."

"*Mother, stretch*—same thing. I'm the *mother* of the Grange." She pauses as another container appears and moves by them, heading back into the complex. "The chancellor said that you were orphaned at a young age, a time when a *mother* is important to a young girl. That must have been hard."

It's as if the softly spoken comment were a blast, removing all of Luci's emotional armor, and now she's naked and vulnerable.

She wonders if this is another of Macer's mind games and doesn't answer.

Bru quickly closes the gap in the conversation. "I used to come down here quite a bit in the 'old' days. That was before Councilman Cavazos convinced the Directorate to install those damned smelly cybos down here. Those things unsettle me." She pauses and shakes her head. "We have never been forced to have anything like that before. I mean, I get it . . . everyone is just so on edge with Gicul on the loose out there somewhere. But I think Pol is exploiting the situation." Luci follows her gaze as Bru looks away from the vortex at the motionless creature in the guard box fifty yards down the walkway.

"Have you met him?" Bru asks. "Pol Cavazos, that is?"

Luci adjusts her headdress. "No. Well, sort of. I saw him talking to the chancellor. Macer thought it best to keep my presence in this interval a secret, at least until Gicul is stopped."

"That's true, but there are four members of the Directorate that know you are here: me, the chancellor, Cavazos, and one other." She withdraws the arm around Luci to point a warning index finger at her. "Listen, if you can do your duty here and return to your interval without crossing paths with Security Minister Pol Cavazos, consider that a good thing."

Before Luci can ask why, Bru adds, "He is very dob-dash."

The quizzical look from Luci forces Bru to select another term. "He is *sneaky*. He makes your skin crawl, making you want to use a month's worth of shower allotment after you have been in his presence for very long." She turns back to the vortex as she says, "Anyway, just trust me on this."

Luci commits the term *dob-dash* to memory and joins her companion in the arrival of the next container. "So this is non-stop, twenty-four hours a day?"

"Yes, my lovely. It has to be. It is the lifeblood of Relicus City, and like your own circulatory system, it must continually flow or you expire."

"Again, it truly is amazing what you've got going on here," Luci remarks.

"Success is not optional; if any part of this slows or fails, someone back home starves, and I cannot live with that."

Another plasti-crate emerges from the nothingness.

"You play a very important role in what happens to Relicus City and the future of mankind."

Luci feels a mix of embarrassment and shame. "I still can't get over the idea that *Hi no Kawa*—"

Bru cuts her off sharply. "That does not matter anymore, my lovely." She puts her arm around her again. This time, Luci isn't startled by her affection. "Remember what we spoke of about Alfred Nobel."

"I just don't know how to even begin to approach the task. It's such a colossal thing, and what if I can't—"

She spins to look her in the face. "Luci, you *will* do it and make it work, because you have to." Her voice is as strong as steel, devoid of doubt.

Bru closes her hands over Luci's hand without the avocado case. Her touch is warm. "You are just like me, so success is not optional for you. Doctor, you have to achieve and solve the task presented, just as I do here, every day, year after year." Her eyes penetrate Luci's heart. "You are required to perform great things because the world is counting on you, one solitary woman for such a time as this to embrace her mandate and shine."

Bru's words and the intensity of her expression force Luci to pull away from her fleshy grip. "I don't think the reason the chancellor brought me here was to see any of this production."

"So you believe this was all a waste of time?" she asks with a confused expression.

"Oh, no, that's not at all what I mean," Luci replies, shaking her head. "I suspect there's a reason that Chancellor Macer brought me here instead of showing me some hologram training video about the farm and processing plant here."

The older woman remains guarded. "Go on then?"

"Don't you find it odd that he went off and left us, me with you?"

"He is a very busy man," Bru replies as if out of reflex.

"Busy. What's more important than saving humanity's only food source from being cut off by a bunch of terrorists?"

Bru tilts her head slightly and squints at her young guest. "What are you saying, dear?"

It's Luci's turn to take the older woman's hand in her free one. "He brought me here to spend time with you. All of this, though spectacular as it is to view, doesn't get me any closer to drift pattern equations, but you, my friend, have touched my heart today and inspired me."

A smile as bright as the chrono energy rings rippling behind them lights Bru's face.

"Director Mandal, may I hug you? It's something that my *stretch* and I used to do." Luci sets the case on the ground. "To feel your strength."

A soft, satisfied expression forms on Bru's face as she leans in. "Why *yes*, my lovely. By all means, do it."

SEVENTEEN

March 22, 2191
Relicus City
[6.217012/127.792969/4.603.388.823/1932:36:27]

RELIKUS SITI

MΛ₵ 22, 2191

"Yes, Director Mandal is a pretty remarkable woman," Luci says, looking out the curved window of the top floor of the chancellor's residence. The reflection of moonlight on the ocean flickers like shards of dancing silver. She breaks her self-induced trance to turn and look at Macer across the room.

"I felt like it was important that you see what we're defending from Gicul," Macer says. "And now that you've flown over the city and visited the Grange, you get a sense for what's at stake. We'll begin tomorrow and, depending on how quickly you work to come up with a solution, will determine how soon we return you to your interval."

Frustrated that something is still being withheld from her, Luci tries a more subtle approach to get information from her "host." Her new strategy is to speak of nonessential drift-pattern project topics in hopes of bigger truths slipping out through casual conversation. "Bru mentioned that she worked for your father, Waleen."

Macer nods from his chair. "This is true. We've depended on Bru for a very long time, but she was a teenager back then, if you can believe it." He holds his own drink to the side of his face to cool himself. "You know, I don't think I've ever seen her out of those yellow farm clothes." He smiles. "Not even the few times when she takes a leap skip to the city for ceremonial Directorate business like she did earlier in the week for the presentation."

The mention of clothing makes Luci appreciate the more modern apparel that she was able to bring back from the Grange, and she adjusts the collar of her blouse. "Royse didn't seem too thrilled about leaving you when we returned."

"Yes, well, he often protests when I send him away on an errand, but sometimes I need to be away from him," Macer says. "Don't worry, we're safe enough in here, and he'll return in a couple of hours to escort you across to the guesthouse."

"He made it seem like he was always at your side."

Macer cups his hands around his mouth, imitating a mock whisper. "I think it may injure his pride that sometimes, his services to me are more for presentation than need. Certainly, when I move about in public, it's better to have him than one of those foul-smelling cybos."

Luci considers this as she walks over to an older-looking longchair positioned on the side of the room. She raps her knuckles on the almond-colored shell. "Why do you have this?"

"Ah, yes, that old thing," he says, standing up and moving toward her. "That is something of a relic by today's standards." He pauses as if remembering something. "It was my father's originally. He had two of the first prototypes, in fact." He points at the cockpit window. "Notice the roomier design inside? A much more elegant art-deco scheme than what's used today." He slowly runs the fingers not holding his glass along the contoured curve of the transport. "It's a little memento that I kept from him." He turns to look at her. "Of course, it's offline from the Spike. Normally, possession of leap-skip technology away from the Spike or the Grange would be illegal, but this is one of the few *perks* that's afforded me."

Luci thinks of the avocado that Bru grew for him.

Before she can mention that as another perk, Macer adds, "*Uneasy lies the head that wears a crown, and so on.*"

"King Henry IV, right?" Luci questions. "From the Shakespeare play. Henry says the line in response to assassination threats to his life. The king is overwhelmed with rebellion; he's tired and sick." She purposefully omits the word "guilty" from her speaking, though she's not certain why. Still, she can't help but notice the odd choice of character comparison. "Enos, do you view yourself as king of Relicus City?"

His bushy eyebrows rise as he makes a tsk-tsk-tsk sound. "A bit cynical, my dear Luci?" He smiles and shakes his head. "A king?" He pauses as he takes a drink. "No, not a king … that's not what I mean. Don't read too much into what I said. For what it's worth, Malom and Cyphor do not wish to assassinate a king—or dethrone me, if you will. They want to undo the entire world that we've built here. I just happen to live in it and hold a high position. Nothing personal." He snaps to, and in what Luci regards as his politician showman's voice, he says, "But speaking of royalty and perks, come in here. I want to show you something before Royse returns."

Luci curiously follows him into a small antechamber with a high ceiling. The temperature is a few degrees cooler. When the auto lights activate, the sight of the room's main fixture takes her breath away. "Is that what I think it is?"

Macer nods proudly and positions himself to the side of the enormous statue. "King David, in the flesh, or I should say, *in the marble*. Carrara marble, to be exact. Although, now that I think of it, Michelangelo rendered him here as he was about to fight the Philistine giant, so technically not a king. This is the shepherd boy on his way to becoming king."

The pedestal base of the statue is sunk deep into the floor, making the figure appear to be standing on a short riser no taller than a street curb.

Luci's eyes well up at the magnificent sight. "He's so much bigger than I imagined."

"Yes, he's a big boy alright—weighs as much as eighty men or more."

She gasps in awe and is suddenly embarrassed, but Macer's smile only widens at this.

Luci extends an uncertain hand. "May I . . ."

"Certainly. He's survived a broken arm in the 1600s by protestors and getting his foot knocked off by some maniac with a hammer in the twentieth century. I'm sure that he can withstand the touch of your hand."

Even though he's granted her permission, Luci moves cautiously, softly pressing her palm against the cold marble. She looks up at the figure's face, staring over their heads. A nervous laugh escapes from her, and tears stream over her cheeks. "It's wonderful," she whispers in reverence. "I've only seen it—*him* from a distance in the Galleria dell'Accademia." She lifts her other hand to touch as well and bites her quivering lip to still it. Without a doubt, it is the most beautiful thing that she's ever beheld. She speaks softly as if David were alive. "So perfect."

"Actually, his right hand was deliberately rendered out of proportion. It's a little larger than it should be, and Michelangelo made him squint slightly to be less perfect than a Roman." The inflection in his voice is like a proud child showing off his accomplishments. "I even have his warning stare facing in the direction of Rome, just like it was in the original installation."

"Thanks for sharing this with me, Enos. It's . . . it's marvelous."

"My pleasure. The way to identify a master sculptor is by the way the hands are rendered. You see, a novice can't quite get the . . ." His sentence is interrupted by a sharp intake of air followed by a series of staccato grunts.

Luci turns from the statue as Macer braces himself on the edge of the pedestal. His eyes close tightly.

"Enos, what's wrong?" she shouts, her voice louder than expected in the confined space.

He shakes his head from side to side but doesn't answer verbally.

Luci rushes around to support and prevent him from smashing his head against the marble base. "Enos, what can I do? How can I help?" She spots the Viatorio on his ear and pinches it between her fingers. Yelling into it as if it were a microphone, she shouts, "Someone help! The chancellor's having some kind of seizure. I don't think it's epileptic, but—"

Macer pushes her away. "No, Luci . . . just . . . wait."

She repeats the action. "Send somebody, please!"

"Please *stop* yelling in my ear," he grunts in frustration while attempting to right himself. "It's not a seizure!"

Relieved to hear him speaking, she pulls back, nearly bumping into the cylindrical robot that's arrived. She pleads with the hovering concierge, "You've got to help him. Something's wrong." She steps to the side to allow it clear access to the master of the house, but the bot only cleans their spilled drinks and whisks away again.

"Luci, it's okay . . . I'm fine . . . just need a moment. Catching up. I'm not in danger."

With the robot gone, she crouches to where Macer is sitting on the floor. "Catching up? What does that mean?" She recalls Bru's comment about heightened security because of Cyphor Gicul and wonders how long it will take Royse to arrive. "You're not poisoned or anything, right?"

His eyes finally focus on hers. He's back, but his expression is weary. "I'm alright. I just need a minute."

She remembers the trio of cybos guarding his home but decides against wrangling one of them inside for fear they might see her as a threat. "You're sure you're okay?"

He nods. "Just a minute is all. It'll pass."

She makes it to her feet. "I'm going to get you some water, okay?"

He flicks his hand in acknowledgement for her to go.

The concierge bot has already stowed the glasses they had used, forcing Luci to tap sliding cupboards to find more.

She finds another, but it takes an eternity for the glass to fill. As she waits, a horrifying question about what will happen to her if he dies pops into her head. The notion that any harm would come to her is quickly squashed when she realizes that Relicus City would still need her to complete her task and return to her time to reveal DPM.

Luci finally returns to the statue nook and hands Macer the drink.

"Thank you," he says between gulps. "I usually feel those coming on, but that one—whew."

When he's finished, she asks, "What exactly was that?"

"Nothing to trouble yourself with," he answers, allowing her to help him to stand.

"Too late. I'm already troubled—and it hardly looked like nothing. What did you mean by *'catching up'*? Is that some weird jetlag or something from the skip?"

He waves the question off. "I don't know what you mean."

"Enos, you said you needed to *catch up* or something."

"I never said anything of the sort," he snaps. "I'm fine."

Luci lets out an exasperated breath. "Really, so that's it? You never said *anything of the sort?*"

He shakes his head, feigning innocence. "Just help me into the other room, please." The argument is getting nowhere, so Luci chooses to shelve the incident for now. Though she is considerably smaller than the older man is, she manages to maneuver his semi-responsive body back into his chair in the other area. As she plops him down into the oversized seat, she gets the final word in. "Okay, but I know what I heard."

She doesn't know if he's lying about the incident because he's embarrassed and prideful or if it's because Macer just lies about everything. She knows she's not going to get a straight answer from him and wonders if she can come up with a reason to contact Bru or Shar to learn if they've ever witnessed anything like that with him or anyone else.

After a minute or so, Macer has returns to himself, though he doesn't leave his seat. Luci realizes that he's deliberately changing the focus when he asks, "So you really like sculpture?"

She reluctantly plays along; tricking him into inadvertently spill unfiltered data to her is key. She'll allow whatever unguarded verbal meanderings he relays for a subconscious pathway to the truth. *"Keep 'em talking Luci G,"* she tells herself.

"I enjoy all art from the Renaissance period," she says enthusiastically. "Dominick and Matt, these two retired seniors that I know, regularly stay in Florence for months at a time. They say it's spectacular. I was thinking about going with them sometime, but now here I am." She takes the seat next to his, studying his face for any trace of a relapse. She returns to her game of attempting to get him to slip up about some non-essential thing. "When did you get it, the David statue? Did Florence survive *Hi no Kawa*?"

Macer's expression contorts as his bushy eyebrows rise. "Unfortunately, it did *not* survive, but there's an interval in a courtyard a few blocks away the week of the annihilation."

An all-too-familiar wave of guilt descends on Luci, and all she can answer is, "Oh, but that doesn't explain how you got—"

"December 19, 2067 P.H." His face is stone as he speaks. "That's the date the first ESTA, a weather drone enhanced with short-time leap skip capabilities, was launched into low-level orbit."

"December 19, 2067 P.H.?"

"P.H . . . pre-*Hi no Kawa*. After the *Hi no Kawa* years, the world . . . what was left of it, shifted to MBC dating, the UNI-FON calendar developed by twentieth-century statistician Moses Bruine Cotsworth." The statement comes out clinically cold. "You'll need to account for the differences in the calendar when you do you drift-pattern calculations. We'll get you started on that within the next day or so." He takes a sip. "Anyway, as I said, the satellite drone was released to overwhelming interest. Though humanity couldn't exactly control weather patterns, the ESTA removed all faulty precognitions. It became a literal window into the future, give or take seventy-two hours."

He pauses and fidgets with his fingers. "As I said last night in the warehouse, foretelling meteorological occurrences with 100% accuracy became the norm. But as with any tool, there's always a dark side; the same blade that can prune a plant like those you saw back at the Grange can also be thrust into someone's heart, ending their life." Macer pauses as if to summon something up inside to continue.

"What happened?" Luci encourages nervously.

"It only took a few months for the warring governments of the world at that time to see the ESTAs and DPM as something that could be militarized. A country from long ago like China could view troop formations days before the fighters would actually arrive. They could rearrange their own deployments to counter, and so forth. In time, treaties were signed amongst the world's nations to ban the use of DPM."

Luci studies his face as he speaks, captivated by the dark pupils staring back at her.

He sighs. "History tells us that many of the original ESTAs satellites were recalled and lowered back down to Earth to be decommissioned, and a few of them were even blasted out of the skies. All this was done in an attempt to prevent military hackers from selling black-market future information the highest bidder. It's suspected that most of the ESTAs were neutralized, but it would've been easy to false-log a deactivation and leave the machine or machines intact. The sky is a massive hiding place for something so small, and the will of a warring nation with the resources . . . well, you know."

Luci's chest tightens.

Macer finishes the cup and examines it by thoughtfully turning it from side to side. "Treaties were signed, and treaties were broken. Everyone wanted just a little more, just a little bit." He shifts his eyes from playing with the cup back to her. "You know, Luci, a reasonable person would think that with nowhere to hide, ESTAs and drift-pattern mathematics would have shut down all military activity. There should've been world peace among the nations." He scoffs. "How can it be that with the ability to know, beyond any doubt, a conflict's undisputable outcome . . . something viewable days in advance of said attack, how is it that the nations would still war with each other? It's ridiculous, but man's bloodthirstiness couldn't be quenched. If anything, generals having the ability to see into the future only made them scramble for more extreme demonstrations of power until—"

Luci finishes the thought. "Until they went with nuclear options and annihilated nine billion, nine hundred eighty-seven million of the planet's population."

As if trying to console her, Macer says, "Not that many in the actual war. The fire only took—"

She waves him off. "That was the end result. Who cares how the death toll is reached, whether it's those that perished in a nuclear blast, starvation, or murder in the aftermath? The tally is still the same."

Macer solemnly nods in silent agreement.

"I feel sick," Luci says, rushing to the kitchen. She barely makes it to the sink disposal in time to vomit up the meal she'd eaten after the tour of the Grange.

Macer gives her space, only approaching as she begins to cry.

She sniffs. "It's so awful. I still can't get over it . . . all those people, all the animals." She looks up from the sink at him through eyes made blurry with tears. "I love animals. I do, I love them. I'd even considered being a vet before the accident with my family."

She realizes she's on the verge of hysterics and forces herself into a routine that has calmed her anxiety many times before. She closes her eyes to focus on complex mathematical computations. The numbers help serve to insulate her mind, forming a wall and blocking out unwieldy thoughts, bringing them under control.

She mumbles dizzying calculations with the speed of an auctioneer, multiplying numbers, subtracting and squaring them, turning them inside out and over again and again. The act serves as a harness or lasso, allowing her to constrain ideas and emotions that result in fear, snapping the brittle necks of bad thoughts. Numbers are *always* faithful, they *always* behave and act orderly, and a calculation *always* delivers the same unchanging answer. They are *always* absolute—they can be trusted when life can't be. When life pulls the rug out from under you, numbers are a net to catch you—a handrail, something solid to grab onto instead of falling all the way down to the bottom of the stairs. When everything else is uncertain, numbers *are* certain and predictable and have been since the birth of the universe. She wraps her mind in numbers and the offspring of their quotients.

After a few moments of this self-distraction, she reaches her "special" number and opens her eyes. Macer is studying her with a concerned look. He places his hand over one of hers that's clutching the edge of the sink.

She surprised that the warmth of it is comforting. "I'm okay . . . just a little panic attack, but I'm alright now."

Some of the tension drains from his face. "I won't tell anyone of your episode if you won't tell of mine."

Even in an emotionally weakened state, she can't resist exposing his earlier lie. "I thought you said it was nothing. Plus, a panic attack is very different from whatever that thing was with you."

A devilish grin flashes across his face, and he abruptly changes the subject. "*Hands* . . ." he says, giving her hand a firm pump before pulling away. "The rendering of hands is what separates a merely good sculptor from a great one."

"Huh?" she asks, failing to realize that he's returned to the topic from the conversation in the other room. She wipes her mouth and activates the sink to clean itself. "Oh, okay, I guess that makes sense," she answers, playing along as if the last few minutes never occurred. She's embarrassed, but at least Royse hadn't witnessed her panic. Macer was bad enough, but he'd had his own freak-out, or whatever it was.

"It's all in the hands." He lifts his in the air like display models. "Hands are very difficult to render well for most artists. My father told me that."

Nearly all the wooziness is gone. "Was Waleen an artist?"

"Waleen? Oh, yes, a dabbler. Certainly, he could have been a great sculptor had he allowed the time for it." Macer's look is far away in a memory. "He and his colleagues were devoted to rebuilding the world, a noble preoccupation indeed." He pauses and slyly adds, "But I found a way to service both my art and my duty to the city, unlike him."

"You're an artist, Enos?" The question comes out more jagged than Luci intends.

His response is equally guarded. "Is that so hard to imagine?"

"No," Luci answers, turning her palms to him. "Nothing like that. I think it's great. I'm glad to know there's art being done in the future. It's important. Other than the Michelangelo in there, I haven't seen any art in Relicus City or at the Grange."

Macer's expression relaxes slightly. He gestures to the Viatorio on his ear. "All of the art posted around the city is catalogued and seen through here. You'll be able to see our art soon enough. There is *one* thing that I can show you now though, something I'm especially proud of. A sculpture piece of my own. Do you want to see?"

"Something of yours?" Luci asks, extra softly to make up for her earlier response. Keeping with her plan to catch him in an unguarded state in hopes of gathering information, Luci jumps at the opportunity. "Of course, I'd love to see your work."

Macer lights up with excitement, and he nearly leaps from the chair. "Come, I have a workroom on the bottom level."

As Luci follows him down the spiral staircase in the center of the room, she says, "I thought the appreciation of art may have ended with *Hi no Kawa*, that maybe your society consisted of more utilitarian ideals."

"How do you mean?" Macer asks as they pass through a level that's clearly his office, judging by the desk and furniture layout.

"I don't know, I'd considered the very real possibility that art may have been discarded, being viewed as impractical. You can't feed a statue to a family or use a painting as a water filtration system." The authenticity of conversation surprises her.

She's pleased at how natural it feels. If nothing else, maybe his art will give her some insight into him and a weakness that she can exploit later.

"True," he answers, stepping on to the bottom level. "But thankfully, that's not the case here. That might be the case for those New Australia barbarians, but not here."

Responding to their arrival, the overhead lights activate. Luci is surprised that this area is uncharacteristically cluttered with all manner of materials and supplies, in contrast to the rest of his home.

Luci scans the work area looking for sculptures, but nothing is in sight. She looks back at him in confusion. Macer maneuvers through the mess to a gray plastic table. As he shoves two small modeling figures off a stack of raggedly bound sketchpads, he explains, "This is very rare here in Relicus City."

"You mean paper?" she asks, cautiously making her way through precariously balanced containers of art tools and materials. "You don't have paper here?"

"Not usually. Well, most people don't."

"Well that explains the bidets here and at the Grange," she says.

"It's kind of like the avocado thing, one of my perks." He presents a large sheet with a charcoal-sketch figure in each hand. "I made something for the city and had someone leap skip to an interval to bring back these supplies. I told them that I wanted to do it the old way by sketching by hand, none of the V modeling . . . nothing digital. So they got me real paper pulped from tree remains."

"This is what you wanted me to see?" Luci asks, receiving the large sheet drawing from him. It's a crude charcoal sketch of a man. One hand holds a shield while the other extends a curved disc above his head. Closer observation reveals the scribbles on top of the disc represent fruit—the romantic figure of a man is lifting a bowl of food of some type to the heavens. Small numbers on the side of the figure indicate dimensions. "This is quite good. You did this?"

Macer smiles, and his bushy eyebrows dance. "That's just a study. I probably did twenty or thirty of those to get everything right. This is what I really want you to see."

Though it's twice as large a device as the coaster-sized hologram projector Shar had in the warehouse, Luci recognizes the tech. Macer exchanges it for the sketch she's holding. "Press the green tab and twist the base of it to the left."

The disc responds with a few clicks as it telescopes in two directions. "You may let go," Macer explains. "It'll hover now."

Though she saw a similar manifestation the night before, it still boggles her mind to see the object float on the air before her.

"Now, depress the button with a plus sign on it," Macer instructs.

Instinctively, she steps back as a full-sized version of the statue in the sketch appears. The gasp she makes embarrasses her and delights him. "Better than the sketch, right?" He addresses the overhead lights with a command. "Medium illumination." With the lights lowered, the details of the hologram sharpen into focus becoming more opaque.

"You sculpted this?" Luci asks. "This is amazing." She moves to look at the image straight on.

"I'm glad you approve of Waleen Macer," Macer says proudly. "The shield represents protection of Relicus City. The bowl of fruit, the pioneering of the Grange's food-growing technologies."

"This is of your father? It's remarkable how much you resemble him," she says. "You could be brothers. You're like twins, except for his moustache, of course."

"I rendered from source material of him from when the city was founded in 2108. He was forty-nine then."

"And you are?"

He pauses before answering. "Over a decade older. I'm sixty-two," he says with raised eyebrows.

"Hmmm . . . you wear sixty-two well."

"You're very kind. My stretch died of Fitchner's when I was a teenager, and then I became very ill with it shortly after. My father stayed in quarantine with me for years until the disease went into remission. He was a great man and leader."

Her heart sinks at the idea of losing his mother around the same age that hers was taken. Daydreaming about how life would've been if her father had survived eases some of the resentment she feels toward the chancellor.

Macer continues, "He became something of a recluse the final decade or so of his life, conducting all business from his home through his Viatorio. This was good, in a way, for me, as I got to spend a lot of time at his feet learning statecraft. This representation is him during his finest hour. I call it *'Deliberate Humanity.'*"

Something about all of this doesn't add up for her; she's heard of older men having children late in life, so that's not what's bothering her, and the dates work, but something nags at her mind the way numbers and unsolved complex equations sometimes do. She glances at the curious inscription at the base of the statue.

'DŪ NOT ULO HU PAST

TŪ DIS±D HU FŪTꓤ'

~ W. H. MꓥSꓤ 2059 – 2147? ~

"What does the plaque at the bottom say?"

In a proud voice, he says, "Do not allow the past to decide the future." He clears his throat. "It was a comment that he always made, though I've adopted it as my own now too."

She remembers her dad's quirky and less-elegant catchphrase about the future. *"The future isn't what it used to be."* She asks, "What are the numbers?"

"Ah, that's his date of birth and death."

"But why is there a question mark following the 2147?" Luci asks, stooping to get a better look. "And why is it written in that weird way? I recognize most of the letters, but a few are unfamiliar."

"Ah, yes, I forgot. It's UNIFON, so it would be slightly different from the alphabet that you're used to." Macer moves to adjust the floating projector disc. The image of the rectangle with the embossed letters enlarges to fill the space. "Many of the characters in the UNIFON alphabet are similar to the twenty-six letters of your twenty-first-century texts, but we have forty glyphs to represent the most important sounds of the English language. Interestingly, UNIFON was developed in your time, back in the 1950s, I believe, but it never saw widespread usage until the rebuilding after *Hi no Kawa*."

He squeezes the Viatorio on his ear. "I'm putting in a request for you to have a Unifon alpha and Unifon calendar converter program loaded into your Viatorio for your work. Of course, conversions could be done manually, given enough time, but the extra effort is pointless when we have these." He points to the Viatorio.

She nods her understanding and asks, "Everything in Relicus is written this way, with fourteen extra characters?"

"Yes, of course," Macer answers. "The principle of one letter per phoneme, one standard language. Don't worry, though. UNIFON is only letters. Numbers aren't affected in any way."

She clicks her tongue off the roof of her mouth. "Yeah, you can always depend on numbers to be a constant. Is the question mark a part of the UNIFON convention?"

"That? No, that's there because of the uncertainty of the date of his demise."

"How's that possible? How do you not know the year he passed?"

Macer examines the nailbed of his thumb. "As I mentioned, my father had become a recluse the final decade of his life, only attending meetings online. He was a shut-in, which made me a shut-in, since I was the only one who he'd allow to care for him." He massages his temple as the words come slowly. "It was the least I could do since he had done it for me years before, but I learned a lot from him and how to govern by observing his practices. When his health began to fail, he took the other prototype longchair he had and did a leap skip to an unspecified interval to die. The prototype chairs don't have tracking capabilities, so it's anybody's guess as to where he may have ended up."

"Is it a common thing for people to skip to a different interval to die?" Luci asks.

"No," Macer says, looking back up at her. "Actually, it's forbidden, but he *was* and *remains* a hero of the city, so certain allowances were made for his behavior. Ironically, his departure just adds to his legend."

"So no one ever found his body or the prototype longchair?"

Macer folds his arms. "Nope, never did."

"Is it hard for you . . . to be his son, to live in his shadow?"

A curious smile forms on his face as he returns the view of the hologram to the actual size setting. "I cast my own shadow. I'm not competing with the ghost memory of Waleen Macer, despite his greatness." In a voice full of bravado, he announces, "*Do not allow the past to decide the future.*"

Something about Macer's father going rogue is off. A thought pops into her mind, an incredibly distasteful idea: *What if he is Cyphor Gicul?* Luci recalls Bru's theory of how too many leap skips can destroy the mind. She does her best to excuse it, knowing how much Waleen is revered in the city, but the objectionable notion still hangs in her mind. She searches for the best way to tactfully approach it. Deciding that a direct question is too confrontational, she opts instead for something less brazen. "Do you know if your father had any dealings with Malom Roderick?"

At first, he appears confused. "Malom is younger than I am, so *no*, the two of them would never have met." The suspicious look forming on his face confirms that he's wise to her thinly veiled innuendo.

She tries to cut her losses and backtrack. "Sorry, I don't know anything about Malom Roderick to know his—"

"If you're insinuating that my dead father is somehow Cyphor Gicul, you couldn't be more wrong." Macer scoffs and his eyes dart around looking for something to focus on. "The very idea of it is impossible. The stated mission of Cyphor and his group is to basically destroy everything that he, myself, and many other dedicated members of the city have accomplished." His pupils finally lock onto hers. "I know better than anyone that my father *would* never and *could* never be Cyphor Gicul."

"Sorry, I didn't mean anything by it. I was just exploring a potential—"

"There's nothing there," he blurts dismissively, ushering in an awkward silence.

Luci shifts the conversation back to the art piece. "His hands," she says. "You masked the figure's hands here." She points to the shield. "You told me that a sculptor should be judged by how well they render hands, and you've hidden this one behind the shield he's holding." She gestures upward. "You can sort of see the fingers on that one holding the bowl of fruit in the air, but only a little."

Macer regards her with a deadeye stare.

"You did that intentionally, right?" She studies his face, attempting to determine if his reaction is an aftereffect of the seizure on the other floor. Finally, a smile forms under his big beak of a nose, but she can tell it's not authentic. He must know this because Macer laughs and snaps his fingers in faux amusement.

"Ah, you got me, my dear Luci." He moves over to her, his face disappearing from view as he steps through the opaque hologram image. She's startled as he emerges and grabs her hands in his. "No one ever noticed that I did that until now."

Luci resists the urge to yank her hands free. "Well, probably the only reason that I did was because you alerted me to the hand-rendering thing upstairs."

The dark eyebrows rise as he squints to look into her eyes. "No, I think you are clever enough that you would have caught it without my help. You are very clever, Doctor, and we are very fortunate to have you with us . . . very fortunate, indeed."

She shakes off a shiver creeping up her neck. In an effort to appeal to his vanity and return to a sense of normalcy, Luci asks, "Where's the real one? The statue, I mean. May I see it in person?"

Her ploy succeeds, and Macer releases his grip to turn and admire his handiwork. "Ah, I wish you could. We had the unveiling of the real thing four days ago. The actual sculpture is at the foot of the Spike." He faces her. "Remember the tall building with the longchairs?"

She lets out a nervous laugh. "Of course. Other than your guest house across the way, it's the only other place that I've been to in Relicus City."

He frowns for a microsecond, but then the smile is back. "Yes, of course you do. Anyway, the statue is at the base of that building in the common area for all to see, so you'll understand that we can't take you to see it in person, as much as I'd like to." The smile melts. "Security reasons and all, you know. We must keep you safe. No more excursions until your work is done."

Shar's final words to her before leaving the guesthouse echo through her mind to *be safe*. Luci bites her lip as she looks at the hovering device projecting the hologram. She's grateful that the tension from before continues to dissipate. "Chancellor . . . er, Enos, I need to ask you something." It's still obvious that he's holding things back from her, though the reason isn't clear. Her mind races to find a way to convince him to let her in on what he's fighting to conceal.

"Of course. What is it, my dear?" he says in a gush that makes the hairs on the nape of her neck bristle again.

She hesitates, picturing Shar handing the recording disc to him the night before and gets a different idea. "The room above this one, the one on the middle level … that's your office, right?"

"My home office, yes," Macer replies, shutting down the image of the hologram statue. "I have another in the Spike building, and you saw the one at the Grange."

"But the one here, that's the one the recording was made in, right?"

"Which recording? What are you talking about?" he asks, retracting the device into its compact form.

"The video where I talk about the doll that I almost won for my mother in the third grade."

He massages the wrinkles on his forehead. "Ah, yes, that. What about it?"

"When was that recording made by future me?" Luci asks.

Suspicious eyes run over her face as he tilts his head slightly. Finally, Macer pinches the end of his bulbous nose and sniffs. "Well, right now, in fact."

She bites the inside of her cheek to mask that she knows he's lying. She expected it, remembering Shar's slip that the recording was made a lot longer than a few days ago, longer than Macer implied in the warehouse.

"Follow me," he says.

The two move up the staircase, Luci trailing behind and contemplating the potential outcomes of what she's about to try.

EIGHTEEN

THE CURVED WALL OF WINDOWS encircles the room like dark mirrors blocking the dim starlight outside. Not that it matters. Like the guesthouse, only the den area on the top level is above the waterline of the ocean outside. Fluorescent light shines up from the plastic grid floor as in most of the city's interiors. In contrast to the art room on the level below, everything is orderly and in place.

Positioned far back from the twisting stairwell opening sits a large metal desk with two guest chairs. In the table's center is a large bowl of liquid with softly hissing bubbles. The ceramic container is a quarter of the size of the one in the den in the guesthouse but larger than the individual ones at the longchair station. As the two of them approach the desk, Luci points at the stand on the desk holding a straw-like apparatus and asks, "What is that? I saw those around in the station and one at your guest quarters."

Macer takes his seat behind the desk. "It's called a pull basin. Late into the twenty-first century, before *Hi No Kawa*, inventors and scientists developed I.I.R."

"What's I.I.R?" Luci asks.

"It stands for Ingestible Information Relay; the common slang is 'sipping.'" Macer clicks the Viatorio. "Pardon me while I summon the domestic attendant to record us." Macer reaches in the desk drawer and produces something that looks like a set of black rubber brass knuckles similar to the item that

Benold Jesper used. As he slides his fingers into the openings, he says, "These are WIBs, short for Wearable Input Bands." He points at the bubbling liquid. "And this is a substance called Jardon. Think of it as liquid information." Detaching the straw and tube from the holder stand, he explains, "A sipper. The user operator drinks a small amount of the Jardon through a sip tube like this."

Reading the confused look on Luci's face, he waves the thin tube around in the air like the baton of an absent-minded conductor. "In your time interval, most people take in information through their eyes. A few learn through auditory means, but most learn through the visual ports of the eyes."

"Yeah, it's called reading," Luci says. "It's been around for thousands of years."

He ignores the sarcasm. "We read glyphs too, like the UNIFON language that I told you about, but just imagine if you could learn about a subject simply by ingesting it in small doses over a brief time, to know something by absorbing it into you. Today, the technology of instantly knowing a topic allows learners to become a master of a static discipline almost instantly. This is going to save an enormous amount of time in you getting up to speed with DPM that the slightly older version of you wrote about in the twenty-first century."

Macer shoots a glance at the floating concierge bot as it enters the area and then returns his gaze to her. "Luci, the days of classroom teaching have long been abolished; there simply is no need to spend countless hours of adolescence to early adulthood in formal instruction. In Relicus City, there are no students, only sippers."

"Bullshit!" Luci exclaims, half-laughing in disbelief. "My lecture clocked in at seventy-two minutes last night. You're saying that a teaspoon of juice from this magic bowl would've relayed everything instead of them listening to me speak?"

"It's called a pull basin, and there's nothing magical about it or the Jardon. And it's been scientifically proven that the information is retained longer because it physically becomes a part of the person as if they experienced it first-hand."

The idea is astonishing. "Show me," she demands, reaching for the sip tube. "I want a demonstration."

"Soon enough, but first we have to—"

"If this Jardon works the way you say it does, I want to see it. Pick any topic. It doesn't matter to me."

Macer pulls back before she can snatch the tube from him over the desk. "That's not a good idea." He gestures to the guest chair. "Have a seat."

"Why can't I sample it?" she asks reluctantly, plopping down in the seat.

"You're not ready. Measures have to be taken to isolate sections of the hemispheres of the brain, and you have to have a Viatorio to be able to search and access files. Without establishing virtual partition compartments in your mind to receive and stow the information, it would be like turning a kachoti blender on high without a lid—very messy and very dangerous. One could die from it."

Luci studies his eyes, but she can't tell if he's lying. "The neural pathways must be identified." He points to the device on his ear. "I've scheduled to have you fitted with your Viatorio and cerebral modifications in the morning. It'll take the better part of the day to get acclimated to using it, but you should be able to begin drift pattern work before sunfall tomorrow."

"Whoa, are you talking brain surgery?"

He shakes his head. "There's no cutting of tissue or skull. I assure you that the process is routine."

She squirms in her chair, attempting to stifle the growing fear. "But there's risk involved. Every procedure has some level of risk, no matter how small."

"Actually, that's not true. The method by which the arom-nanobots perform an installation is flawless, a 100% success rate. They're just inserted in and—"

"Absolutely not." Luci shoots up from her seat, pushing her palms down on the cool metal desk. "If something were to happen to my brain, it'd be bad for both of us." She shakes her head defiantly. "You'd lose your shot at stopping this Cyphor Gicul guy, have no chance of shutting down his resistance, and I'd return home not able to do calculations—or worse, go back as a vegetable. No, it's too risky." She pulls back from the desk and crosses her arms. "Point me in the direction of your science libraries, or if you insist on protecting me, send the books up here and I'll begin in the morning first thing."

When Macer doesn't respond, she wags an index finger. "But nothing goes in my brain."

Macer exhales through his big nose in mild exasperation. "First of all, every text we have is transcribed in UNIFON, so that would take a very long time for you to decipher—time that we don't have. But more importantly, we have no physical books. There is no library. Everything—and I mean everything—all collected knowledge is in the well drop. Back at the warehouse in Baltimore, you asked me if Relicus City had something like the ARPANET of your interval. This is it. The Jardon flows throughout the city from the well drop into these pull basins." He adjusts the WIB on his left hand. "I've shown you what's at stake here, and this back-and-forth between us on every single issue is tiresome."

"There has to be another way," she says in desperation. "Please, Enos."

"There's not, and as I said before—"

He clicks his Viatorio and is in another conversation. He holds his palm up to pause the discussion. He asks the caller, "Of course we're back; otherwise, how would you be speaking to me right now?" Macer glances back at Luci, then up at the ceiling. "How can you not know how long it's been gone, Pol?"

Though the response isn't audible, Luci knows that someone is "speaking" directly into Macer's brain through the Viatorio bud. She wonders how common a name Pol is here and whether or not this is the Security Minister, Pol Cavazos, that

Bru had warned her of, the man that had argued with the chancellor in the hallway outside the guest home a few hours before.

"Yes, she's here with me now," Macer says, stealing another glance at Luci.

She shudders as Macer informs the unheard voice, "I'm arranging for that tomorrow."

There's more silence, but the pause allows Luci to remember the reason she wanted to come in the office in the first place. So distracted by talk of pull basins and altering her brain, she'd forgotten what she'd planned to do on the recording. Her body tenses at the prospect of altering her answers on the video they're about to make. She wonders if she'll be sucked at blinding speed through a portal back to a rainy Baltimore night or some other unexpected result.

"Don't be stupid, Pol. Put everyone on alert for what? If somebody's in an interval that Gicul decides to destroy, it's not like you can do anything to prevent it, not until we understand how he's doing it, and that's what we're working on over here." He massages his veiny forehead. "All that you'll do by spreading news like this is inciting a panic, and that won't do anything for us, not yet." He shakes his head. "Double or even triple your cybo counts around key areas if you like, but don't officially announce anything. I'll speak to you about it in person in the morning."

Macer doesn't attempt to mask his frustration after he disconnects. "I'm sorry." He pauses to find his smile. "Where were we?"

"What just happened, Chancellor?" she probes cautiously. "Did another interval go dark?"

The fake smile fades, and Macer sighs. "The skip node of Poland 1952 apparently was destroyed a couple of days ago. We had five sitters in the interval." He shakes his head in disgust. "They'll be stuck there now for the rest of their lives, and they'll have to survive all alone so as to avoid contaminating the residents of the interval."

She bites her lip and responds in a soft voice. "Sorry. What were they doing there if all the food is at the Grange?"

"They were setting a trap for Gicul, but it failed. We're running out of time before he targets all the intervals." His voice is somber. "He's a madman. I just hope we can beat him when it comes down to it." The intensity of his eyes on her could ignite a fire. "You've got to figure this out. You've got to beat Gicul."

She debates whether now is the best time to go through with her impromptu experiment. It may not work anyway. As is always the case, her curious nature gets the better of her and forces her to press on. "We were about to make the hologram recording that you showed me in the warehouse last night."

"Ah yes," he says. "We do it under one condition: you go through with the procedure to install your Viatorio. No more resistance, no hesitation."

The notion of him *not* making the recording is preposterous to her. She reasons that if no recording is ever made, Shar has nothing to give him to view ... that is, unless something else is going on here. "You drive a hard bargain," she says. "Where I come from, you'd be quite the businessman."

The statement seems to perplex him. Even so, he offers a witty response and, of course, his signature politician's smile. "I *am* a businessman. I'm in the business of the human race." He leans forward. "So, we have an agreement?"

"I'll do it," she lies, convinced that if what she is about to do works the way she thinks it will, none of this will matter anyway. She'll be back in Baltimore headed to Atlantic City and won't even know anything about the *Hi no Kawa*. If Macer really did set up the lecture to grab her, she'll be somewhere else, but someplace safe—anywhere but here. "Yeah, I'll do the Viatorio thing tomorrow," she says confidently.

"Great, then let's begin," Macer says.

Luci notes that his shoulders relax slightly.

He commands the floating robot behind Luci, "Concierge, record meeting—activate."

She turns her head as the device hovers into position. After several banal questions from Macer, he leans slightly back in his chair and makes a comment about the importance of people being clear. It's the line that Luci's been waiting for. She begins the story of how when she was in the third grade and Lakeview elementary had their "Fun Day."

As she relays the story, her stomach knots up. It constricts in the way it would riding on a rollercoaster that's ascending that initial agonizing climb before the first steep drop. She tells of the doll she's going to win for her mother, but this time she switches the number she wrote on the slip of paper from ninety-nine to sixty-six. She holds her breath after she delivers the alteration to the story and grips the arms of the chair.

Her heart is racing, and she's afraid to open her eyes prematurely.

After a few tense seconds, a question comes. "Doctor, are you feeling alright? Are you having another panic attack?"

Her stomach continues to somersault. Wave after wave of confusion envelops her as she opens her eyes. Nothing's changed. She whispers to herself in a daze, "What am I still doing here?"

"I don't understand. Are you feeling okay?" Macer's bushy eyebrows climb, his expression confused.

She mumbles, "You're still here. I changed it. It should have changed the recording and therefore altered what I did in the warehouse, nullifying . . ."

He squints giving a suspicious look. "Whatever are you going on about?"

She gazes blankly at the metal desk, attempting to work out why her revision to the "script" hasn't changed anything. What had he called it in the warehouse? Macer used a term, something like identity convergence—yes, that was it. What had she done wrong? She closes her eyes again on the off chance that the result isn't instantaneous. She struggles to recall Macer's comments about how the longchair U-curve would overlay a previous version of a timeline.

She opens her eyes again to Macer's perplexed expression that's growing into a scowl. Either she has no clue as to how this time travel stuff works or the recording was never her in the first place—it was the Luci from before, the dead Luci. "Ninety-nine to sixty-six," she stammers, still processing. "It didn't change anything."

"Are you okay?" he asks. "What do you mean?"

She twists in the seat for a look at the hovering robot and then slowly turns back to Macer.

He's interrupted by another alert to his Viatorio. "What now, Pol?"

Luci isn't willing to wait this time. She blurts out a question, "What happened to the other Luci? Who killed her?"

Macer shoos her away with his hand while continuing the other conversation. "Absolutely not. I expressly forbid it."

Luci stands, every muscle tensing in her body.

Macer shrugs apologetically to her as he continues in a low voice. "Pol, I'm aware of your and Malom's private grudge, but the whole point of putting him in there is isolation." There's a pause, and then Macer also stands to pace behind the desk. "No, under no circumstances are you to leap skip to his Carcerium, and you're definitely not taking . . ." He looks at Luci while detaching the sipper tube and sliding it into in his breast pocket. ". . . our *asset* there with you so you can gloat over him."

Being referred to as an *asset* infuriates her. Being patronized for her mathematical abilities was bad enough, but relegated to some sort of playing piece on a chessboard is too much.

It's obvious that Macer is struggling to restrain himself from laying into the man in front of her. Luci is not surprised when he makes his way to the base of the stairs to continue the conversation on the upper level. His words become increasingly terser the further away he goes from her. "Pol, he didn't give us any information when you sentenced him. I guarantee you that he won't reveal any more now."

She suspects that he doesn't wish to reveal his "true self" to her in dealing with this insubordination. This is confirmed in that the veil concealing Macer's agitation falls away with each step takes up the stairs. "Put him through cybo conversion and have him be your private protector if you like, but no more interrogations; it's counterproductive, and we don't have time for games like that."

When he's finally out of sight, Luci eyes the large bowl of bubbling liquid. She already regrets agreeing to allow for the brain enhancements in the morning. She wonders if Macer lied about this too. How much control will they have over her mind after the Viatorio is installed? Would they send her back to her time as a prisoner to do their bidding? Would the procedure result in her forfeiting the ability to think for herself? Has everything that she's encountered over the last twenty-four hours been part of an elaborate ruse to put something in her brain by this man? Are there different levels of cybos?

Maybe Macer's plan is to convert her into some type of math-zombie of sorts, a tool that he can control. The notion would've seemed too implausible a day ago, but now, anything is possible. Her thoughts circle back around to the confusion of the ninety-nine to sixty-six revision. Why hadn't that worked?

Macer rattles on the level above. He's saying something about no benefits to the "shock value" of whomever this Pol person is debating him about.

Luci takes a step forward, extending her open palm over the bubbling Jardon fluid. So many lies and half-truths have been told to her since meeting the chancellor, but the answers—*real answers*—are right before her in the form of the gurgling liquid, beckoning her. Macer's warning is likely a lie, just another attempt in a long line of ways to restrict her access to information.

She needs answers.

There's no doubt in her mind that he'll put blocks on the Viatorio device, blocking anything outside the scope of the DPM project. This may be her only chance to access the truth.

Macer's voice coming through the ceiling sounds muffled, but she can tell the argument with the city's security minister is far from over.

Ever so slowly, she lowers her hand closer to the mysterious substance. She finds it curious that her heart is pounding as she allows the top of the liquid to lap at her outstretched hand. It's surprising that the Jardon is tepid; Luci expected it to be cooler. She brings her dampened palm to her face for inspection. The notion that the small dew-like drops contain information in them is a concept as outlandish as the idea of time travel itself; nevertheless, she *is* here, and this is a time different from her own.

She sniffs at the moisture on her hand, but it's odorless. When Luci presses a few droplets to her bottom lip, she experiences a mild tingling sensation like a low-voltage buzzing. She gasps and spins to look back at the stairs.

An anxious giggle erupts from her as she imagines herself as Lewis Carroll's Alice clutching a tiny bottle labeled *"Drink Me"* on it. The noise of Macer on the floor above is dying down.

It's now or never—if she ever expects to learn the truth.

"I need answers," she says aloud as if justifying what's she's about to do to the basin itself, "and the truth around here is in short supply."

After convincing herself of the necessity of taking a sip, she contemplates if she should draw from the center or outer rim of the basin. She looks into the bubbling liquid, realizing there's no possible way to determine what'd be best. "I won't use the old man's sip tube in case there's a way he can tell."

With her left hand, she grabs the side of the basin to brace herself as she leans in. She cups her right hands and dips in. She hadn't noticed before, but the liquid shimmers in her palm like watered-down mercury, if there is such a thing. Unexpectedly, the fluid feels alive. Luci gives herself a pep talk, "Don't back out now, Luci G. Just take a swig. Swish it around a bit. If it burns or something, just spit it out. No one will know." She takes a deep breath. As she exhales, she says, "Okay, I can do this, and then I'll know what's really going on around here."

She brings her trembling palm to her lips and cocks her head back as if taking bad-tasting medicine, but there's no taste—nothing at all. The inside of her mouth tingles. The Jardon *is* alive. Before she can react, the substance swims down her throat, and thousands of microscopic nano-bots hurry to do their work. She knows this, because in this instant, she knows everything.

The experience is both as exhilarating and as terrifying as trying to swallow the mass of the sun. It feels as if every cell in her body is a light switch, and all of them, trillions of cells, have been turned on at this precise instant. She's pulled through countless numbers of doorways, information passageways that mercilessly keep expanding until she feels as if her mind will rip apart.

Already weary and overloaded with knowledge, she's bombarded with facts and information like a never-ending hailstorm with no cover in sight. Even her glorious numbers betray her repeatedly, skewering the fabric of her mind like mile-long needles. It's like every recorded fact in human history has been designated its own video screen in her mind's core, and as she falls toward them, the dissonance rages, but she can't look away, she can't close her eyes, she can't hide.

She's unable to focus on a single aspect; there's too much to process and nowhere to store it even if she had the time. Her head is on fire and throbbing, but even this fact has to compete with the strain of all other input.

There's no release.

No shadow, only the glaring light of information.

There's nowhere to escape to.

It just keeps coming, more and more, layer after suffocating layer of information.

Time distorts like taffy on a hot summer afternoon, and though it feels like hours or maybe even days or weeks, the entire exchange only lasts 2.8 seconds. Then Luci Gaudiano's mind snaps.

PORT II

(Part II)

ONE

March 23, 2191
Relicus City
[6.217012/127.792969/4.603.388.823/1957:19:07]

RELIKUS SITI

MΛ₵ 23, 2191

"So thirsty," Luci croaks as her surroundings blur in and out of focus. She shields her eyes to block the light. While this helps with the stinging pain in her eyes, her head still feels as if her brain has been replaced with molten lava. Something happened—something bad—but she can't recall what exactly.

She hates to cry, but she can't stop it. Her head feels on fire from the inside. The way the hot tears stream sideways down her face alerts her that she's on her side. Disoriented, Luci spreads her fingers apart in order to peek through them. Obviously, this isn't Macer's office. She snaps them closed again. The memory of drinking from the pull basin surfaces; clearly, she should've listened to Macer and not sipped. Of all the times for him to be telling the truth.

She calls out to him, "Water, please." It's agonizing to speak, much less shout, but she ignores the pounding pressure in her head to repeat, "Enos, I'm so thirsty." Maybe he can give her the thing that Shar used that took her pain away from before.

Something brushes against her mouth. She pulls back, startled, and the jerking motion ushers another wave of pain. Luci cracks her eyes as a machine similar to the concierge bot extends a thin, flexible tube near her mouth. There's a soft chime tone followed by a soothing female voice. "Drink." It doesn't sound like Shar; it has a pre-recorded quality to it.

This time, when the plastic spout touches her lips, she doesn't resist. A small stream of liquid begins to flow. Luci gulps greedily, sucking on the tube, but the fluid dispenses in the same controlled trickle. Her head still pounds like the mother of all hangovers, but she's becoming more acclimated to the environment. She's lying on a couch, and to the left of the robot is a white trouser leg. Luci can smell herself, and that's never a good thing. She smells like she's run a marathon, but her clothes are completely dry. Even in this stupor, she's able to reason that she's been out long enough to drench her top in sweat and allow time enough for it to dry. Pulling the tube from her mouth, she asks, "Enos, what happened to me?"

"I'm sorry, Dr. Gaudiano, but the chancellor had to leave several hours ago."

The unfamiliar male voice blasts a shockwave of fear through her. Luci jerks up to a sitting position on the couch. The movement triggers a fresh surge of agony that makes what she's experienced to this point feel like a shadow to this new wave of pain. "Arrgh," she moans, making it worse. "Who are you?"

She cradles her aching forehead in both hands as if to mash the pain into submission.

"I'm Ish," a slender, dark-skinned face answers as he bends down into her field of vision.

Luci wipes her eyes and studies this trim stranger. In her time period, he'd make for an excellent basketball pick; thin but muscular, not brawny in a bodybuilder way, and not a brute tank of muscles like Royse.

"What's an Ish?" she asks, shoving herself back on the sofa away from the man. "Are you a nurse or guard or something?"

A bright, toothy smile contrasts the dark complexion of his skin. "Neither. I'm a technician of sorts." He had a face for smiling, if there could be such a thing. "Ish is my name. Ish Moyta."

"Ish, like *Wish* without the 'W' . . . As in I *wish* my head would stop aching?"

"It's short for Ishtar, a Mesopotamian deity of some sort, something to do with irrigation and agricultural fertility."

"You're named after a fertility god? That's rich, given what's been done to me by dragging me here."

"Ishtar was a goddess of fertility, not a male god."

She impatiently waves off the correction. "Where's Macer?"

The smile fades slightly. "I told you, Chancellor Macer had to leave. We're the only ones here. Are you alright?"

She winces and closes her eyes. "It feels like a jackhammer is tapdancing on my head."

"I'm sorry. I don't know those terms or what that means."

"Of course you don't," she says with a sharp exhale. "Wait, where are we . . . where's here?"

"The chancellor's visitor lodging," Ish says, taking a knee before her. "You've been recuperating for some time now."

Panic grips her. "Recuperating? What kind of a technician are you?" Her fingers nervously scan her head for anything out of place—patches of missing hair or shaved spots. She's grateful to not find any. "Did you do the procedure while I was asleep? Did you implant me with a Viatorio? Is that why I feel this way?"

A confused look crosses his face. "I'm sorry. Again, I don't know what you mean."

Luci tugs at her earlobes for a Viatorio. This sends a sharp pain ricocheting around her brain, but she's relieved there's nothing there.

Ish studies her. "They said the chance of any long-term damage is low."

"But *did* you do the process on me, Technician Moyta? Did you implant nano-bots or whatever into my brain to install a Viatorio later?"

He looks relieved to finally understand. "Oh, no. I'm not that type of technician. I calibrate longchairs and have a background in skip point interval determination and chronal convergence point expansion."

The answer throws Luci off. She tries to focus, but it feels like an electrical storm in her mind. "Just answer me. Did they do anything to my head?"

"I don't think so," he says, rubbing his smooth, angular chin. "I mean, I wasn't here when the accident happened, but I don't think there would've been time enough to—"

"Accident? What accident?" she asks, feeling queasy. "Who else is here? Is there a physician?"

Ish's eyes widen, revealing an alluring hazel instead of brown. "No. I told you, it's just us." He speaks slowly and deliberately. "Dr. Gaudiano, they said that you had an accident, that you accidentally ingested Jardon from the pull basin without any of the Viatorio partition barriers."

Though her throbbing is non-stop, she notes something in the younger man's eyes, something unexpected—a tender kindness.

"You could've completely shorted out your mind and been cudded." In a voice barely above a whisper, he adds, "You could've died." He returns to his feet and gestures to the bot. "As for your doctor, it's this unit here."

Luci closes her eyes. "Shit."

"Do you need me to help you to the lavatory upstairs?" The hushed tone he asks in is comical since it's just the two of them here, if he's being honest with her.

"What? No, that's not what I . . . never mind." She massages her temples. "So what are you here for, Ish, if there's no longchair for you to calibrate?"

"Well, I'm a little more than that, actually. I'm to be your assistant at the behest of the chancellor."

"Assistant, huh?" She coughs and regrets it instantly as the pressure of it forces her to wince. "I feel like I'm having the mother of all hangovers here. Can you get me a coffee?"

The black man's face is blank. "Coffee? That's a pre-world beverage, right?"

"Pre-world?" She massages her closed eyes with her fingertips. It's slightly soothing, and she'll take any measure of comfort that she can get. "Yes, it's a drink made from coffee beans."

"So you want to drink bean juice?"

She opens her eyes. "You people have no coffee? How can you be civilized without coffee?" She grumbles to herself. "I'm in Hell." Luci yanks the med-bot's tube, and after a few more drinks of water, she asks, "So Ish, how exactly are you to assist me?"

"The chancellor sent for me to help you with DPM." He looks at the floor. "To teach it to you, since you can't . . . sip it now."

"So, you're an expert with drift pattern?" she asks.

He answers with humility, "You're the expert, Dr. Gaudiano. I'm just here to help you relearn it . . . I mean teach you the . . ." He shifts his gaze to her. "It's my great honor to serve you. Mathematics is my prime recreation, and when I learned that you had done a leap skip from your interval to help us—"

"Are you for real? *Prime recreation?* Do you mean your hobby is math?"

A quizzical expression forms on his face. "I don't know this term, *hobby,* but I routinely sip DPM writings by you, Chhabra, Müller, and the Conte 5 theorems of Rabinovich."

"Sip? Like the Jardon thing?" Luci asks. Receiving and processing new information slightly distracts from the pain she's experiencing. "I thought anything one drinks from a pull basin became a part of you instantly, that the knowledge meshed cerebrally with the sipper."

He nods. "This is true, but in the same way a memory can fade or distort over a long period of time, so is the case of I.I.R. sip learning."

"Interesting." She adjusts her sitting position on the couch, catching a glance at the pull basin behind Ish. She chastises herself for taking such a stupid and unnecessary risk in drinking the Jardon relay.

A terrifying idea strikes her.

Wondering if she may have burned out synapses in her brain, Luci performs a self-assessment by rattling off ratios. She begins a form of her self-soothe process. "The square root of pi is 1.7724538090. Log e to the base ten is 0.4342944. The square root of ten is 3.16227766." Next, she moves on to the multiplication of a series of random numbers. She stops when she reaches nine digits. Next, she mumbles out four more, then divides the first number by this, and then subtracts various prime numbers from the total until she reaches her "special" number. "Thank God," she says with a sigh of relief.

Ish, who's been silent this entire time, finally comments with a wide smile, "That was . . . *amazing.*"

She massages the crick in her neck and is increasingly self-conscious about her body odor in front of this man who could pass for a male model back home. "I didn't do it to impress you. I did it to check that everything still works up here." She points to her forehead. "Also, doing math decreases a cognitive resource called working memory. That's the short-term memory system that helps you organize information to complete a task."

He doesn't say anything, which makes Luci feel the urge to explain more to dispel the silence. "It utilizes the temporary memory of the brain, which works to calm me down sometimes." Her hand moves from her neck to her hair. "Something I discovered when I was a kid."

"I see," Ish says. "I'll have to try that."

For the first time since waking up, she realizes her clothing is different. Someone has dressed her in a khaki-colored pair of shorts that end at the knee and a matching oversized tank top blouse. She squints and asks disapprovingly, "Hey, you didn't dress me while I was asleep, did you?"

It takes him a few seconds to understand the implications of her question. He answers emphatically, "Oh, no, Doctor. That's what you were wearing when I arrived."

If not for the dark skin, she was sure his face would be a blush of deep red, based on the tremor in his voice. She takes another sip from the tube. "Uh, okay," she says, thinking it could be worse if Macer or Royse dressed her, or that Security Minister Cavazos guy.

"Hey, Ish, there's not like any residual side effects to the Jardon, right?"

"None, really." His eyebrows raise. "Other than if you drink too much, Jardon turns your urine blue."

"What? Jardon turns . . ."

The mischievous grin on his face tells her that she's been had. She begins to laugh, but the motion triggers more of the aching aftereffects. "Don't make me laugh, my head's still too sore," she says, clutching the sides of her skull.

"Sorry, Doctor. I thought a little levity would—"

"No, it's okay," she says. "You're funny. It's just that I'm concerned about that stuff giving me some sort of weird relapse. I've heard of LSD users that . . . never mind."

"I don't know how it affects someone without a Viatorio. Like I said, my expertise is more along the lines of the leap-skip technologies, not neurological medical care." He pauses and then offers reassuringly, "I'm sure that you're going to be alright, though."

"Based on what?"

He pauses. "Well, there'd be no reason to send for me to work with you if you were not . . ."

"If I wasn't what?"

His hazel eyes drift to the couch. "If you were not mentally up for it." Changing the subject, he looks back at her and asks, "A moment ago . . . the calculations, those were random number sequences, right?"

She nods slightly, noticing the pain has subsided a small amount.

He rubs his chin in contemplation. "Why'd you stop? The number, 2012. Why'd you stop on that one? Is 2012 special to you?"

She admonishes herself for being reckless and revealing something so personal to a stranger, even if it was unintentional. "Just a random number that I chose to stop at," she says, avoiding his eyes. "It doesn't mean anything . . . it could've been anything." She forces herself to look at him to see if he accepts the lie. "Hey, listen, do you mind sitting down? My head is pounding, and it hurts to look up at you standing there."

Ish nods and takes a seat on the curved sofa, leaving a respectful distance between the two of them. "How's this?"

"Perfect. Thank you." Luci glances at the hovering medical version of the concierge bot and then back to the man. "Ish, I'd like to ask you something. What do you know of Cyphor Gicul?"

The abrupt change in topic seems to surprise him. He tilts his head and says, "Same as everyone, I guess, which is to say not much." He pauses again. "There are even some who suspect that he's not even real, just some propaganda that the Directorate made up and leaked through the city." He's quick to add, "That's not what I believe, of course, but the fact that he's never been seen makes him a sort of myth to some."

"But you believe he's real?" Luci asks, attempting to get a sense for this man. "Based on what?"

There's another pause, this one longer than the previous ones. Ish pinches his chin between thumb and index finger a few times before he begins. "I'll admit that I wondered myself whether Gicul was real or not. That was until this morning when I got the Level One V.I. from the chancellor's office that I'd be working with you. If you, the actual Luci Gaudiano, are here from the past, then the threat must be real. The chancellor would never take the risk to bring you here risking chronal offset unless something was really happening."

She thinks on this. "Do you know if it was public knowledge that I had skipped here from my time before I . . ." She searches for the right phrase. "Before I had my *accident* with the Jardon?"

"No, Doctor. Like I said, I was alerted to the assignment just this morning. I don't think you being here is public knowledge. I'm fairly certain of that. I can check the pull basin if you'd like to see if there are any updates."

"No, that's alright for now." Luci notes that Macer had been truthful about that at least, and if he's keeping her hidden, her being here isn't a publicity stunt staged to garner political support against his enemies.

Ish continues, "I didn't know anything about your visit until several hours ago. They sent for me from the Grange, and an hour and a half later, they had me leap skip back here to Relicus."

"The Grange? Are you like a farmer there?" Luci asks, remembering her visit with Bru.

"No, my expertise lies in other areas outside of the food harvest and distribution." He frowns. "Dr. Gaudiano, are you having any issues with short-term memory loss? Do you remember how I told you about my background in longchair calibration and chronal point expansion?"

"What?" Luci scoffs, a little offended. "Yeah, I remember. I just don't know all these titles and things." To combat the unconvinced expression on his face, she adds, "I remember that this place doesn't have any coffee—or bean juice, as you call it. I remember that Ish is short for the fertility goddess, Ishtar. I remember that you like to tell piss jokes. Does that prove to you that I'm 100% here in the conversation?"

A relieved smile forms. "I'm glad that you're alright. We've got a lot to cover, and if your memory were faulty, I don't know how we'd—"

"I told you I'm fine," she answers curtly. "I made a mistake is all by drinking the Jardon. I wanted to find out what was really happening with Cyphor and his man, Malom Roderick. I tried to take a shortcut by sipping from the basin, and I regret it." She closes her eyes to massage them again.

"I see," Ish says. "Although I don't have much in the way of information about Gicul, Malom Roderick is an entirely different case. Everyone knows that he was sentenced to Carcerium for crimes against Relicus City several years ago."

She opens her eyes. "Carcerium—Bru and Royse told me that's like prison, right?"

Ish shakes his head. "Oh, it's much worse than that. I'd rather be reconditioned into a cybo than deployed into a Carcerium chamber. Anyway, like I said, you're here, which means Chancellor Macer believes that you can put an end to whatever Gicul is up to, whoever he is."

Luci, still suspicious of her assistant-to-be's alliances, puts it all out there. "I want to ask you about Enos Macer. Do you ever feel that he's hiding something? When you talk to him, doesn't it seem that there's something just beneath the surface? Something that's a little off there? Have you ever seen him have a seizure-like thing?"

"Oh, Dr. Gaudiano, I would not mislead you into thinking that I've ever spoken to His Excellency."

This forces her to reconsider that maybe she was hasty in pegging this grinning boy scout as an inside man for Macer. "Really? You've never met him?"

"Well, I did meet him at a ceremony once." He looks at his hands as he fidgets with interlacing his fingers. "I made some adjustments to the chrono portal vortex the crates are sent through at the Grange and on this side at the Spike."

She notes the uncommon humility in his achievement and says, "Yeah, I've seen that. You're talking about the intake vortex in the chronal canal that those huge plasti-crates flow through, right?"

He beams with pride. "You've seen it? The calculations that I did there allowed us to expand the apertures and send larger containers through."

"Larger containers equal more food to the city," she points out before he has the chance.

"Exactly, Dr. Gaudiano. Exactly. I received an award from the chancellor for that."

His exuberance is contagious, and Luci finds herself smiling, though not as wide as his toothy grin. Her head still aches, but she feels calm in the presence of this stranger. Her mental acknowledgement of this fact puts her mind at odds with what the rest of her feels. Why should she believe anything he says if he's been placed here—or better said, *installed*—by Macer? She considers if more Jardon may be working through her system, clouding her judgement about him. Where was Shar? Why wasn't she dispatched here like before?

"How often have you been to the Grange?" she asks, attempting to stay on point and probe for information.

"Many times," Ish answers. "In fact, I'm working on a special project there for the chancellor, or at least I was until my assignment was changed this morning."

"Ah, Macer and his special projects for everyone," she says sardonically, crossing her legs. "Got you working on making a giant avocado or something?"

"What? No," Ish answers, confused at first. "I'm sure that I can tell you, since it's sort of related. The chancellor received approval from the Directorate to reinforce the Grange vortex."

"How is that related to what I'm—" Luci stops short as the answer comes into focus. "I get it. If I can't stop the skip points from being destroyed, there's only one point or interval portal that really matters. If everything else is lost, the food supply remains unbroken from the Grange because the vortex is different from longchair skips."

Ish bobs his head slowly, the smile gone from his face.

Luci bites her lip. "It doesn't demonstrate a lot of confidence in what I've got going on here with DPM." She plays the scenario out in her mind. "Are people able to go through the vortex, or just the food crates?"

"I don't know," Ish says. "If not and only the vortex remains open, it could mean that workers would be trapped there forever."

Ish points at the long scar on the calf of Luci's left leg. "What happened there?"

Luci self-consciously rearranges the way she's sitting. By crossing her legs the other way, she's able to conceal the jagged injury from the car accident from long ago. "It's nothing," she says, "just something that happened when I was a kid. It's not important."

He taps his index finger to his chin. "Something happened to you as a child?" It sounds like a question, but it's not. He's working through something in front of her. "I sipped a pre-*Hi no Kawa* history file while you slept. You were born at the turn of the twenty-first century, in the old calendar year of 2000." Again, it's not a question.

"Nineteen ninety-nine," she corrects. This is so annoying. Luci bites the inside of her cheek to displace the odd twinge creeping up the nape of her neck. If he "read" a sip about her, then he knows what happened—probably even knows the date of *it*.

Ish stops tapping his chin, and with the same finger aimed at her, he proclaims, "It was 2012. That's the number from earlier, the one you said was random. But it's not random, is it? Something happened to you when you were in 2012."

His elation is off-putting to her. How dare this stranger pry into something so personal.

"I'm right, aren't I?"

She feels raw and naked before this grinning man. Who did this guy think he was? She'd tell Macer she couldn't work with this guy the first chance she got, and he'd put him back on the vortex project and send somebody else—someone who's not as nosey. Maybe she can ask for Shar.

Luci downplays Ish's conclusion by offering an answer in the most uninterested voice that she can fake. "Just a number," she says. "You know—2012, 16096, 8048, 4485—they're all just random numbers, and they don't mean a thing."

All of his perfect teeth display in his widened grin. She doesn't mask how perturbed she is. "What now, Ish? What is it, *Mr. Moyta*?"

"Multiples, Doctor," he says as if it were a game. "Those numbers are multiples of 2012." He corrects himself, "Well, except for the 4485. That's the square root of 2012. To be exact, it's—"

"Yes, 44.855322984," she blurts out rather than give him the satisfaction of telling her. "It's the square root of 2012."

She's never known anyone who could match her talent for numbers, and now that she's met someone who can, she doesn't like it. She stands up. Her equilibrium is off a little from whatever Jardon is still swimming around in her system. "Look, I don't have time to play number games with you right now. My head is killing me, and I smell like a wet dog with mange, though you probably don't even know what a dog is around here."

"I know what a dog was," Ish interjects, his expression serious now.

"Anyway, I'm going upstairs to shower and lay down in that bed if it's still there. You can do what you want, but no more with the inquisition, all right? I'm not in the mood. Okay?"

Ish takes on a subservient posture by bowing his head slightly. "Dr. Gaudiano, I'm sorry. I didn't mean anything by it. You can trust me. Do you need any help making your way up the stairs?"

She gives him an incredulous look, wondering if this goody-goody boy scout act is for real. "How can you help anyone up a spiral staircase?"

He shrugs.

She turns her back to him and lies, "And *no*, I'm not upset."

TWO

LUCI IS BEGINNING TO FEEL herself again. The migraine is nearly gone now. She suspects that this is mainly due to the extended shower she took. It's the first time she's spent on herself since before the night of her lecture in Baltimore.

After adjusting the shower temperature to as hot as the regulator would allow, she stood in place for what felt like a blissful eternity. When she finally rinsed the soap from her body, she caught sight of the scar that zigzagged down the better part of her leg. Luci admitted to herself that she'd over-reacted to Ish's questions about what had happened to her. She should act more professional since if what he told her is true, they'll be spending time as colleagues on the DPM project. He does have a talent for numbers.

She finishes reminding herself of the possibility that there could've been some leftover Jardon in her system making her overly sensitive to him seeing her scar. Either way, she tells herself to go easier on the man until she knows more about where his allegiances lie.

With wet hair dripping down her back and shoulders, Luci emerges from the shower refreshed and with the headache more manageable. She glimpses her image in the video mirror reaching for the perfectly folded stack of towels on the corner of the counter. Her skin is pinkish-red enough to make any Maine lobster proud—pre-*Hi no Kawa* Maine, that is.

She rummages through the various clothes hanging on the rack in the bathroom's cubby. Luci selects a pair of dark pants this time—no shorts—and slides them on with a blouse to match.

The sound of voices coming from the den area on the level below get her attention. She quietly steps through the door to get a better listen, and out of habit, she pulls wet strands of her hair over her ear. What's being said still isn't clear. Cinching the drawstring on the loose-fitting trousers, she creeps to the edge of the staircase for a better listen below.

Though the conversation is still muffled, she recognizes Macer's voice and would know Royse's deep baritone anywhere.

Luci slowly descends the spiral staircase to find Ish transfixed on something beyond her line of sight. Opposite the staircase landing, Macer and Royse cover up the curved windows of the dome. She realizes that they must have arrived shortly after she began her shower because they've managed to cover nearly half of the curved room's area stretching from the floor to about six feet up.

Ish glances over his shoulder, quietly informing her, "It's paper, real paper. All of it."

Luci is disinterested in the material and more concerned about the reason for it. "Did something happen while I was upstairs? Are they afraid someone will see us in here or something and are blocking the view?"

Royse, the ever-vigilant watchdog, stops hanging a sheet and turns to face Luci and Ish.

Her reflection distorts like a funhouse mirror in one of the curved glass panels that hasn't been covered yet. Luci realizes Royse must have seen it too; he stops his work. No one could ever accuse the guard of being slack at his job, even with a cybo outside the front door.

The big man nudges Macer to turn around. "How does your head feel this morning?"

"Like shit," she answers, "but most of the throbbing has stopped."

Macer says something quietly to Royse while handing him some type of adhesive wand tool.

Royse nods and returns to sticking sheets of oversized paper to the outer glass wall. Macer pulls down the sleeves of his royal blue Nehru jacket as he makes his way to her and Ish. "Well, you'll get your wish after all," he says in an acrid tone. "There's no way now to fit you with a Viatorio."

The brief sense of relief at this revelation is quickly shattered and hijacked by guilt. Luci remains silent and feels like sinking through the floor.

"Your little stunt last night could have led to the starvation of millions and thereby resulted in ending the human race. Is that your goal? Did your DPM not do enough damage to the world the first go around with *Hi no Kawa*?"

She swallows and still doesn't answer. For once, she doesn't feel up to debating him. It took nearly everything she had to circle around and around the staircase. Ish's posture stiffens, and his head lowers as Macer navigates his way around the pull basin pit centered in the circular couch area.

Macer continues to berate her, taking agonizingly slow steps toward them as if to draw out the reprimand. "It's a miracle that you didn't fry every brain cell in that stubborn head of yours. As it is, the irreversible damage that you've done to yourself prevents you from ever sipping from a well basin, thus slowing us down. Hopefully, this costly delay won't afford Gicul enough time to carry out his plans."

Unlike Ish, who's staring at the ground now, Luci locks on to Macer's glare, refusing to flinch. At least she has that.

"Why did you do it, Luci?" he asks in a voice that genuinely sounds hurt. "I thought you had a good visit with Bru at the Grange. I thought you enjoyed my Michelangelo. You seemed so sincere. Was it all an act? When are you finally going to believe that I . . ." He shakes his head in disgust. "That I saved your life from those who want you dead? There is word of a real plot against your life and this time's very existence."

Macer stops when he reaches them. He turns to look back at Royse, who has quit hanging the paper sheets to witness her castigation. Upon seeing Macer looking his way, Royse spins around and returns to work.

Macer gestures to Ish. "You there, go help him finish."

Ish bolts from the area his feet have been frozen to. "Yes, sir. Of course, Your Excellency."

Luci searches herself. "*Why feel embarrassed about being scolded by Macer in front of Ish? Who cares what this goody-goody thinks in the least?*"

With Ish safely across the room, Macer sighs. "What do I have to do here to get you to embrace this project, to make you want to invest 100% of yourself? Are you going to wait until you actually witness the citizens of the city starving, rioting in the streets with cybos, fighting for their next meal?"

Luci quietly answers, "I'm sorry. You're right."

"What did you say?"

"I made a mistake, and . . . I'm sorry," she says louder and swallows hard.

Some of the tension drains from Macer's face, but he still looks old this morning. Maybe it's a trick of the light, but he looks older, as if the lines on his face tripled overnight. He has the same overgrown eyebrows, bald head, dark black marble eyes, but enough wrinkles to lend a map of rivers. There's a weariness to him that she hadn't noticed before.

After a long, awkward pause, he answers with a slow nod, "You know, I believe you. I think that you truly regret what you've done, what you put at risk by disobeying my instruction. I'm glad to hear you say it. I had hoped that you would come to your senses."

His hand disappears into the inner pocket of his impeccable jacket. "I've brought a token of good faith with me today." The fingers return with a bright orange envelope. "You may recall how Shar mentioned that we are lucky. Normally, intervals don't fall that closely to each other. When they do, we call them juncture twins."

Luci takes the envelope from him, remembering Ish's astonishment at seeing paper. "What is this?"

A genuine smile forms on Macer's face, displaying a surplus of even more creases in his face. "Open it."

She does and wills her eyes to leave his gaze to peek inside. She gasps at the realization of what she's holding, which makes his grin grow larger when she shoots a look back at him. "A ticket from East Timor," she says in a breathy voice. "It's the place that Shar said . . . the fish market where the skip point is. It's an airline ticket back to the states from there." Part of her feels stupid for saying this aloud, since he obviously knows what he's given her, but she continues anyway. "And my passport . . . or at least a fake one that you had made for me."

"It'll pass inspection in your interval for an authentic document," Macer says, nodding approvingly. "Like I said, we are lucky that the twin leap skip juncture in East Timor occurs close enough to when you left. Everyone in your time will simply believe that you were at Ventnor City in New Jersey the entire time, the location that you told Royse on the way to the warehouse."

She's impressed that he's remembered the details of where she was headed before the abduction. "I guess you've thought of everything," she says, wondering if it's a farce somehow.

He softly cups his hands around hers. "This is only waiting for you to finish the project. It'll be as if nothing happened."

She resists the urge to remind him that the skips in time have rendered her sterile. She holds a fragment of hope in her hands and just answers, "Yes, thank you."

A large sheet of paper falls to the ground across the room. Macer releases her hands to turn to face Royse and Ish. "Don't be stingy with the adhesive. We need those to stay up there for a while."

"Yes, sir," Royse replies as he snatches the wand tool from Ish's grip and retraces the glue lines.

Luci and Macer make their way around the basin area in the middle of the room. "What's with all of this, anyway?" she asks. "Is it to block Gicul and his crew from spying in on me?"

"No, you don't have to worry about anything like that," Macer says.

Royse pauses using the glue wand to face her. "There's no way they can get a drobine within a quarter mile of this dome." The pride in his voice is unmistakable. "We've got patrols in the sky and on the water, as well as that cybo you saw yesterday is still stationed outside of the entrance into here."

"So what is this, then?"

"Improvisation," Macer replies in what Luci has come to regard as his carnival barker personality. "Luci, no offense—I know that you can solve highly complex number problems in your head—but it's going to take more than that. I daresay that what's needed to calculate DPM and stop Gicul from destroying every leap-skip point out there is even beyond your capabilities to do in your head. So, since you forfeited any chance of using a Viatorio to sip DPM tutorials and there's not a way to install a UNIFON language converter into your mind, you and technician . . ." Macer snaps his fingers impatiently for someone to fill in the blank.

Royse gestures with the glue wand for Ish to answer the chancellor.

"Oh, Moyta, sir. Chronal Technician Ish Moyta is my name."

The older man nods approvingly at his eager subservience. "Technician Moyta will be forced to work out the problems the pre-world way—on paper."

Ish breaks protocol, asking in a disbelieving voice, "Sir, you want us to mark on it . . . on the paper?" The word *paper* is delivered with a mystical reverence.

"Son, I know how rare paper is, but due to the doctor's recent act of noncompliance, I'm left with very few options." Macer turns to address Luci. "You may recognize the materials from my drawing room basement, what I used to design and sketch out the statue. I can have more for you in a few days or so."

"Seriously," Luci begins, "you guys don't have white boards here in the future that you can mark on and erase?"

Macer points to his Viatorio and shrugs. "All virtual because of resource consumption." He raises his voice, intending to instruct both Luci and her new companion. "I'm counting on both of you—strike that, the entire *world* is counting on both of you to utilize everything at your disposal to put an end to what Gicul is doing." He moves to the covered wall to press a drooping corner back into place. "The way I see it is that this can be done one of two ways. The defensive approach is to figure out how he and his followers are destroying the intervals and somehow block and prevent him from doing so, or you can take an offensive stance and figure out when and where he's hiding so that we can capture him and lock him in Carcerium. I'd consider either solution a fulfilment of your duty here, Dr. Gaudiano, and allow you to return to your interval to begin constructing your DPM theorem there as you promised."

She tucks the forged passport and ticket into her pants pocket.

Macer says, "Now, I need to briefly discuss something of with Technician Moyta here, so if you'll excuse us for a moment."

Royse steps back from the wall to admire his handiwork with Macer and Ish. When he moves to apply more glue to one of the sheets first stuck to the wall, Luci moves to join him.

She looks back at Macer, who's engaged in telling something to Ish. The younger of the two nods *yes* like a bobble-head doll.

"Royse, I need to ask you something about the chancellor."

"What is it?" he asks with a grimace, apparently finding it distasteful to talk behind the boss's back.

"Last night, when he and I were alone, something happened. He had this weird attack . . . not a fainting spell and not a seizure exactly, but—"

The big man's eyes widen, and he puts a finger to his lips. "Who did you tell about this?"

She's relieved that he knows and believes. "So, you've seen it?"

"Who did you tell?" he demands.

Luci scoffs, which temporarily attracts the attention of Macer across the room. When he returns to instructing Ish, she responds in an aggravated whisper, "Seriously? Take a look around, Royse. Who am I gonna tell?"

Royse acknowledges his dumb question. "Yeah, okay." In a low voice, he says, "The chancellor's been under a lot of pressure lately with this Gicul thing."

"It's something more than that, trust me," Luci says. "This was really weird. I've never seen anything like it. One of my foster mothers, Mrs. Joyner, had an epileptic seizure once, but it wasn't like this. This was more eerie."

Royse steals another quick glance over at his boss. "So, what do you want me to do about it?"

"I don't know, you're his protector guy and all. I thought you should be informed, and I wanted to ask if that was his first episode or if this was a common occurrence."

Royse pauses, and his pained, confused expression clearly shows that he's trying to figure out a way to avoid betraying any confidences. Finally, he gives in. "The seizures, or whatever they are, what you saw was not the first, but it's not a frequent thing." His eyes scan the floor. "I've heard stories of how he was sickly as a child, living for many years shut in away from everyone but his father, only communicating through Viatorio. It's public knowledge that his mother died of Fichtner's disease when he was very young, leaving Waleen Macer to care for him."

"You never answered me," Luci says, committed to pressing him for the answer. "Have you ever seen one of his episodes or not?"

He moves his eyes from the ground to hers. "I've only seen it a handful of times. He's always alright after." He points to the medical bot hovering near the pull basin area. "They always gave him a good health report like two or three hours after one of those incidents, so I don't know what it means, but what I do know is that he gets very irritated if you talk about it with him. So I just avoid it altogether."

"Well, again, I just wanted you to know."

For the first time ever, Royse looks at her without a hint of resentment or aggression. "I appreciate that, I really do." He extends one of his massive hands to her shoulder. "For what it's worth, I'm glad that you're okay after the Jardon thing." There's a pause as he pulls away. "Though it was a very stupid and dangerous thing to do."

Luci thinks to herself, "*Well, so much for our budding friendship.*"

She points at the curved glass being covered bit by bit with the paper. "Those glass walls, have you ever heard of them leaking or anything?"

"What do you mean?" Royse asks.

"It seems like a lot of force from the ocean out there pushing against the glass of the dome. Ever hear of one cracking and letting water in? We'd all be trapped in here . . . under it."

He eyes her in disbelief. "Dr. Gaudiano, this is probably the safest place in all of Relicus City. The glass will hold." He scoffs, "Why would you even ask that?"

Her answer is feeble. "I dunno." She crosses her arms. "I had a bad experience with water as a kid. It just kind of makes me nervous, all that water pressure, you know."

He spaces the words of his response out evenly. "The-glass-will-hold."

Macer gestures to him, indicating they should leave.

As the chancellor and bodyguard head for the door, Macer says, "It's time to get to work, you two."

Ish says, "Yes, sir, of course, Chancellor Macer," as Luci wanders up to join him.

Royse enters the code in the door panel, and it slides open. He exits into the hallway, presumably to check for attackers. Luci wonders why there would be the need to do that if what he said about the patrols and the cybo is true. She dismisses it as a force of habit, or maybe to show Macer his dedication to protecting him.

Macer stands in the threshold of the doorway and says in a full voice, "Good luck, you two. Everyone is counting on you. I know you'll do your best."

Luci softly jabs Ish in the ribs before he can offer his canned, "*Of course, sir, yes, sir,*" response. He looks at her quizzically.

The door slides shut.

"What were you and the chancellor discussing, Ish?"

He shrugs a little. "He was just relaying expectations."

"I see," Luci says. "Expectations of what? Do you have different duties than I do? Are you to report back to him about me like a spy? You know that term, right? *Spy?*"

He shakes his head and fidgets. "The chancellor didn't mention anything like that." He takes in a breath and releases it slowly. "He did the same thing for me that he did for you."

"What did he do for me?"

Ish looks embarrassed to admit it. "He gave me an incentive like how he gave you an incentive to finish the project."

"What did he promise to do for you?" She's surprised. "What's your incentive? Isn't saving the world enough?"

The only door into the domicile slides open with the pneumatic hiss, startling them both.

Macer announces from the opening, "Dr. Gaudiano, you've probably already figured this out on your own, but just like how I said there are two ways for us to defeat Gicul, he has more than one way that he can win without attacking the Grange at all."

"You nearly scared us out of our wits just now!" Luci protests.

Macer shrugs with indifference. "It should be obvious to you that if he were to execute you during your stay at Relicus City or murder you back at your own interval before the DPM groundwork is released, everything ends. But Luci, have you considered what happens if he destroys the skip point juncture that you go through to return to your interval, the one you have the air vessel ticket from? He may not know where you are here, but learning the interval coordinates is as easy as reading lines on a map."

He pauses, and Luci is uncertain if this is for dramatic effect or if he's awaiting a reply from her.

She chooses not to respond.

Finally, he adds, "So believe me when I say that we're in a race against time here. Now go get busy."

This time, the door zips shut before Ish has the chance to offer some kiss-up reply.

THREE

ISH WASTES NO TIME IN sharing the fundamentals of drift pattern mathematics to his solitary pupil. He only pauses every now and then to sip Jardon from the pull basin to ensure that he hasn't glossed over any part of the theorem mechanics that he may mistakenly assume she already knows.

Luci devours the information with an insatiable lust that surprises even her. She marvels at the intricacies of the formulas and imagines herself much like the member of a lost Aboriginal tribe hearing a Beethoven symphony performed by a world-class orchestra for the first time, a cascade of music notes pouring over the enraptured listeners' eardrums.

At no time does she feel that DPM is her creation and that she deserves credit for it; rather, its beautiful complexity and its simple arrangement of mathematical architecture humble her. Just as one discovering a magnificent vista from which to view a sunset cannot lay claim to the millions of pink, orange, amber, blue, and green hues displayed, she is unable to truthfully assert any ownership here. She counts herself as nothing more than the metaphorical mountain climber who turned the bend at the precise moment the sun dipped into the horizon, exploding in color.

At one point, Ish explains that some unknowns remain with DPM. He refers to these exceptions as *"porous"* number compounds or *"limber DPM numbers"* in which varying abstractions perform double duty and thereby alter fixed outcomes.

Though he admits that these occur extremely infrequently, Luci is intrigued and thrilled that there is more to discover in this field.

So enamored is she that after many hours of lecture, Ish informs her that they've skipped lunch and he needs to stop for a dinner break. Luci reluctantly complies, quickly eating the pouch meal from the food printer while staring at the notes she's transcribed on the paper affixed to the glass walls.

When Ish's voice begins to give from the strain of instructing almost non-stop for the entire day and late into the evening, Luci accedes to allow him to return to his home.

"You promise to be here early though, right?" she asks like a child forced to wait one more day before opening presents.

He chuckles, and in a thin voice that's ragged and on the verge of shutting down, he answers, "My Viatorio tells me that it's 2:38 AM now. I've called for an automated transport to collect me in five minutes to take me home. With the added security surrounding this place, it'll probably take ten to get here, so I'll be in bed by 3:00." He yawns and rubs his eyes. "Can we say that I'll be back over here by 10:00? That'll give me at least six hours of sleep."

"No way to make it 8:30 or 9:00?" Luci bargains, still buzzing on everything she's learned.

"You're insatiable," he says, comically collapsing to the couch. He yawns again, removing the rubber WIBs from his fingers to crack his knuckles.

"We can make it 9:30 then," she says. "You can nap here on the couch until you're ride comes to the door."

With closed eyes, he says, "It's an auto-transport. There's no driver. I wait on the platform outside. For security reasons, the chancellor won't allow anyone to come down here."

Still negotiating, she offers, "I'll wake you in a few minutes, but we begin at 9:30 tomorrow."

He waves his hand sluggishly and mumbles, "Fine, 9:30."

"Great," Luci says, grabbing his flailing hand to shake on the deal.

AFTER ISH LEAVES, LUCI JUMPS back into work for another hour or so. She reviews in detail all that she and Ish covered in their first session, and excited butterflies flutter in her stomach just as they did hours before.

Luci steps back to review the sheets that they've filled up throughout the course of the day's work. She slumps down to the sofa for a more comfortable viewing. Though her heart still thrills with excitement, her eyelids droop as she scans the curved wall of numbers and related formulas. "I'll just close them for a moment," she mumbles to herself as she dozes into a heavy, dreamless sleep.

<u>FOUR</u>

March 24, 2191
Relicus City
[6.217012/127.792969/4.603.388.824/968:49:31]

RELIKUS SITI

MΛℂ 24, 2191

A WARM SHAFT OF SUNLIGHT shining on her closed eyelids nudge her from slumber. She rubs sleep crust from her eyes and is in mid-yawn when she realizes she's not alone.

"Dr. Gaudiano . . . Luci?" Ish says softly.

She jolts to an upright sitting position. "What happened? Did your ride not come?" An unpleasant taste in her mouth causes her to swallow a few times. A mild burst of adrenaline from the surprise of seeing him stare at her pushes back any remaining grogginess.

"No," Ish says. "Actually, I overslept a few minutes this morning. I'm sorry that I'm late." He advances to the curved sofa across from hers to take a seat. "Wait, did you stay down here all night?"

"All night?" Luci repeats, recognizing for the first time the brilliant beams of sunlight pouring in through the dome glass as the indicator of a new day. "No, of course not," she lies to cover her embarrassment. "I came down here a few minutes ago, but you weren't here . . . and I took a nap is all." Luci massages the crick in her neck as she stands to her feet. "I'll be right back."

She makes her way upstairs to the bathroom. It only takes a few minutes to change, use the toilet, quickly straighten her matted hair, and brush her teeth. As she splashes water on her face, Luci sees a small, ragged post-it-note-size scrap of something leaning against the edge of the mirror. Remembering the rarity of paper here, she delicately picks up the curious item. Had it been here yesterday? Had she missed it with all the commotion of her pull basin "accident" and the excitement of learning the fundamentals of DPM? She unfolds it to reveal a jagged, handwritten scrawl of unfamiliar letter characters:

U OR BƗIИ LⱠD TU

Luci flips it around and back again. She's certain that it wasn't here yesterday—she would've seen it. She dismisses the notion this is a joke from Ish like the "Jardon-blue-urine" thing. He would have prompted her just now to learn if she'd seen it; plus, the characters are printed with more skill than his awful chicken-scratch penmanship. No, her gut tells her that this is something different.

A dull ache begins to throb in her head, calling back to the Jardon migraine from the day before. She steadies the shaking hand holding the note to examine it more closely. The paper stock they've been using from Macer is of a different grade. The strip in her palm was torn from a linen paper, a fine bond like the stock used for letterhead back home, not the coarse, butcher-block-like paper plastered on the curved walls of the den.

She recognizes the use of UNIFON characters from the inscription at the base of Macer's statue from two days ago. "You," she says running her finger under the first character. "Or biin," she continues, less certain, hoping that context will inform her. "What is 'L' plus or minus 'D'?" She closes her eyes, allowing her mind to recall the formula "$L = (1/2) d\, v2\, s\, CL$." It flashes across the blackboard of her mind, the lift formula that determines aircraft lift capabilities. She opens her eyes to study the paper again and says aloud, "You or bi in, the tangent of the glide angle related to the ratio of the drag, D, of an aircraft vessel to the lift? Is it about the drobine?"

She grits her teeth and crumples the note in her fist. "Argh! Come on, Luci G. Why can't I get this?" She resists taking the note downstairs to Ish. He'd be able to relay the message instantly to her, but could he be trusted not to prance off to Macer with the news of it? What is his stake in all of this? Other than the obvious *"saving the world"* and all, where are his allegiances? Something inside tells her that he may be more than Macer's lackey and won't betray her confidences, but what if he's not? She wonders if that was the point. What if the handsome man downstairs was deployed here because Macer had identified some blind spot in her? What if the future version of herself had somehow revealed a weakness about her to the chancellor? How can she test Ish to verify which side he truly serves?

She acknowledges a bitter possibility—does her hesitation to share this with him stem from her pride? Does she resent that he'd be able to read the UNIFON writing without effort while she stands here struggling to make sense of it? She doesn't like seeing this side of herself. For so long, her abilities set her apart from others. She allowed her talent in mathematics to define who she was. It allowed her to succeed in the world. It served as her "ace in the hole" more than once. In time, everyone accepted that she was the brightest bulb in the room, but now Ish encroached on the safety of that unconscious barrier.

Has this sliver of darkness always been present in her heart? Had this attitude constrained the life she could have enjoyed with Michael, her ex-fiancé, relegating it to nothing more than an undemonstrative stalemate? Her head is pounding now. Until this moment, Luci has never realized how alone she's felt all these years. She has been by herself emotionally since the accident on the bridge.

She watches the video reflection of herself. A disturbing question forms in her head as to whether the video mirror records its subjects or is monitored in some way. Did it record her discovery and the audio of her trying to phonetically work out the message just now?

She moves out of viewing range of the mirror and sits on the closed lid of the toilet. Uncurling the note, she's fairly positive that the last word is "*to*."

She quietly repeats the words to herself as the headache subsides. "You or bi in L plus D to." A familiar rush of endorphins releases into her brain. This is the natural drug that she lives for—she's solved something. Though she sounds it out again as if she's doing an exaggerated impersonation of a southern belle, the first part of the line makes sense to Luci's ears: "You *are being* L plus D to."

The discovery and euphoric release push the twinge of loneliness into the background. "You are being *blanked* to," she says softly. "It's not a plus sign," she mumbles. "*Lied* to." Another wave of satisfaction flows over her. "*You're being lied to*," she whispers. Turning the note over to the back, she says in normal volume, "Well, duh. Not much of a revelation there."

Though the guesthouse is technically Macer's, Luci still feels the anger welling up in her at the violation that someone snuck in while she was unaware. Despite this and a half dozen other unproductive feelings, she's able to remain clinical—she must remain objective and approach it logically. She flips the note back over.

U OR BⱵIⱱ LⱵD TU

Taking a calming breath, she reasons that whomever left it knows a way around the city's security and can get past the cybo standing guard outside the front door. That's a big deal and very scary. She wonders if it could be infiltrators from New Australia.

Working from the assumption that it wasn't left yesterday when she was at the Grange, whomever it is walked right past her on the sofa to place it in here. She swallows, ruling out that they're obviously not from *L'inversione* or they would've killed her in her sleep. Also to be considered is whether or not the intruder knew of her episode of drinking the Jardon. Did they contact her on paper because they knew the fried-out areas of her brain would prevent the usage of a Viatorio for her, or were they being cautious and avoiding any digital message that could be traced back to them?

She exhales and massages her temples to ease the pain. One thing is certain: if they have answers that she can't get from her keepers, she must keep Macer and Royse out of the loop until more is known. The unresolved question from a few minutes ago resurfaces. What about Ish? Does she trust her heart and bring him in or play it safe by siding with logic until she can prove him out? It's more of a conundrum than who left the message and why.

She emerges from the bathroom, creeping softly with the slip of paper cupped in her hand. She squats to peer down through the stair railing at Ish, who is sitting innocently. Luci studies him sipping from the pull basin before returning to the bedroom. It's no surprise to find that there's no would-be-culprit in hiding. She imagines the intruder or intruders to be long gone by now, waiting to make their next move.

She makes her way downstairs to where Ish is sitting. He smiles. "Ready to get started?"

"You ever feel like you're being lied to?" she asks, studying him for a poker tell.

His expression is a quizzical smile as he stands. "About what?"

Moving in closer to study his eyes, she says, "I'm just asking do you ever feel like . . ." Luci quotes the note verbatim, "*You-are-being-lied-to.*" Her fingers flex around the paper in her pocket, waiting for any twitch of betrayal on his face.

Either he's a master of deception or he's oblivious to this new development. He chuckles and says, "I feel like I'm missing something here."

Her body relaxes as she takes her seat to begin. "I'm sorry, there's just a lot going on in my head right now."

He waives it off. "I know we've covered a lot of material, but for what it's worth, I'd never lie to you, Luci."

EXCEPT FOR ANOTHER JARDON HEADACHE flare-up a few hours later, the rest of the morning and afternoon continue without incident. Ish delves back into his tutelage of his solitary pupil, and each new layer presented is like opening a new door of a vast mansion to her. Luci eagerly rushes into each concept as if it were a new chamber in a glorious castle of knowledge. It's no surprise that she leapfrogs over many of the ideas to the point of finishing Ish's sentences.

The thrill she experiences of these new re-evaluations is there, but the undercurrent of who left the note and its purpose taints some of her excitement. Her brain does double duty as she takes in the DPM information while scrambling to run over every scenario involving the cryptic message.

As a brilliant orange-gold sun sets on the shimmering ocean outside the guesthouse dome, there's an unexpected noise from the front door. Both Ish and Luci tense up and spin around to face whoever is entering their math sanctum.

Luci recognizes the man strutting through the doorway like a fat king—Pol Cavazos. He struts around the place as if deciding if whether or not the area is worthy of his presence. The last time she saw the security minister, his boss, the chancellor, was chewing him out in the hallway beyond the door. Now with Macer gone, there's nothing to hold Cavazos in check from lasciviously looking Luci over.

Luci is used to quiet, pervy glances from some men. It not right, but it's just the way it is. Some men expect women to dismiss their awkward gazes as a prerequisite of being a twenty-first-century woman, like a kind of toll that they expect from women for the involuntary shapeliness of their bodies. Most of the gawking usually only lasts for a few seconds, and then they meekly look away as if nothing happened, as if it is beyond their ability to control. Maybe a secret peek would be stolen later, but it'd be more surreptitious than straight-on ogling. This had been the way of it for as long as she could remember, going back to the days of her training bra in the sixth grade.

Then there are the others; the predators, the ones that ogle unashamedly; men she's encountered over the years that leer at women unrepentantly, without reservation. This type of loathsome creature never looks away, acting as if they can pluck her from the vine and greedily devour her until they have their fill, because women are theirs for the taking, like property. Cavazos is this second type of being—she knows his kind well.

Luci crosses her arms, pressing them against her chest as he unashamedly eyeballs her on approach. He frowns and then struggles to bend for one of the large sheets of sketch paper on the floor. Cavazos crumples the edge of the page in his plump fist, bringing it to eye level.

Luci seethes with anger at his hubris. "Do you even know what any of that means?" Her hands ball up into knotted fists wedged tightly in her armpits. "Do you understand any of it?"

He scrunches his nose up at the handwritten figures before allowing the sheet to fall to the floor like a dry dead leaf from a tree. With an unblinking glare, he says, "I don't have to know what it means, but numbers on the page *better* mean that we're getting closer to stopping Gicul." He sucks a bit of air through his teeth. "I understand that, and that's all that I need to understand. The question is . . . do you understand?"

Two cybos shamble through the doorway with equally awkward gaits and take their positions on the left and right side.

The sight of their reanimated forms makes Luci squeamish even before their smell wafts to her nostrils. She shoots a glance to Ish, who's also grimacing. "Do they have to be in here?" she demands.

He smirks wickedly. "You are a valuable commodity, Miss Gaudiano. They're here for your protection." He saunters over to her. "My name is Pol Cavazos—"

"I know who you are. What are you here for?" she asks curtly.

Cavazos snorts and steps forward to run his index finger along her arm. Repulsed, Luci reflexively snaps her arms to her side. She retreats from him, accidentally stepping on one of the blank sheets of paper, tearing its edge.

"Careful now," Cavazos says, pleased about how off-balance he's made her.

Ish bows, looking at the floor in silence like a statue. Luci wonders if his allegiances will prevent him from stepping in if this man goes too far. Would the cybos protect her against Cavazos if she were to call out? Could she run past them out of the guest home and make it to the elevator in the corridor beyond? She's not at the right angle to give him an old-fashioned Chicago-style knee to the groin if he grabs her.

She wonders if it's a tactic. Could Cavazos's sexualization of her be an attempt to diminish her control in this interaction? Her heart skips a beat when her fingers brush against the note in her pocket. She'd forgotten to hide it away from a few hours ago. Luci knows that she can't "number soothe" herself in front of him, because he'll know something's up. She swallows hard and does her best to look disinterested in contrast to the fear that she's really experiencing.

"It appears that you left any of those twenty-first century manners back in the interval we brought you from," Cavazos says snidely. "Well, before your rude interruption, I was introducing myself. I'm the city's minister of security, and you're under my protection. You'll be safe in here—"

Luci takes a step closer to Ish as her fingers tighten around the hidden note. She goes on the offensive. "We're safe unless somebody figures out a way to fool or hack your cybos over there."

Cavazos scoffs, "Impossible. There is only one way to neutralize a cybo, and that would be with this." He produces a thin, black onyx rectangle as long as his index finger and playfully wags it in front of her face. He lifts his bulbous shoulders in a shrug as he tucks the device back into his vest pocket. "It's the only one of its kind, so I don't think we'll have to worry about that anytime soon."

Ish jerks his gaze from the floor. "Minister Cavazos." His voice begins slightly shaky. "I know your time is valuable, especially with the threats to the city by New Australia and the radicals in *L'inversione*. What can we do for you today?"

Luci looks at him, wondering if he is intentionally creating a safe space to deflect the minister's advances. Either way, it works—for the moment.

Cavazos cocks his head as if attempting to size Ish up. "Well, you two can solve this DPM issue before it's too late. I would think that's obvious." Cavazos cracks the knuckles of his fat, stubby fingers. "The other reason for the visit was that I wanted to see her up close and get a sense of who we're dealing with." He glares at Luci. "While she possesses some desirable qualities, sometimes a bad personality can negate them."

Rejecting the obvious attempt to shame her by his scolding, she asks, "Does Macer know you're here?" Her extended index finger is shaking as she points at him. Turning to Ish, she commands, "Contact the chancellor on your Viatorio and tell him that—"

"You'll do nothing of the sort!" Cavazos shouts. In a more refined tone, he says, "Miss Gaudiano, I come and go as I please, and furthermore, while you are here in Relicus City, you are under my care and protection."

"I'm your prisoner is more like it," Luci spouts.

"Call it what you will, but I am in control," he says, self-satisfied. "And by the way, the work you're doing here, Mr. Moyta, is extremely confidential, so don't go spreading what we're doing here in splash forums to try and get yourself some combi."

Ish replies in a formal tone, "Of course, sir. I'd never do anything like that."

"What's combi?" Luci asks.

"Coitus," Ish answers as if back in instruction mode for her.

"Combining sexual organs together," Cavazos adds with a satisfied smirk. "I'm sure that not too much has changed from the twenty-first century until now in that regard. Perhaps when you're done with this drift pattern thing, I could—"

"You disgust me," Luci blurts out, feeling her heartrate increasing.

The statement rolls off him. "Suit yourself, but you may be surprised." Turning his focus back to Ish, he says, "So no splash forums, and nothing said to family members."

"I have no living relatives, sir. I consider it an honor to be selected for this and will do my utmost to reach our goals."

Cavazos waves his hand dismissively. "Relax. You've already got the job through the chancellor, Mr. Moyta, and your points account will be rewarded handsomely." He plops down on the couch with a grunt. "Chancellor Macer requested that I update him regularly as to your progress, so you'll be seeing a lot of me over the coming days . . . hopefully not weeks."

While Luci's grateful to move on from the subject of sex, she's ready for this creep to leave. "We need a list of all skip point junctures."

Cavazos looks to Ish for confirmation.

Ish nods. "Yes, sir, and we'd like to have that as soon as possible along with the ones that have been destroyed and the order sequence that each of the junctures were destroyed."

"Hmm . . . Okay, what do you hope to learn from that?"

Luci answers for him, hoping to speed the visit to a close. "Our approach is twofold. Mr. Moyta here is familiarizing me with the fundamentals of DPM. While he's doing that, we may also be able to reverse engineer the destruction and learn something about the targets chosen to date."

Ish jumps in. "It may be nothing, but we've got to start somewhere, sir."

Cavazos examines the nails of his left hand. "Agreed." He interlaces his plump fingers. "How long do you think this is all going to take before Cyphor and his crew are blocked or captured?"

Luci and Ish exchange a look.

She answers again, "We honestly don't know. It's too soon to tell."

Though Cavazos frowns, the nodding of his head shows his resignation to this fact.

Ish helps him off the couch as Luci stands clear of him. There is no way that she will voluntarily touch this beast of a man. She realizes that she's unconsciously returned to a posture of covering her chest with her arms. As he shuffles to the front door, she remembers Bru's words to her about wanting to bathe after being around him. With his back to them, Cavazos announces as the cybos follow him out, "I'll be in touch. In the meantime, carry on. The future depends on it."

"Yeah," Luci mumbles under her breath, "*but the future isn't what it used to be.*"

"What does that mean?" Ish asks as the door across the room slides shut.

"Nothing. Just something my father used to say." She sighs. "Hey, thanks for distracting him from me a few minutes ago. That guy makes my skin crawl."

He nods. "I don't care much for him either."

Luci raises her eyebrows in surprise. She tilts her head, but before she can speak, Ish anxiously responds, "I mean, I respect the office of the security minister for the city, but I don't care for him personally."

Her fingers curl around the note in her pocket as she contemplates bringing him in on the discovery.

Her hesitation causes him to ask with a puzzled expression, "What is it? What are you thinking?"

Snapping her empty hand out of the pocket she says, "Nothing. I just . . . this is just a new side of you that I haven't seen before is all."

FIVE

March 26, 2191
Relicus City
[6.217012/127.792969/4.603.388.826/1168:18:11]

RELIKUS SITI

MΛℂ 26, 2191

Two days later, Ish arrives to encounter Luci already hard at work testing herself with formula problems. "Hey, you're just in time," she says, handing him a sheet folded in half with calculations. "I want you to check these to see if they're right."

Ish tosses a satchel that he's brought with him onto the pull basin sofa, the area that's become their unofficial lab. He slides the WIBs on the knuckles of each hand and taps his Viatorio. "How do you feel this morning?" he asks.

"Much better. The headaches are coming less frequently and more bearable with each episode." She points at the sheet. "Anyway, I picked some random time coordinates to play with," she explains, "and then advanced these pretend skip point junctures ahead using UNIFON calendar treatment dates by incremental decades like you showed me, and then I reversed the process into the past by doing the same thing back to 1901." Luci tries to be patient as he looks the exercise over, but she's too excited and adds, "I'm working on doing the same thing based on the Gregorian calendar, but it's a little more messy than UNIFON."

He nods but doesn't look up from the sheet.

"I just used made-up start points," she says. "Their conversion and destination conclusions on there." She points to a row of figures on the sheet. "Much of the chronal transposition and TNA points I did in my head."

Still transfixed on the calculations, Ish mumbles equations to himself while pressing his Viatorio for confirmation.

Luci studies his dark, slender face, tapping the sides of her thighs in anticipation. When she can no longer stand it, she asks, "Well . . . they're solid, right?"

He utters his first words of the morning to her. "Hold on. I'm not as quick as you."

Half a minute later, the toothy grin that Luci has come to admire over the last few days forms on his face. "Amazing. Absolutely amazing."

Luci claps her hands and pumps the air with her fist. "Yes! I thought it was right, but I have no way to check it against anything."

He hands the sheet back to her. "Oh, they're right, and the fact that you're able to do this without pull basin access or a Viatorio is just . . ."

"Is what?"

"It's . . . it's marvelous," he answers enthusiastically. "You're marvelous."

Her face begins to flush, and she softly punches him in the arm. "I have a good teacher."

He picks up the satchel. "I have something for you . . . for us." He lifts the flap and removes the paper sheet he left with the night before. "Minister Cavazos sent me a sip last night of the juncture points that we asked for a few days ago." He lets the satchel slide to the floor as he eagerly unfolds the paper. "I transcribed them for you to see." It's his turn to point at markings. "There's over eighty known skip point junctures there. I've circled the nine destroyed by Gicul."

Her eyes run greedily across the data. "I see that." She shakes her head. "Your penmanship is atrocious. It's even worse than . . ." She catches herself before saying, "*whoever left the note.*" It's a secret that she doesn't want to keep from him, but she rationalizes it away since it was two days ago that she found it. She's even rationalized to herself that it could have been a previous guest that didn't approve of Macer's political policies or something. With everything that happened when she first arrived, it's possible that it went unnoticed if left by the previous occupant of the guesthouse.

"Worse than what?" Ish asks playfully. "My handwriting is worse than what?"

Luci quickly recovers. "You remember conversations about missing my rescue dog, Marcus H? Well, he has better penmanship with his gimpy paw than you."

Ish nudges her. "Well, you should know by now that nobody handwrites anything in Relicus City, so . . ."

Turning her focus back to the page of skip point junctures, she asks, "There's a lot here. How long did it take you to do all of this?"

"Most of the night." As if to demonstrate, Ish yawns. "I'll be all right though. I got a couple of hours of sleep."

His yawning is contagious, and Luci covers her mouth with the page as she sits. "This is great, Ish. Hopefully we can get to the bottom of this with these. You have out-nerded me for once."

"What is *nerded*?"

Luci laughs and gestures to the sheets pasted to the walls marked up with formulas. "This . . . this *here* is nerd nirvana. We're both math nerds to the tenth power."

Ish smiles. "That sounds good to me. What got you into mathematics anyway?"

She rubs the back of her neck. "I've always had a knack for numbers. Even from an early age, I'd notice patterns and quirky things—odd things like how all of the squares slots on a roulette wheel add up to 666." She makes mock horns placing her index fingers on the side of her head. "The devil's number."

Ish mashes his Viatorio. Half a minute later, he cautiously corrects her, "Actually, the original number of the beast is 616—*hexakosioi deka hex*—but due to several scribal errors that were ignored by second-century pre-*Hi no Kawa* translator Irenaeus, Bishop of Lugdunum, it went into the text as 666. It's interesting that some pre-*Hi no Kawa* people actually developed an irrational fear of the number."

Luci raises her eyebrows at this, which Ish answers with a shrug before adding, "Number of the beast or not, they were superstitious of the wrong number."

Luci slow claps. "Wow. You sir, are lord king of the nerds."

"I like numbers," Ish says in playful defense. "I told you the day we first met that it was my prime recreation." As if to shift the focus away from himself, he asks again, "So, what was it? What got you interested in pursuing a life in mathematics other than seeing patterns of things in everyday life?"

Luci hesitates.

"Well?" Ish asks, playfully nudging her.

She looks past him at the numbers transcribed around the room. She feels as if she's back on the stage at the lecture hall in Baltimore looking out into the sea of faces, the numbers transforming into the multitude of spectators before her eyes, every digit a witness and participant to her past—both accuser and defender.

"You can trust me. Anything you tell me, I'll keep safe." Ish nudges her again.

"Stop pushing on me."

"I could tell you what the sip files say, but I don't know how accurate—"

She raises a hand to stop him. "No, I'll tell you." Luci takes a deep breath, and the figures scribbled around the room return to numbers. "Something happened to me." Her body stiffens as she contemplates how much to share with him.

After a long pause, Ish asks in a reverent whisper, "The accident?"

She slowly nods, calculating the time from then until this moment. "Exactly 65,242 days ago." A lump forms in her throat. "When I was a young girl, I loved animals—every type of animal, but especially dogs." She stops short, deciding to approach the topic from a different angle. "We—my parents and I—we were on our way to an animal shelter, one for dogs across town, a place where we volunteered occasionally." Luci pauses to sit on the sofa.

Ish takes his seat beside her. "Yes? Go on."

Luci looks down at her feet. "Anyway, there was this girl, a seventeen-year-old messing on her phone, not paying attention, and her truck plowed into us head on." There's a sharp intake of air as Luci plays back the sound of metal and glass exploding in her mind. "I never even saw it from the back seat. The first part, I mean." She shakes her head as if attempting to wake from a nightmare. "They say the girl panicked, an inexperienced driver who mashed the accelerator instead of the brake after the impact." Tears stream down Luci's cheeks as she returns her gaze to him. "That's what did it. That's what pushed our car through the already mangled guardrail and off the bridge."

Ish shakes his head in unison with Luci while softly putting a hand on her shoulder. "You don't have to—"

"No . . . no, let me finish."

He slides his hand away.

"I need to finish. I *want* to tell this to you." Her throat constricts, and Luci feels like she's going to suffocate, as if getting the words out will make room for much-needed air. She needs air just like before, under the water, trapped inside a sinking car. "My mother . . ." She modifies the term. "My *stretch* screamed my name as we fell to the lake below." Wiping her cheeks with the back of her hand, she says, "Everything moved in slow motion, taking forever to hit the water. If I concentrate, I can play back the whole thing in my mind."

She swallows hard. "I can still hear it . . . her shouting my name, stopping the second the car slammed into the water." Luci sniffs and gnaws at the cuticle on her thumb. "You know, I don't even know if my father was still alive at that point or if the original crash had killed him. The coroner's office said they couldn't tell." She shakes her head studying the concerned face of Ish and exhales. "Maybe they just withheld stuff from an orphan girl, I don't know. It probably doesn't matter. Still, I've always wondered." There's a pause, but when the silence is worse than speaking, Luci resumes. "The water roared at me, rushing in so hard. The front windshield was pretty much gone, so nothing could stop it from coming in at that point. It was so cold . . . I remember that. It felt so cold for August." She sighs.

Ish is as still as a statue.

She says flatly, "The teenager driving the truck that killed them was considered a minor, so nothing really was done to her, no jail time or anything that I know of."

Luci sniffs and forces out a fake chuckle. "Anyway . . . *math!* That was the question, right?" she asks, manufacturing a counterfeit cheeriness. "Math was always a constant—never changing, always the same. You always say that I can trust you. Well, one can always trust math. Two plus two always equals four no matter which orphanage or foster home you're in."

"Foster home?" Ish asks delicately with widened eyes, also tearing up.

"Yeah, it's kind of like surrogate parents. In my case, it was always temporary." She mulls this over. "Most of them were good to me, but I was a teenager. I think they really wanted younger children to raise. Foster parents want to be there to see the child grow and develop, I guess, and I was pretty much past the 'fun' stuff."

"There were no other family members?" Ish asks a little more boldly.

Luci pinches the bridge of her nose, rubbing at her eyes. "Somewhere out there, I guess. I'd never met them, and if they knew about what happened, they didn't come to the funeral. My parents were given a double ceremony. That used up any life insurance the two of them had."

She allows the bitterness boiling up inside her to fuel the conversation to the end. "I don't know how it works here in Relicus City, but people in my time can be stupid and cruel to each other."

"Stupid how?"

"My father was Italian Catholic. My *stretch* was from a Jewish family. You have religion here, right?"

"Yes, of course," Ish says.

"Well, the sides of their respective families disavowed them both long before I was born. The chasm of differences in belief was too wide for either family to accept, so . . ."

Ish nods, urging, "People still find stupid reasons to block others out of their lives."

"The fact that the families of both of them were rumored to live outside of the U.S. didn't help anything either." She runs her fingers through her hair. The clamminess she was feeling a few minutes ago is dissipating.

"Anyway, I abandoned any aspirations of working with animals, probably out of some subconscious guilt that I was unaware of at the time or something. I shifted my interests to academia. When I was high school, Iranian mathematician Maryam Mirzakhani became the first woman in seventy-eight years to be awarded the Fields Medal." She diverts to explain, "It's kind of the Nobel Prize for math for people under forty. She died three years later of breast cancer while in the midst of doing some fantastic work. There also was a young American physicist from Chicago, Sabrina Gonzalez Pasterski."

Ish nods. "I know. I sipped that Gonzalez Pasterski went to Harvard for her doctorate, and Mirzakhani was a professor at Stanford."

Luci is surprised at first and then realizes how Ish has had a lifetime to study up on her past. "Yes, Dr. Mirzakhani—she's the reason I went to Stanford and joined the Department of Mathematics. As corny as it sounds and though our fields of study were very different, I sort of followed in her footsteps, even winning the Fields Medal myself." The talk of Luci's accomplishment eases some of her tension. She uncurls her fist and holds up her index finger. "But I won mine at twenty-four."

Ish bows his head as he smiles. "I know that."

"Of course you do."

He shrugs and extends his hand, gently resting it on her shoulder. "Please don't take this the wrong way, but I, for one, am glad that you pursued mathematics instead of the animals."

The soft weight of his hand is comforting. Luci remains as still as possible so as not to frighten it away like an anxious butterfly. "I still love them—animals, that is. It's hard for me to get used to the idea that they're none here in Relicus City. Does the Well Basin info on me mention anything about that, how I love animals? How a perfect day for me is to get to work early to do computations and take an extended lunch at the zoo, eating PB & J sandwiches?"

"No," Ish answers, showing that her point is taken. "Your sip-node files mainly document your achievements and major life events."

She sniffs and risks placing her hand on top of his, careful not to touch the rubber WIB input. She's surprised at how warm his flesh feels. "Ah, so I still have a *few* mysteries to you, Mr. Moyta?"

"Should I say that there are aspects about you that are as unknown as every *limber DPM number* that we've encountered?"

"That's good for starters."

This inspires a welcome chuckle from him. "Then just like those yet-to-be-resolved porous DPM number compounds, I'm certain that you contain within you a world of *impenetrable* perplexities that I could spend the rest of my days working to solve." He draws his hand back to himself as he stands. "I think that I'd like to warm up with something easier first, like the drift pattern, than all of your complexities."

She stands, nodding acknowledgment that he's matched her verbally. "Yeah, I guess we better get started."

"Thank you though," Ish says while handing the sheet to her. "For trusting me with all of that. It was good."

She considers this. "I don't know about it being *good* and all, but I don't usually talk about it—not since I was a kid, at least." She sighs. "Anyway, yes, let's get to work."

SIX

THE REST OF THE MORNING is consumed by Luci and Ish plotting out the chronal coordinates from Cavazos's data. They begin with the most recently destroyed interval juncture of Poland 1952, September 22nd between 8:03 AM and 11:39 PM. Working in intense silence, they reverse engineer each precise leap-skip portal address from its location in time and space back against the other attacks. The work is mentally grueling. Luci feels like a prizefighter in the ring, delivering blow after blow while also being bombarded by an onslaught of more unanswered equations. She refuses to let on to Ish that her head is pounding again, promising herself she'll lie down as soon as they have a breakthrough.

When they pause for a quick lunch late in the afternoon, Luci admits, "I still can't see the common denominator between any of them." She takes another sip from her straw pouch. The meal is something that's been engineered to taste like chicken soup without any chicken and has an odd aftertaste. She asks, "Why are some skip point junctures obliterated while Gicul ignores others?"

Ish shrugs, taking a few gulps of his own meal. "Maybe he only destroys the ones that have something of worth."

She lowers the plastic broth container to pick up a small scrap of paper. "No, see this? This is near Antarctica in 1832. There's nothing there. I mean, why even bother? It's Antarctica."

Ish nods in agreement. "I could check to see if the untouched intervals have some resources that could be used for something."

"Yeah, maybe. Though I can't imagine what he would need and why." She runs her fingers through her hair. "It just feels off. It's like the reason for the destinations that he's picking is just there staring us in the face, but I can't see it."

She halfheartedly sips her soup. "It really drives me crazy."

After a brief silence, an idea pops into her head. "Wait a minute!" she exclaims. She scrambles to retrieve Ish's hand-written transcription from the night before. "Is it possible that these are symbolic in nature?" Luci snatches up the paper from across the room and returns, waving it. "I'm not from around here, so obviously, these targets wouldn't mean anything to an outsider like me, but . . . maybe they represent something to your culture."

Ish crumples his now-empty meal pouch. "Represent what?"

"I don't know," she says, forcing the sheet into his hand. "Back in my time, when I was just a baby, there were some guys that crashed planes into these two buildings to make a statement. The buildings themselves were just really tall structures in New York City, but what they represented in the world at the time is what made them targets for the terrorists."

Ish examines the paper with a newfound concentration.

Luci studies the intensity of his expression. "Do they mean anything to you?"

"Not right off, but—"

"But what?" Luci asks, attempting to conceal her impatience.

"Have you noticed that the list only has two junctures over the last three centuries on the continent of Australia, and both of those were during the Spanish-American War?"

"You're right, no skip points after June of 1898," she says, a little embarrassed that she overlooked this. "What do you think that means?"

He shrugs. "Maybe nothing. I just found it interesting, considering how they're our enemy now."

"Yes, definitely." Luci nods as his eyes return to the page. "So, what does that tell us? We can't skip to the Australian continent. What does that prove? Do you suspect it has something to do with those *limber numbers* that defy everything we know of DPM?"

He hands the sheet back to her and shrugs. "I don't know. It's probably nothing."

Luci throws her head back in exasperation, letting out a loud sigh. Rubbing her closed eyes, she shouts at the curved glass ceiling, "Why can't I figure this out?" She chides herself returning her gaze to Ish. "What is wrong with me?"

"We'll get it, Luci. We'll figure it out."

Part of her appreciates the encouragement, but she resents it a little at the same time. "Just let me sulk a minute, will ya?" she asks, beginning to pace. "I'm not used to all of this." She circles a finger in the air. "I'm not good at being under house arrest, or whatever you want to call it. I'm a prisoner here. You get to go home every night, but I stay. I stay right here. When I was in my twenties, there was a global virus outbreak called Covid-19 and everyone was quarantined for weeks and weeks inside their homes and that nearly drove me mad. I'm getting it here again—cabin fever—and that's not good for the project."

She stops walking and realizes that she's pointing at Ish now. She lowers her hand slowly to her side. "Sorry. I know it's not your fault, but it's driving me crazy." She slumps onto one of the stools, resting her elbows against the kitchen counter. "Back home," she begins, "in my interval, if I got stuck on something, I could go to the gym." Luci massages the back of her neck as she searches the empty counter before her. "I'd exercise until my body was exhausted and it forced me to rest. It'd reboot me. I'd wake up hours later, refreshed in my mind, and often solve the piece I was working on." She springs from the stool. "Or bowling—the delicious geometry of bowling," she says, pantomiming bowling.

"Bowls?" Ish asks quizzically.

She ignores him. "Or dancing—I love dancing," she says with a slow spin that terminates in a curtsey before him. "You guys may not have bowling here, but I'm sure you dance, right?"

When he hesitates, she takes a step in his direction. "Dancing?" She pauses. "Maybe you call it something different here?"

Ish crosses his arms as he shakes his head. "I'm sorry, I understand exercise, but bowls and—"

"Dancing," Luci blurts out, snapping her fingers while giving a shimmy. "You know, people getting together, moving about."

Ish smiles, relieved. "Splash forums."

"Is that what you call it?"

"It's when people gather in here," he says, pointing to his Viatorio. "It's a community get-together. The entire city is welcome, in fact."

"So it's like an online thing?" Luci asks, confused. "You gather online for social events and things? I don't think that we're talking about the same thing."

His face brightens, and there's excitement in his voice. "Yes, we gather in V-space online and view a demonstration together with our pep avatars. This week's demonstration is a man who's going to paint a large orange wall blue."

Luci shoots him a sideways glance and mumbles, "No, that's not dancing—not even close." Intrigued to learn more about the culture here, she tables the dance conversation for now. "Let me get this straight. At some point this week, everyone will log onto some virtual reality thing—"

"Through their Viatorio pep," Ish offers.

"Right, everyone logs in to watch some guy paint a wall—not a mural or anything—just change it from one color to another?"

"From orange to blue." Ish nods, oblivious to Luci's ridicule. "Yes, since bots normally do city painting and restoration, it's intriguing to view a human painting it. Since it's virtual, you don't get dirty at any of the events."

"Seriously, that's a good time in Relicus City," she scoffs. "Going online to watch some guy paint a wall? You're telling me that you people literally think that watching paint dry is fun?" She tilts her head, raising her eyebrows. "And I thought basic cable was lame."

The remark is lost on him. "Well, it's more than that," Ish says, rubbing his chin. "It's mainly a reason for people to gather. It's rare for large groups to meet in person in Relicus, probably a safety thing, I guess. In fact, the chancellor's statue unveiling a few days ago was the first time in a long time that a large crowd gathered in a physical environment, so we meet in V-space."

Luci playfully taunts him. "But you're *not* really meeting. The people going online to witness the event aren't actually meeting in person, right? If you go there to pick up someone like a date, you can't even touch them to hold their hand."

He slides his hands into his pockets, leaving only his thumbs exposed. "We meet in person when there's an official courtship period between two people."

These odd wooing parameters fascinate her, and talking about something other than DPM is a refreshing break, so she continues. "How long is that usually?"

His shoulders rise. "I don't know. A few days in person, though it can be as long as a week or more."

"A *whole* week, huh? Wow." Luci doesn't attempt to mask her sarcasm as she wonders what the divorce rate is here, if there even is such a thing.

Attempting to justify the practice, Ish adds, "Well, the couple would've been to V-Space with the other person for a lot longer before meeting in person—maybe six months to a year—and then after a few in-person encounters, you oath."

"You *oath*?" Luci asks. "You mean you're married?"

He crosses his arms. "Yes, you oath by repeating the words."

"Which are?" She's enjoying making him squirm—this is fun. She finds him cute trying to balance the role of being an information source to her while relaying something that is obviously socially taboo to discuss with a member of the opposite sex. His uncomfortableness heightens her curiosity.

"Dr. Gaudiano, I can't say them here . . . now, to you. It's inappropriate. The words are to only be heard by one's combi."

"*Doctor* Gaudiano?" She smirks. "Why so formal all of a sudden, *Mister Moyta*?" In a playfully mocking tone, she does her best Scarlett O'hara impersonation. "Well, by all means, we don't want to have you do anything . . . *inappropriate*."

He doesn't comment on this, but he shifts the conversation back to the main topic. "Three weeks ago, there was a good one—splash, that is. The performer-organizer stacked a bunch of poly foam cubes up very high. It took her about an hour or so to arrange them in a pattern. The cubes were different colors. When she was done, a brief intermission was taken, and we were allowed to virtually stroll around inside and on top of it. When the splash resumed, she knocked it down. It was very satisfying to view and participate in."

"Sounds stupid to me," Luci says. "Everyone knew that she was going to knock it over at the end?"

Still undaunted by Luci's ridicule, Ish does his best to explain. "Of course. That's why it's so satisfying. The outcome is defined early, whether it's painting a wall or something like with the blocks. So when it happens, it's very therapeutic and you get to meet a lot of people in the city that you may not normally interact with."

She shakes her head. "It's just very different from the entertainment of my day like movies, sporting events, plays, books, streaming shows, museums, dining out." She points at him. "And just so you know, your painting wall thing or foam blocks falling down . . . that's not dancing, not even close."

Ish presses his Viatorio and heads to the well basin.

"What's going on?" she demands, trailing behind. "What are you doing?"

He produces his sip wand and bends over the bubbling liquid. "Learning about your dancing," he says in a matter-of-fact tone.

"I don't think that you—"

He holds his hand up to pause the conversation.

Luci makes a show of disapproval of being silenced and plops down on the sofa next to him.

After a minute or so of him using his WIBs to type in the open space before him, Ish says, "Okay, so our music here is mostly slow-moving tonal sounds designed to soothe the listener. I understand how organized sound would stimulate the brain's reward centers in people. I also read how the chemical dopamine would be released to better control movement and coordination in a person."

"Seriously?" Luci asks, raising a skeptical eyebrow.

He nods, still reading. "Rhythmic auditory stimulation also often results in the issuing of the serotonin hormones."

Luci shakes her head and rises to her feet. "That sounds dreadful."

"Is that not correct?" Ish asks defensively.

"I don't know about all the serotonin and dopamine stuff." She reaches for his hand to pull him up with her. It feels warm in her grasp. "I just know that it helps to clear my head, and since there are no bowling alleys around here . . ."

Ish stands with trepidation, and Luci notices how much taller he is than her. She guides him around the sofa to an area that's not cluttered up with huge sheets of Macer's unused sketch paper. "It's about letting loose. It's about having fun, feeling alive and having a good time. Here, I'll show you." Luci lifts his left hand with her right and places his other on her back beneath her shoulder blade.

He pulls his hands away. "But . . . there's no musics."

"It's okay, I can hum," she says, returning him to his dance stance again. This time, she interlaces her hands together behind his neck. "I'll just show you some basic steps. Do you trust me?"

He nods but looks terrified. "I don't think that I—"

She does her best to calm him. "That's perfect. *Don't* think. Let your body think for you. Let your feet and hips do the talking for you." Luci moves to the rhythm of the tune she's humming. "We're just going to make a box pattern with our shoes: Left foot forward to second corner, right foot to the right to third corner. It's like a math equation. Left foot joins right at third corner, right foot back to fourth corner, left foot to the left, returning to starting corner. Right foot joins left, and repeat."

It's clumsy at first, but her partner is a quick study. The awkwardness begins to wane to a manageable level. After a minute or so of this wooden exchange, Ish stumbles and abruptly pulls away.

Luci freezes in place. "What's wrong? What did I do?"

His slowness to answer makes her self-conscious, and she wonders if she's violated some social etiquette. "Ish, what is it? What's wrong? What did I do?"

His expression is as if he's miles away. Her heart skips a beat as she flashes back to the odd seizure-like episode with Macer.

Ish lifts his hand. "It's alright. I'm okay. I just can't see."

She grabs his arm in a panic. "You can't *see*? What happened?" she shouts. "What do you mean?"

His voice is calm as he wrangles free of her to reach his Viatorio. "It's alright. Give me a moment to report."

She lets her hands slide off his arm. "Report what . . . and to whom?"

"An alert has gone out," he says as if reading or watching something that she can't see. "There's an attack."

The words make her heart race. Luci spins around, scanning the room for signs of danger outside of the glass dome. "Is Gicul here?" she demands.

"No, it's not him or *L'inversione*," Ish says, groping for the sofa edge behind him. "It's marauders from New Australia."

For the first time since her house arrest, Luci is grateful to have a cybo stationed outside the front door. "What did they do, and why can't you see? What did they do to your eyes?"

"I don't know yet," he answers, distracted by something in his virtual vision.

A sense of helplessness envelops her, making her wish that she had a Viatorio to know what is going on. "Is this a common thing from them?"

"No—well, not that often," Ish says, exasperated. "Give me a minute to report in and get this turned off." He states to some unseen entity, "Confirmation Code 1729."

She forces herself not to bombard him with every question bubbling up in her brain.

A minute or so later, Ish softly grabs her shoulders. "Everything is okay now. It was just that some attack boats from New Australia were spotted on the edge of the city."

She gulps. "We're under attack?"

"No. The vessels were small, and they've been destroyed. We're safe here. It was on the opposite side of Relicus, and they didn't have a chance to do any damage before they were sunk."

She tries to relax, but too many questions remain. "Were there any survivors, someone who can be interrogated?"

Ish releases his grip on her. "If there were, they'd be converted to cybos. But either way, they won't be causing any more problems. You're safe here."

"Wouldn't they question the enemy before that though ... before making them into those cybo things? I mean, maybe there's a connection to *L'inversione* and New Australia or something."

He shrugs. "Yeah, I guess so. I'm sure there are protocols for getting information from them before any conversion."

Luci wonders if the cybo stationed outside of the guesthouse door originated from New Australia. "It seems strange to have an imminent threat that no one knows anything about. Don't you think that's weird?"

With a puzzled expression, Ish asks, "What do you mean? The city's security knows how to handle these things."

"In my time, the government is held accountable." She studies his face for a reaction. "The people are informed. There are oversight groups to ensure that human rights are not violated."

"The right to do what?" Ish asks blankly.

She struggles about how to relay the concept of an organization like Amnesty International to him, choosing to save it for another time. "How did the Australians blind you?"

"Oh, that wasn't from the attackers. That's an internal security thing."

She's stunned by the revelation and the casualness of Ish's statement. "Someone in the city did this to you? Doesn't that bother you a little?"

He shakes his head slowly. "No, it's alright, and I didn't exactly go blind." He sighs. "It's just a red band covered my vision until I reported why I wasn't where I'd normally be."

"Sounds like you were blind to me," she fires back. "If you can't see, that's blindness. Why would Relicus City do that to you?"

"Like I said, it's a security protocol. Everyone in the city who wasn't in their predesignated quadrant would've experienced the same thing. That way, if there's anyone working with the enemy, they're incapacitated." Ish offers a weak smile. "But I'm okay. I just reported in and the system administrators confirmed that I'm allowed to visit the chancellor's guest house and everything is fine."

She squeezes the back of her neck and scoffs, "I can't get over the idea that you're okay with them taking away your sight. Why not just take the Viatorio off your ear when that happens?"

"Well, first of all, these can't be removed very easily," he says, tugging at the device affixed to his earlobe. "And if it was removed during a Red Out, it would leave the red band permanently blocking the wearer's vision."

When she gasps, he adds, "Not only that, but doing that could cause mild brain damage."

"It seems like a huge strategy fail to me. A better plan is to allow Relicus City citizens to see if there's an attack from an outside enemy. That just makes sense."

"They only suspended it for a moment, and it's for the protection of the city, so I don't mind if it keeps us all safe from infiltrators."

Luci still can't believe it. "This is the first I've heard of any of this. Is that a problem, sympathizers for New Australia living within the city? Why would anyone do that?"

He offers open palms to her. "Luci, I'm not a political person. I'm a technician. I'm like you. I deal in math, not revolutions."

Luci picks up her lunch dishes and heads over to the sink. "You people are weird here. Really weird."

SEVEN

RELIKUS SITI

MAȻ 24, 2191

LUCI IS UP AND SHOWERED before sunrise. She's still kicking herself for dancing with Ish the day before as she heads downstairs to the kitchen pod. It was a foolish and highly unprofessional thing to do—one doesn't dance with their colleagues in the middle of a project, regardless of what century it is. How could she have been so stupid? The stress of everything that's happened plus being confined is beginning to take its toll on her. She'd never done anything as foolish as that back home. What's happening to her?

Fortunately, they both manage to ignore her lapse in judgement and work the rest of the day without incident—not that it matters; they are no closer to understanding the connection between Gicul's interval targets than when Ish first arrived at the guest house four days ago. Her mind drifts to how odd it is that Ish didn't mind his sight being temporarily suspended during the attack from the New Australians. How can he be so docile about something like that? For once, she's grateful not to have a Viatorio wired into her brain.

As she manually inputs the code into the food printer for her morning protein, she's forced to concede that the destroyed skip point junctures may have been selected at random and bear no connection to each other. The idea that they may have searched in vain for something that doesn't exist is disheartening—they're running out of time. She can't shake the feeling that there's something in common between the skip point junctures, but what could it be? Maybe they should devote more time to cracking what Ish calls limber and porous DPM number compounds to see if the solution is hidden within those anomalies.

The meal fabricator dispenses an orange-and-brown lukewarm mash onto a plastic plate. Luci pokes at it unenthusiastically with her curved fork. She taps her forehead with the butt of her palm and says, "Come on, Luci G., you can get this. The answer's in there somewhere. Just sort it out." She forces a few bites of the mush into her mouth more as a perfunctory act for brain fuel than anything else.

Then she spots something. As she makes her way to the table from the kitchen pod, the plate slips from her shaking hand onto the glossy, illuminated floor with a plop. Her heart feels as if it could burst through her ribs, it's beating so quickly. She knows what the quarter-folded sheet on the table is even before she reaches for it. The note is neatly arranged like a tiny paper tent in the center of the table, beckoning for her to read it. Luci extends her hand to it but pulls back, scanning the room for the intruder who left it.

Her throat constricts as she calls out, "Hello . . . hello, are you here?" Her voice cracks. "Hello?" Luci swallows hard while continuing to turn in a slow circle, searching for any movement. Any morning grogginess has burned away like gasoline on a fire of adrenaline. She feels the hints of a Jardon headache coming on. "Not now," she chides herself, clutching the sides of her head. Every nerve is alive and ready, but no one is in sight. Her blood runs cold that this intruder is able to come and go as they please. She is trapped in the guesthouse with no way to escape or contact anyone.

"If you're in here, you need to come out right now!" she shouts with a manufactured authority and confidence. "Security Minister Cavazos is en route for a status update." It's a lie, but it's the best that she can manage. "He'll be here any minute . . . and with a bunch of cybos, but I can hide you upstairs." She's not eager to meet the trespasser, but at least if they come out into the open, she'll know what she's dealing with, and that blasted curiosity of hers always wins out over what may be the most prudent course of action.

After an intense silence, Luci snatches the note from the table. She unfolds it, cupping it in her hands. The writing is in the same unstable penmanship as the first note.

SUMΗIИ UBΘT NU ΛSTRΛLYU IZUNT R±T

The word "*Australia*" instantly jumps out at her. It doesn't take much to determine what precedes it is the word "*new.*" This note is easier to decipher than the previous one. She reads it aloud. "*Something about New Australia isn't right.*" The sound of the door sliding open at the other end of the area startles her. Luci jerks from the table, knocking the stool back against the curved glass wall behind her. Without thinking, she grabs it by the metal rungs. She spins it around with its legs pointed outward like a circus lion tamer warding off a vicious beast. "Who is it?" she yells, giving the stool a practice lunge forward, testing its weight in her grip.

As small as it is, the kitchen pod blocks her view of the entry door. She gnaws at her lip as she cautiously advances for a better angle. "I said, who's there?"

Ish rounds the corner of the cubicle-like food prep area with a perplexed expression. "You said you wanted to start earlier today, right?"

The stool feels heavy now. Luci allows it to sink to the ground before her. "What?"

He cautiously moves closer. "What's going on here? Are you alright?" He cautiously eyes the fallen plate and splotches of her meal. "What happened here? Why is there food on the floor?"

"Another one," she says. "They left another one." All at once, she feels the fatigue in her muscles and sits on the stool for balance. She grabs the sides of her head, feeling the onset of another one of those blasted headaches. "I thought you were him."

"I was *him* who?" Ish asks, moving more briskly to her. "What's going on here? Was Minister Cavazos here this morning?"

She shakes her head and points over her shoulder. "On the table . . ."

Ish looks her over with a worried expression. His mouth opens for a question, but he opts to go for the table behind instead. Coming back around into her line of sight, Ish holds the note up. "I don't understand. Who is this from? Who was here?"

"A few days ago, there was a note in the bathroom that said I was being lied to," she explains. Luci runs her fingers through her hair and sighs as she looks up at Ish. "I didn't tell you about it because—"

"Because why?" he asks sharply while demonstratively waving the note in the air. "If someone has figured out a way to subvert the security systems of this place, you're at risk. The entire project is at risk. The whole world is in jeopardy. If Gicul manages to destroy all leap-skip passage by destroying the juncture nodes, you'll be trapped here like the rest of us, and if you don't go back, then—"

She avoids Ish's eyes burning into her. "I know, I know. Maybe that was the plan all along, to trap me here to prevent DPM from ever being presented to the world." Her gaze returns to the blobs of food scattered on the floor in a crude circle. The biggest mound is in the center as the others are arranged around it.

She shakes her head. "I didn't know—"

"Know what?" he demands in a voice mixed with confusion and pain.

"I didn't know if . . . if I could trust you." The words tumble out like a stone. She opens her mouth to apologize but quickly snaps it closed. She resents the idea that she should feel bad for something here. She's always had a problem in her time with the concept that women should act contrite when something went wrong for their male counterparts. *She* was the one abducted from her time, not him. She has nothing to apologize for here.

"How could you not trust me? What have I done to you?"

The concierge bot begins cleaning the orange and brown splotches on the ground.

"Nothing. You haven't done anything wrong. I just didn't know whose side you were on."

"Whose side I was on," he scoffs. "Whose side *would* I be on? I'm on your side. You're on the side of humanity, so I'm on your side."

"But I don't trust . . ." She exhales a frustrated sigh. "I don't trust the people that you trust. They brought me here against my will. Royse drugged me and abducted me. I'm not like you, just accepting things like when they blocked your vision yesterday." She pauses, allowing her words to take root. "Your leaders have some messed up ways of doing things to people in the interest of the greater good. How can you blame me for withholding information like this? How am I able to trust any of you?"

He considers this in silence as the robot does its duty. Instead of scooping up the individual morsels of meal one by one, its extension arm pushes the smaller piles to the one in the center.

"You're right. I'm sorry. I've always trusted those in authority over me. It's just the way of the Relicus people."

She frowns at this admission but remains silent.

He cautiously asks, "So you trust me now?"

"Yeah, I guess so," Luci answers.

"What changed?" he asks, studying her face.

"I don't know," she says. "I've gotten to know you better. Things are different between us now. I feel as if I know you more. You don't seem like the others. To them, I'm only a solution—a mechanism to a means to an end. To you, I feel like I'm something more, something different than all of that. Sure, we're partners on the project, but there's also something else . . ."

Ish nods in agreement. "When was the other note left?"

Luci's relieved when he doesn't ask her to define what the difference between him and the others is, because she's not certain that she's able to quantify an answer.

"Did they leave the other note yesterday morning before I got here?" Ish asks more insistently.

There's a comfort in seeing the analytical side of her partner coming to the surface. She shares the ability to compartmentalize the emotional side of things to focus on an unknown. "No, it was the day that Cavazos came here."

A high suction noise whirs from the machine as the extender claw uncoils a small plastic tube.

"We've got to inform Security Minister Cavazos."

Luci looks up at him in alarm. "Ish, please, let's consider our options here. Once we tell the others about this, we lose all control. If someone is trying to help me—help *us*, turning the messages over will shut the door on that permanently. Macer and Cavazos will probably lock us away in a dungeon at the bottom of the ocean somewhere, and the situation here is already claustrophobic enough for me."

What she'd give to see his warm grin, but his face is set and tight. "Luci, you're not safe." His eyes narrow to slits. "Everything is at risk. If something happens to you . . . if someone can get to you, we will lose everything."

She looks away from him down to the concierge bot. It's cleaning up the last of the mess, streaks of orange and brown left behind on the floor.

"Speaking of trust, do you trust me?" she asks. "Whoever this is has been here *twice*. They've gotten past the cybo out in the corridor *twice*. Neither time did they harm me when they obviously could have." She omits the detail that the first note could possibly have been left while she was away at the Grange visiting Bru Mandal.

The bot whisks away, making her spill from a few minutes ago just a memory.

"Luci," Ish says, pleading. "We can't afford to—"

She stops him with a wave of her hand as the door in her mind opens. Remembering the arrangement of spoiled food, she has an epiphany. It was always assumed that Relicus City was the starting point. She inhales sharply before blurting out, "That's it! We've been looking at it all wrong."

"Looking at what?" Ish asks, attempting to keep up.

She closes her eyes, picturing how the mess on the floor looked like a wheel with a dozen or so jagged spokes converging in the center. She's giddy when she looks at Ish again. "I propose that we've been looking at the wrong thing, or rather the right thing but interpreting it in the wrong way."

"What are you saying?" Ish asks from across the room. "Don't change the subject about what we're doing with the notes. I'm not done talking about that."

"Okay, okay, but let me show you this first." She nearly knocks him over scrambling past to the kitchen pod. "We've been using the wrong common denominator. Here, I need another plate." She turns her back to him, mashes the code into the food printer, and turns back to Ish as the processer begins assembling another batch of breakfast. "How do you know when a skip point juncture is destroyed?"

Ish walks slowly to her. "Why is that important?"

"Just answer the question, Ish."

"Well, the way we can tell that they're destroyed is because their FNS-8os and Bine Shadow data return to zero; plus, their trace magnetic signatures go out." He pauses. "It's like a star going dark in the night sky. It's simply not a viewable object any longer on any monitoring equipment—that and any long-chair or similar leap-skip transport wouldn't be able to access it."

"What would happen if someone tried to leap skip to a destroyed interval portal?"

"Nothing," Ish explains. "In order for a corridor to activate, both origin and destination points have to correspond and be live. I still don't get what this has to do with anything."

The meal printer beeps a short tone, alerting that it has completed its task.

Ish pinches his chin. "We still need to discuss what we're going to do about the notes."

Luci raises her index finger. "We will, I promise. Just give me a sec." She makes her way around the counter and crouches with the plate. "So, look at this."

Ish looks horrified as she smears a perfectly good meal on the illuminated tile. "What are you doing? Are you having a Jardon relapse wasting food like that?"

She realizes why the act is so disturbing to him and the cultural faux pas that she's committed. "I'm sorry. I know how valuable food is here, but just watch."

There's a scowl on his face, but he silently nods for her to finish.

Luci scoops more from the plate like an artist dipping a brush into her pallet. She finger-paints a crude circle. "So, every calculation tracking this stuff that we've done uses a Bine Shadow of 0.1573 or, in some cases, rounded up to Bine 0.2, right?"

Ish nods with an intense expression. "Yes, that's correct. So?"

She recreates the image from before that looks like a bicycle wheel. "But that's because we've presumptuously selected Relicus City as the initial leap skip point originator." Luci plops a big glob in the middle to illustrate a hub.

Ish groans his disapproval.

Looking up at him, she asks, "But what if it's not? The chronal points don't change, but the STMO corridors would be vastly different. They'd have to be." Halfway between the mound of food representing the hub and the outer rim of the wheel shape, she places a slimy chunk of protein and gestures at it. "What if the leap skips begin from somewhere else, near Relicus City's time but not quite?"

Ish's jaw drops as he kneels beside her. He whispers in astonishment, his eyes transfixed on the crudely rendered diagram in food. "Of course. The calculations would be completely different." He rubs the back of his neck in astonishment. "If we reverse engineer the fixed termination spots into the past, eventually, they should intersect, and that may tell us—"

"It might show us where he is, or at the very least where Gicul has been operating from."

Ish stands. "We may even be able to determine where he'll hit next."

Luci scrapes the food from her fingers on the edge of the plate, returning to her feet. "Which means that I'll finally get out of here and go home."

The brief elation on Ish's face fades to a stoic expression of acceptance. "Yes, you'll be able to leave this interval and return to your time."

An awkward silence descends between them. Luci believed that except for the dancing incident from yesterday, they were past the stage of uncomfortable pauses. She is grateful for the distraction as the concierge bot zooms in to clean up the new food mess. "That's how I figured it out," she says, pointing at the busy bot cleaning like it's a command performance from earlier. "Watch how it does it. It pushes as much of the food to the center before it sucks up the pile." Luci points. "See how it leaves streaks? They looked like bicycle spokes to me at first, all of them pointing inward at the hub."

"You have an amazing mind, Dr. Gaudiano. Only you could solve the mysteries of the universe by staring into a spilled plate of mush."

She tilts her head playfully. "Is that a compliment or an insult?"

"Just don't waste any more food. It's very valuable around here." His mouth forms a thin line. "You know, I'm still disappointed that you didn't trust me. I get that things have been hard for you here, but I'm on your side."

"I know, but please know that it was never my intention to hurt your feelings." She rubs the side of her cheek with the knuckles of her clean hand. "What if we don't turn the notes in and you stay here tonight?" She feels her face flush and is quick to qualify the question. "I mean on the basin sofa down here, of course."

"Right," Ish answers. "I assumed that's what you meant—down here."

His hesitation causes her to blurt out, "I mean, that's not weird, right? I mean, culturally, that's an okay thing, right?" No matter what she asks, the words feel clunky and wrong, and she feels her face heating up.

"No," he stammers. "It's fine. No one even knows a woman is even staying here, much less famed mathematician Luci Gaudiano."

The room suddenly feels stuffy and too warm to her. "You could stay here on the sofa tonight, and we catch them in the act when they come back and we find out what this is."

Ish is slow to respond, too slow for comfort. "Well, I kind of—"

She nervously wipes the remaining particles of sticky food from her hand onto the side of her pants leg. "Oh my gosh, I never even asked if you had a family. Do you have someone at home?"

He shakes his head. "No, I've never oathed."

She's prying now, but she can't stop herself. "Is there a reason that you've never *oathed* anyone here in Relicus City or at the Grange?"

His hazel eyes don't blink. "It's a very serious thing, not to be taken lightly. I just want to be sure it's right, with the right person. They are the most sacred words two people may say to one another, a very private and intimate thing."

"I'm sorry. It's none of my business, and I shouldn't have asked you to stay."

"No, it's alright." His eyes shift to the floor. "It's not that, it's just I have to meet someone for . . . there's this thing that I'm kind of doing tonight, but I can stay tomorrow if you—"

Luci cuts him off, hoping for a speedy end to all of this. "It was a stupid thing to ask of you. There's probably one of those splash forum things where the splasher people knock down painted blocks or whatever that you want to attend with someone." Nervously running her fingers through her hair, she dismisses the request. "The note guy probably won't even be back again tonight anyway. There was a two-day gap between the deliveries of the last two of them."

He corrects her, "Three days between them—it's been three days."

"Huh? Oh, yeah, right. Three days." She never got things like this wrong. "Yeah, so three days, so I'm probably alright with whatever this is," she says, trying to convince herself.

Ish looks at the note again. Luci suspects that his sudden rekindled interest in re-examining it is due to tension in the air.

There's a sound at the door, and Ish places himself between the unseen entrance and Luci's body. "Who's there?" he shouts in a booming voice noticeably lower than his normal speaking one.

"Special delivery," Macer announces as he and Royse enter from around the side of the kitchen. The big man follows a few steps behind, carrying a colossal roll of butcher-block paper on his shoulder with ease.

Luci's eyes freeze on the note in Ish's hand in front of her. She mouths the words to him, "Please, Ish."

There's a flash of torment in his eyes as he turns to her, but he slowly slides the message into his pocket.

Macer is full of life as he announces, "Sorry, there aren't any more flat sheets, so you'll just have to tear it off the roll." He gestures for Royse to set it down, and the bodyguard leans it against the sidewall of the kitchen pod. Macer turns in a semicircle, surveying the markings filling the sheets in the area. He concludes with a several sharp snaps of his fingers. "From the looks of things, it appears that we're just in time."

Luci cringes, noticing that Ish's hand is still in his pocket on the intruder's note. If he tells Macer or Royse, it could change everything. Her stomach tightens at the thought of being confined in a small, windowless room somewhere in the bowels of the city indefinitely.

"So, where are we?" Macer asks in an oddly peppy voice. "Are all of these writings an indicator that you two are getting close?"

Praying that Ish will remain quiet about the notes, Luci steps from behind him to control the conversation. Speaking quickly, she informs Macer, "Actually, we did have a break-through this morning." She takes a deep breath and exhales it as she says, "For the last few days, we've been searching for commonalities between the destroyed leap-skip intervals at their outermost termination points utilizing Bine Shadow originator STMO corridors of zero sum approximation of where—and more importantly *when*—we are here in Relicus City."

She's nervously rambling, but she can't stop herself. "Instead of allowing the data to inform us, we had been working to overlay a presupposed conclusion with the initial leap-skip originator for the XgM chronal point arrays. Of course, this results in a contaminated calculation bias and can't tell us anything, so now that we've realized what we were doing wrong, we can modulate the stream cores accurately to reveal the EMG ratios."

Everyone is silent.

Macer pivots to Royse and then slowly to Ish.

Finally, he looks back to Luci and shakes his head, confounded. With furrowed eyebrows, his tone is exasperated. "What?"

Luci moves over to the roll over paper and tears off a scrap. "Here, let me show you." She grabs the charcoal pencil from her pocket, presses the paper against the half-wall of the kitchen, and begins to scribble out random directions. When she's finished, Luci hands it to Royse and places the pencil behind her ear. "Here, follow these steps." She hopes the exercise will distract them long enough for her to get the note back from Ish.

Royse looks it over before shoving it back to her. "I can't read any of this. It's old-world script."

Ish hurries over to take the scrap. "I think I know what she's doing." He takes his place next to Macer. "Your Excellency, if you please . . ."

Macer nods but frowns. "Only if it will help make sense of what she said."

"I think you'll see that it will, sir," Ish says with a confidence that Luci hasn't seen him demonstrate in the chancellor's presence before. "So, Dr. Gaudiano has written directions for us to follow with these numbers and arrows. This says to take two steps forward and turn to the left, take one step backward, turn to the right twice, and finally three steps. If you do that, sir, you'll arrive at a specific location in the room."

"If you will, sir," Ish says, urging Macer. The older man begrudgingly follows in Ish's overly dramatic footsteps as he reads the commands a second time.

Royse whispers to Luci, "The chancellor doesn't have time for your silly games."

She ignores the rebuke, concentrating on Ish's pocket with the note in it. She says softly, "I need to ask you something."

"No more talk about seizures," Royse responds curtly.

She peels her eyes away from Ish. "No, nothing like that. It's a security question."

This gets his attention. "Humph. Really? What?"

Ish and Macer have completed the instructions and ended up on the other side of the room.

In a loud voice, Ish tells Macer, "So now, if we were to follow the same steps she's written from here, let's see what happens."

Maintaining a whisper, Luci asks Royse, "Is there a security log of who enters this guest house?"

When he ignores her, Luci presses, "Is there a log or not?"

Royse does his best to keep from moving his lips when he answers, showing his reluctance to the question. "Normally, there would be one, but it's been deactivated. Also, the cybo video log is disabled because the feeds from both would show *'a special guest'* from another interval was staying here, and that wouldn't be very smart."

Ish leads Macer around the area again. The chancellor looks even less happy about another round of it, but he plays along.

Luci fidgets, wondering if Ish will break and alert Macer to the break-ins. She continues in a soft voice, "Is there any way that someone could subvert the security protocols?"

Royse faces her with an incredulous scowl on his face as if she's insulted his mother. "Impossible. Only someone granted access can go through that doorway. Need I remind you of what happened when you tried to pass through to go to the Grange? We've programed in everyone's Viatorio who's been granted access to the guesthouse while you're here: me, the chancellor, Security Minister Cavazos, and your helper friend over there."

Something about the statement is off, but she can't puzzle it out right now. She's too busy making sure that Ish doesn't betray the revelation of the note.

Royse adds, "You're safe here and have nothing to be concerned about, Doctor."

It's so tempting for her to tell him of their secret if only just to see the smug expression on his face disappear at the news that someone has figured out a way to beat Cavazos's security measures.

"I get it now!" Macer exclaims across the room to her. "A different starting point leads to a different conclusion and vice versa. Why didn't you simply say that?" The politician's cheeriness has returned to him. "The mistake was made by assuming Relicus City would be Gicul's starting point. I count it as nothing more than the learning curve that you had to work through. This is actually great news. You two will be able to determine where Cyphor Gicul is hiding soon."

She answers cautiously, careful to deliver reasonable expectations. "We're fairly confident that we'll at least be able to tell where his been operating from, whether or not he's still—"

Macer cuts her off, "It'll take a while to work backward from the skip point junctures to likely origin points. I imagine it's similar to descending a ladder that's a million miles long one rung at a time, but now we know how to look for the enemy. You'll find him, I'm sure of it!" He snatches up Ish's hand and lifts it victoriously. "This is a great day for the future of Relicus City. With Gicul and his accomplices in *L'inversione* brought to justice, we will usher in a new age. There will be no more fear of terrorists, and we'll be able to rule unencumbered."

Before she knows it, Royse has mimicked Macer's gesture and has her hand lifted in his.

She manages to pull away. "Don't do that." She remembers him drugging her back in her interval in Baltimore.

Royse frowns. "What's your problem?"

"Just don't touch me, alright?" she says, backing a few steps away.

"Is there anything else that you two require?" Macer asks her, moving from Ish in her direction.

"No," she says. "The paper you brought is helpful."

Macer nods. "Okay." He turns to Royse. "Mr. Timmons, let's leave the doctor and her colleague to their work."

"Oh, there is *one* thing that I'd like," she says.

"Anything," Macer says, turning to face her and brandishing his politician's smile.

"I'd like to take a stroll outside. I'm beginning to feel a little cooped up in here. It'd do me good to get some of the sea air in my lungs and feel the sun on my skin even if only for a few minutes or so each day."

Macer looks over to Royse, who cracks his knuckles and shakes his head.

"Hmmm, that's a little different request than I expected." Macer folds his arms. "For obvious reasons, we can't jeopardize your safety, especially in light of your recent discovery." Pointing at Royse, he says, "I can allow it if he goes out with you and you conceal yourself so as not to be identified by any illegal long-distance drone cameras."

Luci breathes out an exasperated sigh. "The whole point is to relax a few minutes in private. I'd rather do it surrounded by a trio of cybos than to stroll with Royse here."

"That can be arranged," Royse bites back sarcastically.

Macer raises his hand to curtail the bickering. "We're all on the same side here. I'm sorry, Luci, but as a consolation, it appears that we're very close to ending all of this, and you'll be returned home. And thankfully, there have not been any more attacks for over a week."

"How can that be? I thought Minister Cavazos reported that the Poland 1952 juncture was destroyed."

Macer nods. "That's true. It was obliterated seven days ago on March 20th, two days before your arrival."

She tries to reconcile this new data. "So, what does that mean? Has Gicul and *L'inversione* stopped?"

"For the moment, it would appear so, though we don't know why."

A knot forms in her stomach. "Has he stopped because he knows that I'm here?"

Macer shrugs, and the air becomes thick with tension. Of all the faux expressions that Luci has seen this politician wear, the current one gives her a chill. There's a genuine look of dread in his eyes. He hesitates to speak, as if uttering the words aloud will conjure up an irrevocable consequence.

"What is it?" Luci probes, uncertain she truly wants the answer.

"Let's focus on the positive, shall we?" The politician's mask is back and firmly in place. "We should capitalize on your recent discovery, use that momentum to—"

"Why have the attacks stopped, Enos?" Luci cuts him off. "Please tell us what's going on here. Knowing may help us in some way."

Macer massages his temples, slowly informing her, "Pol Cavazos believes..." He sighs. "The security minister believes that the attacks may have stopped because..." He stops and looks to Royse, who offers a feeble shrug.

"Just tell us," Luci says, encouraging the older man. "We should know. We *need* to know."

Finally, he relents. "We believe that Gicul and *L'inversione* are preparing for a final assault against Relicus City."

Nothing more is said as the two men turn to exit through the doorway.

EIGHT

LUCI'S APPETITE IS GONE, BUT she knows her body requires food in order to perform the day's calculations. She returns to the food printer and makes her third request of the day from it. Maybe she'll get to finish this meal. "You want anything?" she asks Ish.

"A number fourteen, please," he answers, stretching the rubber WIBs around his fingers and clicking his Viatorio.

Luci sets the meal processer's program. "Hey, thanks for your help with that, showing the chancellor what we found. I've spent so much time working with you, I must have forgotten what it's like to try to speak with laypeople about limit theorems for Betti numbers of random simplicial complexes and Coboundary expanders."

When the printer chimes that the meal is complete, she removes the plate to make room for Ish's pending request. "And thanks, you know, for not telling Macer or Royse about the note."

She bites her knuckle in frustration. "Ugh, Luci G."

Ish stops his air-typing to look at her. "What is it?"

"I wanted to ask him about yesterday's attack from New Australia."

He shifts his weight on the barstool. "There's a pull basin post stating that there were four marauders from New Australia who were trying to gain access to the city's western side—three men and a woman eliminated by a squad of cybos with churkas.

She chews a mouthful of breakfast. "How many cybos are in a squad?"

"I don't know."

The machine behind her sounds out again. She slides the plate across the bar to Ish. Handing him an eating utensil, she says, "I don't get why the attackers wouldn't be captured and interrogated. That and Royse told me the other day that cybos are often 'made' from enemies of the city. Why would they shoot these people instead?"

"That's a good point. No one really knows much about the cybo process—government secrets and all, I guess."

She thinks about the creature stationed outside the door. "Your society has too many secrets if you ask me." Luci forces in another bite and wipes her mouth. "May I see the note again?"

Ish leans back in the barstool away from the counter. "Why? What for?"

She sighs. "Just let me see it, please."

His eyes narrow. "You're not going to destroy it, are you?"

She retrieves the original note about being lied to from her pocket and puts it on the counter between them. With hand on hip, she says, "I want to compare the penmanship."

"The what?" Ish asks.

Luci mumbles to herself, "Of course you don't have that word in your vocabulary. Why would you?" She turns the note around to face him and taps it with her index finger. "I want to look at them side by side, at the way the letter characters are formed to try and determine if we're dealing with more than one intruder."

Ish takes the most recent note from his pocket. He unfolds it but doesn't put it on the counter. "I want this back."

"Why?" Luci asks as she leans in and tugs slightly on it.

"Because I haven't decided what to do yet," he says, tightening his grip.

"Well, the notes were left for me, not you."

He frowns. "Just don't destroy them. We may need them later for something."

"I promise I won't," she says, tilting her head to the side. "Now give."

He yields, loosening his hold and she takes it from him.

"Thanks," she says. "I promise to give it back."

Luci turns the notes to face her. It doesn't take long to determine that both are by the same hand. As a gesture of good faith, she scoots them to Ish, who anxiously regards her. "I want you to keep these for us." She doesn't comment on the look of embarrassed relief on his face. Instead, she says, "The same person wrote both of these."

Ish holds them both up for examination. "How can you be so certain of this?"

The light shines through one of the paper scraps, and Luci sees something she missed before. "Wait . . . let me see that one again!"

Ish is taken aback by the force of the command but then hands them to her.

Luci's interest is only in the second note as she holds it above her head to the light. She reads the "ghost letters" shining through the paper stock and exclaims, "Strathmore!"

"What's a strathmore?" Ish asks, leaning in for a closer look.

"It's a paper company from my time . . . from my interval. They produce fine papers for letterheads, resumes, and whatnot." She comes from around the counter and angles the scrap above his head. "This has a watermark. See how, when the light shines through it, you can see the paper bond name?"

Ish squints and asks uncertainly, "So, what does *Strathmore* mean to us?"

She tilts her head back for a second look. "It means that we can narrow down that the intruder or intruders who's been leaving these are from the late twentieth century to the mid-twenty-first century."

She grabs him by the wrist. "Come over to the pull basin. I want to know of every skip point juncture in that range."

Ish follows, but he doesn't sit when they reach the sofa. "That's going to be around five to six dozen or so at the very least." He continues his objection, "Minister Cavazos granted me technical access to review leap skips and sitter archives, but even with these special permissions for the project, there is likely to be hundreds of activity files with . . . I don't know how many individual sitter personnel."

She presents the basin's wand and takes the sipper straw from his top pocket to hand it to him. "So, what if you only search the industrialized areas that would use fine linen paper? You can eliminate any odd junctures like the ones that appear in areas that are inhospitable like the middle of oceans or high in the mountains. Just stick with cities."

He frowns but fastens the straw to the apparatus. "Even if I cross-reference to get the name of every longchair sitter, it doesn't mean that we'll be able to find who is doing this."

"Why not?" she asks.

For the first time ever, there's an annoyance in his voice. "Because I doubt that Gicul and *L'inversione* report their leap skips and sitter activities to the technicians at the Spike command center."

"True," she says pensively as she studies him, "but consider this: If we do decide to turn the notes over, wouldn't it be better to have already come up with the names of a few suspects? Who knows? You may even get promoted up to work for the security minister after I'm gone."

He scoffs, "That's unlikely."

"Why do you say that?"

"I'm not the right shade."

Luci's surprised by the inference. "Racism? Is that even a thing here?"

"It is for Security Minister Cavazos," Ish answers.

Luci remembers the darkness of Bru's South Asian skin and mumbles the term "dob-dash" to herself. "I'll begin work right now on transposing the STMO corridors and chronal points. You can do the variable origins after looking up the possible skip point junctures of where the paper could have come from."

"We're not security detectives, Luci," he protests.

She dismisses his reluctance. "I'm faster at doing rote calculations anyway." She gestures for him sit and partake of the bubbling Jardon before them. "It's the least you can do since you won't spend the night here to catch whoever this is."

He sighs. "I'd stay, but I . . . I'm working on something," he says, breaking eye contact.

"Working on what?"

He sits. "It's not DPM related, just a thing I'm doing. I'm working on a thing for somebody, something for a . . . friend."

"Okay, fine. But what is it?"

Ish shakes his head as he dips the wand into the liquid of the large round ceramic receptacle. "I can't really talk about it, not yet. Just trust me. I'll do your research."

Though she's convinced him to search out the Strathmore paper mystery, the accomplishment is hollow when put against the fact that he is deliberately withholding something from her. She crosses her arms and looks at him coolly. "Fine. Okay, I'll go ahead and get started then."

He's already typing on his unseen keyboard in the air as she turns to go to the galley. Luci constructs a makeshift clipboard out of a food plate wrapped in a swath of butcher-block paper and begins to work.

A FEW MINUTES LATER, SHE'S interrupted by Ish mumbling something. Luci lowers her homemade pad and speaks across the room. "What did you say?"

The question breaks his concentration. "Huh? Oh, what? I was just speaking to myself."

She crosses the area to him. "About what?"

He lowers his sip tube. "Well, like I said, the paper could have come from many different junctures as the company was in existence for 175 years—until *Hi No Kawa*, of course."

"So, what is it?" Luci probes. "What did you discover then?"

"Well, unrelated to all of that, I came across the skip point junctures during your lifetime before and after DPM."

"Yeah, and?" Luci asks, trying not to prod him too hard.

"There's one when you were three and a half months old in Macau on the south coast of China that has a duration of fourteen and a half hours. There's another when you're nineteen, but that's only open for forty-eight seconds in the Pacific Ocean. We know of the corridor that you went through to get here, the interval in a place called Baltimore in the northern hemisphere of America. That one stays open for two hours, twenty-three minutes, and thirty-three seconds. And then there's the anomaly of the twin that the chancellor mentioned. That one occurs in East Timor in Southeast Asia that has a duration of seventeen minutes, thirty-eight seconds."

"Yeah, yeah, so?" The mention of this skip point juncture excites her, and she rubs the folded ticket and documentation that she's carried in her pocket for days. "Go on. Macer mentioned there was one in Luxembourg two years before my lecture. He claims that he went there to fund the meeting."

Ish nods. "Yeah, that checks out. The interval is only open for ten hours, six minutes, and fifty-one seconds. I didn't mention it because he was the only sitter, and we know the notes aren't coming from him."

"So, what is remarkable about all of this that made you perk up?"

Ish clicks his Viatorio. "You know how you were brought here the first time when you are forty-five years of age?"

"Yes, I was told that I develop DPM four years before I was brought here. The first deployment of a physical DPM object isn't—or rather *wasn't*—until 2063."

"Right," Ish says. "To conceal your presence here, the chancellor would never have you listed on the sitter manifest. So, while I can't prove it, the closest one would be an opening that happens in a place called 2045 New Mexico, again in the northern region of what was America."

"You mean *North* America."

"Huh?" Ish responds. "Oh yeah, North America. Anyway, the skip point juncture remains open for six hours, thirteen minutes, and fifty-one seconds."

"Okay," Luci says, running her fingers through her hair. "I don't get it. Why is that a big deal?"

"Two sitters—a man and a woman—definitely came back to Relicus City though the New Mexico skip point juncture in tandem as the record shows." Ish wiggles the WIBs on his fingers, manipulating some unseen data hovering in the space between them. "What's interesting, as best as I can tell here, is that the man and woman didn't skip from Relicus City to 2045 New Mexico. They only returned through it."

He pinches his chin. "They both went from Relicus to 2044 Thuringia, Germany, a duration opening of seventeen hours, thirty-two minutes, and eight seconds."

Luci still struggles to draw a conclusion from all of this. "I want to clarify what you're saying here. Is it kind of like how I came to Relicus City through the portal thing in Boston, but I'll return through the skip point juncture in East Timor?"

"Yes, except the two sitters came over to the skip point juncture in Thuringia, Germany 5,952 hours and 12 minutes, 42 seconds before the first moment that they could bring you back—the 45-year-old you—through the New Mexico interval to Relicus City."

"So, 5,952 hours, 12 minutes?" She does the math. "That's two hundred and forty-eight days. They were there for nearly eight and half months? Is that common for sitters to remain in an interval for that long other than those serving at the Grange?"

"No, it's not," Ish answers. "And that's what caught my attention."

Luci lets this sink in. "That's plenty of time to obtain Strathmore paper. Who were they and what were they doing?"

"I assume they were there to bring you—the *older* you—back to Relicus City. The woman is someone called Shar Ryson."

"I know her. Shar came with Macer and Royse to get me from Baltimore. I think she told me that she was involved the first time too. Was Royse the other one with her?"

Ish extends his hands before his chest and activates the WIBs. He types for a few seconds before looking up at her. "No, it wasn't Royse Timmons. It was someone by the name of Noah Beaumont who did the leap skips with her."

<u>NINE</u>

March 28, 2191
Relicus City
[6.217012/127.792969/4.603.388.828/9452:24:19]

RELIKUS SITI

MΛȻ 28, 2191

AFTER A LONG DAY OF recalculating and transposing the work that they've labored over for the past three days, Luci retires to her bed. She dreams of developing formalisms with Ish and constructing thresholds for integer homology in random d-complexes.

In the wee hours of the morning, her imaginings transform into things more abstract and surreal in nature, and she dreams of a family car ride on a deserted two-lane highway off a coastline somewhere. Who's driving is unclear, since her vantage point is from the backseat. She gazes out the side window at the surf hungrily lapping the shore far below the cliff's edge. The overstuffed vinyl seat is a comfy perch for her. She gently sways with the motion of the vehicle as it maneuvers along the serpentine asphalt and ascends the mountain. Luci presses her face against the window's cool glass as the car engine purrs a mechanized hum of contentment.

Then, without warning, she experiences a sense of weightlessness. The piercing shriek of her mother calling out her name shoots through Luci like lightning. Luci also screams from the backseat, but her tormented yell can't be heard over the anguish of her mother's wail.

The impact comes with an impossible darkness. The only sound is Luci's racing heartbeat. This is the drumbeat of becoming an orphan, a cadence that she is all too familiar with.

She's drowning again, sinking ever downward into darkness and the abyss.

Luci springs up to a sitting position in bed. She's covered in sweat, hyperventilating in the dark; it feels like a jackhammer is tap-dancing on her skull. After self-soothing with math equations which contain some variant of Luci's 2012 number, she rises from the bed in her shirt and panties. She heads downstairs for a cup of water to shake off the nightmare and get some relief from the Jardon migraine.

The sensor mechanisms must be malfunctioning, because she gropes her way to the stair rail without any of the low lighting coming on as it usually does. A soft rain taps on the outer glass dome far above her head as if to explain why the skylight doesn't offer any moonlight from above.

Luci yawns as she begins her descent, gripping the cool metal railing in the dark. Her free hand rubs the sleep from her eyes. She hesitates to squint in the blackness. At first, she thinks the glow is from the concierge bot, but the movement of the narrow beam below is too erratic. Someone's in here with a flashlight, and it's not Ish.

Though every nerve in Luci's body comes alive, she remains completely still. Her sense of flight or fight kicks in, demanding that she escape to the bedroom, but the logical part of her brain insists that there's no way out of that dead end, and the only option is downward. She swallows the knot in her throat and suppresses the urge to call out to the intruder. Her curiosity demands that she investigate. Extending her bare foot to the next step, she tries to ignore her body's quaking. The soft scraping of her foot on the step should be relatively noiseless, but to her ears, it sounds like it's been amplified a thousand times. She freezes in place again.

The beam of light moves along, bouncing on the floor with each step the intruder takes toward the exit of the guesthouse. The notion that he's getting away forces Luci into desperate action, and now she takes the stairs two at a time.

Before she knows it, she reaches the bottom and stumbles forward. The flashlight beam shifts from the floor to the palm reader near the door. A soft pink glows around the silhouette of the intruder's hand against the pad of the reader.

The door slides open with a swoosh due to the change in air pressure. The light from the corridor pours in, displaying the cybo on duty on the other side. The intruder is short and dressed in a dark, non-reflective hooded jumpsuit of some sort. The figure steps through the door and turns to face into the area.

Luci scrambles toward the opening. Before she can get a good look at the intruder's face, the figure reaches into the hood, no doubt activating their Viatorio.

The door zips shut the same instant the lights in the lower level reactivate. Even though the illumination is set to a low level, the sudden change forces Luci to wince as her eyes adjust.

Luci rushes the door. "Come back!" she shouts, pounding it with her fists. "It's okay, come back here!" She leans her ear to the cold metal while attempting to slow her breathing to listen for any movement outside. "Come back, you bastard!" she yells, pressing her face against the door. She realizes the futility of doing this—the door is at least eight to nine inches of metal.

She's too late. It's over.

Luci is completely helpless with no Viatorio to alert anyone to what just happened. She imagines Ish a few miles away asleep in his bed. It will be hours before he arrives and she's able to relay any of this to him. Even if Macer is home in the structure adjacent to this one, there's no way for her to signal to him or Royse to come over. In all her life, she's only felt this trapped once before.

FOR THE SECOND TIME THIS morning, she begins to self-soothe with math, but this time, she stops short of reaching her special number of 2012. "The note," she says aloud, rushing to the dining area. Just as the day before, there's a folded sheet of paper waiting for her. Luci snatches it up and takes a cleansing breath on her way to the sink.

DON'T TRUST MΛSꓤ
WƗV GOT Δ PLAN Tꓴ BRΔK ꓴ FRƗ

A confusing mix of exhilaration and trepidation floods her heart as she fills her cup from the faucet. Sipping the cool water on the way to the couch around the pull basin, she contemplates how close she and Ish are to achieving a DPM solution. The note is right that Macer shouldn't be trusted; even so, she has a ticket from him to go to East Timor tucked under her mattress—a ticket home, a ticket back to her gimpy dog Marcus H., back to her cosmetics, back to steaming cups of coffee and real food, a ticket back to her life away from this madness. Everything will be as it was before, except she will return barren. Despite this, what can this note-leaver guy offer that can compare with any of that?

There's an odd, unrecognizable feeling as she acknowledges that either way, she doesn't have much more time with Ish. Though they've only worked together for a few days, it's difficult to imagine never seeing him again. The notion feels like a heavy stone in her stomach. Out of everyone she's collaborated with over the years, he's the only one who can keep up with her talent and skill. There was that, but then there was something else, something so much more. She shakes her head to prevent being overtaken by sentimentality. This works for the most part, but she's left picturing her partner's unassuming grin.

She sighs. Ish was right all along. She should've turned over the first two notes, but the notion of involving Pol Cavazos irks her. She could live without him prancing and sniff-ing around. She contemplates telling Royse and determines that a better alternative, but how can she contact him without a Viatorio?

She bites her lip, knowing that she and Ish will reach a DPM conclusion within the next few days and all of this "liv-ing in the future" will finally be over for her.

"Papa always said that the future isn't what it used to be." She yawns, the nostalgia of saying his words aloud to herself is comforting. "Little did he know how right he was . . . little did he know. The future is not what—"

Excited, she drops the cup to the floor and barely notices the puddle it makes. "Sweet God in Heaven, Cyphor was never hiding from us in the past—he's in the future! He's got to be there!" Her head darts from left to right, taking in the tapes-try of numbers and calculations plastered on the curved glass walls. In her haste to grab something to write with, she bumps the concierge bot floating over to clean up the spilled water. "Move!" she shouts, though it's no good without a connected Viatorio.

She tears off a sheet from the paper roll and snatches up her pencil. She can't write fast enough.

MANY HOURS PASS, AND THE storm outside picks up in its intensity. Luci hardly notices the dome enclosing her being pelted by sheets of rain.

"Uh, Luci?" Ish calls to her.

She looks up from her writing. "Oh, hey. You startled me."

He approaches, carrying an armful of equipment. "Where are your pants?"

For the first time since waking up from her nightmare and the encounter with the intruder, she is aware of her physical appearance. She never got dressed. Luci frantically pulls the roll of paper to conceal her bottom half. She shifts to adjust it to cover the long scar running down her leg. With her other hand, she attempts to arrange her matted hair, but to no avail. "Sorry," she begins, "I kind of lost track of time."

Ish lowers parts of unrecognizable equipment components gently to the couch. "How long have you been working?"

She sighs and answers in a matter-of-fact tone. "Um, since about 3:00."

He looks around the room cluttered with new sheets of figures strewn about. "It looks like a whirlwind in here. A late-night epiphany? Did you figure out the mystery of porous number compounds?"

"No," she begins. "Well, *no* to the limber number thing, but *yes* to the late-night epiphany question . . . well, sort of."

Luci quickly relays the pre-dawn events to him: spotting the intruder, the latest message, and the concept that Gicul may be operating from a skip point juncture in a future beyond Relicus City instead of one located in the past.

Patiently and silently, Ish listens to it all. When she's done, he says, "I'm sorry, I should've stayed like you wanted. We've got to alert someone about these break-ins. We can't go on like this."

Luci begins to stand until she remembers her bottom half is wrapped in butcher-block paper. "Yeah, we'll do that later, alright? You're missing the bigger picture here—Cyphor Gicul is hiding in the future. I'm certain of it. Can you sip the Jardon to get a list of skip point junctures in the future?"

His solemn expression changes to wide-eyed curiosity. "How far into the future?"

Luci stands up, and the tan paper around her makes a crinkling sound. "I don't know. Let's start within a century or so and see where that gets us. I've almost completed inverting everything that we did yesterday, turning the metaphorical 'spokes' from pointing inward to extending outward to future date corridors. Just hold off for a little longer about notifying anyone about the intruder and the notes. We're so close, I can feel it. Just a little more time to finally solve all of this, and then we can tell Macer everything about what's been going on around here." Before he can argue, she adds, "I'll take responsibility for everything so you won't get in trouble, I promise."

"I'm not worried about any of that. I'm worried about *you*."

"I'm fine. I'm certain they're not coming here to harm me or they already would have, and they're definitely not going to try anything while you're here with me, so we have time to figure out the future skip points today, alright?"

He pauses to scan the sheet. With raised eyebrows, he asks, "You really did all this in five hours this morning?"

She's relieved the conversation has shifted back to the work. "What can I say? I was in the zone. Anyway, I still have a few XgM arrays to convert, but you getting that list will allow us to define viable termination points."

He nods. "Yeah, alright. I get where you're going."

She smiles and carefully tears the paper she's connected to from the roll in such a way to keep her bottom half concealed. Taking small, constricted steps to the stairs, she announces, "No more of this 'pin-the-tail-on-the-donkey' shit."

Before he can ask the meaning of the colloquialism from her time, Luci turns back to him and says, "I mean, we know what we're looking for, and more importantly, how to find it. I'm going to get dressed and clean up while you sip."

TEN

EAGER TO RETURN TO HER work, Luci bathes in less time than she ever has in her life. It's more of a quick rinse than a shower. She looks forward to taking a long, steamy bath when she returns to her interval, which should be soon by her estimation now that they'll be searching in the future instead of the past.

She quickly dresses and heads downstairs and is surprised that Ish isn't at the pull basin doing a sip. "What's wrong?" she asks.

He lowers the large sheet of her numbers that he's been reviewing. "Oh, nothing's wrong. It just that the information is restricted."

"You're kidding, right?"

"No, I 'm not. I guess it's because it's illegal to leap skip to a forward juncture."

Luci continues to brush through her damp hair as she takes her spot on the sofa. "Yeah, why is that a thing anyway, illegal to go forward? I was brought forward."

Ish shrugs. "It's always been that way with us in Relicus City." He slides the sheet to her. "I think I've got this one ready."

His penmanship is improving. His numbers are at least uniform in size now, even if there's a slight tilt to them. Luci nods. "Yeah, these are good. Only two more to go."

"I contacted Security Minister Cavazos to send us information about the future skip point junctures," Ish says.

Her eyebrows raise, but she keeps her protest to herself. "He sounded like he needed to get approval."

"Approval?" she scoffs, picking up one of the plastic components. It looks like an oversized TV remote from when she was a child. "Approval from whom?"

"Probably Chancellor Macer, I guess."

Luci shakes her head. "Even in the future, bureaucracy survives." She picks up another component, this one shaped like a small p-trap kit for a sink. Holding the two items up, she asks, "What is all this stuff?"

Ish looks down at the floor. "It's just something that I was going to show you."

"Okay . . ." Luci begins curiously as she slides closer, thrusting the two parts at him. "So show me."

Ish takes the pieces, placing them on the couch between them. "Later would be better."

She laughs, cocking her head back. "You should know me well enough to know that I'm too curious of a person to accept that." She grabs the parts and extends them again playfully. She wiggles them at him. "Don't be shy. Just show me." She remembers something and pulls the pieces in to her chest. "Wait, is this the reason you didn't stay here last night?" Before he can respond, she asks, "Is this the special project that you've been working on? Am I the *friend* that you were doing the *thing* for that you were so guarded about yesterday?"

His arms cross, and he looks as if he wishes he could turn invisible.

Smiling, Luci prods, "Well?"

His answer is as soft as it can be while being audible. "Maybe."

She's relieved that the secret person wasn't another woman but her. She finds it oddly curious just how much of a relief this news is.

Ish finally makes eye contact. "I had an idea for something, but it seems silly now. Maybe I can show you some other time."

"Absolutely not," she says firmly, gathering the three remaining components to hand to him. "I've been stuck under house arrest for five days now without any internet, my phone, coffee, TV, gym, crowds to people watch . . . nothing but DPM. Whatever this is or does is a welcome distraction. If you deprive me of this, I swear I'll go crazy. So set this up or whatever you've got to do here. You said that we have to wait until Cavazos transmits the data to your Viatorio anyway." She pushes up from the sofa and heads for some paper. "I'll work on the two remaining inversions while you assemble whatever this is."

Ish doesn't move.

"Are you going to do it or not?" Luci asks, feeling a twinge of regret at how aggressive she sounds. "Please?"

Even from across the room, she can tell he's perturbed. He makes a flicking gesture. "I'm doing it. I'm summoning the concierge is all."

Luci feigns interest in working out the final equations of this phase, but in truth, she keeps stealing peeks at what he's doing to the bot.

She realizes that for the first time in as long as she can remember, the lure of mathematics has taken second place to something else. She smiles and gnaws the side of her pencil, wondering where the Luci G. that she knows went off to.

She finishes before Ish and furtively sits on the couch on the opposite side of the pull basin.

"I can feel you watching me," he says without looking up from fastening one of the components to the side of the concierge bot.

"I'm not watching you," Luci protests and makes a point of stretching. "I'm just taking a quick nap. Let me know when you're ready." She demonstrates with an overdramatic yawn to sell her fib. Through the slit of her right eye, she still watches, but what he's working on remains a mystery.

"I'VE GOT IT READY," ISH says, nudging her awake a few minutes later.

"How long was I out?" she asks, realizing her hair has dried. She must've been more tired than she thought.

"Not too long," Ish answers. "It's ready if you still want to see it."

Luci sits up and does a stretch of her arms that would make any cat from her time interval envious. "If I still want to see it? Of course I do."

"Come around here," Ish instructs, motioning to behind the circular sofas. "We'll need some room."

Luci complies. After another yawn, she asks, "So what is it?"

Ish bends to the floating bot that's now "wearing" the different components he brought. He presses a button as he announces, "Dr. Gaudiano, would you do dance with me?"

She doesn't correct his use of the phrase as the music begins to play somewhere from within the hovering robot. Answering with a nod and a smile, she clasps her hand in his and leans in. "Of course I would."

A majestic intro with an exuberant brass section, snapping snare drums, and high-pitched flutes echo throughout the room. She laughs but doesn't pull away. "This is a marching band. It's not—"

The wounded look on his face stops her from telling him that the tune isn't conducive to slow dancing. They move stiffly to a driving beat written for high stepping marchers. Luci concentrates to block out the music as she manipulates the stilted body of her dance partner. After three minutes and fifteen seconds, the recording repeats.

She cautiously asks, "Do you have . . . is there anything else, other music, or just this recording?"

Even though the question is presented delicately, Ish's face tells all—he's mortified. "I'm sorry, are the musics inappropriate? Did I choose a combi theme?"

"Combi?"

He releases her, quickly dropping to one knee to stop the bot from playing. "Combi . . . a copulation musics theme or something."

She lowers to his level to look into his eyes. "Oh no, it's nothing like that. It's a very good song, it's just that it's written for a bunch of people to sort of *dance* on a football field." She knows she'll never be able to accurately explain this, so she tries to humor him. "What's it called . . . the song?"

His mouth is a straight line. "It's called 'Army of the Nile.' It's from pre-*Hi no Kawa*, 1941. My research on this file says it was performed by the Regimental Band of the Coldstream Guards." His face bears a confused expression. "I thought you'd like it. It was difficult to get from the archives."

"Regimental Band, huh?" She takes his hand, and by standing, brings him upright again. "I like it very much, but for dancing—*slow* dancing—it's just a little too formal for my taste."

"What do you mean?"

"Let me show you." She returns his hand on her back shoulder and begins to sway with him as she sings: "*Love is real, real is love . . . Love is feeling, feeling love . . . Love is wanting to be loved.*"

Feeling some of the tension leave his body, Luci gently presses her head against his chest. "*Love is touch, touch is love . . . Love is reaching, reaching love . . . Love is asking to be loved.*"

After this verse, she arches her neck back to look into his hazel eyes. "Better, right?"

"Your . . . your voice is beautiful," Ish says in astonishment.

She shrugs and dismisses the comment. "It's a song from a great writer of the twentieth century named John Lennon. The song is called '*Love*'."

It's raining harder now, pounding on the pinnacle of the dome roof above their heads.

"Do it again," Ish requests. "Sing *Love*, please."

"There's another verse and bridge," she says, feeling his restrained strength.

As Luci finishes the song, she slows the motion of their steps until they're standing still, holding each other in silence. "See, a much better song to dance to than one intended to be played by a high school marching band." She qualifies her words, "But I think what you did was very sweet, and I appreciate the thought. Thank you, Ish."

Luci leans in to give him a peck on the cheek, but Ish pulls away. "Sorry," she says with embarrassment.

"No, don't apologize," Ish says. "I just wasn't ready is all."

She leans in for the peck for a second time, but he shifts, positioning himself to engage her lips. The moment is both electric and terrifying. She feels his body tense up against hers and wonders if he can feel her heart racing. The rational part of her mind rises up with the explanation that this illogical response must be due to sleep deprivation. No other reasonable answer exists.

But it feels so good, so warm, despite the nonsense of it all. She feels whole in a way that she's never experienced with her ex-fiancé, Michael.

The kiss tapers off, and Luci's eyelids slowly open to Ish's brilliant hazel eyes. She gently caresses the side of his face. "You may not know much about dancing and music, but you sure know how to kiss."

He replies with a soft press of his lips against her open palm. "I think I'd like to stay here tonight, if that's alright with you." He sheepishly adds, "You know, in case the intruders come back."

"Huh? Oh yeah, alright. In case the note guy returns, right." She'd forgotten about her early morning mystery correspondent.

She presses the side of her face back against his chest. With her eyes closed, she concentrates on the steady strength of his heartbeat. Luci chuckles and looks back up to him. "I just realized that *Army of the Nile* is going to be our song."

"Our song?" Ish says with a quizzical expression. "I don't know what that means."

"I know you don't," she replies, locking onto his open mouth with abandon. It's even more exhilarating than the other kiss, and a delicious shiver runs through her body.

"I seriously don't think you'll find Cyphor Gicul in your assistant's mouth, Miss Gaudiano," a nasal voice says from across the room.

Both Luci and Ish snap apart like a spring-loaded trap.

Cavazos's words ooze with sarcasm as he toddles toward them. "Hopefully you're celebrating because you've got it all figured out. Am I right?"

Ish's dark skin hides his blush, but Luci feels her cheeks burning up.

Two cybos dripping with rainwater flank the heavyset man on his left and right, their putrid stench coming off in waves.

"So, have you figured anything out or not?" Cavazos asks, making his way to the sofa to sit.

Luci's heart sinks a little as Ish takes a couple of steps away from her in submissive retreat. She studies the two cybos that have halted at the edge of the couch behind Cavazos, specifically their churkas at the ready. "Hey, I don't want them in here," she grumbles, still self-conscious about being caught with Ish.

"Need I remind you that you are a visitor . . . a visitor to *my* city?" the hefty man responds snidely. "You really don't have a say in the matter."

Ish crosses his arms as he addresses him, "Sir, I can—"

Cavazos raises an eyebrow in mockery. "Mr. Moyta, you wouldn't be stretching your work release out here, would you now?" He asks in a way so lecherous that it sickens Luci. He adds with sickening delight, "I'm sure it would be considered a crime if it were to be discovered that you're lengthening the project to have combi with our distinguished guest. Is that what you're doing here, boy?"

He stammers, but before he can respond, Luci sharply says, "You're a pervert."

Seemingly amused, Cavazos gives her a wink. "More than you can imagine, my dear Miss Gaudiano." Waving a plump hand in the air indicating for them to return to business, he says, "All kidding aside, you've been working on this for almost a week. Are you any closer to stopping these terrorists than when you first began?"

Ish studies his own shoes, but Luci looks over to the lethargic beast of a man plopped down on the sofa. "We believe . . ." she begins but stops short, knowing that all they have is conjecture that Gicul is hiding in the future, no hard evidence to support the theory.

"Yes?" Cavazos responds, irritated by her pause. "You believe *what*?"

Ish peeks up at her, catching her eye. She shakes her head. "We . . . we don't know. We need a little more time. We need the coordinates to the future skip junctures that Ish asked you for this morning."

"Yes, that's partly why I'm here. The chancellor approved the request but restricted the transmission to a one-to-one relay."

Luci tilts her head at the new term.

"It requires us to do it in person," Cavazos explains, "not a broadcast over the Viatorio or Basin networks."

"So a closed-circuit type thing?" she asks.

"Something like that." He clicks his Viatorio and addresses Ish. "The data file will only be viewable to you for a little over an hour after you launch the packet, after which it will re-encrypt and 'evaporate' from your V-posit viewer, so don't waste time once you open it." He snidely adds, "I'd rather not have to come back here again. In fact, you're lucky that I was already headed here this morning."

"Headed here for what?" Luci asks, folding her arms against her chest.

Cavazos grunts as he makes the effort to move his heavy frame to stand erect. "We're going on a little trip." Vertical now, he fidgets with the small, flat onyx rectangle dangling around his neck. "You're coming with me."

She wanted a break from being sequestered in the guesthouse, but not like this . . . not with this man. Ish's eyes are as wide as hers. Looking back at Cavazos, she protests, "No, we need to stay here. We need to sort the data out. You said we only have an hour before it—"

"Not the two of you," he says, shaking his head while snapping on a set of WIBs on his fingers. "He stays, just you."

This was exactly what she wanted to avoid by keeping the notes secret. Now she and Ish are to be separated. "Ish, you've got to contact Macer or Royse and tell them that—"

"You'll do nothing of the sort," Cavazos interrupts, his pinkish face turning red.

"You can't do this," Luci says. "We need to stay together."

"Why? So you can finish doing what I walked in on?" His voice raises. "Would you have me and my cybos wait outside in the corridor for fifteen minutes for the two of you to complete that 'task'?" He shoots a look over to Ish. "I'm a generous person. Perhaps I'll give you twenty-five minutes with her. What do you say to that?"

"That's uncalled for, sir," Ish answers through gritted teeth.

His assertiveness surprises Luci. From the day they first met, he's always recoiled in the presence of his superiors. He has to know how dangerous standing up to him is.

Before she can stop him, Cavazos retaliates in a huff, "Uncalled for, huh? I don't know DPM like the two of you do, but I don't think that was it."

"Look, that doesn't matter right now!" Luci shouts. "What's important is that we need to get started on that new data— both of us together. You can't just come in here and separate us on a whim."

"Oh, but you're wrong. I can do anything I please. *Anything.*"

"You can't," she objects.

Cavazos moves uncomfortably close to her. She can feel the heat of his sour breath as he says, "In the brief time that I've known you, I've gotten a glimpse into your interval's behavior, your stubbornness, your tempestuousness always ready to fight first, to argue and bicker, resist any semblance of decorum. Absolutely no respect for leadership." He extends his fingers to touch her hair, but she bats him away. He shrugs with indifference. "You act like a child, Miss Gaudiano, a spoiled child who hasn't gotten her way. If I didn't know any better, I might think that you—"

"Stop it!" Ish shouts, startling both Luci and the man. "Minister Cavazos, please . . ."

Luci's heart skips a beat, witnessing this side of him. She doesn't know if it's anger or fear or a mixture of both that is making Ish's body shakes as he says, "Luci isn't like that, and I demand that you stop verbally attacking her."

An incredulous look forms on Cavazos's flabby face. It's turning redder by the second. "You demand? You dare to demand something . . . demand something of *me*?" Cavazos lifts his hand high, preparing to strike him.

"Stop it!" Luci screams with such a loud shrill that it makes her throat raw. "If you hit him, I will never finish the project for you . . . *ever!*"

Cavazos freezes in place, contemplating his next move.

"I swear it," Luci says defiantly, moving to put her arm around Ish's waist to lessen his shaking. "I swear it on my parent's graves that I won't do a single thing." Hot tears of anger stream across her cheeks. "You see, the dirty little secret of all of this DPM stuff is that you and Macer *have* to send me back, because if you don't, this place will never exist."

Cavazos reluctantly lowers his arm but continues staring daggers into Ish.

"That's more like it," Luci says, pointing her finger in his face. "So, I'm the one in control here . . . doing you all a favor."

Cavazos speaks with words laced with venom. "You overestimate yourself and your position here, Miss Gaudiano. It's a dangerous game that you've begun this day."

"It's not a game!" she shouts, moving to place herself between the two men. "So leave us alone to work on the new skip junctures."

He shakes his head, jowls flapping loosely for emphasis. "No, you're coming with me, and you're coming with me now." A tap on the onyx rectangle activates the cybos, and they both take two steps forward. More rainwater leaks from the folds in their plastic coverings, collecting in tiny puddles on the floor.

Luci swallows her Italian pride and suspends her loathing of this man to attempt another tactic—a softer approach. "Minister Cavazos, please." With upturned palms extended out to him, she pleads, "We're close . . . so close. I can feel it. Just give us another twenty-four hours with the skip point information, and then we can go see the chancellor."

"Chancellor?" he scoffs, pressing his Viatorio. "I never said we were going to see Chancellor Macer. No, Miss Gaudiano, I'm taking you to see someone else."

PORT III

(Part III)

ONE

March 28, 2191
Relicus City
[6.217012/127.792969/4.603.388.828/9461:37:31]

RELIKUS SITI
MΛ₵ 28, 2191

"I LIKED WHAT YOU HAD on before better," Cavazos says, breaking the long minutes of silence with a sickening smirk.

Luci ignores the remark, gazing out the window of the automated boat. She wonders how she ever complained about not getting time away from Macer's guesthouse. *Careful what you wish for, Luci G.*

The small vessel climbs and falls on the ocean waves. The choppy motion forces her to clutch the handrail of her seat. It's the fourth time in the few minutes since they left the guesthouse that she's had to do this to prevent falling face-first onto the floor. She wonders if Cavazos purposefully plotted this course over turbulent waters to make her seasick. Luci silently vows that if she *is* to vomit, she'll attempt to do it on her would-be captor.

"What's going to happen to Ish after he transcribes the data you gave him?"

"Your little boyfriend will be fine," Cavazos says with indifference. "I had a good chat with him while you were changing upstairs. He knows what's expected of him and will comply."

"So he'll remain on the DPM project with me, right?"

Cavazos examines his cuticles. "The project isn't finished yet, right?" He looks Luci over from the seat opposite hers. "Don't worry, his participation is still of value to us. Your Mr.

Moyta will still be at the chancellor's guest home when we return."

She nods, exhaling a slight breath of relief.

The slick, gaudy red décor of the interior of the small six-seater vessel makes Luci wonder if Cavazos suffers from color-blindness of if it's simply a case of bad taste. She gazes back out the forward cabin windows at the beads of rain trickling down the thick glass. Three cybos stand at attention on the other side of the window facing outward in the direction the speedboat is going. The deluge of pounding rain and the nauseating bobbing up and down of the craft doesn't affect their stance.

"Where are you taking me?"

A Cheshire-cat smile forms on Cavazos's face. "Let's just say that we're headed to a private party with an old friend."

The term *"private party"* unnerves her, given his predatory nature. "If you dare lay a hand on me, I swear that—"

"Settle down," Cavazos cuts her off. "No time for any of that. We're headed to the longchairs at the Spike." He clicks his tongue on the roof of his mouth, saying to himself, "So dramatic, this one."

Luci's relieved by the answer, but this raises more questions. "The Spike? Why don't you have a drobine like the chancellor?"

He shifts his weight, placing his plump, meaty hands behind his head. "I have two drobines, in fact," he says proudly, "but I don't care for heights. Is it so odd that I travel by boat? I mean, we *do* live on the ocean, don't we? Plus, this doesn't require a pilot." He points to his Viatorio. "The craft is completely automatic, going off of commands from here."

Luci asks, "You're not afraid of someone commandeering the boat's navigation with a Viatorio or something and hijacking it? I mean, it's seems like someone could just take command of it somehow."

He leans forward. "Let me be clear. I'm the one in command. I am the one who takes over, not the other way around."

Luci shrugs, sensing an opportunity to probe his loyalties. "I thought that Chancellor Macer was in command."

He scowls, waving a dismissive hand. "You know that's not what I mean."

She remembers eavesdropping on Macer's side of the argument with Cavazos the night she ingested the Jardon in his office. "Does he even know that I'm with you ... that I'm not in the guesthouse working on DPM?"

Judging by his sour expression, the question irritates him. "You'll be back before he even knows about it. Plus, it will give Moyta time to transfer the data you asked for to paper without being *distracted* by you."

She disregards the insinuation. "You said we're seeing an old friend?"

Cavazos sits back and crosses his arms. "Yes."

"Someone I know?" Luci asks.

Eyebrows rising, he pauses before answering. "Yes, in a manner of speaking, you could say that you know him."

Another tumultuous break in the waves lifts the vessel and slams it down with a smack. Luci's grip white-knuckles the rail. "Flying is scarier to you than all this?" she protests after a gasp. "We would have already been halfway there by now if we'd flown."

A vindictive laugh bellows from Cavazos's Buddha-like belly. "We'll be there soon enough, dearie, soon enough. Plus, I like watching you bounce."

"That's such a pervy thing to say!" she exclaims, feeling dirty while keenly aware that she's trapped in a boat with this man far away from Ish or anyone else who could help if he decided to make a move. The water's too rough outside if she dove overboard, and she's got a thing about swimming anyway. She's desperate to steer the conversation and his thoughts as far from her body as she can. "You said we're going to the longchairs at the Spike?"

"Yes, that's right," he answers, sounding bored with her question.

"Do you think it best to skip somewhere right now while there's the possibility that Gicul and his crew could destroy the juncture portal and trap us there? We wouldn't be able to get back home." Two thoughts collide in her brain: the unappealing concept of being trapped *anywhere* with this misogynist oaf and how she just referred to Relicus City as "*home.*"

"I know you think you're smart," Cavazos says with a scoff as he repositions himself on the red faux-leather seat. "And I'll admit, in some areas, you are very intelligent and have proven yourself to be so, but there's plenty that you still don't know about Relicus City—*my* city."

"Understatement of the year," she mumbles under her breath, confident that he can't hear over the storm overhead. "Then enlighten me. How do you propose that we ensure that we don't end up like the five longchair sitters that Macer said are stuck in Poland 1952?"

"Because we're not going to a skip point interval like that," he says in a loud voice, competing with the rumble of thunder. "We're going to pay a visit to someone that resides in the ultimate solitary confinement, not an interval as you have come to know them."

This ignites memories from Bru and Ish. "You mean a Carcerium chamber?"

Cavazos's eyebrows rise again. "I'm impressed. Seems like you've learned something of our city after all, even without sip basin access."

Her mind races for the name that Bru mentioned. "There's a guy there. You used to work for him." She snaps her fingers repeatedly trying to recall the conversation. "A guy named . . . Malcolm something."

"*Malom,*" he corrects. "Malom Roderick was a member of the Directorate, and I *never* worked for him. Chancellor Macer himself signed off on his 'incarceration.'" Cavazos interlaces his fingers. "Did anyone tell you what he did? Why he's locked away?"

"Bru and Royse said he was punished for crimes against the city."

This elicits a wry smile from him as another wave bounces the craft. "That's certainly one way to put it. I'm curious, did they share with you how Carcerium chambers work?"

She glances through the glass at the trio of cybos in the rain. Remembering Ish's comment, she points at one and says, "I was told it's more merciful to be transformed into one of those things than to be sentenced to Carcerium, but I don't know why."

Cavazos chuckles malevolently. "I see word has gotten out about the cybo process. That's a good thing." He leans forward. "Imagine a stark, white prison slightly larger than your bedroom at the guest house. Now imagine the room completely devoid of furniture, vidscreens, windows, no sip basin—nothing but an empty white cube that time resets every fifteen minutes or so. Everything inside the enclosure is on a repeating time loop, so the occupant never ages more than a quarter of an hour except for . . ." Cavazos delights in this part and pauses to draw it out. ". . . their mind. Their thoughts don't reset, but the rest of their physiology does."

Luci covers her mouth in horror at the implications. "That's—"

Cavazos adds delightfully, "We discovered it quite by accident. The subject could be in there for centuries in their mind but won't age more than a thousand seconds before it reset again."

"Only a thousand seconds?" She does the calculation. "That's nearly seventeen minutes. It's torture." Luci wants to slap the smirk off his face.

He shrugs. "Torture is a relative term. No physical damage is administered to the subject, they just stay in there—indefinitely."

"But how often do the prisoners . . ." She stops, realizing the answer to the question before asking. "Since the room resets nearly every seventeen minutes, you don't have to feed them or take suicide precautions."

"Or waste cybos guarding them," Cavazos adds, the smirk expanding to a devilish grin.

She feels sick and gazes down at the floor. "How long has Malom Roderick been . . . 'cycling' in there?"

"Technically, for many, many years to him, but don't tell him. Part of the agony is not being able to discern the passage of time."

"That's ghastly. And he's never seen anyone in all that time? No one goes to check on them?"

"There's no need, but today, we make an exception. We're fairly confident that Malom Roderick is—or rather *was*—Gicul's second-in-command. I fully expect that when he sees you in my custody, he will divulge *L'inversione*'s plan and what they hope to achieve by destroying skip point intervals. From that, we will develop a strategy to stop all of this. You will help me break him."

The boat climbs and falls again as Luci tries to process everything that she's been told. "Death," she says, shaking her head.

"Excuse me?" he responds.

She looks up at him. "Death—what does it change? Why does it make us sad? We're sad and experience loss because death takes away our ability to interact with the person who died."

"Yes, so what of it?" Cavazos asks, gazing out the window at the gathering storm.

"That person—the deceased—doesn't stop being a parent in the past for a child or sibling for a sister or brother. It doesn't erase the experiences we have with a co-worker or neighbor who has gone on. We're sad because there are no more chances to interact with them. We need to interact with others. It's a basic human need. Your Carcerium chambers remove the subject from everyone as if everyone in the universe has died."

She swallows as an intense homesickness overtakes her. She pauses, reminded of how everyone she's ever known back in her interval has been dead for a long time. Luci gnaws her bottom lip, forcing herself to go on. "Your prisoners in Carcerium have no contact at all with anyone or anything. Even hermits have some basic interaction with the land, but what you describe is nothing but void. It's maddening in a way that you and I can't imagine."

"Precisely! That's the point," he says, irritatedly looking back at her. "It's intended to be the ultimate deterrent. It's a fate worse than death. It's designed . . . hell, it's even promoted through our back channels in Relicus City to be that way." Cavazos crosses his flabby arms. "I don't expect someone from your interval to understand the measures that we've been required to take, but sometimes, extreme situations require extreme measures."

There's something off about it all that Luci can't put her finger on. "But why am I going and not Macer or Royse? I don't have any interrogation skills." Convinced this is a waste of time, she adds, "I really should be working on DPM." She releases the handhold long enough to make air quotes with her fingers. "What *'extreme measures'* are you talking about? If this guy hasn't already gone insane, how can introducing a mathematician into an interrogation intimidate a terrorist?"

"You underestimate your value in this effort," Cavazos says. "I know what I'm doing, and when the time comes, I will inform you of everything you need to perform your role."

"Perform my role? Fine, have it your way." Luci knows him well enough to recognize that he thrives on controlling information. She won't get a straight answer from him until he loses interest in toying her with his secret scheme, whatever it is. She attempts to concoct every scenario in which Cavazos presenting her to a prisoner results in the slightest influence on the convicted man and comes up empty at every turn. There has to be something she's missing here. She looks him over. There's something he's not telling her about all of this, some important piece that links it all together, but what?

The waves lift and lower the boat a few more times before Luci breaks the silence between them. "I still don't get what someone has to do here for you to feel the need to lock them away in solitary confinement . . . literally forever."

Cavazos's face reddens. "Don't presume to lecture me. I keep the city safe! I don't have the luxury of being sentimental about the feelings of those sympathetic to Gicul's plan to erase six million lives."

A different number flashes across her mind: nine billion, nine hundred eighty-seven million. The guilt of *Hi no Kawa* presses down on her. She's quiet for a mournful pause while she tries to get her bearings again. She goes on the offensive, asking, "What about the people of New Australia? What about their numbers too? Or don't you care about their people?" In an odd way, it's soothing to attack him for being so callous toward human life not under his jurisdiction. "You don't care about New Australia enough to even count or consider their people in your total. I'm sure there are innocent women and children just trying to survive like the people of Relicus City."

She's shocked when Cavazos erupts into an unbridled chuckle. The laughter grows until it shakes his entire body. He manages to sputter out, "Women and children . . . there are no women and children, no innocents."

Luci grits her teeth. despising that something she said has filled him with so much perverse joy. "What do you mean? How do you know they don't have families there? Their people could be starving."

He waves her off as if making him laugh is a deliberate attack. Cavazos's face is even redder than before when he was angry. Between breaths, he declares, "They're . . . they're not starving." His own statement sets off another round of laughter.

Rather than compete with whatever has him so amused, Luci turns to peer out the side window. Dozens of illuminated dome structures of various sizes pass from the left side of the glass to the right as the speedboat continues along the watery pathway to the Spike. Through the heavy rain, the distant building looks like a frozen bolt of lightning through the darkness of the storm. Without looking back at Cavazos, she finally says, "The people of New Australia come over here to steal your food resources. Why would they dare such a journey across the ocean if they weren't starving over there?" She turns to him. "Why is it so difficult for you to comprehend this?"

He manages to reclaim himself but doesn't answer.

"What is it? Why are the civilian deaths of your enemy so funny to you? Have you no heart at all in that obese chest of yours?"

This triggers an enormous knowing smile from him. "I have more heart than anyone in New Australia has, of that I can assure you."

"What does that mean?" She sits up in her seat, processing the possible ramifications of his words. Her lip quivers. "Did you . . . Did you kill them all or something with an attack strike?"

The smile reverts to a pensiveness that she wasn't expecting. There's a pause as Cavazos contemplates his words and the boat bobs up and down. Finally, he concedes, "I guess there's no harm in telling you since you're not going to be around here for much longer anyway." He leans forward to her, and in mock whisper, he announces, "It's all manufactured."

She studies him attempting to gather his meaning. "What are you saying? What do you mean by that?"

He casually slouches back in his seat, arms behind his head. "Just what I said. There is no New Australia—it's all made up." In a matter-of-fact tone, he adds, "The people needed an enemy, so I manufactured one for them."

The revelation is nearly too much for her. In a way, a military victory over them would have been more palatable than this. Her mind flashes back to the intruder's note about something being off and Ish's blindness during the attack, but she never dreamed of a sham like this. The gut-punch admission forces her eyes to scan the craft's tacky interior in a near panic.

When her gaze returns to Cavazos's grinning smirk, he boasts, "Pretty good, right?"

"New Australia is a hoax?" She feels sick, and the choppy waters aren't helping.

"Every bit of it," he answers, delighted.

She's briefly considered that the mystery messenger may have been from New Australia, but this news cancels out that possibility. "But why go to the trouble?" she asks, shaking her head, her mind still attempting to reconcile the concept. "The resources wasted to perpetrate such a—"

He cuts her off, "Again, I doubt that you can understand what it takes to govern a city of six million lives. It is important to maintain order at any cost."

"You're right about part of that," she scoffs. "I don't understand how you can possibly believe that a deception—a hoax of this scale and magnitude—can offer your citizens anything."

He condescendingly enunciates every word, saying, "The one that controls the chaos controls the order."

She scoffs. "Yeah, and that would make a great bumper sticker for this boat." Her forehead furls. "Do Macer and Royse know about all of this?"

"It was his idea," he answers gleefully. He clarifies, "The chancellor, I mean. His bodyguard is just as clueless as everyone else."

Luci nods, thinking, "*Everyone except the people who left the note.*" She struggles to accept it all, though Cavazos's enjoyment of the revelation validates the truth of it. "So Cyphor Gicul and *L'inversione* wasn't a big enough enemy? You had to stage fake attacks?"

His enjoyment seems to be waning. "In fairness, we had the New Australia thing going long before Gicul, and New Australia will continue long after *L'inversione* is caught and converted to cybos."

She shakes her head. "You're both monsters."

"You're wrong. The city enjoys peace. Sure, every now and again, they get a jolt of fear and excitement. This works to squelch any ideas of leaving the city to colonize somewhere else for fear that marauders will destroy them. It also promotes a sense of nationalism when there's a perceived threat, even if it's manufactured."

The boat slows and gradually turns, headed for a small dock under the massive structure of the Spike building. "You'd rather have people live in fear? You'd rather have them cowering, afraid of marauders coming from across the ocean to get them?"

"Fear is simply another tool," he answers smugly. "I am security minister, and as paradoxical as it may seem to you, I use every tool. I use fear to make the people feel more secure and live better lives."

The repetitive tap of the pounding rain stops abruptly as the boat crosses under the canopy threshold and proceeds to an alcove under the building.

Still, she struggles to process what she's just been told. "But your whole society is built on lies."

"Every culture is balanced on a foundation of falsehoods," Cavazos says, pointing an accusatory forefinger. "And fear is a common device whether deliberate manipulation or unintentionally deployed."

Flashing amber light fills the interior of the craft as it approaches an empty section of the dock. Cavazos's boat dwarfs the others in comparison, most being single or two-person craft while his is easily three times their size.

A thought rushes to the forefront of her mind. "Wait . . . the thing about sterilization, is that true?"

"What thing?"

That he doesn't instantly know what she's referring to gives Luci a glimmer of hope that this, too, is a construct. "Is it true that when someone takes a leap skip, even one trip, it renders them infertile?"

"What, that?" Cavazos says. "Yes, that's real, the dirty little unavoidable consequence of moving through time."

Luci's heart sinks, and she bites her lip. She shakes her head in disgust. "I still can't get over it. The attack from New Australia two days ago was completely fake? Staged for what?"

His eyes squint to slits resting on bulbous, fleshy cheeks. "You don't have sip basin access. How do you know about that?"

"Ish went blind," she explains. "He said he saw a red band over his vision until he checked in."

Out the window behind him, enormous pincher claws extend to receive the boat. A mechanical clank is felt more than heard as the apparatus snaps securely on to the craft.

"Oh, yes, I forgot about your 'assistant.' Were you in combi when it happened to him? Did I time it so as to interrupt a moment of intimacy between the two of you?"

Her face heats up. "No, and I'll not have you bring up anything like that again."

"Really, you think that you have any sway over what happens to him after you're gone from us? You'll be back at your interval, but he'll remain here . . . here with me."

His words send a shudder through her. Though she managed to stop Cavazos from backhanding Ish in the guesthouse, she knows he's right and doesn't respond, choosing to look at the bright crimson floor instead.

The docking mechanism completes the task of pulling the boat into its locking position. After a couple of grunts, Cavazos stands, indicating it's time to leave. "By the way, if you share any of what I disclosed to you about New Australia or mention anything that is said in Carcerium to Moyta, I'll see to it that he becomes a permanent occupant there like my dear friend, Mr. Roderick."

Two of the three cybos waddle from the craft to the platform and stand at attention while the third maneuvers to the stern of the boat, rainwater dripping from its ready churka.

"I promise that I won't say anything to him," Luci responds. "Please don't do anything to Ish. I'll only talk DPM with him."

As the vessel's door slides open, he turns to face her with a snide expression. He nods. "I'll know if you don't, and this is my promise to you. I'll have no problem locking him away forever."

TWO

The cool saltwater air is damp, and the metal flooring is slick with grime that looks to have been left unattended for a long time. Luci follows Cavazos through the dock area in a trance-like state. The combination of the threat to Ish's safety and Cavazos's admission about the New Australia scam has her head swimming.

For once, the repugnance of the two cybos accompanying them doesn't register in her mind as she tries to sort everything out. Cavazos dispatches the third cybo to return to guard his boat. The four them move single file in silence through the empty low-lit area. Luci trails Cavazos as he follows the largest cybo. The second guard marches behind her with his churka weapon ready for any sneak attack from the rear.

After a few minutes, they reach their destination. Cavazos presses the Viatorio on his fleshly earlobe, and the doors of an enormous service elevator slide open with a clank that echoes through the area. The bright fluorescent lights sting Luci's eyes as the four of them take their place inside. "This is bigger than my kitchen at home in Chicago," she says, snapping back into the moment.

"This will take us straight up to the longchair area floor without stops along the way," Cavazos explains. "And there's enough room in here that I can do this with them." At the click of the thin onyx device around his neck, the two cybos shuffle over to the far side of the wall from them. "Believe it or not, I find their smell as disgusting as everyone else," Cavazos says with a shrug. "We're working on it, but reanimated flesh has its challenges."

Luci nods and answers absentmindedly, "Yeah, that'll be good."

"When we get there," he begins, "you'll need to get in the front of the longchair. That compartment is smaller than the back where I'll be seated." He pauses as if waiting for a rebuttal from her, but she's silent. "Anyway, you'll need to enter the chronal coordinates in manually. This is something that has to be done with extreme care, so don't mess around with it."

"Longchairs have manual function capabilities?"

He nods. "They do, but no one ever dares to do that because of the danger."

"What danger?" Luci asks, feeling her chest tighten.

"When a longchair travels to a juncture, the numbers have to be precise. If off even a fraction of a second, the transport and passengers could materialize into a solid object or arrive with solid objects inside of their bodies from the destination's surroundings. No skips are ever done manually anymore."

She swallows. "But that's why you have technicians at the Spike . . . to run the math, right?"

He's slow to answer. "Well, yes . . . normally. But there won't be any technicians when we get up there."

The service elevator travels so smoothly that Luci forgets that they're climbing over eight hundred meters in the air until her ears pop due to the pressure change.

"I made up something about New Australia to clear the longchair area out so we can travel without logging our destination. Due to the recent attack, I told them that a scan-sweep was going to be performed to make sure that the area was safe and free from any explosives from infiltrators."

"Of course you did," Luci says sarcastically. "Who doesn't want to be safe?"

"You catch on quickly," he says, making Luci feel a little slimy as if she's somehow complicit in his deception.

"If Carcerium chambers are truly outside of time, how can anyone ever find them?"

Her ears pop a second time; they must be ascending faster now. She opens her mouth wide and massages her jaw. "I mean, how can you locate a place that doesn't exist in a chronological linear timeline and, more importantly, make your way back without being lost in the void forever?"

Cavazos answers, "Yes, where we're headed is a place outside of time, an anomaly, like a bubble swirling around the drain spout. There won't be anything out in non-time for us to crash into or to crash into us."

"You didn't answer my question."

The elevator doors open, and the sudden movement of both cybos lunging at the elevator's exit startles her. Royse was right about their quick reaction speed.

"I have the chronal coordinates for where the chamber quad cluster will be for the next hundred and eighty-six minutes. It's proprietary information that only I and the chancellor possess."

Once outside the compartment, the lead cybo makes a stiff nodding motion to its master, indicating the area is clear of potential threats. Cavazos waves him off, choosing to remain inside. "Like I said, besides me, only Chancellor Macer has access to the mechanism that is able to predict where the compartments will be," he explains with pride.

"So, the group of chambers just randomly appear at various points in space-time?"

He scoffs. "I'd think that you of all people, given your background, should know that nothing in the physical universe occurs with any true randomness."

She suspects that his intent is to insult her, but she doesn't care. She has to know more. "So explain it to me, then."

Cavazos sighs as if answering an over-inquisitive child. He pulls the lanyard around his thick neck over his head with an effort that Luci tries to ignore. He begins dangling the thin, rectangular, onyx device before her like an old-time magician attempting to hypnotize a volunteer from the audience. The small controller sways to the left and right like a shiny black pendulum. "If Carcerium was the cybo controller swinging at the end of this chain, how could you find a way to get to grab it a hundred percent of the time?" Cavazos spins it in a circle now, still maintaining a wide sway. "Look, what do you see?"

She studies the object, trying to predict the changing, circling paths.

"Come on, girl," he chides. "Don't be daft. You're supposed to be a mathematician's mathematician. Where's the one point that you can predict with certainty that remains constant?"

She inhales sharply and feels her ears burning. She knows the anger stirring inside her blocks productive reasoning, but his gloating makes Luci want to slap his fat face. She's aggravated with herself that she can't figure this out. The twinge of a headache threatens.

Then she sees it clearly.

She unballs her fist and points to his thumb and forefinger pinching the top of the chain. "There," she says. "It doesn't matter how much the end of the it moves. Where you're holding it remains constant in its position, relatively speaking."

"Exactly," Cavazos says, pointing with his free hand at the near-motionless end of the chain. "We only have to determine this point." He stops the spinning until the chain becomes a vertical line that he slides down with his fingers. "And then we travel down this *corridor* of sorts to Carcerium here."

"I understand," Luci says as Cavazos slides the lanyard back over his head.

"You should know that this will not be as pleasant as skipping across to an interval, so don't begin screaming or panic and start pushing the panel buttons, sending us headlong into oblivion."

"Different how?"

He pushes his way past her into the elevator vestibule ask he speaks. "The darkness lasts longer. In fact, the journey will be in almost all darkness. You'll feel a little inebriated, but the feeling will pass."

She follows him and the cybos down a dimly lit corridor, another area off the beaten path of other city members.

AFTER A COMPLEX SERIES OF twists and turns through the industrial maze of hallways, the four of them pass through a corridor of normal width. Luci halts as Cavazos gestures for her not to speak with his index finger pressed against thin lips, and the bigger of the two cybos enters through a door. She sighs disapprovingly and leans against the wall while rubbing her temples to massage out the pain of another Jardon headache. Soon after, the shuffling sound of the cybo's tattered boots grow louder as it returns to them.

"We're clear," Cavazos states as they enter.

When she was here a week ago to go to the Grange, she was dressed like Maid Marian, and the control room bustled with activity. Now, there is an uneasy stillness save for the miniature well basins gurgling away in each of the empty operator cubicles.

Eight of the fifteen longchairs remain, giving Luci pause about the five sitters reportedly trapped in Poland 1952.

Cavazos makes his way to the platform stairs. The larger of the two cybos stands at attention facing the door they entered through in the back of the chamber. The cybo behind Luci breaks off to guard the side door.

"Speed it up," Cavazos commands while activating the longchair to open the glass coverings of the pod.

Luci hurries past the cybo in position at the stair edge. Cavazos grunts and huffs as he awkwardly descends into the back of the longchair. Luci doesn't say anything, but it's obvious that he's ceded the front seat to her because the compartment is too small to accommodate his enormous girth.

Back-to-back in the seats, Cavazos instructs her over his shoulder, "There's a panel in front of you. Slide it open and press the orange button."

The plastic drawer sticks when she tugs at it, causing Luci to wonder when it was last opened, if ever. Pressing the flashing orange button, she asks, "Okay, now what?"

The glass covering snaps into place, sealing them in with a short hiss.

"Give it a moment," Cavazos answers.

A soft computer-generated voice comes through the longchair's inset speakers. "Manual override initiated. Enter nine-digit one alpha NBSI destination code using control pad."

A thin slot beneath the orange button opens and extends a metal keyboard slightly thicker than a Tupperware lid out to her midsection.

Luci begins to panic. "I don't know UNIFON letters," she says over her shoulder to Cavazos, who faces the opposite direction.

"Calm down," he answers, peeved. "It'll be all numbers followed by a multiplication sign." He pauses before he adds, "But you have to get it exactly right or you'll kill us. And in a weird way, you'd be doing the job of *L'inversione* for them, so pay attention."

She nods even though he can't see her. "Yes, I understand," Luci says, fidgeting. "I'm ready for the number."

"Alright, punch in 194576001X."

She takes her time and slowly enters the numbers one by one, repeating them aloud for Cavazos's benefit.

"Now press the orange button again to lock in the destination."

When she does this, the automated voice states, "Warning: You have entered a destination point that is not associated with any verified skip point juncture. Please confirm NBSI destination code 194576001X."

Her palms sweat. "What do I do? Should I reenter the number?"

"Just press the orange button, but hold it this time."

Luci inhales and extends her index finger. This time, the keyboard returns to the slot and vanishes from view with a sharp click.

She breathes a sigh of relief.

"Chronal destination acknowledged," the voice responds.

Waves of static electricity gently wash over Luci's skin, but there's no mention of obeying interval laws and customs by the automated voice like when she went to the Grange. She realizes this is because the place they're headed to doesn't exist. One can't break a law or accidentally influence an interval if it's nowhere.

The system pressurizes a thin layer of air around the pod, causing a muffled pop on the outside. Luci closes her eyes in an attempt to relax a little, but a burst of bright light explodes through her closed eyelids. She opens her eyes to impenetrable darkness, remembering her previous skips. Cavazos's claim that it would last longer is true. What he failed to mention is the extended period of weightlessness too.

This is what it feels like to be nowhere, to be outside of time.

She doesn't like it.

They don't converse, but Luci wishes that she'd thought to ask him how long this will take. The intellectual part of her knows that she could ask him right now—it's not as if the long-chair is being piloted by either of them—but a strange dread prevents her from speaking to him. It's an odd fear, a caution ... the silence of two trespassers in some restricted part of the universe, a place humans were never intended to go, like invading the backroom of the workshop of the cosmos.

Luci begins to self-soothe with her special number, 2012. To further distract herself, she adds a layer of complexity by including the month and day of her family's accident to it.

AFTER COMPLETING FIVE ITERATIONS OF random calculations that terminate in the number 892012, a bright, quivering ring of aqua blue-green light envelops the longchair.

The sudden change startles her, instantly ending the "number game." She listens for the popping sound confirming their arrival, but there isn't one. There's only a faint hum oscillating in time with the pulsating ring of light shining in through the overhead glass of the compartment.

"Why isn't there a pop?" she asks. "Is there air out there?"

As the hum grows, the rippling ring of light begins to brighten.

"It's all different here," Cavazos says loudly over the growing crescendo of the hum. "Everything resets here, including the air."

The sound of the hum fades as the glow brightens into a large, white chamber.

Luci breathes a sigh of relief, knowing they've reached their destination. A million questions bombard her mind about the science of what they've just done, but she shuts them out for now. She wonders again about her role in all of this. What about her was important enough to this interrogation to warrant yanking her off the DPM project? Even if only for a few hours, the interruption doesn't compute.

The overhead glass of the longchair slides open, but there's no hiss this time. She stands on the cushioned seat in the pod, the walls of the craft coming slightly above her waist. Before she hoists herself out of the compartment, she scans the room. Save for their transport, it's an empty a cube roughly double the size of a three-car garage back home. The entire white ceiling is one solid sheet of soft lighting.

Each wall bears the neon outline of a doorway to a passage that isn't actually there—three in amber yellow and one slowly pulsating in crimson red. The air is odorless and stagnant.

Cavazos, already out of the longchair, beckons to her. "Come on. We're on a schedule here, remember?"

His voice is strange in her ears; it's him, but something is off like it's been through an audio processor. She grunts as she exits the longchair and lands on the pristine white floor. This, too, sounds odd. "What's with the—" She stops short, hearing the peculiarity of her own voice.

"Don't worry about it," Cavazos says, headed for the wall with the red rectangle. "You'll get used to it in a few minutes. Something about sound waves and there not being any echoes in here with the way the time in the chambers reset."

It's unnerving to hear his voice detached from the source. It's as if she's listening to his response through headphones, not from a few feet in front of her.

He grins at her confused expression. "There's something else. Shout something . . . shout your name." He waits before prompting her again, "Go on, shout it."

Luci eyes him suspiciously but shouts, "I am Luci G!" She's stunned when the volume doesn't match the sensation in her throat. To her ears, it sounds as if she made the declaration in a normal voice.

With eyebrows raised, Cavazos bows his head slightly. "Now whisper it."

She does this too, and although she can detect audible differences in the pitch, the volume is identical. Her gaze drifts to the slow pulse of the red outline of the door as she tries to quantify the experience. "I don't . . . I don't understand this." She looks back at him. "How can this be?"

He shrugs, amused at how she's perplexed by the phenomenon. "It was explained to me once, but I don't remember the technical reasons. The main thing is that it's important to remember this when we get inside: don't whisper anything that you don't want Roderick to know, because he'll hear everything you say."

She points at the white space within the neon-ish red glow. "He's in there?"

"In the flesh—at least he'd better be, or we've got a big problem," Cavazos answers, amused. "Currently, he's the only occupant here." He gestures to the three non-pulsating door outlines in amber. "That's only until we apprehend Gicul and his henchmen." A mischievous smile forms on his face. "Has anyone told you what Malom did to earn this prestigious honor, to be a guest here in Carcerium?"

A bead of sweat runs down the back of Luci's neck, but she doesn't wipe it. "Crimes against Relicus City," she says, following up with, "He formed *L'inversione* with Gicul."

"Much more than that, I'm afraid," he says, motioning for her to approach the keypad. "I want you to enter the validation code." The smile changes into the devilish smirk that she's grown to hate. "What could it be? What would someone have to do to have the chancellor agree to allow me to lock him away in here forever?"

When she doesn't move, he says, "Come on, now. I want you to open it."

She's wary of him. Something about the way his countenance has morphed into something more malevolent. Luci shakes her head. "No, you do it. I did the longchair code thing." Her mind races through reasons why he wants this: *Is it booby-trapped? Does he not want a record that he was here? What's he up to?*

He glowers. "You seriously think I would have you do something that's dangerous to your person?" He lunges at her and snatches her by the wrist.

Luci screams, but the sound is flat.

Cavazos manages to forcibly extend two of her fingers to the pad. "In case you've forgotten that little speech of yours back at the guesthouse, we still need you."

She resists and tries to wriggle away from him, but his grip is stronger than she expects.

"Five, two, zero, eight, nine. See? That wasn't so hard now, was it?"

He releases her, and she steps back out of his reach, massaging her wrist.

"Why must you make everything difficult?" He shakes his head in disgust. "I wanted to have a little fun is all."

She can't figure out his game here, but she knows that he's definitely up to something. She stumbles as she takes another step backward from him. "What's fun about this?"

His eyebrows rise again as he offers a mock shrug with palms extended outward. "Aren't you a little curious about Malom's crime? You said it yourself that you couldn't imagine what someone could ever do that would fit this punishment."

Two flashing buttons the size of silver dollars appear, one orange and the other blue.

"Let's just get this over with so I can get back to working on DPM," Luci says, exasperated.

"Press the blue one, and all will be revealed, my dear." Cavazos makes a mock bow and distances himself from the panel to allow Luci to approach.

She's fed up with this. She wants to get back to Ish. She marches up to the keypad. Staring at Cavazos, she mashes the blue button, keeping her finger on it. "Satisfied?" She's surprised that the door doesn't open. Wondering if it's not responding because she doesn't wear a Viatorio, she shoots him a nasty look. "So, what's the gag here? Why isn't this working?"

His smile grows, exposing the gaps between his teeth. "Oh, it's working. Of that I'm sure. Press it again and I'll tell you Malom's major crime."

Sensing something's off about this, she pulls her hand away. "Just tell me so we can be done with all of this bullshit."

"Very well," he says, his eyes wide with enjoyment. "Malom Roderick was banished here because of a heinous murder he committed, a murder that had far-reaching ramifications for the common good of Relicus City."

She can tell he's paused, awaiting her response. She reluctantly gives in to his game. "Okay, I give up. Who did this guy murder who was so important to get thrown in here?"

Cavazos clasps his hands together and gleefully announces, "The one and only time-traveling visitor Relicus City has ever hosted. He murdered you, Dr. Luci Gaudiano."

THREE

```
Nil
Carcerium Chamber
[0.0000000/0.0000000/0/0:00:00]
```

KARSЯΞUM ℂΔΜBЯ

— — — — — — —

LUCI LEANS AGAINST THE WALL in order to maintain her balance. Cavazos's revelation stuns her more than any other shock over the last week since her abduction. It dazes her more than when she learned that she will become the mother of time travel or how her formulas will inevitably pave the way for *Hi no Kawa*, the end of the known world. A Jardon headache flares up, and Luci clutches the sides of her skull. "No . . . no."

"In the short time of our acquaintance, have I lied to you about anything?" Cavazos asks with a saccharine sweetness. "If anything, I think you'd have to agree that I've been very forthcoming with information, even about things like the New Australia farce . . . about how traveling in longchairs kills reproductive cells." His eyes gloss over as if he's somewhere else. "I can hardly wait to see the look on Malom's face when he sees you with me."

She glares at him but is forced to admit to herself that there's a sadistic logic to his perverse plan. Malom Roderick being forced to confront his murder victim may be dramatic enough to cause him to slip and reveal information about Gicul's objectives. It's a desperate Hail Mary of a plan, but she plays along in case anything of note is said that may help her and Ish save some steps on the DPM. "Just for the record, I don't enjoy being your pawn in all of this." Her head is splitting.

"A pawn?" Cavazos shakes his head emphatically. "Not a pawn, my dear. In the game of chess, you are the queen. You're our salvation." He raises his hands demonstratively and mockingly makes the sign of the cross. "You're our Joan of Arc leading the way, and today, we'll find out what Gicul is planning so we may put an end to this once and for all."

"Joan of Arc, huh?" she asks, her tone bitter. "When it was all over, Joan of Arc was burned at the stake." Before he can offer a rebuttal, she says, "Yesterday, Macer said that you feel Cyphor is gearing up for something big and that's why there's been a break in his activity." She pinches the back of her neck multiple times in various spots to increase the circulation of blood in hopes of easing the impending migraine.

He nods. "For whatever reason, you've cast me as your adversary, Luci, but I assure you that we're on the same side—the side of the people of Relicus City." He takes a cautious step in her direction. "You don't have to like me to do what's right here, but when we go into the chamber on the other side of this door, it's important that we work together as a team against him. We'll only have a little over fifteen minutes in there before the room resets and traps us in there with him, so let me do all the talking until I give you a sign."

Luci lowers her hand and fidgets as she contemplates contingencies. "Do you have a churka weapon or something to keep him from attacking me?" Her heart skips a beat as she pictures half a dozen possibilities in which the encounter can go bad. "I mean, if he strangles me, then he'll achieve the goal of *L'inversione* and none of this will—"

He waves the idea off. "Don't worry, he's in restraints. He won't be able to harm you ever again. When we go in, be quiet and stand behind him out of his line of sight until I motion for you."

"Constraints?" Luci scoffs. "Why constrain him at all? He's in nowhere."

Cavazos's sadistic grin reappears as he moves to press the blue button. "So that we may do this."

"I thought that was supposed to open the door," she says, feeling apprehensive. "What does it really do?"

"You could say that pushing it alerts him that he has . . . *visitors.*"

"How, Pol? How does it tell him someone's out here?" she demands, fearful of the answer to come.

He presses it one last time as a demonic grin forms on his face. "It sends a shock through his restraint coils—nothing lethal, just enough of a charge to make him puke himself."

Fury and guilt swell inside her. Her ears feel like they're on fire. "You sick son of a bitch. There is something *very* wrong with you."

He shrugs, unfazed by her diagnosis. "Remember, we're going in here on behalf of six million people in Relicus City. Pay attention and follow my cue." Cavazos reaches to press the orange button and, with his free hand, puts an index finger against his lips, indicating silence. An opening appears where the bright red glow was, and the fat man enters the smaller chamber.

Luci is still fuming at him for tricking her into unwittingly torturing a prisoner—even if it is the man who killed her older self. Cavazos turns back in frustration to motion her into the area. She reluctantly follows, telling herself that they will have words about this later. For now, she must focus.

Metal coils extending from the ceiling and floor secure the prisoner in place in the center of the stark white room. Malom is dressed in a white jumpsuit and resembles Leonardo da Vinci's Vitruvian Man the way he's positioned with legs and arms spread to their maximum reach in the shape of an X. Thick, bronze coils envelop the wrists and the ankles of his bare feet. His voice is rough like gravel. "Hello, old friend," he begins, though he's facing away from them. "A little much with the shocker entrance. It gave you away, *Councilman.*" He accentuates Cavazos's title mockingly.

The sound waves act in the same strange manner, making it sound as if his voice is in Luci's head.

Long salt-and-pepper-colored locks of hair pour down over the captive's shoulder. "Torture isn't really Macer's style, right, Sol? He's more into total domination . . . likes to get right to the point."

Cavazos struts like a prized peacock into Malom's restricted field of vision. "Consider it a systems maintenance check to ensure everything is in proper working order for your *extended* stay."

"You're not half as amusing as you'd like to be, Pol."

"Maybe that's true, but that's still twice as humorous as you."

Malom tugs at the coil restraints, which barely give.

Luci is as still as a statue as her eyes bore into the back of the man's head who saw fit to end the life of her other self. She seethes, wondering about his motives. Was it because of *Hi no Kawa*, or was there something else between them that made him feel he had to kill her? Was it out of simple sadistic enjoyment?

Though she despises Cavazos, she obediently waits for his cue, the exact moment to present herself and show this man that, for whatever the reason he did it, he failed, because *this* version survived. She will memorize his face, and when he comes for her in *her* future, she will be ready for him, an advantage that her other self never had. Her eyes follow Cavazos as he paces back and forth in front of her killer. She wonders how long Roderick has served time in here . . . served time in his mind.

"We've captured Gicul," Cavazos declares, leaning in closer to bound man before him. "He is to stand trial. Enos has agreed to grant you leniency if you will testify against him and his crimes against the city. I am here to determine if you have anything of value to relay."

"Enos? Leniency?" He laughs. "And what would that be exactly?" Malom responds caustically.

Cavazos crosses his thick flabby arms. "I don't know. Maybe you'd be allowed to leave this place. It depends on what you tell us."

Luci holds her breath, hoping that Malom will fall for the lie.

The prisoner takes his time in answering. Finally, he says, "I think I'll pass, Pol, but I do have a question for you. Ever wonder how Macer managed to catch me and lock me in here? Where did he say he found me? Which interval? You'd never believe where I've been and what I've seen there."

Luci is surprised by Malom's causal demeanor. Is it an act, or has this place truly driven him out of his mind? Either way, she feels the same loathing toward him.

Judging by Cavazos's jitteriness, Malom's lackadaisical attitude has him a little thrown off too. "I could arrange a special public execution, a one-time event in the splash forums."

"Seems a little macabre even for you, Pol. No, I think that I'll just sit tight here with my coils. Plus, it gives me time to discuss with them all of the ways I can kill you . . . and there are so many delicious ways of ending you, Pol."

The statement hits Luci in her gut. She's antsy and not certain how much longer she's willing to wait for Cavazos to gesture to her.

"Talking to your restraints? You can't be serious about staying in here," Cavazos argues. "That's crazy."

"If I'm crazy, this place made me this way, *old friend.*" Malom rattles the coils around his arms for effect. "Remember when we used to play chess through our Viatorio linkups?" He tries to lean forward toward Cavazos, but he can't move more than a few inches. "You were predictable, Pol. You were then, and you still are now. I know that you haven't captured Cyphor Gicul, because if you did, you wouldn't be here. You'd never come here."

Luci is frustrated that Cavazos is allowing this man to dominate the interrogation. She wants to scream at him to bring her in to confront this jerk.

"Pol, you can still do what's right, despite everything between us," Malom says. "Macer has to be stopped, and you can play a key role in that. You have access to him."

He sounds so sincere that Luci wonders what this madman thinks he knows about what's going on in Relicus City.

Cavazos scoffs. "You've lost what little thinking capacity that you had before coming in here."

"I have proof of what and who he really is and what happens if we don't stop him."

"Proof? What proof?" Cavazos scoffs, shaking his head. "I don't see any such thing in here. You have no proof of *anything*."

"I sent it back to Relicus City when I was captured by Macer's goons in the future."

"The future? Then where is it? Where's this proof? Regardless, *Hi no Kawa* can't be avoided. You can't just reset the world without consequences."

The image of Ish's face flashes across Luci's mind. She wishes he was here right now, or better yet, she wishes she was with him and far away from both of these madmen.

Malom answers, "It kind of sounds like something Macer would've said—*Waleen* Macer, that is." Even with the peculiar effect on their voices, his sarcasm is unmistakable. "You have no idea what he's up to, do you? He is still chancellor, right? Or has he set himself up as pharaoh or something while I was away? That's his end game to all of this, but you can help us stop him before it's too late. Set me free and join us. I'll show you everything."

Luci has heard enough and waves to get Cavazos's attention. She points at herself and mouths the words, "*Bring me in.*"

Malom must see Cavazos looking at her, because he says, "By the way, I have no idea how long you've imprisoned me, but it must've been long enough to solve what made your cybo henchmen stink so bad. I know you've got one behind me. I heard it come in with you." He makes a comically long sniff at the air. "I can't smell that unmistakable odor that they used to have. Is it a member of Relicus the Great's new military?"

Luci stiffens and takes a deep breath as Cavazos finally motions her over.

"Actually, my *dear old friend*, it's not a cybo. In fact, it's the person who was shocking you in the foyer before we came in."

She's surprised there's no vomit running down the front of his white shirt until she realizes the room reset the moment they entered. Malom has a beard stubble growth of a week or so that matches the salt-and-pepper locks of hair. His intense blue eyes sparkle like perfectly mounted sapphires. He studies her, and then he bursts into laughter, displaying perfectly aligned teeth a size too large for his mouth.

His delight infuriates her, easing some of the guilt she felt at shocking him. "What's so funny?" She crosses her arms tightly. "Yeah, ha ha, jerk," she shouts, but the volume doesn't change. "The woman you killed is back to confront you, you murdering bastard."

He regains his composure. "I'm sorry, Luci. I can't believe he brought you here to me. It only proves that he doesn't know what he's doing. Pol, there's still time to change sides."

She fights the urge to step backward when he says her name with such familiarity. She regroups and points defiantly at him. "Yeah, I bet you didn't expect to see me ever again."

"Well, you got me there," he says, still smiling. "Welcome home, Luci. I left the place exactly like you had it." He shifts his gaze to Cavazos. "Although she may have been in one of the adjoining chambers. Pol, do you recall which one you put her in?"

Luci spins to look at Cavazos. "What's he talking about? What does that mean?"

He shakes his head, flicking his hand. "He's lying. He's just trying to pit us against each other, that's all. Don't fall for his lies. Don't let him inside your head."

She studies Cavazos before turning back to Malom. She's got to play through the ruse; she can't allow herself to be distracted. There's too much at stake here. She shifts her weight from one leg to the other. "You're surprised to see me? You know what me being here means. Like Security Minister Cavazos said, Cyphor Gicul is in custody."

Malom shakes his head slowly, making a clicking sound with his tongue. "The very fact that you are here, Doctor, assures me that my friend Pol is lying. You don't have Cyphor Gicul." He turns to face him again. "In fact, like I said, him bringing you to me is quite possibly the dumbest thing he's ever done." He winks at her. "And that's saying a lot, because he was behind some very inept decisions when I served with him on the council."

Without warning, Cavazos strikes Malom, causing Luci to jump back. A mix of emotion floods her mind; she wants to scold Cavazos for hitting a defenseless prisoner while part of her wants to slap Malom too for his smugness.

He tongues his split lip, dribbling blood onto the white of his garment for a tense few seconds.

"They say you murdered me," Luci says. "Why'd you do that?" Her fingers curl and lock into fists. "Why did you kill me . . . the other me, the older one?"

He glances over at Cavazos and then back at her. "Do you know who G.K. Chesterton is?" His Viatorio catches the light.

Luci's certain the device is deactivated in this time loop environment. Even if it wasn't, he can't reach it to press it anyway. "Just answer me."

"Chesterton said that idolatry is not merely the setting up of false gods, but also setting up false devils; by making men afraid of war or economic law when they should be afraid of spiritual corruption and cowardice."

Luci glances at Cavazos, wondering if he's referring to New Australia. She takes an uneasy step up to Malom. "Answer me. Why did you do it?"

"We'll get to all that, but first tell me, Luci, did he throw a bag over your head and bring you here like a hostage or did he give you more like the grand tour and show you the works?" He pauses and looks up at her in a way that makes her feel uneasy.

They're supposed to be getting answers from him, not the other way around. "Did you see everything, my dear Luci G?"

Something is off about the question. She looks to Cavazos, who's shaking his head. "Enough of all of this, Malom. Do you accept my offer or not? You tell us what you know about Gicul's plans and I'll take you out of here."

Malom looks back at Luci. "You know, I've spent a lot of time with these coils around me. They've become my only companions for the duration of my stay here. I've even taken to naming them and giving them personalities."

Luci subconsciously steps back, absorbed by the intense look in his eyes. "Luci, I've given every one of them the name of a friend or family member." He wriggles his hands and legs, rippling the coils for dramatic effect, and chuckles.

She shoots a nervous look back to Cavazos. This is completely going off the rails, but he gestures to her to keep the lunatic talking. She can't imagine how pursuing this line of conversation will lead to anything, but Cavazos knows him better than she does. "Yeah, so you name them. Who cares?" she asks sharply. "So this little piggy went to the market, and this little piggy stayed home . . . so what?" She forces herself to close the space between them to show strength, though all she wants to do is run from this guy. "For the last time, I want to know why you killed me and where Gicul is and what he's doing. I don't really care about your coils."

As if he hasn't heard her, he says, "See the sixth coil from my left hand? That one's you, Luci G. Do you want to know who the coil next to it is?"

Her fists clench, and she fights down the nausea swimming in her belly. "I thought you only named friends and family."

He nods. "This is true. The one next to the one named Luci is '*Newt.*' Not really a person, Newt, but I made an exception and named it after an old-world animal." He studies her again.

She's silent while wishing she had a better poker face. It feels like the wind has been knocked out of her. She thought she was prepared for anything, but how this man knows such an intimate detail about her childhood floors her.

"You remember that animal, right? You remember . . . *Newt?*"

Her entire being stiffens as she tucks her hands into her armpits.

"What is it?" Cavazos demands of her in an anxious voice. "What's he talking about? Is it code for something?"

Luci looks down. "No, Newton . . . Newt was my cat when I was in foster care." Her head is spinning. She never expected this man—her killer—to know anything as intimate about her like this. She has to keep it together. They have to regain control of this interrogation.

Malom continues slowly and deliberately, "After your accident on the bridge, you lived with the Joyners for a time, I believe." He adds delicately, "You named the animal after Isaac Newton, right?"

She can't believe what she's hearing. The room won't stop spinning, and despite her better judgement, she plays into his hand, asking, "Why would I have . . . the other version . . . why would I have told you that?"

His response flows quickly like a tactical assault of information. "But you did. You told me that the animal went missing, and you, my dear Luci, as a fourteen-year-old girl, were afraid and heartbroken. You said that you posted fliers all around the neighborhood, even went door to door alerting everyone to the creature's disappearance. After a day or so, you were convinced that Newt had been attacked by some other animal or it had been killed somehow."

She's stunned.

"This is pointless, Roderick," Cavazos cuts in. "Do you accept my offer or not? We're running out of time here."

Malom continues willfully, "Newt wasn't dead, though, and Newt wasn't a he. Newt was female, and it—*she*—had been hiding in the backyard—"

"She was delivering kittens," Luci says, finding the stagnant air even more difficult to breathe. Remembering the sterilization side effect of every leap skip she's taken, she answers between gritted teeth, "Delivering her babies."

"Hidden in plain sight the entire time," Malom finishes, blue eyes smiling.

She manages to recover partial composure. Taking a deep breath, she asks, "I suppose I told that to you before you murdered me?"

"You did tell me about that and your love of animals," he says stoically.

She presses her teeth into her bottom lip, forcing herself to focus. "You still haven't answered my question. Why was it necessary to murder me? Did Gicul order it?"

"One of my favorite passages in Shakespeare is when Ophelia says in Hamlet, *'We know what we are, but not what we may be'*. The question is, do you know who you are, Luci? Who you *truly* are?"

She inhales sharply. "I know who *you* are and that you want to destroy Relicus City, and that's all I need to know."

"Luci, I want to save the world. These men that you're entangled with are ten thousand times more dangerous than I could ever be to you."

"But you were dangerous enough to kill her." Cavazos waves his plump index finger in Malom's face. "That's quite enough talk of the words of Shakespeare and pre-*Hi no Kawa* creatures." His face is bright pink. "Time's up. Tell us where Cyphor Gicul is and stop playing around. This is not a game, damn you!" A burst of spittle erupts from his mouth, though the volume of his words remains the same. "Over six million lives are at stake. Tell me where Gicul is!"

Malom leans in, allowing his chest to brush against the other man's extended finger. "Ah, but it is a game, Pol, only the side I'm playing for is fifteen hundred times six million. When we win—and the fact that you've come here today tells me we must be getting close to winning—all of this will go away, and the world will at least have a chance of not experiencing a *Hi no Kawa*, despite what you say about taking drops of water from the sea. We will win for the past and the future."

"Win by killing me," Luci says, feeling tears welling up.

His face changes to a solemn expression. "You have to trust me that something bigger is happening here, something better than Macer's plan for the future."

"We've got to get out of here," Cavazos says, pointing at the counter in the sealed spot where the entrance materialized a few minutes ago. "We're almost out of time."

"Can we go out and come back in?" she asks, irritated that Cavazos has allowed Malom to hijack this interview. "He hasn't told us anything of use."

"You're wrong," Malom says, shaking his head. "I've told you everything."

"We can go out and let the chamber reset," Cavazos says, making his way to the wall with the large blue digital numbers counting down. There's under two and a half minutes remaining. "It only takes a few minutes, and then we can return to continue."

Luci hurries to follow in Cavazos's slow, waddling footsteps.

Even though his back is to them, Malom still speaks. "Pol, you know history has seen plenty of good leaders and bad leaders. The same with rulers, presidents, pharaohs, monarchies. They all share one thing in common, a common denominator that no matter how despicable or tyrannical a regime may be, there's always one saving grace. Care to guess what that is?"

The heavy man turns to look back at him. "What's that?"

Luci is antsy as the numbers on the wall count down. "Save it until we come back in," she urges, giving Cavazos a mild nudge. "He's trying to trick us into being trapped in here with him or something."

He flicks his hand away from her dismissively. "What's the thing rulers share in common?"

"They always—and I mean without fail—they always die off. Eventually, social systems self-correct. It may take a few generations after someone shouts '*let them eat cake*' or something idiotic like that, but eventually, they even out, and life is bearable again."

The countdown displays 126 seconds.

"Come on," Luci pleads.

Malom continues, "But what if the bad weren't removed from power? What if they didn't die off? What if their rule of tyranny lasted forever? That would be a pretty hopeless existence for those who were not in power."

Cavazos presses his Viatorio, and a blue rectangle the size of a door reappears on the white wall to the left of the digital numbers. "Well, Malom, I'd recommend that one be on the side of the ones with the power rather than the bourgeoisie."

The opening finally materializes for them to pass through. Not that Luci ever would expect him to be a gentleman and allow her to go through the doorway first, but he moves so slowly, it peeves her.

A flood of relief fills Luci's heart as she exits the chamber into the longchair area.

Malom calls from within, his voice still sounding close in Luci's ears, "Release me and I'll take you both to Cyphor. No churka weapons, no cybos, just the three of us, and I can show you both what's really happening here and in the future." He pauses. "For you to make an informed decision."

Cavazos pauses and turns to look back inside the room and then to Luci beside him. His expression of frustration and contempt for her is undeniable, and she resents it. It was a stupid plan for him to bring her here. She's about to remind him that she did everything he told her and it's not her fault. He should've known that Malom wouldn't be jolted to slip up at the sight of her. It's his miscalculation, not hers.

Before she can argue this, Malom calls to him again.

"Pol, you and I have been at odds since we first met, serving alongside each other on the Directorate long ago. I'm asking you one last time to abandon your pride, let go of any past conflict between us, and let's start over. I'm offering you a chance to do the right thing here for the human race."

"Look around, Malom. You're not in a position to offer anything to anyone. I gave you a chance to end this here, and you refused."

"You're making a big mistake. You made a mistake in bringing her here, and if you don't agree to help us right now, I will kill you the next time I see you. I promise I will, just on principle."

"Somehow, I don't think so," Cavazos answers, and with a press of his Viatorio, the doorway turns into a wall with a neon red rectangle in its center.

"WHAT DID HE MEAN ABOUT me being here before?" Luci asks. "Was the older me put in Carcerium?"

"What? Oh, that. That was nothing. He was just trying to distract you."

She recalls Cavazos's claim that he's never lied to her and wonders if that's still applicable as she searches his eyes.

He looks away, making his way to lean against the longchair. "He was lying. What do you expect?"

"I don't know. He didn't seem like he was lying, and what was that stuff about the future?"

"He said that he named one of the coils after you. The man is insane. If he seemed sincere, he probably was, because he's obviously out of his mind."

Luci considers this. "How long until we can go back in?"

"His Carcerium chamber reloads in two or three minutes or so, and then we can—" His normally pink, ruddy face turns white as a sheet.

"What is it?" Luci asks as Cavazos clumsily slides halfway down the side of the white longchair.

He points behind her, but his hand is trembling so violently, it's impossible to determine what he's pointing at. "Yell . . . yell—"

"Yell what?" she asks, rushing over to help him up from his slouch on the floor. "The volume is all the same in here. Shouting won't—"

"Yellow," he says, shoving her away. "It's not red."

"What's not—" And then she sees it. Each of the four walls has a yellow neon outline of a dematerialized doorway, including the one that had been red seconds before—the chamber that Roderick was confined in.

FOUR

"Could it be a malfunction?" Luci asks, stumbling backward from the sealed doorway. "Maybe he's still in there?"

"We've got to get out of here," Cavazos says, beginning to hyperventilate as he struggles to return to his feet. "Did you hear him? He said he's . . . been fantasizing . . . about ways he can kill me." His eyes open wide with fear.

Luci replays their entire visit in her mind. She's rattled, but her curiosity forces a wary step toward the neon yellow outline. "He said something about my cat Newt hiding in plain sight." Her thoughts race in contrast to her slow advance. "Maybe it's a trick. Maybe he's still in there like how the cat hadn't really left the backyard. Maybe that's what he meant by all of that."

"Let's go before he comes back with *L'inversione!*"

"I . . . I have to see." Her heart skips a beat as she rallies the courage to enter door code 52089. She presses the orange button, and the space in the wall instantly reverts to the opening again.

The chamber is empty, and Luci fights to keep her weakened knees from buckling.

"Come on," Cavazos pleads, wrangling a leg over the edge of the longchair until he's standing inside the pod. "We're not safe here. He knows exactly where we are."

Luci swallows the lump in her throat, trying to convince her mind of what's before her. She takes a timid step into the chamber. A second later, she's compelled to pivot and rush to join Cavazos at the longchair.

As she runs to him, his expression of terror unnerves her even more. He gestures frantically with his hands. "We'll figure out how he did it later. Hurry up." And then he says a word that she thought was absent from his vocabulary. "*Please.*"

By the time she hurdles the side of the longchair, Cavazos is already seated with his back to her. Only the top of his head is visible. "Orange button . . . press the orange button . . . and let's get away from this place . . . before it's too late."

She slams down into her seat, hand trembling as she enters the launch sequence that brought them here. The covering slides into place, and they're away.

LUCI WELCOMES THE DARKNESS, BECAUSE it represents safety, at least for the moment. She runs through all of Malom's statements, doing her best to sift the lies from the truth. The entire experience was a tangled ball of confusion, and Roderick didn't even flinch at the sight of her, not what one would expect when confronting their future murderer. Even worse than that, Cavazos's childish behavior demonstrated beyond any doubt to her that he's clearly inept for the challenge they're facing. In fact, in a perverse way, it was his presence in the chamber rather than Malom Roderick's that was unsettling at the end. Could anything this murderer said be true?

Still attempting to resolve his escape, Luci asks in an uncertain voice, "Could *L'inversione* have skipped a longchair in Malom's chamber after the door was sealed? I know it'd be tight, but I think one could probably fit in there."

Weightlessness returns to the longchair compartment, and with it, the auditory anomaly is gone. Their voices sound normal again.

"Impossible," he grumbles, his breathing finally beginning to settle down. "We'd be dead. The whole reason for the foyer is to have a safe area to rest the longchairs. If you put a longchair into the actual chamber . . ."

Luci prompts him when he hesitates, "What? What happens?"

He scoffs. "You obviously don't know anything about variable SD phase values and receding gain loops."

"Receding gain loops?" she asks, her mind running through the concept. "So it would cause some kind of temporal feedback cycle and that would keep repeating until—"

"Until the chamber imploded in on itself," Cavazos finishes snidely. "You can't have longchair chronal displacement in the same place where time doesn't exist."

She thinks on this. "One can't divide by zero, and Carcerium is an anomaly—technically zero on a linear timeline."

"Exactly, dearie. It would destroy the entire area," Cavazos declares. "So, again, *no*, you can't put a time-travel device in a Carcerium chamber when the room is engaged if you want to make it out alive." He adds, "Someone had to know the NBSI destination code, someone on the outside to break him free."

There's a brief silence as she runs through the permutations of nine-digit plus one alpha character combinations. There are 141,167,095,653,376 possibilities, so it's not feasible that someone could have guessed this even with a computer. Luci doesn't relay the figure to him, but she asks, "Does the chancellor know the code?"

"Of course he does, but are you implying that he had something to do with this?" Before she can answer, he dismisses the notion. "You should give us a little more credit. He wouldn't share something as important as the NBSI with anyone."

"Not even with Royse Timmons?"

He scoffs. "He doesn't tell that tug of a guard anything important."

Recalling her conversation with Royse about Macer's odd seizures, she's convinced that this is likely true.

"He had to have help," Cavazos says. "It's the only explanation. It's common knowledge that he was one of the few that had been banished here."

"Where are the other prisoners then? All of the chamber door markings were yellow."

"The other two went insane in short order and were brought back to display on a splash forum. I had it broadcast as a deterrent to potential offenders before dispatching them to the cognitive realignment station for cybo conversion."

"That's ghastly."

He ignores the rebuke. "Don't tell Chancellor Macer about any of this."

She turns her head, though nothing is visible in the black void they're hurtling through. "What? Are you crazy? Malom has already killed me once, and he's got bloodlust to off you too. This isn't like your New Australia thing. This is for real. Macer has to know." She catches herself, recognizing that there's an opportunity here. She speaks slow and deliberately. "I'll make you a deal."

Finally, Cavazos asks, "Deal? What kind of a *deal*?"

She swallows. Sure, it's extortion, but with everything that's been done to her, she doesn't mind cashing in on Cavazos's screw up. She didn't want to come in the first place, and with this major blunder hanging over his head, using it to even the scales feels justified to her. "Back at the Spike, you tried to threaten me with hurting Ish after I return to my time interval." Saying it aloud gives the words traction. Yeah, blackmailing this creep doesn't bother her in the least.

She waits for him to respond, but there's no answer. After an awkward pause, she continues, "If you'll promise me that you won't do anything to him after I'm gone, I'll not tell Macer or Royse about us going to Carcerium and Malom's escape." She adds, "Or we could say that you took me there, but the chamber was empty when we arrived. Either way is fine with me, whatever you decide, but you've got to promise me that nothing bad happens to Ish after I'm gone."

Again, there's no answer.

"Do you promise or not?" For the first time ever, she wishes that she could witness his facial expression. "Answer me. Do we have a deal or not?"

His voice is emotionless. "I can do that."

Though it's what she wants to hear, the answer doesn't bring the relief she thought it would. She prods, hoping to ease the queasiness in her gut, "Say it then—we have a deal."

"Nothing will happen to Mr. Moyta after you return to your interval."

This statement feels hollow as well. She considers if a promise from a man who's lied to millions about New Australia can hold any weight, but she's got to play the hand she's dealt. If only there was a way for Ish to return to her time interval with her when all of this was done, then she'd know he'd be safe. As if to lock in the flimsy agreement between them, she says, "Then I won't tell the chancellor about what happened."

She still doesn't trust him, but to push it may only provoke the man to do something against Ish simply out of spite. In the tense silence, her mind drifts to him. She pictures Ish with his sip wand sitting on the sofa scribbling down future skip point calculations for her to review. The daydream is shattered as she realizes that he's completely unaware that Gicul's second-in-command is loose and that he may be a target too.

Her body stiffens, and she's about to call out to ask Cavazos if a cybo stayed behind to guard the guesthouse when she remembers something. Only she, Cavazos, and Ish know about the visit to Carcerium. Her blood runs cold at the idea that Ish may have been captured and even tortured by Gicul's crew to learn this from him. Is that how they got the Carcerium access code? The analytical portion of her brain quickly reconciles that even if someone apprehended and interrogated Ish, they wouldn't be able to extract a code that he doesn't know from him. It makes no sense, but the impossible has happened somehow.

Another horrifying thought invades her mind that is even more distressing. What if Ish *is* somehow connected to *L'inversione*? She just as quickly dismisses the notion; if Ish had been sent to assassinate her, he could have done so before she ever woke up from her Jardon blackout. She convinces herself of how ludicrous she's being by recalling the hurt look in his eyes when he learned that she'd kept the first note a secret from him and how he held her before Cavazos interrupted them. That moment was authentic, she's certain of it.

She daydreams about the completion of the project, picturing Ish receiving formal accolades from Macer. This time, the chancellor *will* know his name, unlike before when he was rewarded for his work at the Grange. What did he tell her about it on the first day they met? She still had so much Jardon floating around in her system, it's a wonder she can recall anything at all from that day. He mentioned something about the canal at the Grange. She strokes her forehead, struggling to recall his words.

It takes a minute, but finally, the memory of it slowly comes into focus. Ish told her how he figured out how to enlarge the aperture of the vortex time portal that the huge plasti-crate containers of food were sent through. She mouths the phrase he'd spoken: *"intake vortex in the chronal canal."* After her exposure to DPM, she understands why figuring out how to expand a chronal point is a significant achievement. Her thoughts drift to math, as is her tendency, as she contemplates how amazing it is that the skip point vortex can be manipulated at all.

An epiphany ignites her mind like the light of a thousand suns, and she leans forward in her seat as if a bolt of lightning shot through her. "Oh, sweet God in Heaven!"

"What's wrong up there?" Cavazos demands.

"Uh, nothing. I just . . . I bit my tongue is all."

Satisfied with her lie, Cavazos scoffs.

She forces herself to remain quiet, but inside, she's exploding with excitement. Never once had they considered that the skip points may still be there but only reduced in size ... not until forty-five seconds ago.

Her concentration races over the ramifications of this possibility as bright fuchsia and aqua blue-green rippling rings of light envelop the longchair. Gravity returns, making her feel heavy again, and waves of static electricity gently wash over her skin. They've returned to Relicus City, but she's still tackling the concept of shrinking skip point junctures when a pressurized, muffled pop sounds on the outside.

She remains in the longchair as the covering slides open, wondering why they didn't think of this before. Everyone just assumed that Gicul had been obliterating the openings to other time intervals. But what motive would Cyphor have for doing such a thing? She needs more time to write out the formulas, to view them before her eyes.

Obviously, believing her hesitation in exiting the longchair seat to be a result of fear, Cavazos reaches down to her from the platform above. "Come on," he says with a furrowed brow. "Roderick's not in here. We're safe."

The statement brings her back. "Yeah, okay," she says, waving off the arm extending into the cockpit to her. Allowing Cavazos to touch her, even like this, is something she wants to avoid. She stands and gives a quick scan of the area. It's a relief that everything is just as they left it, including the cybo guards. Cavazos is already heading down the platform stairs. It's good to know that he can move quickly when their lives are on the line.

They hurry back through the labyrinth of restricted-access hallways and narrow corridors, Cavazos wheezing and huffing along the way. There's a brief pause in a long hallway before they make it to the bank of elevators. Luci believes they've halted for him to catch his breath until a side door opens and another three cybos join the original two. Quickly after, the seven-member party enters the enormous service elevator, but this time, the cybos stand front and center with five churkas aimed at the door as it slides closed.

"Where are we going?" Luci asks, panting.

Cavazos pauses before he replies through labored breaths, "I've got to return you to the guesthouse before the chancellor knows you're missing, then I'll head to my fortified office."

"The guesthouse? It's safe from attack, right?"

"It's safe," he answers, seemingly annoyed by her questioning. "It's why we put you there. The chancellor's home is right across the way from it, and both are in a remote, highly secured area on the edge of the city that's difficult to get to."

Luci briefly considers mentioning the notes that the intruders have been leaving and how she nearly came face-to-face with one of them during the early hours this morning. Before she can alert him to this, the elevator doors slide open and the group returns to scampering through hidden corridors and passageways of the Spike building.

When they reach the dock, the cybos immediately fall into a defensive formation with two in the front of Cavazos and Luci, one each flanked on the left and right, and one following up the rear. The cluster is so tight that Luci's field of vision is restricted to Cavazos's massive backside and the cybos on either side of her. The group moves quickly around massive support column beams and dripping pipes of the Spike building.

They reach Cavazos's boat, the lone cybo standing at attention just as they'd left her. The docking mechanism releases its hold on the boat with a clang that echoes throughout the vast underside of the building structure. The boat rocks slightly under the extra weight of the cybo guards as they board the vessel. They return to the formation outside the cabin, one behind, two in front, and one on each side.

Cavazos presses his Viatorio from a sitting position while Luci remains standing. "Do those things ever fall overboard? That railing is only waist high, and it's pretty narrow out there where they stand at attention."

"Lower center of gravity," Cavazos explains as the boat's engines fire up with an immediate purr of assurance.

For the first time, Luci considers the speed of the craft. She wonders if it can outrun any vessel that Malom Roderick and *L'inversione* may have stolen to intercept them. She studies the onyx controller on his necklace. In her mind, she questions if *L'inversione* has technology like that, something capable of controlling cybos, something that could turn them against their master.

"What is it?" he asks. "And where was it found?"

The questions confuse her. "What do you mean?"

Cavazos gestures to his ear to indicate he's speaking with someone else. "Has the chancellor been notified? How many of them were killed?" He pauses. "Good, but you don't know what you took from them. Is it an explosive device?"

Luci sits, enthralled by Cavazos's side of the conversation.

His eyebrows furrow. "How can you not identify the components? Is it longchair skip tech or not?" He mumbles to himself, "Multiple chrono signatures?"

Another pause as his expression grows sour. "Here's an idea," he begins sarcastically. "The next time you confiscate technology from a band of *L'inversione* terrorists, find out what it is and its purpose before you kill them all, regardless of how old it looks."

"Ask them if Malom Roderick was with them," Luci interjects.

He waves his hand dismissively, and Cavazos's scowl at her makes her sit back in her seat. He obviously doesn't want her input. "I've just arrived at the Spike from my home," he lies. "I can meet you in the lab in the north wing to determine what we're dealing with here. Yes, yes, bring those as well." He disconnects from the conversation as he rises to his feet with some effort.

Luci asks, "What is it? What did they find?"

"They don't know yet," he says, headed for the door. "Some old tech of some kind. But whatever they found was enough to have more than a dozen members of *L'inversione* guarding it."

He turns and points out the cabin window at one of the cybos, the smallest one of the group. "I'm leaving that one with you."

"What do you mean? I'm going with you to check out what they found."

He shakes his head. "You're a mathematician, not a long-chair skip technician. You'd be in the way. Plus, I don't have the time or energy to explain to anyone who you are and why you're here."

"Okay," she concedes, moving back to take her seat. "I'll wait here. How long do you think it will be?"

Cavazos activates the onyx controller around his thick neck. "You misunderstand." The boat sways slightly as four of the five cybos evacuate the vessel to the dock. "You're returning to the guesthouse. You only need one cybo for that, and the craft is programed to take you the quickest route."

She jumps to her feet as he turns and exits for the deck. "Wait! You're taking four of them with you and only leaving me one while Malom Roderick is still at large?"

The cybo assigned to her moves around to the door of the cabin to block her. She peers around it, trying to view Cavazos, but like a football huddle, the four cybos flank him, blocking her view. She shouts to him anyway, "You can't do this! You can't just leave and—"

As if to assert that he *can* do this, the boat engines rev once, causing the vessel to lunge forward on the water. Luci is thrown down to the gaudy red floor. When she makes it back to a standing position, the craft is throttling away from the underside dock of the immensely tall Spike building.

FIVE

March 28, 2191
Relicus City
[6.217012/127.792969/4.603.388.828/9462:17:31]

RELIKUS SITI

MAℂ 28, 2191

THOUGH THE RAIN HAS SUBSIDED to a mere drizzle, the swollen skies through the transparent roof of the boat remain dark grey. Luci steadies herself against the sway of the speeding watercraft by alternatingly grabbing the headrests of the seats as she moves to the bow of the vessel. Outside, the cybo sentry patrols back and forth, unaffected by the tumult. The only thing in the cabin that isn't a burning bright hue of red is a console. It has five angled touch screen displays of different sizes. Though she is not a sailor herself, she understands the function of many of the nautical readouts: the compass, wind speed, water depth, knot speed, and time to destination. There's even a grid of the floating city with pinprick flashes of light. She suspects the numbers beside the dozen blips to be the call signs of other boats currently on the sea.

She swipes her finger across the various screens in hopes of manually overriding her present course. It's quickly evident that nothing is going to happen without a Viatorio interfacing with the system. "Damn Jardon,"she grumbles aloud. She corrects herself; while it's true that her mishap in ingesting the Jardon nano-bots made it impossible to ever install a Viatorio, the mistake *did* bring Ish to her.

Once again, she imagines him on the couch occasionally dipping his sip wand into the bubbling pull basin. A bittersweet melancholy rises in her heart as she thinks on how it's just a matter of time before she leaves Relicus City and returns to a place beyond him, beyond time, and outside of any quantifiable distance. She'll never see him again once she leaves this place.

She shudders at the realization that he's completely oblivious to Malom Roderick's escape, how that madman could be headed to the guesthouse at this very instant. Everything happened so fast, there was no time to react. She didn't think to have Cavazos alert him with some kind of Viatorio transmission.

Instead of self-soothing with random calculations, she puts her thoughts to better use by thinking on the project. She and Ish must stop Gicul from destroying Relicus City. What they've managed to construct from the ruins of her civilization is a marvel. Luci bites her lip and mulls over the word *"civilization"* and wonders: what was so civil about it? All the great minds of the twenty-first century weren't able to keep mankind from destroying itself over her discovery. A familiar sick feeling begins to take hold within her. She is Pandora that the Greek, Hesiod, wrote of, the woman credited with the suffering of mankind.

She stares out the front window of the boat. The lone cybo moves back and forth as if on an unseen track. Luci shakes her head, quietly uttering the word *"no."* She rejects this self-condemnation. "No, it's *not* my fault," she says, pressing her teeth into her bottom lip. This last outpost of humanity, though only a handful of survivors, still fights among itself even after the near-annihilation of the world. She sighs heavily. Is there any cure for mankind's unquenchable lust to hold another down, to subjugate that person to their will? Is it an inevitable result, the factor flaw of the species? Are we all numbers doomed to this final equation?

Luci shakes herself. These concepts are too much for right now. Contemplating man's self-destructive tendencies will wait. She needs to turn her attention to the matter at hand, something that she *can* solve: the idea of skip portals being reduced down like the aperture of a camera lens.

She does a quick scan of the cabin for boat charts to write on and thumps her forehead. "Duh, Luci G. No paper, remember?" She leans forward to fog the window with her breath. "Well, we'll just have to improvise now, won't we?" She scribbles some figures on the glass and stands back to review them. While she's certainly capable of holding abnormally long strings of calculations in her mind, there's something about feeling quotients and integers moving through her hand and wrist that aids the process. It's a welcome physicality that connects her body to a formula. She wipes the small section of window; it answers with a delightful squeak and she repeats the process with a new set of numbers. For the moment, she suspends her thoughts from the reason why Gicul would shrink skip points to focus on whether it's something achievable.

She looks past the most recent set of numbers at the cybo on the other side of the glass. The guard continues mechanically pacing with a churka at the ready. It takes a few steps to one side along the narrow walkway, scans its head up, down, right, and left, then turns around and repeats the motion after marching in the opposite direction.

Luci pauses to watch the cybo perform the series of movements a few times. It has the emotionless precision of a second hand marching itself around the face of a clock. She realizes the necessity of this solitary protector to remain vigilant, constantly moving instead of standing at attention like when there was a larger group of them. "That coward Cavazos," she says aloud with a sour disgust. On top of that, he left her the smallest one of the lot, though this cybo's garments appear in better condition than the tattered rags of the others.

She returns her concentration to how small of a skip portal can be shrunken down to without collapsing in on itself.

The craft hits a pocket of choppy water, forcing her to brace herself.

After a minute or so of Luci's sequential fogging the glass, writing calculations with her index finger, wiping them clean, and repeating the process, she feels lightheaded from all the rapid exhaling. She takes a seat, allowing the spots before her eyes to clear. "So, 0.1938821254," she says to the empty cabin as she massages the back of her neck. "That's barely the size of a freckle." A larger question arises in her mind. "But where does the energy that was holding the portal open go? Energy can't just disappear."

She stands to return to her calculations, using the new number as a base. This time, when she goes to fog the glass, something about the cybo catches her attention. "That mark," she says, transfixed as it continues through its paces. She questions if she really saw it. When it cycles back through the routine, she's waiting this time.

The cybo turns, revealing a faint but unmistakable mark running from his chin to his cheek roughly in the shape of an upside-down question mark.

"No!" Luci screams, slapping her open palms against the glass. She wants to believe it's not true, but the pit in her stomach confirms the horror, and she mournfully says his name aloud. "Benold."

With tears welling in her eyes, she rushes through the cabin door. The narrow walkway is slick as she makes her way to the monstrosity that once was technician archivist Benold Jesper. Just a few days ago, he was alive, overseeing activities in the longchair room of the Spike. She screams, "No!"

He turns as if on a swivel, ruffling the plastic sheeting covering his torso. His advance is so quick that it startles Luci, sending her stumbling backward. The boat hits a dip in the waves, and Luci loses her footing, slipping over the waist-high rail. She screams, anticipating being swallowed by the cold water of the sea, but the scream lasts too long.

To her amazement, Benold has snatched her by the wrist at blinding speed. He gradually lifts her dangling frame back over the side of the craft. The vessel bobs on the water like it's at war with the sea; nevertheless, the creature deposits her on the walkway smoothly while never letting go of the churka in the other hand.

She pinches her nose with her free hand to block the strong ammonia-like smell wafting off him. He releases her and returns to a hunched position, the default stance for cybos. She uncovers her nose long enough to rub the soreness from her wrist and then wipes the tears and spray from the ocean from her face for a better look at him. The faint taste of salt-water is on her lips as she bends to ask, "Benold, can you understand me?"

She studies the greyish face before her for any hint of acknowledgement but finds none. As she delicately moves in closer to him, the cybo maneuvers the end of the churka weapon clear of her approach.

"Benold, can you hear me?" she asks, tears flowing now. "I'm so . . . sorry," she says, extending a shaking hand to touch the fading port-wine stain birthmark. "I'm so sorry that they did this to you."

Again, the creature offers no reaction.

The tips of Luci's fingers connect with his face, and she gently traces the mark. The texture of the exposed grey face is slick and feels like rubber instead of skin. She pulls away in anger. "Damn you, Pol Cavazos." She sniffles. "And you too, Enos Macer." She looks to the sky as if they can hear her through the clouds somehow. "This is not right!" she shouts with her fists raised. "You can't do this . . . you can't do this to people." Emotionally exhausted, she collapses on the narrow walkway. This triggers the cybo into action for a second time, and what was once Benold Jesper lifts her up with inhuman strength. Despite the stench of chemicals, she doesn't resist as he carries her back into the safety of the cabin.

<u>SIX</u>

LUCI'S HEART IS NUMB FOR the remainder of the return trip to the outskirts of the city. She watches absently as cybo-Benold marches again from side to side, searching for enemy combatants that never appear. Part of her wishes that his enhanced cyborg reflexes were a fraction slower and that he wouldn't have caught her stumbling over the side. She fantasizes about Cavazos being forced to explain to Macer about her unnecessary extraction from the guesthouse if she'd drowned. No doubt he'd resort to converting Cavazos into a cybo or sentence him to a Carcerium chamber of his own.

Then she remembers that without her, none of this exists—none of it. If she's removed from the equation, there's no *Hi No Kawa*, which, in turn, means no timeline containing Relicus City, the Grange, or any of this. Maybe Malom Roderick and *L'inversione* are right to eliminate her after all. How different would the world be if she couldn't be revived the day of the car crash? What if she'd drowned like her mother and father?

All she knows is that she's done playing these games with Macer, with Royse, and especially that creep Cavazos. The stench of cybo chemicals on her skin and clothes serve as a reminder of the evil lengths these people are willing to lower themselves to in the name of serving the populous.

Seeing Macer's home come into view through the boat's window, she determines the thing she must devote her attention to is getting out of this place with Ish. They must find a way to reprogram the cybos. She remembers the master controller around Cavazos's fat neck. If only they could snatch it from him. Then she and Ish could commandeer a longchair to skip back to her time's skip point juncture in East Timor. Once that was accomplished, they'd have to go into hiding long enough for her to pursue a non-mathematical existence to avoid creating DPM. The notion of vanishing from public academia is harder for her to imagine than assuming an alias and living off the grid, but it could be done. It *had* to be done if there was any hope for humanity in the future—a future better than this.

Her main concern is about what will happen to Ish. Can he survive travelling back in time if Relicus City is never formed because *Hi no Kawa* never occurs? How does this type of thing work, and more importantly, is there a way to test it in advance? She recalls every cheesy sci-fi flick in which a grandfather paradox twists time into pretzel loops, only in this scenario, she and her time interval in the twenty-first century play the role of the grandfather.

The craft auto-docks. The armed "house cybo" peers down at the boat over the balcony's edge of the walkway. Luci's eyes run along the elevated path he's standing on, following it back to Macer's larger domicile. She wonders if he's in there or back in the city with whatever Cavazos's security detail has confiscated from *L'inversione*.

Cybo-Benold rigidly motions to her to get up. Seeing no other option, she exits the vessel, stepping up to the slick metal rungs of the service ladder that lead up to the top level of the walkway. When she finally lands solidly atop the platform, Benold and the boat below speed off in the direction of the city. Like a grotesque, foul-smelling mime, the house cybo makes a lumbering gesture for her to walk before it to the elevator bank. Soon, they're moving through the underwater corridor back to the guesthouse entrance.

Luci dashes through the door before it slides completely open to the point that she's forced to duck to avoid bumping her head. Spotting Ish dutifully working away on figures at the sip basin, she exhales a sigh of relief. "Oh, Ish, I'm so glad you're safe." She embraces him before he even has a chance to lower the large sheet he's marking up for her.

The paper crinkles between their bodies. "Why wouldn't I be safe?" he asks, confused. Then his expression contorts to anger. "Wait, where is Security Minister Cavazos? Did he do something to you?"

"What? No, nothing like that," she answers, pushing back to look in his eyes.

He sniffs. "What's that smell on you, and why are your clothes damp?"

Luci's self-conscious about the cybo odor coming off her like a toxic perfume. She grabs his hand, pulling him to the kitchenette. "I have a lot to tell you, but I'm famished."

Luci hesitates, contemplating what to share and what to hold back from him. She shakes her head and decides to chance it and go all in. Disregarding her promise to Cavazos, Luci quickly runs down everything that's transpired over the last few hours between hurried bites. She forces herself to ignore how the taste is tainted with the smell of ammonia from her person. She tells of the farce that is New Australia, the fate of archivist technician Benold Jesper, meeting the murderer of her future self, and his escape from the Carcerium chamber. Ish looks more dazed with each revelation.

He only reengages when she presents questions to him about shrinking skip point junctures instead of destroying them.

He rubs his forehead. "Hmm . . . yes, I think that it can be done, but where would the chronal energy go? I mean, what you suggest is theoretically possible, but the energy would have to be deferred to somewhere."

His answer excites her. "Yes, exactly. That's what I was thinking. The only thing I've come up with so far is if there were some way to confine it into a receptacle of some sort, a holding space."

"Confining all that energy into a repository would be very dangerous," he says, hesitating to raise his spoon to his mouth. "And at best, one would have a single blast of chronal energy that could puncture sequential paths in the future."

"Or in the past," she adds, studying him for confirmation.

"Yes, I guess so," he says tentatively. "But if not done properly, it could dislocate stable junctures—"

She finishes for him, "Leaking chronal energy out like ripples on the surface of a pond that a stone has been tossed into."

He nods slowly. His eyes betray his fear at the concept. "I don't want to even consider how many things can go wrong in attempting something like that." Ish slides his finished plate forward. "Even with the experience that I gained from expanding the vortex at the Grange, it would have to be someone who knows a lot more about this than I do . . . for certain, a lot more."

"Someone like Gicul?" Luci asks.

He nods, and a pensive silence descends.

When Ish breaks the quiet with a sigh, she softly asks, "What's wrong? Is it the New Australia red-out thing again?"

"No, nothing like that. I still can't get over they do that though." He shakes his head. "It's so wrong to put that kind of fear on people. It's just wrong." An intense expression forms on his face. "Do you believe him, all the stuff he said?"

The question catches her off guard. "Do you mean Malom?"

"No, Security Minister Cavazos. Do you believe what he told you?"

She sighs. "I honestly don't know what to believe in anymore . . . Malom, Cavazos, Macer, Royse. Everything is so—"

"Me. You can believe in me." He grabs her hands. His touch is surprisingly warm. "You believe me, right?"

She nods, but the gesture alone feels awkward, so she says, "Yes, of course I believe you." A short while ago, the perverse thought that he may be connected to *L'inversione* in some way had seeped into her mind. Looking into his eyes, she wonders where such a notion could have come from. "I know that I can trust you." Simultaneously, the analytical part of her questions if she's simply made a choice to believe him because it's easier. Hormones and lack of sleep mix into a dangerous cocktail.

As if to demonstrate, Luci leans in a gives Ish quick peck on the cheek. To seal her commitment to trusting him to herself and to Ish, she says, "I want you to stay here tonight. Malom Roderick is on the loose, and it's too risky for you to be out there without cybo protection."

"Yeah, I thought we'd already agreed that I'd stay here before you left." He quickly adds, "Because of the intruders . . . whoever has been leaving the notes."

"Oh yeah, I forgot about all that," Luci says, surprised at herself.

His posture stiffens. "Speaking of forgetting—before you burst in here with all of this stuff that you've found out, I was going to tell you . . . I found something. At first, I thought it was a mistake because there's nothing else like it."

"Nothing like what?"

"I found a point, but it's not like other skip points, so it's not really a point at all, and whatever it is—"

"Yeah?" she prods, staring into his hazel eyes.

"Well, whatever it is, it's different from how the vortex works at the Grange, but there are similarities. It's like a hybrid of the two manifestations. It possesses the chronal architecture of a vortex but the temporal qualities of a skip point. It's really strange and definitely not a natural occurrence. That's why I originally thought I'd made a miscalculation, so I went back and checked and rechecked using different set B6 parameters."

Luci asks, "A manufactured skip destination? How can there be a non-organic skip point occurrence?"

"That's just it—I don't know. There's this weird anomaly that I came across in looking at the future skip points. It appears in Antarctica."

"Ok, go on." She feels her heart speeding up at the revelation.

"It . . ." He searches for a term. "It . . . *manifests* in seventy-two hours."

"Wow, Okay. Seventy-two hours from now?" Luci's eyes dart around the room in excitement. "How can—"

Ish shakes his head. "No, what I mean to say is that it is constantly seventy-two hours ahead of us here in Relicus City, cycling in real time."

She shifts her weight on the barstool. "You mean in the way the vortex at the Grange never closes?" She clarifies, "And this one is continually opening seventy-two hours from now . . . extended out before where—or better said *when* we are right now?"

Before he can answer, she abandons the barstool and begins pacing. It feels like the energy inside her will explode if she doesn't move. The next questions pour from her mouth. "What's the size of the chronal anomaly? How large is it?"

"A distance of one hundred meters in all directions."

She pauses her pacing, staring at the floor. A desperate urgency courses through her veins like a drug. "I want to see it. Your figures. I want to look at them."

He tucks his barstool under the counter and finds the sheet he was working on. "What do you think it is?"

Luci holds up a hand, and Ish gives her silence for her to rummage through calculations they worked out earlier in the morning. She crosschecks the figures.

Ish's eyebrows raise. "So, what do you think?"

Luci tilts her head and gives him a wink. "Chronal Technician Moyta, I think you just may have found where Cyphor Gicul is hiding."

SEVEN

"**Well, it doesn't solve the** mystery of the porous and limber number compounds for DPM, but it's definitely an artificial skip point, if that's the right way to classify it," Luci says, looking across the sip basin at Ish. He's typing with his WIBs on the open space before him. Luci adds, "And it appears that the anomaly has only existed for a few years, maybe even a lot less." She grabs another sheet of figures, feeling excited. "Someone has made this happen, and I'll bet you that someone is Gicul."

Ish lowers his hands to his side. "But why Antarctica? If one is to manufacture a skip point or vortex type thing, why there? What's in Antarctica for him?"

"I think it may be more about what's *not* in Antarctica, which the answer would be *everything*. The perfect place for him to hide is in a place everyone would consider a big nothing. I don't blame him; given the choice of desolation, I'd choose snow over a hot, sandy desert every time. It's completely controlled. Plus the fact that I suspect he doesn't have too many walk-up visitors there." She lowers the sheet and sighs. "Who knows? It also may have something to do with it not being an area affected by *Hi no Kawa* radiation fallout."

Ish nods his understanding. "By the way, I've been running the numbers of the affected skip points for the last fifteen minutes . . ."

"And?" Luci asks expectantly.

Ish smiles. "You're brilliant. Every one of them that I've tested has conclusively come back the same. They're still in the same sequential locations and completely intact, only the transfer apertures have been minimized. I've done all but the most recent two. Should I continue?"

"Yeah, but wait." Luci says.

"What is it?" he asks.

A lump forms in her throat. "Ish, I want to ask you something."

His silence makes her even more anxious. "Have you ever done a leap skip to anywhere other than the Grange? I mean, would you ever consider going with me to my interval in the twenty-first century?"

He clicks his Viatorio. "I don't understand. Why are you asking this?"

Her mind is a flurry of ways to present the idea of escaping Relicus City with him, but none of them sound as good now in her head as they did in the boat ride from the Spike. "I don't know," she stammers. "Ish, this is not . . . this place here, Relicus City and what humanity is becoming is not a good thing. This is not a good place."

He slides the WIBs off his knuckles as he stands to go to her. "What are you saying? Do you want to abandon what we've done here? We're so close to catching him. We finally know where Cyphor is operating from, or at least where he *was* operating from."

"I know, I know. I just don't trust Macer." She takes a few steps to meet him, grabbing both his hands in hers. "Cavazos has this controller thing that operates the cybos. If we could lure him here by telling him we know where Gicul is, you could grab the controller and use it with your Viatorio to get me past the cybo guard at the door, and then . . ."

His crumpled brow tells her that he's not convinced even before he asks, "But then what? That sounds dangerous for you—too dangerous."

"I don't care. I can't play a part in all of this. I just can't. The world is the way it is because of something that I discovered, but I have the chance to alter that. I can change everything." Her voice is soft. "And I want you to be with me, to change it with me. I want you to come back to my interval and experience a better world than this." She states matter-of-factly, "Sure, it's messed up and we have more than our fair share of stupidity and plenty of problems, but on our worst day, we have more than Relicus City. We've got, or at least we *had*, hope." She sees her reflection in his eyes. "Ish, let's finish this thing up and figure out a way for you to return with me, and I will stay away from DPM forever." She leans in to embrace him. "We can save the world. We can give it a second chance." She pulls back to study his expression. "But Ish, my lovely, Ish . . . I can't do it without your help."

He pulls her in to him. "I'll do it."

Her heart skips a beat, and he goes in for a deep, long kiss. Afterward, she says, "Help me finish these last two skip point proofs and you can summon Security Minister Cavazos here to tell him that we think we've found Cyphor Gicul."

"Why finish if we're just luring him here to get the cybo controller?"

She avoids admitting to him her compulsion to complete the equations and irresistible need to finish the project. Instead, she gives him a quick peck on the cheek. "We've got to make it believable, right?"

He acquiesces, giving a small nod. They take a seat next to each other. Luci looks over a sheet of numbers and begins calling out calculations to him.

WHILE WORKING ON THE LAST affected skip point, the front door of the guesthouse slides open. Luci turns to Ish with a frown. "Did you already contact Cavazos?"

Ish shrugs. "No, I was waiting until we were finished so we could ambush him."

Both turn as Royse enters, accompanied by three cybos taking position off to the side. "Time to go, Mr. Moyta."

Luci shoots up from the sofa. "Ish, what's going on?"

"I . . . I don't know," he answers, looking as confused as she feels.

Luci turns to Royse, who's closed the space between them in an amazingly short amount of time. "What's going on here?"

He grabs the back of Ish's shirt, partially lifting him off the ground. "Like I said, he's coming with me. Something he did at Carcerium." He shoves Ish hard enough to cause him to stumble as he shouts, "Now!"

Luci hurries around to grab the big man's forearm. "Royse, wait . . . just wait. He wasn't there, I promise. He's been here the whole time."

With the same force that he shoved Ish, he pushes her aside. "Stay out of this, Doctor. It's city business."

She stumbles, only preventing herself from smashing face-first into the floor by splaying the palms of her hands. Fear and anger mix in her thumping heart. She gives anger the priority. "Stop, Royse! Stop it now!" she shouts from her position on the floor. She's surprised when he halts to face her. He looks her up and down. Ish bounces in the grip of the larger man. He looks like a ragdoll fighting to break free from the jowls of a bloodhound. "Doctor Gaudiano—" Royse begins in an exasperated voice.

"Why are they doing that?" Luci butts in. "Why are the cybos' weapons fixed on him?" She stands, taking a cautious step in the direction of Ish and Royse. "Whatever Cavazos told you is a lie. Ish hasn't done anything wrong. Please let him go." Guilt engulfs her. She should've known Cavazos would double cross her and told Ish to hide upstairs. They shouldn't have been working out in the open. "Royse, you're being lied to."

He shrugs unintentionally, lifting Ish in the process. "I've got my orders, Doctor."

Doing her best to ignore the adrenaline surging through her, Luci wipes wayward strands of hair from her eyes. "I want to see Macer. I want to see the chancellor, now. Right now—I demand it!"

Royse shakes his head as he turns in the direction of the door. "He's unavailable. You can talk to him later."

Luci follows, keeping a wary eye on the cybos shifting between Ish and her. "We figured it out!" she shouts at Royse's back. "We know where Gicul is. I need to see the chancellor immediately."

This gets his attention for a second time. He turns to study her with a suspicious scowl. "You're bluffing. If you had solved it, you would've already contacted someone."

"We . . . we were about to!" she shouts, regretting how desperate she sounds.

Ish makes a sound other than a grunt for the first time since the raid. "She's telling the truth. We just figured it out, and we were re-checking the math."

Royse releases him to take a step back and activate his Viatorio. "So where is he?" He gestures to his ear. "Beam the skip point to me right now, and I'll forward it to the chancellor and Security Minister Cavazos."

Ish looks over to Luci and then back to Royse. "It's a little more complicated than that. We need to see Minister Cavazos in person."

Royse scoffs. "Yeah, I thought so." He grabs Ish again and resumes manhandling him toward the entrance.

Luci pleads. "Royse, we really did it. I need to see Enos immediately. It's a matter of life and death."

"Mostly death would be my guess," he quips.

"If you take him, I . . . I'll stop work on DPM," she says defiantly.

"Yes, you will," Royse answers with a smug expression. "Anyway, you just told me that you already know where Cyphor Gicul is hiding. Which one is it?"

The door is open. Royse didn't bother closing it when he and the cybos burst in. For a fleeting moment, she envisions running past him and the guards. They're focused on Ish instead of her. How far down the corridor could she make it? Surely they wouldn't shoot her in the back—or would they even know what they were doing?

A malevolent smirk forms on Royse's face as he says, "Oh, by the way, the security minister wanted me to tell you something about keeping his word."

Luci gnaws her lip, wondering how to prevent Royse from taking Ish away.

He backs through the opening with Ish in tow. "He wanted me to tell you that he *is* keeping his promise. Mr. Moyta won't be harmed after you leave, but then again, you're still here and haven't left yet."

"Please, Royse, don't." There has to be something she can do here, but she can't figure out what will stop him from taking Ish. "Royse—"

The cybos do an about-face in unison and exit through the door a split-second before it comes sliding down with a chilling thud.

She collapses to the floor screaming, "Noooooo!"

EIGHT

LUCI STARES AT THE STEEL door in despair. Through vision blurred by tears, her eyes trace the defiant half-dollar-sized rivets outlining the frame of the only entrance and exit of the guesthouse, her exquisite cage. The rational part of her knows that striking it is fruitless, but her emotional side demands a release. Letting out a frustrated scream, she pounds and slaps at it until her palms and fingers sting. This pain is a distant background compared to the agony of her heart. Even an attempt at self-soothing with her special number from childhood can't bring Luci's thoughts into submission. Her emotions rage raw like a forest wildfire, engulfing any attempt to calm herself.

She's reminded of a term a professor introduced to her: *"Ultimate Tensile Stress,"* the maximum stress an item can withstand before it breaks. She now has intimate knowledge of this definition. Luci has been pushed to the brink of imploding from the events of the last six days. A tug of war rages in her mind about where they may have taken Ish and what they're doing to him. She's desperate to convince herself that Cavazos won't do anything rash with him, but a darker part of her knows that despite Ish's value to the project, these people are capable of boundless evil. They could easily toss him into a Carcerium chamber if only to buy them time to sort everything out later.

It dawns on her that she knows the NBSI destination code to travel to the Carcerium quad. She rises to her feet, saying the code aloud as if practicing it. "One nine four five seven six zero zero one X." Luci wipes the tears from her cheeks and begins to pace. She wonders if the door codes match the one used for Malom's cell, which she remembers as well. She shakes her head. What difference does all that make if she's trapped in here? She stops pacing when she smells the stench of cybo on her clothes. Her eyes swell with tears again at the horrifying thought of Ish being converted into one of those hideous braindead creatures.

"No!" she shouts to the air. "Please, not that." She rushes upstairs to change as if ridding herself of the spoiled garments will somehow protect Ish from this fate.

It only takes a moment to shed and replace her outfit and return down the spiral staircase. She looks across the area at all the work they've done together plastered on the walls. The sight of it ignites an odd mix of nostalgia and melancholy. His unsteady scribbles look like rickety fence planks aside her perfect block letters and numbers. She gravitates to a set of calculations that he wrote out exclusively and traces the numbers with her index finger and swallows the lump in her throat. The end of the section joins another sheet plastered against the glass containing DPM formulas from them both.

She thinks about how leap skips through time have rendered the two of them infertile, but this, all these numbers . . . this is their *baby*. This serves as their union, their overlapping contributions fusing together to become a single thing, a conscious effort made by both of them intended to produce a specific outcome. She contemplates if the essence of a child at conception can be reduced to the simplest mathematical equation: one ovum plus one tiny sperm cell equals a zygote. From there, it's the ultimate display of division, cells dividing over and over again, splitting millions of times, igniting chemical chain reactions until something is formed where there was nothing before.

The concept is humbling to her, but thinking about it does something that her self-soothing from a few minutes before failed to do: it gives her clarity. She looks around the room at their "baby."

She knows what she must do. Excluding Cyphor Gicul, Luci suspects that she and Ish are the only two people alive in this interval capable of calculating DPM to determine his hidden location in Antarctica. Luci shakes her head, knowing what must be done. It has to be destroyed, all of it. All of this beauty, all of this loving union, it has to go. The only leverage that she has for getting Ish back safely is plastered around the room. She only has one move to play, and she knows it. She must ransom the work they've done together for his sake if she hopes to ever see him again.

With laser-focus concentration, she methodically studies the formularies and notes that they've transcribed together over the last five days. Starting on the left side of the area, she begins to make a slow 360-degree rotation, capturing all the scribbled data into her mind. Like an actor memorizing lines in a play or a virtuoso musician compartmentalizing musical moments in their head, she takes her time to methodically "store" the computations.

Only once does Luci pause when she feels the twinge of the onset of a Jardon headache. She cradles the sides of her head in her hands to block out the pain. "Not now," she says defiantly.

Next, she moves to the various sheets strewn about the room. She memorizes these too, stowing their number relationships in her mind as if her brain is a repository of file drawers. But even she has her limits. She closes her eyes for a long time as she "rehearses" recalling the figures back up at will to make certain she can do it. She knows that everything depends on her ability to retrieve the calculations upon demand. She was never into meditation, but she slows her breathing with deep inhales through her nose and out the mouth to help focus.

Satisfied, she makes her way to the kitchenette. "This had better work, Luci G.," she says aloud between greedy gulps of water. She examines the empty glass, turning it in her hand, reflecting the light. "Yeah, this had better work." She steps a safe distance away from the bar and hurls the glass at it with all her might. The impact resonates like a movie sound effect. Luci picks through the glass remains, selecting a suitable utensil for what she's about to do, one that won't slash her palm.

The concierge bot is dutifully on the scene disposing of the remaining glass fragments. "I've got a job for you to do, little fellow," she says while wrapping a hand towel around the end of one of the larger and more manageable shards.

Making her way back into the main room, Luci looks at a series of figures for a skip point juncture in Banja Luka for the winter of 1973 one last time. She sighs before slicing it to shreds. While the act makes her sad, it's empowering at the same time. As if Macer is standing in the room beside her, she says, "This is for kidnapping me and making me sterile!" She moves to another sheet and repeats the destruction of what she and Ish made together. "Enos, this is for the cruelty of what you did to Benold Jesper."

As anticipated, the concierge bot devotedly cleans up behind her. It scoops up the scraps that fall to the floor like giant strands of confetti ribbon and incinerates them.

"This is for the lie that is New Australia," she proclaims with another jagged downward slice. The rhythm of her pace speeds up with each successive tear she makes. "This is for keeping me under house arrest!" she shouts. "And this is for coercing me by threatening to do things to my friends back home!" Each proclamation is more liberating than the one before. It's as if a valve inside her is being twisted open, fueling an untapped well of rage from the depths of her subconscious. Though increasingly frantic in speed, her movements become more efficient in obliterating the assignment that brought her to this place. Luci isn't speaking in sentences any longer as she slashes, just shouting guttural words like "*Malom Roderick*," "*cybos*," "*Hi No Kawa*," "*Cavazos*," and the like.

An odd recollection of something she read about the Sistine Chapel in college flashes across her mind as she continues her ballet of destruction. It was reported that a frustrated Michelangelo destroyed his work by splashing paint onto the art at one point. She acknowledges the parallel of how he, too, was forced to use his creative gifts in a government project against his will. Luci pauses to directly "feed" the hovering bot by her side scraps of math scribblings to burn. She addresses the robot as if it put the memory of the artist in her head. "No, the difference between Michelangelo's work and the DPM here is that he went back and finished it for the pope. I'm done with this until I get Ish safely back." Even though she knows she can't communicate to the concierge without a Viatorio, she continues, "He wasn't a painter anyway; he was a sculptor."

The concierge bot devotedly receives another scrap of precious torn calculations from her. Despite the fumes making her eyes water, she tells herself that the harsh fragrance of burning paper in the machine's internal incinerator is the incense of Ish's soon-to-be freedom—if only someone comes for her before it's too late.

"Not even a painter," Luci mumbles. She thinks about how the artist's greatest achievement, the statue of David, is not even a quarter mile from her in Macer's domicile. The idea that he has such a thing of magnificent beauty hidden away from everyone but himself reignites her fury. "So selfish," she says louder, returning to an unspoiled sheet glued to the glass wall. She moves her cutting shard to the other hand for a bit. "Hands! That stupid speech about how sculptors render hands!" She doesn't know if she should be grateful or worried that it's been a while since he's come around.

AFTER A FEW MORE MINUTES of demolishing all she and Ish have accomplished, Luci wipes her brow with her sleeve and drops to the sip basin sofa.

Now all she can do is wait.

It's sad to her that nothing remains to show that Ish Moyta was ever in this place, not a trace. She shudders at the realization that if he doesn't come back, he will only exist in her memory.

"No, that's not right."

She springs from the sofa, remembering their first and only dance. Rushing up the stairs, she grabs the components that Ish attached to the concierge bot to play music for her. Luci takes her place on the egg-shaped bed and presses the pieces against her chest as if he inhabits them. She hums the song she sang for them and closes her eyes. "Oh Ish, come back to me. Please come back."

A soft chime abruptly interrupts the moment, followed by the swooshing sound of the front door. Luci's eyes pop open, and she's on her feet, rushing for the balcony stairs before she realizes it. "Ish?" she calls out with all hopefulness.

But it's not him.

She gasps at the sight of the hooded figure in the black jumpsuit moving down below. She recognizes the height and gait of the intruder from the early hours of this morning. Luci ducks down behind the edge of the balcony, wondering what they're doing coming here during the day. Her heart thumps violently as she realizes there's nowhere for her to run. She swallows, wondering if the intruder heard her call out Ish's name. That was a stupid thing to do.

Her only hope is to crouch at the top of the stairs and when the invader comes up, kick them with all her might in the chest. She tells herself that the timing has to be flawless and she'll only have one chance. She tries to steady her breathing as she scrambles into position.

"Luci?" a female voice calls out from below.

She's confused, questioning the number of intruders. For all she knows, it could be all of *L'inversione* attempting a "Hail Mary pass" of a plan to execute her. For the first time ever, she wishes Royse and a group of cybos were here, despite him taking Ish away.

"Luci," the voice repeats, moving around the room. "Luci, it's alright. It's me, Shar."

"*Trap*," Luci thinks, now fearful that the young girl may be a hostage for whoever is down there—if it's really Shar at all. She tries to ignore the sound of her own pulse thumping in her ears as she strains to listen for the footsteps below. Her plan to kick the assailant is gone; she can't fight a squad of prowlers. She tries to listen for crosstalk or shuffling footsteps to gauge how many of them have come for her.

"Is something burning?"

It really does sound like Shar's voice, but Luci waits.

"What happened in here?"

It takes all of Luci's resolve to force herself to peer over the balcony's edge. She's shocked that there's only a solitary figure, not a troop of churka-wielding fighters.

Shar looks up at her. "Are you alright?" She pulls down the hood, revealing her platinum bobbed hair. "It smells like something's burning. Was there a fire?"

When Luci is too dumbfounded to answer, Shar takes a few steps to the base of the staircase. "What happened in here? This place looks like a wreck. Are you alright?"

She still can't believe it, and though her intellect refutes the danger that she was feeling seconds before, the adrenaline still courses through her system. "Shar? What are you doing here?"

"I'm here to help," Shar says, motioning for her to come down. "But we have to hurry."

More confusion. "Help? Help with what?"

"Just come down and we'll get started," Shar replies. "Luci, I know you've been through a lot—"

"Call Macer," Luci blurts out, remembering her plan to extort Ish's safety. "On your Viatorio. Contact him and get him here now."

She frowns. "I can't do that. I can't contact the chancellor, Luci. I'm sorry."

"I don't care who he's meeting with. I've got to speak to him right now before it's too late."

"He doesn't know that I'm here."

A jolt of panic surges through her. "Why not? What are you doing here?"

Shar answers, "I'm here about your assistant."

"My assistant? You mean Ish?" Luci's stomach turns queasy, and she takes the stairs two at a time. "What have you done to him? Is he okay?" She makes it to the bottom level in record time. "Where's he at?"

"My uncle will be here in a few minutes, and he knows where he's at."

"Your uncle?" Luci asks. Although she's confused, her heart rejoices that Ish is still alive—there's still hope. "He's bringing him here? Ish . . . your uncle's bringing Ish here?" Her legs feel weak.

"Not exactly," Shar answers. Motioning to the couches that encircle the sip basin, she says, "We need to talk."

"Talk? Talk about what?" Luci demands until she realizes Shar only said the uncle knew where he was at, not that he was alive. The image of a slain thin black man appears in her mind. "Oh no, has something happened to him? Is Ish . . ." Her mouth won't form the word.

Shar grabs her hands. "No, he's alive, but we need to hurry and get you away from here."

Though she's still slightly dazed by all of this, she's relieved again to know there's hope. She allows Shar to steer her to the couches.

As they sit, Shar explains, "Like I said, the chancellor doesn't know I'm here, nor does Royse or Security Minister Cavazos."

Luci nods but still struggles to understand. "I don't follow. What is it then?"

"My uncle has a friend. I've never met them, but anyway, this friend of his figured out how to restore my access from the other day."

"They hacked you into here? I don't understand."

Shar pulls Luci's fingers to the Viatorio peeking out of her platinum hair. "They modified this in the system. He said because I had the access before, they were able to turn it back on. They'd never be able to grant access—there's too many security protocols—but switching an existing account back to operational status can be done without triggering signal alarms."

Luci lowers her hand from the device fused into the girl's earlobe. "But how did your uncle know about Ish being taken? Why send you today?"

"I've been back several times," Shar says with an expectant expression.

"Several times? Back to what?" Luci's overwhelmed. "Are you talking about taking leap skips?"

"I'm talking about that I left you the notes."

Luci scoots back on the couch as if she's been sucker-punched in the gut. "The what?" she asks, half-laughing, shaking her head.

"The notes," Shar says. "You got them, right? It was me. I left them for you. *'We've got a plan to break you free.'*"

"What . . . what did you just say?" Her head is swimming, but her stomach's somersaults turn twice as fast.

"I left you the notes, the ones about breaking you out of here and not to trust Macer." She tilts her head and looks at her quizzically. "You got them, right? My notes?"

Luci's mouth dries up like cotton. "The notes . . . you? That was you in the wee hours this morning?" She feels sick. "I don't understand. What are you doing here?"

"My uncle sent me to get you out of here, and—"

Luci prods at her hesitation. "And what? What?"

"I . . . I wanted to see you one last time," Shar says, eyes widening. "One more time before you go." She presses her teeth against her bottom lip. "I need to tell you something."

Luci nods, taking note of Shar's black jumpsuit and flashes back to the hooded figure she encountered less than twelve hours ago. It really *was* her. She can see that now. "Why the notes?" Luci asks, still perplexed, her thoughts whirling like a feather in a tornado.

"Sorry the notes were so cryptic. That was my uncle's idea. He told me what to write. He said that I should see what you would do first."

"What do you mean?" Luci asks. "Was he afraid I'd tell Macer?"

"He said that we couldn't take the chance that you'd involve the chancellor or report it to security." The tone in Shar's voice changes. It's less guarded, and the words spew from her like a fountain now. "Luci, I've been so worried for you. It broke my heart that I couldn't help you with what you were going through. It's been tearing me up inside that I couldn't speak to you. I couldn't even sign my name to the notes for fear they'd realize that I had access to the guesthouse again."

Luci senses there's something more to this. "Shar, the time before, with the other version of me, the older version of me . . . Did you and I become friends?"

Instead of answering, Shar reaches for her Viatorio.

"What is it?" Luci asks in a near panic. "Is it about Ish? Has something happened?"

Shar removes her hand from the device. "No, it's just a timer I set. We only have a few minutes before my uncle arrives with the bnanti."

"Who are the bnanti?"

"No, not people. A bnanti is a watercraft. He's coming to take you to your assistant—I mean to Ish. He's due to arrive in eleven and a half minutes. So, you see, there's not much time. We have to switch clothes to get you out of here."

"Who's your uncle, and why is he risking all this?"

"His last name isn't Ryson like mine. It's Beaumont. Noah Beaumont."

"Beaumont? I know that name," Luci says, staring at the cushion between them. "He was with you. Ish said he was with you when you got the older me."

"Yes," Shar answers, pleased. "You don't know him, but in a way, he'll know you since he knew the other one."

Luci thinks about how Malom Roderick knew her older self too, and she doesn't like how she keeps getting into situations like this.

"Most people don't even know we're related," Shar volunteers with a shrug. "He prefers it that way. He's always been obsessed with maintaining his privacy. I even had to call in a favor with a friend of mine in the records division years ago to find out Uncle's birthday."

Shar stands. "Like I said, we have to trade clothes. Cybo facial recognition systems are poor, so this should work."

"Should work?" Luci scoffs, recalling the cybo incident on the first day she arrived in Relicus city. "I don't have a Viatorio. I'll never get past the—"

"We've got that covered. Just undress for now." She slowly unzips the top of her jumpsuit as if to demonstrate. "Don't worry. This is a little big on me, so it should still fit you."

Normally, those words would be insulting, but given Shar's smaller frame, Luci takes her meaning.

"You're only hope of getting past the cybo in the hall is to do exactly as I say," Shar says with raised eyebrows. "Trust me, please, Luci, for Ish's sake."

"But doesn't Cavazos have visual surveillance out there in the hallway in addition to the cybo guard?"

"Chancellor Macer had the camera systems here temporarily deactivated when you arrived," Shar answers. "Uncle says that the chancellor and Security Minister Cavazos wanted to keep the fact that anyone was in the guesthouse a secret. They didn't want anyone to know Dr. Luci Gaudiano was in Relicus City."

"No one except for Malom Roderick," she mutters, remembering Cavazos's failed attempt to flaunt her in front of the man.

"What?" Shar asks with a confused expression.

"Nothing," Luci replies, pulling her shirt over her head quickly. "So, your uncle modified your Viatorio access to get in here."

Shar steps out of the left leg of her jumpsuit, then the right. "After what happened with Malom Roderick from the time before, Chancellor Macer didn't want any trace of you being here in any of the city's systems. He didn't want someone to find out that you were in the city, much less where you were staying." She trades the clothing for Luci's top. "To do this, it required manual input clearance of everyone allowed into the guesthouse so as not to show up in any database activity logs."

Luci removes her pants and offers them to Shar. "Yeah, go on."

"So, the chancellor felt it would be more appropriate to have me by your side while you slept when you first arrived rather than Security Minister Cavazos." Her face contorts into a sour expression. "He has an unseemly reputation."

"That's an understatement."

Shar cinches the waist of the pants that Luci wore a minute ago.

Luci's growing impatient. "And your uncle Noah's friend hacked the system to allow you access to come and go as you pleased. I got all that, but you still didn't answer my question from before. Why? I mean, why risk all this? What happened before, in 2044 with the older me?"

Shar's green eyes dart away. "That time was different, less desperate a situation from when the chancellor, Royse, and I got this version of you from 2032." Shar pauses, and slowly, her eyes meet Luci's again. "The first time, we didn't know about Gicul and how you were at risk, so the chancellor sent me back to 2044 along with my uncle. Our mission was to convince you—the other you—to come to Relicus City."

When she hesitates, Luci prods her, "Go on, Shar."

She shrugs. "Well, since you'd already released your drift pattern theories in 2041, the concept of taking leap skips was already a sound theory to you, but the technology to move a human through time didn't exist yet. I didn't have to do very much in the way of convincing for you to come with us. The other Luci was eager to skip to the future. You're remarkably pragmatic. You decided to get everything in order, since the return skip wouldn't open for another thirteen months. You alerted faculty and friends that you were headed abroad and you'd return in a year or so. I stayed with you while you made your preparations."

Luci's heartrate is finally settling down. "What did the other me feel about playing a part in *Hi no Kawa*?"

Shar looks away, shaking her head. "Chancellor Macer felt that it was best to keep that from her . . . from you. I was forbidden to say anything about it. Plus, you were so happy and excited about visiting Relicus City, I didn't want to deprive you of that."

Something doesn't add up here. "Why did Chancellor Macer want the other me to come? You said there wasn't a crisis like the city is facing with Gicul and *L'inversione*, right?"

"I don't know why he sent me to get her, and I'm not exactly in a position to ask. You believe me though, right?"

She studies her. Luci can't deny that she's felt a connection to her from when they first met in the warehouse in Baltimore nearly a week ago.

Shar reaches for Luci's arm. "We have to hurry. I need two towels, please. Small ones will work best."

"You're holding something back from me, and if we are truly friends like you say, you should tell me." Luci chides her, "If you know me as well as you say that you do, you know that I need to know *everything*."

Shar acknowledges the accusation with a nod. "I've got to do something first, and then I'll tell you."

"Towels are in the kitchen," Luci says, gesturing for her to get them.

When she returns, she asks, "Do you trust me, Luci Gaudiano?"

There's something about the way Shar says her name, and then she notices a blade in her hand. "What are you going to do with the knife?" Luci asks, gulping hard.

"I'm trying to help you rescue Ish," she says, returning to the sofa. She places the hand towels to the side and takes a deep breath. "You might want to look away for a moment."

Luci leans back. "Why? What are you doing?"

"In your pocket, I have one final note for you, the most important thing I've ever written."

Luci can tell Shar's psyching herself up for something. "What are you doing, Shar?" she demands, feeling her stomach knot up. "What's the plan for me to get past the cybo without a Viatorio? Tell me, Shar!"

"My uncle told me this story about a pre-world painter," she says, examining the blade. "Vincent something or other."

The statement confirms Luci's suspicions, and she's horrified. "Shar, don't do it," she pleads as the girl places the knife on the side of the ear with the Viatorio. "Please! There's got to be another way. Don't do it!"

She shakes her head slightly. "He sent his ear to his lover."

"Shit, no!" Luci slides off the couch to her knees. "Please don't. I'm begging you."

She shrugs. "It's your only way out of here, the only way to save Ish. Read my final note to you . . . breast pocket above your heart."

Luci's quivering hand makes it difficult to unbutton it. Her eyes freeze on Shar's doll-like face. Still transfixed on her and the knife, Luci feels around inside the pocket. Her fingers brush against something plastic, not paper, and she pulls it out. It's a rectangle the size of a name badge with a crudely etched inscription on the white plastic face.

⊥L ∧LW∆Ƶ LUV YŪ LU∅Ƈ Ɨ

She understands it all now. Luci's throat constricts, and more tears stream down her cheeks. An unexpected pang of guilt spears her heart. "Please, you don't have to do this."

Shar ignores the words. "I love you. I love you, Luci Gaudiano! The time we spent together a few years ago was the happiest time of my life."

Her expression intensifies. "I can help to save you this time. Last time, I couldn't do anything when they took you away, but this time I can." Shar explains as she moves the blade back and forth slowly against the fleshy lobe. She winces and gasps loudly as if taken by surprise. Even with her eyes pressed tightly closed, tears escape down her cheeks. Shar lets out a wail that pierces Luci's heart. Generous crisscrossing streams of blood flow down the girl's forearm and terminate in thick droplets off the elbow. The curled-up ends of the bottom right side of her platinum white hair turn a speckled red. It looks like some hellish, macabre Christmas ribbon.

Only by sheer will is Luci able to keep down the bile begging to climb up her esophagus. She shakes her head. Between fingers pressed tightly against her lips, she whispers in horror, "No, Shar. Please, no."

Shar's teary eyes open wide as the knife falls to the floor with an echoing clang.

Blood is everywhere.

Luci snatches the towels and mashes them against the side of Shar's self-inflicted wound to slow the bleeding. "Pressure . . . we've got to put pressure on it."

Obviously in a tremendous amount of pain, Shar's words come out in brittle, breathy sputters. "I know . . . this is barbaric, but my uncle . . . he says it'll work. The cybo sensors will perform an identity scan as you go by . . . but they'll see me instead."

Luci's about to compare it to a door access card in an office building until she realizes that the reference would probably be lost on Shar and just says, "Okay, I understand."

Shar sits forward to admire her handiwork beside the blade. "There it is. Take it," she says, motioning to the lobe connected to the Viatorio. "Uncle told me . . . V sensors check for a live . . . pulse every six and a half minutes, so you'd better . . ." She bites her lip. "Better get moving . . . to get past the cybo out there."

Luci looks down at the crimson-colored lobe and the attached device. She thinks to herself that it'll be a miracle if she makes it through this without gagging.

Shar inhales sharply and begs her, "Take it, please."

The sharp odor of blood iron fills the air.

"I . . . I don't know what to say," Luci responds, trying to decide where to grab it as if she were picking up a scorpion.

"I don't . . . expect you to say . . . anything. I just want you to go . . . and be safe, but I had to tell you. I never told the other you how I felt . . . how I loved her, and now she's gone . . . so I wanted you to know."

Luci reluctantly pinches the part of the lobe attached to the Viatorio to avoid clicking anything on the device itself. It's sticky. She lifts it, holding it far from her body. "I'm sorry. This is hard for me to do."

Shar dangles the cleaner of the two towels to her. "Wrap it in . . . this."

"Okay, yeah, that's good," Luci says, receiving the cloth. She rises to her feet while wrapping it tightly in the towel. A thought enters her mind. "Shar, what are you going to tell Royse and Macer about this?"

"I almost forgot. I have a fake message requesting . . . me to come here and saying my access had been restored. The plan is for me to say that when I arrived, you . . . overpowered me and took the Viatorio and my clothes."

Luci runs the scenario over in her mind. She's skeptical it will be believed. There's not enough evidence of a struggle.

"So I need one more favor from you," Shar says.

"Oh, please no more blood," she says, swallowing hard while backing up.

Shar makes a dismissive wave with the hand that's not pressing the towel against her face. "Not that. Hit me."

"Shar, I can't . . . you're already—"

She slumps back into the sofa. "Luci, I fell in love with you . . . a long time ago, and though you don't remember any of it, because it was her and . . . not your experience, you're still you, and for . . . better or worse, I'm still me. I love you, Luci Gaudiano . . . every version of you." She swallows and closes her eyes. "Hit me like my life depends on it . . . because it probably does."

The guilt and turmoil Luci's experiencing feels like she's just doubled down on these emotions. "Damn it," she swears at the circumstances that have brought her to this juncture. She regards the girl before her and wonders if the older Luci had fallen in love with her too or if the feelings were one sided. If older Luci had loved her, it would mean that the dormant seed of that emotion was inside of Luci also. How could she strike her?

"You've got to do it, Luci, for them to believe my story," Shar prompts her.

"I know, I know," Luci says, but her mind is scrambling for an alternative. There has to be some other way, an intelligent option . . . a non-violent option. She wipes tears flowing down her face, reaching an unpleasant conclusion. "Thank you." She sniffs. "Thank you for everything."

"Stop thanking me and hit—"

Luci strikes her hard enough that she only has to do it once. At first, Luci thinks that she may have knocked her out, but then Shar lets out a feeble groan. Shar cracks open her eye that's already beginning to swell. "Yeah, that should do it. That was good."

Clutching the towel folded around the bloody Viatorio, Luci leans in to place a long, soulful kiss atop Shar's clammy forehead. "Thank you."

"The door's still open," Shar says. "You be safe for me, alright?" She runs the fingers of her free hand up and down Luci's face, tracing the path of her tears.

When Shar pushes up to press her lips against Luci's mouth, she doesn't resist. Luci's certain that it won't take long for the authorities to learn what's happened here. If they don't fall for her lie, Shar's punishment for betraying Cavazos and Macer is likely a swift, merciless horror. So yeah, she can allow the girl this indulgence.

Sooner than expected, Shar pulls back, her widened emerald-green eyes staring into Luci's. She whispers, "You've got to go. My uncle will be waiting on the water for you."

Luci wants to comfort her for just a little longer, but Shar shoves at her with her free hand. "Go, Luci. Get out of here."

"Shar, I—"

She cuts her off. "Go rescue your friend and leave Relicus City. Make all of this worth it."

Luci offers a feeble half smile and nods. She forces the lump forming in her throat downward and sniffs, trying to find her voice. "I will, I promise."

PORT IV

(Part IV)

ONE

LUCI MOVES TO THE OPEN door, holding the bloody towel with the Viatorio. She extends it like a priest brandishing a crucifix in a den of vampires. The cybo on the other side of the threshold tilts its head slightly as she passes by, barely taking notice of her exit.

The door hisses as it slides shut with a hollow thud. "Good luck, Shar," she says aloud, beginning to trot down the corridor to the elevator.

Once inside, she drops the towel and its grisly contents, kicking it to the corner of the compartment away from her. The doors close, and Luci exhales a deep sigh. Her stomach throbs like a nest of angry hornets. She steadies herself with her hand against the cool metal wall until she notices some of Shar's already dried blood on her. Jerking her hand to her side, she fiercely rubs it against the thigh of her black jumpsuit until the elevator doors reopen. Luci bolts out like it's the horse gate at the racetrack, and she is standing atop the windy walkway in no time.

But there's no boat, only the rhythmic sound of seawater slapping against the support beams below.

She anxiously scans the horizon for approaching craft, but the water is empty. She runs to the other side of the boardwalk-like platform, chastising herself for not confirming with Shar which side her uncle's boat would arrive on. The saltwater-laced breeze mocks her, lifting strands of hair in all directions as she walks back to the side where Cavazos's boat departed a few hours ago.

Sunlight peeks through a break in the clouds. The top of Macer's dome refracts beams onto the water that sway like thousands of iridescent slivers. She wonders if Royse was being truthful about the chancellor being in a meeting elsewhere, not that she can go to Macer anyway—not now.

She leans against the rail of the walkway, feeling even more trapped than being locked inside the guesthouse. Luci closes her eyes and takes a deep breath. "Sorry, Ish. I'm so sorry."

"Dr. Gaudiano," a man's voice calls out. It sounds as far away as a dream. Luci snaps to attention, scanning for the source as her name is repeated. She's confused that there's still no boat. She turns around and looks overhead for a drobine or some other transport, but the sky's empty.

"Dr. Gaudiano . . . Luci, down here," the voice announces. "I'm down here . . . in the water."

She redirects her attention below the balcony until she sees someone in the water. They bob on the waves like a cork next to something orange and flat that she can't quite make out. Playing it safe, she shouts back, "Do you know Shar?"

"Of course, I do," the man answers, continuing to rhythmically lift and fall with the water. "I'm her uncle."

"Then what's your name?" Luci asks, stalling to look around in case this is an ambush by *L'inversione.*

"My name is Noah Beaumont, and I've been sent here to take you to your partner, Ish Moyta."

Luci's heart skips a beat, trying to decide if she can trust this man or not.

"Doctor, I can't stay above water very long undetected. Come with me now." There's a pause before the man below adds, "Technician Moyta is scheduled for cybo reconditioning."

The confirmation of her worst fear causes Luci's knees to buckle, but her grip on the railing steadies her. "Where's your boat? Did *L'inversione* destroy it or something?"

There's a pause. "I told Shar that I'd bring a bnanti, a two-seater. It's a submersible."

Luci studies the manhole-sized opening of the orange plank beside him and finally realizes that she's looking down at the top of a mini-sub. "Why didn't Shar say it was a submarine?" she mumbles to herself, her heartrate accelerating. "*Why underwater? Cavazos's boat was bad enough.*" Every muscle in her body ratchets up to piano-string tightness.

As if he can read her thoughts, Beaumont volunteers, "We can't risk traveling in the sky or atop the water. Security would catch us."

Luci feels sick as she attempts to hold back the onslaught of images of her near fatal drowning.

Beaumont urges again, "Doctor, please hurry. I need to get the bnanti back under the surface before they find us." His hand emerges from the water to point toward the guesthouse behind her. "We need you so Mr. Moyta knows that it's safe to come with us. He'll believe us if he sees you."

The words puncture her heart like needles. He wants to ask who the "*us*" is but says instead, "I don't think that I can go with you. I have a thing about water."

"A thing?" Beaumont shouts back up to her. "You don't have time to have *a thing*. We've got to get out of here." There's a genuine desperation in his voice. "I've probably already been water-top too long as it is. I can mask scans for the bnanti at lower depths, but on top like this . . . We're exposed if we're up here for too long."

"I'm sorry, Mr. Beaumont, but I don't think that I can do it."

He pleads, "I know of your aversion to water, but think about what Shar did for you." He pauses. "She did that for Mr. Moyta, someone she's never even met."

Luci's throat is dry and raw as she shouts back down to him. "I know . . . I know, anything but water. I had a very bad experience with water when I was young. I just—"

"I know. I remember, but he's going to die if you don't come with me!" Beaumont yells, and Luci knows it's not just to be heard above the din of the waves. "We were told that this person meant something to you."

Her fist tightens as she wonders how he could know anything at all about the two of them. She couldn't feel more violated if she kept a diary and the man below her had ripped pages from it to use against her. Luci's feelings of defilement are only superseded by confusion. How could he—or anyone, for that matter—know about her and Ish? Cavazos had only caught them kissing earlier in this morning, and Beaumont obviously wasn't working with that windbag.

He prompts her again, "Doctor Gaudiano, we have to leave."

"Okay, okay!" she screams, moving to the opening with the ladder. "I'll do it."

"Whoa, wait! Not the ladder. It's got sensors that alert security if someone's climbing up it."

"So, what then?" Luci asks, swallowing hard. "I have to . . . jump?"

"The sensors."

"I can't swim," she says defiantly. "I never learned how." This is the lie that she has told people for so many years that she's nearly convinced herself it's true. "I told you, I have a thing about water."

"You don't have to swim. Jump and I'll get you. It'll only be for a few seconds, and I'll pull you up."

Her mind works overtime trying to find an alternative to all of this, searching for some option that's been overlooked, but there is none. This is the only possibility she has in order to save Ish.

"You'll be safe!" Beaumont calls out, one hand gesturing for her to leap.

"Shut up! Just shut up!" she screeches in a mix of aggravation and fear. "I need a minute, okay?" She holds the rail and leans forward slightly to a dizzying result.

"Leap out and away from the platform to avoid hitting it."

She's certain that she's about to coat the rail with puke. There's no time to self-soothe with her special number, but she's got to settle her breathing or she's going to have a heart attack right here on the platform. She looks upward to the clouds and thinks of her mother and father. The wind buffets her, and the sound of the waves slapping against the structure below grow impossibly louder in her ears. She takes a deep breath and slowly exhales. "Well, shit," she says as she trots a few steps to the opening. She leaps, instinctively closing her eyes on the way down.

Time slows to a crawl as unwelcome images of young Luci trapped in the family car flash across her mind. She's jolted from the terror as her open arms slap against the water with a loud clap. The pain is unexpected, but there's little time to focus on it as a blast of water assaults her nostrils. Out of reflex, she coughs, which triggers her to inhale. She realizes the mistake instantly as stinging saltwater pours down her throat. The sound of bubbles fleeing to the surface from all around her bombard her ears as she sinks downward into darkness. Her limbs tense to the bitter cold temperature of the ocean. She painfully flails about, reaching for the disappearing sky above her, continuing to sink.

A strong, deliberate grip fastens onto her forearm. It hoists her upward at an impressive speed, busting through a weblike stream of bubbles. She reluctantly recalls cybo Benold Jesper doing this for her. Once on the surface, Luci heaves and gasps, feeling as if she's run two back-to-back marathons. Her eyes burn from the salt and tear up from nearly gagging seconds before. With the hood of the black jumpsuit filled to the brim with seawater, its heaviness weighs the back of the garment down. Luci reaches behind to push it out and ease the constricting fabric around her neck.

"You're safe now," Beaumont says, helping her latch onto the handholds near the opening of the vessel.

It prickles when she swallows, and the fatigue in her muscles forces her to lay her head against the cool riveted orange metal of the craft. The ocean mockingly sloshes against her as if to remind her of its power and unforgiving strength.

"There, that wasn't so bad, now, was it?" he asks, pulling himself to his knees on the surface of the bobbing vessel.

She wants to curse him out in English, and when she's spent all those words, switch to Italian, but she's too tired. Instead, she just coughs and spews a string of seawater spittle down her chin. "I . . . I need a minute," she sputters, her teeth chattering due to the cold. "Just a moment, please."

"I know how traumatic water is for you," he says, beginning to pull at her, "but we need to get inside and go under before some security drone spots us."

She allows his help, hoping, in exchange, to barter with him. "Are you're sure that you can't drive this thing above the water and jam a signal or something?" she pleads.

"You go in first," he says, motioning to the portal. "Sit in the front seat. I navigate from the back." He nudges her as he explains, "The scan-blocking device is only for sonar, so it has to be submerged to avoid detection."

Thinking of Ish, she reluctantly descends the waist-high ladder and moves through the narrow, tube-like crawlspace to the front plastic bucket seat. Luci's surprised that the side walls and floor of the tiny submarine are entirely transparent. While she's certain the designers did this for the optimum viewing of the passengers, she would have preferred an opaque interior. If she couldn't see through it, she might be able to pretend she was above the maliciousness of the ocean. She thinks about Cavazos's boat and how he'd never fit in a space this size. This craft could be generously compared to an oversized glass bobsled with a roof or a ridiculously thin minivan. Conscious of her elevated breathing, Luci forces a few deep inhales and exhales in hopes of warding off a bout of hyperventilation; she can't pass out in here. There's too much is at stake for Ish. She's got to keep her wits about her.

Beaumont quickly assumes his spot behind her, and the sub hatch slides shut above them with a muffled thud. There's a pressurized hiss, the sound of them being sealed into this glass-and-metal sarcophagus. Luci surprises herself with a gulp that's a lot louder in the restrictive space. She looks back at Beaumont, but he's focused on the readouts of a glowing hologram screen that's appeared before his face. She recognizes many of the graphics from the display on Cavazos's boat a few hours before. She marvels at how those events already seem like a lifetime ago.

"Here we go," Beaumont announces above beeping warning sounds and a soft automated voice reminiscent of the female speech in the longchairs. As if the change in pressure didn't make it obvious, the voice alerts them to the fact that they're descending.

"Just don't look at it," she whispers to herself. Luci takes in another deep breath and angles her head down at the small puddle of seawater collecting at her shoes until she catches a glimpse of the vastness of the ocean below.

The craft descends rapidly, and Luci is surprised when her ears don't pop due to the sudden change in pressure. This tells her that somehow, the future interval of Relicus City has managed to solve the problem of passengers in diving crafts getting the bends. Normally, she'd have to ask about the science of such a revolutionary technology, but holding her aquaphobia in check requires her full attention. Luci realizes how good she had it as a passenger of Royse's drobine flying over the city's skyline days ago. She's grateful to feel Beaumont leveling the craft off. Still feeling sick and hearing her heartbeat throbbing in her ears, she closes her eyes to self-soothe with her special number, 2012.

It doesn't work.

A crazy thought pops into her brain. As ridiculous a notion that there ever was, it's as if her numbers don't work at this depth, or maybe they've betrayed her by staying back at Macer's guesthouse with Shar. Maybe it was their revenge for her destroying all the calculations that she and Ish did. "You're cracking up, Luci G.," she mumbles to herself between staccato breaths.

"What did you say?" Beaumont asks from behind.

She gnaws at her bottom lip before asking, "How long am I going to be trapped in this thing?"

"This bnanti model can travel twenty-one kilometers per hour, which allows us to move a distance of three hundred meters in less than a minute at top speed. So we should reach our destination in about ten minutes. The craft has been rigged with a mild chrono displacement rectifier that hides our movement to any sonar scans by throwing the bnanti's propulsion registers 172 seconds in the past."

Her reply erupts from inside her. "I don't care about all of those stats. I hate this thing. Do you have to go so fast?"

"Given your feelings about water, I would have thought you'd prefer as brief a time submerged as possible."

She squirms in her seat at the term "*submerged*," and again, she wants to cuss this man out. Deep down, she knows none of this is his fault, but she can't help herself from wanting to lash out at him for subjecting her to this. The image of Shar's once-perfect face, now disfigured, pops into her mind, and she's reminded how this man is the girl's uncle. And for whatever reason that he's agreed to help Ish, Luci is in his debt. "Yeah, you're right," she replies in as pleasant a voice as she can fake. She can do ten minutes or so in this thing for Ish's sake.

"I need to ask you something," he says, displaying a hint of uncertainty in his voice for the first time. "Shar—did you make it look like you attacked her in order to break free?"

She turns to look back at him through the hologram display chart to see if he's crying. She can't tell because his slender, middle-aged face is partially obscured by blinking lights and changing coordinate status mappings floating in the air between them. "Yeah, she did good." Luci swallows the lump creeping up her throat. "And I made it look good to anyone who finds her there," she says remorsefully.

Beaumont nods slowly as if wanting to ask or say something else, but all that comes out is, "Thank you, Luci."

LUCI HERSELF HAS A MILLION questions to ask him such as where they're headed, how they'll free Ish, what's to become of Shar, and the most puzzling question of all, how they knew that Ish had been taken in the first place. These questions and many more clamor around her head, but racing through the ocean like a bullet has her preoccupied. It takes everything in her to keep from coating the glass enclosure around her with vomit. Answers can wait until they're topside again, and she estimates that to be in seven minutes or so.

She's never given thought to what a torpedo shot through open water must feel like until now. While her rational mind knows that they truly couldn't be going nearly that fast, there's no sea life of any kind to focus on in order to properly gauge the bnanti's speed.

She makes a second attempt at distracting herself with numbers. Thankfully, it works for her this time. Given her present circumstance, doing self-soothing calculations down to the date that she nearly drowned as a child isn't very appealing to her. Instead, she invents a new game, something more positive: how many days has she lived beyond the accident? She closes her eyes to work out the problem. Halfway through, she realizes the question has two answers. Because of the leap skip, 65,244 days equal the total number of days that have transpired in real-time since August 9th of 2012, but she's actually only lived through 7,190 days.

She's about to repeat the game for the fifth cycle, this time calculating the hours that have passed since that fateful day on the bridge when the pitch of the bnanti adjusts steeply upward.

"Is something wrong?" she asks, anxiously searching through the sides and bottom glass of the submarine for anyone pursuing them. "What's happening?"

Beaumont responds evenly, "Nothing's wrong. We're almost there."

"Where is there?" she asks.

"Up there," he answers, throttling the engines.

Luci's pushed back in her seat as the vessel climbs toward a red glow of shimmering light in the watery distance above them.

Objects take form overhead as the bnanti shoots through the open water toward the dancing crimson glow. She gauges the opening it's shining through to be approximately the length of a semi-truck, if not longer. The submersible's propellers dutifully thrust toward the underside of a large, flat metal structure of tubes and pipes. Half a minute later, the bnanti erupts through the opening.

Beaumont kills the humming engines, allowing the craft to gently sway from side to side.

Luci swallows, and asks, "Are we where Ish is being held?"

Beaumont clicks off the hologram navigation screen and pulls a lever to release the pressure lock on the hatch. "No, we're at the halfway point to where he is." He moves to the ladder to exit and pauses. "Listen, I don't want to alarm you, but the people out there in the bay—"

"People?" Luci interrupts. "What people?"

"People that are going to help us to get your friend," he continues, slightly agitated about being cut off. "They're a little jumpy right now, so don't make any sudden moves or anything."

"Sudden moves? Who's out there?"

"Friends of mine," he says, headed up the ladder. "You'll see."

TWO

LUCI CAUTIOUSLY CLIMBS THE SUBMARINE'S ladder to the hatch to peek over the lip of the opening. A dank, sour smell assaults her nose, but it's the silhouettes of churka-wielding figures in the dim red light that take her breath away. In a panic, she tries to retreat down into the sub, but Beaumont reaches down from behind and snags the shoulders of her jumpsuit. "Come on," he says, trying to lift her up and out. "It's alright. Like I said, they're with me."

Shooting a glance over her shoulder at him, she protests, "If they're your friends, why are they aiming weapons at us?"

"They just need a minute to check us," he says, releasing his grip. "We're safe here, I promise. We'll have to get back in the water though."

"Back in? Why?"

"This place isn't really a bnanti dock," he informs her, "but I'll help you."

"Great," she scoffs.

Her emergence from the sub makes it bob on the water more sporadically, and the bnanti sloshes a rhythmic refrain from the ocean it's connected to below. She clamps onto the handholds on the side next to Beaumont as if her life depends on it, reluctantly inching her feet down the side of the slippery craft. Cold water from her waist down pricks her skin like tiny ice needles as she re-enters the ocean. She reminds herself that all of this is for Ish and she must press through her phobias.

"Noah?" a gruff female voice calls from the darkness.

"Yes, Ley, it's me," he answers in a voice loud enough to startle Luci into nearly losing her grip on the handholds. "And I've got the doctor here."

"Who's that?" she asks, awkwardly kicking her legs at the water while studying the eight or so silhouettes before them. Luci recalls a phrase from her father about shooting fish in a barrel, and now she knows the perspective of the fish. She spins to look behind at another row of ten or more targeting them from the water's edge on the other side.

Beaumont whispers, "That's Ley, the person that I . . . *report* to here."

Still not convinced of their safety, Luci scans the area for an escape. She's not certain how anyone would be able to make it past the group assembled before them. She and Beaumont have emerged near the end of a trough-like channel. It's a third as long as an Olympic-sized pool lane but three times as wide. Luci winces at the realization that the only perceivable way out of here without taking a churka blast is back down through the water they've just come through.

"You're certain that they'll help us with Ish?"

Before he can answer, the woman's gruff voice from the side calls out again, "What took you so long? Was there a problem with your niece coming through for us?"

Luci scans the row of dark statue-like figures before them for the source of the voice, but she can only approximate that it's coming from the front right.

"Nothing's wrong," Beaumont replies, obviously attempting to sound upbeat while also turning to locate the unseen speaker. "Shar did what we needed."

The unwelcome image of Shar's bloody ear flashes in Luci's mind.

Beaumont continues, "It just took a little longer is all."

Luci takes a deep breath, knowing he's referring to her hesitation to jump into the water back at the guesthouse.

There's a tense pause until Beaumont unhooks one of his hands from the grip to hold it up with fingers spread wide. "I'm shriveling away to nothing here, and this water's freezing. Can we get some towels and get off this blasted thing, please?"

This elicits a few stifled chuckles from the crowd, easing some of the tension. All the weapons lower as if connected to the same invisible string, all but one on the right: the churka extending from a bulky five-and-a-half-foot-tall silhouette. "Go on, Jonn, help them up," the gruff voice commands.

One of the taller dark forms, presumably Jonn, hooks the front end of the bnanti with a long pole. To Luci, it looks a little like the Hulk fishing leaves out of a backyard swimming pool. She marvels at the strength of this guy to pull the mini-sub along with her and Beaumont dangling from the sides through the water.

"Thanks, old friend," Beaumont says as the big man effortlessly hoists him onto the metal platform.

His massive hand pats Beaumont on the back as he says in a baritone voice, "Sorry, Noah. Everyone's got those pre-mission nerves."

Luci clutches the handhold while extending her other arm in Jonn's direction. He bends and places her on the slick metal deck as Beaumont answers him, "Well, two missions means double the anxiety, right?"

"Double the victory, old friend," Jonn replies. "Double the victory and our final stand."

Luci wants to ask about what other mission there is besides rescuing Ish when she notices Ley's churka still pointed at her.

There's a beeping sound from the low, claustrophobic ceiling like a garbage truck backing in reverse. At first, Luci believes it's an alarm of some sort until she realizes that no one is reacting to it. The seawater in the elongated channel sloshes from side to side as a series of great metal panels slide into place to seal the area off from the ocean below. Then the floor quivers as the panels fasten closed with a deep, resounding clunk.

"That's better," the woman with the gruff voice says as the crimson light brightens to a soft pink-white. Ley hands her churka to Jonn. "I'd like to take a look at the great Luci Gaudiano from the twenty-first century."

The relief Luci feels that Ley isn't pointing a blaster at her instantly fades with this impromptu inspection. Ley proceeds to stroll in a slow circle around her as Luci's waterlogged jumpsuit leaks into a puddle gathered at her sopping shoes. The cool, sour air is not as chilling to her as feeling the uneasy mix of a drill instructor sizing up a new cadet. Ley moves like a python searching out any weakness in its intended prey.

Luci stiffens and crosses her arms. "I'm here to help free Ish Moyta. What are—"

Ley, coming back around to the front of her, halts and holds up a finger for her to be silent. "Just a moment, Doctor." Her breath is as stale as the air in this place. "We'll get to all of that soon enough." The pink-white light makes her short-cropped red hair look like fire. This matches the countless freckles spackled across her face and arms. She repeats, "*Soon enough* indeed."

Luci notices something that puts her off, a misshapen deformity with Ley's right earlobe, deliberately severed like Shar's. She shoots a glance to the unmoving crowd behind the woman. While the racial mix is as diverse as the UN from her time, they all share this mutilation. Their disfigurements have had time enough to scar over, unlike Shar's fresh mutilation back at Macer's guesthouse. She wonders if she misunderstood Ish's explanation a few days ago about how Viatorios "tag audit" each resident of Relicus City and the Grange. Shouldn't the system notice the non-operational Viatorios of each person here? She's about to ask Beaumont how these people can operate in the confines of the city without triggering alerts to Cavazos's security when she notices he also shares this group trait. For the first time, she's able to get a good look at him in the pink light, and she can't believe that she missed this on him before.

Ley returns to slowing circling her, assessing Luci. "This, my brothers and sisters, is the woman that destroyed the world."

Before thinking, Luci tenses and responds bitterly with, "No, the world destroyed itself."

She scoffs. "Right. I guess you feel that you only supplied the spark that lit the fuse," Ley says, stopping in front again to face her.

There's an odd mix of awe and contempt in the area as if both Galileo and Adolph Hitler had been transported into the abandoned machine shop. Luci feels their stares penetrating her. There's nowhere to retreat and hide as rage bubbles up in her heart. Normally one who is collected and logical to the point of being labeled a cold-hearted fish, Luci doesn't hold anything back from her accuser. "Can you truly be that obtuse?" she asks. Her face heats up, and her ears feel like smoldering cinders. "That's about as moronic as saying that what the Wright brothers achieved for flight at Kitty Hawk was directly responsible for the Enola Gay obliterating the city of Hiroshima four decades later." Her eyes lock onto a face in the crowd, a young boy of seventeen or eighteen, possibly of Asian heritage. Luci turns away from him, embarrassed for choosing that as an example.

The accusation still stings in her heart though. "My world . . . my interval *was* destroyed by nuclear fire, but not because of me, not because of my discovery!" Her voice is unsteady, but she's got to get this out—all of it. "What I came across is an elegant pillar of the universe, an unparalleled, sublime discovery. And like a beautiful child stripped from his mother's arms—a *stretch*, if you will—it was taken away to be abused and hardened into an unrecognizable creature engineered to kill the world and everything in it. That's what was done with my drift pattern discovery. No, I didn't light the fuse."

Her rant silences Ley, whose stunned expression is an open mouth and raised eyebrows.

Luci capitalizes on her adversary's dumbfound state by adding, "So if you'll cut the bullshit, I'd like you to take me to where Ish is being held so we can get him out of there before it's too late."

The teenage boy from the crowd steps forward, addressing Ley instead of Luci. "I still don't understand why we're going to all the trouble to free a level-three tech." He points to Luci, who is still dripping water onto the floor. "I mean, I get why he may want *her*, but why her assistant? Does this Moyta know something that can help us with the final skip?"

Luci looks to the leader of the group, eager to hear the answer for herself. *Why do they want him?*

Ley doesn't face him, choosing instead to glare at Luci. "Orders, Yuma. Orders. We don't have to know why."

Yuma mutters his dissatisfaction but mildly enough to avoid provoking Ley's ire.

She disengages her glare on Luci and turns to confront the gawkers. "Don't you all have something that you're supposed to be doing right now?"

Ley's caustic question is like flipping a switch, spurring them all into action. The two dozen or so onlookers immediately disband and busy themselves like ants, mumbling all the way.

Though she catches plenty of stolen glances back at her from the group, Luci is grateful to not be the center of attention. Men and women of various ages and ethnicities bustle about, entering and leaving through open doorways on the side and back wall of the warehouse.

Luci gets her first true look at the area, and judging by the numerous boats and watercraft in various states of disrepair strewn about the place, she concludes that it may have once been a mechanical shop of some sort. Moist saltwater air and time have hijacked the forgotten place, converting it into an incubator for rust.

"What are we looking at in terms of security, Ley?" Beaumont asks.

She defers to Yuma, the only one who hasn't scurried off like the others.

He speaks with an assuredness beyond his years. "A handful of us will intercept the cybos as they move him from the containment area to something called a cognitive realignment station. We're expecting a cybo escort of anywhere from five to six of those things."

Luci remembers how quickly the Benold Jesper cybo reacted on Cavazos's boat, and a sense of dread takes her breath. That was only one guard. How could they combat half a dozen of them?

Yuma continues without prompting, obviously relishing being the center of attention. "The processing center is in the same building complex as the holding cell he's confined in, but in order to move a prisoner to there, the cybos have to go through a courtyard area. Floorplans indicate that there are no corridors or tunnels connecting the holding cell to the cognitive realignment station, so we know this is the route that they're forced to take."

The second mention of *cognitive realignment station* gives Luci a shiver.

"It's not a large area, so we'll have to move quickly, but there is a balcony that will shield us." A self-satisfied smile forms on Yuma's face like a dog awaiting a treat for a trick well done. "There's no human security. It's all cybos. There's not even video monitors, just the guards."

To her astonishment, Beaumont nods contemplatively as if this news was good. "It's because no one would have the audacity to attempt something like this."

Before Luci can comment on going up against a squad of cybos, Ley interjects, "Roderick went on to Cyphor to give an update and help with the skip preparations. I'm headed there too in a few minutes with the final ESTA component we snatched from Cavazos in old-world Colorado."

"Roderick? Cyphor?" Luci says aloud in astonished disbelief. Her head swims as she wonders if she heard Ley correctly. She's frightened and embarrassed simultaneously. How she could be stupid enough to be duped like this? The temples of her head pound like a bass drum, and she feels like someone has removed the area's oxygen with a flick of a switch. Luci bites her lip and focuses on Beaumont. Her heart thumps harder than it did on the journey over here. The atmosphere thickens, making it hard to get the words out. "So you people are *L'inversione*?"

Ley answers indifferently, "Among other things."

Luci ignores her, directing sharp barbs at Beaumont. "You tricked me. Shar said that she wasn't with *L'inversione*."

"She's not, but *he* is," Ley answers with a smug expression.

Luci looks past Ley at Jonn in the distance. He and another man carry an old-style steamer trunk. "What's your friend got in the trunk over there, Noah?" She gestures at the two lowering it to a metal platform. "Is that a bomb or something?"

Ley turns to look at the trunk and taunts, "Only someone from pre-*Hi no Kawa* twenty-first century would assume that was a combustible explosive."

Yuma blurts, "It's not a bomb." When Ley, Beaumont, and Luci simultaneously give him the same annoyed look, he shrugs defensively, adding, "What? It's *not* . . . it's not a bomb."

"No, it's not an explosive, Luci," Beaumont reassures her in a familial tone. Luci recalls Shar saying that this man had spent time with the old Luci. Is that true? Had it been a trap from the beginning? Was any of this true? Her stomach knots and re-knots, twisting in every direction at once.

Beaumont adds in the same soft-spoken tone, "It contains ESTA components . . . old, pre-world satellite parts that we took back from Macer's wicked government. Until you came along, it was the only hope for the future of all mankind."

The phrase hangs awkwardly in the air.

"It was . . ." She coughs. "You said it *was* the only hope." She's trembling, partly because she's sopping wet, but mostly at the revelation of who these people are. "So is this . . . is this the place where I die?" She scans the area for a churka she may grab; she's not going down without a fight. While the thought of killing one of them isn't appealing, if she can figure out how to operate the weapon, maybe she can blast a hole in the trunk over there and at least mess up their plans before they take her out. "So this whole thing . . . the rescue of Ish, it was just to lure me here to kill me?" She turns to Beaumont. "Why didn't you just let me drown back at the guesthouse? What's this all about? Am I bait or something? What are you planning to do to Ish when you get him?"

Ley lets out an exasperated sigh as she pulls a metal disc slightly larger than a hockey puck and twice as thick from a side pocket of her jumpsuit.

Though it doesn't look like a weapon, Luci still flinches and pulls back.

Ley chuckles snidely at this. "Relax, this isn't for you. It's not a weapon." She motions to a middle-aged, dark-skinned woman across the bay. "Technically, we don't have to kill you anymore."

As the woman makes adjustments, Luci finally recognizes the device as a holo vid player. The design isn't the same as the one she saw in the Baltimore warehouse, and it's even more different from the one Macer had in his office, but it's definitely the same technology. "We only have to prevent you from going back, Doctor. Macer bringing you here was an unexpected gift to us."

"Is that supposed to be reassuring to me?" Luci asks, unfolding her arms, still dripping saltwater with faint taps onto the floor. "Am I supposed to be okay with being trapped here?"

Ley hands the holo vid player off to the woman she motioned to. "Hopefully, killing you can be avoided, but Gicul has given us some latitude in this regard, so I'd watch it if I were you."

Luci takes a step back and looks to Beaumont, still in a fog of confusion.

He massages his forehead. "Luci, this is not something that we take delight in, but what we do has to be done. You cannot be allowed to present your DPM discovery to the world . . . ever. I'm sorry."

She wants to ask about Ish but instead opts to point out the one major logic flaw in this enterprise. "How do you all see this thing playing out? If you kill me or force me to remain here, *Hi no Kawa* doesn't occur and all of you cease to ever exist and vanish." She knows that it's the same tactic she used on Macer, but the point remains valid.

Luci wants to break Ley's wagging finger as the woman makes a tsk-tsk-tsk sound with her tongue. "That's not so, Doctor. There's a place outside of time that Cyphor says that we all can skip to to 'unlink' our chronal anchor kedge. Doing this will protect us from what we call the 'Undoing Ripple Effect.'"

Tiny hairs on Luci's neck bristle at the mention of Cyphor and Carcerium together.

Yuma, who's been silent since his last rebuke, seizes the opportunity to jump back in. "Even though Relicus will cease to be, the anomaly will allow all of us to skip to the past and live out our lives in a lush world with plenty of pre-*Hi no Kawa* food." He pauses his rapid-fire speaking, searching for a word. Finally, he blurts out an improperly pronounced, "*Iryland.* Old world year 1646, Iryland."

"He means Ireland," Beaumont volunteers on the boy's behalf.

Luci doesn't care. Her mind latches onto the possibility of a way for her and Ish to live beyond Relicus City and the so-called "Undoing Ripple Effect." Her mind for science must be satiated. She has to know how this can be performed. "You know this works? You're certain that you'd survive past Relicus City never being formed because this Cyphor guy told you that's how it works?"

"I've seen it," Beaumont clarifies. "Not Ireland, but the Carcerium. I've been there. Cyphor sent a message with coordinates. We're including that information at the end of the holo vid that we're uploading to everyone in the city. I skipped there myself about ten months ago to break Malom out."

She pictures the blank white room with Malom's empty coils as the revelation rattles her. "Ten months ago? I saw him in there just a few hours ago."

"In your personal timeline, maybe," Ley says, "but many of us spent the last nine months learning to ride equine creatures back in the pre-world, waiting for Minister Cavazos to arrive with the ESTA modules."

"Why is the ESTA so important? It's just old time-traveling weather satellite components, right? What does Gicul need that old junk for?"

"I'm impressed," Beaumont says. "Yes, it was the first use of DPM—before *Hi no Kawa*, even. Cavazos tried to hide it there from Cyphor, but we took it back."

"Where's Cavazos now?"

Ley exchanges a look with Beaumont that turns into a snide expression on her face.

"He's dead," Yuma says before anyone else can answer.

Ley nods, still grinning. "Noah here said that Security Minister Cavazos had a pre-world weapon explode in his face. You called it a *revolver*, if I remember correctly." She mumbles to herself, "Sorry that I missed that, actually."

"You . . . you shot him in the face?"

Beaumont answers, "I wasn't there. Malom did it."

Luci shakes her head in disgust. "Apparently, Malom Roderick is a pretty proficient killer."

"Humph," Ley says. "Too good a death for that rot-throbbing rag fondler if you asked me."

A lanky Hispanic man approaches with two shrink-wrapped packages cradled in his arms. "Pardon me, but you both should change out of those wet clothes. You look cold."

"Thanks," Luci mumbles, examining the contents. She holds up a cowboy hat and a western-wear shirt while allowing the boots and pants to fall to the floor. "Is this a joke? You want me to wear this . . . this *costume*? It looks like I'm going to a hoedown."

The man looks down at his shoes. "Sorry, we weren't expecting you to go out. It's all that we have here that will fit you. It's a leftover from a leap skip that we took."

She glances at Beaumont's bundle, which is more akin to what everyone else is wearing. "I'm *not* wearing the hat."

"He's right," Ley grumbles. "You two should go and get changed. The teams will be leaving in fifteen minutes or so."

The four of them follow the lanky man to the doorway, Beaumont and Luci side by side with Yuma and Ley trailing behind. Luci's compelled to challenge the soundness of the plan, considering how Ish's life hangs in the balance. "Noah, are you sure that you have enough firepower to rescue Ish? Six cybos is quite a gathering of might. They're exceptionally fast. I've seen them firsthand."

"Well, the estimate is actually six to ten cybos. Anyway, we've got this." He tucks his pack of clothes under his arm and produces a small, flat onyx rectangle from his pocket.

Unlike the holo vid device, Luci instantly recognizes it. Her heart skips a beat. "How did you get one of those controllers?"

Yuma races up to them. "It's a PQX inhibitor. It's supposed to be able to freeze any cybos in place in a thirty-meter radius. It belonged to Security Minister Cavazos."

She recalls it being on a chain around Cavazos's fleshy neck. *They really did kill him.*

Beaumont tucks it back into the pocket without slowing his steps. "That's right, so you'll need to stick close to me and not wander off when we get there—for your own safety, of course."

"Wander off?" she asks acerbically. "Wander off to where?"

As if it's his turn to speak again, Yuma volunteers, "Any cybo that is outside of the beam radius is still to be considered operative and can get off a churka blast or grab you."

A realization pops into her mind. Luci abruptly stops in her tracks, bringing the group to a clumsy halt. "You insensitive ass," she says, shoving Beaumont's arm hard enough that he nearly drops his bundle of clothes.

Ley gestures to the man leading them to go on. "It's fine, Miguel."

He nods and eagerly disappears through the doorway, escaping from the drama.

This doesn't deter Luci in the least. "You had that thing with you this entire time?"

Before Beaumont can answer, she scolds him, "You could've used it!" A wave of misplaced guilt finds its way into her heart, fueling her anger. "You can control cybos with that thing, and you let Shar, your own *niece*, slice her ear and force me to take it from her."

"She's not with *L'inversione*," Yuma says. "We can't risk using it until it's needed. He did the right thing."

Beaumont nods. "Once the device disables a cybo or cybos, the disconnect interruption will undoubtedly trigger an investigation into what's going on, so we have to use it sparingly."

"She did it in front of me, you bastard!" she says, letting her clothing bundle fall to the ground. She's so angry, she's shaking.

Yuma looks at Beaumont. "We've all done it. It's no big deal. We've all cut off our Viatorios."

Luci closes the space between her and Yuma. "I've had enough of you. If you don't shut up, I swear I'm going to knock your ass out."

With widened eyes locked onto Luci's fist, the boy stumbles back into Ley.

Luci pivots to face her original target, Beaumont. "She's your own family. You're as sick as Cavazos. You're all monsters here. You should be ashamed."

"I did what I had to," he says. "I've always done what I've had to do. We've all made sacrifices. I don't think that you know what's at risk—"

"Don't you think I know exactly what's at stake here? How dare you!"

The words fly like daggers from her heart. "Let me just review what we've got here. As far as I can tell, the future, at least what remains of it, is pretty much a flaming dung heap, and your precious Cyphor Gicul is wanting to make it even worse by threatening to cut off Relicus City's access to the food harvested at the Grange." Luci scans their faces. All but Ley shield their eyes from her by looking down at the ground or to the side, infuriating her even more. "So am I right? Is anybody gonna explain this to me or not? Or is exactly what all I've heard true? You're all going to starve what's left of humanity just for some twisted payback to Macer and a dead guy you've already shot in the face?" She shakes her head in disgust. "Cyphor Gicul is a coward who doesn't even have the courage to come out into public."

Beaumont looks back up at her. "That's enough, Luci," he says firmly but without raising his voice.

"Is it?" she asks pointedly. "Is it enough?" Her blood pressure spikes again, making her ears throb a rhythmic pulse. "Based on what 'Skippy' over here just said," she gestures dismissively at Yuma, "after you're done extorting the city for who knows what, you all plan to leap skip to Ireland to live out your days."

There's a crowd warily gathering around, but she doesn't care. She's a lit bundle of firecrackers, and this won't be over until every one of them have been burnt through and exploded. "Well, I stream the history net, and I've got news for you. Ireland 1646 sucks when you factor in what Cromwell and the British have planned for you there a few years later. So good luck with that one."

Beaumont looks as if he's about to say something, but Luci doesn't let him. "But yeah, I think I *know* what's at stake, or at least have a pretty good idea of what you're all about." She's on the verge of hyperventilating, spots before her eyes, but she's determined to finish. "From where I stand, it looks like the human race has learned nothing from the destruction in the past. You're still consumed by petty schisms, lusting to be the king of the hill. It's like a tug-of-war, but instead of rope, you're pulling barbed wire through your hands and nobody wins."

"Are you quite through?" Ley finally asks.

Luci sends her a searing look. "Yeah, I'm done. I'm ready to get out of here and go find Ish."

Glances exchange between Ley, Beaumont, and various members of the crowd, but nothing else is said, and a precarious silence descends on the area. Luci feels as if she may retch and comments to herself that if she does, to hit Ley with the full force of it.

Finally, Ley says in a flat voice to Yuma, "Go bring Totti back in here."

"Totti? Why? What for?"

"Just do it, Yuma," Ley says with a scowl that compels him into submission. When he leaves, she addresses Luci who's still trying to calm her breathing down. "I want you to see something, *Doctor*."

"What?" Luci says in a huff.

"You think that you know everything, but I'm going to show you something . . . something you don't know . . . something guaranteed to give your nightmares nightmares for the rest of your days, I promise it."

"I know you've been through a lot, Luci," Beaumont says evenly. "And out of everyone here, I've spent more time with you—the other you—so I feel that I know you reasonably well." He cautiously bends to pick up her garments from the floor and gently hands them to her. "So believe me when I say that there's a lot more going on here than you realize . . . more than growing food at the Grange, more than *Hi no Kawa*."

She clutches the clothing. "What? How can anything be worse than *Hi no Kawa*?"

He anxiously runs his tongue over his teeth before he softly answers, "What the world *can* become."

"What does that . . . what do you mean?"

The middle-aged woman who Ley gave the holo vid player to a few minutes ago returns, unaware of Luci's outburst. "Ley, it's ready to go, and I've spliced in the instructions of how to make the leap skip to Carcerium. We're set to leave for the nexus of the mainframe splash forum node in ten minutes."

"Good, Totti," Ley responds in a tone more civil than anything Luci has witnessed from her thus far. "How difficult would it be to hook up a holo vid projector in this area for one final viewing?"

The overhead pink-white light gleams off Totti's dark features as she shrugs. "I don't know. It's fairly easy. It's just a matter of redirecting the relay port." Though a statement, the estimate comes out like a question. "Three or four minutes, I guess?"

"I want to show it to her," Ley says, indicating Luci. "I want her to see it, what we've seen, all three and a half minutes of it." There's a pause, and then Ley's tone becomes more official. "And it may help for everyone else to see it one last time to remind us all of what this is about."

Totti looks to the side as if contemplating Ley's last phrase but finally nods slowly before heading back out.

Ley turns to Yuma. "Gather everyone up who can break away from what they're doing to watch." Before he can argue, she adds, "We'll make the time."

Luci is still fuming but curious enough about this new development to bide her time and be quiet. What could be any worse than the discoveries and revelations that she's encountered here over the last six days? All that's important is getting Ish back and proving out the validity of Yuma's claim. Can a trip to Carcerium keep Ish from ceasing to exist when this place is gone? Could the answer really be that easy? She closes her eyes to replay the Carcerium NBSI destination code in her mind: 194576001X.

"Gaudiano, second door on the left," Ley curtly addresses her. "There's a changing station that the two of you can use. Don't take long. I want you to see what we've been using as a recruiting video before you leave." The sides of her lips curl up. "Then you *really* will be able to say that you know everything."

THREE

"I'LL CHANGE HERE ON THE left side," Beaumont says, gesturing to the makeshift dressing area. Uneven stacks of rusty party trays balance from floor to ceiling in the repurposed supply room.Dividing the cramped area is a large roll of fire-engine-red plastic sheeting. It's hoisted over a horizontal metal cable, running the length of the area creating an improvised barrier.

Concerned for privacy, Luci discreetly inspects the opaqueness of the plastic tarp as she lifts it to go under on her way to the back corner. She can tell by the rustling sound on the other side that Beaumont has already begun to disrobe.

"What's this video Ley's setting up?" Luci asks apprehensively while flattening the cowboy hat in her hands. She allows it to fall to the grimy tile, steps on it, and begins peeling away her drenched layers of clothing.

Beaumont is slow to respond. "It's the reason that we do what we do." There's a pause before he adds, "It's better if you see it for yourself than for me to try to describe what's on it. I will tell you that Malom Roderick sacrificed himself to obtain this footage. It's the reason he was sentenced to Carcerium."

Thinking she's finally caught him in a falsehood, she snaps back, "I was told that he was put in there for murdering me—my older self."

"No, that's what everyone believes, but it was Cyphor, not Malom, who killed the older you. Malom would never harm anyone."

Grateful to slide out of Shar's damp black jumpsuit, she looks at the swaying partition separating them. Had Cavazos lied to her or was he simply repeating a lie that Macer told him? Or is it Beaumont who is lying to her right now? "Ley mentioned a few minutes ago that you said that Malom shot Cavazos in the face, so he *can* harm someone."

"Well, there's that." This is followed by another pause. "But Pol Cavazos wasn't a very good man—not as bad as Macer, but Malom considered it the right thing to do for the cause." There's a wet plop of clothes on the tile from the other side.

"It sounds like you've decided to give Malom Roderick a pass on certain things." She adds, "I've met him, you know."

"Yeah, he told me about it once," Beaumont answers. "And yes, I think he's a hero . . . not because he eliminated Pol Cavazos. He kinda had to do that to protect the mission. I'm talking about what he did before that. The story is that Cyphor Gicul skipped into a future interval and saw the world to come, what Macer is *really* up to. There's a good reason why Macer made it illegal to leap skip into the future."

"Macer's bodyguard, Royse Timmons said there's some inhibitor put in longchairs that block travel into Relicus City's future."

"Yes, FTTs," he says. "Anyway, Malom says that Cyphor returned and told him everything he saw. Believing that the future under Macer and his . . . 'shadows' was too horrific for a reasonable person to begin to conceive, Malom insisted that they had to get proof to show the people of Relicus. Malom knew that going forward a second time to collect proof would likely get him captured."

After a brief silence, he adds, "Ley wasn't joking about how the holo vid is used as a *L'inversione* recruiting tool, but I'll warn you that it's not an easy thing to watch. Totti edited the footage together and included the skip point information to the Carcerium with a detailed explanation of how citizens can survive the undoing of Relicus City when *Hi no Kawa* is prevented."

Luci finishes buttoning her pristine white Loretta-Lynn-goes-to-the-rodeo-honky-tonk-style blouse and tucks it into her pants. "You really believe that the world can be saved, that the events leading up to *Hi no Kawa* can be averted?"

"As sure as I'm standing here, or what would be the point of any of this?"

"These boots are not going to work; they're too small," she announces, slipping the squishy wet shoes back on to her feet. "Why do you think Gicul wants Ish rescued? What does he have or what information does he know?"

"It's a mystery to me, but Malom trusts Cyphor, and I trust Malom, so that's all that I need." His knuckles gently tap the metal door. "Come on, they should be ready for us."

The plastic tarp crinkles as Luci lifts it to exit. Beaumont's holding the door open for her. She's woefully reminded of Shar's sacrifice as her eyes lock onto his scarred-over earlobe again.

"What is it?" he asks.

She's a little embarrassed, but she has to know. "Your Viatorio . . . all of you have removed your Viatorios. I assume this is to move around the city undetected."

Beaumont tilts his head slightly. "True," he says, dragging the word out to allow the end of it to curl up into an inflection.

Someone scurries by outside the open door. Beaumont steps forward, allowing it to close behind him.

"Well, how does that work?" she asks. "I mean, doesn't the security system around here have to account for every one of your Viatorios suddenly going offline? Where I'm from, if 'Bob' is placed under some kind of house arrest with an ankle bracelet monitor and all of a sudden it goes dead, his probation officer, police, or whatever would know about it and go to check to see what was going on."

Beaumont nods. A wry smile accompanies his answer.

"They think I'm in Banja Luka." He pauses before adding, "Banja Luka, pre-*Hi no Kawa* juncture, January 1973. Ley and Totti and some others are believed to be stranded in Poland 1952."

She's confused at first, but then the genius of what he claims they've done sinks in. "Of course!" she exclaims. "You all did leap skips to intervals that everyone thinks had their portals destroyed."

He touches the end of his nose with his index finger in affirmation. "No one's looking for us, because they believe we're trapped in our respective intervals."

She closes her eyes, visualizing the calculations that were plastered around the guesthouse. "There were nine in all. Were the people out there in the warehouse from all of the skip junctures that Cyphor shrunk down?"

"No, only seven. It's another demonstration of Cyphor's genius, just like how he and Malom were able to fabricate a skip point from the warehouse in there that isn't a naturally-occurring chronal node destination."

Luci runs her fingers through her frizzy, partially dried hair again. "Yeah, I wondered about that too."

He reopens the door for her.

"Oh, wait," she says, doubling back under the tarp. "I nearly forgot." Her fingers race over the small pile of wet clothing until they locate a small piece of hard plastic with a crude UNIFON etching. She tucks it in the blouse pocket with the ornately embroidered rose and returns to Beaumont.

"What did you forget?"

She contemplates telling him everything that Shar revealed about her feelings to her but instead answers, "A special note from a friend." She stops short of the door. "What about your niece . . . what about Shar? She doesn't have a Viatorio now. She can't view any alerts in the splash forum because she has no sip basin access, can she?" She doesn't mention that Shar is trapped at Macer's guesthouse.

Beaumont looks at the ground and lets out a long, dejected sigh. "The plan has always been to alert as many people as we can about what Macer is preparing to do." He presses his hands together, sliding the palms over the other, unsuccessful in finding a comfortable fit to rest them. "We know that not everyone will survive what's coming today, but it's all that we can do."

Luci can't believe she's hearing this. "But if Shar can't make it to Carcerium before Relicus City evaporates from the timeline, it will be as if she never existed." The statement comes out of her louder than expected. She overcompensates by whispering, "Noah, she's your niece! You should value family above all. I'm telling you this as a person who lost their family in an instant. You can't just leave her in the city to disappear, especially after what she's done for you . . . what she did for me."

He looks up at her but rubs his forehead, shielding his eyes from hers. "I . . . we decided . . . there's no other way."

"Does she even know what's about to happen here?"

He looks up at her sharply. She mistakes his contorted expression for hateful anger until the hurt in his eyes match the tears swelling in them. "Luci, we're focused on the ones that can be saved. You will see why on Malom's holo vid. There will be sacrifices in Relicus City today. Not everyone will make it beyond here, we know this, but we can't allow Macer to do what he plans to do." His voice teeters on breaking. "We must find a new and better path."

Beaumont exits the area swiftly before anything else can be said, leaving Luci to find her way through the door on her own.

THE AREA THEY RETURN TO is charged with anxious energy manifested in a low, constant roar of mutterings. An even larger crowd than before has formed a crude semicircle and paired up in informal groups of three and four. Luci estimates nearly thirty people have gathered. The atmosphere is a contradictory mix of excitement and dread under the low rafters of tubes and electrical wiring.

Luci and Beaumont weave through the crowd on their way to the center of the area. She catches snippets of conversations from the clusters, including musings about the final Ireland skip point destination, seeing Cyphor for the first time, and a disconnected punchline to a joke that incites nervous laughter. Each group briefly suspends their speaking as the woman blamed for the end of the world passes through their midst.

They reach the center where the bnanti was a few minutes ago. In its place is Totti kneeling in a dry spot inserting a thick cable into a makeshift metal box on the floor. Luci searches the crowd for Ley and finds her against the back wall with the trunk containing the ESTA next to Yuma. She's barking out some instructions to Jonn, who nods submissively.

Luci comments to Beaumont, "This is so intense. The stress in here is thick enough to cut with a knife."

He nods and says solemnly, "There's a lot at stake. You'll see in a moment."

Totti stands to her feet, wiping her hands on the legs of her trousers. "Can you blame them? Everything we've done . . . years of preparations comes down to what happens over the next hour or so. Getting this Technician Moyta to Cyphor is an unexpected last-minute addition. Of course they're nervous."

Beaumont gestures to a jumpy-looking teenager compulsively giving her churka a weapons check for the umpteenth time. "Most of these people have never seen any battle. Their biggest offense to date is clipping their Viatorio." He gives a long sigh and shakes his head. "They simply answered the call for a new and better path."

Without missing a beat, Totti repeats the mantra, "*For a new and better path.*"

"But you've got the cybo controller from Cavazos," Luci says. "If Yuma over there is right, there shouldn't be any fighting to free Ish. You just deactivate the guards."

"There's always risk, even with an airtight plan," Beaumont says. "And not all of them are going with us. Most are going with Totti to splice the holo vid into the splash forum."

Totti points out the obvious issue. "And there's only one cybo controller."

The din of the crowd begins to quiet in waves from the back as Ley treads with purpose to the center. *L'inversione* members part to give her a wide berth as she passes through them.

Yuma abandons what he's doing with the ESTA trunk to follow through the opening that Ley has made in the throng of people.

A grave hush falls, leaving only the slow, repetitive sound of dripping water echoing through the area.

Ley positions herself in front of Luci, Beaumont, Totti, and the recently arrived Yuma. She clears her throat and begins, "So, I know that we've gone over this a dozen times or more, but here it is one final time: Everyone is to meet back here after their respective tasks are completed."

Luci's eyes bore into the back of Ley's head as it slowly turns from side to side addressing the warehouse occupants. "It's important to note that we won't be able to wait for stragglers, so stay with your team and don't wander off after you're done." Sounding like a military commander, her voice booms off the hard surfaces. "All of the skip-freight barges along the walls in here are set to skip seventy-two hours from now to Antarctica."

The mention of the leap-skip destination excites Luci—she and Ish were right about where Gicul was hiding. If only he were here right now to know it.

Ley slowly lifts her hand and lowers it again. "The barges can comfortably carry six to seven standing up. We're doing a leap skip to an enclosed area that's climate controlled, so the stitch we're wearing now is fine. We'll be able to change into more interval-appropriate garments later."

Luci glances down at her conspicuously decorative blouse and then returns her gaze to the back of Ley's head. "We will finally meet up with Gicul in the Antarctica skip point and go in groups of eight to the temporal anomaly."

She unexpectedly thrusts both hands victoriously into the air and shouts, "And then we leap skip to Ireland!"

The crowd erupts with such exuberance that Luci takes a step backward, bumping into Beaumont. For the first time, she considers just how free historical information is to the common Relicus City citizen in the splash forums. She wonders how they can't know of the problems facing their supposed Ireland paradise.

Ley begins to pace. "Expect all hell to break loose when things get going on this side though." The excitement of the crowd shrivels up like a wilted flower, but Ley continues, undeterred. "Someone in the city's system security will likely 'red out' the citizens' vision once everything starts happening. Because of that, there should be no trouble from anyone getting in your way to make it back here. Except for Noah's team going to get the technician, we're doing small groups of two and three because small groups are less conspicuous—we're not trying to be seen. Everything we want the city to know is on the video that Totti's team is uploading into the splash forum. The end of the broadcast relays instructions on how citizens can leap skip to the Carcerium anomaly to save themselves before this timeline ceases to exist. What they do with the information from there is up to them."

Ley pauses as if she's allowing her instructions to marinate in the minds of her audience. She resumes somewhat more somberly, "*L'inversione* has always survived best in the shadows, and today is no different. Do your task and make it back here to skip to Antarctica as quickly as possible. Malom has requested that I bring the final ESTA module to him and Cyphor immediately, so I'm headed there now and will begin the final preparations for all of us to skip into the past one last time. Before we go our separate ways to complete our tasks, let us take a moment to remember those of *L'inversione* who gave their lives for us to make it this far."

There's a mournful half-minute pause. Though it's different from what Ley says to lament, Luci reflects on the fate of Benold Jesper and Shar Ryson's sacrifice for her. She runs the tips of her fingers over the etched plastic in her pocket and sighs, wondering how she can convince Beaumont to take her to Shar when this is over. She'll even be willing to risk another bnanti ride if that's what it takes.

The silence concludes with Ley lifting both arms upward again. "Just know that in a few hours, each of us will have a new life in a pre-*Hi no Kawa* world, and we will establish a memorial for our fallen."

A smattering of applause erupts and catches like wildfire with manic shouts of, "*For a new and better path.*"

Something about it all feels off, but the prospect of Ish safe with her even in seventeenth-century Ireland is enough to appease Luci for now. "*One step at a time,*" she tells herself.

Totti steps forward and, speaking loud enough to be heard over the noise of the crowd, informs Ley, "It won't have sound since the audio is for virtual view on the splash forum."

"That's fine. We all know the narration. Go ahead and start it up."

This hovering disc is considerably larger than the one from Macer's office with the statue hologram, and though it's Luci's third time to witness this technology, she's still astounded by the sight.

Yuma instructs Totti by pointing at the hovering device. "When you get it hooked into the mainframe, you'll press this, then this, and here. The upload to the splash forum will send out notifications to everyone in the city and, a minute or so later, copy over to the TmR server receivers at the Grange." Pride seeps into his voice. "I've got it configured to where system administrators shouldn't be able to track the transmission origin back for at least three minutes—five if we're lucky—so get out of there once you see this little light flashing."

Ley nods to Totti, saying, "Give the ones on the extraction team thirty minutes after you get there before manually activating the holo vid at the nexus." Ley turns to Beaumont and sandwiches his hand between both of hers. "I'll see you shortly, Noah."

He acknowledges with a slight bow. "For a new and better path."

She releases Beaumont from her grip with a nod. "Please relay what's happening on Totti's video to . . ." her eyes shift to Luci, "our *guest.*"

The crowd's anxious clamoring dies down as Ley traipses over to the skip barge bearing the trunk with the ESTA device. She lifts a lever on the lectern-like control panel; there's a brief atmospheric pop, and she and the transport vanish a second later.

Luci turns to Beaumont beside her. "It's like a longchair?"

"Yes. Same leap skip technology but designed as cargo movers used by the Grange for larger loads." There's a pause before he adds, "Except in this case, the cargo will be all of us going to Antarctica."

She's still astounded that a leap skip can be performed from a place that isn't a natural chronal node and makes a promise to herself to learn how such a thing can be when Ish is safely rescued.

The holo vid begins. Totti has set the hologram parameters to display the image a meter or so above their heads and as long as a sports car. UNIFON letters appear under the image of the city's chancellor: "*Waleen Macer.*" Luci is amazed by the likeness to his son, Enos. They share the same big nose and bushy eyebrows feature. "So, that's what Waleen looked like? I saw the resemblance in the statue of him, but he and Enos could be twins."

Beaumont's deadpan response is off-putting. "No, they're *both* Waleen."

She scoffs at hifs joke in bad taste. Forcing her eyes from the image to Beaumont, she asks, "What did you say?"

He faces forward like an unblinking mannequin. "They're both him . . . they're both Waleen"

With her mouth agape, Luci looks down at her still-damp shoes. Like a battering ram splintering the fortress of her mind, the concept finally smashes through. "No," she begins as one of her Jardon headaches creep in. "How can he be—"

"There is no Enos Macer, only Waleen," he says, turning to gauge her shock.

She barely registers him looking at her, her mind running through the implications of what this means if it's true. Luci replays every interaction she's had with him all the way back to the conversation inside the limo on that rainy night in Baltimore.

She remembers him lying to her about identity convergence writing over a future self. Then she recalls Royse telling her how Macer's mother died of something called Fichtner's

Disease when he was very young, leaving Enos to be raised by his father, Waleen—all lies! None of it was true. He must have thought her an imbecile when she suggested the possibility of Waleen being Cyphor Gicul. She flashes back to the conversation with him about the "66" and "99" number thing for the doll for her mother. He had explained how identity convergence occurs and U-curve overlays. It was a lie—it was *all* a lie. Her heartrate's up, and the words come sluggishly from her dry mouth, "But . . . but that would have to mean—"

Beaumont nods and points at the changing image, but it's Yuma who interrupts. "It gets worse. Watch."

Younger Waleen and the chancellor morph into a third and final face. It's still Macer, but he wears an intricate headdress of deep red. It's not as tall as the papal tiara that the Pope wears, but it's easily as tall as a top hat from her time.

Luci's legs feel weak, as if all the blood has raced from them into her pounding heart. She moves to shift her weight in hopes of balancing. Totti places her arm around her shoulder to steady her.

The image of this Macer pulls back as the camera does a reverse zoom. He's clad in an ornately stitched red robe. His mouth is moving, and though it's obvious he's passionately speaking, there's no sound.

"What's he saying, Totti?" Luci asks. "What's going on in this part?"

She shakes her head somberly. "He's declaring himself a god to the people below."

Luci looks to the left at Beaumont and Yuma for confirmation.

The older of the two answer, "It's true. At some point, Waleen discovered that by visiting specific skip point junctures that he knew he would find himself at, he could bring another version of himself back."

"This is bad," Luci says to no one in particular.

Still shaking her head, Totti says, "We're still not sure if this was something he discovered by accident or if he deliberately sought out to extract 'shadows' of himself out of his linear timeline." She pauses and gently turns Luci to face her. "But what we do know is that Waleen was able to reinsert them . . . himself . . . into the future."

Yuma peeks around Beaumont at Luci to add, "No one even knows how many shadows Waleen has made of himself."

Luci asks, "Shadows are what you call copies of him . . . copies of Macer?"

Her self-consciousness sets in that only the four of them have been speaking. All the other members of *L'inversione* remain reverently still as if at a funeral.

The "camera" image gradually pulls back from Macer behind a golden lectern. There's an enormous crowd, easily over ten thousand docile spectators in attendance.

Beaumont offers in a hushed tone, "Malom said this was an address that Macer, here calling himself *'Relicus the Great,'* gave in our future. He said it was some sort of religious indoctrination ceremony."

By now, the figure on the stage is too small to see, but massive video screens as tall as five-story buildings hovering on opposite sides of the stage clearly display Macer's contorted shouting mouth.

Luci recognizes the building. He's standing in front of the Spike, and it's adorned with flags that bear a pictogram of Macer's face in an intense expression of determination.

"Malom did the leap skip three centuries into the city's future," Totti says, withdrawing her arm from around Luci to gesture to the massive hologram. "This is 328 years from now."

Luci tries to swallow, but her throat feels like sandpaper on the inside.

Beaumont informs her, "Malom told me that he believes that Macer reinserts himself periodically every so often on these religious holy days."

"So Macer never dies," she says, remembering Malom's rant back at Carcerium. "And since Macer barely ages between visits to them, the people can believe the lie that he truly *is* a god."

"All time travel in the future will be abolished by him," Beaumont says. "Technical information destroyed when he ascends to power, and to even suggest the possibility of leap-skip time travel will be considered blasphemous heresy against the god, Relicus the Great."

Any doubts as to which side was the good one in this battle between *L'inversione* and Macer are squelched in Luci's mind. While she's still unable to reconcile why Gicul is sending a deployment to retrieve Ish and that whole matter of murdering her other self still lingers, she decides to trust these people, even that snooty Ley.

The image does a sweep pan over the crowd. Posted at various points stand stocky figures with modified churkas. Their facial features are identical and stoic.

Luci points at the reflective red armor bearing a large "R" insignia on the chest plate. "Who are they?"

Beaumont shrugs. "Malom wasn't certain, but we believe those are a variation of the cybos that we have today."

"But they all look the same," Luci observes.

"I don't know," he answers. "Maybe Macer . . . or 'Relicus the Great' has figured out a way to shadow them as well. We can't be certain, but Malom said that they're definitely Macer's militia." He pauses as if he's waiting to add something.

Yuma breaks the silence. "They're the advanced cybos of the future that captured Malom as he was making this video."

The comment triggers Beaumont to continue. "Knowing he'd be apprehended, Malom programed the video drone to leap skip back here to Relicus City the moment he was captured and connection to the device was lost."

"Here it comes," Totti says with a voice that makes the hairs on the nape of Luci's neck prickle.

The image abruptly switches from the mass outdoor ceremony to a wobbly handheld shot of Malom in a poorly lit low-ceiling area. She feels odd about seeing the face of the man whom she despised just a few hours ago, believing him to be the murderer of her future self.

Luci senses a shift in the room. While completely still and quiet, everyone collectively tenses up in unison as if bracing for something. She wonders what could be more horrible than the oppressive rule of Macer as an undying deity. Managing to choke out a question slightly louder than a whisper, she asks, "What's Malom saying in this part?"

Totti answers, "He's saying that he's taking the drone into the vortex of the Spike, the one on the Relicus City side."

Luci recognizes the area from her visit earlier in the week. "What's wrong with it? Why have all of the machines stopped? None of the crates are moving. They're all bunched up like boxcars from a derailed train." The aftereffects of her Jardon incident make her head pound. "I don't understand."

Then something chills Luci to the core. The drone image pans across the slain body of a dark-skinned older woman on the ground. Only the upper torso is visible beneath one of the massive food crates. While the woman's dying expression is one of agony, that's not what makes Luci gasp and call out, "Totti, back it up, please! Back the video up a few frames or whatever."

When she doesn't immediately respond, Luci pleads with Beaumont. "I have to see something. Have her back it up . . . please."

He shrugs and then nods to Totti.

The image pauses before playing in reverse for a few seconds.

"There! Stop it there!"

"On the crushed worker?" Totti asks in disbelief.

Luci nods emphatically, her eyes never leaving the image. "Yes, please."

Beaumont says, "It's one of the workers from the Grange side of the vortex. Somehow, they came through with the crates into the Relicus juncture."

She feels sick as the image freezes on the old woman under the container. The fallen Grange worker wears an unmistakable bright yellow jumpsuit—it's Director Bru Mandal, or at least it was a long time ago. Luci wants to die, but she can't look away from the expression of anguish on the grandmotherly woman's face.

"I know her," Luci says in an unsteady voice. "She gave me a tour of the Grange when I first arrived here." The only consolation that she can make to placate her emotions is that this hasn't occurred yet. This is a shot from a future event. Bru is alive somewhere—probably at the Grange, in fact.

She wipes her eyes as she wonders if Bru was attempting to escape something on the Grange side or if she came through to the Spike processing area to warn the people of this juncture about something. She sniffs, saying, "You can start it up again, Totti."

After a few chimes from the projector, the video resumes.

Luci says, "I don't understand why Macer . . . 'Relicus the Great' or whatever would intentionally destroy the city's access to their food source."

"Control," Totti says. "Cutting off the vortex channel to the Grange gives him complete control over the protein supply in the city, which, in turn, grants him absolute control over its people."

Luci shakes her head. "But that doesn't make any sense. If he—"

Yuma takes a rigid step forward and says stoically, "There are other sources of protein."

Luci spins to Totti. "What does that mean?" Her stomach knots up as she addresses Beaumont. "What does he mean? I was told that nothing could be grown here." There's an answer gathering in her mind. It's like an unending shrill behind a door about to collapse on its rusted hinges.

Many of the occupants of the warehouse look away and to the floor as glistening images of wet meat being processed display.

Beaumont confirms what Luci is piecing together but rejecting at the same time. "One thing grows here . . . the one thing that has always grown here."

"No . . ." Her lip trembles. "No."

Yuma clarifies as if the footage leaves any doubt, "The flesh is harvested . . . human flesh." He points as the holo vid shifts to a wide shot of rows of foggy, cocoon-like compartments, each containing someone unconscious.

Luci collapses to her knees. She forcefully wipes the tears from her eyes in order to take in all the footage.

Beaumont comes to her side, gently lowering his hand to her shoulder. "That's enough, Totti."

The image freezes in place again, this time on one of Macer's modified cybo centurions' shiny red armor.

Totti is the first to speak. "As Noah mentioned, we have reason to believe that Waleen Macer imprisoned or murdered anyone with knowledge of leap-skip technology. The obvious result would allow him to be the only one with the ability in the future to move through time."

Luci instantly thinks of Ish and the crew in the longchair station in the Spike. She thinks of how Macer did this exact thing to Benold Jesper just a few days ago when the tech questioned his comings and goings. "He has to be stopped. I don't care about the cost. This cannot be allowed to happen. I can't let this happen."

Beaumont helps her to her feet.

Shaking her head, she addresses the warehouse in a defiant voice, "This . . . this cannot be the future of humanity, here or anywhere . . . at any time." Luci pauses, attempting to recall the phrase. She turns to Totti. The dark woman's determined expression looks as if it were chiseled into stone. Luci turns back to the members of *L'inversione*. Their faces look equally set. "I will help you . . . I and Technician Moyta will help you achieve your goal *for a new and better path.*"

Luci isn't surprised that the mantra is repeated back to her several times. The tone is less jubilant and more mournful as if the words carry the burden of the charge within each syllable.

In a low voice that only she can hear, Luci proclaims, "We're coming to get you, Ish. Just hang on a little longer, my love."

FOUR

THE ROOM SWIFTLY SPLITS INTO two groups. The majority pair up with Totti to upload Malom's edited drone video footage to the splash forum while the remaining half dozen fall in under Beaumont's command.

Luci is pleased the tall man named Jonn strolls up from the back to join the team to rescue Ish. She imagines that strength is always a valuable asset when heading into a potential fight, and she suspects it will be needed, despite Yuma's overconfidence in the cybo controller. She's less impressed that busybody Yuma remains by Beaumont's side instead of prancing off to bother the splash forum video group. She's about to say something about him when Beaumont hands the onyx cybo controller to the teen. He passes Yuma another item, a black device that resembles an office stapler, though she knows that would be ridiculous.

"What's that do?" she asks.

Yuma slides the thin onyx controller into the opening of the device with a click. "Well, to put it simply, it will do what a Viatorio does when the time comes."

It's difficult for Luci to tell if he's boasting or being condescending to her—probably both.

He informs her, "You may have noticed that none of us have Viatorios anymore. I invented this to mimic V-commands to the security minister's controller."

She looks around at the other four members that have assembled in the group and then back to Yuma. "And you know for sure that it works?"

He confronts her skepticism without hesitation. "Without a doubt, Dr. Gaudiano. Don't worry."

"I *am* worried. Everything depends on that thing nullifying the cybos guarding Ish. Judging by what was said earlier, you haven't tested that on an actual cybo yet, so there's no way to know for certain that—"

"Luci," Beaumont interjects. "It's alright." He grips her shoulders and gently turns her to face him. "Yuma knows his tech; I trust him. If he says it will work and stop cybos, then I am confident that it will suspend them long enough to free your friend."

She glances back at Yuma, who looks like he's awaiting a verdict from her.

"Trust me," Beaumont says.

Jonn chimes in from behind him in his low, booming voice, "Yuma is really good at things like this, Doctor."

Miguel, the man who brought dry clothes to Luci and Beaumont, says apologetically, "I looked for a work apron in the shop to make you look less conspicuous, but I couldn't find anything."

"Thanks," she says. "At least the clothes fit well." Luci recognizes the awkward twenty-something as the one nervously checking her churka from before. "I'm Luci."

She nods. "My name's Sari." The girl falls in beside Yuma, studying his every move with big, doe-like eyes.

Beaumont gestures to a muscular, light-skinned black man in his thirties who is nearly standing at attention while waiting to be acknowledged. "And this is Cline. He's been with us from the beginning."

Cline responds with a slight bow of the head. "Dr. Gaudiano."

"And coming this way with the remaining churkas is Danica," Beaumont concludes.

At first, Luci thinks it's Ley who's returned for some reason. Only as Danica moves closer can Luci tell that the spikey-haired woman is taller and not as stocky as Ley, though she could pass for an older sister or cousin.

As Cline and Miguel break from the group to retrieve their churkas from the approaching Danica, Beaumont addresses Luci. "So, outside of this building is an auto-transport hauler that Yuma has programed to take us near the sector that Technician Moyta's being held in. Though it's a decommissioned model and a little worn from use, the hauler shouldn't draw too much attention to itself."

Yuma butts in, saying, "I've set it to take a route off the main lines and then a direct path for the return back here, since we anticipate the city going red after Totti's upload to the splash forum."

Beaumont lifts a patient hand, silencing the teen. "Yuma, Jonn, and Cline have cleared out the cargo container for us to ride in there. It'll be cramped, but we're bringing light, and the ride is only a few miles from here." He places his hand on her shoulder. "Where we are is an industrial part of the city—a low traffic area, so we shouldn't encounter too many people as we make our way to the hauler a few blocks over."

Luci nods, impressed by the thoroughness of the strategy. "You came up with all of this in the short time after Ish was taken?"

"Well, yes and no," Beaumont answers humbly. "We've been using the hauler transport to move around the city in secret for some time now."

She gnaws her bottom lip. "Hey, I want to apologize—"

Beaumont tries to wave her off.

"No, I came down pretty hard on you in front of everyone earlier about not helping Shar." She sighs. "I had no idea of what Macer was up to. It's still hard to imagine that he—"

"No apology is necessary, Luci. The evil within Waleen Macer is difficult for any decent person to comprehend. There are some members of *L'inversione* that theorize that he went mad due to taking too many leap skips."

"That's a thing?" she asks, shocked to learn of a potential side effect to time travel. She recalls the odd seizure that he had. "Is that what you believe?"

After a pause, he says, "I believe that the seed of lust for power was in his heart all along." He shakes his head. "No, I don't think doing leap skips had anything to do with it. He just embraced the evil inside of him instead of resisting that part of his nature."

Luci glances over to Sari and Yuma edging their way closer to them. "Sir?" Yuma asks with a respect that Luci thought was beyond him. "We should be going."

"Right," Beaumont answers as if awakened from a dream. He twirls an index finger in the air. "Team, let's head out."

THE EIGHT OF THEM TAKE the shop's solitary service elevator, which, judging by the metal creaks and groans of the gears and cable hoists, must be on its last leg. She's grateful when the doors finally slide open to the street level. Beaumont exits first, scans the area, and then motions to the others.

As she exits, Luci is surprised that it's nearly dusk. The neighboring shop structures reflect deep orange hues of the sun setting on the sea. In the far distance, the Spike building defiantly extends into the sky.

The group moves in a quiet tension, scanning the area while attempting to not be obvious that they're scanning. The narrow, overlapping mishmash of tempered plastic bolted to metal that passes for streets here are empty of people. This is a relief because Miguel couldn't find anything to conceal her loudly colorful cowgirl outfit. Part of the success of the operation hinges on going undetected, and she definitely doesn't blend in with Relicus City fashion like the rest of the team.

As they round the corner, Luci gets her first look at their ride. The hauler is colored lime green and as nearly as long and tall as a city bus. It's curved like a giant metal shark with the dorsal fin and tail removed. A metal pipe twice as large as a truck axle runs the length of the cut-away midsection. This suspends a corrugated steel container that Luci would not give a second look if she saw it on a railway cart back home.

Yuma races ahead of the group to the harsh, blunt front end of the hauler.

Beaumont drops back in the formation to instruct Luci. "He's initiating the sequence. The container will open for us, and we'll go in."

"Yeah, okay," Luci nervously answers as if she's done it a thousand times before and all of this was a part of her daily routine.

All but Yuma congregate before the steel container, dangling from the center beam of the vehicle in anticipation.

"What's wrong, Yuma?" Beaumont asks, scanning for onlookers. "Why isn't it opening?"

Luci tenses while surveying the area for signs of an ambush, aware that she's the only one without a churka.

"It's worked before—many times," Yuma proclaims nervously. "Nothing's wrong. It just—"

"Obviously, something's wrong," Danica argues.

Luci notes that it's the first time the woman has spoken. While her voice is firm, it's different from what she imagined from her, not gruff or raspy like Ley sounds.

"Nothing's wrong," Yuma protests again but walks over to strike the container with the butt of his churka.

The sound startles Luci, and she jumps. Her insides churn nervously at the notion that this inept crew is in charge of rescuing Ish from a squad of cybos. "We're wasting time here," she says.

"She's right, Noah." Miguel begins moving beside Beaumont. "You know that we can't stay out in the open like this for very long. It's not safe."

Luci mistakes a loud beeping sound for an alarm until she realizes it's an alert from the container that the wall panel is lowering. She sighs. This is the second time in less than an hour she's mistaken this type of sound for a danger notice. As the panel continues to lower, she glances over at Beaumont, who offers a shrug.

"See, I told you nothing was wrong," Yuma declares.

Groans echo through the group at his remark, but Cline confronts him. "I don't want to get trapped in there, you understand me, little man?"

Yuma backs away from him, protesting, "We'll be able to get out. It's just old, that's all." Still on the defensive, he adds, "It's the first time it's ever given us any problem in all the time that we've used it."

Creaking like a drawbridge over a castle moat, the steel wall is two thirds of the way down.

"Old or not, I need to know that this box is going to open for us when we get there."

Jonn joins in, and as if he needs to point it out, he says, "I'm a big guy, Yuma. I don't like being confined into small spaces. Cline is right."

The beeping continues, occasionally punctuated by pneumatic hisses as the panel lowers.

Beaumont intervenes, "Before I signed on at the Spike, I used to work freight. There's a manual-override wheel located in the front panel of these models. It's a safety put there for someone who may be working alone. We're not going to get trapped inside."

The lip of the panel touches the street, making a connection with a slight scraping sound. The beeping stops, and what was the side of the transport is transformed into a short ramp inside.

Satisfied with Beaumont's assurances, Jonn and Cline hurry to follow Sari, Miguel, and Danica into the pod container while Yuma fiddles with a device.

Luci keeps time with Beaumont as he grabs Yuma by the arm.

"Sir?" Yuma replies in a voice that could be mistaken for a whine.

"When we get there, leave the panel down in case it's slow to respond again."

"But it's not my fault. The regulator is—"

"I know, I know, but every second counts, Yuma. Just leave it down, ready for us to re-board."

"Yeah, alright," Yuma acquiesces as he steps onto the steel slope of the ramp.

Beaumont helps Luci in as he says for only her to hear, "It really will be alright, I promise you."

ONCE INSIDE, CLINE UNFASTENS THE front panel to confirm the manual-override wheel that Beaumont mentioned. To her, it looks similar to the apparatus in every submarine movie she's ever seen when the sailors have to seal off an area. The strong smell of vulcanized rubber and a faint hint of citrus fill the container, though there's no sign of any fruit or tires. Luci wonders about what the previous cargo hauled in this thing.

Cline snaps the covering back into place and positions himself in the corner.

The beeping alert from the ramp wall rising back into place stops, and the vehicle engages. Yuma and his eager would-be assistant Sari have fastened four slim magnetized lamps to the steel walls of the compartment for light.

Luci wonders if Yuma has even the slightest awareness that the girl is sweet on him. It's probably the reason she took this detail instead of going with Totti's larger group.

She thinks of Ish and wonders what could be going through his mind, wherever he is. It all must seem hopeless to him. There's no way he could ever imagine that she's headed toward him involved in a rescue mission at the behest of Cyphor Gicul himself.

Sari studies Yuma with puppy-dog eyes as he checks and rechecks Cavazos's PQX inhibitor device. Luci shudders to think that if Yuma's tech misfires or is delayed like the container opening, they'll likely all be dead by cybo churka fire within the hour.

One thing that Beaumont failed to mention to her is how the container isn't bolted to the carrier transport. To compensate for the swaying from the left to the right of the compartment, all but Cline, Jonn, and Beaumont have slid down to a sitting position on the bare steel bottom. Obviously, the inside was constructed for maximum cargo loads, not for the comfort of hidden passengers. As the container dips and swings in response to corners taken by the hauler, the two bigger men of the group look as if they're engaged in a balancing contest with their legs spread wide like surfers. Beaumont crouches but hasn't yet yielded to sitting flat.

Yuma pauses his inspection of their cybo-salvation mechanism to look up at her. "What you said back in the warehouse, was any of that true?"

"Is what true?" Luci asks, attempting to sift through the tangled memories of everything she's learned today about Relicus City.

"pre-*Hi no Kawa* Iryland, 1646." Yuma shifts his weight to straighten his back against the container wall. "You called him *Cornwall* or something."

"Cronwall," Sari volunteers incorrectly.

"Oliver *Cromwell*," Luci answers. She pauses to consider what the world must be like for this young man just getting his start and the horror that is to come if Waleen Macer isn't stopped. Tears swell in her eyes as she swallows the lump in her throat. She bites her lip; the mild self-inflicted pain focuses her. "Yeah, well . . . it does get pretty bad."

Both Sari's and Yuma's wide eyes gape back in confusion and distress. A previously unknown source of compassion bubbles up from inside her toward them. Sensing their emotions on the verge of heartbreak, Luci consoles them, "Cromwell's army is brutal to the Irish, but the worst of it will occur a few years after the leap skip there. I don't plan on sticking around." Luci forces a smile that unexpectedly turns genuine for her. "You and Sari should join Ish and me. When all of this is done, I'm going to have him travel from Ireland and head to Florence, Italy. I speak enough Italian to get us by."

For the briefest of moments, the sway of the container doesn't bother her. Her voice is sincerely cheery. "I understand that there's a lot of great art happening in that part of the world around that time; plus, it would be interesting to visit Arcetri where Galileo lived out his remaining days." She knows that if they haven't heard of Cromwell, it's doubtful that they know where Arcetri is or why Galileo is important, but it comforts Luci to say these things, and self-medicating with a little hope of her own can't be a bad thing.

Yuma and Sari both nod as if considering Florence to be a better destination plan.

Luci catches Beaumont mouthing the words "*thank you*" to her where the couple can't see him.

She looks away, slightly embarrassed that he's seen through her attempt to lift their spirits by giving them a hope to hang on to.

"Noah, why didn't *L'inversione* just get me at the lecture in Baltimore?"

"That just shows how desperate Waleen Macer was in trying to get you here to stop Cyphor," Beaumont says. "You lived in a city over a thousand miles from there—"

"Chicago," Luci interjects.

"Right, but the skip point juncture was in Baltimore and was only open for a period of 146 minutes."

Luci recalls the conversation with Macer in the limousine. "He said he sponsored the lecture through Vincent DuPont years before. So that was just to get me to 2032 Baltimore so they could snatch me?"

"That's right," he answers. "We didn't know why he'd done a leap skip to Luxembourg 2030 until after you were abducted and brought here six days ago. You gotta hand it to him, he is very clever at achieving his goals."

Luci mulls this over. "You came to get me—the older me—with Shar the first time?"

He nods.

"That was at the behest of Macer, right?"

"No one knew about him or his plans back then," Beaumont answers. "I'm ashamed that we didn't see the signs of what he was doing back then."

"Constructing his deity of Relicus the Great?"

"We had no idea. Shar and I were following orders of the directorate."

"Led by Macer, of course." Luci adds.

"Yes, the chancellor, who we believed to be Waleen's son at the time, sent us to retrieve you in 2045. In retrospect, we believe that he did this to isolate your knowledge of drift pattern mathematics from anyone in our time."

"Isolate my knowledge? That's why Macer had Cavazos put her in Carcerium?"

"Yes, but Malom freed her from Carcerium," Beaumont says.

"Only to deliver her—me to Cyphor."

There's an uncomfortable pause.

YUMA BREAKS THE SILENCE. "WE'VE got two and a half minutes until we reach the destination."

"Luci," Beaumont says, standing to his feet, "I've never met Gicul myself." He gestures around the pod. "In fact, none of us have, but Malom says that Gicul has told him to bring your technician friend and you back safely to him. Malom says that no harm is going to befall you when we all get to the Antarctica juncture. The only reason that he's not with us in this container is that Malom wasn't sure that you'd trust him, given what lies have been told to you—lies told about him from the other side. We need you to help convince Technician Moyta that it's safe to come with us."

"How can he or I believe anything that you say is true when you never even told Shar, your own niece, what was really going on?"

He sighs and stumbles to the left as the cargo container sways. "My father impregnated a woman other than my stretch. My stepsister is Shar's stretch. It's something that we've been fortunate enough to keep out of city Basin files, and since I'm not on any wanted lists, it's worked to the benefit of *L'inversione*." He pauses. "Shar felt guilty when things went badly from the time before, so when Macer said the circumstances changed and you—*this* version of you—had to be put in a safe place for your own good, she volunteered." He takes in a slow breath. "Malom and I made a judgement call about involving her in what we were doing. While she opposes the use of Carcerium chambers and is anti-cybo at heart, her lack of knowledge about

L'inversione allows her to be able to pass random subconscious V-scan analyses."

"What's that?" Luci asks, remembering the severed earlobe in the guesthouse elevator. "There are random Viatorio scans of the wearer's brain?"

Yuma answers for him, "Yes and there's no way to counterfeit or mimic pure memories in order to avoid detection of someone being involved with *L'inversione*."

Beaumont inspects his churka. "We needed someone on the inside who was authentic. Because of her feelings for you, we were able to test your receptivity to the idea of leaving Macer."

"Testing by having Shar leave the notes for me?"

"I'm not proud of it, but I was instructed to leverage her guilt that she had from before to do that. You know she loves you, right?"

Luci looks away, stopping the reflex to pull the hand-engraved plastic from her front pocket. She swallows and says softly, "Yeah, we spoke."

It's peculiar, but Luci's grateful to feel the transport beginning to slow and come to a stop rather than being forced to speak of the tragic events of Shar Ryson. If all goes according to plan, Ish will be with her soon, and they'll be able to leap skip away from this city once and for all. Maybe the two of them can devise a way to rescue Shar before they travel into the world's past.

Rising to her feet along with Yuma, Sari, Miguel, and Danica, Luci says, "There's one thing that I still haven't been able to figure out about all of this."

"What's that?" Beaumont asks over the beeping of the wall panel being lowered.

"How did *L'inversione* know about Ish in the first place and that he'd been abducted from Macer's guesthouse?"

"Cyphor alerted us through a special non-Viatorio communication," Beaumont answers.

Everyone faces the panel as it lowers. The tension in the compartment ratchets up to ten, though only Beaumont and Luci converse.

"Okay," Luci says as the opening grows before them, "but that doesn't explain to me how Cyphor Gicul would have known anything about him or that Ish was taken."

A puzzled-looking Beaumont looks back to her and away from the panel, which has made it halfway down. "It must have been…" He stammers over the problem. "I guess that he…"

She studies his face as he looks down trying to work it out. He looks genuinely perplexed.

"I don't know," he admits, shooting a glance back up at her. "I don't know how he could have been informed."

The clicking sounds of the team inside the container activating their churkas ring out.

Cline says to a clearly distracted Beaumont, "You ready, sir?"

Luci recalls Malom's mention of her cat, Newt, and all of that hiding-in-plain-sight stuff. "How well do you know Ley and Malom? You don't think that they sent us into an ambush just to get me killed, do you?"

"I trust Malom," Beaumont protests, but his eyes betray his doubt as they dart around, looking for something to focus on.

"How do we know for certain that Ish is even out there?" Before he can offer an answer, Luci asks, "Do you have any idea why Gicul would have reason to kill off the older version of me?"

The edge of the panel connects to the ground and the beeping stops, but her accelerated heartbeat still keeps the time.

"I don't know, Luci. Really, I don't know. I promise I was never told anything about all of that."

Jonn and Cline move down the ramp first with churkas drawn.

The others and Luci follow.

FIVE

THE CARRIER DELIVERS THEM TO a sanitation unloading zone with a dock facing the back of a squat, wide, two-story metal structure. Above their heads is an awning that the transport has narrowly cleared by a couple of meters. The saltwater breeze whips through crevices between the short buildings, gently tugging at Luci's hair like invisible fingers. The closeness of the Spike towering over them indicates the distance they've traveled from the repair shop on the water to here.

Beaumont gestures for her to fall in between Danica and Miguel in the back as he takes the lead with Cline and Jonn. In the middle of the pack, Sari carries both her and Yuma's churkas as he fidgets with the controller, scanning for cybo activity.

Around the corner, three strangers struggle to hoist a large grey plastic container onto an elevated conveyer under lamp light. Without a word, the group flanks the side of the wall to avoid detection by the men. It's too late, though. One of the workers lowers his end of the container, alerting the other two. The box falls to the ground with a thud as two of the men begin to charge at the rescue team, shouting, "New Australians! They're here!"

Beaumont raises a fist to signal and, without reservation in his voice, calls out, "Cline? Jonn?"

Both step forward, lock into a stance, and discharge two uninterrupted blasts of concentrated energy from their churkas at the approaching men.

Luci screams in horror, covering her mouth at the sight of blue beams connecting with their targets. It's her first time seeing the weapons in action, but she expected any use of them to be against cybos, not living humans.

Even before the two workers drop to the ground, Miguel runs to get a clear line of fire at the third man, who remained near the container. The stranger reaches for his Viatorio. Miguel unleashes a blue blast into his abdomen.

The absence of blood surprises Luci. While she's relieved, it's still hard for her to stomach that these men were slain simply for being in the wrong place at the wrong time.

Yuma scurries to examine the closest of the fallen men while Miguel cautiously advances to his victim in the back of the area.

Luci slides her hand from her mouth to cover her nose to block the acrid stench of sulfur filling the area. She fights back the nausea from witnessing the slaughter of the trio of bystanders.

"It worked!" Yuma exclaims, prodding the slain man with the butt of his churka. "The modification works!"

Beaumont sighs. "That's a relief."

"They're alive," Yuma says, overjoyed.

Luci faces him in angered confusion. "They're not dead?"

"No, but each of them are going to wake up with one hell of a headache." He gestures to Jonn and Cline, who maintain their firing stances. "Drag the three of them out of view in case anyone else passes by."

Both men nod and hand their weapons to Luci. Expecting them to weigh the same as extended rifles, she's surprised at how light and cool they are to the touch.

"How long will they sleep?" she asks Beaumont, who's already headed to Yuma.

"An hour? Thirty minutes—fifteen?" he answers over his shoulder. "We don't know for sure."

Danica comes over to her and gestures to Yuma with her churka. "Look at that grin. You'd think he stunned Waleen Macer himself just now."

"He modified these?" Luci asks, awkwardly lifting them up in the cradle of her arms.

Danica takes one from her. "Yeah, but we weren't certain it would really work—the stunning them and all, since it was never tested on a live subject."

"Why not?" Luci asks.

"The scarcity of volunteers," Danica answers with a shrug as she steps away. "Would you want to be the one to test something like that for Yuma?"

"We've got about fifteen minutes until Moyta is scheduled to be moved," Beaumont announces to the group already beginning to reassemble.

Luci gladly passes off the remaining churka back to Jonn, who receives it with a nod.

THE RESCUE TEAM MOVES QUICKLY through a long alley, which terminates into a narrow passageway. They're forced to maneuver single file through a concierge-bot corridor, sidestepping with their backs pressed against the opposing wall and churkas lifted over their heads. More than once, there's a brief pause followed by Jonn grunting near the front of the line to wriggle free of protruding extensions.

Just as Luci feels that she can't stand moving through the cramped space, the area expands into another alley. This one is shorter in distance, and the team is forced to maneuver through several stacked plasti-crates, but it's an improvement over the constricting concierge-bot back pathway.

"We're nearly there," Beaumont says in a hushed voice when all the members regather in a huddle.

Luci's heart is pounding, and her mouth is dry.

"Still no cybo brainwave signatures," Yuma announces, sounding slightly disappointed.

"We're probably too far out from them, which is to be expected," Beaumont says.

"Why don't you let me monitor that for us?" Luci says, extending an expectant hand to Yuma. "I don't have any experience with firing a churka, and it's best to have everyone who can shoot have their hands free to do so."

"Yeah, I don't think so," Yuma snidely replies.

Luci faces Beaumont. "Noah, I *need* to do something here. No one can seem to tell me why Gicul sent me with you other than to say that Ish will go with you if I tell him, so let me operate the damned device or I'm not budging from this spot." She touches his hand. "Please, Noah, let me help. I need to be a part of this or I will never forgive myself if something goes wrong."

Beaumont considers this and nods agreement. "I'll allow it. Our objective is Technician Moyta. Before he left, Malom reported that Gicul told him that your importance as a target has shifted, so—"

"A *target*," Luci blurts. "So you're *not* trying to kill me anymore?"

"I thought that would've been obvious to you by now," Beaumont answers caustically. He faces Yuma but addresses the group. "She's right about one thing: we need everyone wielding a churka that we can have. Give her the cybo blocker."

"PQX inhibitor," Yuma corrects and pulls the device into himself. "But we shouldn't need churkas if—"

"Just show her how to use it," Beaumont commands.

"Trust me," Luci says, "nobody wants this mission to be a success more than I do. It's the only thing I can do to help the team rescue Ish."

Yuma scans the group, looking for an ally other than Sari before finally shoving it at Luci. "Fine, take it."

She receives the device as she looks to Beaumont. "Thank you."

Beaumont tells her, "When we hit the courtyard, you'll need to move to the front of the group to detect any cybo sentries, but don't activate it until the entire squad comes." He motions to Jonn to move out. "Watch for my signal, Cline."

Everyone holds their breath, silently watching as the two of them dart across the opening.

Cline instructs the group's technician, "Better do what the boss said, little man. Show her how it works."

Yuma huffs and grabs Luci's wrist, holding the controller more forcibly than necessary. "See the amber color on the screen?" he asks condescendingly.

Luci pulls back. "Don't be so rough."

Sari gives her a cutting look.

Yuma offers a halfhearted shrug. "Alright, I apologize. Cybos' brainwaves operate at a different . . . um, frequency. When the little screen turns to blue, you know they're in the vicinity and you push the button on the side twice."

Luci turns the oversized stapler-shaped mechanism over to examine it. "Right here?"

"Yeah, that's it. Just press it twice and it will scramble neural transmissions in the brains of any cybos in the nearby radius." He looks over to Sari and back to Luci. "I worked really hard on that, so please be careful with it."

"I will, Yuma," Luci says. "Thank you."

"Let's go," Cline says. "They say the area is clear."

The remainder of the team rushes in twos across the clearing, Luci pairing up with Danica. With everyone in the alcove, Beaumont and Jonn bolt from there to a medium-sized building supported by large two-meter-wide columns. The supports conceal them from any onlookers in the mezzanine courtyard below.

Danica nudges her and says, "Come on."

Luci steals a glance at the device in her hand to make sure they're safe before dashing after her. They press against the closest of the six massive columns, mimicking the other members of the team down the row. Hand signals that Luci doesn't recognize ripple through the group in a round of gestures.

Danica informs her in a clinical tone, "Behind us is a terrace, and at the base of that are steps that lead to a sky bridge connecting the three buildings in this complex together. The second sky bridge segment is where we're headed. The cybos will pass under it, giving optimal wave broadcasting range for Yuma's inhibitor device."

Luci inhales a sharp breath, convincing herself that all of this isn't just an elaborate ambush orchestrated by Gicul. Recalling Beaumont's words about her no longer being a target, she reasons that if Gicul wanted her dead as in the original plan, he could've had Ley or Beaumont do it back at the shop. Whatever is happening here, for whatever reason, will be over soon, and she'll do whatever is needed if there's a chance to save Ish from becoming one of those cybos.

Danica tells her, "Our turn. Here we go."

Luci swallows hard, peeling herself off the wall. "Yeah, okay."

The two of them emerge from the safety of the columns, running at breakneck speed through the vast open area.

DESPITE HER BULK, DANICA REACHES the steps before Luci. Both take them two and three at a time without looking back. Luci's heart thumps wildly in her ears as they speed to the protection of the first sky bridge segment. Both women slump to a sitting position with their backs shielded by the waist-high iron-handrail wall.

Danica is panting as she points to the controller Luci's carrying. "Anything yet?"

Luci turns the device to present it to her, gasping to catch her breath as well. "Still amber, not blue."

"Good," Danica says, carefully placing her churka between the two of them. The woman moves to her knees, where only her head peeks over the railing. After a few accentuated gestures to the team below, she returns to her sitting position. "They're getting in place now." She points to the end of the sky bridge they've just come from. "You and I wait for Yuma and Sari." She gestures to the device in Luci's grip. "You know, if you can't do it, you can give it to me—no shame or anything."

Luci glances at the inhibitor and back up to her. "What do you mean?"

Danica averts her eyes. "If he ... Technician Moyta ... if they've already—"

Luci swallows a dry lump. "If *who* has already done *what*?"

Danica's head lowers, but her eyes look up at her. "If he's already been conditioned and you can't bring yourself to ..."

Luci is surprised by the loud gasp that erupts from within her. "I thought ... I mean, is there the chance that it's already happened to him?"

"Sometimes the intel that we get is incomplete or stale." Danica pauses, no doubt seeing Luci's horrified reaction. She dismisses the idea, offering a forced smile. "You know what? I shouldn't have even brought it up. I'm sure that everything is going to be fine. I made a mistake. You won't have to neutralize him with that, because he *won't* be a cybo. I was only saying that if it came to it, I would do it for you. I shouldn't have said anything."

She studies the woman dubiously to the point that Danica turns away. Luci doesn't know whether to thank her for the offer or be upset for planting the ghastly possibility in her head.

Yuma and Sari arrive, but they're less out of breath than Luci and Danica were. The four of them move as quickly as their crouched bodies will allow until they reach the center of the second sky bridge segment.

The walkway is wide enough for Sari and Yuma to sit flat with their backs against the iron-handrail partition facing Danica and Luci without touching their feet.

"Now what?" Luci asks Danica.

"We wait," Yuma answers before Danica can. "It should only be a few minutes until they bring him through."

Sari has returned to the annoying habit of nervously checking and rechecking her churka.

"Just keep watching for the PQX inhibitor screen to change color," Yuma instructs Luci.

"Yeah," she says, holding it out for display. "I got it—when it turns blue."

THE SECONDS TICK BY AGONIZINGLY slowly for Luci as they wait. She focuses on the small screen before her, praying that Yuma is the technical genius that he presents himself to be and that Danica's crack about Ish already undergoing conversion treatment being false. She catches Danica staring at the device. Luci begins softly, "How did Cyphor Gicul know that Ish had been taken?"

Danica shrugs but doesn't shift her gaze from the screen. "I wondered about that too, but Cyphor sends messages every few days alerting us of the progress that the two of you are making on DPM."

Luci is taken aback. "But how's that possible? How could he have known anything about what—" Then it hits her. She says the thought aloud, not believing her own words. "Ish? He must be a spy." Luci leans forward. Her thoughts race. "Is that why Cyphor wants him rescued? Does he know something?" She shoots a glance across to Sari and Yuma engaged in their own nervous conversation. "Ish must be working for him. It's the only possible explanation."

She shifts back to Danica, who's shaking her head at this conclusion. "I don't think so. I've never met Ish, and *L'inversione* is a small group. We all know each other."

"But you've never met Gicul either," Luci argues.

"Except that Cyphor only began sending messages to Ley and Noah about Moyta a few days ago, after we found out that you'd arrived in Relicus City."

Luci feels the onset of a Jardon headache setting in as another possibility explodes in her brain: Could Ish Moyta be Cyphor Gicul himself? If Enos Macer could be Waleen Macer, why couldn't Ish be the puppet master behind all of this stuff? She feels nauseated as she plays back their interactions together. He knew about Antarctica! He acted like he discovered the anomaly, but he must've known it all along! Her world spins off its axis, taking her heart with it. Did he purposefully guide her along the path, feeding information at precise moments to keep their momentum going? She whispers, "I can't believe that I didn't see the connection." She bites her lip to stop it from trembling. "Could Ish be Gicul?"

Danica places her hand on her shoulder. "Dr. Gaudiano, I don't see how what you say can be possible."

Luci dries her eyes with her free hand. "Why . . . why is that?"

"We received the message from Gicul that Technician Moyta had been taken into custody within the same hour that he was moved from the chancellor's place. How could he send a message about his own captivity?"

Luci looks at the scar tissue dangling from the side of Danica's face where an earlobe once had been. "A message . . . like through a Viatorio system or something?"

"That's not how Cyphor sends his messages anyway," Yuma volunteers.

Danica pulls back from her like she's touched the burner of a hot stove. She points at the device in Luci's lap. "Blue! It's blue!" she exclaims. "The screen is blue!"

SIX

YUMA'S EYES WIDEN AS HE quickly scoots on his knees to her. "Wait until they're directly below us."

The temptation to mash the button is nearly overwhelming, but Luci knows that they'll only get one shot to do this right.

Danica takes point and risks a peek over the side of the railing, her fingers spread wide a meter or so from Luci's face. "I'll tell you when," she says. "Here they come."

Luci's blood runs cold as Danica lets out a prolonged, "Oh no."

"What is it?" Luci demands, feeling the sweat on her palms. "What's wrong? Is he not with them? Have they converted him already?"

"No, he's fine, but there's a lot more than six of those things."

Yuma scoots to the other side of Luci, opposite Danica, and looks over the railing. "Whoa, it's more like twenty or more."

Luci's heart leaps that Ish is still alive—at least for the moment—but the number of cybo escorts send a shiver through to her core. "Do I do it? Do I do it now?" Luci says, looking across at the fear growing in Sari's eyes.

"Not yet," Yuma says, holding up a hand. "I'll tell you when they're directly below us."

The waiting is torture as Luci holds her breath. The tiny blue screen shakes in her hands. Will it work?

The sound of the squad scraping their feet grows louder. These creatures were not produced for stealth. She knows that they must stay out of sight for Ish to have any chance of making it through this. She wishes that she had a Viatorio so she could send him a message that everything is going to be all right, to alert him that they are here and that soon this will be over and the two of them can leave Relicus City for good.

Yuma's signaling hand quivers. Finally, it snaps with a downward motion. "Now! Do it now!"

Luci simultaneously exhales and double pushes the button while picturing Ish's face.

The sound of footsteps below continue unabated.

Yuma reaches for the inhibitor, but Luci pulls it away.

A flash of fear fills his eyes. "Twice! You have to push it twice!"

"I did," she argues. "I pressed—"

Danica aggressively shushes them. "Listen! They've stopped now."

Luci scrambles to peer over the railing and gasps at the sight. Almost directly beneath stand two dozen dingy grey figures frozen in place like pieces on a chessboard. In their midst is a thin black man in a bright red jumpsuit—Ish.

At first, he's as motionless as his immobile captors, and Luci is horrified that the conversion process may have already been initiated. She exhales in relief when he breaks free from their ranks and begins to run.

Her heart skips a beat as if the device she's holding suspended her mobility too. "Ish!" she yells, though he doesn't react from below as he races across the courtyard.

The "ground team" members of the group cautiously emerge from their hiding places with churkas drawn. Ish first spots Miguel and spins to run the other way.

"Ish, it's okay!" Luci yells as Cline begins running to intercept him across the space.

"I told everyone it would work!" Yuma exclaims behind her to Sari.

Luci tears herself away from her perch to head for the stairs with Danica running close behind. A dreamlike feeling envelops her as she races down to the courtyard to reunite with Ish. Luci can't believe that they've pulled this off. She doesn't care what his involvement may or may not be with *L'inversione* and Gicul, only that he's alive. He's alive and he's here.

She clutches Yuma's makeshift controller so tightly that her hand begins to cramp. She doesn't dare risk dropping it for fear that doing so would reanimate the dead minds of the cybos.

By the time she gets to him, Ish is struggling to break free of Jonn's one-armed bear-hug grip just a few meters from the cluster of cybos facing the opposite direction. "Ish, it's okay. They're with me. You're safe now."

Cline mumbles something about how she's technically with them, but she doesn't care. The man she loves—yes, she loves him—is alive.

As if he were a marionette whose strings had just been cut, all of his resistance instantly drains from his body. "Luci?" he asks, confused. "Luci, I don't understand. How did you get here? Who are these people and why are you dressed in that strange outfit?"

She runs to embrace him, and Jonn releases his stranglehold. When he doesn't put his arms around her, she notices his hands are bound in what looks like a high-tech hand warmer muff. Her momentum nearly knocks him backward as she rushes to put her head against his chest. The sound of his heartbeat is the most beautiful music that she's ever heard. "I'll tell you everything on the way back. For now, just kiss me."

He does, and as they kiss, the entire world and all of its problems don't exist. It's impossible, but it feels as if she's known him for a millennium and they've been separated for twice that time.

"We can't stay here long," Beaumont says, approaching them. "The second those things went offline, an alert rang out in some security system somewhere in the Spike, and they'll be sending someone or something to investigate."

Luci nods and forces her body away from Ish's, as hard as it is to do so.

Beaumont instructs Yuma, who's also just arrived, "Can you do anything about his restraints in case there's a tracker of some sort?"

Luci steps to the side as Ish extends the restraints for his inspection.

"Yeah, shouldn't be too difficult."

"Can you do it on the move?" Beaumont asks. "I'd rather not have anything tagging the transport back to where we're meeting up with everyone."

Ish addresses his liberators for the first time. "They deactivated my Viatorio, so at least they won't be able to locate where I am with that."

There's a surreal celebratory vibe rippling through the group as the rag-tag squad gathers around Ish. If she had to guess, Luci would say that they haven't done anything like this in this team configuration before.

Miguel is the only member outside of the circle, his churka scanning for any movement among the statue-like cybos. "Sir!" he shouts over his shoulder to Beaumont. "What do we do with them?"

Beaumont pauses, looks over to Jonn, and then says, "Cook 'em."

Everyone with a churka except Yuma, who is busy working on Ish's restraints, forms a line, shifts off the stun setting on their weapons, and fires into the backs of the incapacitated cybos. After those nearest collapse into smoldering heaps of flesh, the team repeats the act until none of the creatures remain.

The mixed stench of roasted rotting flesh and sulfur forces Luci to cover her nose with her sleeve, but her eyes, having no protection, water from the fumes hovering in the air.

When it's done, Beaumont slowly lowers his churka and announces in a deadpan voice, "Well, if their security monitors didn't know something was wrong with the escort, they certainly will now."

THE TEAM TRAVELS QUICKLY IN a group formation now instead of two-by-two. Beaumont drops back into the center of the pack to speak to Luci. "Keep an eye on that thing," he says, indicating the controller. "We're not out of this yet. I want you at the front of the squad with me and Miguel in case that screen turns blue again. Every second counts."

She looks at Ish. He's flanked by Sari and Yuma as the teenager struggles to keep time with the bouncing apparatus securing Ish's wrists. "Don't jiggle it so much," Yuma scolds him. "I can't work like this."

Ish ignores Yuma and speaks directly to Luci. "I'll be fine. Do what they say."

She and Beaumont double-time it to the vanguard position of the group alongside Miguel. While she's grateful that the need for stealth has been abandoned, she struggles to keep up with the pace set by these two. Even so, she shoots a look at the amber screen in her grip every few steps.

"Ha!" Yuma ecstatically shouts from behind. "Got it."

Luci looks over her shoulder in time to see Yuma victoriously tossing Ish's restraint against the alley wall. She steals another frenzied glance back down at the screen. It's still amber—they're in the clear.

The two men in front round the corner far ahead of her. It's the building with the columns again, but there's no need to hide against them this time.

This marks the halfway point to the transport.

Luci looks over her shoulder to ensure Ish is following. He, Yuma, and Sari move more quickly now he's free from the restraints.

Luci's encouraged that it won't be long until the nine of them are zooming away from this place in the container hauler when she hears a scream—a long scream.

At first, she believes it's from the building that they're racing toward, but the second time she hears it, she stops in her tracks. The voice is from where they've just come from, and it's familiar.

"Jonn!" Danica's voice echoes off the sides of the buildings, sounding as if it's coming from everywhere at once. This agonizing shriek is followed by a long wail. Luci looks back and realizes the team is split up: Danica, Jonn, and Cline have separated from these six.

Beaumont, who had gained a significant lead, backpedals to Luci, yelling, "Press it! Press the button!"

She does, but the screen glows amber, not blue. "Something's wrong with it!" Luci shouts in a panic, holding it up for him before realizing he's too far away to see the small screen.

Yuma converges on her first from behind, scolding, "What are you doing? We're under attack! Stop the cybos!"

She turns and pushes past the teen, trotting back in the direction of Danica's scream. If she mashed the button with any more force, she'd sprain her thumb. She calls out as she runs, "I'm coming!"

Ish manages to snag her and forces her against a crate as tall as he is. "Luci, stop and wait a minute. You're too important to—"

She struggles to free herself from his arms while continuing to mash at the button feverishly. "You don't understand. She needs my help. Something's wrong. We must be too far out of range for this to work or something."

Yuma catches up to her, violently snatching the inhibitor out of her hands. "That's impossible. We're well within range of any cybo brainwave signatures if they're being attacked." He anxiously examines the device. "What did you do to it?"

Beaumont and Miguel reach the three, but they don't stop as they race past them to the source of Danica's wailing. "Run to the alcove on the edge and stay there until we come back," Beaumont commands. "And fix that damned thing."

Sari joins Luci's trio as they duck into the alcove across the way. "I didn't do anything to it," Luci insists to Yuma.

Before the boy can reply, Ish points out, "The screaming ... the screaming from the woman. It's stopped."

"What ... what does that mean?" Sari's voice cracks. "Do you think she's alright? Did they get there in time for whatever ..."

Luci feels sick, but she listens, hoping for another sound to indicate the rest of the team is alright.

Yuma's preoccupied with his device. "I don't understand it," he says in frustration, forcibly shoving Cavazos's onyx rectangle back into the inhibitor slot. "It looks fine. It should be working."

"Oh no!" Ish exclaims frantically, his hand shooting to his earlobe. "It's back on. They turned my Viatorio back on. Red ... it just went red. I can't see anything."

"Oh shit," Luci says. "What does that mean?" she asks, spinning to face Yuma.

"Totti's team must have uploaded the holo vid," Sari offers feebly.

"No," Yuma argues, shaking his head. "It's too soon for that. They're not supposed to do it for another eighteen minutes, allowing us to be clear of this place."

Luci asks, "Can they track an active Viatorio during a red out?"

Yuma's answer comes slowly. "Theoretically, if the convergence relays are—"

"*Yes* or *no*, Yuma?" Luci cuts him off impatiently. "Does Macer know where we are?" Remembering the incident with Shar, she asks, "Yuma, do you have anything that can cut Ish's Viatorio off?"

"If it's removed during a red out, it will blind me permanently," Ish protests, protectively covering the device with his hand.

"He's right," Yuma offers. "Or much worse—do damage to his brain."

Luci tries not to panic, but answers aren't coming quickly enough. "Can he be tracked while this red out security thing is happening across the city?"

"They could, but it might not be as easy as that," Yuma admits in frustration. "I don't . . . I don't know how it works when there's a red out. During normal conditions, *yes*, but I just don't know once a citywide alarm is posted."

She turns to Ish. "We've got to get out of here then. If there's the slightest chance that his Viatorio could be broadcasting our location, we've got to leave now. We can't stay in one place for long."

"Noah said to stay here," Sari reminds them in an unsteady voice. "We're not leaving this spot."

"I'm telling you that we've got to go from here," Luci says, moving to steady Ish, who's groping at the air. "If his Viatorio is being tracked, it's just a matter of time before we're found."

"But we don't know if that can be done during a red out." Yuma looks at Sari, shaking his head. "No, Sari and I stay like we were told. If we leave, they won't know where we are and the team may waste valuable time searching."

"How can you not understand this?" Luci exclaims. "If we stay here, we may *die* here! Noah said to stay before Ish's Viatorio was reactivated. Now that it has, that changes everything. Please . . . if nothing else, make your way to the container transport and wait for us there."

Sari taps into some courage, hidden up until this point, to defy her. "We stay like Noah said."

"Suit yourself," Luci says in aggravation. "But give me one of the churkas. We're going to find out what happened to Danica and the others."

"We're not doing that," Sari protests.

"We can't just abandon them if something's happened. I won't do that! Give me the churka!" Luci yells as she reaches for the one Yuma has leaned against the wall to "fix" the cybo controller.

"I said I can't let you take that," Sari says, sniffling and fixing her own churka on Luci. "Back away or I'll stun you both."

"You little bitch," Luci says, placing herself between the end of the churka and her sightless Ish.

"Why are you doing this?" Ish asks, allowing Luci to take his hand.

"Like the doctor said, things have changed," Sari answers. "It's about survival now, and in order to survive, we need both weapons. She already took Yuma's inhibitor, and by her own admission, she doesn't know how to fire a churka."

Another sound of agony rings out, but it's a lower voice than Danica's . . . a male voice. All four pause to listen for more, but it's eerily quiet.

With one of the coveted weapons cradled in his arm, Yuma turns the amber inhibitor screen to Luci for inspection. "It's not cybos," he says with a nervous shrug. "Look, we'll be here when you check out what's going on with them, and then we'll all leave together. I left the transport on standby mode."

Time is running out. Luci considers reminding these two teens that the objective of their mission was to deliver Ish safely to Gicul, but she doesn't press for fear that they'd hold him hostage and not allow him to leave with her.

Luci runs through a list of unwelcome options she's faced with. Arguing with these two isn't getting anywhere. The prospect of fleeing to escape is preposterous to her—where could she go anyway? She decides that she's been through too much to get here to abandon Ish now, Viatorio tracking or not. The gruesome image of Shar's severed ear reminds her of the sacrifice that Beaumont's niece made for her and how he may need her help now.

Luci moves Ish's hand to the back waist of her pants, lacing his fingers around her belt. "Come on, Ish. Let's check on the others."

SEVEN

TO **BETTER FACILITATE TOWING I**SH behind her, Luci softly utters the word *"step"* to him each time she steps with her right foot and *"pause"* when they need to come to a brief halt.

As they continue to backtrack toward the courtyard, she whispers over her shoulder, "We're nearly to the building with the columns."

A few steps later, Ish pulls at her belt, announcing in a frenzied whisper, "I smell churka discharge. What do you see?"

Luci slows her pace but doesn't completely stop as she peers around another corner. "Nothing yet, but I'm sure we're getting closer." She listens intently for the noisy, foot-dragging shuffle of cybos, but the area is eerily silent save for her and Ish's movement.

"I just pray that we're not walking into a cybo ambush," she says softly, attempting to steady her breathing.

"I don't think cybos hunt," Ish whispers. "I suspect that their programing is too simplistic to employ any cunning skills like that."

If only his words could convince her. It stills feels like they're moving toward a trap. "All I know is that I owe it to the others to see if they need our help. Each of them risked their lives to save you."

Ish doesn't reply, but Luci feels his snug grip tighten around the back of her belt.

IT TAKES A MOMENT FOR her to register the scent of something that's out of place, a new smell that doesn't belong here. The smell of cooking mixed with the bitter stench of churka discharge on the air is the aroma of cooked meat—roasted flesh, in fact.

She's wondering how the wind could've also carried the smell of cybo slaughter all of this way when they turn the corner. At the end of the alley is what she dreaded. She stops abruptly but forgets to whisper to Ish to pause, so he collides into her.

"What is it?" he asks, wildly waving his free hand out before him.

It's difficult to convert the gruesomeness of it into words. "They're . . . dead." She scans for cybos, but other than the smoldering carcasses at the end of the way, there's nothing.

"Who's dead?" Ish asks. "Who is it?"

Her stomach twists into knots at how she mistook this odor for cooked food. The pungent stench of burnt hair compounds the sickening feeling. The strength in her legs wanes as she repeats, "They're dead—all of them." As if reciting a macabre roll call, she murmurs the names in order of their proximity to where she and Ish crouch. "Beaumont, and the others . . . they're dead!"

"Luci, you have to leave," Ish says, violently tugging at the waist of her pants. "You have to leave now! You're too important!"

His words fade into the background as she continues reporting to her sightless companion, "They've all been roasted! Their flesh is—" She collapses to her knees, bringing Ish tumbling down with her. She finds it odd that there's no blood until she realizes that the smoking, mangled flesh of the dead is cauterized. The grotesque sight and smell is more than she can bear, and a hot, sour stream of vomit erupts from her gnarled stomach.

When she's done, she turns to see Ish flailing at the air to find her. "Come on, Luci. You should return to those young people back there and head to the transport. You'll have a better chance without dragging me."

Her chest convulses with the aftershocks of retching. Wiping a string of spit from her mouth with her sleeve, she returns to her feet. She studies her blind companion, rejecting his suggestion. Luci turns her head to the side and back again. The motion, repeated more quickly, transforms into frustrated head shaking. "So what? You're just going to give up? That's about the stupidest thing that I've ever heard you say."

His expression is somberly resigned and placid. "It's for the best."

She's astonished but then grows furious at the suggestion. Luci repeatedly taps her index finger hard into his chest with the motion of a tiny jackhammer. "Absolutely not! That's the one thing I know we're not doing."

Ish doesn't expect the forceful contact and stumbles backward trying to steady himself. "I just thought that if—"

"That would mean that these five died in vain." She sighs. "And I can't allow that. Plus, I need you . . . I need *you*, Ish." She's relieved that he can't see her face. He doesn't witness the tears flowing down the crevice of her nose and cheek. Before he has a chance to respond, she says," Wait here a minute."

Her steps wobble, but she forces herself to advance down the alleyway into the heart of the carnage. She cautiously skirts along the wall past Miguel's corpse as if her footsteps could rouse the man from a deep slumber. His steaming form lies upon a churka. She does a double take upon realizing that his left forearm isn't tucked under his chest but is completely missing from his body. Luci bites her lip and looks away, not having the courage to slide him off the weapon.

She moves instead to Beaumont, who is on his side facing away from her. He's clear of his churka by a safe half meter. Taking a deep breath, she snatches the weapon on the ground beside him. Luci makes the mistake of looking back at his face and instantly regrets it. His distorted visage looks like a candle that's halfway melted in a flame. His only remaining eye looks past her.

She feels the urge to puke again, but her empty insides make the reaction even more painful. The reflex is a painful dry churning and twisting of her already belabored diaphragm and raw throat. Her airway constricts, launching her into a panic—she's got to flee this spot.

She runs back to Ish, whose face is strained as he cups his ears to hear.

"I've got a churka," she says, refastening his hand to the back of her belt. "Do you know how to operate one of these?"

He whispers sharply, "I'm a Chronal Technician—calibrating longchairs and chronal convergence point expansions, remember?"

"Okay, settle down," she says, examining the weapon. "I figured it couldn't hurt to ask."

They're on the move again.

After a few steps, Ish asks "What are you doing?"

He tugs hard at the back of her pants.

"Hey, don't—" Luci spins to face him.

A bulky eight-foot-tall figure armored in crimson hurls Ish against the wall of the alley. The motion is as effortless as a paperboy tossing the Sunday paper on Luci's block back home when she was a kid. She gasps at the sight of the large "R" insignia on the center of the reflective red breastplate. Luci recognizes the emblem from Totti's holo vid as one of Macer's Relicus fighters from the future.

Ish grunts in pain, the sound telling her he's still alive. She raises the churka, but the attacker is too fast. In a single fluid movement, it spins to face her and bats the weapon away with a downward swipe. Luci turns to run, but something locks onto her left ankle like a vise. The world turns upside-down. She's dangling in the air, swinging suspended by the grip of the hulking assailant.

"Run, Ish, run!" she screams, doing her best to wriggle free of her captor's hold. Its face is as stoic and unchanging as the first-generation cybos of this time period.

"What's happening?" Ish calls out from behind her. "Who's here?"

"Just go!" she shouts, batting at the red fighter. She remembers the other two survivors of the team and calls out in desperation, "Yuma, help us! Yuma, please!" It's unlikely that they're close enough to hear her, but she must try, so she yells again.

The red monster points a rod at her. Luci does her best to knock it away, but the creature has already calculated the length of her reach and keeps the object out of her range.

A bright red beam shines from the rod. Luci surmises this must be a modified churka from the future. She does her best to swing clear of the beam, but it's no use; there's nowhere to hide. She braces herself for the anguish of being burned alive.

The beam runs up and down her body. Confusion overwhelms her when her skin doesn't blister or burn.

"Luci, keep talking for me to find you," Ish says. The sound is closer to her than expected, as if he's directly behind them. "I found the churka," he says in staccato bursts.

"Dr. Luci Gaudiano scan identified and subject secured," the red warrior announces to no one in a cold, synthetic voice.

"Run, Ish!" Luci shouts.

"No, I can do this," he protests.

"Ish, you're blind!" she says in horror.

"Describe it for me, where to aim. I'll shoot low."

Remembering how he mentioned only being a chronal technician not even a minute or so ago, she shouts, "How can you—"

A flash of bright blue light illuminates the area behind her. The pungent stench of sulfur fills her nostrils, masking the smell of her vomit from before. The temperature in the alley instantly shoots up as her captor staggers, attempting to right its stance.

Another blast, and Luci's ankle is released from the creature's grip. She drops; her hands catch her, preventing her skull from slamming into the ground. Converting the momentum of the fall into a somersault roll, Luci barely registers the pain due to the adrenaline exploding through her body. She rolls over on her side as the slain Relicus fighter tips and collapses like a tree downed by a chainsaw. Through the haze, she realizes that one of its legs is missing.

There's a third blast, this one a direct hit to the chest as if the R insignia is a bullseye. Luci can't look away from the sight. The creature is unrecognizable as a thing that was humanoid only seconds before.

She's shaking as she brushes her hands against her legs struggling to stand.

"Luci?" Ish calls out. "Are you alright?"

She hurries to him, careful to stay clear of the raised churka. "How did you know where to shoot?"

He stammers clumsily receiving her embrace, "What just happened? I . . . I didn't fire."

There's a figure through the dissipating haze at the end of the alley.

Luci releases Ish, squinting for a better view. "Yuma, is that you?"

The figure approaches. As the shape takes on more definition, she realizes the form is too large to be the boy's or his companion, Sari. She swallows. "Ish, give me the churka and get behind me."

"You're a long way from home, Dr. Gaudiano," Royse's baritone booms as he carefully steps over the massacred *L'inversione* corpses. He carries his churka as casually as if it were an extension of his own body. Royse shakes his head, coming to a stop a few meters from Luci and Ish. "I should've known about you, Moyta. It all makes sense now."

Not certain of what to do, Luci instinctively aims her churka at Royse. "What does he mean, Ish?" she asks over her shoulder, her heart pounding.

He's returned to gripping her belt. "Is that Mr. Timmons? I don't know what he means—I don't, I promise."

Her mind races, wondering about Ish's potential connection to Gicul or if he, in fact, *is* Gicul in some way, despite the earlier conversation with the now-dead Danica.

"Stand aside, Doctor," Royse orders, gesturing with the end of his churka.

For the first time, she sees the open doorway that the Relicus fighter must have emerged from to ambush them. "What do you mean, Royse?" Her voice cracks, and she grips the weapon more tightly with sweating palms. "What should you have figured out about him?"

Ish, hunched over, whispers from behind, "What's happening? What's he doing?"

"He's got a churka weapon trained on us. He's the one that shot the red . . . cybo."

"I'm not aiming at you, Doctor. I'm aiming at him. He's one of them." He shouts, "Now get out of the way!"

She raises her voice to meet his. "No, you're wrong! He's not with *L'inversione*. They—"

"Not *L'inversione*," Royse scoffs, sidestepping for a better angle. "The New Australians. He's with the New Australians. He helped them come through the vortex portal at the Grange he expanded for them!"

Luci is stunned to silence but shifts around making sure to remain between Royse at Ish.

Royse shouts, "The New Australians are in the city right now!"

"No, that's not right," Luci answers. "There *is* no New Australia." Her heart skips a beat, remembering the fate of Bru Mandal on Totti's holo vid. Even worse is the possibility that Relicus City may be infested by more of Macer's future cybos. She forces herself to focus. "New Australia isn't real. It's all a hoax made up by Macer and Cavazos to control everyone through fear."

Royse shakes his head. "That guy that I blasted on the ground over there doesn't look like a hoax to me. He seemed pretty *real* when he was holding you upside down and about to kill you."

She realizes how badly she's trembling by seeing the end of her churka shake. "No, Royse, you've got to listen to me. You've been tricked . . . everyone has been tricked. What you've been told isn't true."

"Tricked by who?"

"Tricked by Macer. He's lied to everyone."

Royse's posture stiffens. Despite what he said, the churka is aimed directly at her now.

"Royse, he's not who you think he is. He's Waleen." Ish gasps behind her as she continues, "He's Waleen Macer. There is no Enos. There is no New Australia. You shot one of Macer's cybo warriors from the future." She swallows. "I don't know why they're here, but it can't be good, and we can't stay in this spot for too long now that it scanned me."

She remembers the objective of the second *L'inversione* team—Totti's mission. "There's a video that shows everything, actual footage of Waleen Macer from the future. It's in the splash forum, or at least it will be uploaded there in the next few minutes. Watch it and see. What I say is true: Macer is a tyrant."

Royse furrows his brow and squints at her. "You lie. I don't know why you're saying all this, but you're lying."

"No, Royse. I'm not."

He shakes his head. "No, no, no . . . you said you saw a splash vid." His right hand snaps to his Viatorio. "That's impossible without one of these." His hand swiftly returns to the churka. "Enos would never lie to me. I know that there are affairs of state that must be kept secret for the good of the—"

"He's not Enos!" Luci screams. "He's an imposter. He set himself up as a god. People in the future are forced to bow and worship him." Pity swells in her heart for him. Her voice returns to normal. "I'm sorry, Royse, but he doesn't care about you, he doesn't care about me, he doesn't care about Relicus City like he's always saying. He doesn't care about anyone." She snatches a quick breath to calm her pounding heart. "Everyone is just a means to an end for him. Everyone."

He looks like he's been gut punched, but he remains motionless, studying her.

Luci's arms grow tired from holding the churka up, but to lower or surrender it would mean certain death for Ish and capture for her. "Royse," she begins softly, "in the future, people are bred for food. Relicus City is forced into engineered cannibalism." She pauses. "It's in the video."

He scoffs and shakes his head more adamantly than before. This time, his voice sounds uncertain and lost. "You're lying. The chancellor—"

"I saw it. They showed me a holo vid," she says, indicating the slain members of *L'inversione* scattered on the ground. "The video that the other members of their group are uploading to the splash forum."

"All splash activity is suspended." He takes a defiant step closer. "The city's in red out because of the attack from New Australia. That's why your friend behind you can't see. The red out is working just like it was meant to, hampering any traitor's vision."

"I'm not a traitor!" Ish shouts, moving in time with Luci as she repositions their angle to the man.

"Move out of the way, Doctor," Royse says between gritted teeth, taking another step in their direction. "Let's get this over with and you back to the guesthouse where it's safe."

"Hold it right there," Luci orders. "Don't come any closer or I'll blast you."

He eyes her but stops. "You're bluffing."

"Bluffing?" She repeats the word as if trying it out in her mouth. "Bluffing?" Saying it again gives her the notion to do it. "These five people that you see on the ground, they thought I was bluffing." She tightens her grip around the churka barrel and strokes her shaking finger against the weapon's trigger. "Why don't you ask them who was bluffing, Royse? Ask them."

He nods slowly as if sizing up the deception.

She remembers how Yuma has modified the group's churkas with a stun option. She steals her eyes away from Royse to look for it on the churka. She doesn't want to shoot this man, but stunning him would allow her and Ish to escape to the transport with Yuma and Sari.

Royse advances another step.

"Stop it!" she screams.

Royse's expression is a dangerous mixture of pain, confusion, and anger. The cadence of his speech accelerates, the words bursting free from him. "You're trying to convince me that my whole life is a lie, that the man I've sworn my allegiance to for all these years is a fraud, that he's broken his own law about skipping into the future?" He takes another step uncomfortably closer. "That he's making people eat each other?" He shakes his head violently, but the churka in his hands barely sways.

Luci realizes that she's got to contain this; it's getting too emotional. She searches for the proper words to diffuse the situation while being truthful. Royse has been tricked and lied to just like everyone else. He deserves to know. "Royse, please listen to me," she pleads in a soft voice. "Think about it for a second. What advantage do I gain by making any of this stuff up? I'm an outsider, a stranger from the past."

"New Australia isn't real," Ish interjects from behind her.

"Ish, please," she orders, keeping her eyes fixed on Royse's wounded expression. Her heart is racing, triggering a faint Jardon headache. "It's all true," she says, swallowing the lump in her throat. "All of it."

Royse's shoulders slump slightly, and his eyes look like he's in another place far away. The tiniest light of hope shines within her heart that she's getting through to him as his churka lowers halfway. Instead of pointing at her chest, it's inattentively pointed downward at her shins now. "I'm so sorry, Royse. I wish it wasn't true." She grits her teeth. "I'd like nothing more than to believe that too, but you've just been blinded by his charm like everyone else—we all have, but Macer is evil beyond comprehension."

"You said that you killed these *L'inversione*, but you also said they showed you a holo vid." He angles his head back up to her. "Which one is it? In fact, how can I know for sure this is *L'inversione* at all?"

He's got her. She should've stuck with the truth only instead of mixing it. "Okay, I didn't kill them. I just said that as a bluff, but everything else I said is true." There's a long pause, and Luci takes in a deep cleansing breath. "Royse, if you'll trust me enough to come with us, I'll show you the proof of what I say. You only need to trust me a little, and you can even bring the churka back to where—"

"No," Royse says softly as his expression intensifies. The lost look in his eyes transforms into a dark hatefulness. "No! I refuse to believe it. No!" With amazing speed and agility for his size, Royse drops to a one-legged crouch and swiftly pivots. Before Luci can respond, his extended leg strikes her left shin, causing her to buckle and crumble to the ground with the force of twin bowling pins. The pain of the impact stuns her as much as the unexpected act itself, but she instinctively rolls to grab her fallen churka.

Royse is already working on returning to his feet. He raises the end of his churka to Ish, who is blindly batting at the air and calling for Luci.

There's no time for her to focus a perfect shot, so she takes the only one she has, at the big man's feet. There's no recoil from the weapon when she pulls the trigger. If it wasn't for an immediate rise in temperature, the bright blue flash of light, and noxious gas cloud, she'd think that the weapon hadn't fired.

Royse collapses to his knees, screaming in agony for the now-missing bottoms of his limbs.

Luci scrambles to her feet while Ish squirms free of Royse in a panic. She winces at the sight of Royse hobbling on the misshapen stubs where his feet were.

This churka clearly wasn't set to the stun function.

"You . . ." Royse gasps as he turns halfway back to her. "You stupid bitch!" The sound of his rapid breathing fills the area. He manages to shamble on the smoking nubs of flesh until he's facing her. "I'm going to kill you!"

"You know you can't do that." Tears cloud her vision, and she sniffs. "If you kill me, all of this disappears."

He lowers his head while letting out a primal-sounding scream. It's impossible to determine if it's due to the pain raging through him, frustration, or a combination of both.

He looks up at her with such contempt that it makes her shudder. "Moyta has convinced you of all of these lies about Chancellor Macer. He's an infiltrator and has messed up your mind." The rapid-fire of his breathing sounds like he could hyperventilate at any second.

She raises her trembling churka to meet his. "No, Royse, that's not true. Please, Royse."

"I'll show . . ." He spits. "I'll show you . . . kill this New Australian, and we'll go to Enos. The chancellor will fix it all!"

"Put it down. Put the churka down, Royse. Please."

"We've got to kill the infiltrator first." He howls again as he hobbles, this time slightly slipping on his sinewy meat stalks as he turns his back on her.

She refuses to shoot him in the back and allows her weapon lower. "No, Royse, you can return with us. We're going to—"

"I refuse to believe the chancellor would lie to me," Royse sputters, pointing his churka at Ish crouching blindly against the wall. "I'm Enos's number one. That's why Moyta must die."

She utters a single-syllable word of defiance so softly that only she can hear. "No." Again, there's no recoil from Luci's weapon; it's the same absence of force as is she's shining a flashlight in a darkened room. She cries as she cooks his flesh with repeated bursts until she's forced to look away from the gore.

The noise of his exaggerated breathing is gone; only the sound of her sobs remains.

HER LEG THROBS WHERE ROYSE kicked her, but she doesn't massage it. She's frozen in place, staring at her feet for what feels like an eternity.

Ish's voice rouses her out of her semi-conscious state. "Luci?"

She allows the churka drop to the ground and moves to embrace him. "I . . . killed him. Ish, I killed Royse. He—"

Ish pulls her into his chest tighter. "I know. I know, but you had to. It had to be done. He forced you to do it."

She shakes her head and sniffs. "I know . . . I know, but it doesn't matter. I killed him."

He pats her back. "Come on, Luci. We've got to get out of here."

EIGHT

A COUPLE OF MINUTES LATER, Luci snaps out of her nightmarish stupor at the sight of the smoldering bodies of two more *L'inversione* members.

Her abrupt stop prompts Ish to ask, "What is it? What do you see?"

"It's Yuma and Sari," she answers in a flat tone and bites her lip, wondering if she'll ever be free of the smell of cooked flesh and burnt hair in her mind.

Ish switches his grip on her belt to the other hand and, in a near-reverent voice, whispers, "Do you think it was that modified cybo thing or Mr. Timmons?"

She sighs. "No way of knowing, but definitely churka blasts of some sort." Her voice breaks. "I never even got to thank Yuma for all the tech he made to rescue you."

"You tried to warn them, Luci. You did your best. There's nothing that you can do."

She nods her head as the teardrops fall. "I know . . . I know," she says, remembering their conversation about Ireland and Florence on the way over in the container. "It's just such a waste, all of it. Such a waste." She turns and wraps Ish's fingers around the churka. "Give me a second, okay?"

"What are you doing?" he asks, making a point to aim the weapon up and away from the sound of her voice.

"Looking for something that may help us," she says, dragging Sari's mutilated form from the top of Yuma. She pauses to turn her head, refusing the bile that threatens to erupt from her. To the side of the Yuma's corpse is what remains of the PQX inhibitor. The device is in two splintered pieces, one shorter than the other, with a small section missing. "For a new and better path," she whispers while wiping her eyes. "A new and better path."

She stands from her squatting position and reclaims the churka from Ish. "The cybo inhibitor is busted," she informs him. "We've got to get to the transport before the entire place is swarming with security and/or those cybos from the future."

They return to their rhythm of Luci leading her blinded companion. He only stumbles a few times, despite the fact that Luci has ceased to call out every step as they move to be move more stealthily.

"Can you operate the transport carrier?" Ish whispers.

She hesitates, wishing she had a better plan. In a controlled environment, she'd even have a backup plan to her backup plan, but this situation is thin on contingencies. Finally, Luci admits, "Hopefully, Yuma pre-programed the carrier to return to the mechanic shop and we can meet up with the others, but . . ."

"But what?" Ish prompts, struggling to keep in time with her steps.

"But . . ." she begins slowly, "Yuma really liked to be in control of things. There's the possibility that he made it where only he can operate it. I just don't know what else to do." She hates admitting this, least of all to Ish.

"Let's check it out," he reassures her. "If it doesn't work, we'll come up with something else."

"Hopefully, it'll still be there," she says, the words bitter on her tongue.

"It'll be there," Ish says. "We'll figure this out."

She tightens her grasp on the churka as she looks over at the building with the large columns across the street. "Let's hope so," she says, adding, "I'm definitely open to ideas at this point."

OTHER THAN A FEW MISSTEPS by Ish, they move through the narrow alleys without incident. Ley had been right about the city-wide red out clearing the streets for them. Even the three stunned men the team encountered on the way to rescue Ish have retreated inside somewhere.

"Wait a minute," Luci says, peering around the corner at the lime-green transport hauler across the street.

"It's still there?" Ish asks in an anxious whisper.

"Yeah, it's still here and the ramp is down just the way Yuma left it, but wait." She scans the area for any trace of disturbance. Luci catches a glimpse of the Spike building in the distance. It's as if it looks down at them like some great foreboding eye, scrutinizing their every move.

"Do you think it's a trap?"

She continues to slowly move the end of the churka parallel to her vision. "It'd be a perfect one if it is. I can only hope that Beaumont's cunning to have Yuma park it so far away from your rescue paid off."

Inhaling a deep breath to calm her raging heartbeat, she says, "I hate this, but there's only one way to find out."

Ish responds with a silent nod. His feet scrape the ground as he shifts his weight preparing to run.

"I just don't know what else to do."

"I trust you," Ish says. "Whatever happens, we'll do it together."

She swallows the lump in her throat as she studies the determined expression on his face. "Okay, let's go."

They scurry as quietly as they can to the ramp of the transport hauler. Once inside the long, corrugated metal container, Luci thrusts the vertical churka barrel to her blind accomplice.

She removes the front panel over the override wheel, letting it fall to the floor with an echoing clang louder than she expected.

"What was that?" Ish asks, stepping backward uncertainly.

Luci answers between grunts as she strains at the wheel, "Sorry, that was the cover to a manual wheel in here that changes the ramp back into the carrier's wall panel." She wipes hands already slick with sweat on her pants legs. "I'm gambling that once it's closed, the transport will automatically take us back to the origin point."

"Here," Ish says, extending the churka into the air between them. "I may not be able to see, but I can turn a wheel."

She contemplates this while wiping her brow. Despite her all effort, the ramp-wall has moved less than a fifth of the way into position. "Yeah, okay," she says, huffing. "Good idea." She receives the churka from him and guides his hands to the metal circle.

The wall mechanism groans its resistance as Ish forces it to submit to his strength. He's grunting now every time he heaves at the dial, but the panel reaches the halfway point in a short time.

Luci's eyes nervously search the area for movement, cybo or otherwise.

Her heart stops as a figure approaches from around the corner on the other side of the street. The red fighter's trot transforms into a full run at the sight of her.

She bites her lip hard while aiming. The churka blast barely clears the top lip of the container as the wall continues to rise. The first heated shot is too far right of target, but her second connects dead center and splits the attacker in half. The citrus-and-rubber smell within the cargo pod instantly gives way to the noxious odor of sulfur.

"They found us!" she shouts back to Ish as if any announcement is necessary. The adrenaline pumping through her veins makes it difficult for her to stand steady and peer through the haze for more of Macer's future cybo-warriors.

Ish's grunting speeds up to match his energy in sealing them in. "Don't worry," he says. "They won't shoot at us. They can't risk hitting you."

She strains her vision scanning for more of the re-animated fighters.

There's a loud clang from the side of the container opposite the rising panel wall. The impact causes the transport to sway, and a surprised Luci and Ish slam to the metal floor.

"What was that?" Ish shouts, attempting to return to his feet despite the pendulum-swinging motion of the area they're in.

Another strike from the same side echoes through the hauler.

"They're trying to come through the other side!" Luci shouts, scrambling to retrieve the churka. "Turn the wheel! It's our only hope. Seal us in!"

There's another loud hit, but this time, light from the outside pours in through a puncture in the metal. Luci manages to snatch the churka back up from the floor. A type of pickaxe tool violently dislodges from the freshly made hole for another blow. "They're making a hole," she reports to Ish, who has feverishly resumed the task of sealing the opposite side of the cargo compartment.

Still on her knees, Luci rocks with the swaying motion of the container. Though she grips it as tightly as possible, the churka moves wildly in the air like a rowboat lifting and falling in a typhoon. The axe tool on the outside systematically continues to widen the rip in the metal skin of the container. This produces bursts of sparks with each ear-spitting strike.

As the container sways backward from impact, Luci catches a glimpse of their assailant; the red armor is unmistakable.

Using the butt of the churka to brace, she clumsily maneuvers herself uneasily close to the torn opening. The hole is roughly the size of a soccer ball now, just large enough to peek outside despite the continual bouncing of the compartment.

She extends her weapon through the jagged hole just as the red fighter deals another nearby blow to the transport.

Its proximity startles Luci long enough for the modified cybo outside to latch on to the end of her churka and yank it. Luci screams as she's unexpectedly jerked forward to the ragged opening. Another two centimeters to the left and the mangled shards of metal bent in from the punctures would've lacerated her arm. Miraculously, she manages to retain her grip on the churka. Her pull against the strength of the red warrior is useless, but then she remembers that she doesn't have to match it in a tug-of-war. She fingers the trigger, and a glorious blast of bright blue light reflects off the inside of the metal container. The pull on the weapon outside goes slack.

"Luci!" Ish calls to her.

"I'm okay!" she shouts while firing again for good measure, though the churka haze blocks any view to the outside.

A resounding clunk from the roof behind her makes her think something is on top of the transport. She withdraws the churka from the gash in the side and aims it upward at this new threat.

"I think . . . I think that's it," Ish shouts, using the wheel to balance.

Luci turns her attention to the side of the container with the ramp wall, realizing the noise overhead must be the pod snapping shut.

"It's closed, right?" Ish asks.

"It's closed," Luci answers. She apprehensively looks down both sides of the long, empty cargo pod. "But why aren't we moving?" She swallows. "Why isn't it going?" she grumbles through gritted teeth. She knows they won't kill her, because they can't without erasing everything from this timeline and their future one by proxy, but she's certain that her presumptuous gamble has forfeited Ish's life. It's just a matter of time until the red warriors make it through to them. Her mistake has guaranteed that Macer's forces will know exactly where to find them—perfectly locked up in a little box. "I'm sorry, Ish." She chides herself, "How could I have been so stupid?"

"What do you mean?" Ish asks, scooting on his knees toward her. "Sorry for what?"

A chilling thought enters her mind. "The hole. Maybe the red cybo wasn't trying to get in but trying to make an opening for a gas canister or something." She moves to see if there's any outside activity through the opening. "Ish, do they use tear gas in this time?" The haze of the churka blasts still hangs in the air, making it impossible to tell if there's any movement.

"Tears of gas? I don't know what that is."

Two sharp thuds resonate from under the cargo pod. Both Ish and Luci fall to the metal floor as the container lurches forward.

"What's happening?" Ish asks in a near panic. "Luci?"

"I'm alright," she says. "Shhhhh . . . listen."

"What is it?" he asks softly, returning to a kneeling position.

"That's the beautiful sound of the transport hauler's engine engaging." She moves to him on her knees, laughing while nearly in tears. "We did it! It worked!" She faces the ceiling of the container, and in drawn-out, jubilant exhilaration, she shouts, "Yuma did it!" She can barely contain her laughter. "Yuma, wherever you are, you're a genius. Thank you, Yuma!"

AFTER A FEW NERVOUS MINUTES of riding, they settle against the wall opposite the hole. Ish reaches for her, and Luci sits with her back against his chest. "You're shaking," he says, draping his arms around her.

She hadn't noticed this before, but now she is self-conscious of her involuntary quivering. "Adrenaline, I guess. This is not something I normally do."

"Yeah, me either," he replies, tightening his embrace.

He's drenched with sweat, and though it takes a bit for her nerves to settle, this is the safest she's felt since her arrival. She thinks on this and determines that despite currently riding in a windowless transport to who-knows-what-end, she can't remember a time when she's felt as safe as she does in this instant—even before her abduction by Royse and Macer.

There is a melancholy to looking across the empty cargo pod. On the way over, it was cramped with members of Beaumont's team. Now it's only her and Ish, Gicul's "prize." She still can't reconcile why the leader of *L'inversione* would even bother with someone like Ish. What is he to him? Is it his technical knowledge about expanding and contracting skip-portal apertures, or is it something darker?

All of this is in the back of her mind as she begins to debrief him on the events of the last few hours. She fills him in on how Shar was the one leaving the notes under Beaumont's influence. She hurries through the part about the girl's gruesome self-mutilation and feelings for her, focusing on the escape instead. She relays her horrific underwater experience on the bnati and meeting members of *L'inversione*. She tells him of Yuma's modifications to Cavazos's cybo tech controller and the news that Cavazos was killed by Malom Roderick back in "cowboy days," which was probably the source of the ridiculous outfit she is wearing.

Ish tenses as she describes the holo-vid of the future of Relicus City and the true nature of Waleen Macer and his multiple shadow copies posing as him in different intervals.

Through it all, Ish remains silent. When she's no longer able to contain it, she says, "There's something else, something that I need to ask you."

"Anything," he says.

She hesitates, uncertain how to proceed. "I need you to tell me the truth, whatever that may be." Her words feel clumsy. She considers turning away from probing him for an answer. Does she really want to force him to reveal something that she may not be ready to know, something that may drastically alter what they have together? Despite her apprehension, the scientist in her wins out. She has to press on, regardless of the consequence.

As she's reaching this conclusion, Ish prompts her, "I'll tell you anything you want to know. I promise you the truth, always."

"Thank you," she says with a sigh that comes out louder than expected. "I have to understand something before we go any further. I have to know why all of those people died rescuing you. Why are you so important to Gicul for him to risk their lives?"

"I . . . I don't know."

She wriggles out of his arms and crooks her head, preparing to observe his reaction. "Ish Moyta, *are* you Cyphor Gicul?"

He scoffs and stammers, "What? No, I am not Cyphor Gicul! Why would you even ask that? How could—Luci, you know me." His blind eyes ricochet from side to side as he asks, "How would that be possible?"

She fires off the next question nervously. "Do you know him or work for him in some capacity?"

"No, never. I work on special projects from time to time, but it's always at the Grange or for the city." His voice sounds hurt. "Why are you asking that of me now? What's brought this on?"

"You really can't think of any reason why Gicul would have *L'inversione* send a rescue team for you? How are you so valuable to them and Gicul?"

His tone is more desperate as he fervently shakes his head. "I don't. I really don't. Until you showed up with them, I thought *L'inversione* was determined to kill you like they did the time before." He pauses. "If I were some mastermind like Gicul, do you think I would have masterminded my way to avoid this?" Ish points both index fingers at his eyes. "I wish there was some way that I could prove it to you. I've never had any dealings with *L'inversione* or Gicul. You've got to believe me."

"Look, I'm sorry I brought it up. It just doesn't add up for me why Beaumont and the team were dispatched by Gicul to get you."

"I really don't know," Ish says. "I truly can't answer that, but I'm glad that you did, and I'm glad that you're safe now."

She resists the impulse to mock his statement that they're safe, saying instead, "I'm sorry for doubting you. Let's just drop it, okay?"

He agrees, but Luci's mind turns the mystery of his importance to Gicul and Malom Roderick over and over for the remainder of the return trip.

NINE

AS **THE HAULER SLOWS TO** a stop, Luci crawls to peek through the puncture hole previously made by the red warrior. In a hushed voice, she tells Ish, "I can't see a thing through here."

"Why is that?"

"It's too dark. The sun's gone down, and the shop is in a semi-vacant zone of the city that's not well lit."

"Are you certain that we've arrived at the rendezvous spot?" Ish asks, steadying himself against the wall panel to stand up.

"There's no way to tell," she answers, shifting to a different angle for a better look. "All I know is we shouldn't stay in here for very long."

Ish fumbles along the wall in search of the wheel. A moment later, the combined sounds of his grunts and the squeak of the wall panel lowering conceal Luci's muffled sobs. The incident with Royse replays on an unwelcome loop in her mind—his shocked expression as she fired upon him and the smell of churka and burned hair and flesh torments her. She glances down at her white-knuckled fingers coiled tightly around the weapon. Luci is grateful Ish can't see it shaking in her hands—glad that he cannot see her tears.

She stands, eager to reunite with Totti and the other team once she and Ish can leave this deathtrap compartment. She shudders at the prospect of having to inform them that none of the members of Beaumont's team survived. Their friends are dead, and she still doesn't know why. Luci is certain there will be a measure of resentment toward Ish—it's only natural—but she selfishly would trade any of them again for the man turning the wheel beside her. Luci shakes herself, resolving that now isn't the time to be distracted by things that can't be changed.

Facing the expanding opening with the churka aimed outside, the only thing in view is the windowless side of a dark-grey building. The clang of the panel hitting the ground jars her, and Luci moves to allow Ish to latch onto her belt again.

The narrow street is empty, and the bright lights of the Spike building looming in the distance offer little help in getting her bearings. After a few paces, she tells Ish, "Wait here." She tucks him into a darkened doorway. "I need a minute to figure out where we are."

She does her best to replay the route that Beaumont's team took as she skims along the side of the building. Her mind is drained, her thoughts lethargic compared to how focused she normally is. She's on mental overload, something she didn't believe possible about herself until today.

Luci stops to look up and down both ends of the street, mumbling her habitual self-pep talk. "Come on, Luci G. You can do this. Just figure it out."

She pauses and closes her eyes upon the realization that she no longer feels her Jardon headache, not even a residual trace. While she's thrilled at this discovery, her mind is spent. This isn't the time to have her thoughts gummed up like taffy in the gears. She's convinced that she just needs a little rest and urges herself to go on a little longer until they're safely with the others in the shop. Then she can rest, and then she'll be herself again.

When she opens her eyes, a jolt of relief shoots through her. She recognizes two doors across from where she's standing. She peers down both sides of the street again before rushing over to them. Unable to contain her excitement, she slides the fingers of the hand without the churka across the cool metal plate. "Yes!" she shouts exuberantly while running at full speed to gather up Ish.

"Luci, what's happening?" he demands, reaching through the air at the sound of her voice. "Did you find the rest of *L'inversione?*"

Her excitement and relief at finding the hideout is unrestrainable. Charging Ish at full speed, she nearly knocks him over with a hug. "I haven't gone down there yet. I came back to get you, but we're going to be okay now."

He nods in relief, but then his smile quickly vanishes. "Something's coming. Listen!"

Luci spins to see a vehicle approaching from the far end of the street. Whatever it is doesn't have lights for her to judge its rate of speed. There's only a split second to decide if the two of them should chance a run to the shop or hide. She decides to play it safe.

"Get down," she tells Ish while shoving him to get under the midsection of the cargo transport that brought them.

As she slides up next to him on her belly, he whispers to her, "Is it cybos?"

"I don't know yet," she says, scooting up on her elbows for a better look at the approaching craft. "Whoever or whatever it is doesn't need headlights on the vehicle to see where they're going."

"Automated transports don't require lighting," Ish volunteers.

"So does that mean cybos or not?"

"I don't know," Ish admits.

The unmarked vehicle slows to a stop across the street. The side door begins to lower, and the light from inside defines the edges of the enclosure. It's a considerably smaller vehicle than the one Ish and Luci came in, but it's clear that it's another cargo carrier by the unadorned interior. She swallows and aims the churka at whatever is about to exit through the growing opening.

Ish asks impatiently, "What is it? What do you see?"

Luci shushes him sharply as her heart pounds. She wants to wipe the sweat from her palms but doesn't dare pull her index finger away from the trigger.

As the vehicle's door reaches the halfway point, a young woman in her mid-twenties with Arabian features peers out cautiously.

Luci releases a pent-up breath with a long sigh of relief and allows her eyes to blink again. "It's *L'inversione*. I don't know her name, but I saw her here with the group from before."

Luci helps Ish crawl from beneath their transport as the door of the vehicle across from them touches down to the street with a clang.

Luci turns to greet the new arrival. "We just got here ourselves, and—"

"Help us!" the woman cries.

"Totti?" Luci asks, dumbfounded at the sight of the younger woman hoisting Totti's lethargic arm over her shoulder. Luci abandons Ish as she breaks into a run to the transport's ramp. "Totti, what happened?"

The two women stumble a few steps as Luci races to steady the collapsing frame of the older black woman by grabbing Totti's other arm and slinging it around her shoulder. Luci wields the churka like a walking stick with the butt of the weapon against the ground.

Totti lets out a groan, and for the first time, Luci sees that the woman's left leg from the knee down is missing and she's in shock.

"They're coming," the girl says between awkward steps, trying her best to steer Totti's movements.

"Luci?" Ish yells from the side of the punctured lime-green transport that delivered them here.

"I'll be there in a minute, Ish. Just hang on."

There's another moan from Totti.

"Who's coming?" Luci asks the girl. "The other members of *L'inversione*?"

"Macer's Red Guard from the future!" the girl answers in near hysterics. "We were ambushed by the cybos from the holovid."

The news nearly causes Luci to drop her side of Totti, for which she quickly apologizes.

"After Miss Totti hooked into the nexus of the mainframe splash node, they were everywhere. It was . . ."

Luci's heart is in her throat. She's about to ask for more details when a red beam washes over the trio of women. She recognizes this beam from her encounter with the red warrior in the alley where she blasted Royse. She yells over her shoulder, "Ish get on the ground!"

"No, this can't be happening!" the girl on the other side of Totti screams. "We're nearly there!"

Luci allows her side to drop in order to fire a churka blast back into where she guesses the origin point of the red scanning beam to be.

In the same instant, a bright blue beam of energy to match her blast fires to the left of her. Totti is gone. Luci knows better than to look at whatever's left of her.

It's clear that the girl doesn't look away though when she lets out a shrill scream.

Luci stares through the churka haze struggling to remember Ish's location, but there's no sign of him.

"Luci, are you okay?" he shouts.

She gasps in relief. "Ish, stay down!" she yells while firing multiple blasts at the unseen enemy through the noxious smog.

There's an uneasy feeling that whoever or whatever is out there hasn't returned fire. Could she be so lucky as to have hit the attacker on the first try? What's going on here? She's even more suspicious that only a single cybo would be dispatched if Totti's carrier was followed here.

Luci chances a glimpse down at the girl on her knees to the side of her. She's weeping uncontrollably. "Hey, what's your name?" Luci shouts, returning to scanning back through the haze of churka discharge for a potential target.

"Banu," the girl answers, sniffling. "I'm Banu."

"Are you hit?"

The response doesn't come quickly enough. "I said, are you hit? Did the blast wound you?"

"No, but Miss Totti is—"

"There's nothing we can do for Totti," Luci snaps coldly, her heart feeling as if it will explode. "Banu, we've got to get out of here, and I mean right now." Luci gnaws her bottom lip as she skirts around the sickening mess of Totti's remains, attempting to block her mind from the reality of what's smoldering before her. There's that repulsive smell again. She grabs the lapel of the girl's jumpsuit hard and yanks it. "Banu, get up and run across the street to call the elevator."

"Ele-va-tor," Banu stammers with a nod. "Yes."

"Go!" Luci yells, forcibly tugging at the material. She releases as the girl makes it to her feet. "Run, Banu, run!"

There's no time to watch even if she could see her that far away. Luci fires another couple of random blasts into the impenetrable haze. "Ish, I'm coming for you. Stand up and call to me."

With the churka haze blocking what dim light the street has, she feels as blind as he is and takes meticulous steps in the direction of his voice. When the two finally connect, there's no speaking. He latches on, and they dart back to the shop.

Banu shifts from a crouch to standing as Luci and Ish arrive. The clunky doors of the service elevator obediently slide open with a noisy, mechanical effort.

"Banu, can you operate the skip barge controls?" Luci asks as the doors slide shut. "The Red Out has blinded Technician Moyta."

The lift begins to lower with an unnerving jolt that forces the three to adjust their footing.

Over the metal creaks and groans of the old elevator's gears and rhythmic clanking sounds, Banu answers, "Yes, a skip barge isn't difficult to operate."

Luci can already smell the familiar damp and sticky saltwater air as the compartment descends. She welcomes the scent as she sighs, "Are you 100% certain that no other members of *L'inversione* are coming?"

Banu faces Luci in the antiseptic light of the elevator. "They're all dead," she says, shaking her head, looking like she's about to have another breakdown.

Luci glances at Ish, standing against the wall of the compartment with a sullen expression. "You're absolutely positive?"

She nods, "All of them . . . everyone."

"All of Beaumont's team too," Luci admits, fighting back tears. Before she breaks down too, she quickly adds, "So, when we first get in there, you take Ish to one of the barges and start it up or whatever you have to do." She thrusts the churka upward, nearly touching the light. "I'll use this to disable the elevator and the shaft from anyone following us down to the—"

A heavy thud above their heads interrupts her. Each of them sends a fearful look upward, including blind Ish. Luci raises a hand for Banu to be silent even before the girl can speak or scream. Luci prays that it's the effect of rickety elevator gears losing their long-time battle with the damp and sticky saltwater air.

A second, more forceful impact overhead quickly dispels that notion, shaking the compartment like a boat tossed on water.

This time, Banu does scream and grapples wildly for the churka. Luci taps her with the end of it hard enough to shove the girl down, causing her to fall back against Ish.

"What are you two doing?" he shouts, attempting to get Banu off his feet.

"Shoot it!" Banu screams hysterically, pointing at the ceiling with widened eyes. "It's coming in!"

The clanking overhead takes on a rhythm, reminding Luci of the red warrior puncturing the cargo carrier that brought them here. "Shit!"

Banu returns to her feet, poised for another attempt at Luci's churka. "Shoot it, please."

"If I fire upward and hit the cable suspending us, we *die*!"

A red, cone-shaped beam runs across her from above. As before, a cold, synthetic voice announces, "Dr. Luci Gaudiano scan identified. Weapon detected. Proceed with non-lethal apprehension of subject."

She freezes at hearing the red warrior say her name. In that instant, Banu lunges for the trigger of the blaster and, with Luci still holding it, shoves the barrel upward at the unseen source of the voice.

The temperature of the compartment raises so high and so quickly that Luci thinks she's been blasted and her skin will boil off her like the other victims she's witnessed. The trio desperately coughs and wheezes to expel the heated sulfuric air from their lungs. Through the elevator's flickering light, a basketball-sized hole can be seen in the top corner. The still-glowing opening allows for a piece of something dark and unrecognizable to smear down the left side wall on its way to plopping to the floor—at least the blast hit something.

There's another violent thud as something else lands on top of them followed by another. The elevator sways with each terrible successive strike.

Though completely sightless, Ish seems to have figured out what's happening too, because he calls to Luci in a raspy voice between coughs, "Shoot out near the bottom of the door. You can climb down the shaft."

The idea is absurd, but she does it, believing it to be better to fire downward than to the ceiling again. "Against the wall, you two!" Luci commands, aiming at the bottom of the door. Another blue blast and the area heats even more, accompanied by more coughing from the trio.

An alarm rings out from inside the compartment as Luci lies flat, looking through the smoldering opening she's made. Harsh red light from the shop shows through, but the elevator is only a quarter of the way down and isn't advancing.

Another overhead thud causes Ish to call out, "Luci?"

She's on her knees. "Both of you, listen to me. This hole is just large enough for us to get through. Just be careful to avoid touching the sides—they're still glowing hot. Ish, you go first, then wait for Banu. I'll go through last since Macer's red warriors won't shoot me."

"Are you sure they won't?" Banu asks with widened eyes.

An overhead thud causes them to pause to regain their balance.

"I hope to not find that out," Luci says, grabbing Ish by the shoulder to guide him. "There's a bit of a drop, so go feet first."

Ish disappears through the opening, to Luci's relief. "Your turn, Banu."

An earsplitting screech and groan of metal scraping against metal overhead forces Luci's eyes up. The horrific sight of the roof of the compartment being pulled back like a banana peel sends screams from both her and Banu.

There's just enough clearance for one of the red cybos to drop into the lift compartment with them. The area sways severely enough to slam Luci against the far wall. Luci looks down at Banu's feet crushed by the weight of the eight-foot creature. The girl's sustained scream and elevator alarm blend into one heinous shrill. Luci brandishes the churka, but there's no shot without hitting Banu in the confined space.

The creature hoists Banu up by the throat, lifting her twitching body near the compartment's destroyed roof. She isn't screaming now, just making guttural sounds as the red cybo's grip crushes her windpipe in its fist.

"Sorry, Banu," Luci says, weeping. She fires a blue blast into both of them. Their flesh fuses together in a smoky blob and collapses toward Luci. She kicks at the steaming mess, shoving it away from the escape opening. She sends the churka through and then follows.

Luci hits the metal floor hard with her rump in a sitting position.

Her groan causes Ish to call out from a meter and a half away. "Banu?"

"No, Ish," Luci says, making her way to her feet and clambering for the churka. "It's just us again. She didn't make it."

His dejected expression in the dim red light matches the somber acknowledgement of his nodding head. "Oh."

As Luci quickly guides him to the nearest of the five skip barges, the slow, repetitive drip of water echoing through the area is punctuated by clanks and thuds from the elevator area. "You can do this, right?" she asks between breaths.

"I'll guide you," he answers. "You said they told you they've been pre-programed to skip to Antarctica seventy-two hours in the future?"

Luci unlatches him from the back of her belt and helps him step up onto the transport platform. "That's what Ley and Beaumont said." She scurries across the flatbed to the front of the craft, leaving him near the tail. Bolted to the scuffed metal flooring in the front is a control panel similar in height and breadth to the lectern Luci gave her lecture from back in Baltimore a few days ago. That night feels like a hundred lifetimes ago.

Ish gropes for a steel mesh container the size of a barrel welded into the structure. At first, Luci mistook it for a cargo item left on the barge until seeing the same metal shape near the stern of the other transports. He lowers to click something, and there's a deep hum felt more than heard through vibrations in the stomach and soles of her shoes. Static electricity makes her arm hairs stand at attention, and she thinks that they may just pull this off after all.

Ish frantically calls to her from the tail section, "If the loader's anything like the ones used at the Grange, there should be a lever that you push forward and a large foot pedal."

She spins her sights back to the controls. "Yeah, I see it. It's like an oversized gas pedal, and there's a metal U-bar like the safety harness on a roller-coaster."

She reaches to touch the galvanized bar with the hand not holding the churka. A sharp pain explodes through her palm, forcing her to wince and instinctively pull away. She lets out a yelp as if she's burned herself.

"What is it?" Ish asks.

Luci's shocked to see a smear of red dripping from the metal U-bar. She turns the right-hand palm to present it to herself in disbelief.

"Luci, are you alright?" Ish desperately calls out to her from the back.

The sight of a puddle of blood forming in her cupped hand stuns her at first. She wonders when this happened and even more how such a serious laceration could have gone unnoticed until now.

"My hand . . . somehow, I've cut my hand," she answers. "In the elevator, or getting out of the elevator, I guess."

"How bad is it?"

She shoves the injured area against her stomach to apply pressure, and her white blouse instantly turns into a bloom of crimson. "I'll be okay," she lies, downplaying the pain. "Just tell me about how we get out of here."

This seems to satisfy Ish, and he returns to his instruction. "You'll activate the foot pedal, and while standing on it, you lift the bar up." He interrupts himself as he rises to his feet. "There should be a number."

"A number?" she says, stealing another wary look across the bay. The assault on the metal of the elevator door tells Luci the cybos aren't willing to risk a churka blast for fear of accidentally harming her on the other side, but how long do they have?

Ish responds impatiently, "A number . . . a big one. Does it end in a 'o' or a '2'?"

Luci moves back from the panel for a closer examination. Imprinted on both sides are two fading digits of large block characters. Using the churka as a pointer, she says, "This one is '35.' Is that bad?" Judging by the look of concern on his face in the crimson shadows, she asks, "What's wrong?"

"It's an older barge. They need more time to warm up for the leap skip."

"How much time?" she shouts back, surveying the elevator lobby area and pressing her palm harder against herself.

"It could take a couple of minutes," Ish answers with a defeated shrug, not exactly facing her.

Seconds later, scores of red warrior cybos pour in through the opening like ants from a smashed hill.

"Here they come!" she shouts to him. "Ish, get down!"

The ground quivers with their approach, and the clatter of their metal footwear on the floor sounds like an endless barrage of marbles striking tile.

Luci fires without taking aim at a specific stoic-faced member of the approaching mob. Thankfully, the cut on her hand doesn't impede her ability to finger the trigger of the weapon. She sways it to the right and left as if dousing flames with a firehose until the churka pauses to recharge. When it does, she returns to applying pressure to her sticky wound.

Ish crawls on his stomach from the back of the barge to her. "You've got to destroy the other transports so they can't follow us to the Antarctica skip juncture."

Through the churka haze, she reviews the effect of "spraying" the attackers with the blast. The creatures that aren't instantly destroyed are either maimed or temporarily trapped behind the smoldering obstacles of burned cybos in the front row.

She counts it as a stroke of luck that the barge that she selected is in the center of the five vessels, with two on either side. Luci aims at the barge farthest out on the right side of them and pulls the trigger back. At first, there is nothing. When she attempts it a second time, the weapon, now recharged, rewards her with a bright blue beam of destruction. The control lectern is obliterated.

She turns the churka back to the hoard of red-armored cybos and spurts random short blasts to hold them at bay. Not knowing how many more of them to expect, she cannot afford to expend any more precious firepower than necessary on them.

Ish, still scooting on his elbows, is nearly to her. He shouts, "Don't fire at the skip-thrust cabinets on the back of the barges!"

Letting loose another blast at the mob, she asks, "Skip-thrust cabinet? What the hell's a skip-thrust cabinet?"

"The squatty canister on the back. It could blow this entire place up."

She swivels to the extreme left side and blasts the far barge there. "*Now* you tell me!"

As the first skip barge burns, she fires on the one closer in. Her accuracy and handling improve with every shot. After another series of short blasts into the growing mound of red warriors, Luci turns to the final barge. A trio of red cybos has managed to sneak around to flank them.

"Stay down!" she orders while cutting through these new attackers. "Shit, that was close."

Once they fall, she has a clear line of fire through the haze at the final control podium.

She shoots, but nothing happens.

"Uh oh."

"What's wrong?" Ish demands. "What's happening?"

There's only a couple of meters between the cybos and the lip of the barge.

"It's going to be close," she says, mashing down the foot pedal of the craft. "When I tell you to, lift the bar up to launch us."

"I'm ready!" Ish shouts, assuming an exposed crouching position at her side.

She pulls the trigger—still no response. The churka is sticky with her blood. "Shit!"

She does it again.

This time, a glorious blue blast lights up the area. Her aim is off, though, and the shot is wide of the control panel. She tries to correct, but the beam slants down. To her horror, it makes a straight line to the only object in the entire space that she had to avoid—the cabinet of the barge transport.

"Now!" she screams. "Do it now!"

In the second and a half that it takes Ish to comply, there's a white light as bright as the sun. This is accompanied by a gust of hot wind that pushes Luci to her back on the barge platform.

THE WORLD OUTSIDE OF THE craft is still. They never hear the explosion.

Looking up, Luci groans as quivering rings of bright violet-fuchsia and aqua blue-green light ripple in her view overhead.

Ish comes into view between rhythmic flashes of the emerald pulse. He awkwardly gropes at the air. "Are you alright?"

"Yeah, but that was too close." Luci lowers the churka to the platform and struggles to tear at the collar of her blouse with her good hand. After several grunts and heaving at the material, there's a satisfying rip. She forms an improvised bandage to slow some of the blood loss. Both she and Ish scoot together into the front center of the vessel. He rests his back against the control stand, and she finds her way against his chest, the same position as before in the hauler.

"We won't fall over the sides if that's what you're wondering. We're in a skip bubble. We can move around in here safely."

"You're certain?" she asks, examining while tightening the cloth around her hand.

"Absolutely," Ish responds. "And this shouldn't take very much longer, since we're only skipping a few days and not centuries."

She lets out a humph while managing to tie off an end of the soaked fabric. "Part of me wishes that it would take longer."

"Really? Why do you say that?"

Luci takes in a deep breath and slowly exhales. "Because on the other side of this skip, Malom Roderick and Cyphor Gicul are waiting for us."

PORT V

(Part V)

ΔNTΛKTIKU

MΛ₵ 31, 2191

THE PRESSURIZED POP ANNOUNCES THE arrival of their skip vessel. Beams of sunlight through an immense skylight dome some thirty meters above force Luci's eyes to adjust to the sudden change in brightness. The vast openness of the area reminds her of a food court of some abandoned mall back in Chicago, except in place of chairs and tables, there's a scattering of unrecognizable equipment, marked-up portable whiteboards, a longchair, a couple of skip barges, and thick cables crisscrossing the floor like a massive spider's web. Her squinted scan freezes on the form of two motionless bodies sprawled out on the floor in the distance.

"I can see!" Ish exclaims.

Luci turns to her left, where he's exuberantly waving his hands before his face.

A rustling from behind the barge causes her to spin around. "Ah, you're finally here." A figure concealed in a dark cloak approaches from a few meters away. A metal rod appears from under the black material folds followed by the bright blue blast of a churka.

Ish's excited voice is silenced. He stumbles off the edge of the barge, clutching his side as he slams into the floor with a thud.

"No!" Luci wails, scrambling for her own churka. Her crude bandage is restrictive, but she manages to aim the churka at the attacker through the noxious haze.

"Stop," an authoritative female voice commands through the swirling cloud between them. "He's only stunned. Put that down. The churka has Yuma's modification."

Luci swallows a lump in her throat and chances a quick look down at Ish on the floor, praying this is true. As far as she can tell, his body is intact—not missing limbs, no sign of damage from the blast.

The stranger continues at a deliberate pace toward the barge. "He'll wake with one hell of a headache, but he's okay—nothing permanent."

Luci does her best to push the abject fear she's experiencing from her mind. With the shaking end of the churka still fixed on the cloaked assailant, she steps down from the skip barge. Placing herself between Ish and the stranger, she musters up the courage to shout, "That's close enough!"

The woman in the cloak slows her advance but doesn't halt. Pointing her own churka upward to demonstrate a non-threat, she condescends, "Easy there now, Annie Oakley. I just want to check him."

The reference to the nineteenth-century female sharpshooter from a resident of Relicus City catches Luci off-guard. "You're mocking my blouse, right?" Luci asks. "Who are you?"

"Time enough for those questions, my dear. For the moment, let me see him."

"You said he was only stunned," Luci says.

"Out of my way or I'll stun you too," the woman says, perturbed, pushing past her. "Either way, I've come too far to have a frightened little orphan from Midpoint Hills, Illinois get in my way now."

Luci wants to ask how this woman knows about her past, but other things are more pressing. Hoping to reclaim some lost control, she steps back, angling for a clear line of fire. If she's forced to blast whomever this is, she doesn't want to risk hitting her unconscious partner. "Those two over there," Luci begins, despising the wavering in her own voice. "Are they stunned too?"

The woman in the black hood pauses, saying in a flat voice, "No, my dear Luci G. They're very much dead."

Something about the way this woman moves is even more unsettling to Luci than the two dead bodies, but she can't pinpoint what it is. Instead, she asks, "How do you know my name and where I come from?"

The bottom folds of the dark cloak spread like the petals of a black flower as she lowers to her knees before Ish. "I have waited for this moment for what feels like centuries."

To Luci's disbelief, the oversized hood of the woman's cloak envelops Ish's face as the figure leans forward. She's enraged when the woman pulls the cowl back, inadvertently revealing her lips pressed against his slacking mouth. "Hey! What do you think you're doing?" Luci moves in to yank at the woman's shoulders. She finally forces her to disengage. "Stay away from him!"

With a satisfied smile, the encroacher announces, "It was worth the wait. My beautiful Ish, I'm so sorry, but everything will be set right soon."

The contours of the woman's features are hauntingly familiar to Luci. She scoots backward in astounded panic and stutters in disbelief. "M-M-Mama?" Her mind flashes back to the last time that she saw her mother on that tragic ride to the animal shelter as a young girl. She shakes away the slow-motion image of their car sinking into the water from her head.

The repetitive motion of the woman's fingers running up and down Ish's chest brings her back. The woman answers in a deadpan voice, "No, she died a long time ago." She tilts her head, presenting her face to Luci. "Look at my eyes. Her eyes were blue. Mine are brown. Brown, just like yours, Luci G."

Her world grinds to an abrupt halt. The air is thick and suffocating. "You're . . . you're me?" The blood pumping in her ears matches the painful throbbing pulse of her right hand.

She nods slowly with eyebrows raised. "*Yes . . .* and *no,* in a manner of speaking. Technically, you are *me.*"

"How can . . . Wait . . ." A thousand questions ricochet around in her brain. "But everyone said the older, post-DPM Luci died, that Malom killed her . . . killed *you,* I mean, and then Beaumont said Gicul did it." The world is spinning, but for the briefest of seconds, there's a clarity. "You . . . you both faked it!" Luci exclaims, putting the puzzle together in her mind. "Macer isn't after you, because he believes you're dead. That what you wanted, isn't it?"

The woman nods. "It was Malom's idea. I wanted to go after that maniacal, narcissistic son of a bitch the second I got out of Carcerium, but Malom said we had to be certain to eliminate the Macer Prime and not risk exposing ourselves by only offing one of his shadows."

Staring at her older self, Malom's words in the Carcerium chamber come back to Luci in a flash. She mumbles the line he quoted from Shakespeare's Hamlet in a pensive whisper, "*We know what we are, but not what we may be.*"

"But I know where to find Macer in the past," the older Luci announces lustfully as she returns to her feet. "Because of you, I know *exactly* where to find that devil—the original one—and make him pay for what he did to me."

Luci gestures across the way. "Did you make those two over there *pay?*"

The eyes of the other narrow to slits, but she doesn't answer.

She knows it may be dangerous to press the topic, but Luci prompts her anyway. "That's Ley and Malom Roderick, isn't it?"

"It *was,*" the older Luci answers between gritted teeth. "Malom and I had a disagreement about what to do with you." Her face contorts into a bitter expression. "And then Ley and I had a disagreement with how I resolved my disagreement with Malom."

Luci feels drained and slightly dizzy. She can't determine if it's due to this woman's detached revelation or if it's due to the blood loss from her wound, and she's going into shock. She wants to ask where Gicul is and if she killed him too, but she must know something else first. "What was it that Malom wanted to do to me?"

"Don't worry, I'm not gonna kill you," the other Luci scoffs. "Give me your hand. I'll show you why."

Luci tightens her grip on the churka and shakes her head. "If you're not going to hurt us, why'd you stun Ish? What do you want from us?"

The older Luci bends and demonstratively places her churka on the floor. "Think about it, Luci G. Why didn't I zap you instead of him? You had the churka. If I wanted to kill you, I'da shot you instead of him, and I promise that it wouldn't have been set to stun."

Luci takes her point but still can't wrap her mind around what's going on here. "Where's Cyphor Gicul? What do you want from me?" The adrenaline coursing through her body makes it difficult to hold the weapon steady.

"What do I want with you? I want to talk. I have the answers to everything that you and Ish have been working on for the last week or so—all of that and more . . . much, much more." She takes a dangerous step closer until the barrel of Luci's churka nearly touches her. "With the exception of our sleeping Ish on the floor over there, you're the only person alive who can even begin to comprehend what I've accomplished, the splendid perfection and beauty of it all." She motions to Luci's quivering churka. "But before all of that, I'll show you why you can stop aiming that at me. It makes me nervous that it'll accidentally go off." She snaps her fingers and commands, "Now give me your hand."

The older Luci produces two objects from inside the folds of her cloak, one the size of a travel toothpaste and the other looking like a miniature curling iron. "Your palm, *please.*" She places both items in one hand. "It'll only take a moment, and then we may move on to more important things—things about DPM that you never dreamed possible. All those limber and porous number compounds that had you and Ish stumped." When Luci doesn't respond, her expression sours and her tone grows more impatient. "It won't do either of us any good if that cut isn't taken care of. So put the churka down or I'll take it from you."

The prospect of some new revelation regarding drift pattern mathematics is distracting. Luci's attention wavers, and that's all it takes. The older lunges at her, shoving the butt of weapon back hard into Luci's chest. The pain shooting through her hand from the shaft sliding across the injured tissue causes Luci to drop it. There's a metal clank as the churka strikes the floor. Luci steps back, clinging to her wound as she screams.

The elder clamps onto Luci's wrist like a vise. "I can't believe that I was ever so dense," she says aloud to herself. Then to Luci, "I swear on Mama and Papa's graves that I'm not going to kill you. I'm showing you why. Hold these."

As the grip eases on her wrist, Luci accepts the two items in her good hand. She winces and bites her lip as her older version unwraps and tugs at the soaked cloth from the wound. Forcing her eyes away from the gore, she looks over at Ish, unconscious in the distance. ""How are you here and where is Cyphor Gicul?"

"Shut up and keep your hand completely still."

Luci feels lightheaded but presses through the pain, refusing to allow the spots before her eyes to distract her. Her heart races beyond any effort to self-soothe with numbers; they won't clot a wound anyway. "What are you going—"

"Old Luci G., always with the questions," the older woman says mockingly. "Well, I'll tell you then." She allows the blood-soaked cloth to fall to the floor as she grabs the metal instrument from Luci's other hand. "*This* is a heal kit."

There's a click, and the wand hums as the woman traces Luci's wound up and down. There's a warm, tingling sensation as a faint violet beam of light from the device mends the damaged skin.

Older Luci informs her, "A device like this would've put plastic surgeons out of business back in our interval. It's really that good at syntha-skin replication."

To Luci's astonishment, the pain becomes more bearable.

"Drink the solution in the pouch and be quick about it."

Luci does what she's told, but the gritty, warm, malt-like solution is what she imagines an ashtray must taste like.

"There are nanobots in there. Drink it all," she orders, making an adjustment to the wand before repeating the back-and-forth motion.

Luci forces down the substance, trying not to think of its contents. As she wipes some of the stray strands of liquid from her chin, she exclaims, "That's amazing!" She opens and closes her hand in wonder. Her palm is still sticky from the blood, but the pain is only a phantom memory.

"Yeah, well, don't get too excited just yet," older Luci replies. She clicks the device off and returns it to one of the hidden pockets within her cloak. "The heal kit has a variety of settings. Depending on the severity of the injury, internal damage, etcetera," the woman says sounding like a product spokesperson, "it also has a cosmetic and non-cosmetic mode, mainly used for emergency situations on a battlefield or something. The cosmetic setting, which naturally takes a little longer, also has multiple modes. When set to the optimum mending selection, it's hard to tell without a microscope that an incision or tear to the flesh was ever made."

Luci traces two fingers over her newly formed scar, looking for any traces of a change in its size. Not certain where the conversation is headed, she asks, "Yeah, so?"

"To illustrate a point, I've left off all of the cosmetic features, disabling the tissue reconstruction application that prevents scaring."

Luci looks up at her, perplexed. "But you said all of that stuff about it being better than plastic surgery of our day."

She raises a hand to silence Luci. "Any moment now, I'm certain to experience a memory overlay of these deliciously traumatic things that you've just encountered, and then you'll—" She stops short, taking in a deep breath with her eyes closed. She stumbles forward and braces her body against the high table. "There it is. Give . . . just give me . . . a minute."

Luci's witnessed this behavior before. It mirrors the seizure that Macer had in front of the Michelangelo statue of David. For the first time, Luci steals a glance at their surroundings. They're in a massive geodesic dome, the sides caked over with snow greying out the walls. Only the top, which Luci originally believed was a skylight, is free from patches of snowfall. That space has a faint pulsating aura that reminds her of the chronal ring ripples back at the Grange. The air shares the same artificial, recycled, too-sweet quality. She bites her lip, remembering the future image of a slain Bru Mandal.

"There's no door out of here," the woman says, coming back from her trance-like state, "if that's what you're looking for. The only way in or out is by skip transport, but no door. Even if you did somehow miraculously puncture your way through the re-inforced glass and ice, the outside is untold kilometers of frozen wasteland in a post-*Hi no Kawa* world."

Luci chides herself for not making a break for one of the two churkas during the short pause. "Why did you—"

She holds her hand up again. At first, Luci believes she's indicating for her to be silent once more until a faint, jagged pink line appears on the skin's surface. Luci is mesmerized like a kid attending a magic show as the scar takes on more definition. As it grows, turning a deeper shade of pinkish purple, the older nods. "So you see, Luci G., whatever you physically commit to ripples across time to me. If I kill you, I kill me." An unsettling smile appears on her face like that of a gargoyle statue as she adds, "And I plan on sticking around for a long, long time."

"You disabled the non-scarring function just to show me that?" Luci hisses. "And now we're both permanently scarred?" An unexpected burp escapes, forcing her to relive the foul taste of the nanobot carrier solution. Turning her head to the side to spit, she exclaims, "That stuff's worse coming back up!"

"I know you well enough to know that you have to have things proven out. You'd never believe something just because someone told you." The woman slowly traces her index finger over the aged scar tissue of her own palm. "Not even if the someone telling you was *me*."

Luci closes the fingers of her right hand, concealing her own scar. She can't dispute this fact. "Why did you stun Ish, and what did Malom want to do to me?"

The older version slaps her own side and points at Luci with a crazed smile. "That's right, Luci G., always so many questions! Ish has had a pretty rough day with all that almost being turned into a cybo stuff and then the red out. I figured he could use a little rest."

Luci's other hand curls into a fist to match the one with the fresh scar. "Why did you stun him?" she demands between gritted teeth.

"I wanted some . . . *girl time* with you first. He'll wake up soon enough. As for Malom, I'll admit that he was a good man . . . some even may say a hero. But hero or not, we reached an impasse: two diametrically opposed solutions about what to do with the past and ergo the future."

"No, you said the disagreement was about me."

"Your naïveté is a lot less charming than you imagine. Of course it's about *you*. You and I are the supposed godmother to *Hi no Kawa*." She sighs. "I'll fill you in on all of that in a bit. For right now, don't you want to know about DPM?" She extends her hands like a carnival barker. "Aren't you curious to know about what you and Ish nicknamed '*Porous compounds or Limber DPM numbers*'?" She lowers her arms and presses an index finger against her temple. "I know what they are."

With a jolt, the older Luci springs across the area to what looks like an inverted steel pinecone that's as tall as a bookcase. A disappointed expression forms when she turns to look back at Luci, who hasn't moved. "Get over here." She motions enthusiastically. "I promise I'll explain it all." She holds up the first three fingers of her left hand. "Scout's honor."

"You were never a girl scout," Luci rebuts.

She nods. "You're right, but come look." She holds up a curved piece of gunmetal grey material larger than a computer tablet but smaller than a miniature boogie board. "This is an ESTA damper panel. Come see."

Still sensing something to be off kilter about the woman, Luci looks for a reason to delay and keep her distance. She holds up her left hand with the healed cut. "I'm sticky. I want to rinse all of this dried blood off first." She looks across the open area to a freestanding lavatory near a hovering concierge bot that's easily the size of a refrigerator. Beside the bot is a futuristic hospital bed with a complex web of weights, pulleys, and arm and leg cuffs.

"What's all that?" Luci asks.

With the older woman's face buried in a logbook of sorts, she turns a page and answers disinterestedly, "Exercise bed." Marking something on the page, she turns to the large, inverted metal pinecone-looking machine hovering to the side of her. "Ever want to skip the gym or track and exercise in your sleep? That's what that does for you. Now stop stalling and get over here. We'll clean you up after I show this to you. I promise you'll be amazed."

Out of excuses, Luci reluctantly complies and makes her way across the vast area. As she passes the bot halfway between them, she notes the number of additional components and extensions from the small one at Macer's guesthouse.

"Macer kidnapping you from my past proves that Malom was right," older Luci announces in a loud voice. "Malom was convinced how desperate Waleen was to safeguard his perverse version of the future." She inserts a curved metal object in the place of one of the missing scale extenders. The mechanism receives the component with a soft chime of acknowledgement. She taps the machine hovering in the air with the tool a few times to punctuate her words. "I gathered 2068 ESTA components from pre-*Hi no Kawa* satellites and made this here, a machine that can sustain an artificial interval oscillator."

Luci halts a safe distance from her, saying, "The ESTA tech from the old twenty-first-century leap-skipping weather drones, huh? That's why this place is seventy-two hours out from Relicus City's timeline, because the original satellites were sent that duration of time in the future to relay data to the past."

Older Luci gives a nod of satisfaction. "But this baby does more." She slowly spins the large steel mechanism around, revealing a plain-looking seat and harness rig mounted in a cutaway section of the metal. "Much, much more."

Luci can't hold her curiosity back. "A passenger? You've converted these old satellite components into a transport vehicle?"

"The greatest ever conceived." She takes a few steps back as if presenting it on a stage. "It is my magnum opus. I have defied space-time with this creation and brought the impossible down to its knees, because this can perform leap skips not restricted to merely skip nodes along the timeline." She pauses, studying Luci's reaction.

Nervous laughter erupts from Luci. "Are you saying that you think that you've actually found a way to slingshot to any moment in time—past or future—and anywhere around the globe?"

She beams with satisfaction. "Ah, there's the Luci Gaudiano that I know."

Luci's head is swimming again, causing her to look down at her feet. This is the answer to the "limber DPM numbers" that eluded her and Ish. "But how do you avoid rupturing organic space-time flow? Doing a leap skip to seventy-two hours in the future to a nonexistent node, while very impressive, doesn't cause the ramifications that would occur for greater skips of a month or more, and the further out you'd go from the origin point, the more unstable the cycle ring becomes until you could potentially fracture the architecture of what holds time together for all of us."

Older Luci smiles. "Not true. That's where the theorists got it wrong. Time is a lot more resilient than that. Einstein was wrong. J.M. Keebler was wrong. They'd have you believe that doing so would be like crumpling a sheet of notebook paper up on itself like a waded ball that would never stop compressing. In truth, it doesn't affect linear chronologies at all, not in the least."

Luci looks back up and wants to rush over and touch the cool metal of the transport, but she doesn't dare move closer to the woman. "How, then, do you avoid temporal disruptions if you—"

She cuts Luci off, "Like I said, time is remarkably resilient."

An orgasmic wave of enlightenment rushes over Luci. "This . . ." She points at the machine. "This serves as both the repository and the chronal trigger? You intend to store the energy from the shrunken skip point portals that you've collected and then '*slingshot,*' to use your term, into anywhere that you wish to puncture in time."

"Well, it's a little more elegant than that, but in principle, *yes.*"

Luci rubs her temple excitedly. "But how do you get back?"

"You don't; it's a one-way trip," her older self explains in a matter-of-fact tone. "In order to launch, the amount of CE confined in the receptacle cells must be tremendous, but the energy can't be compressed without a relay, and the rider—"

It's Luci's turn to butt in. "The passenger can't take it with them and can't be followed by a longchair to a node that technically doesn't exist."

She smiles greedily at Luci's unreserved wonder. "Exactly."

Luci approaches the hovering machine and slowly circles it in reverent astonishment. "How did you ever figure out how to do this? Did you have help from Cyphor Gicul?"

An unexpected laugh explodes from the older Luci. "You might say that," she answers, fighting a losing battle to restrain a wave of belly laughs.

Not getting the joke, Luci studies the ornately stitched clothing that drapes her other self, waiting for whatever this is to subside. After it's taken longer than the woman's memory overlay from a few minutes ago to dissipate, Luci scathingly asks, "Why is the mention of Cyphor Gicul so funny to you? What did you do to him? Did you kill him too?"

This sets off another round from her, this time including a few snorts. Finally, she says, drying tears of laughter from her eyes, "That's rich. I haven't laughed like that since before I was brought to Relicus." She sniffs, shaking her head. "You still haven't figured it out yet? As smart as you are, Luci G., you still haven't connected the dots?"

Luci gnaws her lip. "Haven't figured out what?"

"Gicul." The woman in the cloak shakes her head and begins spelling her name, "L-U-C—"

Even before she gets to the "G," Luci understands that *Gicul* backward is an inversion of Luci G. The revelation sends her reeling making her legs feel like they're made of yarn. She collapses to her knees.

TWO

LUCI FEELS FAINT. HOW CAN this be, and how could she have ever suspected Ish? She speaks aloud—not to her other self, not to Cyphor Gicul—but she speaks, attempting to examine the truth of this woman's claim. Luci stammers, "That's why Malom mentioned my cat when he was in Carcerium, Newt. We thought the cat was male right up until . . . until *she* delivered kittens in the backyard." Her throat feels like it has a marble in it that won't go down no matter how many times Luci swallows. "That's what he meant by being hidden in plain sight the entire time. It was me—or rather *us*—all along. I am Cyphor Gicul."

"Well, not exactly. I am Gicul. You . . . let's just say that you're the raw materials, the ingredients, if you will, for what I will become."

"Did Malom Roderick know this or did you kill him when he found out?"

The amusement leaves her face. "No, he knew from the start. Malom even said it was foolhardy to call myself something so blatantly obvious when dealing with *L'inversione,* but no one got it." As if clarifying a punchline, she adds, "I even put the word '*cypher*' at the beginning of it as a 'screw you' to Macer after what he did to me, but he never got it. Apparently, no one did." She shrugs. "Not even my younger self."

She returns to the metal machine and turns a handle a quarter of the way clockwise. "One of the only benefits of a patriarchal society, even in this interval, is that everyone's eager to assume Gicul is a man. I mean, after all, how could a *woman* pose the biggest threat to someone like Macer's 'Relicus the Great'? Nope, gotta be a man for something like that."

She pauses as she inhales a sharp breath and her eyes roll back. Gicul stumbles, barely catching herself by grabbing onto one of the metal protrusions of the pinecone-like machine. "Give . . . just give me . . . a minute," she says.

Luci looks across the way at Ish, who's still unconscious near the skip barge, wondering what he'll think of her when he learns that she was Gicul all along and what that will change between them.

"Whew! That was the biggest one yet," Gicul exclaims with a soft chuckle. "I guess the shock of learning you've been hunting your future self would create a pretty impactful memory."

"Do the memory overlays hurt when they come?" Luci asks.

"Well, that was more than just one, but no, it doesn't hurt. It's just something like extreme déjà vu on LSD. They've become more frequent since you've arrived at Relicus City, I guess because of the strain and intensity of your encounters here."

Before she can ask, Gicul explains, "Don't worry, I can't read your mind or anything like that, but thoughts become memories . . . at least the major emotional concepts, decisions, or discoveries, and those ripple through time and eventually settle up here." She taps her temple.

"Does it erase your past?" Luci asks, still fighting down a wave of nausea at the revelation that she is the one they've been looking for all along.

"No, nothing like that; it just very disorienting as the memories merge and are combined with what I already know."

"Combined with . . . are your original memories overwritten by what I do?"

Gicul pauses before going into lecturer mode. "You remember reading '*The Shining*' when you—when we were sixteen?"

"Yeah, so?" Luci replies curiously.

"Then, a year or so later, we streamed that old Kubrick film at Michelle Alston's house?"

Gicul waits for Luci's acknowledgement, which comes in the form of a slow bob of the head, before continuing. "The book ends with the Overlook Hotel blowing up, while the movie version ends with the father—"

"Jack Nicholson," Luci volunteers.

"Right—Jack Nicholson running around with an axe and freezing to death outside in the garden maze." She holds her hands out, pantomiming holding each story in her right and left palm. "In the same way that both versions simultaneously exist as fact in your memory..." She clasps her hands together in demonstration. "My past in my thirties and what you're living now exist side-by-side in my mind. The original memories of what I've done aren't overwritten or replaced by any different experiences that you contribute. They have equal weight, so to speak."

Luci stomps her foot in amazement. "And that's how you knew that Ish had been taken away from the guest house! That's how you knew to send Noah Beaumont to get me."

Gicul nods. "Now you're finally getting it."

Luci pauses before asking, "So, then, you know all about Shar?" Attempting to clarify the question, she adds, "Not just the notes and the ear, but the way she feels about you ... about *us*?"

Her eyes narrow, and she sighs. "Shar was an emotionally confused child that our dead friend Ley over there was able to manipulate through the woman's uncle, Noah Beaumont."

"Confused child?" Luci asks, thinking of the inscribed plastic note in her pocket. "Confused how? Weren't the two of you—"

"Shar connected the dots up to be a certain way in her mind, but sometimes, dots are just dots and nothing more."

The coolness of the response shocks Luci, considering what the girl sacrificed for her. "So the two of you never—"

Gicul cuts her off again, obviously irritated that the topic is still going, "People see what they want to believe. Shar Ryson wanted to believe that she was in love with the great Dr. Luci

Gaudiano, but no, it was never anything more than a night of too much wine and false echoes on the wind."

A piece of Luci's heart dies witnessing the callous contempt that Gicul has toward someone who cared so much for her. It unnerves her to consider that somewhere inside of herself, she is capable of such blatant selfishness.

The shock and self-loathing are suspended as another conclusion comes screaming to the forefront of her mind. "Carcerium . . . the code and skip destination information, you got that from me when I went with Cavazos, and then you told *L'inversione* what it was. You knew it because *I* knew it."

"Yes. Cavazos was a fool for doing that, and that's the reason why Malom was so excited to see you there. I wish that Malom's banishment to Carcerium could've been avoided, but he knew the risk. He never hesitated to ensure that others would get the truth. It was fairly certain to him that he'd get caught and be converted to Cavazos's personal cybo or banished to Carcerium, but he went through with it anyway. He's both the bravest and most foolish man I've ever known."

"Was it his plan to return to the past and execute me before *Hi no Kawa*?"

"That was one idea he had, though, as I've demonstrated, that would've been the end of me too. I played along with it, saying that I would allow myself to be martyred for the sake of humanity." Gicul reaches for a different tool. "All of that changed, though, about a week ago."

"When Macer, Royse, and Shar abducted me?" Luci says, her chest tightening at the mention of the event.

"Exactly," Gicul says, pointing a futuristic-looking wrench at her. "*L'inversione* determined that they didn't have to use this to go back in time to kill you. I had the date all set up and DPM mapped out for a specific location in our past, a point in time where I knew exactly where *we* would be. Turns out that all of those calculations weren't needed after all, since Macer snatched you up for us."

Another wave of nausea washes over her. "*L'inversione* figured they just had to keep younger me from leaving Relicus City and returning to the twenty-first century to release DPM later in my timeline."

Gicul slowly and scornfully shakes her head. "*L'inversione*, an assortment of buffoons led by idiots on a grandiose crusade to save the world."

This statement dumbfounds Luci as much as anything Gicul has revealed since she and Ish arrived here. "You can't mean that," she says, looking over at the dead bodies of Ley and Malom. "Isn't the world worth saving? Isn't that what this is all about, why you brought Ish and—"

"No!" Gicul yells as she strikes the floating ESTA transport hard enough with the tool to make it sway. "What has the world ever done for me—for *us*?" Her face is a scowl as the words come out at the speed of bullets. "The world took my parents . . . *our* parents away from us as a young girl and then thrust us into the horror of governmental child agencies with monsters like that Ms. Schofield. Even so, we rose above that tragedy and secured scholarships, but let me ask you something, *Dr. Luci Gaudiano*. Do you ever feel as if you're treated as a third-class citizen in the scientific community?"

Luci presses her quivering bottom lip between her teeth rather than answering.

"Well, tell me!" Gicul shouts "I know I'm right. I lived it, remember?" She scoffs. "I've got news for you, sweetie. Even after I unveiled the drift pattern in 2041, many of my colleagues challenged the validity of it, and that's the way it was for nearly two decades until test trials proved the theorem was sound." She abandons the ESTA and begins taking slow, deliberate steps in Luci's direction.

Luci responds with mirroring steps backward until she inadvertently collides with the massive medbot that's hovered up behind her.

Gicul continues her rant, oblivious to her audience's attempt to retreat, "Then, just as I'm getting my due, a psychotic madman from the future, Waleen Macer, kidnaps me for my discovery and locks me away in Carcerium for time immeasurable just to keep the knowledge away from everyone else."

The metal of the medbot's outer shell is cold against Luci's back. She wonders if it's programed to defend Gicul if she was able to grab a churka to stun the manic woman approaching her.

Gicul stops short, tears streaming down her face. "So *no*, the world hasn't done me any favors along the way. Why should I care whether it gets another crack at surviving itself?"

To Luci's astonishment, Gicul lowers to a seated position a few meters before her. Her ornately stitched cloak spreads out like a perfectly round puddle of black ink on the floor. She mumbles, "I doubt that it would change anything anyway."

The statement perplexes Luci. "What do you mean? If there's no DPM, then there's no *Hi no Kawa* and there's no Relicus the Great."

"Are you sure, Luci G.? Are you 100 percent certain of that fact?"

"Don't call me '*Luci G.*,' and that's what all this was about, right? Bringing Ish and I here . . . wasn't it?"

Gicul lets out a dismissive, "Pfft." The sound is followed by a long sigh. "The sooner that you admit to yourself what we're dealing with here, the easier it'll be for you to accept your role in all of it."

"My role?" Luci asks, tensing up at the words.

Gicul makes her way to her feet but doesn't advance on Luci. Instead, she backtracks across the area to a bank of three portable lockers near the ESTA transport. She speaks loudly over her shoulder as her dark cloak sweeps along the floor with her every step, "Twenty-first-century mankind is poised to obliterate itself. It just used DPM's ability to leap skip into the future by seventy-two hours at a time as the excuse to bring it about. It's the destruction they were itching to do anyway. To hold DPM responsible for *Hi no Kawa* is as ignorant as to blame the science of aviation for the terrorist attacks in New

York City on September eleventh. Those madmen were set in their hearts to do evil things. Only a fool would blame aircraft manufacturers for the deeds the terrorists did."

Luci glances down at the fresh scar in her palm and strokes it with the index finger of the other hand. Looking back up at Gicul, she argues, "That's different than DPM."

Gicul scoffs. "Is it? Do you honestly believe that? Then let me ask you: If Neil Armstrong wasn't aboard the lunar module, if he hadn't gone, if someone had gone in his place, then Buzz Aldrin would've likely been the first person to step onto the surface of the moon. It wouldn't have stopped the mission. The moon landing still would've happened, just different people and different names. The world was primed for that event." She pauses before she adds, "If Adolf Hitler had died in childbirth, someone else would have carried out the genocide that he's known for. Or if for some reason Johannes Gutenberg refused to construct his printing press in the 1400s, do you seriously believe that we wouldn't have printed books? No, the world is a time bomb and will do what it will despite DPM. *Hi no Kawa* is inevitable in some form or fashion."

Luci cautiously follows the path Gicul took. "I think your hypothesis is wrong. It's unproven, and the world deserves another chance to try . . ." She feels emboldened to say the words, "To try and find a new and better path."

Gicul slams her hand against the locker door with an echoing bang. "Oh, that's rich. My memory of what you've encountered today tells me that *L'inversione* slogan isn't even twenty-four hours old to you, and you're ready to get those hollow words printed on a bumper sticker or a tee-shirt. Well, I've spent a lot more of time contemplating the way things *really* are." She glares at Luci.

"A lot longer . . . longer than you can imagine. When Macer first brought me here . . ." She abruptly stops and sighs. "They didn't have a full understanding of Carcerium back then. While they knew that it reset the properties of the room, it was believed that the subject placed inside reset too. Macer's strategy was to confine the one person in the world that was an expert on DPM in there for safekeeping, and he thought that my mind would reset every seventeen minutes as my body would."

A dark revulsion fills her eyes that Luci can't endure to look at. "The amount of lifetimes that I spent in that impenetrable white void of a box is beyond what even I could count." The flat and clinical quality her voice assumes is chilling. "It doesn't take long until the mind begins devouring itself when there is no stimuli. Try to comprehend an existence in which you never go to sleep, you never stop thinking, the light of the mind is always on and burning . . . no refresher from the inevitable fatigue of cognitive thought." There's a pause, her gaze far away. "If not for a mind predisposed to mathematics to occupy me, I'm certain that I would've gone insane in short order."

Luci fights back tears of her own as Gicul recounts the horror.

"Working out what you and Ish have been calling porous number compounds or limber DPM numbers allowed me to float atop the madness like a life raft on an unending ocean. I meditated on this. It's what my mind fed on to avoid turning into mush."

Luci moves closer. "How did Roderick survive it then? I saw him a few hours ago in Carcerium, and while a little loopy, I wouldn't have classified him as someone who's gone insane."

"Eidetic memory," Gicul answers, a bit of melody returning to her voice. "Some people claim to have a photographic memory, but he really does." She corrects herself, "He did have one, a great mind. That, coupled with being the most well-read person I've ever met." Her mouth forms a melancholy smile. "He'd recite Homer and Beowulf verbatim, or Canterbury Tales. Even mid-twenty-first-century soap operas that he'd come across somewhere. About the only thing I could get him on was lyrics from pop songs of our time." The smile brightens. "But a horrible storyteller. He had hundreds, maybe thousands of stories filed away in his brain, but he couldn't tell a story of his own or tell a joke to save his—"

Gicul inhales a deep breath before changing the subject. "Somehow, Macer let it slip at a council meeting, bragging that he had me, Dr. Luci Gaudiano, the woman responsible for time travel and *Hi no Kawa*, in his custody. Malom heard this and devised a way to break me out. Thinking we'd be safe to hide out in the future is how we accidently discovered Macer's true identity and his endless depraved regime."

"You never answered why Ish was brought here. If you were able to figure all of this out, why do you need a chronal technician who calibrates longchairs? Surely you don't need him for his knowledge of how to adjust portal apertures. You've already mastered that."

"And then some," Gicul answers, opening the waist-high locker door. "You're right. I don't need him for any of that."

Luci moves in closer. "Beaumont, Danica, Yuma, Sari, Miguel, Jonn, Cline, Banu—all of them died to bring us here to you in Antarctica with the hopes that all of you would leap skip to seventeenth-century Ireland. What was that for?"

"It's not my fault," Gicul answers defensively as she reaches into the locker. "I didn't know . . . I didn't know they'd all die bringing him here to me."

"But why *did* you bring—"

"Because I love him, that's why!" Gicul shouts as she slams the locker door closed.

Luci gasps at the sight of the churka aimed at her. "Look, wait just a minute here, okay?" She doesn't remember raising her hands. She slowly lowers them halfway. "Let's just remain calm here," she says, attempting to force a non-threatening smile. She knows she can't outrun the blast, and there's nothing nearby to take cover behind. "We can work whatever this is out. Just lower the churka."

"There's nothing to work out," Gicul says coolly while advancing on her. "Though I've only kissed him for the first time myself a few minutes ago, I have loved him for over millennia!"

She lowers her voice, but the quick cadence of her words continues. "Mathematics wasn't the only thing keeping me sane in Carcerium. When you fell in love with him, the memory rippled across to where I was in non-time, and my heart latched onto it and fed on the emotion. My mind has replayed that slow dance in Macer's guesthouse, that first kiss, and the kisses that followed on that day countless times." The intense look in Gicul's eyes sends an icy shiver down Luci's spine. "My young Luci, I love him more deeply, more intensely than you could ever begin to imagine and more than you after a handful of days with him."

Luci's natural jealousy is no match for the fear bubbling up inside her heart. It's obvious to her that Gicul's time in solitary didn't leave the woman's mind completely unscathed. "So, what now?" Luci asks as evenly as possible, attempting to conceal her abject fear. As if to remind the Carcerium-damaged mind of Gicul before her, she softly says, "You know you can't kill me. You won't fire that at me."

"It's set to stun you," Gicul informs as another memory overlay seizes her. This one's brief, and she's back. Gicul repeats, "It's set to stun. I zap you into unconsciousness, and Ish and I leave this frozen snowball for good."

"And what?" Luci asks, tears of frustration swelling in her eyes. "Ish will never leave with you." Her voice is desperate. "He'll never allow you to leave me here."

"He'll never know," she answers smugly.

"How can he not know?" Luci shouts, giving into the panicked anger bubbling in her heart. "Of course he'll know. You're older."

"Again, so naïve to be so intelligent," Gicul says contemptuously, her expression as dark as her ink-black cloak. "I'll drug him before he awakes and then take him to Carcerium for a few brief cycles in there—an hour or so should do the trick." A sickening pride fills her voice. "When I get him out, I'll inform him that coming here was an ambush and that Macer killed Gicul and the others and imprisoned Ish in Carcerium for decades. I'll convince him that it took all that time for me to catch and subdue Macer and avert *Hi no Kawa*." The glee in her voice is sickening. "He'll never know the difference, and we'll leap skip to an interval before all of this mess. It's a flawless plan."

"Flawless except for one thing," Luci says, her heartbeat raging in her ears at the prospect that this facility is about to become her own version of Carcerium.

Gicul chuckles, but the weapon never waivers. "Oh really, dear? And what's that? What one thing have I missed here? Please do tell me."

Luci defiantly extends the palm of her right hand. "You should've never shown me this. What happens to me ripples across time to you. The second I wake up, I'm killing us both."

Gicul shakes her head while making a tsk tsk sound. "Oh, come now, Luci G. You're not a good Catholic, but we both know that suicide is not on the table here for you."

Luci extends the hand even further out to present her scar. "I'd be forgiven if I prevented *Hi no Kawa*."

"There's no preventing, only delaying. We've been over this, and I haven't much more time to get *'sleeping beauty'* over there to Carcerium before he wakes. In the off-chance I'm wrong about this, though, we'll just have to ensure that you don't wake up while I'm away."

The words make her feel as if she's been dunked in ice water. "What . . . what does that mean? What are you planning to do to me?"

Gicul's haughty expression indicates to Luci that she's relishing the delay. Finally, she announces flippantly, "*Nothing*. Nothing will happen to you, nothing at all. Your med bot friend over there will see to that for you."

She looks over her shoulder at the silent concierge floating in place as if it's awaiting the next command from Gicul.

"I've told you the truth. That bed over there." She gestures slightly with the end of the churka. "It does exercise the sleeper like I said, and that sleeper is to be you. You'll sleep peacefully in a drug-induced coma until you reach the age that I was when DPM was published. I'll return here then—without Ish, of course—to take you back to the twenty-first century. *Hi no*

Kawa will occur in a similar fashion as before, but I'll reunite with an unsuspecting Ish hundreds of years before the carnage to live out our days."

Panic overtakes Luci, and she begins to plead, "You don't have to do this . . . any of this. The three of us—you, me, and Ish—can go back and try to stop Macer and stop *Hi no Kawa*."

"No! There is no stopping it! And you're staying here." An expression of disgust forms on her face. "I was doing you a favor by revealing the missing part of DPM to you before Ish and I left."

Something twists inside of Luci's psyche. "You can shove your damn favors." She seethes with anger. "You're just as evil as Macer."

The accusation stuns her older self. She responds defensively, "No, that's not true. Take it back."

For the first time, Luci has a strategy forming in her mind. It's a big risk, but if she can antagonize this woman to engage her physically—to fight without the churka—she may be able to overpower her, being the younger of the two. "You don't really love Ish. He's nothing more than some perverse trophy to you."

Luci shoots a glance over to the skip barge that brought her to this trap. "Ish! Wake up, Ish! Come here!"

Gicul pauses to check the sleeping man. "You have to see the logic in it, how I love him more than you. I've loved him longer because of my time in Carcerium and the memory overlays."

"I don't care," Luci attacks her again with the only thing that riles the woman. "You're just as evil and twisted as Waleen Macer. Your time in Carcerium has made you as cruel as he is and want to change places with another version of yourself."

"No, what would be cruel is to force Ish to choose between us," she says as the end of the churka bounces sporadically. "He'll believe me because he'll want to believe me, and right now, you're the only person in any interval that knows that I'm alive."

"That's why you killed Malom, isn't it?" Luci shakes her head, despising the older version of herself. "He objected to your plan to keep me here, so you killed him. You murdered your friend, the one who liberated you from Carcerium. You murdered him in cold blood. You're sick. Don't you see that? No sane person would do that."

"We're all mad here, says the Cheshire cat," Gicul responds unevenly, giving a shrug that sends a chill through Luci's heart.

She sniffs and wipes tears of anger forming in her eyes. "We should've died at the bridge. We should've never come up from that submerged car."

"Maybe," Gicul says with glassy eyes of her own. "But we *did* survive and I'm leaving with him and there's nothing that you can do to stop me."

There's a finality in her tone that indicates to Luci she'd better do something quick if there's any chance of wrestling the weapon away from her. "Even Macer wouldn't kill his friend, his partner who rescued him."

"You don't have a clue!"

The verbal blow landed, buying Luci a little bit more time. Gicul continues, "He killed his own son."

The revelation shocks Luci. Stupefied, she asks, "He did?"

"Malom told me that Waleen's wife died of Fichtner's Disease when Enos—the *real* Enos—was a teenager. City health records indicate that the boy was also diagnosed with the early stages of Fichtner's, which meant he was forced to remain in quarantine. Normally, the illness destroys the body of the host very quickly, but records report that Enos's quarantine lasted for an extended period—many years, in fact."

She studies Gicul's face for any hint of a memory overlay seizure rising to overtake her. "So why did Malom think that Macer killed the boy?" Luci asks to prolong the conversation until an opportunity arises.

"Waleen was tested and cleared, so exposure to his son wasn't a problem for him. He became the boy's primary care-taker, along with an in-home med bot."

Her eye twitches slightly, and Luci shifts the weight on her legs, preparing for the moment to strike.

Gicul continues, seemingly ignorant to the younger's plan, "But trust me, no one comes back from Fichtner's disease like that. It's a death sentence." Her eyes squint as she shakes her head in disgust. "He did something to that boy, I'm certain of it. Malom told me once that he believed that Waleen—"

This is it!

Gicul's eyes roll back, and Luci lunges to pull the barrel down to where it's angled at the floor.

Gicul still has a tight grip, so Luci does her best to wrangle it free.

A sharp poke from the churka in Luci's ribs causes her to double over in pain.

She's winded and coughing.

"You dare to take away my moment?" Gicul screams like a wild banshee. "You dare to take away what I've earned?"

Luci balances on one knee, spots dancing before her eyes as she fights for breath.

Gicul takes a few steps beyond Luci's reach. Looking down the barrel of the churka, she says apologetically, "You, more than anyone, should understand that I never asked for any of this—*Hi no Kawa*, Carcerium, everything that happened to *L'inversione*, Shar, Ley, Malom—and you being here. This isn't personal."

The words infuriate her. Through clenched teeth, Luci says, "Not personal? Get it over with, you crazy bitch."

Gicul nods somberly as she adjusts the angle of the churka. "As you wish. Goodnight, Luci G. See you in a few decades."

Luci defiantly shakes her head. Refusing to allow Gicul the satisfaction of seeing her growing fear, she clenches her eyes closed, wondering if she'll dream during the extended drug-induced slumber to follow. "Whatever," she says sharply. "We'll settle this when I wake up."

THREE

A BRILLIANT BLUE LIGHT SHINES through Luci's tightened eyelids. There's a bloodcurdling scream, but not from her. The smell of the churka discharge in the air fill her nostrils. Luci opens her eyes to Gicul on the floor before her, whimpering in agony and writhing in pain. It's clear the shooter has nicked her left side, because that much of her is missing from view. Half expecting Macer and a battalion of his red cybo warriors, she peers through the blast haze.

There is no battalion, though. Only a lone figure advancing slowly across the area with their churka drawn—Ish!

Luci shakes off her disorientation, running to meet him. The relief that his being stunned by the churka truly didn't cause any permanent damage is nearly more than her heart can bear.

Cautiously making slow and measured movements, Ish never lowers the churka. His wild eyes remain fixed on his wounded target in black. Ish waves Luci off with the end of the weapon as she attempts to embrace him, warning her, "Watch out—she's still alive!"

She turns to Gicul struggling on the floor and notes the proximity of the fumbled churka a safe meter and a half away from the woman. Luci grabs his sleeve. "Ish, it's okay. You don't understand."

Still not making eye contact with Luci, Ish aggressively jerks his arm out of her grip, continuing his advance to his fallen victim.

She suspects that he's fueled on pure adrenaline, so she shouts, "Ish, don't kill her!"

This finally breaks his concentration long enough for him to regard Luci with a puzzled look.

"Ish!" Gicul calls out to him, shifting the focus back down to the ground a few meters in front of them.

"How do you know me?" His steps slow as he asks Luci in a low voice, "Is that Cyphor Gicul?"

Before she can answer, he stops abruptly. "It's . . . she's . . ." His head snaps around to Luci in pained confusion and then back at Gicul's pitiful condition. "Her face looks like . . ." He pauses as if afraid to complete the sentence. "I . . . I don't understand," he says, trembling. "How can she be . . . you?" He looks back at Luci with a mix of suspicion and fear. He examines his churka as if it may provide an explanation and then back to Luci with tears forming in his eyes. "What have I done?" He swallows hard. "How can she be you? Answer me! What's going on here?"

"She's—" is all that Luci is able to get out before Gicul addresses him.

In a shaky voice, she says, "Closer, Ish."

His lips clench, tears streaming down as he faces Luci for guidance.

She nods, saying, "Give me the churka."

Ish quickly drops to his knees onto Gicul's massive cloak spread on the floor like a prayer rug from another era. There's a substantial burn hole in the fabric from the churka blast. "I'm sorry," he offers in a quivering voice. "I didn't know that—"

The anguish on her face screws into a forced smile as she shushes him. "Got me good . . . my side," she says, wincing while struggling to present her mask of fake joy. "Not . . . your fault."

He shakes his head. "I don't understand how the two of you—"

Gicul manages to feebly place three fingers over his mouth to silence him this time before allowing her arm to collapse heavy to her chest. "I . . . I know. Luci will tell." She slowly allows her head to roll to the side facing Luci.

The younger one wipes tears from her eyes before returning her grip to the churka.

"Have to change plan," Gicul says, followed by a series of coughs that painfully necessitates the closing of her eyes.

"Heal kit!" Ish exclaims, bolting to his feet and scanning the area. "Do you have a heal kit around here?"

His urgency is contagious. Luci frantically points to the area with the futuristic hospital bed intended for her decades of slumber. "Ish, she has a huge medbot over there that can—"

"No!" Gicul shouts with surprising force and volume enough to echo through the area. The act makes her wince again. After another round of coughing, she says in a hoarse voice, "No." She pauses as if to cough again, and Luci is relieved when it doesn't come. Finally, Gicul adds, "Blast sears flesh . . . no way for nanobots to . . ."

"I'm so sorry," Ish blubbers while Luci swallows hard, trying not to visualize what's happened to the woman's organs.

"Two things," she rasps through a cough.

"What things?" Luci asks, kneeling to better hear her while placing the churka on the ground behind her.

"Kiss me," Gicul says, straining to raise her head slightly to Ish.

He looks horrified as he turns to Luci.

She bites her lip and tries to avoid looking into his widened eyes, but there's no escape from them.

Gicul extends her fingers to his cheek. "Please."

Her touch makes him jerk away and dab at the tears in his eyes. He looks to Luci again for a way out of this agony.

She sniffs, contemplating this dying request, and closes her eyes while nodding. "It's okay. It'll be okay."

The sound of a soft ruffling alerts her he's complied. Luci opens her eyes to witness Ish tenderly pulling away from Gicul.

The woman's pained expression is displaced by a look of utter satisfaction. Gicul slowly opens her eyelids to peer up at him. In this instant, Luci realizes that it's the fulfilment of all that her other self ever wanted. *Hi no Kawa* will be averted if Luci remains true to her word, and the man whom Gicul has loved through centuries of Carcerium confinement is sending her off in an affectionate way. What more could anyone ask for at the end of a life, to right any wrongs they may have caused along the way and to go to the next world gently on the wings of love?

She feels conflicted. A few moments ago, Gicul was ready to abandon her, confining her to decades of lonely isolation, but Luci can't bring herself to hate this person before her. She searches to harness the bitter feelings inside, but the only emotion present is a sorrow for the unimaginable torture her other self experienced.

She sighs as Ish returns to slumping on his knees before Gicul. He asks, "What's the other thing? You said there were two things you wanted. What's the other?"

Luci has already forgotten this. She leans in for Gicul's answer.

The woman's face is drained of color, and it's clear she's fading fast. "Macer Prime . . . destroy."

Luci shakes her head. "We don't have to. All I have to do is avoid releasing DPM and thereby prevent *Hi no Kawa*." Her words speed up. "If there's no *Hi no Kawa*, there's no Relicus City, which means no Macer."

Gicul winces and closes her eyes again. "Wrong . . ."

The long pause makes Luci wonder if the slain woman spread out on the ground before them will expire before an explanation. "Wrong? How is that wrong?" she prompts.

Gicul's eyes open to slits. "Waleen . . . Carcerium," she says before a sharp inhale and cough. "Been outside . . . linear time."

Luci tries to grasp the relevance of this. "So you're saying he could go on even if there's no post-*Hi no Kawa*?"

Ish shoots a horrified look at her. "Luci, the chancellor with access to leap-skip technology could achieve the type of godlike status you told me about even without—"

"*Hi no Kawa*," Gicul mutters feebly.

"We have to find him and eliminate him," Ish says flatly as he gazes back down at Gicul.

Luci shakes her head. "But how can we do that? With Royse and Cavazos gone and with what *L'inversione* pulled, he'll be more protective than ever. There's just no way that we can ever get him alone to—"

"Can't allow . . . Relicus Great," Gicul whimpers. "David."

"David? David who?" Luci asks in desperation.

Gicul slowly shakes her head, making Luci wonder if the dying woman is cognizant or experiencing a hallucination involving someone named David.

Ish speaks slowly as he assembles the pieces of his conclusion together. "I suspect that as long as Macer's out there, he can leap skip back and get either one of you *Lucis* and extort you to share DPM. You're not safe. Or he can simply use his knowledge of history to establish himself and, in time, rule the nations in an even worse way than the future he set up for Relicus City."

It's a faint, almost imperceptible movement, but Gicul nods that Ish's conclusion is sound.

Luci whispers "Macer Prime" to herself. "The original Waleen . . . all others stem from." She turns to Ish. "How can we be certain of getting the original version of him?"

Gicul weakly motions. Her voice is a faint whisper. "David."

"Can this *David* identify the true one—the original Macer, *Macer Prime*?" Frustration and alarm set in. "I know that you were planning to kill him after you left with Ish. Where were you going to leap skip to? Where is the Macer Prime going to be for us to find him?"

Gicul feebly lifts her hands off her chest as if to make a gesture, but they just hover there. Luci scrambles to place her ear near the woman's mouth as Gicul whispers, "Macer Prime—

destroy him." The last word tapers off like a weak drawn-out sigh into nothingness. Her hands collapse onto her chest like deflated balloons.

Ish and Luci focus on Gicul's dead eyes in still silence.

"*Subtraction*," Luci thinks with morbid detachment. "*There were three people in here; now there are only two.*"

"She's dead, Luci, and I killed her," Ish says mournfully. "I killed her."

"It's alright, Ish." Luci, still in the problem-solving recesses of her mind, acknowledges him with a nod but says, "What was she doing with her hands? It doesn't make sense."

When he doesn't respond, she recognizes that Ish is in a daze of pain and confusion. For the first time in her life, Luci Gaudiano postpones solving a problem, choosing instead to direct her thoughts to the shattered man before her. She moves to him. She presses against his back, wrapping her arms around his front torso like he's done for her many times. She's intrigued to feel his knotted tension transform tightened muscles into a more relaxed posture as if the stress is melting like a snowbank outside the dome they're in.

Ish sniffs. "I know it's mad to say it, but . . . it's like I killed *you*." He shakes his head slowly. "When I kissed her, it was like . . ." His voice trails off.

"I'm still here," Luci says softly, reaching to caress his cheek. She pulls back abruptly, recognizing it as the exact gesture made moments before by her older self. "You did what you had to. She . . . she murdered Ley and Malom." Luci sighs. "She wasn't whole. Her extended isolation in Carcerium drove her insane and destroyed any trace of compassion. She was going to put me in a coma in order to pretend to be me so she could run off with you."

As if he hasn't heard her, Ish gestures to Gicul sprawled out on the floor. Lifting his shoulders in a shrug, he says, "I saw the churka pointed at you. I was helpless to do anything when Mr. Timmons came at you at the other place, but then we're here and there's this person dressed in black aiming at you and I just . . ." Emotion overtakes him, leaving the sentence incomplete again. Cradling his head in his hands, he winces. "Oh, my head is pounding. I have such a migraine."

"It's from the stun blast. She said that it would wear off after a while," Luci says in a voice that even she finds unconvincing. "Maybe the medbot over there has—"

"What was that about hands and David?" Ish interrupts.

Luci's shocked at his willingness to reengage the topic. "I . . . I don't know," Luci replies. "Do you know any David in Relicus City?"

"No, but if he's connected with the chancellor, we've got to figure it out. We have to end this once and for all, and it begins with locating Macer Prime."

Luci looks over at the skip barge. "Is there any way that you can go *online*? I mean sip Jardon from a pull basin in order to review a directory of Davids listed in Relicus City?"

She feels his back muscles stiffen as he informs her, "The second I sip, anyone monitoring for my reg. number will be alerted."

"Okay, so going back to Relicus for you to access the network is out," she admits. She mumbles her standard self-pep talk, "Come on, Luci G., figure it out. Figure it . . ." She perks up. "Do you know anybody there that can do it?" Spinning around to face him, Luci asks, "Is there anyone that you trust to run a query on all of the Davids in Relicus City? I doubt anything like that would be considered classified information."

Before he can answer, Luci repeats the phrase to herself. "David in Relicus City." In an instant, she knows what Gicul was trying to say. She leans in and kisses his cheek in excitement. "David! I know what she meant."

Ish straightens astonished, "You do? Who is it?"

"David isn't a *he*. David is a *what!*" she announces jubilantly. "Macer has a famous sculpture statue called *David* back in his study. When I first arrived, he showed it to me, bragging about how he'd taken it from a gallery just a few days before *Hi no*

Kawa occurs. We just need to locate the interval skip point in Florence, Italy that happens a few days before the war."

"But what are the hands?"

Luci cycles through her interaction with the chancellor. "Macer spoke about novice sculptors having difficulty forming the hands of their subjects." The combined revelation electrifies her; she proclaims, "We can do this! We can know exactly *when* and *where* the original Macer is going to be!"

ISH LETS OUT A LONG sigh. "So Gicul told you that Waleen murdered his own son, and you believe her?"

Luci looks up from the churka in her lap across the skip barge at his dark-skinned face. He's alternately bathed in the bright aqua blue-green and violet-fuchsia light rings of energy rippling around the outside of the vessel. "Do you think that could be true?"

"I don't know." He shrugs. "It would explain what everybody calls the *'Macer Miracle'* though."

"What's that?" she asks, placing the weapon beside her as she adjusts her posture against the cool metal base of the control panel.

"Well, if city records are to be believed, Enos Macer is the only person to have ever contracted a level-two case of Fichtner's Disease and have it go into permanent remission."

"But how could he pull off convincing everyone that he, Waleen, was Enos Macer?" Luci asks.

His answer comes slowly as if he's assembling the pieces together for himself first. "It may have been easier to do than you think. At some point, the father must've commandeered the younger Macer's sip-basin online presence and began to impersonate him. The story goes that by the time Enos was twenty-four, his system was free from any trace of Fichtner's

Disease, but by then, he had become so accustomed to living as a shut-in that he never went out. There was no public sighting of him until much later in life."

"Macer's age now."

"The chancellor didn't start appearing in public until about a decade or so ago. He said that even though the medical tests indicated he was free of any sign of Fichtner's, he didn't want to take the chance of exposing anyone to some rare dormant strain and cause a pandemic."

"How thoughtful of him," she says sarcastically.

"Right," Ish agrees. "It would be the perfect cover." He places his own churka beside where he's sitting, mirroring Luci's actions. "All I know is that I'm grateful to be away from the interval in Antarctica."

"I know what you mean," she answers. "It kinda felt like doing math calculations in a morgue with the three bodies there." Ish bumps against the ESTA pod hovering behind him, causing it to sway gently. As if she's in confessional, she lowers her gaze, staring at the empty space between them on the platform. "We didn't even figure out where Gicul has that pod programed to leap skip to. We could've spent another couple of hours there working that out—maybe even another whole half a day—but I couldn't stay in there any longer."

"I know it bothered you, because you're never one to leave something unsolved like that," he says soothingly.

She scoffs at herself. "I know. It's definitely a red-letter day when Luci Gaudiano willingly abandons an equation, but it was just too creepy for me." She avoids telling him that she was more troubled by the recently-expired presence of her older self than the other two slain bodies. "At least we're certain the Gicul set the single-passenger ESTA pod for some destination in the past." To change the subject, Luci asks, "How's your headache from the stun blast she got you with?"

"I'm better now," he answers. "It stopped hurting as bad about an hour and a half or so ago, before we loaded the ESTA pod transport onto this barge. It's just a dull ache now." He leans forward slightly. "Speaking of the stun setting on the churka . . . I still think the better option is simply to end Macer and not mess around with stunning him to send him back through time on this thing."

He reaches behind to touch one of the gray ESTA panels jutting out from the mysterious pod transport the barge is hauling. Contact with the hovering structure makes it bob even more. "I think the plan is too dangerous. *He's* too dangerous to mess about with. I think when we see the opportunity, we blast him—no questions asked—and end it once and for all." Ish releases his grip on the pod bracket to massage the back of his neck. "That way, we know another version can't come and find you somewhere."

Luci's grateful the interval destination their barge is leap skipping to is 2068, over a hundred years in the past from Gicul's Antarctic hideout. This gives them a few minutes to discuss her reasoning and state her case. "I don't know if I can go through with killing him when we arrive in pre-*Hi no Kawa* Florence."

"But all of those things," Ish says incredulously, "the things you told me that you saw on the holo vid, Macer can't be allowed to become what you described to me—never!"

She swallows a lump in her throat. "I just can't condemn someone for something that they haven't done yet." She looks up at him shaking his head, his eyes wide in disbelief. "Ish, how can one justly convict and kill anyone for crimes they've yet to commit?"

He scoffs and nods his head. "I can find a way, believe me."

Luci bristles. "It's just that—"

"I'm of the mind to end him since we know what he *will* do. We should end him the first chance we get, no messing around with sending him back through time where he can't do any damage. We end him once and for all and be done with it."

In the week they've spent together, they've never disagreed. There are no arguments in math formulas, no debate over the absoluteness of an equation. His opposition to her opinion about this is frustrating. "You don't understand why I can't," Luci says. "Gicul—"

"Gicul what? Did she say something to you?"

"It's just that..." she sighs and then blurts out, "If you can execute Macer for the acts he will later commit as Relicus the Great, how does that make you feel toward me?"

"What do you mean?" Ish asks.

"Gicul...I *am* Cyphor Gicul, and she merrily admitted that she had shot down both Ley and Malom Roderick without any remorse." Luci sniffs. "She mocked Shar's feelings for her and could care less about the sacrifices made by *L'inversione* to rescue you. She was ready to put me in a comatose state for decades until 'thawing me out' to present DPM so the two of you could run away together. In some ways, she was just as selfish as Macer, maybe more. That stuff..." She strikes her chest with her fist. "That same darkness in her exists in here somewhere."

Ish is quiet.

"Answer me this. How can you be willing to convict Macer and not convict *me* of my future deeds?"

"It's different," Ish says softly. "She wasn't...she...Gicul isn't you."

The intermittent glow of the energy rings the barge is passing through increase in speed.

"She was driven mad, but that's not you. It doesn't have to be you—it *won't* be you."

"But how can you know that?" Luci says, wiping tears.

"Because I know *you*," he says, moving on his knees to close the space between them and embrace her. "She was fractured, broken by her time in Carcerium, but that's not you."

"But the potential is here inside of me to become like her, just waiting like a time bomb."

"The potential for evil or good exists in all of us—it's a choice," he says. "Do you truly believe that by not revealing DPM in your time interval that *Hi no Kawa* may be avoided?"

She sniffs. "Yes, of course. That's what this is all about, the possibility for the world to make better choices—avoid its mistakes."

"So if you admit that a choice, a single decision made by one solitary person, can have far-reaching ramifications, affecting the lives of billions of people to come . . . if you believe that, then you have to embrace the truth that you choosing to be a different version of yourself is also an equally viable proposition."

A nervous laugh escapes from her. "You make it sound so easy."

He nods pensively. His gaze is intense. "Well, it is and it isn't at the same time; in fact, it's likely to be the hardest thing that you'll ever do, that any of us are to ever do."

Luci plants a quick kiss firmly on his lips. "For a new and better path."

"What?" Ish asks, tilting his head slightly.

"It's just something that . . ." She pauses, then says, "Something that some friends of mine used to say: *'For a new and better path.'*"

He nods contemplatively. "Yeah, I like that. For a new and better path."

The partial weightlessness from the skip journey dissipates, alerting Luci they're nearing their chronal destination.

Luci returns to the unresolved topic. "So if there's truth to the possibility of me not becoming like Gicul in the future, the same would apply to this Macer Prime we're headed to see. He may or may not one day become that evil Relicus the Great. We can't execute him for that, not if there's a shred of uncertainty."

Ish silently contemplates this. Finally, he concedes like a chess player bested by a skilled master. "I'll agree to what you ask under one condition."

The vibrating rings of energy transform into a soundless, psychedelic fireworks show around them.

"What condition?"

He sighs dejectedly, acknowledging that her logic has bested him. "When the time comes to strap Macer into the seat on the ESTA pod . . ."

"Yes, go on," she prompts him.

"When we do all of that and we send it to whatever unknown interval that Gicul has programmed it to skip to, I want to be the one to do it—just in case."

Luci shrugs. "Okay, fine with me, but just in case of what?"

"It blows up or something."

She represses her shocked laughter. "Why would it blow up?"

"The ESTA satellite components in this thing are over a hundred years old, and none of this has been tested. You and I spent over an hour back there just trying to figure out where this behemoth is going to skip to, if it even *can* perform a leap skip in the condition that it's in." He takes the controller device from his pocket. "All that we've been able to determine is this thing has to be in close proximity to activate its leap skip function. I'm just trying to . . ."

"Trying to what?"

"Trying to protect you from all of this."

Tingling waves of static electricity run up and down her skin, indicating their impending arrival into the past.

She scoffs. "I don't need you to protect me. I'm completely capable of—"

"I know, I know," he cuts her off. "You're the great Luci Gaudiano." His voice is thin and sounds as if it's on the verge of breaking into a thousand bits. "I acknowledge that you least of anyone don't need me or anyone else to protect you." He brushes something from his cheek, shaking his head. "But something inside of *me* needs you to allow me to protect you, as silly as that may seem." He exhales shakily. "I'll concede to strap Macer in and send this thing to wherever it's set to go, but I'll operate it when the time comes."

Luci collects herself, aware how she's unwittingly injured this person that she cares for so deeply. "I can agree to that if it's that important to you."

He crosses his arms as his eyes narrow. "It is."

FOUR

August 28, 2068
Florence, Italy
[43.7695604/11.2558136/4.603.391.893/5736:25:39]

flORINS – IT∆Lɪ

∆GUST 28, 2068

⊖

PRɪ-Hɪ NꝊ KꝊWU

THE BARGE MATERIALIZES AT THE destination, but instead of the soft pressurized pop that Luci has come to anticipate, there's a sharp crackling of bangs as loud as firecrackers. She instinctively lunges for her churka by the navigation lectern at the front of the skip vessel.

"Miscalculation!" Ish shouts, pointing to the front of the barge while jumping to his feet.

Luci realizes that they're outside in the night's rain as she spins to see his meaning. She gasps in terror at the sight before her. Waist-high, wrought-iron fence pickets jut up through the bow of the barge like a series of perfectly aligned vertical spears, fence posts that weren't there seconds before.

"Luci, it's alright!" Ish yells above the cacophony of noise that roars at them from every direction. "The spikes didn't materialize into anything vital."

She shifts from Ish to the base of a platform that's unnervingly close to the edge of the barge. Her eyes anxiously scan upward through hard rain at the edifice. Drops of rain ricochet off the statue of a cloaked figure in the halo glimmer of streetlights, and there's a constant droning buzz sound overhead.

Luci is completely disoriented, but before she's able to call out to Ish as to where they are, a spotlight from high in the black sky clicks on. The cone of light frantically searches the ground below.

"Over there!" Ish yells. "We can't let them spot us!"

Luci works out the connection between the growing buzzing sound and the searchlight and shouts a single word of acknowledgement: "Helicopter!" Other discordant sounds echo off the building walls. A klaxon alarm blares in the distance, accompanied by the wails and agitated chirps of far-off police sirens, indicating that Macer has already broken into the museum a few blocks from here.

Ish has her by the hand, pulling her over the slick, rain-soaked bricks of the street. On their way to a covered bus stop, they run through a large courtyard past a second skip barge considerably larger than theirs. This transport is situated near a cluster of perfectly arranged trees at the edge of the square.

Ish points out the obvious to her when they reach the canopy of the bus stop. "Macer's here alright."

The rain pelting the plastic covering above their heads sounds like endless applause. Both stop to catch their breath.

Luci tries to wipe the water from her face with an already drenched sleeve, saying in humiliation, "I don't understand how I could have been so off with the calculations." She stands her churka up vertically and tries to contain the shaking from the adrenaline raging through her body. "That could've been us the fence skewered, or the ESTA pod."

Ish peers intensely through the plexiglass wall panel of the shelter at Macer's barge. He responds without looking over to her, "I know, but we're alright. The barge and ESTA transport are intact, so we still have a chance at Macer. Nothing else matters."

Though safely out of sight, they both instinctively duck as the helicopter searchlight shines through the semi-opaque dome of the bus stop housing before moving on. He faces her, saying, "I'll be right back."

Ish dashes through the downpour to Macer's craft, bends, and then disappears behind the vertical control podium. There's the briefest of blue flashes like a flashbulb of an old-time camera. The ground trembles, and then he reemerges, running back to her.

Though it's slightly after 3:00 AM, small clusters of people scattered under tavern entrance canopies point up at the helicopter beam. Some seem unaffected by the commotion, more concerned about staying dry, while other couples huddle under umbrellas, dashing along the slippery sidewalks.

Despite the noise and chaos all around, the voice inside of Luci's head is louder. She castigates herself for rushing through the DPM numbers to get here, horrified at how close they came to forfeiting everything to Waleen Macer's future. That was unnecessarily risky and stupid. No matter how tired she is, they can't take chances like that again.

Ish is nearly out of breath as he ducks back under the bus stop canopy, shaking off excess water. "That ought to do it. He won't be going anywhere without an armillary relay." He turns to listen. "The alarms are coming from that direction." He clears his throat. "You stay here, and I'll go see if they're coming."

"Like hell," Luci says, gathering her churka. "Though I don't claim to be Annie Oakley or anything, I've shot more of these than you." She stops short of mentioning the only time he fired a churka was when he fatally wounded Gicul.

His dripping face looks like he's about to argue for her to remain behind, but Ish sighs and says with a nod, "Alright, but I lead, and Macer's mine. I don't want you getting too close to him or whoever he's brought with him."

"Alright," Luci says. There's a pregnant pause as Ish looks at her while nodding as if on auto pilot. Luci gestures in the direction of the alarms. "Well, let's go."

He advances to her unexpectedly and plants a quick kiss on her cheek while accidentally flinging rainwater on her. "Yeah, let's go."

Thankfully, the copter has moved beyond the courtyard, allowing the two of them to move freely. They rush down the nearby empty avenue. Though she's visited Florence a few times, she's always surprised at the claustrophobic narrowness of the common streets. It'd be impossible for a full-sized semi truck to make it down this avenue without scraping the walls on either side.

As they scurry across the slick pavement, nearly slipping in puddles, Luci feels like she's maneuvering through the valley of an urban canyon four stories tall on both sides. To the right is a corridor of small retail shops with their metal bay doors pulled closed. Each storefront butts up against its neighbor so as not to forfeit valuable real estate to something as trifling as an alleyway. On the left is a waist-high slab of stone with iron bars and columns every few meters extending the length of the corridor out of sight.

Luci ducks at the sound of a muffled explosion up the street.

Ish points to the source of the blast and a new set of wailing alarms. "Here they come!" There's a small, smoldering pile of rubble on the side of the external Accademia Gallery wall.

A bright white beam from a police helicopter finds what it's been searching for up the street. The jittery spotlight cuts through the rain down to the subjects marching in time down the avenue. They move in unison before the twenty-foot object turned on its side—the *David*, no doubt.

Luci wipes rain from her eyes with her free hand, and her voice is unsteady. "I count four or five figures in all, unless there's more behind where we can't see." Two bulky cybos approach, one on either side of the front of the horizontal object. These are not Macer's future Red Guard cybos but the type like Benold Jesper was converted to, so maybe this is really the Macer Prime that Gicul indicated as she lay dying.

A commanding voice squawks overhead from the speakers of the chopper's intercom in Italian demanding the thieves immediately halt.

"They're not carrying it," Ish reports uneasily, his shoes skidding to an abrupt stop. "There are cybos, but they're walking beside it with churkas drawn!"

Luci swallows her heart as she sidles up to Ish. Closer observation reveals he's right. "It's . . . floating," she says in disbelief. "Shit! This complicates things."

The two of them anticipated cybos carrying the massive sculpture and therefore unable to wield weapons; neither of them is prepared for a shootout.

The bouncing police spotlight follows Macer's crew as if it's all some avant-garde stage play of pandemonium.

"Cargo suspensors from the Grange," Ish says. "They're not toting it at all. It's floating on suspensors! I should've guessed. We need a different plan."

As if to demonstrate that the cybos have unrestricted access to their churkas, the one in the back of the procession stops, aims upward, and releases a bright blue blast of fire. The shot, like ground lightning, extends up to the heavens, illuminating the area.

Luci muffles a scream as the beam of energy follows a parallel path up through the spotlight of the helicopter. The cybo shooter doesn't wait to acknowledge that the blast is a direct hit. The creature instantly falls back in line as a red-and-orange ball of heat illuminates the area like a plume of fire.

The twisted bulk of the craft spins until it smashes into the buildings with a deafening impact that rattles the ground. The aftershock of the explosion slams the two of them against a shop wall as fiery metal and glass fragments from the copter rain down further up the street. The area is instantly anointed with the noxious odor of churka discharge and petrol from the craft.

The cybos and their cargo have already advanced safely beyond the flaming spiral of glass, stone, and building mortar raining down. Rubble crackles against the pavement louder than the noise of the storm.

Luci's heart skips a beat recognizing Macer's hooded orange slicker as the same one he left in the warehouse in Baltimore when he abducted her. "There he is!" she exclaims, spinning Ish around to face them.

A new chorus of whining alarms joins the shriek and shrill of the mayhem already in progress.

"There's no clear shot at him behind the cybo in the front," Ish says.

Luci agrees, adding, "And the statue will shield most of him on this side if we wait here."

Both watch in silence as Macer leisurely follows behind the largest cybo on the right side of the hovering art piece. His nonchalance sharply contrasts the bedlam of the scene.

"We can't stay here; we've gotta fall back," Ish finally says. "They haven't spotted us yet. We've got to pull back to the corner."

Luci swallows the lump in her throat. "Yeah, okay."

A half-dozen armed police drones whiz by in formation, firing pellets at their targets. The cybos effortlessly take out the armed devices as easily as shooters at skeet practice. Ish and Luci sprint stealthily down the uneven sidewalk back in the direction of the piazza. The area has emptied out all the night owls as the pub-hoppers have retreated into hiding.

Ish tells her in staccato words as they run, "We'll need to split up, one on either side and ambush them as they walk by. I'll hide at the corner and shoot the single cybo in front of Macer." Finally, as they approach the corner, he leads Luci to an enclave in the wall opposite it. "You crouch and hide here. When the cybos on your side of the street react to me blasting the first one, they'll turn, and that's when you fire into their backs." He looks half-crazed, but Luci nods that it's a solid strategy. He clasps his hand on her cold, drenched shoulder. "I love you, Luci. I'll stun Macer, we'll send him away, and then this will all be over soon enough."

"I love you too," she says. The words are still on her lips as he scrambles to his improvised post across the street. She doubts that she'd be able to see him poised on one knee through the sheets of rain had she not kept her eyes focused on him getting into position.

Luci mirrors his stance, tucking herself into the recess of the gate entrance. She attempts to calm her beating heart, but the ground rhythmically quivers as the trio of cybos make their way down the avenue, approaching her hiding spot. A sense of dread enshrouds her heart like the darkest of clouds, and Luci fights back fearful tears. She shivers, not because of the rain, but from abject terror that encompasses every part of her being.

"You can do this, Luci G.," she whispers, reminding herself. "*We* can do this—they're not expecting it." She oddly finds herself contemplating the second phase of what they're doing here, sending Macer back through time. She's certain that he doesn't know any substantive information about DPM. There's nothing that he'd be able to relay to anyone in the same way that she couldn't instruct the Roman armies of old of how to achieve flight. She knows that wherever the ESTA dumps him is a one-way trip without a longchair to leave. She's certain that the inhabitants there will think him a mad man if he dares speak of time travel.

She knows that sending him away instead of killing him is the perfect solution, but here in this moment, she just wants it all to be over. She just wants to escape with Ish to a place in time before DPM and never think of Macer or Relicus City ever again.

The rhythmic sound of cybo boots scraping the pavement cuts through the discordance all around. She sneaks a peek at their approach, gasping at how near they are to her hiding spot. Luci feels as if she's having a heart attack. It takes everything inside of her to resist the instinct to flee to the skip barge and set it for a destination out of here—anywhere from here.

The first cybo crosses into her line of sight directly in front of her, and Luci holds her breath: stillness equals invisibility in this deluge of rain. She must wait for Ish to fire for any of this to work, and he'll wait until the entire party clears his corner so Macer won't be allowed to flee back down the avenue. The waiting is an eternity of pounding heartbeats.

Slowly passing before her is the floating statue of David encased in a translucent gelatinous substance the color of pale amber. Embedded in the strange goop every meter or so is a brick-sized steel device blinking from blue to orange, which Luci realizes must be the cargo suspensors holding it up. The statue floats by like a balloon in a parade of the surreal.

The top of the base of the statue is before her now, and Luci knows that the success or failure of Ish's plan will be decided within the next thirty seconds.

Unexpectedly, the bright blue, red, and white flash of a patrol car's lights shine off the neighboring structures down the far end of the street. The siren wails down the avenue like an angry banshee as the car rushes toward them past the punctured outer museum wall.

Astonished that any vehicle could even make it past the pile of rubble down the street, Luci sickly grumbles to herself, "No, no, no!" The cybo on Luci's side in the back turns, assumes a firing stance, and unleashes a lightning bolt from Hell into the engine of the speeding vehicle.

The car's momentum carries it a bit closer before the wreckage slams into the closed metal door of a leather goods shop.

A second churka blast from around Ish's corner lights up the area. Realizing he's using the distraction of the police vehicle to their advantage, Luci responds by firing upon the cybo at the front on her side of the statue. The creature staggers and falls with a wet thud into a puddle.

The cybo in the back that fired on the squad car is already moving around the base of the container to protect Macer, but she doesn't have a line of sight on him anyway. Luci aims through the churka haze at the cybo. Her blast connects instead with the suspensor at the base of the statue. Whatever the substance the sculpture is encased in glows bright orange, absorbing the shot. The statue sways on the air like a plank of wood on a turbulent sea and then, starting with the back, comes crashing down with a thud and a sickening crunch.

"Shit!" She locks on to the cybo. Judging by the way it's jerking its leg, the other foot must be trapped under the fallen art.

Luci moves around to what *was* the base of the statue. Macer's gone. A brief confusion sets in as she peers through the rain and noxious haze of churka discharge. She knows he didn't flee this way, and Ish is certain to outrun him if he bolted in the other direction. She faces Ish's corner, but he's out of sight too. Luci fires a blast into the chest of the struggling cybo at her feet and sighs with relief when it goes limp.

A second patrol vehicle arrives, this one coming from the direction of the piazza where the skip barges are. The officer screeches to a halt and throws the door open, crouching behind it as a shield. She shouts in Italian to throw down weapons.

Luci drops to a crouch, pressing against the side of what was a Michelangelo masterpiece mere seconds before. She doesn't have a clear line of sight to stun the officer, but she doesn't need to. The woman isn't looking in her direction but turned more to face the corner. The officer repeats the command.

Though Ish doesn't speak Italian, the policewoman's inference is clear. He reluctantly steps forward into Luci's view, tossing his weapon to the ground. Luci swallows a lump in her throat, whispering, "No," as he raises his hands, falling to his knees in puddles on the sidewalk.

Luci creeps along the side of the fallen statue, careful to remain concealed.

A churka blast burns through the squad car door, killing the policewoman instantly. Luci notes the origin of the shot around the corner and rushes around the heap for a better angle. Her only hope is that Macer is unaware of her presence, allowing her an advantage.

There's a second blast, this one turning Ish's churka on the ground to molten slag. Macer lunges from the shadows. He violently snags Ish by the collar in one hand and yanks him back around the corner. "You'd better not try anything else," Macer threatens, "or I'll melt his pretty face!"

Ish calls out, "Run for the barge, Luci!"

She feels nauseated from the tension. A surprise attack isn't an option. All that remains is the possibility that she can fire off a shot that would stun them both. She gives the briefest of looks down at the weapon to ensure its readiness. Her legs move as if they're filled with lead and treading through molasses. How can she hope to get a shot off before Macer, even if she did have a good angle? Soon, this courtyard will be crawling with every cop in the Florence Police Department, and there's no way that she can drag two unconscious, full-sized men back to the skip barge in time.

"Dr. Gaudiano?" an unseen Macer calls to her.

She swallows a knot in her throat as large as a jawbreaker, taking a cautious step forward, still without a plan. "If you kill him, I kill you," she says, trembling.

Macer unexpectedly delights in her threat. "Ah, so he *is* of value to you. Good to know." He pauses before adding, "We're coming around the corner so I may see you, my dear. Again, don't try anything."

Luci doesn't respond. She takes her stance, intending to stun them both when they emerge. "*Sorry, Ish,*" she thinks. "*Stunned twice in one day.*"

Her heart leaps at the sight of him, but Macer is cautiously to the side, out of view. Only the end of the churka prodding him in his ribs is visible.

Ish calls out, "Luci, run back down the alley and double back to leap skip to your Baltimore!"

"What's a *Baltimore?*" Macer asks over the continual tapping sound of rain.

Macer's question confirms to her that he *is* the one—he's Macer Prime!

A thunder crack lights the heavens.

Macer shouts to her, "I don't know how he managed to break you out of Carcerium, but I'll lock you both away forever unless you do exactly as I say!"

"*Gicul.*" She nearly drops the rain-slick churka at the realization. "*He thinks I'm the older Luci. He only knows of the post-DPM version of me that he hid in Carcerium.*"

Before she's able to figure out how to use this mistaken assumption to her advantage, Macer yells, "Throw down that churka or I'll put a blast through your associate's heart."

"Don't do it, Luci!" Ish pleads. "Get away from here!"

"I don't know who you are, but you need to shut up," Macer growls.

Luci's tears mix with rain.

"Do it!" Macer commands in a guttural yell. "Throw down the churka!"

Her fingers tighten around the weapon.

For the first time, Macer sounds anxious. "Dr. Gaudiano, the skip point here is closing soon, and we've got to leave before any more of this interval's security come and trap us here permanently. *Hi no Kawa* is just a few days away, and this entire spot on which we stand will be turned to smoldering heap of radioactive nothingness."

Luci's eyes lock onto the rain bouncing off the barrel of her churka. Her heart thumps double-time as she contemplates what to do. There's not enough time to explore every option systematically like a math equation.

She's denied even this fragmented moment of concentration, as Macer proclaims, "I honestly don't see a reason why I need him to come with us, Doctor. If you persist in delaying us, I *will* end him right here."

Luci roars a primal scream of frustration, and before she knows it, she jettisons the churka with a lunge. Her heart sinks at the sound of the metal hitting the street and sobs angry, frustrated tears.

Even worse is Macer's twisted praise as he victoriously assures her, "You made the right choice, Doctor." He emerges from around the corner's edge. "Now, let's get you back to a safe place away from here."

Ish slumps his head in defeat.

"I'm sorry, Ish, so sorry," Luci says clasping the sides of her face in her hands.

"No time for *sorry*," Macer barks as the orange hood of his raincoat is pelted by the night's rain. "It's time to go. Now, get in front of us so I may keep an eye on you."

Luci takes uncertain steps as she falls in line before them. The trio picks up the tempo of their steps in their rush to the courtyard. She doesn't bother to slow her trot as she moves past Macer's disabled skip barge, and from the uninterrupted sound of their feet splashing through puddles behind her, he must have spotted the hole that Ish shot through the control panel earlier.

They reach the barge with the ESTA on it, and Macer orders Luci, "I'll give you the skip point coordinates to punch in. Do exactly as I say or you'll kill us all."

"I know how leap skips work, okay?" Luci turns to give him a snide enough look for it to register through the relentless fall of rain. Some of the fire goes out of her, seeing Macer backed up against the ESTA transport with his churka still lodged firmly into Ish's back.

"From the looks of things, you barely made this juncture point without destroying this craft and killing yourself," Macer says scathingly. "That iron fence is dangerously close to your control panel there."

His criticism is uncomfortably valid. Luci turns to the control lectern to avoid showing her embarrassment. "What are the damned numbers?"

"Input NBSI destination code 194576001X."

She pauses after pressing the first three numbers into the keypad. "I know these numbers." She's shaking as she turns to face him. "That's Carcerium . . . You're taking us to Carcerium."

"Normally, I'd be impressed that someone other than my-self and Pol Cavazos would know of that," Macer says, "but in the case of you two, obviously, this one here knew that NBSI destination code in order to break you free from there."

Her mind floods with panic. "You can't take us there. You don't know who I am." She shakes her head violently, presenting the one deterrent that may stop him. "If you lock me in there, Relicus City will never be. I'm not the Luci that you think—"

"I did it before, and the city survived just fine," he says before exploding in frustration and impatience. "Now, finish putting in the code or I kill him!"

The sound of a throttling engine comes from the south-west corner of the courtyard behind the car of the slain female officer. Luci looks over at a large, militarized transport vehicle skidding to a halt. She doesn't know what the Italian equivalent of S.W.A.T. back home is called, but half a dozen armed figures in black pour from it like a cluster of angry hornets.

With no options left and not enough time to reset and en-ter a skip destination of her choosing, Luci completes the code.

She can barely hear the automated voice from the control panel above the sound of the rain and shouting of the special forces police brigade. "Warning: You have entered a destina-tion point that is not associated with any verified skip point juncture. Please confirm NBSI destination code 194576001X."

"Again!" Macer shouts in a panic. "Override it by entering it again."

Luci's index finger shakes so badly that she nearly presses the wrong last two characters of the sequence.

She's both relieved and forlorn as the system accepts the code, confirming, "Chronal destination acknowledged."

Ish, who's been silently submissive since they boarded the barge, makes his move. He spins around on his knees to face his captor in an attempt to tackle his legs.

Luci knows what he's trying to do and understands that if Ish can shove any part of Macer off the barge when the leap skip is initiated, the limb stays behind in this interval. It's a dangerous gamble since Ish faces the same risk.

Macer is ready for the maneuver, because he takes a step back from bumping into the ESTA transport. This sets it into an equally precarious floating bobble. Luci dives forward to complete Ish's attack. Macer unexpectedly advances, causing her face to collide with his shin while her arms grapple at empty air behind him.

Macer brings the butt of the churka down hard next to her. There's a painful crunching sound followed by Ish wailing and covering his face and reeling on the platform base on his side.

"That's enough of that!" Macer shouts.

There's the noise of a gunshot as bright skip flash floods her vision, and then everything goes dark.

FIVE

WAVES OF STATIC ELECTRICITY TINGLE over Luci's soaked and shivering body. This sensation, along with the pulsating rings of light rippling down the length of the barge, indicate that they've left Italy 2068 far behind. As if someone pressed the mute button on a raucous television show, the noise from the courtyard instantly ceases. Painful moans from Ish combined with Luci's and Macer's belabored breathing mix with the sounds of water dripping from them onto the metal deck.

"Those imbeciles!" Macer moans. "Those damned imbeciles shot me!"

A shaky flashlight beam reveals the blood-soaked cuff of Macer's trousers.

Luci thrusts her arms out to grab him a second time until the barrel of his churka burrows into her shoulder like a dull spear. "Sit back down," Macer orders, shifting the light from his wound into her eyes.

She squints as the light piercingly connects with her pupils. "Let me look at it," she says, regretting being so aggressive. "I can help."

He thrusts the end of the churka harder, causing Luci to stumble back into a seated position against the barge's control panel podium. "Not a chance in Hell," Macer says, sounding amused by the attempt. "The shot only grazed me. Anyway, I've had enough of your *help* for one day." The humor leaves his voice. "You destroyed a magnificent specimen of art."

A mild weightlessness descends over the skip vessel.

"You broke my nose with the end of that churka," Ish says, his voice sounding off.

"I should have broken your jaw so you couldn't speak," Macer responds with a growl. "That was a stupid, stupid thing to try," he scolds, shining the unsteady light back onto Luci. "I don't know what you intended to prove by coming to Florence, but you're going to wish that you had taken a leap skip somewhere else instead of interfering with my plans."

He's right. She already wishes they were anywhere but here. Her compulsion for absoluteness brought her and Ish to this moment. Something inside her had to be certain this man was the "Macer Prime" as Gicul said. In retrospect, they could have done a leap skip away after Ish destroyed Macer's barge and not even seen him. He would've been trapped there just as well as if they'd strapped him into the ESTA and launched it into whatever past Gicul had set it to leap skip to. Now, they're the ones trapped, all because of her rigid need to know and ironically not believing her future self's accuracy about who this man is.

Macer says, nonplussed, "Your hair looks different. Some kind of poor attempt to disguise yourself?" The light moves around her features. "In fact, there's something entirely different about you."

"You'd be surprised at how different I am from what you know," she says through gritted teeth. Luci debates if she should reveal that she's not the version of her that he believes her to be. Her mind reels, thinking how she can use this information to their advantage with this lunatic. The concern is once this fact is revealed, Macer may use Ish as a bargaining piece for her to return to 2032. The only thing that's certain is Macer must have her return and present DPM according to history so as not to disrupt the Relicus City timeline.

Then, as if someone switched the channel of her mind to another station, she's no longer on the skip barge in the dark. She's back in Macer's home on that first night. The area is well lit, and he's sitting behind his desk nearly a week ago. Luci's listening to him ramble on when he has a seizure of some sort. At first, she thinks it's a heart attack or stroke, and then maybe an epileptic episode because of the way he's acting. It's just the two of them, since Royse stayed behind a little longer at the Grange. Luci shoots up from his guest chair to help, afraid for him and afraid for herself since the chancellor is her only way back to 2032.

Something is happening to her foot . . . her right foot. It's moving, but not by her. Her consciousness returns like a theater curtain going up on a play. Someone's kicking at her foot in the dark.

Macer shouts, "I said, what's wrong with you?"

"Nothing," she stammers, attempting to reorient herself to her surroundings in the here and now. She hears her own voice saying, "*So real.*"

"What's real?"

"Just a . . ." What did he call it back in his office? "Just a '*catching up*' . . . sort of like a seizure."

"Nice try, Doctor, but that wasn't a seizure," Macer scoffs. "I don't know what you thought that little stunt would do for you, but it didn't work."

Her understanding is returning. The memory of standing before the David statue in Macer's home is being overwritten by a new experience, since the sculpture will never arrive there now. So vivid is the incident in her mind that she finally understands what Gicul was saying about what she called the overlapping. Luci ponders the paradox of how she could have known to find Macer at Florence if she never saw the statue in his home to begin with, but a viable explanation escapes her.

The flashlight shines back on Ish. The hand covering the bottom of his face is streaked with trails of blood from his pinched nostrils. The narrow beam of light moves from his face to his sitting body. Macer taps the butt of the churka against the ESTA pod floating behind him a few times. "What is this clunky old thing?"

Both Ish and Luci remain silent.

"Tell me or I liquefy his insides right here and now," Macer threatens, moving the barrel of the churka in Ish's direction beside her.

"It's too risky," Ish says boldly. "You can't risk the blast going through me into the navigation computer. You know this. That's why you hit me with the butt of it instead of firing."

"We'll arrive at Carcerium soon enough, and I won't have that risk. Now, tell me," Macer orders through gritted teeth.

Luci considers if there may be a way to trick Macer into voluntarily strapping into the ESTA transport. "It's old-world tech, pre-*Hi no Kawa* stuff."

"Okay, but what does it do?"

Still pinching his nose to stop the bleeding, Ish says, "It's a leap skip transport that can travel to intervals off the preset skip nodes."

Luci is grateful that Ish is playing along. It's delicate, but they may be able to convince him to get into the ESTA pod's seat of his own will.

Macer's face is too obscured in the dark to gauge his expression. Finally, he says, "You both lie. That's impossible, and everyone knows it."

"It's true," Luci rebuts, being deliberately economical with her words in hopes of Macer taking their bait.

"If what you say were possible, you could go anywhere— leap skip to any place in history . . . or the future. In fact, the two of you could go anywhere in time, making yourselves nearly invincible. Why would you have ever wasted any effort on me if you truly could 'land' at any point in your personal timelines?" There's a haunting pause, then a sense of awe in his voice as he concludes, "To the rest of the world, it would appear that someone doing this never aged, like they lived forever. If such a thing were true, it'd be . . ." He drifts off into his dark contemplations.

Luci's skin crawls, remembering the holo vid image of him clad in red. She swallows, recalling the soundless video of him shouting from a podium to thousands of enslaved subjects below who believed him to be immortal. Is she responsible for that possible outcome? Is this where that profane idea was conceived in his heart?

He waives it off again. "No, what is it really for? Is it an explosive? Was the plan to strap me into the seat and launch me somewhere to make a political statement or something against the Directorate Council?"

They're losing ground and running out of time.

"It's not a bomb," Luci argues.

"Are you sure about that? Because I can imagine that you'd love to send a high official like me back to the Grange and detonate it on arrival. Doing something like that in the proper way could cut off the city's food source, and then you'd be able to wield power over the leaders and the people of Relicus City."

Luci is taken aback, the seed of Macer's extortion exposed. The evil was in his mind and heart from the beginning. How she loathes this perverse creature in utero, waiting to emerge from his rotting chrysalis to devour what's left of the future world. The depth of the hateful revulsion she has toward him is unsettling to her, and she's grateful that she can't see much of him up close in the darkness. "You are pure evil," she says to the silhouette before her.

This amuses him. "You have no idea of what I'm capable of, my dear doctor."

"You're wrong," Luci says in defiance. "I know *exactly* what you're capable of."

<u>SIX</u>

Nil
Carcerium Chamber
[0.0000000/0.0000000/0/0:00:00]

KARSꓤƐUM ₵ΔMBꓤ

— — — — — — —

As **the skip barge materializes** at Carcerium to the neon amber outlines of the doorways, Macer sarcastically announces, "Home again at last, Dr. Gaudiano."

She'd forgotten how the time distortion properties of Carcerium make voices sound eerily close to the listener. Macer limps a step but keeps the churka warily aimed at Ish. "Both of you stand up and move slowly away from the barge's control panel."

The sight of the churka pointed at Ish weighs Luci's on heart. He still wears the same red jumpsuit he wore when a squad of cybos marched him through the courtyard to erase his mind back in Relicus City. That would have been a more humane ending than what faces them both now in Carcerium.

A small amount of rainwater spills from the hood of Macer's bright orange slicker as he lowers it with his free hand. "Move! Now!" he commands, motioning with the churka.

"*This can't be how it ends,*" she thinks, trading a dejected look with Ish. They comply and reluctantly step off the skip transport onto the pristine white floor. Though the skip barge is only slightly longer than a truck trailer back home, it looks so much bigger to Luci in this confined blank space. It barely fits lengthwise in the white cube of the room and is off-center, closer to the wall on the left side of the vessel.

"You first, Technician Moyta," Macer says, motioning for the door opposite the barge. His shoe leaves behind a bloody footprint, a reminder of the gunshot that nicked the back of his calf back in 2068 a few minutes ago. "Dr. Gaudiano, you move to the corner there to give us some room." His bushy eyebrows raise as he sarcastically adds, "But don't worry, I'll get to you soon enough."

She moves in a stupor. The stagnant, odorless air seems more difficult to breathe than when she was here earlier today with Cavazos. That feels like a lifetime ago, and in a way, maybe it was. How long has she been awake? She reaches the spot and turns to face the men at the amber neon outline of a door that isn't there—yet. Macer's positioned Ish between himself and Luci a couple of meters away. After all she and Ish have been through, she can't believe it's to end like this. But there's only one churka, and Macer has it pointed in Ish's back. And unlike the ones from *L'inversione*, this churka isn't equipped with a stun modification from Yuma.

"Enter code 5-2-0-8-9," he tells Ish, again, his voice sounding like it's in her head.

Luci's stomach knots up. Her mind scrambles to find a way to prove that she's the Luci from 2032 and if he locks her in here, Relicus City will never exist because *Hi no Kawa* won't take place. Maybe that would be for the best, she thinks and then considers that it would mean the two of them trapped in separate chambers for all eternity. The memory of Gicul's madness flashes across her mind. Even she, on her least selfish day, cannot agree to this type of horror.

"Now, press the flashing orange button," Macer instructs.

Ish does, and a brief expression of awe covers his face as the neon glow is instantly replaced by an open doorway into the chamber.

Luci's heartbeat doubles. This is it. She has to do something. "Waleen, I need to tell—I need you to know that I'm not the Luci Gaudiano that you think—"

"What did you call me?" he cuts her off, peeking around Ish. "What did you say?"

The unexpected effect on him surprises Luci at first, but she quickly goes on the offensive. "You are Waleen Macer." She doesn't have a plan yet, but if exposing his ruse puts him off balance, she'll capitalize on this to buy some time for them.

"Why would you say that?" Macer demands. "Who told you that?"

She takes an unsteady step forward. "You're not Enos. You took his place and stole your son's identity in order to pose as him in the government and continue your plans."

He keeps the churka aimed at Ish but moves slightly to the side to address Luci. He nods slowly, pursing his lips, contemplating each word he's about to deliver as if taking time to weigh each syllable an inspect it.

"You know that I'm right," Luci says. "You're no more Enos Macer than I am. You're his father, Waleen."

His words finally come, but slowly as if the admission is something painful in his mouth. "The city needed continuity in order to . . ." He pauses, shaking his head. "In the early days of Relicus, to even call what we were a city back then is a misnomer. We were no more than a fragmented, distressed huddle, each of us scavenging for existence." There's a disgust in his words. He sniffs sharply through his large beak of a nose.

It's obvious to her that he's caught up in his own discourse, which means they may have an opportunity here to overpower him after all. *"Keep him talking, Luci G. Act interested and let him ramble to his heart's content."*

The volume of Macer's voice in her ears doesn't fluctuate due to the audio anomaly of Carcerium. "Sure, the ones that remained were descendants of those who had survived *Hi no Kawa*, but the collective mindset of the people was that of starving refugees, weak nothings." His face contorts into a scowl. "We were no different from the contaminated vermin that we were scrounging to eat, shambling from spent resources until even that food supply was exhausted."

Luci chances another slow step forward, this one more deliberate than the previous one. Her stare is fixed on the placement of the weapon aimed at Ish. She's got to get Macer to aim it away from him.

"Whatever perverse providence that delivered us, though, was more curse than blessing. It's difficult to comprehend the mocking burden of survival when it's easier to quit and die."

Macer strikes his chest with the fist of his free hand, startling Luci into shifting her eyes back to him. The intensity of his gaze sends a shiver rippling down her back. His voice is deliberate. "But I . . . I united us. I gave us an identity. When others were content to scrape by a day-to-day existence, I gave the people a hope for a tomorrow. I gave a reason to believe again. I imparted the vision—the vision that we could escape the spiral of squalor and ruin."

Luci begins to take another step but hesitates when Macer shifts his weight along with the angle of the churka against Ish's side. His delivery speeds up. "I alone held up the banner that we didn't have to devolve into warring tribes pitted against each other."

Another small step forward. Her heart pounds like it will explode. "But you can't deny that others helped you in the rebuilding."

Macer scoffs, "Yes, others assisted, but all under my direction. I transformed myself into a ruthless vessel of change, and through my force of will, various reconstruction councils were formed, each tasked with specific goals. I oversaw them *all*, every bit of it."

She risks a quick glimpse to Ish. He blinks wildly, signaling to her. She nods acknowledgement but is careful to make it appear as if she's responding to Macer's words.

"My mandate required anyone with scientific understanding to forsake everything. I made them stop anything I deemed non-essential activities until solutions were reached."

Ish mouths something that's unclear to her.

"I was the only one bold enough and courageous enough to separate workers from their families for months—even years—at a time until my goals were achieved, goals that built a heaven on Earth."

Luci does her best to inhale smoothly and steady herself in front of Macer. She's not certain what Ish has planned, so she's got to be ready for anything.

Macer speaks with unmistakable disdain. "No one else had the stomach to require such things. Their weakness, unchecked, threatened our continued existence."

Her heart races as Macer's voice tapers off. "I still don't understand," she says, hoping to jumpstart more of his egotistical twaddle while simultaneously signaling Ish her confusion.

"What's to understand?" Macer asks dismissively. "It was *my* goals, *my* vision that rebuilt humanity's final outpost. It was *me* alone to unflinchingly peer down the barrel of oblivion and bend the circumstance we faced to *my* will."

Again, she catches sight of the bloody cuff of his pants leg.

"It was my strength and my resolve that dug us out of the hole that the old world had buried us in. Anything that is good that exists in the world today is because of me. Everything of any worth is by my hand through the sacrifices that I relentlessly demanded of those around me. Who are you to disapprove?"

Luci looks into Ish's hazel eyes when Macer shifts his weight on his injured leg. She understands what Ish is mouthing—his lips repeat two words over and over: "Get ready." Luci raises and lowers her head so minutely that she wonders if Ish even recognizes it as a nod.

She responds to Macer's accolades as non-threateningly and softly as she can to keep the conversation going. "What Relicus City has become is certainly a marvel, but your methods sound very Machiavellian to me. You can't simply discard human dignity for—"

"Yes, I violated plenty of what you'd consider your old-world ethics, but ethics don't get the job done." His words are rapid fire now, his olive complexion turning a burning pink. "The wind does not request permission from the windmill to blow. You cannot comprehend the burden. You can never understand. In time, I was merely to speak, and things came to be. Can you even begin to grasp how that is? If I declare there's need for an additional power plant or refinement center, it becomes so from words alone—*my* words."

There's a sniffle, and it sounds like it's in Luci's ear. She focuses on Ish, who slowly slides his hands up as if he's massaging his broken and bloody nose.

"It was my ingenuity that led to the creation of the Grange, my idea to utilize your own drift pattern mathematics to save the human race by doing leap skips to back into the past where food can be grown."

She watches Ish while addressing Macer, "But you sterilize everyone in the process. Everyone who leap skips can't reproduce."

"Just one more measure that had to be taken. That was the tradeoff. We weren't aware of the sterilization side effect at first, but it wouldn't have mattered if we did. What good is it to be fertile if the children you bear starve to death before their first birthday? I regret nothing!"

Ish sniffs again, and Luci spots what he's subtly doing. On one side of his nose, he has five fingers extended, massaging his inner cheek. On the other side, he's using his index finger. He repeats the process three times: 666.

"*Hexakosioi deka hex*" she thinks. Luci understands that he knows the number's wrong. On the fifth day she was here, Ish informed her the number of the beast was really 616. She slowly nods her agreement to this signal to act, and Ish returns his hands to his side.

Any moment now.

Macer is oblivious to the exchange and seems to welcome someone to confess his prolicide. "As for changing places with

Enos, by that point, he was just one more sacrifice along the way. I was required to do what I did to him to preserve what had been built. I couldn't leave the work of the city half completed, left to naïve plebeians and circular bureaucrats, so I took advantage of the technology to leap skip and present myself as my son for the good of the city."

Luci shakes her head in genuine disgust. "Impersonating him to attain your goals is bad enough, but you admit to murdering him. It's the definition of evil."

Something incredible happens. Macer unconsciously pulls the churka from Ish to brandish it at her. "Your tired, outdated constructs of good and evil are a luxury that wasn't afforded to me back then and still isn't today. Right and wrong are ever-changing. They are, at best, fluid concepts, often standing in the way of progress, and in this case, life itself."

Luci's mind battles with her survival instinct: she must force Macer to keep the weapon trained on her for Ish to be able to act, but everything inside her screams to cower and turn away from the end of the gleaming barrel. She forces herself to stand, though her legs feel unsteady, and resolves to push Macer harder. It's their only option. "I can't believe you honestly feel—"

"At worst, those naïve preconceptions are poison in the bloodstream and most certainly would've extinguished the light that we were so protective of back then. Protective of then and now."

She takes in a deep breath, not knowing how close this maniac is to blasting her for her boldness. "Call it what you will, trying to justify yourself, but murdering your son is always wrong—in any time period, for any reason."

"You impertinent child! How dare you presume to know anything about that. I did him a favor! He contracted Fichtner's Disease from his dying mother and was doomed to a slow and agonizing death."

Ish gestures to the ground, causing Luci to gnaw her bottom lip. The timing has to be perfect or she'll die on the spot she's standing, and possibly Ish too.

"I watched my young wife die like she was being tortured every waking second. I wasn't willing to watch him go through all of that."

Luci prepares to dive to the floor as she extends an accusatory index finger. "I think you're a devil!"

"A devil, huh? The story is that God kills his son, and it becomes a religion. I do it to find a way to serve mankind, and you say I'm a . . . a devil and a monster."

She's confused that Ish didn't act when she blurted what she thought would be the code word: *devil*. Did she completely misunderstand his signal? Then she realizes his intention. Ish plans to somehow drag Macer into the Carcerium with him, to sacrifice himself for her to flee from here. Luci cannot explain how she knows this, but she does, and the idea prickles her heart. She does her best to regroup, forcing herself to scoff at Macer as if the barrel of the churka wasn't poised and ready to melt her insides. "You think you're a god?"

"I honestly see very little difference. Relicus City wouldn't exist in the state that it does without me forcing everything that has come before."

For the first time since they've arrived here, Luci hears the strangeness of Ish's voice in her head. "I love you, Luci." These four words break her heart.

"Ish, please," she implores, her mind racing to come up with an alternate plan that doesn't involve sacrificing himself.

"How quaint," Macer mocks with a sneer on his face, obviously unaware that something's about to happen.

She's trembling due to the flood of adrenaline surging through her body. "I love you too," she answers as tears swell in her eyes. She's forced to admit that there's only one way out of this, and she knows Ish understands and has resigned himself to this fact. She braces for what they must do.

He bows slightly to her. "Find a new and better path."

She nods. They lock eyes, and the next two seconds feel like lifetimes.

"You are no god, sir," Ish blurts out, though the volume of his voice remains constant. "You are the chancellor of devils!"

This is it!

Luci dives to the floor in time to witness Ish spin around and crouch to grab Macer's wounded leg.

He stumbles backward, and as he does, the room is lit with the unmistakable bright blue flash of the churka.

Luci is alone in the antechamber. The sounds of the men's scuffle fill her ears from the open Carcerium cell as if they're directly beside her. Unseen, Ish slams the man against the far wall of the inside chamber. "Seal us in, Luci! Seal the door!"

She leaps to her feet, rushes to the panel, and enters the number as before. The opening disappears, transforming into a wall with a neon-red pulsating glow outline of a door.

And then there is silence.

IN THE STILLNESS, LUCI TURNS her back to the wall and slowly slides down until she's sitting with her knees pressed against her chest. The glow of the neon red pulse through the churka haze keeps time with her heartbeat. She doesn't openly sob, but a small, prolonged whimper escapes from her throat. She crosses her arms, tightly pressing them against herself to forbid the sound. This is not the time for that, she scolds herself. She must figure out a way to free Ish and determine what to do with Macer.

She peers through the noxious haze at the skip barge. She turns away at the sight of the wrought-iron fence pickets poking through the front of the craft, another reminder of a serious miscalculation she's made.

Countless possibilities as to what could be happening in the sealed-off chamber behind her fill her mind. Has Ish successfully overpowered Macer and now holds him at gunpoint within the compartment? Or did he finally fulfil his wish to kill him for the future atrocities that Macer would commit?

She must consider another viable outcome, that Macer has regained control and holds the weapon on Ish. Logically, she must admit that Macer, in his frustration, may have fired upon him and Ish could be dead.

Is Macer dead? Is Ish alive? Have they reached some stand-off? It's a real-life Schrödinger's cat situation.

Another question is whether the chamber reset would restore and bring back someone slain in there. If so, would whoever wields the weapon be forced to fire upon the other every 17 minutes for all eternity? The gruesome thought of either of them repeatedly dying an excruciating death by churka blast reminds her of Zeus's punishment of Prometheus, only in that mythology, the titan was helplessly chained to a rock and had his liver eaten by an eagle only once a day. She does the math—the event here could potentially happen eighty-four times a day, nearly every quarter hour. She must reluctantly concede that Ish could live through an agonizing death millions of times at the hands of Macer, and it's her fault. They should have just left him in Florence.

She's considering all of these things as the churka blast cloud dissipates enough to see where Macer's stray shot connected.

Screaming, "No!" she runs to the destroyed control panel of the skip barge. The unrealistic fantasy that it's only cosmetic damage to the outer casing is short lived. Her examination reveals a smoldering softball-sized hole through the chronal relay board.

She's trapped here—trapped outside of time.

Luci kicks the base of the control panel in frustration and is forced to move backward when part of it folds in and collapses on itself with an odd noise. Recalling the explosion back at the *L'inversione* repair shop hideout, she thinks, *"At least Macer's shot didn't hit the skip thrust cabinet at the back of this thing."* She sighs. *"Although it doesn't matter."*

She sits with her legs over the side of the lip of the barge, burying her head in her hands. Not only is she stranded here, but she doesn't get the benefit of the seventeen-minute reset function that the Carcerium chambers have, meaning that she'll starve here and die alone. Of course, she could release Ish and Macer, but even if she does, all three are trapped here. The equation of death is always like multiplying by zero.

She looks over to the ESTA's single seat, wondering where her future self programmed it to skip to in the past, not that it matters. Ish has the ESTA control module with him in the Carcerium chamber. Without that controller, she can't activate the pod anyway. Glancing back to the side with the wrought-iron pickets from Florence, she determines it's too risky to set it for a random skip even if they *could* launch it.

Luci approaches the neon amber doorway outline nearest the front of the barge. She enters the code, and the opening appears instantly. Maybe it's the idea of having control over something no matter how innocuous, but a tiny spark of satisfaction ignites within her to open it.

She wanders to the other two doorways and repeats the process. It makes the area feel larger, if only by a little bit. She sighs, contemplating a new enigma: if she never makes it home to her time in 2032 to publish her drift pattern theorem years later, then how can she be abducted when she's older by Waleen-Enos Macer later?

It's all too much. The only thing that's certain is she's stuck here and Ish and Macer are locked away behind that flashing crimson glow.

She begins pacing and launches into self-soothing to reach her "special" number of 2012 but stops short. *"What's the point?"* she wonders, disgusted with her childish game.

She faces the blinking red outline.

She allows the rhythmic pulse to hypnotize her for a few seconds and then takes a step. She moves as cautiously as one would approach a bear trap buried below the snow. Forcing her hand to extend to the wall panel, she braces herself. How quickly will she be able to reactivate and seal the doorway if there's trouble? Luci pantomimes the 52089 code in the air centimeters from the panel a few times to ensure the dexterity of her shaking fingers.

She inhales a deep breath to steady herself and depresses the "5" square on the pad, then, somewhat easier, "20" followed by a shaky "8."

Something dawns on her for what she's about to do, a horrific dilemma. If she deactivates the chamber by opening it and Macer was to blast Ish with the churka, his body wouldn't restore in seventeen minutes, because the room wouldn't reset, leaving Ish to die in a similar gruesome fashion as Royse, Gicul, Malom, Ley, and the last member of *L'inversione*, Banu back at the repair shop. She swallows and wipes a bead of sweat from her lip. Her hand falls to her side. Luci pulls back from the panel, unable to enter the final digit.

In this instant, she realizes that she will never see the face of Ish Moyta again and bites her lip hard.

She returns to sitting with her back against the non-doorway.

LUCI'S UNCERTAIN AS TO HOW long she sulks in that posture, but it's long enough for both of her crossed legs to go numb. She braces against the wall to stand, shaking first the left leg and then the right, allowing the blood to circulate again. As she moves, she catches a gleam off the ESTA transport hovering on the back of the skip barge. Ignoring the strangeness of her own voice, she says bitterly, "Cyphor Gicul's greatest achievement and discovery." She shakes her head. "A discovery that the world will never know about."

Luci fights back tears. Gicul's plan to trap her in Antarctica for her to live out her days was a more humane conclusion than what she's ended up with here. She moves to the transport's seat. Luci bumps it as she goes to sit down, causing the floating ESTA to move slightly back away from her. She plops down in it harder than she meant to, causing it to sway gently until the transport levels off.

Staring into the open doorway of the closest open Carcerium chamber, Luci recalls Cavazos's admonition from when she was here before. He mocked her ignorance when she asked about the possibility of *L'inversione* rescuing Malom Roderick via a longchair skip into his chamber. She recalls the terms he said then. "*SD phase values, receding gain loops, and the temporal feedback cycle.*" In the conversation, she simplified it to be impossible to place a time-traveling mechanism in an area that time resets.

The morbid daydream solidifies into a plan of action, and Luci leaps from the seat. With all her strength, she presses against the ESTA. It responds, as before, with a gentle sway like a pendulum. Luci grunts while forcibly rocking the inverted-pinecone-shaped transport back and forth. It was easier to move it onto the barge platform when it was her and Ish.

There's no way to be certain if Cavazos's assertion was accurate about placing a chronal displacement engine in a Carcerium chamber, but it's the only feasible option that she can stomach. She appeases herself that if all goes as expected, the area and compartments will implode on themselves, thereby correcting this time anomaly and removing Carcerium altogether. She and Ish will be sacrificed, if he's not dead already, but the act will guarantee one thing: none of Macer's shadow versions will have a pathway to rescue the chancellor and start this cycle all over again. She can accept that it's her fate to die here in exchange for that guarantee. In fact, it feels like a noble death in some way.

As for Ish, she knows that he knew the sacrifice he was making when he called out to her to seal him in with Macer. The last thing he said to her before his assault of the man was for her to "*find a new and better path.*" He said these words—this plea—even after telling her that he loved her for one last time.

He knew *exactly* what he was saying and what he was about to do.

Though it's tight, she's grateful that the ESTA floats through the doorway without needing to be disassembled. She knows herself well enough to admit that in the time it would take to remove any of the metal "shingles" of the ESTA pod, she'd likely lose her nerve to perform such a suicidal stunt.

With a final herculean shove, Luci forces the ESTA far enough into the chamber to do the deed. She moves back through the doorway, transfixed on the ESTA hovering before her. She regards it floating in the Carcerium cell before her as one may consider some abstract piece of modern art. Luci shares some strange solidarity with the inanimate mechanism. It's like looking into the gaping mouth of a volcano, aware of the inevitable conclusion before erupts. There's apprehensiveness but not fear.

Two contradictory emotions flow through her. On one hand, the ESTA represents death, and every instinct in Luci rages inside her, demanding she push the thing back out into the foyer to postpone her end. At the same time, she experiences the peaceful resolve of knowing that when this thing terminates her life here, *Hi no Kawa* will cease to be along with the future threat of any version of Relicus the Great. A soft smile of acknowledgement graces her mouth. Billions— maybe even more than trillions—one day will have a chance of a life beyond the bleak future of what she's witnessed in the Relicus City interval. "*Today is the birthday of the world,*" she thinks, wiping her eyes. "*A new and better path.*"

The metal ESTA is not a bomb. It's a seed, a hope of life. And a seed must die and be buried in the ground in order to bloom in the spring. She accepts her role in this transformative process for a hope for something better.

Her finger grazes against the surface of the keypad. As she presses the code in for the final time, she says, "I love you, Ish Moyta." Though she knows that he can't hear her voice, it comforts her to say the words. "I hope that we may join again somewhere on the other side of what was this life."

She completes the sequence, and the flashing red glow replaces the opening. Luci closes her eyes to welcome oblivion.

After a prolonged moment of expectation, she reopens her eyes. "Well, shit."

As she reaches to re-enter the code and examine the contents of the chamber on the other side, there's a tiny buzzing in her ear. At first, she thinks it's a fly. She quickly dismisses the idea, realizing that no insects could exist in this environment. The buzz shifts into a low hum. Luci turns to face the barge behind her. The sound isn't coming from there though. She glances at the chamber holding Ish and Macer. Not from there either.

The hum grows louder.

It's not external. It's not heard by her ears at all. It's something from within. A growing vibration accompanies the sound.

Luci steps back from the chamber housing the ESTA. As illogical as it is, a part of her wants to stop what's about to happen. A selfish part of her resists the idea that she has to die in here outside of time. She suppresses the urge, recognizing it as primal programming to survive.

Though there's no pain, her cells buzz with energy. It's not electrical though. It lies beyond sensory quantification. A great pressure descends as if she's deep on an ocean floor, but Luci's more intrigued than fearful. She touches her face, but neither cheek nor fingers register the feeling, only the growing strength of the vibrations.

The sound of male voices fills her head with the auditory anomaly again, but the words aren't clear. Her heart leaps to "hear" Ish. She turns to face the chamber on the side, but it remains sealed. Though she's able to grab snippets, coherent meaning can't be formed, because the phrases spoken are backward. It's disorienting to hear her own voice running back.

She realizes the previous conversation in here is being played back in reverse order, and her body feels fused to the floor. She doesn't recall falling, but she can only see the barge and flashing red doorway behind it out of the corner of her eye.

Macer's backward speech continues in her ears. Luci wonders what will occur when the area reaches the beginning of their conversation. The scientist part of her experiments by attempting to shout. Nothing comes out, only the growing "sound" of the hum and overlapping backward voices.

It's difficult to determine if she's stuck against the floor or ceiling now, and there's an odd juxtaposition, a sense of motion while feeling completely still. Is she falling or are things rushing past her?

As if to answer this, her perspective changes. She sees herself like gazing down at the ground at a photographic negative on the white floor. Her view pulls away from the square with ever-increasing speed, rising higher and higher until the picture is a mere speck that blinks out of vision. The sensation of rocketing upward through the confines of the chamber continue faster and faster. The trillions upon trillions of subatomic particles that joined together in the construction of Luci Ann Gaudiano climb higher, accelerating through bands of ultraviolet radiation and magnetic fields. The ascension, unhindered by any friction, spans an unfathomable distance across the universe.

At its apex, the particles that link Luci's corporeal form together simultaneously lose their grip, bursting in all directions. The eruption isn't violent, but the beautiful plumage of light is so bright and without variation of any kind, it's as if darkness or shadow are only a forgotten myth. For the briefest picosecond, the intellectual awareness of Luci Ann Gaudiano blends into her consciousness, and she comprehends mathematics—all of it.

As if every arithmetical concept fuses together to form a single entity, this essence leans in to kiss her forehead as if she were a newborn child.

And then it's over.

SEVEN

UNSPESIF±D INTƎRVAL MOKƎR DΛNJƎR
10417 NON-KRONAL MXN EVINT

BLUE—LIGHT BLUE, TO BE PRECISE—IS all that Luci sees before her. Noting the air is easier to breathe, she moves a hand in front of her face to confirm that her eyes are actually open. A small speck enters the left side of her frame of vision. The slow-moving dot carves a tiny white scar into the endless light blue as it continues along in a straight horizontal line. The dot moves along its steady path as the end of the white line from its farthest point slowly expands, tripling in size like a soft trail of plumage—a contrail?

Luci's mind is still reeling, but the distant rumble of jet engines confirms Luci's suspicion that the speck is some type of aircraft far above in the sky. Relicus City's air transports are noiseless drobine carriers, so where is she? When is she?

As her awareness comes more into focus, Luci looks away from the puffy zipper of white forming in the heavens. She turns her head sluggishly to the left to see that she's lying on grass. At first, she reasons that she must be in a field as a soft warm breeze tickle tiny hairs on her arms and face, but when she squints, seemingly endless rows of evenly spaced horizontal beams come into focus. She sits up to see bleachers from the base of a stadium—a football stadium. The design of the aluminum bleachers hint at sometime between late in the twenti-eth century and obviously before the events of *Hi no Kawa*, but when and where exactly?

The only explanation that tracks is that she's arrived at the non-interval destination that Gicul programed the ESTA to leap skip to. While it's fascinating to consider how the device managed to win a quantum tug-of-war with the Carcerium chamber she sealed it in, she'll have to postpone her thoughts and theories. Right now, the more pressing issue is the date and continent she's been slingshotted to and why.

Her attempt to stand up is met with instant wooziness, but she manages to perform a full 360-degree scan of the arena. There's no one else here, and it makes sense that Gicul would have programed the ESTA pod to arrive somewhere discreet. The sight of the nearby goalpost and her proximity to it places her at or near the ten-yard line. An equally puzzling sight is the skip barge, intact and unmarred other than Macer's churka blast through the control lectern. Luci marvels at it, noting its exact distance to her as it was back at the chamber. There's no sign of the ESTA, and she swallows a lump, not seeing any trace of Ish or Macer. She shouts Ish's name, and her voice reverberates off the stands back at her as if it's mocking that he's not here.

Luci needs answers not found in a football end zone. The delayed roar of the jet reaches its full strength and decrescendos. It's a relief to see that the ads around the scoreboard are in English. This means she's in a western country somewhere. It's also a bonus to not have to work out UNIFON writing characters for a change.

There's an ad sponsorship by Aydelotte Automotive Repair, but the graphic next to it takes her breath away. She blinks multiple times in astonishment at the nostalgic logo of a fierce cartoon insect with a sharpened stinger. Luci drops to her knees into the soft grass. Through the fingers covering her mouth, she whispers, "Meadow Lake Yellow Jackets."

Luci looks down at a patch of ground, attempting to process this discovery. She turns back to the image of the mascot, partially afraid that it won't be there, that it was some mirage or hallucination, but the logo remains. "Sweet Jesus in Heaven, I'm back." She rises to her feet and walks toward the scoreboard in awe.

"This is Whitfield Stadium. I'm back home and within a few decades of when I left!"

It's almost more than she can bear. Tears of joy stream down her cheeks. The question of which year she's arrived in still nags at her. *L'inversione's* original plan of preventing DPM was to stop her from publishing her findings by any means necessary. Does this mean there's another version of her running around out there somewhere? Is the older version of Luci Gaudiano working at this exact moment on the brink of publishing her findings?

Luci races off the field under the bleachers past the boarded-up concession stand counter. As she runs by, her eye catches something that forces her to stop and turn around for a closer look. Signage on the left and right of the closed snack bar proclaim the Yellow Jackets 2009 and 2011 as District Champions.

Luci has to steady herself, recognizing all of this from her youth. While she never was given the chance to attend high school here because of the family's accident, her junior high played mid-week games here during football season. She attended as many games as she could with her friend, Christine Dade.

The temperature feels like summer. She scales the cyclone fence to leave the stadium, noting the empty parking lot on the other side. Even on weekends during the school year, there would be a sprinkling of cars in the lot for Saturday detention or whatever.

She wipes a tear at the sight of her old middle school across the street, but she doesn't slow her running. The expansive one-story brown brick of her old junior high looks glorious, given this is additional proof of where the ESTA pod's blast delivered her.

As she approaches, an aspect of the campus clues Luci in on the "*when*" question. The LCD lights of the marquee state, "*Welcome Back Students: School starts Tuesday, Sept 4th.*"

Starting with the year she was abducted by Macer in 2032, Luci does the math while sprinting. In short breaths, she calculates aloud, "September the 4th will be on a Saturday, and it's a leap year." Her movements dissolve into a distracted trot, but she doesn't slow. "Tuesday, September the 4th occurred in 2029." Luci scoffs, "Surely the Yellow Jackets would have won something from 2011 in over a decade and a half!" She's panting now, barely running at all as she's nearly to the sign. "Another occurrence of Tuesday, September 4th is in 2018 and again in 2013."

She reaches it and touches the brick of the chest-high marquee. The stone is surprisingly cool relative to the warmth of the day. "Wait, no, that's not right," she corrects. "There was a leap year in 2012 too, meaning . . ."

She jerks away from the sign as if a hot burner on a stove. "*I'm back in 2012? Can that be right?*"

Luci spins around at the noise of an automobile entering the adjoining service road.

Though her leg muscles are beyond fatigued, she makes a desperate dash for the oncoming vehicle. That it's not a self-driving car supports her idea she's been transported back to the days of her childhood.

She knows the year and the season, but she has to know the day. "*Can it be that day?*" she wonders, running directly at the oncoming motorist. She has to make him stop. She has to know if her family's accident has happened yet.

The driver is caught off guard by Luci jumping into the lane before him. Her plan for stopping the driver doesn't work. He pounds the horn while swerving to miss her. Through the open window, he yells profanities and offers accompanying gestures as he barrels past.

It's not a total loss though. He came close enough for her to see the car's inspection sticker's renewal date: *October 2012.*

With the year confirmed, Luci reverts to a brisk walk along the concrete bike path, scanning for the approach of another vehicle. She concocts a safer strategy: she'll stand on the side and yell for help next time.

As she hurries, Luci attempts to wrap her mind around why Gicul would have set the controls of the ESTA to leap skip to an empty football stadium in their past. As the winding sidewalk turns sharply, revealing the tops of five- and six-story buildings through the trees, she has her answer. It's the hospital she was taken to after the accidental drowning of her mother and father. It's the one place in time that Gicul knows with certainty that younger Luci will arrive.

Looking at the tops of the hospital peeking through the trees, she concludes, *"You were going to kill us . . . end us both to prevent Hi no Kawa."* The acknowledgement is a gut punch to her, forcing a brief stop. An ant mound in the ditch catches her eye. The worker insects busily move about, scaling up and down in rows. Luci gives her weary legs a rest and crouches for better inspection. *"Gicul knew we'd be held at the hospital for observation for hours, an easy target for L'inversione or herself to smother the twelve-year-old us with a pillow or do something worse."* She returns to her feet, but her eyes stay on the colony's work in the mud. *"But what altered that plan? What made you switch?"*

"Ish Moyta happened is what. I . . . you . . . we fell in love and abandoned the idea of suicide because you had something to live for. Everything shifted from then—for him." She sniffs, tears welling in her eyes. *"Now he's gone too."* Luci inhales a shaky breath. "All of it is gone."

A faint buzzing sound grows louder. She turns to see someone motoring up the path. "Hey!" she yells at the approaching boy while waving her arms. "I need your help!" His ride is too small for a motorcycle. She guesses it to be a moped of some sort. The high-pitched whine sounds like a swarm of angry bees approaching.

The rider comes closer into view, clearly a pre-teen. He's decked out in baseball gear. The end of a maroon bat extending from the kid's backpack gleams like Excalibur.

"Hey, I need your help," Luci repeats, flapping her arms even harder.

When the kid doesn't slow, she positions herself with her legs and arms spread wide to block the narrow concrete path. Judging from the spotless condition of the scooter, she suspects that he won't risk taking it down into the muddy ditch.

He makes an overly dramatic side skid to avoid a direct collision with her, nearly tipping it over.

Luci ignores the theatrics, demanding, "What day is today?"

He eyes her with disgust. "I don't know. It's a Thursday, alright?"

Luci steps forward, clamping onto the scooter's handlebars. "How do you not know the day of the month?" she asks incredulously. "Okay, you said it's Thursday. Is it August 2nd, the 9th, 16th, or 23rd?"

He yanks the Vespa back to free it from her grip, but it only budges a little. He's clearly no match for her strength. "Let go, you homeless freak," he squeals nervously, looking around for help.

The insult is confusing until Luci realizes that her hair is still mussed from the Florence rain hours ago. At least she'd changed out of the bloody blouse back at Gicul's in Antarctica or the kid would be calling the cops. "Look, I just need to know the date. Do you have a cell phone?"

"Of course I do, but I'm not giving it to you, you crazy bitch," he says with a grimace like he's sipped a cup of sour milk.

She's had about enough of this punk. Luci lifts the end of the scooter up enough to slam it back to the ground to emphasize her point. "I don't have time for this, you little brat!"

In another overly dramatic demonstration, the kid allows himself to fall to the ground, and the Vespa follows, resting on its side. "My stepdad is going to sue you for that, and he always wins."

She wants to remind this little shrimp that if she were really homeless like he said, there wouldn't be anything to sue for. Instead, she acquiesces, "Look, I'm sorry. I just need to know some things." She reaches for him, asking, "May I have a look at your phone? It'll have the date and time. I won't even make a call. I just want to see it."

He crab walks backward away from her, his eyes wide with fear. "I don't have any money, okay? Just stay back! Stay away from me!"

Luci's fatigued body is a reminder of how long it's been since she last slept. She finds herself wondering if in real-time it's been twenty-four hours or more. Every muscle aches, and this kid's yelling is an assault to her senses.

He's made it to his feet and swings the aluminum bat with wide, defensive strokes like a broadsword.

"Come on, kid," she says, careful to avoid his exaggerated swings. "I just wanted to—"

"Stay back!" he shouts, moving away through the ditch.

Luci's surprised when the boy hurls the bat at her like a projectile. As tired as she is, Luci manages to leap out of its path. The aluminum bat strikes the sidewalk with a high-pitched gonglike tone.

The kid holds up the cell phone. "I'm calling 911, you homeless bitch." He places it to his ear, still shouting at her. "They're going to lock you up. I'm gonna tell 'em you grabbed my crotch, and they'll put you away."

She judges the distance between them, wondering how quickly he can run if she tries to snatch the phone. She notes that she'll have to leap over the downed yellow Vespa for any chance of catching the boy. Then an idea comes to her, but is this kid really so dramatic?

Luci coolly walks around the scooter in the direction of the boy. For every step she takes, he takes three or four. Whether real or not, he begins to report into the phone how he was attacked. She pursues a few more steps, forcing his exaggerated retreat from her. When he's an adequate distance, she turns and runs back to the banana-colored scooter.

She hoists it up and straightens the handlebars. If she were told a week ago that she be stealing a moped from a kid, she'd never believe it, but this is better than traveling on foot, and she's got to get some answers.

It's been decades since she's ridden a scooter like this, and the movement is jerky and awkward at first as she struggles with how much throttle and brake to give.

Eventually, this levels out as Luci gets her equilibrium. The Vespa's dial indicates 30 MPH as she opens up the top speed on the concrete path. She only slows to turn off the winding sidewalk to a busier street. The hospital complex is in full view on the other side of the overpass in the distance. The number 413 flashes, unsolicited, across her mind—unlucky number 413. It's the number of the hospital room where her worst fears were confirmed. She can still recall the room's unnatural smell of antiseptic. She still remembers that hag, Schofield, the wrinkled social worker with the weird teeth and bad shoes who flippantly informed her that her parents had died. The woman had callously informed her that *everything happens for a reason,* to which young Luci responded with, "Shove your reason!"

There's a bustling Starbuck's coffee shop on the corner at the base of the overpass. The aroma of coffee on the air is heavenly, even from this distance. It's only been a week since she's had coffee, but her emotional response to the smell resonates to her core—she really *is* back home! Next to the shop is a small branch office of a bank. The bank has an LCD sign that alternates flashing the temperature, time, and date.

Luci stops the scooter for a closer look. She gawks at the display in disbelief.

89°F - 2:38 P.M. - August 9th

The revelation paralyzes her, forcing her to watch the display cycle through a few times. Luci sobs uncontrollably.

"They're alive!" she says, nearly afraid to speak for fear of breaking this moment as if it were a delicate thing that could shatter unexpectedly by the weight of her words. *"I can't believe it. They're alive and we're on our way to the . . ."*

The celebration is interrupted by another revelation. *"I can stop it! I can stop the wreck!"*

Luci revs the scooter, jetting at top speed to the coffee shop with a plan. Not only can she prevent *Hi no Kawa*, but she can erase decades of personal pain in the process. How this change will overlap her current self is something to be determined later. For the moment, the only thing that she can think of is delaying her father from driving the three of them across the bridge over the lake.

She bursts into the shop. The scent of coffee is as heavy as a churka blast cloud. "If I may have your attention, please," she announces. "I need to borrow a cell phone!"

There's easily ten people in the shop not counting four aproned baristas behind the counter. Every set of eyes burrows into her, and all activity stops as if Luci has pressed a pause button on the scene.

"I need a phone, now!" she pleads. "It's a matter of life and death!"

Some of the patrons in line turn their backs on her dismissively as if her temporary spell on them was broken.

"There's going to be an accident!" Luci shouts. She realizes the lunacy of trying to explain how she could possibly know in advance that a car is going to be knocked over the guardrail into the lake and modifies her statement. "There's an accident! Please, help me."

A sharply dressed, middle-aged black man tucks a copy of Forbes magazine under his arm as he stands from his table. "Here," he says, unlocking the phone code with his thumb. "Do you want 911?"

"Thank you," Luci says. "No, I need to call . . . call my father and warn, I mean *tell* him." The sentence feels so strange and foreign to her ears: *my father.*

"Take all the time you need." His baritone voice is soothing as he guides her into the seat he occupied.

The shop returns to a normal level of bustling with the added sounds of patrons murmuring about Luci's melodramatic interruption. She doesn't care what they think. She's been granted the impossible, the chance to fix the worst day of her life. There's a pang in her heart as the conversation with Ish on the skip barge headed to Florence pops into her mind. He said how she had the opportunity to change the outcome of the future. She sniffs, thinking he could have never imagined something like this.

To anyone else, it would be a challenge to recall a cell phone number that they haven't dialed in over twenty years, but numbers are Luci's life. Her thumb shakes as she enters the ten digits on the screen.

The sound of her father's voice on the recorded message is so startling that Luci accidentally tips over the black man's coffee onto the floor. "I'm so, so sorry," she says, scurrying to snatch the cup with her free hand before all of the contents spill out, but it's too late. She's in a puddle of the stuff, but his phone remains tightly pressed against her ear. The warmth of wasted coffee soaks through the knees of her pants as she awkwardly offers the man the cup and plastic lid. "I don't have any money to—"

The phone message beeps, indicating it's recording, but where does she begin? Luci panics and presses disconnect. As she goes to stand, she bumps her head on the table. The impact knocks the phone from her grip into the spreading coffee puddle. "Shit!" she says, snatching it back and frantically wiping it off on her blouse as if there was any way the man hadn't noticed. "I'm sorry, I need . . . I need another minute, please."

The man's expression is not as compassionate as before. He reaches for his phone.

"Please, sir, just one more call. I'm sorry about the mess."

He grimaces and shifts the magazine to his other hand as he rights the chair Luci knocked over. "I'll order another latte, but then I'll need it back."

Luci nods ardently. "Yes, of course." She feels the shop's eyes on her again. "I'm so sorry."

The man sits her in the seat for a second time, but his agitation is clear as he heads to the counter with the empty cup.

Luci stares at the "call ended" display and has a horrifying thought. Did her father not answer because the accident has already happened?

With tears streaming over her cheeks, she mashes the return button until the phone clock displays *August 9th*, 2012 - 2:42 *P.M.*

Luci releases a sharp sigh. "There's still time!" she announces aloud to herself, increasing the volume of the murmur rippling through the room.

She anxiously redials her father's number. "*The police report placed the accident between 2:55-3:00 based on the phone video footage by witnesses on the scene.*" She stops the number short and looks up at the fan circulating overhead. "*He's not answering because he's driving! The three of us are headed to volunteer at the animal shelter across the lake.*" She returns her eyes to the screen of the phone and inputs another number. It takes forever for it to dial. The sick irony of her father not answering his phone to be safe while driving by isn't lost on her.

"Hello?" the female voice on the other end of the line answers.

"Uh . . . hello . . ." Luci sputters.

A pimply-faced worker with a mop approaches, gesturing to the mess on the floor. "Miss?"

Luci rises from the chair to give him room. Her heart pounds as she attempts to compose herself. "Mama, I know this is going to sound weird, but—"

"Mama? I'm sorry, lady, but you have the wrong number. I'm—"

"Wait!" Luci panics. "You've gotta listen to me. You're going to be in an accident. You have to believe me. I'm your . . ."

As she pauses to find the words that don't sound crazy, she hears the muffled sound of her mother speaking to her father. "I don't know, some crank caller or phone spam thing."

The teenager with the mop interrupts, "Miss, the table . . . I need to move the—"

"No, wait . . . listen, please!" Luci screams. The mop handle strikes the floor as the worker abandons it and the Rubbermaid bucket for the safety of the counter.

The woman's voice on the other end is perturbed. "Who is this?"

The strength in Luci's legs drain at the sound of her mother alive at the other end of the line. She braces herself by clutching the back of the chair. "Mrs. Gaudiano, I need to speak with you. Please don't hang up—"

There's a pause when she hears her last name, but she resumes more irritated than before, "How do you have my name? How'd you get this number?"

Luci desperately attempts to construct a reasonable explanation for why her mother on the other end of the line should listen, but the truth is too absurd, and a good lie escapes her.

After an awkward moment, Mrs. Gaudiano says, "Look, I don't know what scam you're selling or who you are, but I certainly am not your mother. If this is spam, I demand that you take me off your call list. I'm so sick of people like you bothering us all the time. You can stop calling anyway because I'm blocking this number. Goodbye."

"This can't be happening." Luci looks at the disconnect screen in horror. She looks around at the faces staring back at her. It's a showcase variety of distasteful expressions of judgement. "I need to borrow another phone." Some of the patrons head for the door, avoiding eye contact.

"Please, can someone just give me their phone? She's going to block this one's number." Her voice is breaking as she pleads while turning a slow semi-circle for any takers. "Please, I need a phone." She knows how the scene must look and forces out a fake chuckle, explaining, "Look, I know this all seems odd, but I'm not crazy. I promise—not crazy."

A stocky, solid-looking guy with a face of thick stubble and Armenian features cautiously approaches. He pulls meaty hands from the pockets of his apron and says in a low but firm voice, "Miss, if you're not making a purchase, I'm afraid that I'm going to need you to leave."

"I . . . just need to make a call," Luci says, sobbing.

The man pauses and surveys the shop. "I'm sorry. You've made your calls." He puts a comforting hand on her shoulder.

Luci recoils from the weight of it and pulls back. "Don't touch me."

He lowers his hands. "You're disrupting the peace in here."

"Damn your peace. My mother and father are about to die!"

Customers scoot away warily as Luci moves backward toward them. The manager closes the gap between them. "Miss, please . . . the gentleman's phone."

She forgot she had it. Luci presses the clock display: 2:46 P.M.

"Miss, please, I don't want to call the police," he says, extending his hand with an open palm.

The device is useless to her now anyway. She tosses it to him as she continues stepping backward from his uncomfortable advance. She addresses the crowd in a loud voice, "Can anyone give me a ride to the bridge over the lake, please?" She motions over her shoulder as she steps. "I saw a pickup truck in the lot out there. I can ride in the back if you're worried about . . ." She scans the room for the customer most likely to haul stuff in a truck to address them directly, but no one fits the profile. "I'm not crazy," she repeats while knowing this is exactly what an insane person would claim.

The manager continues to methodically close in on her space as if he's rustling a boa constrictor.

"Please, I just need a ride to—"

The front door behind her opens with a chime. Luci spins around to see the butch female barista who was behind the counter serving when she first came in. In the time it takes her to realize that the tall woman must've snuck out the back to loop around, the manager lunges and shoves Luci backward.

As she staggers out of the shop, the female server dashes by and pulls the door to her.

Luci finally gains her balance only to hear the sound of the door lock clicking. The coffee shop's windows fill with curious and relieved faces staring out at her. The sound of applause erupts. It takes a moment for her to realize the celebration inside is of how the quick-thinking efforts of the manager and barista thwarted the potentially deadly actions of a raging lunatic.

Luci resists beating on the windows and trying to explain herself—she's running out of time. If her memory serves, the bridge is about two to three miles from the hospital on the other side of the overpass. She glances at the bright yellow scooter leaned against the wall. Maybe there's enough time for her to make it there. It's the only option she's got.

She gets on and rides.

EIGHT

MERCILESS STREAMS OF SWEAT STING Luci's eyes, but she can't pause to wipe them. She zigs and zags in and out of the rolling line of vehicles to the sound of the occasional horn of annoyed motorists. A few near misses of a chrome bumper against the back tire of the scooter make Luci's heart leap to her throat. She doesn't slow, but she chides herself to be more vigilant in choosing when to dart and weave. It won't do any good to snag the Vespa on a fender and be forced to go on foot—she'd never make it in time. Even at the rate she's going, she suspects it's going to be dangerously close.

Leaning hazardously to one side and then the other to lend the scooter momentum, a dark thought enters her mind. If she can't prevent the accident, then what? Is she willing to visit Room #413? Is she prepared to end the innocent life of a freshly orphaned version of herself? Can she do that in order to prevent the end of the world through the nuclear fires of *Hi no Kawa*? Hot tears flow, blurring her vision at the acknowledgment that she may be more like Cyphor Gicul than she wants to admit. *"Hold it together Luci G,"* she thinks, finally dabbing her eyes with her sleeve.

Luci quickly works to replace the ghastly idea with an alternate scenario. Perhaps she could convince the younger version of herself to commit to never releasing DPM. Maybe this will work if she can somehow demonstrate that she's her older self and alert the girl of the horrors to come if things aren't changed. She searches herself. Would she have believed such an implausible tale at that age? What if seeing proof of her older self serves as a catalyst to motivate the girl to pursue DPM and bring about the end of the world even sooner?

People are not as predictable and compliant as numbers, not even when that person is herself. The scooter's unrelenting whine is a sign that Luci's pushing the machine to it limit, but she can't let up—she just can't. The view of the bridge up ahead chills the blood in her veins. The structure stretches out over the water like a malevolent, reclining dragon of asphalt, concrete, and steel. She takes solace in how the traffic is flowing slow but steadily, an indication the accident hasn't happened yet. But how long does she have?

Luci's head pounds, not like symptoms of a Jardon headache, but from the sheer pitiless stress of all of this. Her mind feels like a rubber band that keeps stretching and stretching beyond its limits.

The sinister idea of killing her younger self boomerangs back into her mind in a different form. It strikes her that the young girl in the car with her parents is the "Luci Prime" in this equation. If Luci smothers the child in room 413, she, too, will cease to exist as the pre-teen and will never advance to age 32 as she is now. These conundrums are things that she'll have to work out after she saves the three of them.

She shakes off the thought—she can't accept the idea of failure. "*Stay positive, Luci G. You can do this. You've traveled across time to do this!*" She recalls Ish's final instruction to her to "*find a better path.*" Her overburdened heart feels another sharp pang at the vision of him shoving Macer into the Carcerium chamber.

Luci's right hand on the accelerator threatens to cramp as the scooter vibrates its protest against being handled so roughly. She's not sure how to get the bridge traffic to stop, but she'll strip her clothes off and stand naked in the center lane until the cops come if that's what it takes to save them.

Continuing her near-suicidal roadway dance with the cars, Luci steers the moped onto the turnoff entrance to the bridge.

All the while, her mind strains as hard as she pushes physically. Her thoughts shift to what a successful outcome would look like. What happens to her if the accident is prevented? Did her experience in the lobby of Carcerium as it imploded and the ESTA flung her back to this interval insulate her from chronal changes, or will she simply disappear from existence if she succeeds?

After she whizzes past a makeshift trailer hauling landscaping equipment, she pulls her hand with the scar off the sweaty handlebars. She only allows herself a second to glance at the palm before curling her fingers back around the rubber grip, but it's enough to spark the memory of Gicul's scar manifesting before her.

All this chronal causation is unchartered territory for her. Usually, the unknown of a puzzle like this intrigues her, but not today. There's too much at stake if she gets the equation wrong.

The Vespa sputters in agony as she ascends the pitiless climb of the bridge. Luci can't remember if the family car is headed eastward or coming from the west on their way to the animal shelter. All she knows is that the teenage girl on her cell phone responsible for the collision will be driving a truck—a white one. Luci never witnessed the initial wreck; she only saw the sinister vehicle when the girl panicked and pushed the accelerator after the first impact. This sent the three of them sailing backward over the guardrail into the water below.

Her stomach clenches, and she forces down the bile threatening to spew up from her gut. For years, she wanted to hunt the little bitch down, but because the girl was a minor, the court docs were sealed and her identity forever remained a mystery to Luci. Today will be different though. She fantasizes about how, when this is done, she'll yank the girl from the oversized truck cab and slap her face with no explanation. Luci is surprised again at the shadow of Gicul moving across her heart. Where is this stuff coming from?

So much pain . . .

Luci sobs while attempting to get her bearings. She scans for the new red company car her father received as a part of his sales promotion the month before. He was so happy.

Sailing over the apex of the bridge, she tries to orient herself to which direction each vehicle will be coming. The water of the lake below glimmers and reflects the sunlight like thousands of swaying daggers, hungry water ready to swallow the lives of the most important people to her, not counting Ish Moyta.

A vehicle whooshes by, nearly clipping the scooter—a white truck headed eastward!

"*Oh no!*" She guns the throttle frantically "No! No! No!" she screams as she races behind it. The downward grade mercifully grants her speed to catch up. "Stop! Please stop!" she screams at the passenger-side window to the truck's oblivious driver.

Luci gasps when her hands slip on the handlebars and the scooter nearly swerves into the pickup. Her heart is in her throat as she peers into the cab of the truck. There's the glow of a phone screen as the girl holds it up to view, just like the police report suspected.

Approaching in the distance from the opposite direction, is a car—a red car!

Time becomes elastic, and the seconds stretch out before her. All of Luci's conjectures about what to do fade like vapor, and in this moment, she has absolute clarity.

She is presented with a choice.

Ish's words flash across her mind: "*A single decision made by one person affecting the lives of billions of people to come.*"

The future of humanity rests on what she decides, but the burden is not as heavy as one may expect. There is only one thing to do, only one option that will solidify a new path to be taken. She accepts this, whatever the consequence.

In a blur, Luci revs the Vespa's belabored engine to skim along the side of the truck. She takes a sharp breath and twists the throttle all the way back for one final thrust.

"*This had better work*," she thinks in this final moment.

It *does* work, and for a fraction of a second, she places the Vespa directly in front of the vehicle as intended.

This position is short-lived as the high bumper of the truck swats her away.

Luci's flying.

All sound is blocked save for the racing thump of her heartbeat in her eardrums. Like a discarded shirt tossed across a room into a hamper, the arc of Luci's trajectory peaks, and she returns to the ground with a sickening thud. There's an abrupt bone-snapping crunch. Her body slides across the graveled pavement and finally skids to a stop.

Time returns to its normal state with the screeching of tires in stereo on both sides of her.

She finds it odd that there's no pain.

There's a flash, and she's in the back of a car. Someone is screaming—a woman. Young Luci tosses her Sudoku magazine on the seat beside her to unbuckle for a better look. "What is it, Mama?"

The scream stops. A familiar man's voice from the front seat says incredulously, "That woman just cut in front of that truck!"

The memory doesn't last; Luci is on the pavement again. On her side, she sees the mashed scooter a few meters from her, the front wheel spinning like a misaligned Ferris wheel.

Again, she finds it strange that there's no pain. Shouldn't there be a tremendous amount of pain? But there's nothing, just blurred shapes of people rushing around and the spinning wheel of the baseball kid's moped.

As chaotic a scene as it is, Luci is completely at peace on her side.

The front wheel of the Vespa slows to a stop. She suspects it will *never* be ridden again by her, by that bratty baseball boy, or by anyone.

A man rushes up, blocking the view of the motionless scooter tire. He crouches, putting his face close to hers. His words are indistinct, warped sounds fading in and out. Luci recognizes him, and her heart flutters. Papa? She wants to call out to him, but she can't for some reason. He looks so hand-some, but there's a sadness in his eyes. Why does he look so sad? Her heart overflows with joy. How can she tell him who she is—his little *"Luci-Poo,"* how much she's missed him all those years, how much she loves him? She wants to tell him how she's thought about his death every single day since it hap-pened. How many days has it been in real time since she's seen his face all those years ago? She begins to work out the math of it but then pauses. She'll do it later. She's tired right now . . . so tired.

Another man bends beside him, also with widened eyes. Papa turns to him, speaking quickly and shaking his head. The presence of the other man is frustrating, and Luci wants him to go away, leaving only her father to her. Both stand upright, and all her field of view offers is the bottom of their trouser legs and the occasional pointing gesture. Her father crouches again. This time, she will tell him. This time, she will speak.

She's snatched away again. The overlap memory is of her flinging a deep-burgundy graduation cap high into the air among hundreds of others. The hats return to the ground like clumsy giant confetti. She embraces her best friend, Kimberly Lassiter. Luci knows and simultaneously doesn't know this friend whom she loves so much. What's unmistakable is that she's never been happier than in this precise moment.

She returns to the present. The shriek of faraway sirens pierces the noise of the crowd. Papa has taken a few steps back from her. He's in full view on his cell phone and pacing back and forth. His eyes never shift from hers. He was always a good man, she thinks. He looks so troubled and helpless. If only she could explain to him that it's okay, that it's what she wanted. In this instant, it dawns upon her that she did it—she's saved them and, by proxy, saved the world! Again, her heart is flooded with joy. This elation outshines the graduation-to-be. She thinks of Ish and smiles, knowing that she did it—*they* did it. The two of them traded their lives for the life of the world, for a *new and better path*. They have delivered a second chance to a world that had no hope.

Papa approaches and bends to her again. She wants to re-place the fear in his eyes with joy. She's never seen him afraid; it doesn't look right on him. She wants to tell him a joke, some-thing funny, something corny like he always came up with, to erase the grief on his face. If only she could speak, she would play his old line back to him: "*The future isn't what it used to be.*" She thinks of how he didn't know how right he was about that. Luci smiles—at least she thinks she smiles, but she can't be sure. Whatever her expression is, it causes Papa to stop and regard her quizzically. Some of the tension in his forehead relaxes as he lowers the phone.

Coming up slowly from behind him is a cautious young girl, her eyes wide with astonishment. Luci senses a fair amount of fear in her, but it seems to be held at bay by the girl's power-ful fascination with the scene. She peeks over the top of a Sudo-ku magazine as if it's a shield.

Luci knows this girl—it's her.

Upon realizing his young daughter has snuck away from the back seat of the car, Papa frantically grabs young Luci by the shoulders to spin her around. The issue of puzzle games flies from the girl's grip and falls to the ground. Papa shouts to someone. Mama comes into view but only long enough to snatch their daughter away from the scene. All the while, the girl fights to look over her shoulder at older Luci on the ground.

Another memory flashes. It starts with young Luci's point of view on the bridge looking at a bloody woman on the pave-ment who's been struck by a truck. It jump-shifts to "college Luci" retelling the same story in an upscale bar, explaining how that single horrifying event inspired her to go to medical school. Her three girlfriends scoff at her in good humor, re-minding her that she's studying to become a veterinarian. Luci hears this other version of herself join in with the laughter and explain, "What can I say? I like animals more than people, I guess."

Luci is back, but the younger version is gone, and so is Papa.

A man with intensely blue eyes and bright blue hands is yelling something to her. The blue is a glove; it holds a tiny annoying flashlight that he's shining in Luci's eyes.

There's another ceremony—graduating from veterinarian school. She looks out from the platform. Papa and Mama clap exuberantly, pausing only to wipe tears of joy from their eyes.

The flashlight is back; four blue gloves now, maybe six.

A handsome young man brings a well-groomed husky into the clinic for the dog's shots. Monique at the front desk tells Luci the man's name is "*Haris*—like 'Harris' but with only one 'R'."

Luci lazily gazes upward at the ceiling of the ambulance. Frantic voices shout about losing something, but she doesn't know what they've lost and doesn't care. She finds herself wondering if God, the universe, or whatever will reward her sacrifice today by allowing her and Ish to be together again somewhere.

She has a final memory overlay even more intense than the ones preceding. Twenty-six-year-old Luci's forehead is drenched with sweat, and she can't remember a time that she has been more exhausted than she is right now. She's tired beyond words, but even more than that, from within her heart flows an unending waterfall of love and serene satisfaction. She holds this fragile little person, balancing his tiny slumbering body on her sweat-drenched chest. Without a doubt, he is the most amazing thing that she's ever laid eyes upon. He is the embodiment of hope, a connection to something that will go on well beyond herself, a physical flesh-and-blood promise for the future. She wants to unwrap him and place thousands of loving kisses on his soft, unblemished skin, but the nurses have instructed Luci to keep him swaddled.

The registrar nurse asks Haris for the first name of the child. He turns with a proud smile that only a new father knows.

Looking back to Luci and his newborn son, the husband says, "She wants to know his name."

She uses her final breath to whisper what Luci Prime in the delivery room is saying as the memory begins to fade. "His name? Ish . . . Call him . . . Ishmael."

Luci Gaudiano closes her eyes.

EPILΛG

(Epilogue)

ONE

A SLENDER, DARK-SKINNED MAN SLOWLY makes his way across the deserted cemetery. This interval's custom of inserting its deceased in the ground instead of releasing them to the sea is peculiar to him. Nevertheless, he's grateful for the tradition, thankful to have a location to visit.

He pauses, looking down at the scrap of paper the clerk inscribed the location marker on. Paper reminds him of her, and it probably always will. She's gone now, but the paper remains. A bittersweet smile forms as he muses on how she would've likely found the slot number they've placed her in amusing: 137, the number related to the "fine-structure constant" of quantum electrodynamics.

He approaches his destination, stepping slowing as he attempts to reconcile the emotional confusion in his heart. How do you mourn for one who still lives, albeit a younger version of themselves? He concludes that he is not mournful of her death but the death of her being with him. He's mournful at the realization that he's the only living soul that will ever experience the brilliant mathematical mind of Luci Ann Gaudiano, the extraordinary woman who chose to save the world twice—once from nuclear fire and once from Waleen Macer's future abomination.

He sighs, arriving at the spot where the scrap of paper indicates her remains are laid.

It remains a mystery to him how the Carcerium had deposited him at the sports stadium a month or so ago. The best explanation is that Luci had somehow triggered the chamber to hurl the three of them across time to this non-interval point. A melancholy grin forms as he acknowledges that if anyone could do such an impossible thing, she could. He suspects that he and the body of Macer arrived exactly one thousand seconds after she'd skipped to this pre-*Hi no Kawa* period. Though there was no sign of the ESTA in the stadium, the skip barge was on the field a few meters from where they appeared. Its obliterated control lectern eliminated the possibility of anyone from this period reverse-engineering the tech. He toggles back and forth in his thoughts as to whether she had done this deliberately.

The one piece of Relicus City technology that *did* survive the leap skip is Macer's churka, but he's made sure that's safely tucked away.

While doing duties for the past week in the homeless shelter, the question of what if she'd waited those seventeen minutes after she arrived has weighed heavily on his heart and mind. Would seeing him have stopped her from preventing her family's wreck? Would he have asked her to stay in order to be with her, or would he have encouraged her to go on once she knew where she was?

It's a question that he knows he will never be able to fully answer.

A lump forms in his throat. "*Well, you set the world on a new a better path.*" He wipes a solitary tear defiantly marching over his cheek. "*A new and better path at least for a little while, and hopefully that'll be enough. Hopefully, they'll make the best of the second chance you've given them.*"

He tears up at the sight of the Jane Doe marker and shakes his head.

"And no one will ever even know," he says aloud in a voice on the verge of cracking.

He considers keeping tabs on the young girl and her family. Maybe one day, when she reaches adulthood, he'll approach the woman and tell her how the Luci he knew and loved forfeited academic accolades in order to give the world a second chance. He tries to visualize how to initiate such a preposterous conversation and cannot.

"Then again, maybe it's best just to leave it alone."

He stares at the plaque as if waiting for it to answer back, but it's as silent as the contents of its designation.

He looks up at the sky; it's nearly dusk. The man turns to begin his long walk back to the shelter. He has years to decide if he'll try to tell her.

For now, he'll find his way in this new world he's been thrust into, accepting that this new future's secrets are not to be known . . . not just yet. He carries her love in his heart and decides maybe that's enough for now.

Yes, it will have to be.

ҺƗ END
(The End)

Acknowledgements

. . . My brother Nathan Lee Padgett, who patiently listened for an hour and a half in the wee hours of the morning back in August 2016 as I relayed nearly every plot point of this tale.

. . . My mother Mary, who has been a bottomless well of encouragement that I have frequently drawn from my entire life.

. . . Shannon Winton (The Novel Nurse) for story structure guidance and so much more during a critical time of the writing of this.

. . . A special thanks to Christian Roule: my own private quantum physics guide/instructor and time travel tale 'mechanic'.

. . . The remainder of Team Armageddon (my beta readers and critique group) - Jason Aydelotte, Dominick D'Aunno, Erik Hailey, Hilary C. Ritz, Paige Theriot, and Chris Lewis, and editor Josh Mitchell.

. . . And as always . . . my lovely wife, Sabrina, for indulging me in these adventures.

About the Author

Texas native George Wright Padgett is a multi-genre author who 'grew up' reading science fiction and comic books. After a brief stint writing children's picture books, he turned to darker themes. He now writes a mix of novels and short stories in sci-fi, detective, and horror categories.

His 'non-writing' time is divided between being a husband and father of two, a jazz piano player, a graphic artist, and a playwright.

Connect with George

Email:	georgewpadgett@gmail.com
Facebook:	facebook.com/Author.GWP
Web:	www.georgewpadgett.com
Fan Club:	www.georgewpadgett.com/fanclub

Support Indie Authors & Small Press

If you liked this book, please take a few moments to leave a review on your favorite website, even if it's only a line or two. Reviews make all the difference to indie authors and are one of the best ways you can help support our work.

Reviews on Amazon, GreyGeckoPress.com, Barnes and Noble, or even on your own blog or website all help to spread the word to more readers about our books, and nothing's better than word-of-mouth!

http://greygeckopress.com/review-drift

Grey Gecko Press

Thank you for purchasing this book from Grey Gecko Press, an independent publishing company that focuses on new and emerging authors, bringing readers the best in fiction and non-fiction at reasonable prices in all formats.

With books in nearly every genre of fiction and non-fiction, there's something for everyone, and you can be sure that buying books from us leads directly to the support of independent authors like Susan Adger.

Visit our website to purchase our titles, including special and autographed editions, and pre-order upcoming books at a discount.

And don't forget: all our print editions come with the ebook absolutely free! Email support@greygeckopress.com for your copy today.

Web:	www.greygeckopress.com
Facebook:	facebook.com/GreyGeckoPress

More from George Wright Padgett

Spindown

For over a hundred and fifty years, the rarest and most valuable substance in the solar system has been mined from the only location where it exists in significant quantity: Jupiter's largest moon, Ganymede. For all of this time, the remote mining outpost has been serviced by clone slaves who are drugged into mindlessness, and all of it has been monitored, controlled, and administered by the artificial intelligence known as Prinox.

But what happens when a failed rescue mission causes a small band of escaped clones to begin questioning their lives, their society, and their very existence? Hunted by deadly killing machines, confused and scared, these renegade slaves are about to find out—for better or worse—just what it means to be human.

grey gecko press
http://books2read.com/spindown

amazon iBooks
BARNES&NOBLE BOOKSELLERS kobo

Addleton Heights

New Year's Eve 1901: Six hundred feet above the Atlantic Ocean, the platform city of Addleton Heights balances on massive, soot-covered metal stilts. A grisly double murder interrupts the party in the floating mansion of the city's most powerful man, and for reasons unknown, he coerces detective-for-hire T.H. Kipsey into taking the enigmatic case.

George Wright Padgett weaves a cat-and-mouse mystery through a steampunk, alternate-American history that will thrill readers of Cherie Priest's *Boneshaker* and Christopher Beats's steam-noir *Magnocracy* series. Join Kip as he races against time to unravel the clues that will thrust him across the city, up to the clouds, and into the depths beneath Addleton Heights.

grey gecko press
http://books2read.com/addleton

amazon iBooks
BARNES&NOBLE BOOKSELLERS kobo

Recommended Reading

Absence of Mind

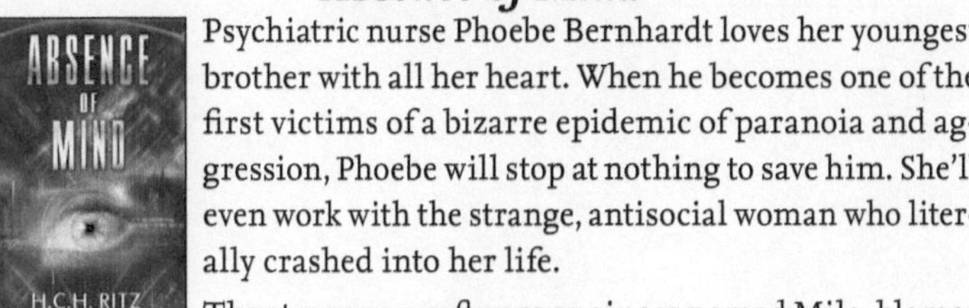

Psychiatric nurse Phoebe Bernhardt loves her youngest brother with all her heart. When he becomes one of the first victims of a bizarre epidemic of paranoia and aggression, Phoebe will stop at nothing to save him. She'll even work with the strange, antisocial woman who literally crashed into her life.

The stranger, a software engineer named Mila, blames the plague on technology . . . but she's hiding something. Is Mila a possible path to a cure – or is she the cause of it all? Or will she just prove to be indifferent to the fates of thousands of people, including Phoebe's brother?

Searching for the answers will force Phoebe to face her fundamentalist religious family and her own assumptions about who she is – and drive her to the brink of death.

grey gecko press
http://books2read.com/absence1

amazon iBooks
BARNES&NOBLE BOOKSELLERS kobo

Invasion at Miratev

If humanity is to survive, the alien T'Kharr must be stopped . . . even if it means sacrificing tens of thousands.

Grand Commander Brandon North and his fleet must liberate a research facility taken by mankind's most ruthless and deadly enemy, the T'Kharr. The new technology developed there cannot be allowed to swing the decades-long war in the enemy's favor, even if it means sacrificing tens of thousands of lives . . . including his own.

Reminiscent of David Weber's *Honor Harrington*, John Scalzi's *Old Man's War*, and John Ringo's *Legacy of the Aldenata*, this thrilling debut novel will appeal to all fans of military space sci-fi, intrigue, and bloodthirsty aliens bent on humanity's subjugation–or destruction–whichever comes first.

grey gecko press
http://books2read.com/omega1

amazon iBooks
BARNES&NOBLE BOOKSELLERS kobo